THE SIEGE

THE
SIEGE

JERROLD
MORGULAS

Holt, Rinehart and Winston

NEW YORK / CHICAGO / SAN FRANCISCO

ISBN: 03-086003-2
Library of Congress Catalog Card Number: 77-138882
First Edition

Designer: Guy Fleming

PRINTED IN THE UNITED STATES OF AMERICA

To my wife, Susan,
for her help, her patience,
her encouragement and, most of all,
her love.

If you run
down the night of your hatred,
mad Sfarad, mad wild horse,
whips and swords
will rein you in.

You cannot crown whom you choose—
                the blood-shedder,
                the traitor, the rapist,
                        the thief,
or him who never piled brick on slow brick
in a temple of his own sweat.
The first thing fire burns
is freedom.

                .   .   .

Oh idol you've carved for yourself,
portrait of your own sickness.

Once, long ago, one day in this our winter,
when this heaven hung low and sullen,
we could see, frightened,
Sfarad's great sin settling into place,
deep in envy's heart:
the infinite sadness of that mortal sin,
a war with no victory,
a war between brothers.

—SALVADOR ESPRIU

(*translated from the Catalan by Burton Raffel*)

Prologue

SPAIN / 1934

SEPTEMBER 22

The Government will declare a state of alarm when the circumstances warrant it.

Epoca (Madrid)

TOWARD THE FORMATION OF A NEW GOVERNMENT! Premier Alejandro Lerroux has encountered difficulties in presenting to the head of State the list of the members of the new government.

OCTOBER 5

I shall allow unlimited attacks on me, personally, but absolutely no attacks on Republican institutions.

Premier Alejandro Lerroux

The monstrous act of accepting the Republic's enemies in the cabinet is treason. We therefore sever all solidarity with the national regime's institutions, and we intend to go to the limit in defense of the Republic.

Manuel Azaña, former premier, leader of the Left Republican party

ONCE AGAIN THE MARXIST ORGANIZATIONS DECLARE A GENERAL STRIKE!!

Epoca

Demonstrators early this morning fired on Civil Guards, who attempted to disperse a gathering in the *Prosperidad* quarter, a Communist stronghold, as workers headed a general strike call in protest against the inclusion of "enemies of the Republic" in the new cabinet of Premier Alejandro Lerroux.

The New York Times

OCTOBER 6

ONCE MORE THE ARMY IS THE SALVATION OF SPAIN!! In Asturias, where military bombers and troops commanded by General López

Ochoa were sent to subdue rebellious coal miners, the situation is well in hand, said Interior Minister Eloy Vaquero.

Epoca

OCTOBER 8

On the Atlantic coast the cruiser *Libertad* debarked an infantry regiment at Gijón to reinforce the Oviedo garrison. The striking coal miners are reported to have fled to the hills and they were bombarded by military airplanes and the cruiser *Libertad* which shelled the hills around Gijón.

The New York Times

OCTOBER 10

With the capture of Azaña, along with the Socialist directors and the separatist ringleaders, the actual subversive movement has been localized in Asturias.

Epoca

The army was awaiting reinforcements before attacking. A column of troops under General López Ochoa was moving into the mining district. They were reported to have encountered centers where rebels had slaughtered entire garrisons of Civil Guard, including their wives and families. More than 400 Guard were said to have been killed.

Associated Press Wire

OCTOBER 12

The troops of General López Ochoa have occupied Oviedo this morning. . . . The Air Force bombed the arms factory where the rioters, who fled along footpaths and trails, were barricaded.

Epoca

OCTOBER 13

War Minister Hidalgo announced today that thirty courts-martial were being held in Asturias where striking coal miners are still fighting troops under General López Ochoa. With the exception of the railroad station, which is serving as a fortress where a strong force of rebels is barricaded, the military have taken possession of Oviedo. Troops took the big arms factory in Oviedo by assault. The Hotel Covadonga where other strikers had taken refuge was burned to the ground.

The New York Times

OCTOBER 16

FIRST REPORT OF THE TRAGIC EVENTS THAT TOOK PLACE IN OVIEDO. . . . The rioters had cannons and machine guns. Among the buildings destroyed were the City Hall, the University, the Hotels Digles and Covadonga, the Ministry of Finance, and the Bank of Asturias. . . . Hundreds of bodies were gathered in the streets.

Epoca

Those sentenced in Asturias to the ultimate penalty are now sufficient in number.

Premier Alejandro Lerroux

Spain / 1936

July 13
On Sunday evening, four Fascist gunmen shot and killed Assault Lieutenant José Castillo. The cowardly attack was committed as the Lieutenant left his home to go on duty.

Claridad (Madrid) (page 1)

Yesterday, at three o'clock in the morning, the leader-apparent of the Fascist movement and ex-Minister of the Dictatorship, Don José Calvo Sotelo, was taken from his home and killed.

Claridad (Madrid) (page 16)

DEPUTY CALVO SOTELO IS TAKEN FROM HIS HOME AND ASSASSINATED. . . . After the crime, his assailants took the body to the East Cemetery where it was left in the morgue. "If we cannot end assaults on individuals, the State will collapse. We cannot allow the citizens to believe that the State is unable to guarantee their safety."

Martínez Barrio

July 15
THE DISSOLUTION OF PARLIAMENT AND THE SUSPENSION OF THE LAW OF PUBLIC ORDER. The Permanent Delegation to Parliament will meet today to approve the extension of the state of emergency. A forceful action by the groups representing the opposition has been announced.

July 16
By the rebellion of 1934, the Left has lost all authority to condemn the rebellion of 1936.

Salvador de Madariaga

BOOK ONE /

A Burning Once, and a Burning Once Again

FRIDAY, JULY 17, 1936: *The Mercaders*

IT IS SAID THAT IN THE BEGINNING God hung the sun directly over the city of Toledo as a sign of his especial favor, and though the sun was later moved the *toledanos* still shake their heads and wonder: if such is God's favor, how fearful must be his wrath?

To the north of the city the plains stretch flat and stiff as a tanning hide, the infrequent wind stirring nothing more than dry yellow grass. Magpies wheel mournfully above the sparse cover, searching for something green. In the distance, toward the Sierra de Gredos in the west and Cuenca to the east, the land lies prostrate under the summer heat, wrinkled, cracked, and blistered. Remnants of thin black clouds hang low and motionless over the endless folds and furrows of the plains, like the last breath of smoke rising from a charred surface. Mesas, flat and black as a smithy's anvil, ride the horizon. Bleached, spectral towns, all whitewash and pale clay, float like mirages in the heat shimmer, the inevitable steeple jutting up sharply from the tumble of buildings, each town thus impaled upon its own church.

The Madrid road twists on in painful passage through these towns, breaking out straight again only when it has shaken off the misery of their inhabitants, and reached the magisterial bleakness of the open plains again. To the north, Madrid, covening with itself just below the horizon; to the south, Toledo, rising bone-white above the clinging Tagus, surveying the empty plains with a despair centuries wise and resigned.

Between Toledo and Illescas on its northern flank, the road dips drunkenly up and down between the sheltering flanks of low hills and, for a moment here and there, the land gives a deceitful promise of green. Trees rise and test the still, hot air, and moist grasses brush the side of the hills with a peacock's brilliant plumage. Tall cypress and low, palmlike fronds sprout hopefully. But in a moment the green is gone again, and the land on either side of the road lies still, with a breath of parched, African death about it. It is not here that the few rich of Toledo have built their homes, but rather on the greener slopes above the Tagus to the south of the city: *Los Cigarrales*. Yet hidden in these verdant pockets, among the cypress and palm grass, there are a few houses, the homes of those who wish to be just that much closer to Madrid and who do not like crossing rivers.

Just out of sight of the city, three miles distant and set at the bottom of a small depression, stood a large whitewashed house, only ten years old. Around it on three sides ran a whitewashed stone wall, along which the inevitable cypress stood guard. The house was low and of a flat, chalky white reminiscent of bleached animal bones. Nearby stood two smaller houses connected by a path of fine gravel. A beaten earthen driveway angled down from the Madrid road, passing between cairns of the same white stones until it came at length upon the house of Francisco Mercader. From the approach, it seemed as though the house had no windows, but upon coming closer one could see them, recessed into the walls and shuttered so that the glass would not be exposed to the heat. It was an African house, not surprising near this city of Moorish ghosts— where a man can so easily become accustomed to the African quality of the landscape which surrounds it.

Overhead, a military trimotor flew on lazy patrol, droning with an anxious, nasal whine, high in the air where there were no clouds at all but only a glassy blue expanse shining like the face of a mirror. Below, no one stirred. A few chickens ran in dizzy circles around the smaller of the two detached houses, screeching and flapping about the carcass of an old black Ford which stood at the end of the driveway near a shed of ash-gray boards which served as a garage.

As the aircraft passed overhead, a stirring far off on the plain caught the eye of Francisco Mercader who was watching from a curtained window on the second floor of the main house. He parted the curtain slowly with his hand, allowing a blade of sunlight to cut through the shadowed interior of his room, and he smiled apprehensively.

On a far ridge a low column of dust was forming where the wind blended the vigorous dust spurts of a horse's hooves into one long trail clearly visible now against the brilliant blue horizon. Even from that distance the flash of spurs could be seen. Only one horse, thought Francisco Mercader, letting the curtain fall back; he knew only one horse that could run like that—his own, and on it—his own as well, his son.

The trail of dust billowed out, and the rider became larger against the blackened earth, took on a shape distinct from that of his mount, a great brown mare now lathered and foaming, her head tossing, her mane caught in the wind of her own motion. The rider clung to the mare's back, his legs pressed against her sides; his body angled forward so that his head was near to the whipping mane.

Slowly, the rider began to slide from the saddle, to lean forward and over the left side, until his shoulders came level with the hollow of the animal's throat. He could see the post about a hundred yards ahead, jutting up out of the cracked earth, just where he had thrust it on his way out, hours before. His garrison cap was still there, the gold insignia glittering in the sun; the reflection spun across his eyes, blinding him for a second, then went shooting off into the sky.

Jaime Mercader tightened the grip of his left hand on the pommel, leaning still farther forward. The ground rocked and lurched before him; all he could see now were the whir of pebbles and the dust churning beneath the horse's hooves and the rush of ground as the mare closed the gap between him and the post on which his old military cap hung.

He remembered the times he had done this in Morocco, with the men of his mother's tribe, with other young officers who had been raised as he had been among the Berbers. It seemed so long ago, and the man he remembered being then was someone else entirely.

He cautioned the mare into an easy, forward glide. Was his father watching from the window? he wondered. Of course. He always did. Jaime felt a twinge, thinking of how he must be tormenting the man. But what was he to do?

No more time; the stake was less then twenty yards away; the mare would cover the distance in seconds. He let his left arm hang down loosely, his fingers curled and ready to snatch the cap away as he passed. It had to be done with precisely the right motion, the slightest grazing of the fingers, then a sudden tightening; too soon or too low, and he could be thrown from the saddle, too light, and he would miss. As he dipped lower, his face now inches from the whipping hooves, he thought, "This is foolish, foolish . . . but what else?"

His hands tensed, one on the pommel, the other curved, caressing the air. Dust and bits of grass struck his face, leaving tiny welts. The stake with the cap on it rushed at him, and he swung his arm back, then brought it forward in a long, shallow scoop. He could pass a lance through a barrel stave at that speed, he knew. The cap was easy.

Then the cap was in his hands, and the forward lunge of his movement had carried him back full into the saddle. He straightened himself and slapped the cap on the pommel, passed his hand over his forehead, and reclaimed the reins.

How long had the cap been there? An hour? Two or three? He could not remember; he carried no watch and had no idea how long he had been gone. He did not feel hungry, but that was no gauge; many times before he had spent days without eating and hardly had noticed it. How his father had worried. But he kept his worry to himself. That was worse, Jaime thought. But how else could it be? If they spoke all that there was between them, there would be no end to it, and it would get them nothing except more pain.

He was near the house now, and the mare, recognizing its surroundings, slowed to an easy canter. Jaime patted the animal on the crest, whistled to it. They had become good friends in the two months since he had left the army garrison in Ceuta and had come to the house near Toledo. "And what have you done since?" he thought. "You ride and you ride and you decide nothing . . . sooner or later your father is going to say, 'Make up your mind, Jaime, you must do something.'" Soon, he knew, they would begin to press him for a decision.

Both the lawyer, Soler, and Tomás Pelayo, from whose bank the Comercio Mercader S.A. took its loans, were becoming anxious about the management of the new oil subsidiary. Francisco, they knew, had his heart set on putting Jaime in charge and, so, ensure his succession. Jaime could see the confrontation as clearly as though it had already occurred: Francisco and the banker waiting for him in his father's study, the calf-skin folders open on the desk, the inkwell uncapped, the pens ready, and the documents prepared for signature. Pelayo would be standing behind the chair as he always did, smoking one of his thin cigars and blinking his owl eyes while Francisco sat there, nervous but determined to have it out. Commerce can wait only so long for the human heart to catch its beat.

He looked ahead, pretending not to raise his head, caught the slow fall of the curtains in the upper window facing him. His father or his mother? They were always watching him. But waiting for different things. How many different forms love can take and with how many different results, he thought. The cap distracted him, the insignia once again netting the beams of the flat sun overhead. Why always the cap, the cracked visor, the dusty brown cloth? Was it the same cap he had worn at Oviedo? That had never occurred to him before.

The mare trotted toward the outermost of the two dependent buildings. A shadow from one of the towering cypress fell across the animal's path. The tree towered above him, and Jaime became suddenly, briefly dizzy.

The stillness about the yard unsettled him; he could hear noises from inside the shed that served as a garage for his father's car, the clank of metal tools and an occasional curse as the driver, Barrera, tinkered and twisted under the hood of the old Ford. Did his father ever use the car? or was it kept there solely for the amusement of the intense, sad-faced man who seemed to bury himself perpetually in its innards?

"Our escapes," he thought, passing the pile of gray boards, the isolated metal grumblings. "I ride; he hides in the coils of a motor." Suddenly he tensed, angry with himself, with the slowness of the horse's gait. He slapped the animal on its flank, and the mare leaped forward, reaching the house at a full gallop, then reared high in the air, its forelegs seeming to hack at the sides of the building. Jaime slipped from the saddle and landed with practiced lightness on his feet. He was covered with sweat, his dark forearms glistening and the blood pulsing in his temples. It had been a good ride, but it proved nothing, brought no answers. He snatched the cap from the pommel and angrily thrust it into his pocket. He pulled a towel from the nearby post, and after he had finished rubbing the animal down, he stood for a moment with his head thrown back, staring into the sun. The sun seemed to him the only fixed point in his universe, the only reality the fact that he had resigned his commission out of anger, that he was still brutally angry and that he had no idea what he was going to do next. He knew that he would ride out again the next day and the day after that and spend long hours on the sun-blasted, breathless plains imagining that he was back in Morocco and trying to discover through that futile deception whether Morocco was in fact where he really wanted to be.

The curtain in the window above him had not moved in the last five minutes. He tried to visualize the face behind it—the silent, gentle face of his father, which showed its feelings precisely when it tried most to hide them; the large eyes, perpetually mobile under those small, almost feminine brows, so unlike those in the faded pictures of his father's father who had been a ferocious man, square and angular. But the face faded quickly, replaced with the shaggy, prophet-bearded head of Colonel Carvalho. The Colonel's eyes seemed to float on the surface of the sun. "But what?" he thought, "what am I to find in those eyes? Certainly not answers to my questions . . . God, how certain that is." Everything had moved from his father to Carvalho, in natural, inevitable progression. He had been passed by his father into Carvalho's safekeeping, and there he had lost whatever faith he had ever had. And now, passed back to his father, he had come full circle. He looked to the south, to the unseen bone pile of Toledo staked out on its bleached escarpment behind the hills; there, he knew, was Carvalho's home hidden away among the ancient ringing houses of that once royal city. How it all turned back on itself; his father, then Carvalho . . . then his father again; but the memory of Carvalho still remained, had survived the second transition. Could he never rid himself of the man's presence? But, he wondered, was that what he wanted?

An emptiness swept through him and he felt dizzy again. His head was steaming hot. His father had warned him about sunstroke, but he refused to listen. He scooped up water from the horse trough and poured it over his hair, letting it stream down and run heavily over his chest, turning his shirt black and showing his narrow ribs through the drenched cotton. Twisted locks of dark hair hung over his high forehead, reaching to his eyebrows. He had let it grow out since he had left the Ceuta garrison in Morocco. It seemed that every day that passed since he had resigned had been spent on the plains east of his father's house, a furnace of a place that could have been the surface of the sun, where days blended one into the other and the mind lost its roots in time. And each day when he returned, his father would be waiting behind the same set of translucent curtains and his mother, too, somewhere in the house, waited behind the loose folds of her *jellaba*. There had been a tension between them from the moment he had come from Ceuta. He knew it, and it pained him as much as did his own memories; she smiled understandingly as he played the Berber and rode out into the vaulting sun each morning, while his father, the quiet merchant, waited patiently, hoping that each day would be the last and the end of it and that his son Jaime would come back, sit down at last at the evening tea and say, "Yes, it's time. And I will come with you in the business . . ." Perhaps even add, "It's what I really want. I've decided."

The last drops of water had fallen from his hair. His reflection stared back at him from the surface of the trough, but all he could see clearly were his eyes, dark and sunken as though embedded in his head by a blow. The rest of his lean face, his long curved nose with its flaring nostrils, the ears with their heavy lobes of which he had always been embarrassed, the rest slipped away on the ripple-furrowed water. It had been such a long time since he had thought of such things as his appearance . . . a long time. "And yet you are only twenty-eight . . . and thinking like an old man already." He scowled at his reflection, patted his hair and dug into his pocket for some sugar for the mare. The animal nuzzled deep into his palm, and he cupped his hand over her nostrils, capturing her warm breath against his skin. The mare's rough tongue took the sugar and she whinnied again, this time in pleasure.

On one of the three balconies facing inward on the patio garden of the Mercader house, father and son sat, silently facing each other. Between them lay a tooled copper tray on which had been set an empty silver teapot and a bowl of *khab el ghazal,* the "horns of the gazelle," from which each of them now and then thoughtfully selected one of the sugary almond pastries, thus excusing himself momentarily from conversation. Even as the blank, whitewashed exterior walls of the house gave no hint of the floral magnificence within the patio, so the emotionless expressions of each man concealed the unrest of his thoughts.

Next to the tray lay the traditional three silver boxes, their lids bearing a whirl of flowers and Moorish scrolls. To the left, between the two men, a small charcoal brazier glowed, the kettle atop it gradually quickening with the mirthful sound of boiling water. Francisco took from the nearest of the boxes a palmful of green tea leaves and sifted them between his fingers into the pot. Still the son said nothing, watching the ceremony with a tense pleasure.

The father sighed and reached with soft, curved fingers for the tiny hammer which lay near his knee. From the second of the boxes he took a loaf of glistening sugar and with a deft, practiced tap chipped off three chunks into the pot.

Then he waited.

Jaime Mercader hesitated until he was sure that his father actually intended for him to take the final step. He was surprised and puzzled; it was the first time since he had returned that he had been given such an invitation. Staring into his father's eyes, he saw only that which had been there before, a look which said to him, "I am patient, and I will wait for my son to make up his mind and to find his way, but pray God that it be not much longer. . . ."

Jaime nodded gravely and with one finger turned back the lid of the last box and removed a bound cluster of fresh mint leaves.

Through the steam now rising from the teapot, Jaime studied his father's face, searching in it for some reassurance that here was indeed his father, that some undeniable tie of blood bound him to this man, something beyond the simple love he felt for him. But now, as always, he found nothing. What had that gentle, moonlit face, with its sad, almost priestly wise expression, to do with him? And how could it be that he had been produced by that man's seed? His own face was his mother's, and his blood, if anything, that of his grandfather who had first taken the Mercaders to Morocco. Yet there in Francisco's eyes was the love and that, he thought, counted for much. His mirror was in his mother, her long, dark features, glistening like a knife's edge. In his father, perhaps, was his hope.

Francisco touched the knot of his tie. Then, embarrassed by the nervous gesture, he dropped his hand to his lap. It was hot, and the steam made the sweat bead on his rounded, balding forehead. The swell of hair above his ears, like wings, the long sideburns, his tiny mustache, all glistened.

The fragrance of fresh mint spread about the balcony, mingling with the scent of tamarisk that rose from the patio below. The sound of the water in the pool, disturbed by the swift movement of tiny golden fish, added a bell-like ripple to the chatter of dry leaves caught in a momentary breeze.

When the tea had been poured into the long, silver-bound glasses, Francisco Mercader looked again at Jaime, as though expecting an answer to a question he had not asked. He extended his ringed fingers and lifted one of the glasses, offered it to his son, looking at the same time hopefully into the young man's fierce, angular face for some reflection of himself.

"*Shoukran,*" whispered Jaime, taking the glass. "Thank you . . ."

Francisco drew a breath. "How Spanish you were once, Jaime," he said with sadness.

"I admired Spain once, Father."

Francisco hesitated. His son had been with him now for over a month, yet he was still a stranger. Only the boy's mother, whose language and customs he now emulated to the exclusion of everything Spanish, seemed able to communicate with him. And their conversation consisted mostly of a knowing silence.

"Then," Francisco said at last, "shall we talk about . . . new things?"

"Time," thought the father, "time to heal, just as my own father healed from his wounds after Tetuán." Only time could possibly ease the bitterness which had set like a seal over his son's heart. Francisco shook his head, "Why does he have to understand, when no matter how much one understands, nothing changes?" Could Jaime ever know why a man must sometimes turn away from something he cannot bear and that the very act of turning away is the deepest imaginable expression of his pain? "How he must hate Enrique now," Francisco thought, bringing to focus a mind's image of his friend's face, the wild, tangled white beard and beak-like nose that seemed forever on the verge of a thrust, the eyes clouded by the incomprehensible griefs he had suffered on the sands of Morocco, before the gates of its towns, Tetuán, Ceuta, and Melilla, and in the ruined, ten-times dead villages of Spain itself. How could Jaime expect to understand all this in a day or he to explain it in a word? He smiled charitably at his own impotence.

A curtain of vapor now hung between them, floating up from the teapot on the brass tray. Jaime lifted his glass slowly and sipped at his tea. His gaze wandered over the tops of the tooled silver boxes and he glanced rapidly toward the doorway leading into the house to see if his mother had passed. But it was only a curtain trembling in the night breeze.

Francisco, a note of resignation in his voice, continued hesitantly: "I'd hoped that this would be an evening to talk of things . . . together . . . of what . . . we might do now, you and I . . . but . . ."

He leaned against the tasseled pillow. At that moment he seemed more the Moroccan, less the Spaniard himself than Jaime could ever remember having seen him before, and the son felt a surge of warmth for that small, delicately boned man who was, so amazingly, his father. Carvalho's face appeared again like a magic-lantern image over his own father's features, the Colonel's expression impassive as it had been on that chill afternoon when they had stood together on the mountain slopes of northern Spain overlooking the city of Oviedo . . . the smell of apples and gunpowder . . . the Moorish cavalry below them on the hillside, grouping for an attack, the artillery batteries pounding the city to rubble . . . dust clouds and sound sundered so that the whole barrage seemed some incomprehensible optical illusion.

Francisco was speaking again with an artificial animation that only emphasized his preoccupation. "Cork was not good this year, and the last few months it's fallen off even more. It seems there's no market for cork these days, but as far as fuel oil is concerned . . . ah . . . particularly fuel oil, that's very good now . . . probably the thing of the future for us. . . . We will set up a special office in Ceuta for the oil alone. Can you imagine? As if there were enough automobiles in Spain to make it matter, but it seems . . ."

"Father . . ."

"You could take charge of that office, Jaime. It would be a fine thing for you. . . . I don't want to go back there myself; I've had enough of that heat. Oh, yes, perhaps for a few weeks, on a visit, for your mother's sake. But you, on the other hand, you want to go back there. I know . . . and it would be such a fine future for you. . . ."

The young man smiled gracefully, a trifle sadly, and said: "What do I know about oil, Father?"

"You could learn. I know you want to go back, so . . . rest a few more weeks, then . . . go. It will be much better for you than riding about on that desert out there, pretending that it's Morocco. . . ."

"I'm not 'pretending' out there; I'm really running. We both know that." He would not let his father take such an easy way out. He had to say that he, too, knew the truth.

"Why, then?" his father said, surprised.

"Because you built this house so close to Toledo and to Carvalho's home. His house is just over the hills, and the whole countryside stinks of him. He loved that house more than his wife. The nights he would spend describing its walls, the doorways, the view from every window. Do you want to know what kind of wood the dining table is made of or how many rails there are in the banister? Do you want to know who fashioned the iron railings on the balconies or how old the iron eagle on the door is? Father, it was obscene the way that man loved his house. I thought he would drive me mad with it. I'm sorry, Father . . . that's the way it was, and that's why I ride. Out there, the stink gets burned away."

"Jaime, Jaime," Francisco pleaded. He understood but could not express his understanding. "You hate him that much, then?"

"He went back there, to Oviedo, didn't he? He let them send him back there, and he went without a word. It meant nothing to him. . . ."

"What else could he do? You, you're young, you can say, 'Here, take back your commission,' and walk away from it. A few years lost, that's all. But Enrique can't do that. Not with his family, his wife and daughters, his son. He's over sixty now. . . . His whole life, in the army . . ."

"All the more reason he should have refused. But it was so like him simply to pretend that nothing was happening. Pontius Pilate, washing his hands, just as he did before." Jaime started to rise, then sank down again, a look of hopelessness on his face. "Explain it to me then, Father. You've known him for a long time. You sent me to him as his aide. . . . How could he go back there . . . after what happened? Doesn't the man have any conscience, any sense of guilt?"

"For what? He did nothing. You've said so yourself."

"That's just it. He did nothing," Jaime said bitterly. He knew that at all costs he must keep from lashing out at his father who had done him no harm, done nothing except try to defend his oldest friend.

"Don't you understand what it was like, being with that man, listening to him day after day and believing in what he said . . . about justice and dignity and how there was to be a new Spain . . . but what he showed me was Spain of three hundred years ago. . . . They made an inferno out of that city, and he stood there and watched it and then walked away. . . ."

"I know," Francisco said, his lip trembling, "that Enrique is a good man and that God's way is something very difficult to understand. . . ."

"*Inch Allah?*" Jaime murmured, hardly aware that he had used the Moslem phrase. "Is that the answer? God's will?" He had become even more agitated, straining forward. "He did it to save himself, not me. He knew I couldn't have allowed those men to be shot, with no more evidence than a bruise on their shoulders. Rifles? Just as well pickaxes or shovels. So what did a bruise mean? No, he was protecting himself, not me. Did I tell you? No . . . I never did, but you're making me do it now. . . . After the trials, when I was relieved, and they were trying to decide what to do with me, I asked them to find Carvalho, and we went up into the mountains together, because he'd disappeared. . . . They took me up with a guard of soldiers, and we found him there, fishing. Just that, fishing. . . . I suppose all of us find our peace of mind in different ways, but . . . Christ's bleeding wounds, fishing . . . Father. Fishing . . . ? And afterward, after he's done the only thing he could do to save his own honor, he acted as if it had meant nothing at all. That was the worst part of it. Not the killing, but the months afterward, trailing him around from Madrid to Melilla and back . . . one reception after another, weddings, diplomatic parties . . . I thought, all the time, 'He's wounded but his pride won't let him show it,' and I tried to forgive him. I even made myself believe for a time that I had nothing to forgive. . . ."

Francisco scowled. He wished his wife would appear and relieve him of this impossible, painful situation. Only she seemed able to soothe Jaime, to calm him. Yet now, he knew, it was up to him to continue, even if he finally drove the boy from him by doing it.

Jaime was still talking though his eyes were almost closed: "I forgave him all of it, Father. I had to or I would have lost my mind. When they ordered us both back to the Oviedo garrison, that was the end for me. But he went without a word. I think that I understood then, for the first time, that he'd been lying to me all the while and that all of his talk was just to comfort him for having been such a fool all these years. You enjoy biblical parallels, Father. Recall Christ's horror when He thought that His disciples had deserted Him and that they'd only pretended to accept His teachings? Now, imagine how it would have been if it had been Christ who had deserted Peter, not the other way around. . . ."

"Jaime . . . ," and the tea spilled from the glass in Francisco's hand. Perspiration glossed the smooth, still firm skin of his face, and the wavering light of the coals accented the rigidity of his features. He struggled against the need to defend his friend, even from his own son.

"Remember what he's been through and don't judge him so harshly. The wars when we were first in Morocco . . . Abd-el-Krim . . . Enrique helped to save all of us then, after the massacre at Anual. You don't remember how things were in those days; you were only a child. He's seen bloodshed all his life, while to you . . ."

"Father," Jaime broke in with a sudden, unnerving gentleness. "This is . . . now . . . not twenty years ago. A man has to be judged today by what he does today. . . . I try to judge myself that way, and I must judge him that way too."

Francisco Mercader ran his hand across the strands of black hair that curved damply down over the arch of his forehead. He thought, absurdly, of the dinner he had arranged for the following evening, the guests so carefully chosen for his son's diversion, to draw him out: Ruperto Barcenas, Dr. Blas Aliaga, Sebastián Gil, even Carvalho's youngest daughter who was staying at the Toledo house while the Colonel followed his course at Oviedo and the rest of his family waited in Biarritz. He saw now what a mistake it had been inviting the girl.

He heard himself say: "Believe him then, even if you can't understand him, Jaime. You owe it to him . . . an act of faith . . ."

"That phrase has certain connotations . . . in this country. . . ."

Francisco drew a breath, held it until his lungs throbbed. Had Carvalho really destroyed what had taken him all of Jaime's life to build? Rather than return to Oviedo, Jaime had resigned his commission as lieutenant of artillery. Where once his son's most cherished hope, the affirmation of his manhood, and his identity as a Spaniard had been for success as an officer, now he had rejected it all with an unrelenting violence . . . all because of one week, one city. . . .

Jaime rose suddenly, stood towering over his still seated father.

"With your permission . . . I want to sleep now . . ."

"You should eat."

"I'm not hungry, Father . . . please . . ." He drew a deep breath. "It doesn't do any good to talk this way, believe me. I know you're only trying to help but . . . but we love each other . . . too much. Excuse me and thank you for being . . . so patient with me."

"All right," Francisco answered reluctantly. "Sleep then . . . be alone. Just like your mother . . . the Berbers are happiest when alone . . . silence, that's her most precious gift to you, and I can't match it with words. . . ."

"Thank you," Jaime said again, thinking of that quiet woman, gliding soundlessly from one room to the other with her delicately tinted veils trailing in an unfelt wind; lost, looking for her home but too loving to speak of it. Jaime had seen it in her eyes, that look of a frightened animal in a strange place. How was it that his father could not see or understand it? . . . Because this harsh plain between Toledo and Madrid was, in the end, his real home? No wonder Quixote had gone mad.

"I may go out again before dawn," Jaime said from the doorway.

"Will you be back by evening?"

"Yes . . . when the sun is down . . ."

"Good. There will be guests tomorrow night," Francisco said. "Tomás Pelayo will be here. We will want to talk about the arrangements for the oil department, the loans, and who will head the office. Think about it tomorrow, Jaime. Also, I think, he wants to talk to you about Luis."

"His son? I haven't seen the boy in four years."

"He's no longer a boy even if he's not yet quite a man either. Tomás is very worried. Luis has gone to the Monastery of San Pedro with the intention of becoming a monk. Tomás is afraid for him, of what may happen if there's trouble."

"Why should he be afraid? Tomás supports the Government, and certainly the government is not going to go about burning monasteries."

Francisco held back, knit his fingers. "Tomás is concerned, nevertheless. He is convinced that the Government will not be able to . . . control its friends and then. . . . Talk to him, Jaime. Perhaps . . ."

"Luis and I were never friendly, you know that."

"Talk to him, nevertheless."

"For you, I'll talk, though what I can say, God knows. . . ."

Jaime walked back to where his father was seated and let his hands linger on Francisco's shoulders for a moment. Then he turned and entered the house.

Francisco remained alone on the balcony, sipping his tea.

FRIDAY, JULY 17: *Santander*

THE WATERFRONT OF SANTANDER had changed little in the half century since José María de Pereda had written of it. The Puerto Chico and the fishermen's quarter lay, a jumble of intersecting derricks, cranes, masts, ladders and cables, rickety bridges and rotting shacks, seemingly thrown in utter confusion at the end of the street. A long stone wall had been built to separate the rows of tar-stained buildings from the Mar Cantabríco. A drenching spray rose continuously above the ragged seawall and washed over the buildings that huddled by its edge; the salt wind ate away at the obsidian faces of the fishermen and dock-workers on the loading ramps and between the rails of the spur lines that crisscrossed the quayside, wore them down at last, just as it had eroded the headlands of the Vizcayan coast for centuries past.

The port of Santander, once the berthing place for stately galleons bound for the Americas, had been reduced by fire, explosion, and riot to a jumble of rotting buildings, slanting one against the other, over blackened piers and stone breastworks all of which seemed to be held together only by a tenuous web of nets looping down from windows, laundry lines, poles, and rusting iron gaffs. Beads of salt spray dripping from rope and cables caught the last rays of the dying sun and glistened ironically with a diamondlike beauty. The faltering light of a drowning sun flung up from the waves the silhouettes of a few last tuna boats returning to port, some riding low in the water, freighted down by a good catch, others floating high, almost off the surface of the ocean entirely.

From the windows of the shapeless fishermen's houses at the end of the Paseo de Pereda and from the *tabernas* came an ominous jangle of sound: the tinny voices of radios blaring, speeches, news, music, and now and then a single human voice, raised in fierce, angry song.

Guitar chords, discordant as barbed arrows, punctured the cacophony, and from the doors of the docker's *tabernas* came the never ceasing crack of mallets struck vengefully against the shells of a thousand tiny sea creatures. A suffocating smell of petrol invaded the air, mixing with the odor of decaying fish.

At the far end of the paseo, a circle of palms waved gently in the wind about a white fountain which sent up plumes of water in faint blue and white jets. Shadows rippled across the iron-balconied faces of the even, five-story buildings that lined the paseo up to the angle where the Puerto Chico and the fishermen's quarter began. A barrier, unpassed and unpassable; strolling couples moved like tiny dolls along the water's edge beyond the circle of palms.

The coming of the Republic had changed nothing, and few thought that its passing would mean more than a spit in the wind either.

In the back corner of the Taberna de las Ballenas, a man of about sixty sat alone, his short, ragged white beard stained by the juices of the *percebes* he was methodically cracking against a round wooden anvil on the table before him. A plate of half-eaten boiled crabs lay near his elbow and a glass of white wine, untouched, stood by the half-empty bowl of barnacles. A black fisherman's cloak, threadbare and spotted with grease stains, enveloped him to the throat, and he held it there with his other hand as tenaciously as though it were the dead of winter rather than the middle of July. His eyes were set in a perpetual squint, and his high, arching white eyebrows gave him the faintly sinister look of a down-at-the-heels magician of the kind found at fiestas and circuses. His long face was dark and leathery beneath a disorder of tangled white hair that flared at the sides and gave the appearance of horns.

With regular movements of his right arm, he raised the hammer and brought it down hard, smiling tensely as the gray shells cracked and the sweet pink flesh was laid bare. After each blow he would lay the mallet aside and twist the flesh loose, slip it into his mouth and chew with a slow, revolving motion, at the same time reaching into the bowl and sliding another barnacle onto his anvil.

Only the muted ticking of his wristwatch anchored him to time and place. Every so often he would pause to glance at the dial and shake his head. Conversations flowed through the low-ceilinged room, as mechanical and meaningless, yet as inevitable as the tide lapping at the seawall outside. From somewhere in the rear, emerging now and then between bursts of static, came the sound of the Madrid radio; a reedy tenor whining his way through *"Mujer Fatal."* Abruptly the radio was switched off, plunging the room into the conspiratorial density of the fishermen's sullen talk and the acrid smoke of their pipes and cigarettes.

". . . the damned *Dato* . . . one good cannon and we could have blown her out of the water . . . ," someone reminisced. It was the kind of talk that one heard everywhere now; the past was becoming the present again, renewing itself.

"That's all history, for the angels now . . . ," another answered.

"I . . . I got away. I was the only one in my group. The only one . . ."

"Your group of what? That's the whole trouble. No damned organization. We didn't have it then and we don't . . ."

"Speak for yourself, Ramón. . . . What the hell do you think is going on now?"

". . . Oviedo, that's where *we* caught it. My sister too . . . the Moors . . . ."

"Let them try it again. Only once a fool, that's what I say . . ."

"Is it true about the *Blanco*? Hipólito says there are three thousand rifles on board her, from . . ."

"Don't dream too hard or you might not wake up."

"God's shit, man, you know, you just *know* . . ."

A waiter passed, glancing at the empty bowl. The white-bearded man nodded quickly, afraid to speak lest his southern accent betray him. He had had enough.

Again he glanced furtively at his watch, a fine gold Bulova. As he did so, a corner of his cuff appeared from under a fold on the cloak; a brownish-olive cuff of rough cloth.

Quickly he covered his sleeve and dropped his hands to his lap. The waiter brought over a plate with the bill and quickly disappeared.

The old man slipped a few coins out of his pocket and placed them on the plate, carefully holding the fold of the cloak over his arm.

A sound: the plangent whine of a bagpipe? The bearded man's forehead creased as though from pain, and he raised a fist to strike the sound from his skull. He thought . . . "Oviedo" . . . the one word over and over again until he realized that the sound was not that of a bagpipe at all but only the distant hoot of a boat in the bay somewhere out beyond the lighthouse rock.

"The bastards," he thought, raising the wooden mallet once more and smashing the last of the barnacles to a pulp on the round board. There was nothing there to eat: he had ground the shell into the creature's flesh. He left the mess on the board and stood up, shuffling his boots on the damp boards. It was time for him to go to meet Blasco Núñez . . . if Núñez was going to come. Fragments of shell littered the floor around his table. Beer froth gradually darkened the wood.

At a long table near the door a dozen other men sat, each one pounding upon his tiny anvil, throwing the shells over his shoulder. The atmosphere was stifling, full of sour cigar smoke and talk. Someone kept rambling on bitterly about the cruiser *Dato* and the landing at Gijón . . . almost two years before.

The foghorn hooted again. The bearded man lowered his head as he passed the long table but no one looked up. He was as filthy and as bent as they were and attracted no attention.

The *taberna* was near the seawall and overlooked the bay. The harbor itself was dark, a forest of masts, cranes, spars, and looping rope ladders. The spars turned mast after mast into a shadowy crucifix, a golgotha of crosses, rising from the waters in lunatic profusion. Boats rolled precariously, pitching on each incoming wave. The wind from the north had freshened, bringing with it a chill that ate through the thin cloak that covered him and through the uniform hidden beneath it, boring finally into his bones.

Colonel Enrique Carvalho y Davilla shivered, walked slowly along the seawall, pulling his cloak more tightly about him.

As a matter of principle he had refused to discard his uniform. His sole concession to caution was to cram his officer's cap into his trouser pocket and to keep the black cloak tight about him. According to the rules, he was a deserter. But it seemed to him absurd that such a thing could be; Spain, its army, had deserted him. That was the plain truth of it.

He had served his country long and, he felt, well. From the day that El Mizzian had first led his Kabyles down from the Riff mountains, he had been there. After the battle of Hadd-Allal-U-Kaddur at which El Mizzian had been killed, the young Lieutenant Carvalho had fought against El Raisuni, leader of the Beni Aros, in the "holy war." How like the present were those distant times, Carvalho thought bitterly, with the plump, wily El Raisuni now harassing the Spaniards, now siding with them against rival chieftains. What strange alliances; Carvalho smiled. The "Popular Front" before its time and just as ephemeral. How many times had Enrique Carvalho bled for Spain in those days? As a captain he had been with General Silvestre when Abd-el-Krim had turned the retreat from Anual into a massacre in which 15,000 Spanish soldiers had died. Escaping by a blind miracle, he had stumbled, crazy with thirst into the arms of a column of Foreign Legion troops headed for Melilla where the Moors were already gathering. He had been awarded the medal of the "Sufferings for the Fatherland" for his part in raising the siege of that city. He had fought for his king, then for the dictator Primo de Rivera, and then for the Republic. But now the Republic was falling apart before his eyes, unable to maintain order, unable even to protect those who supported it. Perhaps he had overreacted during the last few months at Oviedo, but that was something he could not cancel out. He had so compromised himself that he had only two choices now: to stay and fight for whatever the Republic might be today, tomorrow, or the next day, or to admit to himself that there was no hope and flee. No . . . at the Oviedo garrison he had had no choice at all. At Oviedo he could no more volunteer his services to the Republic than a wolf could offer to join the dogpack that hunted him.

"Stop it," he thought. "Stop it, stop it . . . ," angry at the indecisive old man he had become, at Núñez for having given him too much time in which to think, at his son Raúl, far away in Paris, for having pushed him still further toward the Núñezes and their kind, even at his wife and daughters for whom, so he tried to convince himself, he was now risking everything; and mostly at his daughter Mercedes, alone in Toledo, the product of his own "conversion," possibly the victim of it as well. Recognizing his guilt made it no easier to bear, but rejecting it would only humiliate him further, and that he refused to do.

Far to the east, on the outskirts of the city, he could see a dull glow rising from the smelting ovens at the zinc mines. The threatening light outlined dark piles of cumulus clouds which were now building up over the mountains to the south in the direction of Oviedo.

Would Núñez come? Carvalho looked again at his watch. *He* was exactly on time, but where was the other man? The spot had been carefully arranged through intermediaries. He became angry, cursing at himself for not dealing directly, for having to resort to the insignificant, worthless people who ran such errands for anyone who had the price. Above him was the appointed sign: "Carlos y Beltran—Export and Import—Coal and Cork." The wind that rocked the masts as far as he could see rose from the water and frosted his beard with droplets of spray, bringing a bitter salt taste to his mouth. The Altantic wind was chill and the gray-black waters oily and cold as the lid of a dead stove. A sheet of spray gey-sered suddenly from the thrashing waters, drenching a dozen small boats, then fell.

It was already long past time now. Núñez should have been there. Could the delay have been caused by a *Guardista* patrol? "No," he thought, "they're bad enough themselves, the Civil Guard, but the fisher-men and dockers with their scaling knives and baling hooks are worse. The Guard don't dare come down here, that's certain. . . ."

The thought struck him that perhaps Blasco Núñez had been there early, had not seen him, and had left. "Usually you can count on a man to be late, but *do* it and, by Christ's ears, he comes early." The Colonel cursed himself for his self-indulgence. He should not have lingered so long at the *taberna*. How could he explain that? He could have been dis-covered so easily. Two years before, his face had been on the front pages of every newspaper in Spain, and if anyone there had recognized him now, his body would have been floating well out to sea by midnight. Why then, he wondered, had he stayed there so long? And why the uni-form? Why, for that matter, had he chosen Santander rather than some obscure village farther up the coast? He no longer understood himself.

He began to pace, furious at himself for giving in to his emotions. All his life he had done things in a precise, careful way. But now, this . . . relieved of his command in Tetuán and sent to Oviedo, the one city where nothing he had done or said since 1934 could make any difference. The miners had long memories, and to them his name was synonymous with Ochoa, Yagüe, and Bosch, with the horror of the repression. They had been clever, his fellow generals and colonels. Afraid to take direct ac-tion against him because of his position, his respected name, they had nevertheless managed to get him neatly and quietly out of the way. "Sim-ply send him back to Oviedo. . . ." What could be more obvious?

Facing the wind from the sea, he searched among the hundreds of moored vessels, back in the shadows of the shanties and low buildings that spread along the waterfront. A jumble: boats, buildings, slanting walls, and streets, all twisted into an incomprehensible, inextricable whole; a microcosm of the whole country. "Order, order . . . at all costs . . . ," he brooded. "But whose order and at whose cost?"

How long had it been since he'd made his decision? He had been in Oviedo barely two weeks when Manuel Azaña had assumed the presi-dency in place of Alcalá Zamora . . . the same Azaña who had been hunted down and arrested after the '34 risings. How ironic it was; be-cause of Oviedo, Carvalho had begun his move to the Left, not out of sympathy for the cause itself but out of revulsion toward its opponents. Yet the very people to whom he now felt himself most strongly drawn still distrusted him because of his part in the Oviedo repressions, while his fellow officers rejected him because he had moved away from their old ideas of strong, conservative government, of order above all else. Carvalho had at once begun to make arrangements to transfer his family and possessions from his ancestral home in Toledo to Biarritz where, years before, he had built a summer house for his wife. Then he would wait and see what happened, whether the country would choose lunacy and death or reason and life.

Simple enough: his wife was there already, on holiday with his older daughter, Inés, and her French husband into whose keeping the house had been given. Raúl was safe in Paris, an attaché to Azaña's military mission. Which left only Mercedes still in Toledo where she had been quietly supervising the transfer of the family possessions and carrying on her own private course of study amid the ruins of Toledo's ancient churches and synagogues. Once the faithful Onésimo Ramos had left with the last truckload of household belongings, she had only to go to Madrid, as he had instructed her to do, take the train for Barcelona, and join the family at Biarritz. For all he knew, she had left already. Time was growing short; he could read that easily enough in the whisperings and dark looks of the officers at the Oviedo garrison. And all he needed was a few hours, a day or two at most. Then, let them all howl.

A wailing sound rose up from the black pile of buildings behind him, a real bagpipe this time. He clutched his temples, as though waiting for the explosions to follow as they had always done. God! To be haunted so long and so fiercely by something one had not even wished, had in fact tried to stop. He remembered his rage, his indignation, his outbursts against General Yagüe; but in the end, while the butchery went on, while the firing squads worked deep into the night, and the Moors raped and tortured, he had stalked haughtily away from it all, gone up into the mountains to fish in the trout streams. Alone, in the deep forests, exposed and vulnerable to any fugitive rebel who might pass . . . the same thing, in a way, as he had just done at the *taberna.*

The wailing sound stopped and a voice rose, wordless, coiling about the echo of the mountain bagpipe, so out of place at the border of the ocean. A figment of his imagination . . .

He paced the seawall, his cloak weighted with spray, stopping in the shelter of a fisherman's shanty to light a damp cigar. The flame finally took and as the smoke curled up, thick and bluish, he swore murderously.

Perhaps Núñez had abandoned him. What real claim did he have on the man after all? He had met him only once, on the beach at Biarritz; a courier between the Basque Marxists and certain elements of the French party with which Raúl had become involved, a messenger plying his trade in the manner of a nineteenth-century smuggler, his boat, the *Dolphin,* threading its way in and out of the hundreds of coastal bays that lay between Spain and France. A fishing boat. But which one among the hundreds that rocked on the black waters below? Would he even remember him, he wondered? He might mistake any large, coarse-featured man in seaman's clothes for Blasco Núñez.

It all made him uneasy. He hated having to rely on others. Only when he himself was in command, giving orders, directing things, did he feel in the least secure. To rely now on his son, on men like Núñez. . . . "Not even punctual . . . what kind of a man? . . . Look at the time." It rankled like a burr driven deep into his flesh. He continued pacing, his boots sliding in pools of oil, over the skins and flesh of dead fish, stuck in puddles of fresh tar.

A sharp peremptory whistle shrilled from an alleyway behind him; he turned slowly, an arc of sparks from his cigar curving in the wind.

A short, thick-limbed man in a striped jersey, grease-smeared trousers, a leather smock with a curved knife thrust through the ties stepped out into the phosphorescent sea light. The harbor glowed greenish, threatening storm. The Colonel had seen clouds that color before, over Gijón . . . pierced by searchlights from the cruiser *Dato,* illuminating the landing of General Ochoa's troops before the march to crush the rebellion.

Nuñez was precisely, frighteningly, just as the Colonel remembered him: square jaw, his eyes set too closely together in a slightly oriental slant. A pipe clenched between his teeth gave off a rancid odor and a glow that outlined the heavy bones of his cheeks. Carvalho recalled watching the man bathing with Raúl in the waters of the Côte Basque and again on the beach below the flower-tiled house at Biarritz. Blasco Núñez' shoulders and back were covered with thick, repulsive hair, almost like fur. This deformity had earned him the nickname by which Carvalho now incautiously addressed him.

"El Oso"?

The pipe vibrated noisily in the man's teeth; it was obvious that the name infuriated him. "Well enough," Carvalho thought. "It's he all right."

El Oso said nothing.

"Did anything go wrong? I've been waiting for a long time," Carvalho said brusquely, aware at once that his manner was wrong. He was totally dependent on this man, and yet he could not help addressing him in the same tone he would use for the lowest soldier in his command.

Núñez' eyes narrowed and his mouth crinkled in a malicious grin as though to say it was high time that the mighty, the colonels and the generals of this world learned a little of the patience and humility they expected from others. He flourished one hand, exhibiting an ancient, greenish watch.

"The sea air affects even the best of watches," El Oso said slowly, remaining where he was. His meaning was clear enough: the Colonel was to come to him.

Carvalho dropped his cigar and ground it underfoot. He stood there for a moment, staring at Núñez. Each man was waiting for the other to make the first move. Why had he deliberately angered the man at the outset, Carvalho wondered. To test him? Núñez had reason enough to mistrust him without his adding insult to the memory of Oviedo.

Reluctantly, for he now felt both debased and angered by the seaman's surly manner, Carvalho took a few steps toward him. The smell of tar steamed up from Blasco Núñez' clothing.

"That's close enough," El Oso said suddenly.

"You know me. We've met before. Use your eyes, man."

"I don't have as good a memory as you do," Núñez said. "How do I know for sure who you are?"

In answer, Carvalho let the cloak fall open, revealing his uniform. In the glow of the distant street lights his medals caught fire; he had worn them all: the red cross of Military Merit, the Cross of Maria Cristina, the San Fernando, the medal of "Sufferings," . . . all of them.

Núñez whistled, then seemed to reconsider. "Anyone could steal those," he said at last. His hand brushed the edge of the hooked knife.

"I earned them," Carvalho said, "with my blood. Now listen to me . . . if you don't want to do this, then just say so. . . ."

"Prove yourself, that's all I want."

Carvalho took another step forward. Blasco Núñez snorted and touched his knife again.

"I remember you," Carvalho said, "on the beach with my son, Raúl. . . . Your neck and back and shoulders are covered with thick hair. . . ." There, the insult again, but the truth. El Oso . . . but what other name was there?

"Colonel Carvalho then . . . yes, your name is well remembered here."

Carvalho drew a short, painful breath. He had been expecting that. "If I ever was what you think I was, then I am no longer. Times have changed. Men can change too."

"True, of course," Núñez said, smiling. "A convert? Yes, so I've been told."

The Colonel remained silent. This dark, shaggy man was his only way out of Santander; the wrong word, and he could be a body floating face down in the bay among the trawlers and buoys.

Núñez went on, his voice very low. "The holy fathers, may they rot in their own hell fires, they tell us also that the Jews converted once . . . a long time ago. . . ."

"And . . ."

"They converted, so they said, yet there were many burned at the stake. Many who said they'd converted but . . ."

"You don't trust me," the Colonel said. "All right. I don't blame you for that. How could I?"

"You're right there. . . ."

"And I don't trust you either. But do I have a choice? Do you? You have your instructions, man. Are you going to obey them?"

"One day, when there are no more colonels or generals or priests or . . ."

"May that day be soon. But if we stand here like this for much longer neither of us will ever see it. Now, will you take me or not?"

"I could just as easily kill you. It would please many in this city to know that Enrique Carvalho was dead. I could be a very big man here. . . ."

"You'd die with me, my friend." Carvalho touched the butt of his service Mauser and shook his head. "So, you see . . ."

Núñez squinted, studying the Colonel's features, anxious now to cut the conversation short. The pleasure of baiting the older man had evaporated.

"How did you get here?" Núñez asked quickly. "Were you followed?"

"Do I look like such a fool to you?"

"That's not what I asked."

"I drove . . . from Oviedo."

"That can't be true. . . . They'd never let you take a car alone."

"I had my driver with me. It was all very regular. No one suspected a thing."

"Your driver? Where is he now? Did you . . . ?"

"In the bushes about twenty miles north of Oviedo. I forced him out of the car at gunpoint and made him take off all his clothes. Don't worry, he'll stay put for quite a while, unless he wants to be the laughingstock of the garrison."

"All right," Núñez said grudgingly. "You know, I believe you. . . ."

"It's settled then?"

"Yes. Come on, the boat is right over there."

They walked together to the edge of the dock, then twenty yards farther. A small fishing boat with motor and mast, sails furled, rolled against a buoy; the name *Dolphin* was painted on its bow.

Núñez spat again. "That was a stupid thing you did, opening your cloak that way. How did you know I wasn't an informer? And it's stupid wearing that uniform altogether. You haven't been walking around in it, have you?" Again, the compulsion to humiliate, to revenge himself on the accomplice of Yagüe and Bosch and Ochoa.

Carvalho didn't answer but placed his foot firmly on the first rung of the rope ladder leading down to the deck. The smell of tar and caulking compound was heavy in the salt air. The deck was slippery with oil and the blood of fish.

"Get below, Colonel," Núñez said, emphasizing the rank as though it were an insult. "And it would be a good idea if you didn't mention your name. The others might not understand. . . ."

Carvalho turned; why was it that Núñez took every chance to bait and demean him? It was so clear: in Núñez' eyes he could never be anything but Yagüe's butcher. Núñez did what he did solely because of Raúl and the party, and that was all there was to it. Colonel Enrique Carvalho could expect neither respect nor loyalty from these men and, he wondered, was he entitled to anything more? Why should it have taken the bloodbath at Oviedo to break him loose from ideas at which even his own barely grown son had laughed behind his back? No, Núñez' scorn was not at all unjustified.

Núñez stared at him; the slither of ropes being uncoiled and the clink of small chains slipping into the water mingled with the lap of waves and the slap of nearby hulls against their moorings.

"Didn't I say get below? Do you want everybody to see you?"

"What difference would it make? Do I look so different from you? Am I on fire? Do I have a halo of flames? Thank you, I'll stay up here."

A motor began to chug somewhere below decks. The figures of three or four men could be seen, their backs bent, undoing the lines at the rear of the smack.

"Do what you want," Blasco Núñez shrugged, turning away.

Carvalho pulled his cloak around his throat and, in a moment's pause in the breeze, lowered his head and lit another cigar. The aroma freshened him; the tip of the cigar glowed like a cat's eye.

"When we're out of the harbor, we'll use the sails. You'd better get out of the way then," Núñez said.

"I'll know what to do," Carvalho replied. He had been sailing boats, far bigger than this wretched craft, before Núñez was born. He could manage a Moroccan sailing ship as well as any man in Ceuta or Melilla. As he closed his eyes, the thought of those curved, sword-shaped craft with their billowing shell-colored sails cut across his mind, a vision disappearing over imagined horizons sparkling with sun. How long ago had that been?

Slowly, the smack eased out into the Puerto Chico. Far off, as though from the mountains themselves, the bagpipe droned, then faded, its cry blotted out by the rising wind.

JULY 18, 1936: *Santa Cruz de Tenerife July 18, at 6:10* P.M. (*Telegraph*)

The Commander General of the Canarias to the Commander of the East Africa Conscription (Melilla):

Glory to the heroic African Army. Spain above all. Accept the enthusiastic greetings of these troops who join you and other companions in the Peninsula in this historical moment. Complete faith in our triumph. Long live Spain with honor.

General Francisco Franco y Bahamonde

JULY 18

In the face of the grave situation of the moment, the Republic, representing the Law, needs everybody. To her defense!

Heraldo de Madrid

JULY 18

A senseless and shameless action.

Part of the Army representing Spain in Morocco rises in arms against the Republic.

Ground and Air Forces, and the Navy on their way against the rebels to repel the movement with unyielding energy.

The political parties and labor organizations of the Popular Front, and the CNT react with unanimity against the infamous action of the "Patriots" who, abroad, betray the Republic with the very arms she placed in their custody.

Claridad

Evening, July 18: *The Mercaders*

From the landing, Jaime Mercader could hear but not see. He leaned against the banister posts, looking down the stairs to the entry hall with its bands of blue *azulejos* tiles set in the white walls. The entrance hall was cut off from view by the angle of the stairwell, and he had seen only the feet of the guests as they had entered one after the other. Now and then he passed his hand over his hair, smoothing it back, adjusting the shoulders of his stiff cotton jacket and pulling at the knot of his tie, hesitant as a child who is to be introduced into adult company for the first time. He felt as awkward now as he had in his army uniform the day he had first put it on. Time and again, he had decided to plead illness and go back to his room. What was the use, he thought, of going down there and spending an aimless, pointless evening. Among the guests there would be men he had known since childhood: Tomás Pelayo y de Suelves, the banker from Madrid; Pascual Soler, his father's lawyer and lawyer for Pelayo as well; quiet, eager Don Aurelio Aguilera de Tella who had just returned from a trip to Germany; and Dr. Blas Aliaga, who had once lived in Ceuta and now divided his time between his practice in Madrid and his house in *Los Cigarrales*. There would be others he did not know—a certain Ruperto Barcenas who was involved in the export of wine and cognac and a man named Marquina. The idea of meeting men who had known him for years, who still regarded him in their inevitably and unavoidably patronizing way as a "boy," troubled him even more than the thought of meeting new, unpredictable people. He had already assumed that sometime during the evening his temper would get the better of him, and he would give offense. The possibility of disturbing his father pained him, but what could he do? His father had brought it on himself.

Since dawn when he had left the house, he had not seen a living soul. Not even a single mule had passed in the distance on the Madrid road. During the course of a day he would normally see at least two or three aircraft overhead; not so today. Returning just after sundown, pale and streaming sweat, he had avoided everyone and gone straight to his room, sleeping for a few hours, then bathing and preparing for the guests. Now he touched his forehead, searching hopefully for a fever but finding nothing. His head was as cool as the blue-flowered water pitcher that stood on his bed table.

The smell of coriander and saffron floated through the house. Once more he pulled at his tie, squared his shoulders, and descended the stairs.

His mother's voice rose above the murmur of conversation below. The doors to the kitchen must be open, he thought. There, in the kitchen, among the steaming pots and the sizzling coals, his mother would find her voice, now ordering the cook Xaviera, now taking part herself; trilling laughter as she would cry out mysterious phrases in Kabyles that even Jaime did not understand, bringing down curses on an underdone chicken or urging a lemon sauce to perfection with a persistent clucking of her tongue. At all other times, she would pass through the house in silence, her beautiful high-boned face smiling out of a dimension where no words were needed to express love but only the gentleness of a look or the flicker of her dark hands against the white of the *jellaba* she still wore so often.

Jaime reached the bottom of the stairs and paused. He knew that it had all been arranged just for him. "To take your mind off . . . things," the cook Xaviera had told him that morning. Xaviera's stolid face had been already dark with forebodings of the meal to come and Señora Mercader's advent in the kitchen. Mistress of the straightforward, hearty Basque dishes that had widened her to her present girth, the cook had dire suspicions about the spices that Señora Mercader sprinkled so liberally over everything. She would cross herself protectively and mumble about spells and potions. Even the sight of the silver cross Jaime's mother always wore did not pacify her.

Jaime stopped in the corridor just short of the front room. He could not help thinking of the last diplomatic reception he had attended with Colonel Carvalho, in Ceuta, just before the posting to Oviedo had come. The new khalifa, the Sultan's delegate, was being installed that evening, an old yellowed man wrapped in yards of white cotton, bejeweled, his stained teeth set all evening in a frozen smile. "Remember that smile . . . go thou and do likewise," Jaime thought. He turned into the main room, sweating heavily and acutely conscious of his own acrid odor.

The front room never seemed quite as big as it did when there were people gathered there. In the huge, unconquerable spaces, each of the guests seemed wholly and hopelessly isolated. They stood, ranged about the room from the high, arched windows covered with Moorish faience to the stone fireplace, now cold and dusty with summer ash. There was a tension in the air which each of the guests seemed to be doing his utmost to ignore, as if even to acknowledge it were to participate in some unspeakable sin. Dr. Aliaga stood near the dead hearth, twisting the end of his spade-shaped beard and flipping the ribbon that fell from his pincenez. He regarded the man next to him with the expression of amused tolerance that is the exclusive property of men who spend their lives watching the sufferings of others. "There's nothing so ridiculous," the doctor would say, "as a man in pain. Healthy, we pretend to be gods. Sick, we are utterly without dignity." Dr. Aliaga was not paying the slightest attention to his companion, though the other man was sawing the air with his hands and talking volubly and at great speed. The name *Skoda* emerged every so often like a small explosion. The second man was taller, younger, also wore a sort of goatee which made him look like a figure out of a Goya painting. He punctuated his discourse by enthusiastically slapping his palms together, pausing from time to time to translate the conversation to his wife, a handsome blonde Scandinavian woman in a bright orange print dress who stood next to him, pouting with annoyance each time her husband returned to his native tongue, a language of which she obviously understood not a word. Dr. Aliaga's wife, a heavily masculine woman of about fifty with hair the color of petrified wood, was busy listening to Señora De Tella explain what had happened to her in Madrid that morning.

Not far off, and visibly annoyed by the stranger's intrusive clapping, stood Tomás Pelayo y de Suelves, a small, trim man with a large round head and the expression of a disgruntled owl. His hair, still black by the aid of dye, was combed smooth over a domelike forehead upon which wrinkles appeared each time the name *Skoda* erupted behind him. The banker's usually placid exterior, designed to create confidence in others, was gone, revealing the face of a truly unhappy human being. That afternoon he had been to visit his son, Luis, at the monastery of San Pedro, a few miles south of Toledo and had been unable either to convince the boy to reconsider or to reconcile himself to the boy's decision. He had not mentioned the news that had been coming in over Union Radio from Madrid since the early morning hours. Several times he had been on the verge of coming out with it and putting it to Luis in the bluntest of terms: "Give up this absurdity or risk being a martyr to something that I, your father, know perfectly well you do not really believe in." The only people in the room who knew of his ordeal were Jaime's father and Pascual Soler, their lawyer, next to whom he was standing.

Soler, with the tact of his profession, remained silent. Soler was a compact man, both in physique and thought. He dressed simply, in black, and avoided jewelry of any kind. His face was square and healthy, his mustache trim, and his features of a kind which preserved anonymity rather than announcing an individual.

His fingers, tracing rapid patterns on his lapels, revealed his own particular distress. Having come to the dinner with hopes of concluding arrangements with Pelayo for the financing of his host's new fuel oil venture, he found both principals sunk in worry about their sons and in no mood to talk business.

Glancing briefly at Jaime, he noticed the young man's obvious nervousness. Had he heard something just now on the radio? Soler wondered. He wished that Francisco or someone else would suggest turning on the receiver to see if there was any news. All afternoon the radio in his office in Toledo had been broadcasting only popular music . . . "meant to buoy our spirits as the flames mount, no doubt," Soler had thought. "Well, they might have picked something more appropriate than these endless paso dobles. The Republic is certainly no bull—a steer more likely—though it may be going to the same end."

Jaime moved slowly into the room. It was as though a corpse were lying in the center of the room and everyone was pretending that it was not there.

It would be better, he thought, to find two complete strangers if he could; he would be less likely to lose his temper then. He had no desire to get into a conversation with either Pelayo or the lawyer. Both of them knew what had happened at Oviedo.

He passed by Dr. Aliaga and his wife without a word and walked across the room to the window where his father was standing, talking to a second unfamiliar guest.

Don Aurelio Aguilera de Tella looked on, waiting for an opportunity to intrude into the conversation with a remark or two about the pharmaceutical plant in Germany which he had visited. His wife, a stout woman of forty whose coloring was precisely that of Don Aurelio's beloved apricots, greeted Señora Aliaga's descriptions of the crowds of shouting workers in the Puerta del Sol that morning with gasps of excited disbelief. The mild, retiring Don Aurelio looked away, embarrassed by his wife's piercing voice. How was he to have guessed, surveying the placid orchards that were to form such a large part of her dowry, that she would become quite so irrepressible? He kept glancing back at Dr. Aliaga, thinking that perhaps a medical man would be more receptive. But Señor Marquina, with whom the doctor was conversing, would not let up for a second and continued to extol the virtues of Czech heavy industry at the top of his lungs. He, De Tella, knew better; the Germans were the wave of the future, clearly. "Once they're self-sufficient industrially, they'll get over their childish excesses," he was fond of saying. "No need to put on a show of strength once you're really strong."

As Jaime approached, Don Aurelio gave up all thought of joining in either conversation and simply held out his hand.

"It's good to see you," he said, and Jaime shook his hand in a perfunctory way, anxious to reach his father.

"Are you well?" Francisco asked, turning away from the man with whom he had been talking in order to address his son privately. "Where have you been all day? Out on the plain? Of course . . . then you don't know what's happened, do you? Well, it makes no difference. It will all be over before I can tell you. . . ." Francisco began to speak very rapidly, still keeping his voice low. "We've had reports of some trouble in Morocco. General Franco, they say, was on the radio before dawn with some kind of proclamation of rebellion but Madrid assures us that no one on the mainland is involved. . . ." Despite what Madrid radio said, there were rumors that Cádiz, Córdoba and even Jerez had been taken by rebel army units and Civil Guard. The entire south was said to be in arms. Jaime stared at his father in horror as the story unfolded. He had known all along that it was coming, but with that same incredible suspension of truth that enables men to avoid recognizing the fact of death, he had never believed that it would actually arrive.

At that moment the man standing next to Francisco broke in cheerfully: "There are also rumors that the garrison at Sevilla has been overcome. Can you imagine it? At Sevilla? But . . . of course . . ."

"Señor Ruperto Barcenas," Francisco said, "my son . . ."

Barcenas extended his hand but Jaime was barely aware of the contact.

"Don't be concerned," Barcenas said, "it will all be over quickly. It's nothing at all. . . ."

But Jaime was not listening; his gaze was fixed on a tiny black and red rosette in the man's lapel. He felt a wave of cold discomfort. The corpses that had lined the road into Oviedo had worn rosettes like that too . . . corpses all dressed in new suits looted from store windows, their old clothes discarded in piles by the roadside; the empty trousers and jackets had more of the appearance of humanity than the stiff bodies of their former owners turning blue in the cold rain slanting in from the Mar Cantabríco.

Jaime moved quickly to his father's side as though for protection.

Barcenas was a head taller than Jaime's father though about equal in height with Jaime himself. His head was a trifle too large for his body, and his chin jutted out assertively. His eyes were narrow, his brows heavy, and he squinted unhappily into the smoke from the curved briar pipe clamped between his teeth. Despite the warmth of the evening, he wore a woolen sweater of contrasting color beneath a tweed jacket of discernably English cut. Barcenas' Spanish, too, was colored by a trace of the English accent which he had absorbed from his associates in London and Manchester at the other end of his cognac business. He went on, in a nasal voice of wide tonal compass.

"Yes, yes, your father's told me a good deal about you."

Jaime stiffened and Don Aurelio coughed discreetly, thinking that perhaps it was a good time to mention the excellent apricot crop in his orchards this year. He, too, knew what had happened to Jaime and how the young man would react if it were made the subject of discussion.

Barcenas puffed on his pipe and said quickly: "You are . . . an officer in the army . . . the artillery . . . isn't that it? Well, an excellent time to be home, I'd say . . ."

"I *was* in the army. No longer."

"Oh . . . ? So very young to be retired." Barcenas winked and was surprised to see Francisco return his smile with a scowl. "So many were retired in '31 . . . you don't look old enough for that."

"He resigned," Don Aurelio offered. "That's all. . . ."

"Well, we all have our reasons."

"I had mine," Jaime said.

He glanced at his father. Francisco was already upset. A few words, and already an incident was in the offing.

Don Aurelio screwed up his courage and said a few words about his orchards. Francisco was relieved and even Jaime could not suppress a smile. He had always liked Don Aurelio though he had little admiration for the sybaritic life he led. Yet the man was harmless, inclined toward stupid ideas but too weak to ever put them into practice. In short, he was a kind, well-meaning man and sought to harm no one.

"When you came in," Francisco said, "we were just saying that the situation is becoming . . ."

"Unsteady," Barcenas interrupted, puffing smoke. "A bit like the market for our cognac . . . unsteady. Well . . . we've all seen it coming for months. Madrid is getting to look like a set for one of those American gangster films. But here, thank God, wise counsel . . . yes . . ."

Don Aurelio's eyes widened. "You should have seen it this morning," he added. "We were there, you know—on the way back from a week's visit with my wife's uncle. The Puerta del Sol was packed with workers. Oh, thousands and thousands, from building to building, and all shouting for rifles as though the Moors were already at the city gates. It was absurd but frightening, too. Of course Quiroga had given orders not to distribute arms to anyone and the duly constituted organs of public order and Azaña . . . *mirabile dictu* . . . supported him. I wouldn't be surprised though, if we had a new government by morning. My wife's uncle, Don Diego de . . ."

Jaime cut him off. "What you say can't possibly be true. If it were, you couldn't be standing there like that. . . ."

"Don't be so concerned, Señor Mercader," Barcenas replied. "We've seen all of this before, many times, even if you don't remember it too clearly. Of course, you were young then . . . but, believe me, it's all in the nature of things. You have to keep a cool head and try to evaluate it all in a scientific manner as I do."

"A scientific manner?"

"Yes, science. Logic . . . premises, or if you prefer, hypotheses, theses, antitheses . . . syntheses. . . . So . . . thesis: the military takes matters into their own hands because the disorder has become too great, yes? Thesis number two: that neither the Anarchists nor the Communists are fools. Well then, add a third thesis . . . a little irregular but necessary . . . that nothing whatever is done in the *usual* way in this country. Remember . . . the key word is *excess* . . . everything here is done to *excess*. So . . . a fourth thesis then . . . that the generals aren't fools either. Synthesis next. An even balance results. The Anarchists, both the CNT and the FAI, know that they can't win against the army and the Civil Guard combined and that they simply haven't enough equipment or arms . . ."

Jaime stared at Barcenas, amazed. How could a man wearing the Anarchist emblem in his buttonhole be talking like that? It made no sense at all unless the rosette was simply another affectation, like his English pipe and tweeds.

"Suppose," Francisco Mercader said, "that the army is not united in this? Suppose a portion of it, say a substantial portion, remains to defend the government . . . what then?"

"Precisely. You see my point before I make it. The generals, for their part, also are unsure. A rising is always a risky business. If they don't carry it off at once, if it takes time, then what? They may face not simply the government, however weak, but a real revolution. The Republic has many 'friends' who are not its friends at all but are waiting only for the right time to upset everything. . . ."

Jaime could not restrain himself any longer. "Excuse me, Señor Barcenas, but that rosette . . . and what you are saying . . . I don't see how . . ."

"This? Yes . . . in theory I'm with them. A little deceit. I do believe in the principle. In practice though, I'm afraid that . . . well then, you see, as I was saying . . . nothing is very certain, and everyone is afraid of what the others will do. So where are we then? Ultimate conclusion . . . no one can really make a clear gain from such a situation, so no one will move. Don't misunderstand me. My sympathies are all here. . . ." He tapped the emblem. "But logic compels me to admit . . ."

"Yes," interrupted Dr. Blas Aliaga, thrusting the point of his beard into the group. "That's all very well, but it has already happened, hasn't it? The generals don't seem to agree with your analysis or else they are all fools, which I very much doubt. So . . . what do you make of that?"

"Nothing," Barcenas said laconically. "Whether I'm talking about hypothesis or reality, it's all the same. In any event it will all be over in a few hours, one way or the other. As I say, no one can risk a real revolution, neither the Republic nor the army and one or the other will have the good sense to back down in time, you can be sure of that."

"Do you play chess?" Dr. Aliaga asked suddenly.

"Chess?" Barcenas repeated.

"Yes, chess. Of course you don't, do you?"

"No, I don't, but . . ."

"You see . . . and neither does anyone else in this country. Too bad. It helps a man refine his way of thinking. . . . It should be played more in this country of ours. But then that's our trouble, isn't it? We tend to perpetual *excess,* as you say. Too much emotion, too little logic . . ."

"You're wrong," Don Aurelio interjected, smiling good-naturedly. "Reason will prevail. What better combination than reason buttressed by self-interest?" He smiled, pleased with his choice of words. "Not everyone is implusive as . . . say our General Quiepo de Llano or your bomb-throwing Anarchist friend Durruti . . ."

"My friend?" Barcenas looked genuinely surprised for a moment. Then he glanced at the rosette as if he had never seen it before, and his mouth wrinkled in a sour smile.

Don Aurelio's good-humored expression changed instantly to one of consternation. He had not meant to say anything offensive. . . .

Jaime was by now flushed with anger. His father tensed, waiting for the explosion he knew was coming and which he was powerless to prevent.

"Even a blind man hears a bull coming," Jaime said, "but you . . ."

Barcenas smiled with patrician forgiveness. "So young and so frightened. Listen, young man, a word of advice . . ."

"I've had a great deal of advice in the last two years."

"Not mine. Not my advice. Mine is good, solid—the result of scientific observation, logical deduction . . ."

". . . in a country that burns people alive to cure them of heresy?"

"Come now . . . that was a long time ago . . ."

"As long ago as fifteen months. I saw it, so don't tell me about it. Priests hung up by their heels from lampposts and burned alive, and miners doused with kerosene and a match set to them. You couldn't possibly understand . . ."

Barcenas' eyes glittered, within each iris a point of fear as precise as a nailhead. Jaime knew it all . . . the old fear of doing anything, a terror of any motion, either forward or back. "Understand? It's you young men who don't understand, I'm afraid."

Then the words became lost in a deluge of sounds: the garbled voices of Don Aurelio, his father, Dr. Aliaga describing the man who had been shot in the foot near his office in Madrid the week before. The sallow Marquina and his reiterated syllables, "Sko . . . da . . ." Jaime heard his name called . . . was vaguely aware of speaking, first to his father, then to Tomás Pelayo. Old men, Jaime knew, standing about and testing the fabric of the air with the sharp edge of words.

". . . a nice balance. Everyone's afraid of everyone else . . ."

". . . everyone?" Don Aurelio, forever hesitant except in the matter of apricots.

"Yes . . . if you see how neatly it all . . ."

Barcenas, distracted: "We'll crack the English market with our cognac just as we have with our sherries . . ."

"I, myself . . . you? All of us here?" Pelayo said, catching the tail of a conversation, misunderstanding.

"We? Well . . . we have nothing to do with it. We can only observe and chart our courses as best we can . . ."

I've been in Madrid all week, with Señor Kovarovic who was good enough to accompany me . . . he's lodged in the hotel just down from the Ritz . . . and . . . yes, all week, and we can't get in to see anyone. I'm simply amazed at their stupidity . . . there are so many things to be done, and they insist on doing them all in the oldest way possible, the least efficient . . . now you, Señor Pelayo . . . Francisco tells me that you have the automobile of the assistant minister of labor and perhaps . . ."

Soler, chiding the cognac dealer: ". . . don't you feel . . . impotent?"

"Strange choice of words . . ."

Dr. Aliaga coughed, put on his best clinical expression.

". . . helpless then . . . ?"

"Helpless? To do what?"

"To do . . . anything . . ."

"We do . . . by doing nothing . . . which is all we *can* do . . . ," Soler said.

"Who can . . . then?" Don Aurelio's smooth face wrinkled in confusion.

"Why . . . ?"

"Someone must be able to do something . . . certainly . . ."

"Not true at all," Dr. Aliaga said, replying to a remark dropped by Augustin Marquina. "Contrary to what you obviously believe . . . a revolution is the last thing that the Leftists want . . . look at how successful they've been with their other tactics . . . why, they're becoming civilized, . . . just like us. . . ."

"A revolution will accomplish nothing here . . . we're not Russians. We can solve our problems without murdering half our population. . . ."

"But what else," said Barcenas, "will clean away five hundred years of . . ."

Jaime stood there, sweating, trying to shake loose, feeling that if he remained another minute he might start smashing things. If he could only survive the dinner, he would find some excuse to go up to his room, even if he had to feign sickness.

". . . sunstroke?" He heard his father speak, then felt a slide of fingers across his forehead. "No, it's cool . . ." A whisper, "Jaime, you're sweating horribly . . . are you all right?"

Jaime shook off his father's arm, turned, his head down. The pattern on the carpet beneath his feet, swirls of yellow across which diagonals of red diamonds paraded with military precision, began to move, and he could not keep his eyes focused.

"Why do you subject me to this?"

"You must not allow yourself . . . control . . . come, we'll talk to Pelayo about financing the fuel oil subdivision . . ."

Jaime stared at his father, incredulous. But it wasn't his father's fault. The men in the room, his father among them, simply did not share his world of experience, and he knew he could neither expect them to sympathize with his concerns nor understand how it was that they, in all their innocence, had created what was, to him, a horrifying and mad world. As easily expect a country priest to comprehend an artillery ballistics problem or a Moroccan foot soldier to fathom Christian theology. Even if they had once known, he thought, then they've forgotten. . . . Known what? How to act . . . like men . . . imperative to act, yet how could a man act when he was surrounded by those who perpetually took refuge in their own helplessness? Which was worse, to act without reason or, through reason, not to act at all? One as pointless as the other, he knew, and equally as destructive. And now this room full of old men, each embellishing his impotence with carefully turned phrases. "But," he thought, "some do move and force us to move too . . . who are *they* and from what do *they* draw their strength? . . . my God . . ."

Jaime caught a shuttling movement by the entrance, between the flanking bookshelves full of uncut Unamuno and well-thumbed novels by Alarcón y Ariza, Pereda, Palacio Valdés, and Bazán.

A large, flaccid man of about fifty, dressed in a rumpled suit of black linen entered the room, two women close behind him and almost obscured by his wide shadow. On his right arm, Jaime noticed a black band of mourning. In his narrowed eyes, sloping down at the outer corners, a startling look of pain was lodged.

The man paused, hesitant to subject himself to the indignity of such company, then entered, his head lowered in resignation. The skin over his high, balding head was reddened in patches, his black moustaches the only luxuriance left on what must once have been a floridly vigorous face. Cheeks slack, his sideburns almost down to his jawbones in the style of the old military etchings in Sandol's *Enciclopedia Española,* his true expression seemed hidden. His clothing hung loosely on him, and he gave the impression of a man who has begun to melt away without even noticing it; in time there might be nothing left of him at all. Jaime recognized him without ever having seen him before: Sebastián Gil, proprietor of a shop in Toledo where phonograph records and electrical parts might be purchased, the husband of Alicia Sandoval, the pianist, whom Jaime remembered being taken once to hear as a child. The arm band—had she died then? When? His father had not mentioned it.

"Sebastián . . . ," Francisco moved to greet him, his hand extended.

"I'm late," Gil said. "The trip was difficult for me . . . the car . . ."

"Don't pay any attention to him," said the young woman to his left, "he's just making excuses for me. I wasn't dressed when he came for us, so he had to wait. . . ."

"Mercedes . . . Señorita Carvalho . . . ," Francisco cast a quick, nervous glance at Jaime.

"Who would not wait," Dr. Aliaga said, with half-irony, "for such a beautiful one? . . . a lovely woman may always take her time without fear of reproach. . . ."

"The truth is," the girl said, a barely concealed edge in her voice, "that it was announced that Ibarruri was to make an address on the radio at nine-thirty, and I wanted to hear her, that's all. 'La Pasionaria' won't tell us the truth about what's happening either, but her untruths will at least be in the opposite direction so that one may get some ideas of what's really going on by striking a balance. . . ." She laughed suddenly and, Jaime thought, harshly. "But she was late, so very late, that I just couldn't keep Señor Gil waiting any longer, so I gave up and went down to the car. What a waste of time. . . ."

Jaime started to move back toward the fireplace. Carvalho? It was impossible. He would have remembered her. . . . The Colonel's daughter? There were two of them. One was married to a Frenchman named Luccioni, an agronomist whom the Colonel detested. They lived permanently at the house in Biarritz, and the Colonel was forever grumbling about the greenhouse the man had built and the smell of his soybean plants. Then it had to be the other, the youngest one. No, he'd met her two years before, and this was not the same girl. . . . He closed his eyes, caught up in a rush of images and remembered sounds: the lobby of the Palace Hotel in Madrid, the concierge in his stiff carapace of a jacket, the porters drifting by in their gray uniforms; from the back of the main lobby, the elevator operator's sonorous voice, calling off the floors as the gilt cage slid up its web-work of cables; the muted whine of a string orchestra, the waltz from Lehar's *Eva* . . . the room in the rear, down the forked corridor where the wedding guests had assembled. He himself, Lieutenant Mercader, fidgeting with his white gloves and waiting for his Colonel to arrive. Anxious to return to the ferment of the Puerta del Sol, now sealed off by the hotel's granite walls, the musty velvet draperies, and the curtain of notes flung up by the violinists and the young pianist who played with his gloves on. The Colonel's entrance, recognition, a few words of introduction . . . Major Figuera, and Colonel Hirsch, all acquaintances of Carvalho's friend Valle-Riestra, the bride's father . . . impossible to recall their faces now . . . the girl's mother, covered with black lace, a high comb rising from abundant hair, a woman as imperious as the Colonel but not half as imposing. Behind her, a plump, blandly pretty girl, no more than seventeen, eager and full of absurd, foolish questions. Jaime tried to sharpen the blur of faces, superimpose that one image onto the stronger, leaner face of the young woman now advancing toward him across the room, but the faces did not match at all. The girl at the Valle-Riestra wedding only two years before had been all too aware of her own ignorance, had tried to hide it by being cheerfully impudent. Her hair, he remembered, had been done up in imitation of her mother's perilous coiffure, and she had toyed with her fan until her father's angered gaze had finally caused her to snap it shut. But this young woman before him breathed a quiet firmness. Her blue-black hair was pulled tight away from a high forehead and clasped severely at the nape of her neck. Her eyes were wide, slightly larger than they should have been, and heavy lidded, her expression redeemed from sullenness only by the upturned corners of her mouth. Her nose was perfectly arched, and her cheek bones rose high almost to the corners of her eyes, softly shadowed.

She held out a hand to Dr. Aliaga. As he brushed his fingers in a parody of a bow, the man with the mourning band coughed and looked displeased.

Don Aurelio, gentle as ever, touched the doctor on the shoulder and smiled approvingly. The two men laughed as the others advanced to greet her. Only Jaime hung back, but in a moment he had been propelled forward by his father.

"You haven't seen each other in quite a while, have you?" Francisco said, his voice touched by a note of special pleading.

Jaime replied under his breath. "It was two years ago, father . . . We'll talk about this later . . ." Then, aloud: "Excuse me Señorita Carvalho . . . I hardly recognized you."

He suffered himself to be introduced, held out his hand and stiffly brushed the girl's fingers. How could his father, knowing how he felt, have done such a thing to him? He felt as confused by events as poor Pelayo who was still muttering about his son in the monastery.

"He really doesn't remember me," Mercedes Carvalho said lightly. "Should I be insulted?" The older woman who had come in with her adjusted her shawl and coughed nervously into her hand, then sat down without a word in a corner near another bookcase.

The two young people stared at each other. "Where," thought Jaime, "is the resemblance? She looks no more like her father . . . than I do like my own."

They stood there, he with a brooding, resistant silence, she with an amused and scarcely concealed curiosity. Mercifully, an argument erupted a few feet away, and they both turned toward it.

"Not all of the financial interests are with the CEDA," Dr. Aliaga was saying. "Take Señor Pelayo, for example . . . you don't mind, do you, Tomás? With all the funds at his command . . . and our host too, with his new oil interests, they're still with the government. However bad it may seem now, it's better than what we had. That's the point we can't forget. You can't improve things by tearing down everything the second it doesn't go exactly the way you'd like. That's what the Anarchists have got to learn, just as well as the Right. No . . . now is the time for us to compromise our differences and recognize our common interests in the face of . . ."

". . . never should have allowed women to vote . . . that's what's caused all of this. Without them, the priests would never have gotten back into the saddle . . ."

Pelayo was heard to mutter something at the mention of the "cura." He looked for a second with beseeching eyes at Jaime as though to find in the young man's face some understanding for the plight of his own son. Jaime did not turn away his glance. It was clear that the man wanted to talk to him. After dinner perhaps . . .

"Women?" Mercedes was saying. "It's so easy to blame everything on us instead of yourselves, isn't it? One election and it's all the women's fault."

"He didn't mean *you*. Of course, it was the vote of women like you that helped bring the Republic back to its senses last February," Dr. Aliaga interrupted smugly. His slit eyes winked behind his pince-nez, giving him an uncommonly conspiratorial look.

"If only," Mercedes said, "you'd all given us something to vote *for* instead of simply something to vote *against* . . ."

"The señorita's meaning? I don't understand," Barcenas said.

"Only that we voted . . . *I* voted, and I can only speak for myself . . . that *I* voted *against* what we had for the last two years, the stupid bloodletting, the disorder, the repressions. . . . Now, will you show us something better? If you don't, you men, where shall we turn next?"

"Magnificent, magnificent," Soler broke in. "Just like her father."
Jaime turned away. Like her father? Did the man know what he

was saying? He caught Pelayo staring at him, smarted under the man's understanding gaze.

Jaime was barely listening; they were talking now about the murder of the *Asalto* officer Castillo. Soler had been at the funeral and was describing it with grand oratorical flourishes. His sympathies lay with the Left, as did those of every man in the room, but he had no patience with their ceremonial excesses any more than he did with the pomposities of the Right. Jaime looked away. He saw in that room a pitiful assemblage of well-meaning, self-deluded fools, full of the echoes of their beliefs but lacking the will to turn those beliefs into acts. Don't they care? Jaime wondered. Or is it that they understand their impotence only too well and are simply trying to fool each other with this show of indifference? Knowing his own imperfections, Jaime had from childhood struggled to find the redeeming element in every man, even as he had tried to find some way to forgive Carvalho for his betrayal . . . perhaps, he realized, as a kind of insurance against the day when he, too, would betray himself . . . but now, he despaired of discovering anything at all.

His mother entered and became at once the center of attention. She gave Jaime a furtive smile, and he nodded quickly in thanks as she began to guide the guests away toward the dining hall, taking the Carvalho girl first. Francisco, disturbed and confused by his son's behavior, lingered by the book-flanked arch and stared at him with imploring eyes.

"Have I done you so much wrong . . . again?"

"Later, father . . . it's not the time . . ."

Jaime, shamed by his mother's understanding, moved to join the others, following with his eyes not his father's movements but those of the girl and her duenna, Rosa, who were both just passing out of the room. The girl's head was cocked to one side. For a second she caught Jaime's eye. "It's only natural," he thought moodily, "I'm the only person in the room anywhere near her age." But then she shrugged and pretended to listen to Barcenas' wearying discourse on the meaning of the women's vote. An expression of disdain passed over her face; Jaime saw for a second the profile of her father, the same bird-of-prey shadow, the familiar darkness welling up behind the superficial sparkle of her eyes. Everything was as it had to be, as he had expected it to be. Colonel Enrique Carvalho was not far off at all.

The table was covered with crisp white linen and set with fine crystal that flamed in the light streaming down from the rows of wrought-iron candelabra on the walls. The guests ranged themselves quickly in what were clearly their accustomed positions.

The soup course was brought in steaming from the kitchen by the stout Basque, Xaviera. She eyed with longing the tureen in which the poached eggs swam languidly in the clear onion broth amid thick slices of the onions themselves, knowing that it would be the last familiar dish to emerge that evening. Everything else to come would be of Señora Mercader's devising, not hers.

Mercedes had seated herself across from Jaime and had immediately engaged herself in conversation with Gil and Dr. Aliaga. Nettled by her attitude, he leaned forward. He had hardly expected her to ignore him simply because he had indicated a desire to be left alone. She had measured him all too quickly, he thought. He listened as the guests continued their multiple monologues on the fate of man in troubled times, but barely heard what they were saying.

At last, Dr. Aliaga's voice cut through the babble. "Has it not occurred to you," he insisted as the cook began ladling out the soup, releasing clouds of mace-scented steam over the table, "that the murder of Robles may not have been simply an act of revenge but rather a planned act of provocation? That it would have happened with or without the Castillo affair? Consider . . . an excuse is needed to make the Right react in a way that it does not want to react. An outrage is required which will provoke an even greater outrage and in turn provide a pretext for revolution?"

Sebastián Gil shook his head. "We must learn to leave each other in peace. Then, given enough time . . . time . . ." he said. Then his mind seemed to wander, and he left his sentence unfinished. Mercedes' expression grew serious. Jaime tried to catch her eye but she refused to acknowledge him, and he felt properly rebuffed.

"Better the kind of peace we have at El Escorial, I'd think," said Dr. Aliaga. "That's what it will all lead to anyway, what with all this shooting and indiscriminate killing . . . why a man was shot down in the streets near my office just last week. A watchmaker, he was . . . had nothing to do with politics. He was on his way to visit his grandchildren with an armful of presents for a birthday party, and a car came by, and they shot him in the leg. A broken shinbone. Who knows why? So it grows worse and worse. The lion may lie down with the lamb, as they say, but not in this country. You should know that, of all people. One day, I'm sure, you'll open the paper and find that your friends have murdered each other right before your eyes. . . ."

Gil smiled insecurely. "Each of them knows I am a friend of the other . . . and they . . . respect each other . . . and me . . ."

"A fine respect . . . ," Aliaga said.

The girl broke in: "Why are you so positive that they must oppose each other? The Civil Guard, after all . . ."

". . . is reaction personified," said Ruperto Barcenas. "Just wait."

"They may yet stand with the Republic. They did in '34, didn't they?" Gil shot back, his face flushed.

"In '34 it suited them. The Right was 'the Republic' then. It's hardly the same thing now."

"Señor Barcenas, let *me* remind *you* . . . that at the same time, the same year, the FAI in Toledo *also* stood with the 'Republic' . . . at least, let me say, it did not rise. The Anarchists here heeded Torroba's advice and refused to make a bad situation worse. If only the Asturians had been as wise, we might all have been spared. Well then . . . why can't we expect the same now? The Civil Guard may be in the same position as Torroba's people were two years ago. Why assume that they have not profited by the lessons of history . . . ?"

"The only thing that we learn from history," interrupted Soler, "is that we learn nothing from history."

"Cynicism does not become a man of your learning, Pascual. Oh, yes, they're very amusing, your epigrams. Very clever. But look at it seriously for a moment. . . . What has the Civil Guard to gain by taking the part of the military clique? If they stand by the government, which is the soul of the country today . . ."

"Bravo, bravo . . . ," cried Barcenas, clapping his hands. Francisco Mercader looked embarrassed.

"I was talking to your friend Colonel Venegas, not about the Guard in general, and certainly not about the Anarchists who learn nothing from anyone. They are like children, and we needn't concern ourselves with their naive beliefs. So . . . ," Aliaga said, "too bad that Manuel Torroba isn't here tonight. We could ask him, and . . . being as honest as you say, he'd tell us. . . . Of course, he's intelligent. No one doubts that. The leaders are always intelligent, but there comes a point, remember, when the leaders don't lead anymore. They only think they do. . . ."

"He has control here. And Madrid has absolute confidence in Venegas. Just the other day the Civil Governor . . ."

"Until the first reverse," Barcenas said, as though he had not heard Gil at all, . . . "the first mistake. Then we'll see about this 'confidence.' "

"As long as order is maintained, nothing will happen."

Dr. Aliaga laughed and sat back. "That's just it. Do you call two important murders in a week 'order'? And how many others will there be like my watchmaker and his smashed femur? Why do you think I've come out here, away from the city? I don't want to join my watchmaker, that's why. Now look, an important *Asalto* officer, then a Calvo Sotelo . . . shootings in the streets, the Falangists and the Anarchists battling for a year now, and the great Prime Minister Azaña openly encouraging this sort of thing? Yes, this is certainly order. . . ."

Sebastián Gil regarded his soup sullenly and chewed back his words.

Francisco Mercader, from his place of command at the head of the table, intervened. He cleared his throat, hoping at least to restore order at the table. "He's right, Sebastián. It can lead to no good, these dangerous friendships of yours. Colonel Venegas . . ."

"Why single him out? Why not say just as well, 'It can lead to no good, this friendship of yours with Torroba?' Isn't that what you mean?"

"No it is not," Francisco said. "You know that I respect both of them, as they do you. But . . . you can have one or the other, not both at once. Can't you see that?"

Jaime could not help a faint smile. His father loved so to play the peacemaker, a role which gave him the greatest pleasure when the two sides seemed most irreconcilable. How fragile those "truces" were, Jaime reflected, and how helpless Francisco really was. Surely he understood by now his own weakness. But he went on, nevertheless.

"And can you tell me with any degree of certainty what Colonel Venegas will do if there's trouble? I don't know and I don't think he knows," Gil was saying. "It will depend . . . they may even find themselves with a common cause, he and Torroba. As for me, I'm not involved in that sort of thing. You know that. We simply have our evenings of music, that's all."

Jaime found himself staring at the girl across the table, seeing more and more strongly the image of her father impressed on her features. "That look in the eyes. Perhaps he has actually told her. But she hasn't said a word to me about him. That's important. If she doesn't know what happened, then she would have asked me why it was that I was here while he was . . . in . . . Oviedo." He felt a curious relief. If she did know, then he would be able to talk to her, perhaps even to discover some clue to her father's behavior. And if he dug long and hard enough there might be . . . just possibly might be a reason, an explanation, something that would enable him to forgive and at the same time would restore both his lost faith in the man and his faith in himself. For a moment, he caught a clear glimpse of himself as a man not so much tortured by the destruction of his faith in others but outraged by the simple fact of his own betrayal. In seconds, his inner vision had dimmed, and he shook himself loose of the awful implications of that revelation.

He looked frantically about the table. The *tadjin* was steaming before him. He had not even seen it placed there . . . great chunks of lamb and prunes covered with an aromatic white sauce. Compliments on the food flowed about the table as the wine was brought in.

The girl's voice kept distracting him, even though she did not address one word to him throughout the dinner but rather let him sit there, silent and sullen. Her deliberate avoidance began to anger him.

After the *tadjin* had been consumed and the wine had gone round a second time, Jaime looked down the table to Pelayo who had been trying to attract his attention. Pelayo's stricken expression left little to the imagination. There was no need even to talk to him after dinner. Would Jaime speak to his son, try to convince him? Jaime nodded; a few hours at the monastery, in a different kind of quiet, some time with another young man who had also turned his back on the world around him, for what reasons . . . ? It might at least provide him with another way to look at his own problems.

Pelayo looked relieved, signaling his thanks in a secret, self-conscious way, as though he wanted desperately to make sure that no one else had seen him.

It was strange, Jaime thought, how warmly he now felt toward Tomás Pelayo who, though he had known him for twenty years, had never been close at all, while he felt for Carvalho only a seething bitterness. It was, he knew, precisely that distance between them that allowed him now to feel such compassion, whereas with Carvalho it had been just the opposite; he had trusted the man and had, inevitably—it seemed—been deceived. "Trust only those you can afford to have become your enemies."

He raised his glass of wine up for the first time. Through the curve of the bell, he saw the distorted image of Mercedes Carvalho as she leaned toward Barcenas, keeping her eyes carefully averted from Jaime's side of the table. He seemed to hear her through the deep garnet-colored wine, as though her voice were coming from a sea—deep, full of muted echoes. He squinted; as she moved, ever so slightly, her image fanned out, lost all human shape. Only the profile, with her father's curved, hawk's nose and the same mass of thick hair curving like an armored cap around the skull . . .

He brought the glass to his lips. The *valdepenas* was sharp and bitter, and he let it sit in his mouth a long time before he took his first swallow.

"I'm expecting a new recording of the Mozart clarinet quintet on Wednesday," Sebastián Gil said. "Any of you who might care to visit me, why of course . . ."

EVENING, JULY 18: *Toledo*

IT WAS A CHEAP ROOM, NOTHING MORE than a large closet with a roof of tin and tar paper which still steamed and crackled from the day's heat. All around the building bubbled the sounds and smells of *Las Covachuelas,* the workers' district: odors of cooking, fat, the barbarous clangor of radios and of loudspeakers strung up from lampposts, the wires a hazard to the birds that flew about the streets in hunt of manure and a speck of grain here and there.

From the window, Anton Vitolyn could see nothing but lengthening lavender shadows of the Alcázar on the high ground of the city, cutting across the sun as it dropped heavily in the southwest. The street below was narrow, cobbled, empty of people. Everyone had retreated to the shelter of their hovels, their bars, and their brothels.

Vitolyn had nowhere to retreat but within himself, and he found that a poor refuge indeed.

He had taken off his shirt, but he was still covered with a cold, chilling sweat which oozed down continually from his neck, making everything he touched elusive and slippery. There was nothing left to take off. "My skin?" he thought, wishing he could strip that off as well. He rubbed his face in his hands as though to erase his features but his face remained the same: thin, emaciated, with a large, hatchet-shaped nose and an Adam's apple that rose and fell constantly along almost the entire length of his long, crane's neck. Once, he recalled, people had said he was the image of Karl Radek. That was before Radek had been branded a second time as a Trotskyite and a traitor. No one made such comparisons any more; they would have been in poor taste. But now, Vitolyn thought acidly, there was even better cause. He *was* in fact what Radek had been accused of being. The resemblance now was complete. He examined himself clinically in the mirror, taking stock of each feature, and comparing it not only to the image of Radek that haunted all of his hours but to the face of the man he had seen the day before in the *taberna* two streets away. How ironic that his own face should be his mark of Cain, and yet at the same time, and by the same absurd chain of accident that had led him to Toledo in the first place, might now be his salvation as well. He had always had an almost photographic memory, had been able to retain the complete contents of lengthy documents at one reading, had committed to memory long lists of figures, codes, and ciphers. His memory had been one of his most important assets, at least as far as the Vienna group was concerned. Now his life might depend on it.

A bottle of cheap hair dye lay on the table near the bed. An enamel barber's bowl full of reddish brown rinse stood nearby. His scalp tingled, burned in places as though eaten by lye. Now his bushy hair was the same reddish brown color as the other man's. . . . "Roig," he had caught the name . . . "César Roig." Vitolyn's skin, reddened by too frequent shaving with dull razors, had gradually acquired a prickly discoloration that counterfeited perfectly his intended victim's sun-scorched complexion. Only the eyeglasses were different—Vitolyn's rimmed with tortoiseshell, Roig's more austerely bound in plain steel. The resemblance would be very, very close, he thought . . . pleased.

He lay down on the lumpy cot and rubbed his sweaty back into the sheets, gaining little comfort. He wondered if the man Roig had any idea of what he was planning. The world, he reflected, is so full of stupid people who can't see what's going on right under their noses. Zipser, for instance . . . had it ever occurred to him that he was as good as cutting his own throat by allowing him to escape? Poor, trusting Zipser. It was an effort, but he managed to think of the man in cutting, sarcastic terms; it was the only way to avoid the crushing burden of guilt he really felt, even for a moment. "Scorn turneth away truth," he said to the ceiling. "But not for long . . . well . . ."

He lit a cigarette, one of his last; soon he would have to smoke the foul Spanish brands. Perhaps he might try balsam cigarettes; he had managed to fool himself about so many things, why not about cigarettes as well? *"Cigarellos Balsamico,* Dr. Andrews," said the advertisement in the newspaper. For a moment, he let the smoke swirl luxuriously in his lungs, then exhaled. Pushing aside the curtains at the window, he looked out. Across the narrow street was the house in which Roig was staying. He could see the window of his room clearly. For three days now he had been watching; the man's movements were astonishingly regular. Exactly at three o'clock each afternoon he would come in, patting his stomach from lunch, sometimes wiping bits of food from his lips with his handkerchief and go upstairs to his second-floor room. Then he would sleep until four-thirty; after which he would go out again, returning every night just after twelve. What he did, where he went, Vitolyn didn't care, though he knew that he was often at the El Bronco where he had first spotted him.

What more did he need to know, after all? That the man came home at three and slept for an hour and a half, drugged by his heavy lunch was quite enough. Between three and four-thirty would be precisely right. No one would notice; Vitolyn could never get used to the sepulchral calm that settled over the city, over every Spanish city he had ever been in, at that hour. Even in Madrid the streets suddenly became vast, empty canyons, inhabited only by the gray water trucks that sprayed away the morning's accumulation of trash.

And in the three days he had been watching, he had never seen a single visitor mount those stairs to Roig's room. How convenient that the curtains on the windows were only light muslin and almost transparent. Had anyone come up, he would have been able to see him. During those hours, between three and four-thirty each day, Vitolyn had sat by his window, smoking his vanishing supply of Austrian cigarettes and watching, each day more satisfied with what he saw.

The irony of it forced a laugh into Vitolyn's throat. History and the lives of men have such a way of repeating themselves, he thought, as though life were a film that one was forced to sit through over and over again until one went mad from boredom. He had once refused to kill and then had stolen to justify his refusal. Now, because of that refusal, he would kill without qualm . . .

"What a descent," he reflected, "from idealist to common thief . . . but then there's little difference in the end . . . a murderer, now there's something . . ." He could still hear Baumgartner there in the cellar, shouting about honor and loyalty until his walrus face was puffed and apoplectic from the strain. He could hear his own insulting laughter which had, in the end, so infuriated Baumgartner that Vitolyn had almost been killed right there on the spot. He recalled poor August Zipser again, Zipser and his mushrooms, and wondered what had happened to him once Baumgartner had discovered that the old man had let him escape on purpose. And what would they have done to him if they had known that he had really kept the rest of the money, not destroyed it as he'd proclaimed? It was just insane enough a story for them to believe, and they had . . . even Baumgartner who was normally a much shrewder judge of men. But he, too, had been confused. The order to silence Stoplinsky hadn't been of Baumgartner's making . . . "Poor man," Vitolyn thought, "yet, he had to carry it out. I wouldn't, but he *had* to. That was the difference. And how ironic it was . . . Stoplinsky had wanted a rising and, so, had to be silenced to avoid bringing the police down on their heads. Then the order comes from, God knows where . . . Moscow, or wherever such stupidities ritually originate. . . . 'Have a rising.' In the meantime, I steal. I escape, and there is the rising anyhow. All my reason for doing what I did, all Baumgartner's reasons for having humiliated me, all his reasons for wanting Stoplinsky dead, have suddenly been turned on their heads . . ."

Vitolyn held the cigarette out in front of him, the glowing tip toward his face, and gazed at it as though it were an eye he was trying to stare down. He smiled bitterly; Baumgartner had been right all along, and Stoplinsky wrong. The rising had been a disaster; Dollfuss had crushed it in days and sent the surviving "comrades" running for a dozen countries. . . . But *had* Baumgartner been right after all? No . . . "right" only because he was following the right order. "He'd walk off a cliff, that man, if the right person told him to. So . . . he was wrong, but acted in a way which was correct, as it turned out, while I . . . was right, but acted in a way which was incorrect . . . then, everything is reversed and wrong is right. . . ."

Vitolyn laughed aloud and returned the cigarette to his lips. Was Baumgartner still alive? For a moment, he felt a twinge of guilt, not over the blind jackasses who had hounded him out of Vienna, but over the act of having looted the party treasury. Had he really done it simply to prove a point as he'd insisted or had it been revenge coupled with—or even eclipsed by—greed? And had his theft cost lives during the rising? Perhaps, if the money had been there, all the thousands he had stolen could have been turned into rifles, machine guns . . . the disaster averted?

The tin box under his mattress, locked. So small, yet it contained so much. All of it in bills of enormous denominations. He tried converting the Austrian schillings into pesetas . . . turned the numbers over and over in his head. It was his now, not flushed down the toilet, not spent, not burned, as he had lied . . . and so life had become one constant escape. Nine countries had played him unwilling host in as many months. He wondered if, after the bloody massacre in Vienna, anyone was left to hunt him, if there was a man alive who even knew what he had done? Yet he kept running . . . and soon, he knew, he would come like a lemming to Portugal and the sea. And what then?

He had made his way to Spain deliberately, hoping to find a resting place, at least for a while, a place where he could regain his strength and try to understand what had happened. It had seemed so natural; at the time he had escaped from Vienna, Spain had been under a right-center rule . . . Gil Robles of the Catholic Center Party, the CEDA, was at last in the government, and each day the country seemed to be heading back more rapidly to a sort of somnolent authoritarianism in which Vitolyn could at least find shelter if not comfort. The Communist party was small, almost nonexistent. But no sooner had he arrived than the general elections had swept the latest of Europe's Popular Fronts into power and with it a resurgent Communist power. For the moment, in Anarchist-controlled Toledo, he was safe, but if civil war broke out, if the generals moved—as it was obvious they would sooner or later—then he would have to get out. He would have no choice.

It was his final chance; in each country, in each city, in each town, the process had been repeated: first he would arrive, gray, defeated, weary from his travels, and would lie alone for weeks in some bare hotel room, eating out of cans, mistrusting even the night. Then, when he could no longer stand the seclusion, he would venture out, timidly, knowing what the end result would be, but unable to stop himself. They would be there, the "comrades," the small, tight clusters, huddled together. They were never hard to find, and he would flit hesitantly about them like a moth about a kerosene lamp. Then something would warn him . . . and he would pack his suitcase and run again. Always toward Spain, the logical, only choice, where he could speak the language passably enough, where there was none of the dreadful efficiency that his own people applied to the hunting down of a man. . . . But it had all been a mistake, he thought. History itself was a mistake, or he a mistake in history.

He sat up straight, wrenched suddenly from his thoughts. Someone was moving in the hallway outside the room, heavy-footed and clumsy. He rose almost soundlessly from his chair and in one step had reached the bed. His hand went out to touch the butt of the revolver he had thrust under the bare mattress. He felt reassured at once; a bullet from it, with the end filed crisscross, could make a hole the size of an orange in a man's chest.

The sound of steps grew nearer. Two fingers, then three curved around the butt of the gun. He could feel another lump under the mattress—the tin box crammed with schilling notes; he was sitting directly on it.

The shuffle halted outside his door. Vitolyn could hear heavy, asthmatic breathing. He waited; if he did not move, the sound would depart.

Then there was a light knocking.

"Yes?"

"I brought you something," came a woman's voice from the hallway.

"Who is it?" Vitolyn said slowly, trying to pronounce as carefully as he could, yet slur at the same time . . . to make it very natural.

"María Florez . . . I brought you something . . ."

It was the woman to whom he had paid his money for the room. "All right . . . the door is open."

The woman pushed the door open with her foot. She was heavy, worn, so creased by work and worry that it was impossible even to guess at her age. The clothing she wore was dark and shapeless, a collection of fringed rags. In her hands she held a brown clay bowl from which a curl of steam rose, half obscuring her face.

"You looked hungry when you came in, so I brought this up for you."

Vitolyn stared at her. Who had asked her to interfere? If he was hungry, what business was it of hers?

"Thank you," he said, thrusting one hand into his pocket. How much would she want for it? The mess stank but how could he turn her away?

"No," she said, seeing his movement. "There was plenty. This was left over. You eat it . . . it's not much, but it will fill you up."

"All right," Vitolyn said. "I'll eat it . . ."

"Good for you," the woman said. "It's not much but . . ."

"It has a good odor . . ."

"A good taste too, you'll see . . . ," Señora Florez smiled. Vitolyn wondered whether she had singled him out for some special reason, whether she was really spying on him. He could not understand such generosity in the poor. It was something Baumgartner and the others had always preached as an ideal. To actually come upon it made him extremely nervous.

"Are you sure I can't give you something . . . ?"

"An empty bowl," she said. "That's what you can give me. I'll come back for it later, or in the morning if you want. Now eat. You look so hungry . . ."

She put the bowl down on the foot of his bed and laid a wooden spoon next to it. "I'm sorry, there's no table here . . . you see . . ."

When she had gone, he sat down, his head in his hands, the bowl of beans reeking on the bed next to him. He knew he would not be able to bring himself to eat; one spoonful and his stomach would explode in protest. Yet he had to have something. She was right; he hadn't eaten all day, and it must have shown.

He picked up the spoon, his nose wrinkling in anticipatory disgust. When he had learned their language at the University, read Cervantes and Lope de Vega, Calderon and Unamuno, he had never dreamed that someday he would have to eat their wretched beans as well. Now, for the first time, he thought he understood what Unamuno had meant by that curious term *abulia* . . . the loss of willpower, which he blamed for all of Spain's ills. But which, Vitolyn wondered, came first? The loss of will or the grinding poverty? He had no desire to pursue the question, only to get out . . .

He picked up the bowl in both hands, thinking to move it to the chair where there would be no chance of spilling the sloppy brown mixture on the mattress. His hands trembled; he was weaker than he had thought.

Pulling the chair up to the bed, he began to eat.

"*Abulia* . . . ," he thought, pronouncing the word over and over again until—as any word will do when mouthed repeatedly—it lost its meaning, became a garble of sounds, comic, absurd.

He ate slowly; the beans were very, very hot.

JULY 18
The Permanent Delegation to the Cortes met yesterday morning.

This Parliamentary Committee was summoned to approve the extension of the state of emergency.

El Sol (Madrid)

JULY 18: *Biarritz, France*

A STATUE OF THE VIRGIN ROSE SHARPLY at the end of an abandoned breakwater that Napoleon III had intended as the beginning of a great harbor. Silhouetted against the swinging beam of the lighthouse at the tip of Cap San Martín, it stood, above the wind-furrowed waters on a pedestal of jagged rocks like a pagan sea goddess, shadowy and unreal, alternately appearing and vanishing in the tunnel of light from the beacon.

Just to the east of the wooden causeway that led out to that mournful statue, the *Dolphin* dropped anchor. Núñez had no desire to round the Atalave promontory and come within sight of the bathing beaches and the Casino Bellevue. In the darkness of the Port Vieux area, with its three thrusting fingers of land and its rushing waves, he felt safe. Without lights, he could not be spotted.

Núñez pushed his cap back from his forehead and wiped away the spray that frosted his forehead.

"You can go ashore now," he said brusquely. "That's your house up there, if I remember." He pointed to the cliffs and hills sweeping up above the sheltered scallop of beach known as the Côte Basque. The outlines of the white Andalusian house with its Portuguese tile front were visible against a slate-blue night sky lightened now by a shower of stars and a full moon.

"You're not coming ashore?" the Colonel asked, surprised.

"No," Núñez answered. "I don't want to risk it. Not now . . ."

"And the boat?" Colonel Carvalho asked, nodding angrily at the rowboat then being lowered from the stern of the smack. Was the man actually telling him that he was to row in by himself?

"I'll pick it up next time we're by here," said Núñez, sourly.

"So . . . I understand you perfectly, señor . . ."

"You do? How surprising."

Carvalho could hardly control himself; the arrogance of the man was overwhelming. Yet what more could he expect? Though he had tried as best as he could to wash it away, the blood of Oviedo still stained him. Could he really blame this somber man of Santander for his suspicions and distrust? "Order," "discipline," the words flashed through his mind, and he held his tongue.

"Give my regards to Raúl," Blasco Núñez said. "Tell him I was glad to be of such . . . service . . ."

The Colonel turned away with a perfunctory nod and went to the rope ladder that led down to the rowboat now rising and falling on the crest of the sea below.

He began to climb down into the boat. One of the seamen held the rope steady. Water sloshed against his boots, and the smell of dead fish and tar poisoned the air. He took the oars, set them in their sockets, and held them aloft.

A gaff slid down from the side of the *Dolphin*, touched the rowboat on its side; a rope was loosened, and the two craft slipped silently apart. Enrique Carvalho lowered his oars, struck one deeply, angrily into the swell, and wheeled the prow of the boat around toward the shore; then he began to row, digging into the water as though each stroke were a knife driven into Núñez's throat. Was it for men such as these that he was risking his life, his position, everything he had built up in forty years of service to Spain? But there were others, the dead of Oviedo, those who would soon become the dead of Seville and Madrid, of Toledo and Bilbao, who also laid claim on him.

He continued to row, the strokes more rapid now, and the boat shot forward, cresting the waves which grew heavier as he neared shore. The heat of his exertions made him feel young and gave his anger a joyful quality he had not experienced for a long time.

Turning his head, he could see the lights of his house through the sea spray and the mist that rose along the shore. Damn his arrogance, but Núñez had picked the best possible spot to let him off. He would beach just at the foot of the gray wooden steps that led up the embankment to his house.

High on a hill overlooking the beach, accessible only by that long flight of splintery wooden stairs, the house itself was almost hidden among the stand of dark green elms which rose above a farther fringe of tamarisk that he had had planted there years before. He had built the house thirty years ago, just after he had married, to compensate his wife for the loss of the fresh Atlantic breezes off Cascais and Belém. It was to be her consolation for the African furnace heat of Tetuán to which they had been consigned and for the summer smolder of Toledo where the Carvalho family home had stood for over two hundred years and to which, whenever he could, Enrique Carvalho liked to return to contemplate his heritage and try to find that lost tie that had once bound him to Spanish soil. The house in Toledo was his, but the house toward which he now drove the rowboat was his wife's, really, and no part of himself. He had given it over to the keeping of his older daughter, Inés, and her French husband who tended flowers and raised hybrid plants in a greenhouse behind the rear gardens. It was their house and his wife's, and he came only as an exile.

Sand grated under the hull; he swung up the oars and let the waves thrust the boat onto the sand where it wedged firmly, the prow digging deep into the beach. The strength of his movements surprised him as he jumped from the boat, his boots barely making an indentation in the firm sand. He strode quickly across the stretch of beach that led to the stairs, thinking, "The devil with the boat . . . let it float away. . . ."

Climbing the stairs, again more quickly and with less effort than he had imagined it would cost him, he found himself wondering who would be home, whether his wife would be there alone or whether his daughter and the pallid Frenchman husband of hers would be there, too. Since his older daughter had married, he had been totally unable to communicate with her. Something the Frenchman had done to her, he concluded: infection of the mind. Always pottering about with his plants and smiling a condescending smile when anyone brought up the subject of politics, as if to act instead of to think was the mark of the barbarian. The day would come, he knew, when he would order Hector Luccioni out of his house. But Inés? What of her? He gritted his teeth and took the top steps with a leap that carried him onto the cliff's edge. He turned and at once looked back toward the churning sea. The *Dolphin* had hoisted sail again and was wheeling back in the direction of Spain. They had not even waited until he had gotten to shore safely.

He turned again; the house was closer than he had expected. He could see the blue-and-white tile facing—tile brought long ago from Lisbon by Francisco Mercader, especially for him, the result of a bad deal in cork which had left Mercader with credits that could only be paid off with such things as tile and ornaments. Mercader had made a present of them to Carvalho's wife, and with them they had completed the house.

The two front windows above the graceful wrought-iron balconies were smudged with soft light. Candles within, not electricity. Gravel crunched underfoot. He had forgotten that he had built a driveway to connect with the main road that led into the town proper. As he crossed the roadway, a dog began to whine, uncertain of the scent. Carvalho could envision the animal, his daughter's, but could not remember its name.

At the front door, he realized that he did not have a key and began to pound heavily on the oak panels ribbed with steel bands. He could hear the sound of footsteps on the stairs, someone coming down to the front entrance.

The bolt slid back and the door swung open. Against the dim light that flowed from the rear of the house, the figure that stood in the doorway was for a moment only a vague silhouette.

He let his cloak drop quickly to his feet. The woman, seeing his uniform, found in it what she had not been able to find in his face, the identifying mark.

"Father . . ."

"So, it's you Inés . . ."

"What's happened?" Her voice was immediately full of alarm. Of course, he had not had time to let them know he was coming, and it would have been impossible to do so, even dangerous. "We weren't . . ."

"Shall I come in, or do I stand here like a statue?"

The woman backed away, and as she turned the light caught her face, accenting the round, soft features; she was plumper now than he remembered her being. At least the agronomist was feeding her properly, he thought. That was something.

"Your mother?"

"She's asleep . . . shall I wake her?"

"What do you think?"

The woman flushed. At that moment there was another sound, a door opening, the shuffle of slippers on the stairs. Inés' husband, Hector Luccioni appeared on the landing. He was small, with the pinched face of a man twice his age but without the wrinkles. Heavy glasses, sandy hair from which the color seemed to have been meticulously bleached. He squinted, trying to see, turned on the flashlight he was carrying and swept its beam across the doorway.

"Tell him to turn that damned thing off," the Colonel shouted at Inés in Spanish. Though Carvalho could understand French and speak it after a fashion, he refused to do so in the presence of his daughter's husband. His one attempt, years before, had led to disaster, a violent fight over politics . . . violent, at least, on the Colonel's side. Hector Luccioni firmly believed that all the world's ills could be solved by developing soybean plants. The Colonel had given up; better to let Inés serve as a filter.

The woman, frightened, cried in French to her husband who immediately switched off the flashlight.

Colonel Carvalho scraped his feet, dislodging cakes of sand, and slammed the door behind him.

"Can we have some light in here?" he said angrily, aware that he was taking out on his daughter and the inoffensive Luccioni what he had been unable to take out on Núñez and his crew.

Luccioni, now at the foot of the stairs, began fumbling for switches. In a moment, the front hall and the main room were fully lit. The Colonel advanced into the living room, making damp marks on the rugs, his daughter following behind him with a frightened look on her face.

Abruptly, the Colonel stopped. Standing next to his favorite chair was a table on which sat an antique telephone. He waved once again at his daughter. "Can you get me something to drink? I'm exhausted. Brandy or coffee, it doesn't matter. And something dry to wear . . ."

She nodded. "Shall I wake Mother?"

"Not now. There's no need. She'll know about it all soon enough." He settled deep into the chair, his feet thrust out. He thought for a second of removing the soaked boots, then caught sight of Luccioni standing by the archway leading into the room, the flashlight still in his hand; the man was wearing a striped bathrobe that made him look like an escaped prisoner. Even behind the thick glasses he could see the consternation in the Frenchman's eyes. He had been careful to keep everything from them. How surprising his appearance must have been . . . risen like Poseidon from the sea.

Then the woman was back with a bottle of cognac and a glass, passing her husband who still stood where she had left him, uncertain of what to do, no longer master in his home. "Perhaps he'll run out to his hothouse," the Colonel thought, "like one of those rabbits he's always chasing away from his plants. . . ."

"A full glass," the Colonel said as Inés poured. "I've been at sea for a long time and it's cold . . . did you find clothes?" He drew himself up in the chair and took the glass, draining it in one long swallow. The alcohol burned fearfully. It stiffened him and brought him back to life. The anger returned to his eyes, and he searched for an object. Luccioni, still by the doorway, useless. "Harmless but useless," he thought. "Núñez, useful and harmful. . . . What a world. . . ."

"Tell him to come in and sit down . . . ," Carvalho said, pulling off his damp boots. His feet stank from sweat, seawater and fish guts; the boots he kicked under a nearby table. "I'm not going to hurt him. . . ."

Inés turned to her husband and beckoned him in. As he came slowly in he spoke softly, comfortingly to Inés and turned a reproachful glance on the Colonel.

Behind him, other sounds, another figure: Amalia Carvalho coming down the stairs, a robe over her nightgown. . . . The Colonel stood up suddenly as his wife entered the room. She stopped, her bland face suddenly flushed. Her hair was loose, her eyes ringed with sleep, crease marks on her face from the pillow. She was still a handsome woman, black-haired and firmly fleshed. But that damnable blank look . . . thirty years of it was enough . . . it was the way she had looked the night he had come raging back into their house at Ceuta only hours after Abd-el-Krim's final defeat, furious over the bloodshed, his body aflame with excitement. The night, he was sure, Mercedes had been conceived.

"Amalia . . . ," was all he could say and he said it almost angrily, as if he would have been happier if she had remained asleep. He did not care to explain, to sit and comfort her. There were things to be done that did not need women to listen. . . .

He walked across the room and took her in his arms in a firm, powerful way that said simply that he was there and that nothing more need be explained.

"I didn't want to wake you," he said softly as though no one else were in the room.

"I couldn't help it. . . . I heard noises . . . Enrique, I wasn't asleep. But how can you think that I wouldn't want to be wakened?"

"All right, that's fine, I understand," he replied hurriedly. "Now tell me, has Mercedes gotten here yet?"

"No . . . ," Amalia Carvalho's eyes opened in surprise. "I didn't know anything about that. She's coming, here? Why didn't she write?"

"She didn't write because I told her not to. She was simply supposed to take the train to Barcelona as soon as the last load of furniture left, that's all. Well then, has Ramos gotten here yet? That would be some indication."

"Not yet . . . I don't know what's keeping him. He should have been here by now. I had to clean out the whole shed in the back so there would be room. Why did you have to send it all now, all of it at once?"

"Forget about that . . . the important thing is, why isn't he here yet?" Carvalho said. His wife's voice seemed to irritate him beyond measure.

He looked about the room. "Do you think your son-in-law can get me Paris on the phone?"

"At this hour," Hector Luccioni volunteered in awkward Spanish, "it would be extremely difficult. The switchboards . . . the connections . . ."

"All right, in the morning then . . ."

"You want to call Raúl?" his wife asked.

"Yes, I do. I assume he's still in Paris, isn't he?"

"Yes, he's there."

"Good, then he should stay there. But I want to talk to him, about . . . never mind . . ." He had begun to formulate vague thoughts concerning his return to Spain. Not an hour across the frontier and he had begun thinking about going back. Not because he wanted to, but because there were so many things that could happen that would force him back. And if he had to go, it would be better to have some insurance of safety. How ironic it was that he should have to look to his son for such guarantees. Two years before, the boy had been on the verge of a spectacular political career; his patrons were seriously proposing to run him as a deputy in the next elections, certain of overwhelming support from the moderate Left, the *Izquierda Republicana*. Then had come the Asturian revolt and Oviedo. The name Carvalho had emerged stained with the blood of ten thousand miners, and Raúl had retired, bitter and brooding, to the Embassy in Paris. He had never forgiven his father for what had happened though the two never spoke of it. In Paris, in virtual exile, he had cultivated many important people, among them men high in the French Communist party apparatus. Now, in the time of the Popular Front, such friends could be of enormous help in counterbalancing the hate the Anarchists had for the name "Carvalho."

The Colonel slumped back into the chair and took another sip of brandy and pulled the blanket around him. How long would it be now, before the generals' rising? . . . a day or so, a week? . . . . He had gotten out just ahead of the dogpack. Had he stayed in Oviedo, the outcome would have been the same regardless of who had come out on top; either his own fellow officers would have shot him as a Republican or the Anarchists would have shot him for what had happened in 1934.

Luccioni was earnestly trying to explain how much better the telephone system worked in the morning; that was the time to call. . . .

"Well," Carvalho said, taking another sip, "that's what comes of letting the French run their own phone system. In Spain we're intelligent enough to let the Americans do it for us. . . . Yes, you've got to understand your own limitations and not fight against them the way you people do. Instead of batting your heads against the wall, let others do it for you until you've learned how. That's the secret. . . ."

"Perhaps," he was thinking, "Raúl can find someone to go back with me . . . Prunier or Lachine or even Saint-Luc. . . ." At any rate, the brandy tasted good. Better, he had to admit, than the *fundador* he was used to in Oviedo.

He rose, took Amalia by the arm.

"Now . . . I want a hot bath and then some sleep . . . wash the fish stink off if I can . . ." He stopped short, looked at her full in the face. "When Mercedes gets here, we'll have a celebration." He tried to smile. "We'll have dinner at the Chanticler and then go to the casino. What d'you say to that?"

She nodded, put an arm around his back.

"Now, all of us, upstairs and to bed," he commanded. As he passed Hector Luccioni, he held out his hand. The Frenchman, surprised, took it. For a moment they stood there in an unaccustomed attitude of friendship as the Colonel became aware that he really had nothing against the man other than his soybeans and his quiet ways.

"A good night's sleep," he said, as he began climbing the stairs with his wife . . . "A night's sleep for us all; then in the morning . . . at six, I think, yes . . . six . . ."

From the French windows that opened onto the narrow bedroom balcony, Colonel Carvalho could see a dark slice of sea and the solitary beacon at Cap San Martín. By turning his head slightly, he could also see, in a gilded mirror hanging on the wall just to the left of the French windows, the reflection of his wife sitting in bed, a light coverlet drawn up over the bodice of her nightdress, a cup of steaming chocolate balanced on a saucer which she held with both hands. She had taken the chocolate only to humor him, not because she really wanted it. The trip on Núñez's smack had chilled Colonel Carvalho to the bone, and in addition to the cognac he had taken two glasses of hot water and lemon to warm him. She must feel the cold, too, he insisted, and though he apologized to her for keeping the doors to the balcony open, he would not close them and thus ordered Inés to prepare some hot chocolate for her mother.

"Is it too hot for you?" he asked listlessly, seeing her sliding the cup back and forth on the saucer.

"It isn't that," she said.

"You don't have to drink it."

"Perhaps in a little while." She set the cup down on the nightstand and crossed her hands over her breasts. The image in the mirror was of a handsome woman with searching eyes, a vast net of still dark hair. How they could have enjoyed each other, he thought, if the times had permitted.

She seemed to be talking to herself: "If only you could find some way to speak to Inés and especially to Hector . . ."

"I know. I'm unnecessarily cruel with him. It's not his fault, but what can I do?" He began to pace in a tight circle. It had become very important that he see a light on the ocean somewhere; it was a game with him, since his childhood. "If a leaf falls from that beech tree in the next minute, then everything will be well the next day." He had proposed to Amalia that way too. They had been in Madrid, on the Castellana. He had said to her, quite suddenly, "If a blue automobile passes in the next five minutes, you will marry me." It had, and she had smiled and said yes, of course she would. He was only a captain at the time and stationed at Melilla.

If there was a light on the ocean, Mercedes would arrive the following day and everything would be all right.

"Hector is such a gentle man," his wife was saying. "I know it's difficult for you to understand such a person, but you can try, I know you can try. And Inés loves him, really, don't forget that. They're so happy together. If only Mercedes . . ."

The Colonel shivered in his dressing robe; the damp wind from the beach seemed to penetrate his bones in spite of the cognac, the hot water and his robe. If only a light would appear out there, a passing sailboat, even an airplane would do. He longed for his younger daughter with a longing which was at that moment intensely physical. Had he done the right thing? Now he had begun to doubt. During the years of the Rivera dictatorship, years which saw the Socialists cooperate with a military junta and the ideas of reform, of meaningful change become twisted until he could no longer recognize them, he had dreamed of the coming Republic. And when the Republic finally arrived, he had sworn loyalty to it in a way which seemed now to have ignored so many realities. He would serve the Republic regardless of whether he agreed with what those in power at the moment were doing. It was the Republic itself, abstract, supervening, which compelled his loyalty. "That's what it's all about," he had tried to explain to Raúl after the '34 repressions. "The idea of elections, of rule by free choice. The people have chosen to go this way for the time being, and it's not up to us to say no. After all, you can't believe in democracy only when the particular results please you." No, Raúl did not see. The Colonel's adherence to that abstract notion had ruined the young man's political fortunes and turned him toward stricter disciplines and the French Communists who hung around the Paris Embassy. The Colonel had once overheard Mercedes trying to explain him to her brother. How proud of her he had been, so proud that he had not dared mention to her that she had been overheard. "He's a Republican above all else," she had said. "That's his faith and that, by his definition, implies constant compromise with those who are in power at the moment. That 'compromise' is an article of the faith just as much as the Trinity is an article of Catholic faith. You've got to believe in some things that you can't understand, even you, Raúl. . . ."

In '34 the Colonel hadn't approved of the results of the elections either, of the resurgence of Rightist power, but it had not been up to him. It was true, the Left hadn't made much of its opportunities and perhaps the people were correct in returning a right-wing majority. The important thing was that there were elections and would continue to be elections. He had even defended the Asturian repressions once, shouting at his son and hurling a glass paperweight against the wall of his room. "You can't revolt simply because you don't like the results of elections. Oh, it's all very well and good when things go your way, but if the elections go against you, then the Fascists have subverted things, is that it? Well, damn them all, if anyone's subverted things its been the Left, by their own incompetence. And now, you have the gall to defend them?"

"What are you looking for," his wife said, her voice very calm and conciliatory. If only she did not love him as much as she did. It was a burden on him now because he felt he could never return that love. He had almost rather she had drifted away entirely than to inflict such a love on him. At such moments he felt as though his life had been neatly divided, that he had existed on two planes separated in time. Once he had been a man, but now he felt himself more a priest, able to think only in terms of his dogma. It was unfair and he loathed himself for his lack.

"Can I help you?" she offered. He heard a rustling. She had slipped out of bed, thrown a shawl over her shoulders, and come to stand next to him by the window.

She smiled. "Are you waiting for a light?"

He remained grim, his brows furrowed.

"What will happen if you see the light out there?"

She knew him far too well. How could one person understand another so well and yet not be understood in turn? It was to his deep shame that her thoughts, her feelings, remained to that day as much a mystery to him as they had been in the years before they had married.

"Mercedes will come tomorrow. . . ."

She touched his arm, "And if there's no light?"

He hesitated, then said: "She'll come anyway."

"Of course . . ."

But the sea remained black, the only light the pale yellow funnel that sprang from the Cap San Martín beacon. It picked out furrows of foam near the beach, probed the ragged waves that had been stirred by the north wind and now came slicing in to chew away at the shore.

It had grown so dark that Carvalho could no longer tell where the sea ended and the sky began.

"Of course," he echoed.

JULY 19

Sectors of the army in Morocco and Sevilla rebel and are fought by loyalist forces.

Mr. Azaña grants power to Martínez Barrio.

The Popular Front supports the constitutional government.

El Sol (Madrid)

SUNDAY MORNING, JULY 19: *San Pedro Monastery*

THE SACRISTAN'S FINGERS would not obey him; no matter how hard he tried, he seemed unable to release his grip on the iron gate. Across his face a multitude of varied expressions flickered, predominant among them—envy . . . of the young man who was passing just then out of the monastery garden and off, God knew where, but at least out of that worried place. For a second, the sacristan fixed Jaime with an accusing stare. Its meaning was plain enough: "Señor, how can you leave us here to die? At least let us have the solace of knowing what is to happen to us, and why."

Jaime paused just inside the gate of the San Pedro Monastery. Somehow, it seemed that it would be much easier to talk to the sacristan than it had been to talk to Luis Pelayo. But he was out of words and so angry at the banker's son that he could do nothing more than bite his lip.

The sacristan had by now worked one finger loose. Behind him, inside the garden and under the arcades beyond the flower beds, cassocked figures passed to and fro like shuttles through a loom of shadow and hot silence.

"Is there . . . ," the sacristan began haltingly . . . "any news, at all? Anything we can . . . *believe* . . . ?"

How strange it was to hear the word used in such a way in such a place. *Believe?* Was there any doubt here what to *believe?* Jaime thought. But he knew that it would be unforgivably unkind to say such a thing then. From the moment he had ridden up that morning, the brothers, the few priests, had talked of nothing else. God's business? Well, they have every right to be concerned, though Toledo is a priest's paradise and there's no real reason to worry. They should be on their knees and thanking God that this isn't Ciudad Real or Murcia . . . or Oviedo, for that matter. . . .

Jaime shook his head as he heard the question repeated in a lower, more urgent tone. He was irritated both by the persistent questioning and by the fruitless talk he had just had with Luis Pelayo. Now, he deeply regretted having come. For what? He had only upset himself.

"You've got a radio out there, haven't you?" the sacristan asked. "Tell me, what's really happening. . . ." He cast an anguished glance back at the brothers in the garden. "They'll have us all killed," he said. . . . "All of us . . . and in the name of the Church." His fingers traced a sad cross over his lips. "I don't want to be a martyr, señor. . . ."

"It's nothing but rumors," Jaime lied, passing through the gate. Rumors? It was a good deal more than that now. The very insistence with which Madrid radio had been claiming all morning that the rising had been crushed gave weight to the reports that the rebellion had in fact spread and was rapidly gaining momentum.

The sacristan's expression contrasted violently with the flushed look of exultation he had seen on the faces of the priests earlier that morning. He had assumed that they were already welcoming a triumph of the rising and the restoration of the Church to its "rightful" place. Could it be that he had been mistaken, that what he had seen was really the look of expectant martyrdom?

He turned away from the gates, leaving the sacristan standing there, sadly shaking his head.

Walking quickly across the burning shale of the hillside, Jaime considered his fruitless talk with Luis Pelayo. Neither anguish of spirit nor vocation had brought Luis to the monastery, Jaime had realized rapidly enough, but simply a taste for piquant new experiences. They had stood under the eucalyptus trees in the monastery garden and conversed haltingly for over an hour. Jaime had had to pretend that he did not know of Tomás' visit the day before and, worse still, to pretend that his own visit was accidental, that he had heard that Luis was there and had ridden over simply out of friendship. As they had never been particularly close before, it was obvious that Jaime was lying, but both men pretended to believe the story. Luis, his bulbous head with its oddly pinched cheeks quivering now and then with amusement, had laughed often, a high, annoying laugh, and he had molded the air with his hands as though he were caressing a woman.

As long as the brothers indulged him and no irrevocable commitment was made, what did it matter? He seemed completely oblivious to both the danger he was in and to the pain he was causing his father.

"The 'truth' of it is," Luis insisted, "that my father doesn't care at all about me. It's only that I've embarrassed him and ruined his plans for me, isn't that it?"

As Luis talked, Jaime became more and more convinced that it was the young man's irresponsibility rather than the moral implications of his acts or even the possible danger that had so disturbed his father. Luis seemed to take positive pleasure in the fact that he had upset his father, and Jaime could not help but feel that if only Tomás had ignored the whole matter, his son might have been home by then.

The two parted as they had always done in earlier years, neither understanding what moved the other. Jaime, surprisingly, had found within him no reserve of good feeling for the boy . . . the "boy," he persisted in thinking of him as the "boy" though Luis was only three years his junior . . . but only sorrow for Tomás and a penetrating scorn which made him feel both angry and superior.

He kicked at the stones underfoot and turned back to look once more at the monastery. The mountains behind it were almost the same bleached ocher color as its walls, and the shape of the low sandy buildings could barely be made out until that point in their rise where the bell tower pushed free of the mountains and jutted suddenly into a glittering blue sky, as smooth as glass.

Somewhere within the monastery walls a deep bell sounded twice, and the scraping of metal pannikins was borne aloft. A pulley groaned, and a bucket could be heard clattering up the walls of a well. The faint rustle of the eucalyptus trees in the garden reminded Jaime of how false was the calm that the monastery seemed to offer and, again, of the boyish foolishness of Luis Pelayo. "But," he thought, "how different are you? You've gone and shut yourself up inside the monastery 'San Mercader,' and you won't come out either. You'd better have a good reason, I warn you. . . ."

He recalled the last dead priest he had seen at Oviedo, a charred corpse, one leg still tied to a telephone post. He wondered whether the adventure would be worth *that* to Luis.

The mare was tethered near a clump of scraggly brushwood and was nibbling forlornly at a few sparse shoots of green. Beyond her, over the crest of the hill, the land curved away, toward the replenishing Tagus in long, endless furrows, yellow and barren as volcanic ash hardened by a pelting rain.

The few trees, poplar and a single twisted cypress, that grew about the monastery only served to increase the atmosphere of loneliness and sterility. Only the day before, that aching vastness had pleased Jaime. On his long rides he had found his sole comfort in the clangorous contrast of blazing blue sky and the yellow plain. Now it made him tremble unaccountably.

He mounted, and for a moment sat rigid in the saddle, surveying the hills, the buildings behind him, the slope glittering with mica and heat, the fall of the plains to the north toward a Madrid he could not see and did not wish to see. The Tagus ran like a curved mirror wound around the sprawling stones of Toledo, a sinuous winding of life through a landscape of perpetual death. Its banks were brushed faintly with green here and there as though an artist had only just begun to tint the slopes but, driven mad by the heat, had given up the job.

The heat had begun to anger him, and he gazed longingly at the river. Gently urging the mare forward, he guided her down the shallow rock-strewn hillside and onto a level stretch of plain that ran between the monastery of San Pedro and the next rise. Beyond that rise lay Toledo and the Tagus. As the mare broke into an excited gallop, the spires of the distant cathedral slipped suddenly down behind the breast of the hill directly ahead of him, and all he could see was the tip of one tower of the Alcázar on the southernmost cliff above the river. Again, the impulse overcame him and the landscape resonated with memories and longings. The mare whinnied with pleasure and lunged forward, leaving a trail of white scars on the ground where her hooves had carved out her passage. He could see only the ground spinning beneath him, the ridged yellow earth rushing by under the mare's hooves and the sky, pressing him down farther and farther until he felt himself inseparable from his mount. The wind swirled by him, struck against his teeth. He tried to shout against it but could only emit a grating, arid croak. It was well, for it had always been that way when he rode in Africa. . . .

The mare slowed, pawing up the rim of the hill and coming to an expectant halt above the Tagus. Toledo sprang out of the vibrant sky before them, the towers of the Alcázar and the taller, solitary spire of the cathedral thrusting up in accusation toward the uncaring sun. The city itself was gathered at the height of the hill, held nailed there like hide by the twin spikes of Church and Army, while the smaller buildings tumbled down along the rough, dry slopes. The bluffs and precipices vainly strove to reach the river. Low, dessicated houses, white, ash-colored, here splotched with a terra-cotta roof, there with darker earth, crawled down toward the Tagus, dwindling until the city itself seemed to give up in exhaustion. Far to the left, the waters of the river quivered suddenly, taking on an unexpected urgency and cascading silver over the rocks and earthwork obstructions in a torrent. But there before him, the water had the pale green color of the sickly trees that hugged the river's banks. Reeds moved in a breeze that Jaime could not feel, giving the water, even at that distance, an inviting motion that contrasted violently with the stillness of the sun-blasted city. It was as though Toledo had died of thirst trying to reach the river, and its bleached skeleton now lay broken over cliffs which, in the end, it could not overcome.

Jaime looked farther up the bank, toward the east. There he could see four or five people bathing. They splashed in and out of the shallow water just at a point where the current quickened and the surface of the water began to show traces of froth as it rushed over unseen stones and through passages between sunken boulders. Jaime pressed his knees into the mare's flanks, and the horse shot happily forward, trotting along the edge of the slope until she found a path down to the river's pebbled edge. As Jaime descended, he passed a lone stand of poplars and heard a fragile whispering sound as the breeze lisped among the leaves.

He watched the river carefully, as though he might divine beneath its surface the secret of what was to come for him. It was the same way that he had stared at the sea the day he had taken the packet from Ceuta across to Algeciras and begun the long trip to his father's house. The dawn-gilded sea flowing by him that early Monday morning—and he remembered that it had been Monday just as he remembered everything else on that day which seemed to divide his life like a wall—the sea had seemed deeper than he had ever seen it before. He could recall the walk to the dock, buying his ticket, climbing on board as clumsy derricks swung nets full of crates over his head into the ridiculously small ship's hold, and the mail coming on board later, the color of the few automobiles that had been on the wharf. There had been a reek of salt, fresh and bracing and somewhere above, the pungent odor of burning charcoal as puffs of smoke erupted into black semaphores against the cloudless sky, floating away like balloons.

Across the river toward which the mare now eagerly descended lay the city of Toledo, full of its Moorish ghosts, the lament of the exiled, the smell of rancid frying oil and refuse . . . across the sea . . . Algeciras, a glassy expanse of water, its faint ripples furrowed with gold, the sun raising a haze around Gibraltar and a mountain of mist rising from the water, and beyond it the coastline of Spain, low and still, as though not yet roused for the day.

His body had begun to respond to the throb of the ship's engines, and he had begun to sway gently against the rail . . . the rocking motion of his mount, the horses flank's shifting as the muscles expanded, then contracted, the powerful legs gathering in the distance . . . leaned into the salty wind that rose from the ship's wake, his eyes squinting against the spray. He seemed to see himself then as a tiny figure at the end of a spyglass. Not far off, the ship's only other passengers, two men, one a Moroccan in a stained black suit, the other a small, sun-withered man wearing a white linen jacket.

"Do you think it will all come out all right?" the man in the linen jacket had asked. From his hand dangled a bulging wineskin. He spoke with a thick Portuguese accent. Words had drifted back along the rail with the smoke. The Moroccan had turned away and grunted. The other had persisted: "There's something brewing back there," he had said spiritedly. "Everyone knows it . . . surely . . ."

Jaime had turned away and stared at the nearing coastline, trying to make out the shapes of the port, the black docks, the hills. A light mist trailed over the water, obscuring the shoreline.

The mists had parted for a second, and he thought he saw the outlines of Algeciras clearly. Then . . . nothing.

The Portuguese voice: "Everybody knows it, eh? So why pretend, you and I?"

One of the ship's officers had passed far toward the stern and shouted something.

The man in the white jacket had said: ". . . brewing back there . . . half the generals in your army have got their pointy beards in the stew . . . no? Well, let's change the subject then, eh? Can you tell me, of course you can . . . in Málaga . . . are there any bullfights this time of year?" He had raised the bursting wineskin, offered it to the Moroccan. The man had taken the skin and raised it to his mouth, and at that moment the ship had lurched suddenly on a swell and the jet of wine had splashed across the front of the man's shirt. He had let out a short, harsh cry.

Jaime remembered that, and the sacristan's words even though now he could not remember his face. The wine, a red blotch on the Moroccan's shirt, dripping down to the deck at his feet . . . the railroad cars at Oviedo, dripping blood, the miner against the wall . . . sharp crack, blotch . . . the same color. Man's blood and wine. He could not dislodge the image. Then the Moroccan had gone, leaving the Portuguese leaning by the rail, the wineskin still slung over one shoulder . . .

The tops of the high grass and the fronds brushed his legs. The mare slowed down, feeling for her footing as the ground grew softer. A stand of reeds rose from the water in biblical profusion just ahead of him. He could hear the voices of children, the echo of the Portuguese voice, the sacristan mumbling disconsolately to himself.

The bluffs upon which Toledo had died rose steeply above him, casting a purple shadow across the water. He seemed to be directly under the walls of the Alcázar. He could see a few soldiers strolling lazily about under the walls, along the esplanade that faced the river and the gorge. He wondered, had they heard the rumors, the reassurances that order had been maintained which meant quite the opposite? Now and then the sound of a voice would float down from the escarpment, a hundred feet or more above him. He could not understand what they were saying. On the top of the wall, near one of the towers, a flash of light attracted his attention. Someone was searching the southern plain with field glasses.

He slipped from the mare's back and stood in the damp riverside earth, watching the toes of his boots sink into the sand. The air was refreshingly cool and he was glad that he had come down to the river and away from the sun even though he loved the sun and the smell of his own sweat and the horse's lather. The men he had seen before had moved down along the curve of the river and though he could hear their voices, he could no longer see them. The sun sparkled in the little pools of water where their feet had left depressions in the soft earth between the runs of white pebbles.

Jaime drew off his shirt and threw it across the saddle. The mare bent her neck and began nibbling at the tender ends of the rushes which grew about her forelegs. Jaime patted her on the rump, pulled off his boots, and hung them from the forked branches of a small tree nearby. He walked out into the shallows. The cool water swirled by, darkening his trousers. Something flashed through the water not far from where he stood, a little farther toward the deep where the channel plunged and the current was faster and more powerful. A fish . . . slim body twisting through the water. How much more life there was there when you could see it close up, he thought. From the distance, the river was only a mirror, disguised by the reflections of sky and hillside. But once you were in it, it was something different. He bent forward, gathered up handfuls of water and splashed it over his body, felt the caked dust wash loose and run down along his ribs.

The sound of a girl's voice came tumbling down the hillside. He looked up, his head dripping. High on the side of the bluff, just under the walls of the Alcázar, he could see two girls in bright cotton dresses, blue and green. They carried amphoras of water on their hips and held peeled branches hung with white china cups, two, three or even more, if they had been successful selling water in the past.

The words "agua . . . fresca . . ." splashed into the river below like raindrops. He wished he could see their faces. Perhaps they would remind him of someone . . . the girl who had been at his father's house the night before. But he knew he needed no reminding; he had thought of little else all night and all morning, though in his thoughts she was often her father, and her father often her. He found himself wishing to talk to her as he might have wished to talk to her father. If he listened long enough, if he let her answer all the questions he wanted to ask the Colonel, perhaps he would understand why her father had done what he had done.

To recapture his lost faith in the man, that was the most important thing "Or to ease your own injured pride?" he wondered. But he knew he would ride out to see her tomorrow.

He thrust his hands into the waters again. A tiny fish leaped through his fingers and arrowed into the rills a yard beyond him. He flung himself headlong into the current, and swam with strong thrusts of his arms out into the middle of the river. The mare whinnied in alarm and raised her head from the stand of rushes.

He shouted back at her, turned in the water, and swam back against the current.

It surprised him . . . he had almost laughed.

JULY 19: *Toledo*

THE TRUCK DRIVER Onésimo Ramos and his helper, César "of the strong back," stood in the empty front hall of the house, shuffling their feet in the dust and waiting for Mercedes Carvalho to tell them what to do about the harpsichord. There was still room for it in the back of the truck, and they were anxious to get under way.

Mercedes seemed not to notice the two men at all. She was lost in contemplation of the harpsichord, a beautiful inlaid instrument of the time of Carlos III, all mother-of-pearl and fine exotic woods. Not even the keys had yellowed. It had been one of her mother's favorite pieces. Yet, she considered, no one in the family really knew how to play it. It had sat there, a relic, beautiful but useless, for so long. Was there any point in sending it? Raúl had once tried to master its keyboard but had given up in disgust at the pale, almost inaudible sounds it made and turned instead to the guitar which he had never learned to play either.

"What shall be done, señorita?" Onésimo Ramos finally asked, twisting his cap. The longer the partially loaded truck stood outside in the street, the more certainly it would attract some attention. The things going on in Toledo made Ramos uncomfortable, even though they seemed not to bother the slender, soft-spoken young woman at all. He felt embarrassed at showing his nervousness before her.

"In a moment," Mercedes said, still not turning. She touched a finger to her lip, still unable to decide and for a moment turned her gaze away from the harpsichord and let it wander about the room, the empty walls of ivory stucco, marked with lighter squares of bone white where pictures had once hung. Dust had begun to gather on the floors since the carpets had been removed, and the curtains billowed now and then in infrequent gusts pushed in from the hills across the river. The dust spun, then settled again.

It's useless, she thought again. But would her father have wanted her to take it? How would he have decided? It was a fossil, she knew, beautiful as the hairline skeletons embedded in rock she had studied in her geology classes, but of another age, a time which had nothing to do with her. That her mother, that anyone should insist on clinging to such times, to such objects infuriated her.

No, better to let it stay there.

She turned at last, her skirt clinging tightly to her legs. She caught her own reflection in the lenses of César's glasses; she was slender and very striking, her face long, cheeks high-boned, her nostrils flared perhaps a trifle too much. A wave of glossy black hair poured over her head and onto her shoulders. She preferred it loose and would never pin it up or wear a shawl. It was an intense face; she was not vain of her appearance, but knowing that men would turn and look after her gave her a certain pleasure. Knowing that she was more intelligent and aware than most of them amused her even more.

"Onésimo," she began, "take the chest at the foot of the stairs instead. It's full of books, and it's very heavy. . . ."

"But your mother . . . ," Onésimo began cautiously. He had been with the family for a long time and knew about the harpsichord. While he was disturbed by the girl's answer, he was relieved not to have the responsibility of seeing the instrument safely from Toledo to Biarritz, across all the bumpy roads, the rutted lanes and hills they would have to traverse.

"Don't worry about that. I'll tell her all about it when I get there. You just say that I told you not to take it and that's all." Mercedes smiled, and there was no replying to that smile. César, "of the strong back," plucked at his companion's sleeve, and the two men went to the staircase to fetch the chest of books.

That was the right thing to do, Mercedes thought. Her father would have preferred saving the books; they at least would be read while the harpsichord would sit for another twenty years, unplayed.

But she could not leave it alone completely and went over to it, raised the lid over the keyboard and struck lightly and at random at the keys, drawing forth a few faint, plucked notes. She knew that under a master's hands much fine music could be coaxed from that frail instrument; Sebastián Gil had often looked at it longingly though she knew that Gil could not play it either. Perhaps, before leaving on the train to Barcelona, she would give it to Gil, and perhaps he would learn to play it himself, now that his wife was dead. It might give him some pleasure. She resolved to call him during the day or, if she could, to walk by his shop and tell him herself. It would only take two men to move the instrument, and Gil could certainly arrange that easily enough.

Only the huge portrait of Colonel Carvalho, done by Benaventa Onis years before, when her father was still a major, remained on the wall. It was life size and executed in earth colors which, as they had faded because of the bad turpentine Onis had used, had blended into the walls so that Colonel's likeness now seemed an excrescence of the masonry itself. Mercedes stared critically at the face: the long, equine bone structure, the bushy eyebrows and the explosion of thick graying hair just above the crown, the beard, trimmed to a spade, the ends of the mustache turned up and slightly waxed, and most of all the glaring eyes which always seemed to flame with indignation. Her father had changed little since that fierce portrait was committed to canvas. It was as though the withered old Onis had seen into the future and painted the Colonel not as he was then but as he would be. She had seen that very look on her father's face in late May when he had stopped at Toledo on his way to his new posting at the Oviedo garrison. Lieutenant Mercader had not been with him then, and in the most casual manner she had asked after the aide-de-camp. The expression of dismay that had clouded her father's features at the mere mention of Mercader's name had been warning enough, and she had not mentioned it again. The Colonel's visit had lasted only two restless days, and they had spent much of their time together walking along the rim of the river. He had seemed to be looking for something in the water below, but she knew that a physical appearance of searching was only his way of expressing a deep confusion of which he was too ashamed to speak. She, alone of his children, shared a real intimacy of thought with him; he had raised her as though in resentful atonement for all his failures with her sister Inés and Raúl, perhaps for his own failures as well, though they never spoke of them. He had taught her a kind of rootless humanism which she found comforting, but increasingly difficult to practice. Once or twice she had felt him on the verge of explaining Mercader's absence. A young officer from the Alcázar's summer staff had passed them near the cathedral and, for a second, he had reminded them both of the missing young man. Colonel Carvalho had started to say something, then recovered and lapsed into a morose silence. Then they had gone to the city's main square, the Zocodover, and had a glass of lemonade at a café by the Arca de la Sangre, the stone portal that pierces the left side of the Zoco and lets in a brief glimpse of the plains across the river to the east. "He wouldn't come with me," her father said once. And another time, "I don't know 'what' happened to him or why," but his tone told her clearly enough that if he did not know "what," he at least did know "why." Then he had packed and gone off in the staff car which had brought him.

After that she had had no word from him until the first of the cryptic messages concerning the furniture. She had wanted to ask Mercader about it the night before, thinking that perhaps he might be able to explain why her father, in Oviedo, would suddenly order his house stripped and the contents shipped to Biarritz and why, for that matter, he had instructed her to take the train from Madrid to Barcelona and thence to France herself as soon as the last load had left. But Mercader had been as taciturn—and belligerent—as her father, and she had quickly decided not to even mention it to him. Obviously there was something very wrong between the two men, and she knew at least enough of her own father to understand that time and patience, not questions, would be needed before an answer would be forthcoming.

She went upstairs to her room, the only room in the entire house in which there was any furniture left. On the wall was a large, silver-bordered mirror and beneath it a chest on which she had piled a few possessions—books, a number of bracelets and earrings, and a folder of old photographs. From her window she could see across the river toward the hermitage of Nuestra Señora de la Cabeza. A delicious fragrance of thyme came with the breeze, riding over the gathering heat.

She took her sketch pads from the almost empty shelves next to the bed. She had been making detailed drawings of the tiles in the Tránsito nearby and of what still could be seen of the plasterwork on the walls and the spandrels high on the ceiling. The custodian had been terrified when she had first asked for a ladder and had mounted to the ceiling to copy the designs, but he had been equally afraid to refuse her. The name "Carvalho" was still something to conjure with in Toledo, even though since '34 there were many in the city who would have liked to have seen the Colonel and all his family dead. The series of drawings done in pastel chalks was almost complete now. She could not remember what had prompted her to begin copying the designs or why she had chosen the synagogue of El Tránsito other than that it was near the house and had always given off an attractive air of sad mystery. She had no idea what she would do with the pictures once they were finished; certainly neither her mother nor her sister would understand why she had made them or what they were . . . fragments of a history that seemed in some unfathomable way closer to her than the reality she saw about her.

She gathered the chalks and the last of her pads together and put them in the straw basket she had been using for her work. In the street below, Onésimo and César were just finishing with the truck, tying the ropes around the tailgate so as to make sure that the trunk of books, the last thing to be loaded, would not fall out. How many of the books she had read were in that trunk? she wondered. How much of herself . . . ?

The two men got into the cab, and Onésimo, seeing her leaning from the window, waved. She waved back with her handkerchief. The motor kicked over, and the truck lurched down the narrow, uneven street, disappearing shortly around a bend.

Now she was alone. Although Onésimo and the other man could be trusted with furniture, she could understand why her father had sent word for her not to go with them on the last trip but to take the train instead. Who could tell how they might react on some lonely mountain road or out on the plains? She laughed to think of being attacked by Onésimo whom she had known from childhood, but the other one, César, who rarely spoke, was another matter entirely. Her father had been wise not to trust them too far.

She went downstairs again, carrying the straw basket, and out onto the street in front of the house, pausing only to lock the door behind her with a key from an iron ring which she dropped into the basket next to the chalks. It was only a few minutes from the house to the synagogue, and the custodian, Acosta Matteu, was bound to be found lounging on the paseo overlooking the Tagus, fanning himself as he usually did with a copy of the Madrid paper *Ahora* and drinking his inevitable bottle of *magnol* which made him forever faintly redolent of lemon and anise.

She turned a bend in the street, passing between two walls of shadow broken only by a spray of bright purple flowers on a window ledge just above her head, then came out onto the wider street bordering the paseo. A breeze was rippling the upper branches of the trees that overlooked the gorge and, below, the insistent rush of the river water could be clearly heard as the flood leaped the weirs and splashed down into the next watercourse.

Flies buzzed, and not too far off Mercedes heard the clopping of a horse's hooves. Down the *calle,* in the direction of the church of San Juan de los Reyes, a figure on horseback passed, his patent-leather tricorn glistening in the morning sun, his rifle jutting up like a cutout above his shoulders. The Civil Guard rode hunched over the saddle. Then he vanished behind a building.

She could see Acosta Matteu asleep under a tree near the low stone wall that separated the paseo from the cliffs leading down to the river. She watched the regular rise and fall of his chest for a moment, almost decided not to wake him. Then the man stirred to wave at a fly which had settled on his forehead. He saw her and, knowing what she wanted, got slowly to his feet and came toward her, swinging his iron chain of keys.

She would spend an hour or so. Perhaps she could almost finish the sketches. Tomorrow morning she would come again. On Tuesday she would pack her things and the next day begin her trip to France.

"My poor father," she thought, "how afraid he must be . . . of people, of himself. Why should he want me to go? What is there to harm us here?"

Acosta Matteu nodded his head in "good morning" and smiled.

"Buenas dias," she said and followed the round little man toward the somber, peaceful building in which the ghosts of the long-departed jews still cast shadows over friezes inscribed with glorifications of Pedro el Cruel, the arms of Castilla and of Trastamaras.

She let the basket of chalks swing loosely from her hand while Acosta Matteu grunted and twisted the key in the heavy iron lock.

"Only for you, señorita . . ."

"I understand," she said. "Thank you, Señor Matteu. . . ."

"My pleasure."

She stopped inside and was at once overwhelmed by the cool, musty shade. She felt very much at peace with herself and quietly began to take out her chalks and her paper, leaving the basket near the door. She glanced once at her watch. She had almost the entire morning to herself.

She began sketching, forming a light-blue tracery of lines across the surface of her tablet. Behind her, she heard Acosta Matteu's footsteps as he headed back to the paseo for his second *magnol* of the morning.

July 19: *Toledo*

Hanging around El Bronco was dangerous but it had its rewards. The owner could only afford two electric bulbs which he judiciously hung close to the entrance so that potential customers could see that there were actually people inside, drinking and talking. Vitolyn would go in and sit in the back where it was darkest. There, he would have a bottle of sweetish beer or the dark, faintly bitter wine of the region, would drink quietly, keep his head down and listen. But he would often find himself not so much listening as daydreaming, imagining himself back in Vienna with a "decent" glass of beer in his hand. Wrenching himself periodically from his reveries, he would turn his attention to collecting information, listening and fitting together the scraps of talk which passed by him like debris on the surface of a sluggish river.

The factory workers and the *campesinos* would talk mostly about women or sports. They never seemed to tire of predicting the outcome of the French cycle races, or putting up extravagant bets on the wrestling matches at the Circo de Price. The favorite that week was Alfredo Koch whom the papers called *"El Cientifico* Alemen." *"El Tigre* Stresnack" was another favorite whose name was much bandied about, and after a while Vitolyn began to wonder if, in fact, there were any truly Spanish wrestlers at all. But to wrestle meant the chance of defeat in full view of thousands of spectators; losing, it seemed, was an activity best left to bulls and to foreigners who did not have to live the rest of their lives with their neighbor's memory of it.

There was some talk of films, which the habitués of El Bronco knew more from the reviews in the papers than from the actual viewing of them. There were only two cinemas in Toledo, too expensive for the men of *Las Covachuelas* and still showing films that were two or three years old. The bullfights were a subject that Vitolyn tried to shut out whenever they were mentioned. There seemed to be particular concern over a fight scheduled for the following Sunday in Tetuán in which six novice matadors were to make their first appearances. Betting was heavy on how many would be gored. The more politically conscious, well aware that the Republic frowned on bullfighting, remained obdurately aloof and silent whenever the subject was brought up.

"You don't listen to the priests when they tell you not to screw, so why listen to the shit the government spouts about bulls?"

"Listen, man, it's a different matter, don't you see?"

"Bulls are bulls, that's the truth of it. And anyone who tries to mix them up with politics is a fool . . ."

So Vitolyn listened, straining to catch anything of value. News of the

rising was so mixed with obvious untruth that one could do better by ignoring it all and making up whatever one pleased. Workmen from the
Fábrica de las Armas insisted that the Russians had already landed two
divisions on the coast near Gijón and were on their way to "aid" the Republic. Others opted for the French as though the matter were a soccer
contest or a boxing match. The Anarchists swore loudly and called the
rising a good thing; the State would be destroyed, both Left and Right,
and men could get on with the business of being men. Vitolyn endured it
all in silence, raising his head only to check on new arrivals.

The man "Roig" usually came in around ten in the evening, often
stayed well past midnight, eating there as well as drinking. On each such
occasion, Vitolyn was obliged to hide behind his newspaper, a subterfuge
that by itself might just as easily have caused comment. There were few
papers in El Bronco, and Vitolyn's, spread wide in front of his fact was at
least . . . conspicuous.

A group of workmen engaged in renovating the vaults of the sacristy
of a nearby church were joking loudly about some remains they had
found in the underground chambers when Roig entered that evening.
"After all," Vitolyn thought, hardly noticing his quarry's arrival, "if
death can become a ritualized event in this incomprehensible country,
why should we respect it just because the dead are human beings rather
than bulls?" The Spaniards' easy conversance with death disturbed him
immensely. The cheerful bantering about skulls and skeletons, coffins
and crypts made him very uneasy.

"It's the beer," he insisted, peering around the corner of his paper to
see if Roig had left yet. The pistol was tight in its holster in his jacket
pocket and he was, for once in his life, absolutely ready. What little real
information he had been able to pick up had led him to the conclusion
that there was no time to be lost. He would have to get it over with and
get out of Toledo as fast as he could. The mood of the workers whom
he saw in the streets was growing nastier by the hour and, experienced
as he was in such things, he knew that it would take very little to spark
the situation. It seemed to him that something would have to happen in
Toledo soon if the government was to retain control. If the Republicans
didn't move, then the FAI would; and if the anarchists did take to the
streets, the "comrades" would not be far behind. It would be Stoplinsky
and Baumgartner all over again, only this time on a mammoth scale.

César Roig was sitting at the other end of the room, smoking a long
cigar. He had just paid for his wine. No one had spoken to him; he always appeared just a bit too neatly dressed for the rest of the men in
the bar who instinctively mistrusted anyone who looked the slightest bit
more prosperous than they. Roig seemed oblivious to it all, and Vitolyn
could not help wondering who the man was and what business he had in
Toledo; certainly he was not a native. More likely he was traveling for
some unimportant commercial firm, poor himself, but trying to give an
"impression" . . . hence, the overly fastidious dress. From his few days'
observation, Vitolyn knew only that Roig's existence was both lonely and

extremely regular. Once or twice Vitolyn had lost track of him but Roig always turned up at exactly the same spot and at exactly the same time.

It was almost midnight; Roig finally got up to leave, and as he made his exit, Vitolyn lowered his paper with a sigh of relief. His arm muscles had become almost rigid from the effort. He pulled his cap firmly down on his head so as to decrease the resemblance between himself and his quarry as best he could. He also had left off his glasses which made it difficult for him to see, but he managed, nearsighted as he was, to get out of the smoky bar without incident. Two nights earlier he had accidentally knocked a man from a bench and the ensuing quarrel had nearly led to disaster. The passing of a Civil Guard patrol had ended the squabble abruptly, and Vitolyn had made a quick, safe exit; but it was an experience he was not eager to repeat.

He had watched Roig so long and so hard that it was difficult not to have a certain liking for the man—a liking which was, he admitted readily enough to himself, a kind of narcissism. After all, what did he know of Roig other than his appearance which was so like his own? Too bad, but he would have to go through with it. What a combination of bad and good luck, to have been in Toledo and encountered César Roig just at the moment when events had determined that he must get off the Continent entirely. Now, he needed papers and now, for the first time he might be able to obtain them. It was one thing to go scuttling across land borders at night, from country to country without papers, and quite another to get passage on a ship to Africa or America. He had heard that the Portuguese were very particular about such things and their jails were the worst on earth.

The street was full of a musty, rancid darkness; the stink of cooking oil hung like a ground mist over the glossy cobbles. Ahead, Vitolyn could see Roig making a turn into one of the innumerable narrow alleys that ran through the one-story brick hovels of the quarter.

He turned into the alley . . . but what street in Toledo was not an alley? The workers' houses which made up the shapeless, monotonous jumble of *Las Covachuelas* cowered like hunchbacked dwarfs against the earth, fearing God's whip.

Vitolyn hurried up the street, trying to make as little noise as possible. He was vaguely conscious of heading south, uphill, toward the center of the city, toward his own room and Roig's. Heat, that was what he was most aware of; Roig's shape proceeded ahead of him, a smear of darker shadow, his head down, walking with a loose, disjointed gait; he would have to remember that walk, try to imitate it. There were few people on the street. Though no one looked at him, he still felt conspicuous. Since he had arrived in Spain he had been acutely conscious of what he felt was his out-of-place appearance, but he had come slowly to realize that there was no such thing as a "typical" Spanish face. The races, mixed and mingled, produced a million contradictions, and the only real common denominator was the hair oil and the dark, scorched look of the skin. If Roig was Spanish, then why could not Vitolyn be . . . Spanish as well?

He felt the weight of his pistol, an unpleasant reminder. He preferred to think of himself as out for an evening walk, a stroll along the
gray Donau canal such as he used to take so often.

Vitolyn squinted up the twisting *calle;* they were almost there. Roig
was still unaware that he was being followed. Vitolyn smiled, trying to
imagine what the man's reaction would be if he knew that he was being
followed by a man who could be his own reflection.

Suddenly he stopped short; Roig had pulled himself into a doorway.
At the head of the street, where it turned into the slightly wider road on
which the house of Florez and the other opposite it lay, four men had
erupted without warning from the front of a two-story house, only
slightly grander than the hovels which it overlooked.

"Pío . . . get that bastard out here, now. . . ."

Vitolyn flattened himself against the building, watched the men and
the indistinct shape of Roig, also watching. . .

"He doesn't want to walk."

"Help him a little." Some laughed, angrily.

There were five men in the street now. Two of them were carrying
pistols, and one had on a shapeless cap onto which had been fastened a
strip of black cloth. They formed an aisle to the door of the house. Then
a sixth man came stumbling out, his face covered by his hands, and behind him two more men, both with pistols. One of them struck the stumbling figure in the small of the back, a vicious swipe which caused the
victim to reel and fall to his knees.

"Get him on his feet," someone said.

The man on his knees kept saying, "Please, please" through his crisscrossed fingers.

"Don't beg, Rubén. You may as well be a man for once."

Two of them took the beaten man under his arms and yanked him
to his feet; he stood there swaying, refusing to take his hands away from
his eyes. He was shaking his head violently.

Inside the house a woman was screaming. It was the first time that
Vitolyn had noticed the sound, though she must have been screaming all
along.

The victim suddenly lowered his hands. His face was streaming
blood from cuts along his cheeks and scalp.

"Go ahead," he said, pulling in a breath so deep that it made his
whole body shudder.

The seven men drew into a circle around him. "But no one will
shoot," Vitolyn thought, watching transfixed. "Impossible to shoot a man
who is in the middle of a circle. The bullet might pass through his body
and hit somebody else." He'd seen that happen once before, during a
street fight.

Then he became aware of another sound, the scuffling of shoes on
the cobbles behind him, along the street in the direction from which he
had just come.

The first group heard it, too. They drew away from the man in the center of the circle and stood there, frozen like the cutout silhouettes that old men make at village fairs. . . .

The men at the end of the street, four or five of them, began walking slowly toward the first group.

The man who had yelled for Pío shouted: "That's far enough . . . who the hell are you . . . ?"

"Regards from Tierres," came the reply. They continued to close the gap, and as they passed the doorway in which Vitolyn was hidden, he saw each of them clearly; two youngish, anonymous-looking men, one heavy, fleshy man, round as an olive, a massive peasant and, in absurd contrast, a slim, fortyish man with a wasted face and sunken cheeks. Two men carried pistols, one a crowbar, and the last a baling hook.

"Far enough" said the man who had called for Pío. "Far enough."

"We don't want this," said the heavy man. "You're not doing the right thing."

"Together . . . we should be . . . together . . . ," the other answered.

"In the grave, maybe. Where else? But we certainly don't need the Guard here, so we'll settle this later. . . ."

The wasted man emitted a high, abbreviated laugh.

The seven withdrew, backing down the street, leaving their intended victim standing alone between the two groups. When the seven were almost at the end of the block, he staggered forward to join his rescuers.

Then, suddenly, from the end of the street, one of the first group shouted, "Bastards . . . ," through cupped hands, and then one single pistol shot exploded. The bullet slammed off a wall, very high, and the first group bolted around the corner.

The wasted man laughed again. The shot had been so badly aimed that it was only an insult, nothing more. None of the six moved to follow or to fire back.

Someone went into the low building and brought out a sobbing woman wrapped in a blanket. Although it was steaming hot outside, she was shivering under the blanket. Then, the seven of them continued up the street and vanished around the corner.

Vitolyn stepped cautiously from his hiding place and looked up and down the street. Roig was nowhere in sight. No matter. He would turn up at the house in a few moments. The shot worried him; it was loud as a cannon. Someone had mentioned the Guard. He hadn't seen many of them around that day, mostly in the Zoco and in front of a few public monuments, but there was always the possibility that the shot might bring some kind of investigation or a roundup.

He hesitated, then doubled back and took the long way around to Florez's house. He was not sure what had happened, but he dimly recalled having heard the name Tierres in El Bronco, and the leader of the first group had been wearing an FAI emblem on his cap. Vitolyn was terrified by the implications.

He went in the front door quickly, not even looking across the street to see if Roig had arrived ahead of him. Rather, he went straight up the short flight of steps to his room. Only then did he go to the window and look across the way. There was no light in Roig's window.

He let the curtains fall. The sweat ran down along the angles of his thin, almost emaciated body, wracked now with cramps and diarrhea from the tainted food he'd been eating for days. He took the pistol out of his jacket and laid it on the bed, directly over the spot where he had hidden the flat tin box containing the schilling notes.

Just then there was a clatter on the street below. He went back to the window in a panic. A group of Civil Guard were hustling along the *calle,* headed toward the spot where the shot had been fired. One Guard took up a position at the end of the street while the rest went on. He stood there, leaning against the wall, his Mauser cradled in his arms and his black tricorn catching the wink of an oil lamp across the street.

At that moment, someone struck a match in Roig's room and lit the lamp. A scarecrow shadow leaped across the wall, its outlines blurred only slightly by the flimsy curtains.

It was impossible now . . . not with the Guard standing there. "Perhaps, later . . . if he goes away . . . ?"

Vitolyn sat down on the bed and held his head in his hands in the classic posture of grief. He knew that he would do nothing that night, nothing at all . . . not if the Guard went away, not if Roig came out on the street and offered himself up, not for anything.

He kept thinking about the two groups of men, about the name "Tierres," and the black emblem, and about Stoplinsky the Trotskyite and Baumgartner the "true believer."

"Bakunin wrote that all men are good, and we must destroy everything which keeps that goodness suppressed which means . . . *everything* . . . we say . . ." He stopped short . . . "*We?* Do I, after all that has happened, still feel myself a part of that *we?*" The thought took him by surprise, and he shuddered.

He stretched out on the bed and tried to sleep.

JULY 20
The Government has controlled the military revolt.
The Loyalist forces in Madrid have seized all army posts.
General Goded surrendered in Barcelona, announced his defeat over the radio, and advised rebels to stop fighting.

El Sol (Madrid)

MONDAY, JULY 20, 11:00 A.M.: *Toledo*

THE CALLE DEL MORO, like nearly all the streets in Toledo, seems to have lost its way; it knows neither consistent direction nor vertical attitude. At some points it becomes so narrow that it seems in danger of losing its identity altogether, of being crushed by a vise of stolid, low houses whose facades, innocent of windows, face unknowingly onto the wretched streets they strangle. It is the unique ability of these houses and those within them to turn their backs on such poverty and to find comfort within their own embowered souls that alone permits their survival. As if in revenge for being ignored, the streets outside plunge angrily up and down in a determined effort to exact retribution from those who must climb them. The Calle del Moro is such a street, its irregularity seeming more the result of some long-past volcanic disturbance than of human design.

Toward eleven in the morning Sebastián Gil came through the unbolted door of number 15, Calle del Moro, and began walking slowly up the angled street toward the center of the city. The building he had just left was two stories high, with an iron-railed balcony jutting out from the second story, built long before when there had been no building across the narrow street but only a small horse fountain beyond which one could view the hills across the Tagus to the south, *Los Cigarrales,* spotted with small trees and apricot orchards and often bathed in a velvety purple at sunset that was beautiful to see.

Gil paused for a moment in the street outside his house and reached into his pocket for a handkerchief. A freshly laundered mourning band encircled his left arm. As he walked, he dabbed alternately at his forehead and the back of his neck with the handkerchief but was unable to stanch the flow of perspiration. He tapped at the pavement with the end of the long walking stick which he always carried when he walked from his lodgings and his shop, though he had no real need for it.

He struck with particular viciousness at an oval stone which seemed to him to have the same shape as Ruperto Barcenas' head. Never before had he been subjected to such an attack. "A man's friends are his own business and no one else's. . . . I should have put him down instead of just sitting there. It's only because of Francisco that I didn't. I have too much respect for him to insult a guest in his house, but I see that some of his other 'friends' don't have the same decency. . . ."

Ever since his wife's death, Gil had kept more or less to himself, receiving visitors in the safety of his own apartment but rarely venturing out. It had only been because of Carvalho's daughter that he had accepted the invitation, and if anyone else had offered to escort her, he would gladly have stayed at home. Hadn't the Colonel stopped by on his way to Oviedo, using precious time that he could have spent with his daughter? "Look after her, will you, Sebastián?" he had said, with a distant, distressed expression that foreclosed refusal. They hadn't ever been that close. . . . "It's impossible with a man like that who is . . . let's put it bluntly . . . just never 'here'. . . ." But he had always admired the Colonel in much the same way that he admired men like Torroba and Fernán Venegas, not so much for what they had done in life but simply for the courage they had shown in going ahead and doing it. The girl seemed to him to have many of the same qualities and because of this he thought it almost laughable that he should be asked to "look after" her. "More likely the other way around," he thought in rueful recognition of his own weaknesses.

The city seemed quiet, and the morning paper, *Claridad*—Large Caballero's Socialist daily from Madrid—carried reassurances that the military rising had already been put down and that justice would be meted out to those responsible in short order. Content with what he had read, all of which seemed confirmed by the orderly, even peaceful tempo of life in Toledo, he had not even turned on the radio; the brassy, martial music which Union Radio in Madrid had been playing for the past two days grated terribly on his nerves, and he could see no point in subjecting himself to anything so irritating without good reason. Besides, how many times in twenty-four hours was even a good Republican expected to listen to Riego's hymn without beginning to feel ill? It was, after all, a wretched piece of music to start with.

He felt, rather, an intense desire to be in his shop, to soothe his troubled nerves with . . . with, it did not matter . . . any one of the records on the crowded shelves would do. He could blot out everything with Boccherini or Mozart.

Few of the houses which he regularly passed on the way to his shop had windows that faced the street; most showed only blank walls of stucco or stone. But as he walked, he noticed that those few windows which did break the monotony of the rough, featureless facades were now shuttered, the rooms behind and their occupants hidden away. It made him vaguely uneasy not to see even that small evidence of life behind the walls, not to see the pots of basil and carnations that usually stood on the sills, the trailing greenery that hung down now and then from the door lintels to decorate the stone. Why were the windows shuttered? He had never seen such a thing in all the time he had lived in Toledo. Where were the children running and playing in the alleyways? Where was the strong, pungent odor of people in those crowded houses to bring back to him the memory of his own childhood?

He would have to speak to Torroba that evening, if he came. . . . Torroba would know. He passed a small café whose facade was usually bright with a clutter of wooden enamel signs promising wines, beers of various kinds, roast pig, cheese, and olives. But the signs and the window were hidden, covered by a corrugated metal armor, the iron shades drawn down tight over the glass. The doors had been fastened with heavy padlocks. No wire chairs had been placed on the sidewalk though it was well past opening time. All the other shops along the way stood similarly shuttered and desolate.

He glanced with increasing concern down each street that intersected his route but saw nothing, no one. Only a few cats on the lookout for mice, prowling among the garbage cans. Fresh horse droppings, brown as earth in the morning sun, steamed on the stones. But he saw no horses.

Gil continued on, tapping his stick against the cobbles. As he neared his destination, his confusion intensified. Emptiness and silence seemed no longer a unique phenomenon to be observed on a particular street but a raging epidemic infecting the entire quarter.

Quite suddenly, he heard—almost with relief—a clattering noise close by him. He turned just as a heavy wagon drawn by two yoked horses rumbled out along the Calle Zuraban directly behind him. The street was barely wide enough for the broad-beamed wagon to pass. It was loaded with mattresses and crockery. Blankets of bright colors and stripes hung over the side, giving it a deceptively festive air. A thick-limbed woman sat amid piles of pots and bundles of clothes, two small children encircled by her sunburned arms. She kept glancing about, peering into doorways and along the edges of rooftops, as though expecting something to be thrown out at her. The driver, a Civil Guard, surprisingly unshaven, his tricorn dulled with dust and his rifle slung, muzzle down, over his back, wielded a prod against the horses' flanks and urged them on up the street. The wagon nearly ran Gil down as it went by.

The Civil Guard glanced at him but said nothing. His lips, Gil noticed, were trembling slightly, his gaze uncertain and apprehensive. It was an unusual expression to see on a Guard's face.

Another wagon, similarly laden, suddenly entered the street about thirty meters farther up. From the direction they had taken, Gil guessed that they were headed toward the Zocodover, perhaps even to the Alcázar. It made no sense, unless something terrible was going on. Why should the Civil Guard be coming in from the countryside and bringing their families with them?

Gil turned away, pressing into a narrow alleyway, the shortest route to his shop. All at once, he could hear the sound of wagons coming from every direction. The whining of small children rose above the creaking of wagon axles and the labored wheeze of old automobile engines sounded from somewhere farther up the street.

Emerging from the alleyway, he found himself within yards of his shop. There were the green-shaded windows with "Sebastián Gil" in gold across the front, the door with its latticework of iron to protect it from vandals. He lowered his eyes toward the latch, the pendulous lock. The walking stick dropped from his hand and went rolling over the cobble-stones.

Spread out on the cobblestones in front of his doorway, lay the body of a man about forty, roughly dressed, in baggy trousers and rope-soled sandals. Blackish blood ran sluggishly into the street. The man's eyes were wide open, his body rigid, arms flung out, stiff as a crucifix. The man was a complete stranger; Gil had never seen him before in his life.

The street itself was otherwise empty. Gil took another step forward. It was a warning, what else could it be? What Barcenas had said to him once was true: "You can't expect everyone to understand the delicacy of your motives. . . . Neither the workers nor the army, as far as I know, care much for Mozart. . . ."

He rushed back to the alleyway. There was no telling who else might be about, hiding in a doorway, waiting behind a window to see what he would do, how he would react. He would have to tell someone. "Venegas," he thought, "right away . . . Venegas. He'll do something about this. . . ."

He began to run, lurching against the walls of the narrow alleys, trying to get his bearings. The Plaza Mayor near the cathedral . . . which way? . . . to get lost in that labyrinth of streets . . . no, not now, not this time . . .

Neither of the two sentries flanking the entrance of Civil Guard headquarters tried to stop him; one of them, in fact, recognized Gil and waved him on. Gil entered the building, his clothing sopping wet with perspiration. He was barely able to breathe. He had run all the way from his shop.

The interior of the stone building was cool and smelled of dust and lime. No one was about. The ground floor hall ran, twenty empty meters ahead of him, armored by a succession of closed office doors. A few paintings of past military governors hung on the walls. Through one of the few nearby windows fell the reassuring shadow of the cathedral spire, casting a triangle of black across the hallway just by the foot of the stairs that led up to Colonel Venegas' office.

It had been a long time since Gil had come to this building. Torroba had warned him against it. But what was there to do now?

He tried to mop away the perspiration, braced himself, and began to mount the stairs with stately deliberation. More pictures of historical figures had been hung along the stairwell, past Guard commandants and photos of Civil Governors of the province, going back to the time of Alfonso XI. Another Civil Guard, a Corporal Morales who enjoyed tuba music and had asthma, stood at the landing, just around the curve of the hallway. He too recognized Gil, raised a hand in brief greeting, grinned, and went back to rolling his cigarette. Gil shuffled by him without a word. Morales shrugged. He was used to such things. Twenty feet more and he would be in Venegas' office.

Still another Guard, an unfamiliar, heavily built man with a square face and a brutal, bored expression was leaning against the wall by the door.

He looked up and shook his head brusquely. "No, señor . . . no."

"I must; I insist. Tell the Colonel that Sebastián Gil is . . ."

"The Colonel has given strict instructions," the Guard began. . . . "No one should even be on this floor now . . . how did you come up here? How is it? . . ." The Guard noticed the black mourning band and seemed puzzled.

"Don't you understand at all? I must . . . tell him. He'll see me."

Even as the Guard thrust out a calloused hand to stop him, Gil pushed by and entered the room.

Colonel Venegas' office was not large; it only seemed so to Gil because of the sparseness of its furnishings. The walls were blank, and there was only one small, almost empty bookcase in a corner and a few old wooden chairs. Venegas' desk, a large trestle table with drawers, stood near the window. It was all so like the man himself: austere, self-effacing, self-righteously harsh. The room was full of sunlight, bright and blinding. Gil blinked. Behind him, the Guard on duty protested loudly and tried to pull him back through the doorway.

Two men were in the room: Venegas and another man in civilian clothes seated in front of the desk, his back to the door so that Gil could not see his face. Venegas, who had been engaged in low conversation with the second man, looked up and saw Gil and the Guard struggling by the door. He waved sharply, snapping out a word that Gil did not catch. The Guard stepped back and closed the door quickly.

"Sebastián . . . what is this? Didn't Sergeant Cruz tell you . . . ?" Fernán Venegas began, visibly annoyed. The collar of his tunic was open, and a cigarette lay fuming in a white glass Cinzano dish by his elbow. His round, almost bald head seemed to have swollen in the heat, making his pinched features look even smaller than they were, the vagrant puffs of graying black hair over his ears more pronounced. He pushed his glasses up on his nose and leaned forward, supporting himself on outthrust palms.

"I'm busy, Sebastian, can't you see . . . ?"

"But you don't know what's happened," Gil began. He could think of nothing but the body in front of his shop.

The man to whom Venegas had been talking hunched down in the chair and did not turn. Venegas said, "All right, quickly then, Sebastián . . . whatever it is . . . quickly . . ."

Gil tried to stop his trembling, braced himself against the wall.

"They killed a man and threw his body in front of my shop. . . ."

"So . . . ?" said Venegas. "An accident? Or not. Whatever difference it makes. We've had our share of killings these past few weeks. In front of your shop? So what? I'll send someone to get rid of him. . . ."

"But that's not it . . ."

"What then?"

"My shop . . . why my shop? . . . it was a warning, I know it. . . ."

Venegas sat down heavily, looked away. "And what do you expect me to do? I warned you about Torroba. Now, see what it's gotten you? You can't play both sides, Sebastián. . . ."

"Then you think it *was* a warning. . . ."

"I didn't say that."

"But you think . . ."

"I don't think anything. Only what you've told me: that someone dumped a body in front of your place or that he was killed there. See López on the way out. He's the one at the foot of the stairs. He'll send a few men to clean up." Venegas got up and walked around the desk to where Gil was still standing.

"Look," he said. "I know this isn't very helpful to you, and I can see how upset you are, but later, please Sebastián, later . . . you shouldn't be here. This is very dangerous for you, more than you could imagine. . . ."

Venegas put a hand on Gil's shoulder, squinted up at him, through his heavy glasses. "You have to understand, Sebastián. This was a foolish thing for you to do . . . very dangerous." Words drifted by as he was pushed into the corridor, gently, so slowly: ". . . things you don't understand . . . don't worry about all of this, I'll see to it . . . now, please . . ."

The corridor, darker than before; Gil and Venegas standing there next to the guard. The door closed again and the shadow of the man who had been seated in front of Venegas' desk was thrown against the glass panel of the door.

"Sergeant . . . ," Venegas was saying to the Guard at the door. "Take him to López and see that a squad goes with him. No, better yet, he'll give you the address and you send the men ahead. He'll follow after you . . . yes, you can leave your post here for a minute." He took Gil's hand. "Any other time but this. Try to understand, Sebastián. In a half an hour, come back. I can talk to you then. Close the shop and come back. . . ."

Gil followed the Sergeant down the hall quietly. Come back in a half hour? How idiotic. They would remove the body. Well and good, but what about him? How many more bodies would there be? And why? What had he ever done to anyone?

They had carried the corpse away on a stretcher, a blanket thrown over it so clumsily that the feet stuck out at the bottom. On the way up the street, one of the Guards almost stumbled on a slippery mound of garbage, and the stretcher pitched wildly. Some children on a nearby wall had shouted in derision, vanished when the other Guards had thrown pebbles at them. No respect for the dead, when death is a commonplace of life. A man who's dead is simply a man who's been caught at something and didn't have the wits to escape. A fool, in other words.

There were only two men outside now, Corporal López and another who was throwing water from a bucket onto the stones, trying to wash away the blood.

The pinkish water began to seep under the door and into the shop. Gil pushed a wad of newspaper up against the crack and went behind the counter. A soft, almost subterranean light filled the room. The shop was at the bottom of a narrow street, and neither the heat nor the full light of midday had yet found its way through the drawn blinds, the shades and the grille with which Gil attempted to cut himself off from the outside world.

Gil loosened his tie and sat down behind the counter. Next to the counter, on a low table, stood an electric Gramophone and a pile of records. Under the counter, easy to reach from where he now sat, was a telephone. Gil reached for it slowly, as though expecting it to explode at his touch.

He spoke the number quickly; the voice at the exchange, distant, dispassionate, grated against his nerves. "How can she be so calm?" . . . Then a series of clicks, another, different voice at the other end. If Venegas would not help him, who else was he to turn to?

"Manuel?" Gil said, recognizing the voice.

"Yes? Yes? Who is it . . . ?"

Gil began to speak very rapidly, the words rushing one over the other, not giving Torroba a chance to answer. Finally out of breath, Gil stopped but before Torroba could say anything, he added in an accusing tone, "Why me? Why should you do this to me?"

"We didn't. I swear to you, Sebastián. It was not one of my people."

"Who else then? . . . Tell me, who else?"

"The FAI aren't the only ones in Toledo who . . . have to kill sometime . . . you know that. . . ." His voice was hushed, as though he was ashamed.

"Why me?" Gil insisted, as though he had not heard Torroba's denial.

"I can't talk to you now, Sebastián. . . ."

"Not now, not now, not now," the words echoed. All the same: Venegas, Torroba. Opposites, but the same. He felt a choking heaviness in his chest and tore open his collar as though it were a lack of air rather than of understanding which was strangling him.

"If you could come over, just for a few minutes . . . this is a terrible thing, Manuel . . . you don't know . . ."

"A corpse? We have too many of them these days . . . Sebastián. . . . If I could stop it, you know I would, but what can I do? If it was one of our people . . . I could help you, but what am I to do about the Communists or the blue-shirts, or the plain *pistoleros* that are running loose now? You tell *me* that? It's all coming apart now . . . the news from Morocco; it's all true. Sevilla and Jerez and . . ."

"Please . . . ," Gil began to cry, hardly listening to what Torroba was saying.

Torroba cut him off. "If you want my advice, it's still the same. Stay away from Venegas. Maybe it's too late already. It seems so. Now you'll have to take your chances . . . what can I say? Tell me, what do you want me to say to you? . . . Stay in your house, don't go out if you can help it. . . ."

"Manuel, please . . . ," Gil repeated. What did he expect the man to say? Why had he called him? Gil could see Torroba there in the granary the Anarchists used as headquarters, trying to talk without revealing who it was he was speaking to. He could deny that his people were responsible for the body all he wanted to, but what did it matter if he wouldn't do anything to help?

"Look . . . I'll try to come tonight or tomorrow," Torroba said. "We can talk then. Now I must hang up, do you understand? Do that for me, Sebastián. Understand . . ."

A click at the other end. *Understand,* the same word Venegas had used, the only word of their conversation he seemed to remember. Gil fell back into his chair, let the receiver dangle by its cord. After a moment he reached out and turned on the fan. He looked about: the door was bolted, the grate drawn. A narrow slice of light entered through a tear in one of the shades, permitted him to look out into the street as well. The *calle* seemed empty, but how could he tell?

A breeze swept the shop as the fan oscillated noisily, sending the dust up in swirls from the cluttered shelves. He sank back into the chair, lit a cigarette, and took a record from the top of the stack and placed it on the turntable. He set the needle to the grooves and began to move his hands, shaping the air into sound, as though he were conducting. He had not even looked to see what was on the record. The gentle, longing music that emerged washed over him, soothing and perfect. He no longer thought of the corpse as something specific, having to do with himself, but only of death in the abstract. His wife's death, his own . . . someday. It was a mood he found congenial, even reassuring. The voice floated from the tinny speaker, filling the room: Fleta singing *"Nostalgia Andaluz."* Slowly, Gil began to relax. In the rippling accompaniment, the tolling of bells under the winding voice, he heard, then saw his wife at their own piano:

> *Triste toque de l'oración*
> *Muere'l dia, tambien mi amor . . .*

What did any of it really matter? Venegas, Torroba, the corpse, Gil himself? Death in the end, the death of the body, the death of love. One and the same . . .

Outside, far up the street, a muffled explosion resounded. The creaking of overburdened axles answered like the protest of a dying animal.

The phonograph needle had jumped the grooves. Gil reached out, moved the needle back to where it had been before the explosion.

"If only one could move time back as easily," he thought. "What a blessing . . ."

He closed his eyes, wondering if Torroba would really come in the evening as he had promised. Fleta's voice rose, weighted with passion, fell again.

> *"Muere'l dia . . . tambien mi amor . . ."*

MONDAY, JULY 20, 11:30 A.M.: *Toledo*

HE APPROACHED THE CARVALHO HOUSE from the east, crossing the San Martín bridge on horseback and then leaving the mare with a stableman near the Church of San Juan de los Reyes. Passing under the somber gold walls and into the shade of the cypress that bordered its approaches, he paused to look up at the chains hanging slack from the walls overhead. It was just as well that the chains had been left there; sooner or later someone would find a use for them again.

A pack of dogs with swollen bellies and stark, protruding ribs ran by. Two ragged boys chased after them, shying stones. The crack of rocks bouncing on the cobbles and the pant of the dogs' breath were the only sounds in the street. The sun was resting heavily in late morning fullness above the city. The alleys and narrow twisting *calles* were airless and full of dust motes. Flies buzzed through fresh manure that marked a mule's passage up the street toward the ancient synagogue of the Tránsito.

Jaime moved forward hesitantly. He knew precisely where the house was, had no need to ask directions of any of the black-clad women who passed carrying huge baskets, straw brooms, their faces seamed with the miserable acceptance of their own humanity. More dogs passed, snarling and tumbling, and far ahead, where two of the cramped streets jostled each other for command of a crossroads, a Civil Guard on horseback glided by, hunched low in the saddle. He wore his cape even in the sweltering heat, and his face was as dark as his tricorn. His Mauser was unslung and clamped rigidly under his left arm.

The street curved past the synagogue, away from the paseo and the river, and ascended toward the center of the city which rose to the northeast like a great ant mound. Jaime pushed his hair back, wiped the sweat away, and peered down the *calle* before entering. The open street leading from the San Juan had been white with sunlight. Here, the buildings suddenly leaned together, casting a thick umber shadow over everything. Ahead, where the walls of the houses on either side climbed even higher, the shadow turned to purple, an unaccustomed cool color on the hot palette of the city.

He had no idea what he would say to her but that seemed to be of no importance now. He simply had to go there, if only to look at the house, to say a few insignificant words to the girl, perhaps ask her out onto the paseo for nothing more than a look at the river. The rest, if there was to be a rest, would come later. He had not felt so sure of himself in a long, long time.

She was his way back to Colonel Carvalho. The *calle* widened a little, and the Carvalho house came into view less than thirty meters distant. It was a simple, two-story building, not much wider than those around it, but with patrician simplicity of design. He went straight to the front door, a heavy set of panels studded with typical Toledan nails and emblazoned with a double-headed Hapsburg eagle made of wrought-iron. As he raised his hand to knock, he saw that the door was open. Puzzled, he lowered his hand and looked up and down the street as though expecting to find someone who had just gone out and was hastening back to lock the door after him. No one.

It was not at all clear to Jaime whether he was hesitating simply because of a natural reticence to enter the Carvalho house uninvited or because he was afraid that someone might see him. Certainly, he no longer feared the house itself. The appearance of the girl had changed all that; like so many fears, it had assumed an entirely different aspect once he had actually confronted it.

He pushed the heavy door open and stepped inside.

The front hallway was empty. Dust stirred on the floor. He could see light outlines, bleached squares and marks on the darker floor, where furniture had once stood. An old newspaper blew across a threshold. The walls were bare. Farther in, he found a scattering of carpet tacks where the coverings had been lifted. The front room was empty too. An old candelabrum had been left on the floor in a corner, next to a harpischord over which a shroud had been thrown. On the wall, hung Carvalho's old picture. It and the instrument were the only traces of his ownership.

Jaime could not make it out at all. The girl had been to his father's house only two nights before and had mentioned nothing about leaving. But then, he had barely talked to her. How could he blame her for not saying anything? And, besides, what right had he to know? Twelve hours before, perhaps even less, he would have recoiled in anger, had anyone suggested that he come to the house of Carvalho. But now, perhaps because of yesterday's visit to the monastery, perhaps . . . there were so many possibilities . . . he had at last recognized the stupidity of hiding. He had thought that solitude, withdrawal . . . in his own way . . . was not only the answer but the end in itself. Seeing Luis Pelayo, grasping another, equally pointless kind of solitude had made Jaime realize how foolish it was. The best mirror in which to glimpse one's own stupidity is the face of another who is doing the same thing.

He walked through the empty rooms, stopping now and then to make patterns in the gathering dust with the toe of his boot. The house smelled of desolation, of unfulfilled expectations. A trace of scent, a woman's perfume, lingered near the stairs. He called out but no one answered.

Without quite knowing why, he thought suddenly: "He's deserted. It was all a lie, going to Oviedo that way. Now he's deserted and left her here, that's the only explanation. And he's got the cruelty to strip the house down around her, even to make her do it for him. . . ." Often he would arrive at a conclusion and then have to stop and trace his way back through a labyrinth of unstated reasons to find out why he had decided as he had. This time the way was short. How often had the Colonel spoken of the house, dreamed of it, looked to it as his anchor in a world which, as he put it, "never had the decency to leave him in peace," . . . all this until the house was more the man than he was himself. Jaime knew, without ever having seen, each and every piece of furniture in the place, every carving, every picture on the wall. The Colonel had never tired of describing them. Strange, but he had seldom talked about his wife or children in that way, and their faces always came as a surprise, as Mercedes' had two nights before.

As he worked his way back to the explanation for his sudden understanding, Jaime grew flushed with anger. It was the same thing that the Colonel had done to him. "Worse, because she is his own daughter. . . ." But did she realize what had happened? he wondered. Of course not; it had taken him almost a year to understand the extent of his betrayal, and this woman was the man's daughter. How much slower, then, the process of understanding. He felt a strange sympathy like a wound opening in his chest. He had come to the house to face down his phantoms and perhaps find an explanation for the Colonel's acts, and he had found his explanation in their repetition. Now he had only one course: to help the girl and make her realize just what her father was, to shame him in her eyes and, in a way, to take his place with her. It gave him a deep sense of satisfaction to know that he might accomplish both at once.

He walked back through the halls, pausing once to look at the shadowed portrait hanging tilted on the wall above the draped harpischord; then he went back out into the street.

He followed the sloping cobblestones to the paseo near the Tránsito. A few empty benches and a soft drink vendor in overalls, pushing his cart away from the poplars that bordered the gorge. Across the way, a short man of about sixty was reading a newspaper, pausing now and then to push back a cap which kept slipping down over his forehead. He was puffing determinedly on a wrinkled cigarette and exhaling streams of evil-smelling smoke. As Jaime came out of the street and onto the paseo, he looked up and nodded.

There was no harm in asking and, besides, if he was a regular on the street, he might have seen the girl pass by, . . . know which way she had gone. Jaime walked over to him.

"Señor . . . ," he began. "*Buenas* . . ."

MIDDAY, JULY 20: *Toledo*

ALTHOUGH HER HAND HAD BEGUN to tire some while before, Mercedes Carvalho continued to work until the last drawing of the series was completed. Then she came down from the short ladder which Acosta Matteu had left there for her use and stood on the dusty floor, looking up at the rows of arched windows which were not windows but simply openings onto recesses of stone, scalloped and wound round with twining designs of stone vines. Between them, set at regular intervals, were carefully sculpted pillars and rosettes which formed false arches within and between the real arches; above it all, running just under the ceiling beams, stretched an endless row of graceful Hebrew letters, only a few of which she could decipher. Acosta Matteu, who was learned in such things by virtue of the long years he had spent as custodian of the Tránsito, had once translated some of them for her, but she had forgotten most of what he had said.

She had been right; she had had neither strength nor time enough to finish the drawings on Sunday. These few more hours on a quiet Monday morning had been necessary to bring the series to a conclusion. Now she could think about packing, about leaving Toledo for France.

Looking about the tranquil, high-ceilinged room, it seemed incredible to her that her mother should have decided to move permanently to Biarritz and that her father would have acquiesced and remained at his post in Oviedo. The few letters she had received had been cryptic, as though the Colonel had been afraid to commit anything to writing but the simplest, most innocent of directions. Why, she wondered, had he been so maddeningly cautious? It wasn't like him at all. She tried to think of other things, of the beach at Biarritz, the casino. She would follow his instructions now that the last truckload had gotten off, go down to the Zoco in the afternoon and buy her ticket for the bus to Madrid. Train connections were still open; there hadn't been anything on the radio about train service being disrupted, and with any luck at all, she could be in Biarritz in two or three days.

She could not help thinking of her father, of Oviedo . . . though she had never been there and had seen pictures of it only in magazines and newspaper supplements. It occurred to her then for the first time that it was not just another post but rather a kind of purgatory for him to return there. He had never spoken much of what had happened two years before, but she understood more of it than he cared to have her know. She had tried to convince herself that reason would prevail, that everyone understood him as she did and knew that the things that were said about him, about what had happened during the miners' rising, were lies and that he was a good man who had been simply overmatched by events. But it didn't always work out that way, not in this country, she thought.

"We don't often think with the nice reasoning of the English," she had said to him once in response to some now forgotten question, and he had stopped his stern inquisition abruptly and rubbed his beard. "We don't have the appreciation for the subtleties of logic that the French have or the feeling for endless convolution that the Germans cherish, so what can we do but think with our hearts?" She could not remember what he had said after that, but it was true. "With our hearts and with our bodies, but rarely," she thought, "with our heads." Everything was determined along the simplest of lines: death, loyalty, death, faith, death, revenge, death, beauty . . . all inextricably linked by the one constant re-frain: "death," celebrated in tradition and in every act of every day so that it became a commonplace. The horribly bleeding polychrome Christ carried in the feast-day processions made one's own body ache and one went to Mass burdened not with the suffering of God's son but with the pain of one's own suffering. Everything had to be directly experienced. It was, she thought, just as in the ancient, anonymous sonnet that she could never forget and that seemed so full of hidden meanings for her:

"It isn't the heaven that You have promised me, my God, that moves me to love You, nor is it the hell I so fear that moves me to cease my sinning, *You* move me, Lord; it moves me to see You nailed to that Cross and despised; it moves me to see Your body so wounded; the in-sults You have suffered and Your death . . . moves me. . . ."

Nothing could be explained; it had to be felt. Perhaps, then, in the end . . . her father was right. The only question was, what would he do?

She gathered her chalks together in one hand, took up the pad in the other, and walked across the empty, high-ceilinged room, under the heavy beams, past the fifty-four arches. Under her feet, the tombstones of the caballeros de Calatrava, to whom the Tránsito had been given after the expulsion, added the echo of a name to each step. She would have to come back and make drawings of those stones, too, though it would be much dirtier, more exhausting work. In the fall, the weather would be cooler. By then, she would be back in Toledo.

During the morning, she had heard footsteps behind her many times, heard the door open, close, a few whisperings, the jingle of coins in pockets and, once or twice, Acosta Matteu's heavy breathing. But no one had come in. She pushed open the door. The day outside was bright, almost stunning in the flat glare of the sun on the tawny stones of the street. The breeze had vanished and the leaves of the trees hung perfectly still as though pinned to the dazzling blue sky that showed through the fretwork of their branches. Everything seemed very quiet, and she could not even hear the usual clop of horses' hooves or the shouting or innocent children at play in the ruins that tumbled down the cliff banks to the edge of the river.

Matteu was nowhere in sight. It was very hot, and the hills across the river seemed to glow, the rocks sparkling in the sunlight, and the scrubby trees vivid green though they drew little water from the rocks. How they survived in such a climate, in such terrain, she had often wondered. At the end of the low stone wall along the edge of the paseo, about thirty yards away, a young man was standing, his back to her. . . . She could not see his face. His shoulders were bent slightly as though he were either very weak or very tired, and his head was lowered. A wide black strain of perspiration blotched the back of his white shirt, and he stood with one leg crooked, his foot resting on a projecting stone.

There was no one else in the paseo and no one on the street beyond. From the distance now, she heard the muted sound of a radio, a thin, metallic voice, the words almost incomprehensible: ". . . under control . . . the situation . . ."

She began to move toward the distant figure, but before she had gone more than a few steps, he seemed to hear her and turned. It was the young Mercader. He gazed at her with a profound sadness that made him look much older than he was. She stopped, waited until he had come up to her. He was unshaven, and there were dark circles under his eyes. His black windblown hair hung loosely down over his forehead, giving him a wild look that contrasted oddly with the gentle expression of his eyes. She watched him carefully, as though the slightest motion might explain what he was doing there.

"You don't mind my being here? I came to . . . see you . . . ," he said. His voice was calm, weighted with that same odd weariness that clouded his eyes. How strange, she thought, that anyone, particularly such a young man, should seem so tired. And at a time like this. Things were happening all around. Events would carry her along, and she welcomed the flood; they seemed to confirm everything that Raúl had promised, that her father had sworn by for the last five years, ever since the Republic had been proclaimed, since Primo de Rivera had died. She remembered that day clearly, the surprisingly cruel light of satisfaction in her father's eyes. How much he blamed on the dictator, how much on King Alfonso. Now it would all be swept away. Finally. Yet this young man seemed almost broken.

She said, "Why would you want to see me? What would we have to say to each other?"

"I don't know. . . ."

"I didn't mean it that way . . . but the other night . . ."

"I know. It was my fault, and I apologize to you. I don't ask you to understand, only to forgive me."

"That's simple enough. I'm not a priest. I don't have to pretend to understand before I can forgive."

He smiled in a tentative way. "Your house . . . it's almost empty."

"You were at the house?"

"Yes, I went there to find you." He paused. "What's happened to the furniture?"

"It's gone to Biarritz, all of it. My father sent word."

"Sent word? Where from? Where is he now?"

"At Oviedo, I think. At least I don't know that he's left there for any reason."

"It will be bad for him, staying there."

"Is that why you're not there, too?"

"Yes . . . it would have been bad for me, and it isn't good my being here either, but it's worse for him there."

"Why?"

"You don't know? You really don't know any of it? Hasn't he told you anything?"

"What should I know?" she asked cautiously.

"That it's dangerous for him . . . in two ways . . . as the priests say . . . for the body and for the soul. For me it was the . . . soul . . . I could have taken the other risk. . . ."

"Sit down here . . . now . . . ," she said pointing to a bench by the wall. It was a spot shaded by a stand of poplars. "Because of the rising? Is that what you mean?"

"Yes, that's what I mean. The generals sent him up there to get rid of him. And he knew it. In Madrid he could have remained with the Republic if that was what he wanted . . . but up there, they'll kill him first. They won't even ask whose side he's on. But he went anyhow, knowing that. That's what I don't understand."

"And you . . . ?"

"I couldn't go. I just couldn't go. Not even for him. It wouldn't have been so dangerous for me. I'm just . . . I was just . . . a lieutenant.

Nobody remembered me or cared. But I couldn't go there. . . ." He stood up, nervously twisting his hands together. "Listen . . . can we walk a bit, and you'll tell me about the furniture?"

She shrugged and stood up with him. "There's nothing to tell. It's gone, that's all. You saw . . . I'm going to go to Biarritz too, in a few days. That's what he wants. . . ."

"Your father?"

"Yes . . . he sent me letters."

"Are you sure they were . . . from him?"

"Don't you think I know his writing? Yes, of course they were from him. . . ."

"He must be in Biarritz himself then . . . that would . . . make sense. Yes, he wouldn't tell you . . . not in a letter that someone else might read, but . . ."

"You're wrong. He's in Oviedo."

"He couldn't stay there . . . and he hasn't . . ."

"Believe what you want," she said with mounting irritation. She choked it off; he meant no offense, was only trying to tell her something that she had sensed herself before, when her father had been there. The implications of Mercader's words began to shake her. If her father really was in Biarritz, then he had deserted. She hadn't even considered such a possibility.

"I'm sorry for behaving so badly," he said, as though he had not understood her question at all, ". . . the other night . . . the guests . . ."

"You don't have to be sorry. . . ." It was simpler to return to meaningless commonplaces than to talk further about her father. She slipped back into a superficial tone with relief. "I hate people like that myself. They're frauds, all of them, I think. They talk in one world and live in another. . . ."

He was silent, then said: "It wasn't that. It was you . . ."

"Me? What do you mean?"

"You were there and so was your father. That was all. You and your father . . ."

It was back again. She had to accept it: "But you came here today . . ."

"I know."

She stood there, shaking her head. The wind had come up again from the river and the hills of *Los Cigarrales,* driving the heat before it.

Her eyes grew darker, her features more highly animated. Nothing about her face was perfect, nothing too imperfect. She resembled her father very strongly, the same long nose, flaring nostrils, the same intense eyes. Not at all the way he remembered her from the wedding. He remembered more details of that night now, seeing her again. The Colonel had proposed a toast to Azaña who was then in prison. Another officer at the table had refused, and the men had gone outside into the hallway to quarrel, leaving Jaime alone at the table with the girl and her mother. The orchestra had been playing the *Eva* waltz. He remembered that, and she had asked him if he knew the song.

Jaime watched her carefully. Neither quite trusted the other, yet neither really disbelieved the other either.

"Aren't you afraid," he said at last. "You've heard the reports on the radio . . . the rumors?"

"Why should I be afraid? My father will serve the Republic, and there isn't even a garrison here to revolt. Only a few cadets at the Alcázar. Besides, it's all nothing . . . only rumors, and you've heard, the situation is . . ."

". . . under control? Do you believe that? I don't."

"No matter what happens, I'll be all right, and . . . then . . . I'm going to France in a day or two."

"If what Señor Barcenas said the other night is true . . . do you remember? If there's a real revolution, do you think anyone will care for the truth? No one else does. You're Enrique Carvalho's daughter, remember?"

"You can't tell the Anarchists from the priests here. . . ."

"They both wear black. . . . They'll both wear red too."

She tried to laugh but it came out forced and insincere. "You're so serious . . . ," she said. "Did you come all the way here to talk about such frightening things?"

"No . . . I don't know why I came. I was riding, and it seemed that I should come. . . ."

"Then you wanted to see . . . me?"

"In a way," he replied. "May I come again tomorrow? If you would take lunch with me in the Zocodover . . . the old woman would come, of course."

"Tomorrow?"

"Yes . . ."

"My father would want it. Yes, then."

"We can talk about him tomorrow," Jaime said. "I would like to hear about how he was when you were a child. I have . . . great respect for him. . . ."

Just then Acosta Matteu came by, clinking a few coins forlornly in the palm of his hand and carrying an empty *magnol* bottle. He was angry because the vendor of bottled drinks had gone off for lunch with his cart, and there would be no more lemon soda until much later in the afternoon.

He looked suspiciously at Jaime whom he had directed to the Tránsito only a little while earlier.

"Is he bothering you, this man? If I had known, Señorita Carvalho, that he would bother you I would not have told him how to find you . . . even for a few coins. I'm no Judas. . . ."

"Don't be concerned. We were just talking. He's a friend."

Acosta Matteu considered her answer for a second: "If he begins to bother you then . . . which may be expected, God's curse on such young men who do not know how to behave before women, all you have to do is call out. I am in the habit of listening carefully to what goes on around me and I assure you, I will hear . . ."

"Thank you, Señor Matteu, but we were only talking. . . ."

"Talking, now," Matteu persisted. "But later he may bother you. If so, there is a Civil Guard, Pablo Cruz, who is sitting now with Pepe Cintron and playing cards, just up the next street. He should not play cards, I know, but he's a good young man, a *gallego,* not so much like the others," and he made a stern face to express his scorn for young men who took themselves too seriously . . . "a very young man who hasn't soured yet . . ."

Mercedes smiled. "Thank you for your concern. Now . . . Señor Matteu, the ladder you gave me is in the corner by the door. I left it there for you . . ."

"It might be stolen," Acosta Matteu said, wrinkling his nose. "So I'm glad you told me. Will you be using it again today . . . ?"

"No. . . ."

"Then I'll see that it's put with my other ladders where it will be safe. These days nothing can be considered really safe. They'll be wanting to make my ladders everybody's property one of these days, and your drawings too, Señorita, and your house too. Listen to me . . . I know what I'm saying."

He turned away from them, distracted by the chatter of a few ragged children who were throwing stones against the wall of the Tránsito. He moved off, kicking sullenly at the ground.

"Tomorrow?" Jaime asked when Matteu had gone.

"Yes," she said.

"*Buenas dias,* then," he said. "Tomorrow at this time . . ."

He touched his forehead in what might almost have been a brief salute and walked away across the paseo and down the street.

For an instant, she wanted to run after him. Her mind was filled with contradictory thoughts. Nothing seemed to make sense. His gentle, sad mood had infected her with uncertainty. She had that same sensation of questions left unasked, of things bursting to be said but somehow stifled that she had experienced during her father's visit. "No, it isn't gentleness," she thought . . . , "It's resignation . . . my God . . ."

She stood there under the motionless trees on the paseo, looking into the shadows beyond the second ancient synagogue, now called Santa María la Blanca, for any trace of the Lieutenant. But he had gone now.

The river in the gorge below sounded louder, more insistent, and she could hear the shrill piping of magpies in the rocks and low trees across the Tagus. Acosta Matteu was just emerging from the Tránsito, carrying his ladder. He headed toward the house of Carlos Blanco with whom he played cards. He always lost and often he would joke about it;

the world would come to an end the day he won, he would swear. She wondered how he would do today.

JULY 20, 2:00 P.M.: *The Mercaders*

"TOMÁS PELAYO CALLED ME just after noon. He said you'd been to see his son yesterday, and he wondered why you hadn't stopped by to see him as well . . ."

Francisco Mercader had been walking along the whitewashed stone wall that enclosed his lands when Jaime had ridden the mare in, this time coming from the main road that led to Toledo. Francisco had been surprised but had said nothing about it.

It was two in the afternoon, and the sun was at its strongest, bringing the air almost to a boil and making it impossible to breathe. Used to the Moroccan heat, Francisco survived the swelter even better than the natives of La Mancha. He was in the habit of walking about his lands at hours when others had retreated into the shade of houses and taverns. Passersby could often see him from the road, dressed in a loose white jacket and carrying a twisted stick, walking along the wall and through the groves of cypress and olive that dotted his lands. Sometimes he wore a cap from the back of which he hung a handkerchief, spread to keep his neck from burning, after the fashion of the French Legionnaires whom he had always admired, especially in the films. Today, however, he went bareheaded in the sun.

Jaime studied his father. "If Tomás Pelayo knows I was there, then he must also know what took place," he said. "There wasn't anything to tell him so I wanted to spare him the disappointment. It's too bad he knows that I was there."

What he said was only partly true. After leaving Mercedes Carvalho he had gone to the center of the city and to the Banco Toledano, hoping to speak to Pelayo. He had even gone inside, past the Civil Guard at the door and into the cool stone front offices, but then he had turned about and left as quickly as he had entered. The Guards at the door had stared after him, and Jaime realized that, in fact, it had been the Guards' faces, their presence, that had caused him to leave so suddenly, without even asking whether Pelayo was there or not. The Guards seemed to him like the dead, mummified images that stand upright in the Mexican catacombs he had read about: they were infected with the same cancer that was killing him. Did it matter to them for whom they raised those ugly Mausers? . . . in whose service they pulled the trigger? One government demanded that they kill Asturians, another that they slaughter Moroccans; yet another government required that they defend the Pelayos and the Solers against . . . whom? . . . The generals who had risen against disorder and threatened to create still more? the Anarchists who lay in the shadows waiting to take advantage of events? the weak-willed Republic itself, unable to keep its identity for even a day? What mattered was that men would kill, and there would be no real reason for it. He had tried, and staked everything on doing what he thought was right. It had accomplished nothing except to humiliate him and had almost cost him his life. Against such irrationality, what could a man do?

Jaime became aware that his father was talking, taking up the thread of conversation at precisely the point where he had stopped speaking before. He had said something about Luis . . . about Tomás . . . "It's too bad that he knows I was there. . . ." Was that it?

Francisco was answering him: "Luis told him, so you see . . ."

"That's odd," Jaime said, hardly concentrating. The conversation with Luis Pelayo had faded almost entirely from his mind, and the mention of it brought back only a dim memory of the monastery, brooding dark against the mirror-blue sky. "Why would Luis tell him?"

"Tomás didn't understand it either. It seems that Luis thought you were very 'amusing'. . . or at least that's the term he used to his father. . . . What did you two have to say to one another?"

"A great deal which meant nothing at all." He turned away from his father for a moment. Even with Francisco, only one out of every thousand words he spoke had any meaning. He twisted off a twig from a nearby tree, heard his father draw a breath in protest, but Francisco said nothing. "That's the way it is," Jaime thought. "He objects, but he won't say anything. That's the way they all are . . . can it be that to grow older in this world simply means to accept more and more things that outrage us? Is that the answer to Carvalho's behavior?"

"Tomás was very disappointed. He had hoped . . ." Francisco began dimly, walking along the wall with his head down. He took out a handkerchief and mopped the back of his neck, which was beginning to redden. ". . . that Luis would talk to you but instead, it seems, Luis was . . ."

"Just as much of a fool with me as he is with his father . . . ," Jaime said. The mare whinnied, and he turned back; something had caught her attention up on the main road. He heard the grumble of a car's engine, and through the trees that shaded the road at that point, he saw a passage of brown, a flapping military pennant mounted on a radiator cap, a cloud of dust thrown briefly into the heavy air, then falling.

"I saw that same car go by last night, just at sundown," Francisco said. "There's very little traffic on that road this week . . ." His voice trailed off. "Would you go and talk to Tomás, nevertheless? He's very upset."

"Talking to me would only make him worse. He'd better forget about Luis and look to more important things. You've been at the house this morning?" he asked with sudden urgency. "What's the news?"

Francisco pretended he had not understood, then said, finally: "Madrid says simply that the situation is 'under control.' Oh, yes, now they admit that more than Morocco was involved. We've all heard about the slaughter at the Montaña barracks, so they can hardly deny that. But they insist that the rising has been put down, and who are we, out here, to argue with them?"

"So . . . and do you believe them? Would you stake your life on it?" Jaime muttered, shaking his head. He believed nothing and no one anymore and hardly knew why he persisted in asking questions. He had come to see that real truth is the most unattainable of all things; man's greeds and his prejudices never fail to distort it no matter what his intentions. The more vigorously a man attempts to tell the truth, the more likely he is to end up lying. "The city is . . . quiet . . . ," he said. ". . . So far, at least . . ."

"Of course. And it will remain quiet . . . nothing will happen, Jaime."

"But have you thought of what might happen if there is trouble, here? That is what is bothering Señor Pelayo. Toledo may be full of priests today, but it could be full of priestly corpses tomorrow if . . ."

"Jaime . . . Jaime . . . must it always be the same with you? Can't you believe that your . . . experience . . . was just that, an isolated event, something which . . . happened, and can never happen exactly that way again? Certainly, terrible things happen occasionally, but there's nothing to fear here. You know how many friends I have in the Government . . . the Ministry . . ."

"I know, but you should make plans anyhow." Jaime could contain himself no longer. "You must know, Colonel Carvalho has deserted. He's run to France."

Francisco turned on him in shocked anger. "How could you know such a thing? It can't be true."

"I was at his house. I went there. Don't ask me why. It came to me yesterday that I should go there and talk to the daughter, that perhaps I could exorcise this horror I have of him by simply facing up to it. As you said, I can't spend the rest of my life riding back and forth from Toledo to Illescas. So I went, but I didn't find her there. Instead I found the house open, the door unlocked, and everything gone. He's had the furniture shipped to Biarritz, and he's told the girl to go there as well."

Francisco looked relieved and smiled, nodding his head. Francisco said, "If that's all . . . well, how do you come to such a conclusion from . . . that?"

"Don't you see it? I thought you knew the man."

"I do. It's you who . . ."

"Don't tell me. It's as plain as anything could be. That house is his anchor, the furniture, the pictures, all of it. He's been running all his life and always, let me tell you, always, he speaks of that house as though his soul lived there, not in his body. Now he's had it stripped, transplanted to another country. No, I don't need any more than that to tell me. He'd never have had them do it if he were still in Spain."

Francisco considered what his son had said. "And you want . . . what?"

"I want you to do the same. He knows what's happening. . . . It wasn't just his own skin that made him run. Whatever else he may be, he's not a physical coward. It's got to be more, and if it is, we haven't any choice. . . ."

He wondered if he really believed what he was saying. Was there any real excuse for refusing to accept one's responsibility to act? But if everyone else ran, if events were so overpowering that a man alone could do nothing, then why sacrifice everything simply to assert one's self? He knew, deep down, that *there* lay the key to what Carvalho had done; he was certain of it, and that if he thought about it long enough, perhaps with the girl's help, he could come to understand. Might it be that the only real courage lay not in doing something one knew was foredoomed to failure, but in refusing to become involved at all?

Francisco pursed his lips, then shook his head and looked up into the branches of the olive trees under which they were just then passing. "And leave all of this? Do you think your mother could stand another . . . dislocation? I know how much she suffered when we left Ceuta. Don't insult me by accusing me of that kind of insensitivity, Jaime. I know what I did to her . . . but there was no other choice. We had to come here, and I've tried to make it easy for her. I think she may come to like it after a while. . . ."

"What has that got to do . . . ?"

"I won't uproot her again. Come, let's not talk about such things any longer. Look there, have you seen how well the cypress are growing this year . . . and on such little water too. I . . ."

"Father . . ."

"I said, we won't talk of such things anymore. Look at the cypress, Jaime."

He let his gaze be directed across the field to where a line of cypress grew tall yet mournfully across the distant prospect of the Sierra de Gredos. The ground around them was, as his father had said, arid and bleached white by the sun, yet the trees grew and grew, reaching high into the sky.

Father and son stood for a moment simply staring at the trees. It all tied together; if the Anarchists could wrongly blame Carvalho for the slaughter at Oviedo and, God, while he had been unable to stop it, at least he had tried . . . then who could tell what might happen if their anger were unleashed again? And was his father, his family more immune? Who, upon seeing the clean white house, the fenced-in lands, the evidence of well-being, would stop to think that here was a man almost unique among his fellows, who had come by it all honestly and without trampling on anyone else . . . or had he? . . . The truth, Jaime thought: could he even tell the truth himself or was he as blind as everyone else?

His father, face seamed with discontent and his eyes narrowed, was pacing among the small gray stones by the whitewashed wall.

"Will you ride back, Jaime?"

The son glanced over his shoulder. The mare was watching him, paying no attention to the sweet grasses between her hooves. She sensed his agitation and responded to it with the closest she could come to compassion.

"No . . . we'll walk back. Will you wait here for me? I'll bring the mare."

It was over a hundred yards from where they now stood to where Jaime had tethered the horse.

"I'll walk ahead," his father said. "You can catch up."

"He senses it, too," Jaime thought, "how far apart we've become. Well, it doesn't matter. He may not understand any of this, but it's still my obligation."

He walked back across the parched yellow field, keeping close to the stone wall, thinking that it had always seemed his responsibility to act when no one else would. This, at least, was something he could do. First he would get the mare, then he would have to see about a car. If the Colonel had gone to Biarritz, and he had no doubt at all that that was what had happened, then the situation must already be completely out of control. What else could have made a man who had accepted in silence an insult, no, a degradation, like his return to Oviedo without protest, pick himself up now and desert? The air smelled of lies and the stink of procrastination rose up around him. He tried to imagine what was happening in that city by the Mar Cantabrico. He could see its streets and its skeleton buildings, gutted and running with rats, but he could not people it; the vision hung before his eyes, empty and as desolate as the plains between Toledo and Illescas.

For a day, he had been free of it. Now it was coming back, and it spelled out a message of what was to come loudly as the braying trumpet that begins a corrida.

He wondered, was he the only one who heard it?

Monday Morning, July 20: *Biarritz*

The radio lay, smashed to bits, on the floor where he had thrown it the evening before. The dial was shattered; tiny slivers of glass lay about, as thin as the pointer which now struck like an arrow across the room, indicating the sea. Colonel Carvalho could not help noticing it. The glass crunched underfoot, and he kept glancing down, back and forth between the carpet, its Byzantine designs frosted over with powdered glass, and the sea beyond the window where the sun could be seen sparkling peacefully above the horizon.

He would not believe it though he had predicted it months before. Now that it had actually happened, he found that he could not credit either his own predictions nor the reality itself. And to make matters worse, Mercedes had not yet arrived. Nor had the call to Paris gone through; the connection had been made but Raúl Carvalho was not to be found. Messages had been left, but no return call had come.

9 3

How much of what he had heard before smashing the radio could he believe? Certainly not the Madrid station, weak as it was, that kept insisting that the uprising had been contained in Morocco and that no one on the mainland had any part in it, and then, by evening, was insisting with equal vigor that the rising had been crushed everywhere, even "in Sevilla." The Communist deputy, Ibarruri, La Pasionaria, had made a speech late in the evening, and at that point the Colonel had thrown a bookend at the radio, smashing it to bits.

He had slept fitfully, waking from dense, hot dreams in which the colors red and brown predominated, to walk about on the balcony outside his bedroom, watching the beacon at the tip of Cap San Martín revolve endlessly over the sea. Amalia, his wife, said nothing to him though she was not asleep either; she knew better than to try to talk to him when he was in such a mood and had, in any event, little to say, having heard only the very first broadcast before being waved out of the room.

He breakfasted lightly, a cup of bitter coffee and some figs, and went at once to the balcony off the main living room, where he sat, his back to the telephone stand, watching the ocean. The day was unexpectedly cool and bright, the sun beaming but without its usual heat. Below, beyond the curve of beach at the foot of the cliff, the Atlantic rippled like silk under a soft eastern breeze. Gulls wheeled in arcs like time itself suspended on the sky. The froth on the beach sparkled, and far away a commercial ship sledded through the open sea, leaving a low signature of smoke across the brilliant azure horizon.

Shortly before noon, the agronomist Hector Luccioni came timidly into the room, his hands covered with dirt from the greenhouse where he had been working. He had a radio in his greenhouse on which he liked to listen to dance music while he puttered with his soybean plants and hybrids, and he had kept it on all morning, listening to the news from Bayonne and Toulouse. On a pad of blue-lined paper, he kept jotting down notes of what he had heard and comparing them to the items that had come over the Spanish radio the day before. He found the Colonel pacing up and down in front of the high French windows that opened onto the balcony, his head sunk on his chest, his hands clasped at the small of his back.

Luccioni bumped into a table; the Colonel turned suddenly with the look of one who is being attacked, his hand jerking out to grasp a bookend from a lamp table nearby.

Luccioni coughed in protest, trying to find the right words in Spanish to express himself.

He stopped abruptly, seeing the bookend in the Colonel's hand. The bright sea light hurt his eyes after the tropical gloom of the greenhouse, and he began to blink rapidly behind the thick lenses of his glasses. He held a short trowel in his hand and had made footprints across the Moroccan rug by the entrance hallway.

Carvalho faced him angrily. Though it was well past noon, he had not yet dressed himself completely. His uniform at the moment consisted only of his trousers, boots, and undershirt. The room was heavy with the acid blue smoke that poured from a Cuban cigar clenched between his teeth.

"Well, for the love of Christ, what do you want . . . coming in like that?" He had been absorbed in speculation, trying to compensate in some way for the fact that he neither knew nor could do anything about his youngest daughter's continued absence. The agronomist's sudden intrusion, his disarray and "filth," as the Colonel saw it, angered him. The fact of his own incomplete dress seemed wholly irrelevant: he was master in his own house.

"What is it, damn it," he shouted in Spanish, making no concessions.

"*Es verdad . . . ,*" the words burst out of the recesses of Hector Luccioni's brain and he began to grin foolishly like a schoolboy who has suddenly discovered that he has, after all, prepared his lesson well enough. "The radio . . . in the greenhouse . . . ," he began. "It's all true, all of it."

Carvalho stood still, the bookend in one hand, the other thrust deep into the pocket of his uniform trousers. "The radio?" As Luccioni rattled on, Carvalho stared at him angrily. What right had such a . . . creature . . . to be telling him things like that? No Frenchman had the right to confront a Spaniard with such bloody truths, and particularly not such a man as his son-in-law. Was he doing it deliberately? Did the Colonel detect a note of relish in Luccioni's voice as he reeled off the names of the cities and towns that had already fallen to the military rebellion . . . Sevilla, Cádiz, Melilla, Jerez, Algeciras, Córdoba, Tetuán. . . . Anger within, but not at what had happened, only at the messenger who dared bring confirmation of what he already knew. Of course it had had to come, but why so quickly? It had only been seven days since the body of Calvo Sotelo, the Monarchist leader, had been found in a cemetery in Madrid, two bullets in the back of his neck, a reprisal for the killing of a Lieutenant of the Assault Guards, which was in turn a reprisal for the killing of the Marquis of Heredia at the funeral of a Guard who had been killed during the fifth-anniversary parade, which, in turn. . . . The events appeared in Carvalho's mind as a trail of fly specks on a long string that arched over an immense horizon yet seemed to be visible continually. There was no beginning and no end; everything was interconnected. But even so, it was all superficial, the manifestations of a condition so unbelievably complex, so ruinous that it defied analysis. How rarely, though, do major decisions depend on major events; the death of one man may spark a cataclysm while the sufferings of an entire nation may continue for years without causing a ripple. We live, Carvalho thought, in a world where we seem to need excuses of the moment for everything we do. Like children. God . . . how much like children! . . . He rolled the name Calvo Sotelo over in his mind even as Luccioni was relating the events of the preceding days, the uprising of the military in Morocco, the radio declaration of war by the generals from the Canaries; Sotelo . . . better that he should have lived to a ripe old age than to have been assassinated. Now the excuse had been provided. Hesitation gave way to a cry for vengeance cloaked as a demand for order. The pattern was so familiar. The country had had a century of practice and the army would move through its paces automatically and with absolute certainty that God was on its side.

He heard himself say: "Are you sure of that?" but did not even know which detail he had questioned.

"The radio . . . not yours. Ours. It comes from Paris."

Carvalho bristled at the implied insult, but it was true enough. What one heard on Union Radio from Madrid could be discounted, but Paris could not be denied.

"The fools, the imbeciles . . .," Carvalho thought, turning his back on his son-in-law as though he did not exist. He slammed the table below his right arm with the bookend he had picked up, cracking the veneer. Hector Luccioni stepped back, frightened by the sudden display of violence.

Hours—a day at most—remained. The troops were probably already on the move from Morocco. Who would be at the helm? the vain, aged Sanjurjo? Yagüe of the Foreign Legion? Quiepo de Llano? Franco? Mola? . . . who? He turned the possibilities over in his mind with slow, painstaking effort. The troops would stream in from the sea, and the Moors would land again as they had at Gijón and Oviedo and Mieres, and every city in Spain would become a slaughterhouse.

"Get Inés and my wife in here," the Colonel commanded, not even turning. He walked quickly out onto the balcony, leaving Luccioni standing foolishly in his dirty coveralls and fidgeting with his trowel. He went out at once.

Mercedes had not arrived yet. The thought suddenly tugged at him with an unexpected violence. If she had left when Ramos had left, with the last load of furniture, she should have been here by now. But Ramos had not appeared yet either. Suppose something had happened to them. He realized that he had no idea of what had occurred in Toledo during the last forty-eight hours or even if the trains were still running between Madrid and Barcelona or, for that matter, between Barcelona and France . . . and Raúl, what of Raúl in Paris? Surely he should have called by now. But if the risings had already started, perhaps something had happened at the embassy as well. Raúl was known for his associations, his Leftist friends. If the generals had taken over the embassy, then Raúl might be in the basement, under arrest, or even dead by now. The uncertainty of it all made him furious, and the pacing increased. He went from one end of the terrace to the other, first in twenty steps then in fifteen, finally in eleven.

He heard a vague turmoil in the house behind him but did not turn, rather found himself thinking of his friend Francisco Mercader and his white Moorish house just outside of Toledo, of the young man, Mercader's son, who had once been so close to him but was now so distant that it was only with difficulty that he could recall his features. Mercedes was everything the boy was not—clear-headed, practical, always ready to obey instructions and to sort out the reasons afterward. Of course, she had done as he had instructed her to do; no doubt she was on her way now, probably even over the border by now. But the boy, Jaime Mercader? Perhaps he had fled to the mountains already. Hadn't he, Carvalho, done the same thing after the bloodbath at Oviedo? He remembered the mountain forests, his self-reproaches, the swiftly rushing streams alive with fish, the hope that someone would kill him there, on the spot. But they had found him up there and brought him back to deal with the furor raised by Mercader's dismissal of charges against a dozen men the Civil Guard had brought in for trial. It was unheard of, unbelievable. A court-martial meant the firing wall. Once accused, a man was presumed guilty, had to be guilty, otherwise why accuse him in the first place? But Mercader had refused. "No evidence. There is simply no evidence to convict these men. Worn shoulders on their jackets, that's all? Look at you. You've got a worn patch on your jacket, too. From what? From a fishing rod, that's what."

The Colonel nodded to himself. How unlike Mercedes the boy was. She would have done as ordered and then reasoned out the justifications later. Not so Mercader. He had saved the young man from a discharge and possibly even a firing squad. Yet it had not been a gratuitous act or one simply born of loyalty to his aide or even to Francisco Mercader. There remained the gnawing truth that the boy had been right and that had he not come to his defense, his conscience would have troubled him for the rest of his life. As it was, he still experienced a certain uneasiness over the fact that it had been Mercader and not he who had done what should have been done. And while he had been fishing, turning his back. . . . He slammed one fist into his open palm, a characteristic gesture which seemed to sum up all the useless violence of which his life had been made.

The sound of voices at the front of the house increased in volume and excitement. He glanced through the window. A truck had pulled up in the driveway and he could see Onésimo Ramos and Amalia Carvalho standing there, seemingly in the midst of a violent argument.

He crossed the room and went out.

"Onésimo . . . at last," he said. Ramos' head was bandaged, and there were purple bruises on the side of his head. "Where is César?"

"Colonel . . ." Ramos said, looking embarrassed. He touched his bruises. "You should never have trusted César . . . these . . . you see.

There were bloodstains on the running board of the cab.

Amalia Carvalho was saying over and over again; "But the harpsichord, where is the harpsichord?"

César apparently had tried to talk Onésimo Ramos into stealing the truck and selling the furniture. When Ramos had refused, they had fought, somewhere north of Guipúzcoa.

"He said to me, 'Why not? Why shouldn't we do it?' He said to me, 'What do you owe the Colonel after all?' And he called you names which are not true . . . about '34. I know they are not true," Ramos said, but his eyes were wide, his expression that of a man desperately seeking affirmation.

"It's all right," Carvalho said. "They are not true and I thank you for knowing that."

"It was not all right," Onésimo Ramos answered. "He should not have said such things. It made me angry, much more angry than his idea about stealing the truck. I said to him, 'We are not thieves,' and he said to me, 'Well, Onésimo, we are not . . . butcher's assistants either'. . . ."

"And?"

"He's in a ditch," Ramos said. "He was a good man, believe me, Colonel. I didn't want to hurt him. Maybe he's still alive. I don't know."

"The harpsichord, make him explain about the harpsichord," Amalia insisted.

The Colonel turned angrily and ordered his wife inside. To Luccioni he gave the task of seeing that Ramos' wounds were properly dressed. "You're a man of science, and medicine is a science too . . . so the doctors insist . . . now go . . ."

Before he vanished inside the house, Ramos received from the Colonel a wad of bank notes which Carvalho had not even counted before taking them out of his pocket.

"This is not to make you forget," Carvalho said, "but to make remembering less painful."

"I don't want . . . ," Ramos said, drawing back.

"Go . . ."

When he was alone in front of the house, Carvalho began to stare again at the sea, waiting and watching. He could hear the voices of his wife and daughter within the house. He kicked at the tailgate of the truck and walked fitfully up and down the driveway.

Minutes passed, and his head swarmed with angry thoughts, none of which would take on definable shape and, so, deviled and eluded him at the same time.

Suddenly he became aware of a sharp, jangling sound from inside the house; the telephone was ringing. He could hear everything through the French doors he had left open.

His wife was speaking animatedly to someone. The Colonel stood for a second longer, regarding the peaceful breast of the Atlantic, then, abruptly he tore himself away and went back into the house.

"Here . . . here," Amalia Carvalho urged, seeing him and holding out the phone. He seemed not to be able to focus on her face, only on the ugly black instrument she offered him. Only a few words penetrated the dense barriers his preoccupation had thrown up around his consciousness of external things.

". . . Raúl," she said ". . . from Paris . . . you've been waiting for . . ." Her face instantly swam into focus; his wife, who had seen him through Melilla, the years in the outposts on Morocco, the defeats, the victories, and the humiliations in those same victories, all the disgrace of his twisted life which he had come so bitterly to regret, his wife who now understood . . . he realized . . . as little as he did but who wanted so desperately to help.

He took the phone. Terrible interference, crackling as bad as static on the radio, a dim, unreal voice behind a veil of electrical noises . . . a voice unsteady, faintly bored . . .

"Father?"

"Raúl . . . ? Is that you? What . . . ? Woke you? Are you an old man now or drunk, which is it? Well, first of all, are you awake enough to answer me?"

"Yes," came the voice on the other end, faintly sardonic. "I'm quite well awake . . ."

"Then tell me, first of all, what do you know of what's been going on? The French radio says . . ."

The Colonel listened: it was all true. The embassy was in an uproar but nothing more had happened. Raúl, at least, was perfectly safe where he was.

Crackling from the phone; "Christ's blood . . . this connection . . . Yes, I can hear you . . . who's that? Lachine? Yes, I was going to ask you . . ."

A dim, metallic voice: "I'm ahead of you, father. The moment I heard the news. Of course, I also heard about your deserting from Oviedo."

"Deserting?"

"Two days ago it was called 'desertion.' I'm sure I can arrange things. Don't worry." A tinge of sarcasm. The Colonel felt his chest tighten. If at that moment he could have struck his son full in the face. . . . "It will be a little delicate. I'm not sure they understand quite yet why you did it, but I'm sure that you did the right thing and that it will all turn out . . ."

The Colonel cut his son off: what about Lachine? Of course he would help and in return . . . ?

"He'll smooth things over for you, if you want him to," Raúl said.

Carvalho contained his anger and managed to speak calmly; all the while his wife was watching him closely with a pained expression on her face. She knew the tone. Father and son had been warring for two years. Ever since the disaster at Oviedo.

"By the way, did you know . . . your friend Ramón Linares has been elevated. I think he's in line for a post at the Naval and Air Ministry if Prieto has his say . . ."

"Fine," Carvalho said stiffly. He had no interest in Ramón Linares at that moment, only in himself and his position.

"I only mention it because I think you should see him. If there's any difficulty."

"You will clear up any difficulties I may have."

"Yes . . . of course . . ."

"Now, what does Lachine want in Toledo . . . you'd better tell me."

"He'll tell you himself. It has to do with . . . money. Isn't that amusing?"

"Very . . ." But Lachine had the soul of a banker. He had always thought that. Whatever the man wanted, it was certainly fortuitous that he should want it at that particular moment. He would have preferred Saint-Luc, an older man with a more outgoing personality, but Lachine's connections were, if anything, even better.

"He'll be flying in," Raúl Carvalho said through a burst of line interference. "In a day or so . . . and another man with him, Emilio Portillo, also from Toledo. . . . you remember—I wrote to you about him and . . ." More interference. All he could hear was ". . . POUM, I think . . ." A short laugh, harsh and vicious. "But this is the time of the Popular Front, isn't it? The Stalinists will lie down with the Trotskyites . . . Well, what can you expect . . . ?"

Damnable, but the static cleared at the most unimportant parts of the conversation, rose up again, as though deliberately, as Raúl began to explain what was happening at the Embassy.

A few more sentences, that was all. The Colonel replaced the phone in its cradle and silently surveyed his family gathered around him. He felt love, pity, and most of all helplessness. Once Mercedes was safely in Biarritz, he might go back and to go back he would need Lachine or someone like him. "Smooth things over?" The phrase nettled him, but it was true; that was precisely what was required. How frustrating to be a man of good will in the midst of such a scheming pack of fools. . . .

"You heard?" he said sharply to his wife.

"There will be a plane, perhaps soon," Carvalho said. "Amalia . . . do I have a clean uniform here? I don't want to meet our guests in this condition. . . ."

"I sent the clothes you came in to be cleaned," his wife said. "We haven't any servants now. . . ."

"That won't be soon enough. Upstairs . . . is there anything upstairs?" He had suddenly become embarrassed by his disarray, reached up to his beard and began yanking at it, to untangle the twisted strands. The wind on the balcony had rushed through his hair and given him the look of a fierce but aged Mephisto. A glimpse of himself in trousers and undershirt, his white beard and hair bristling from his long skull brought a momentary smile to his face.

"Whatever you can find," he called after his wife. "Any kind of jacket. I have my cap." He would be damned if he would meet the plane in civilian clothes. He had not deserted the Spanish Army; it had deserted him.

By the time they heard the plane pass over the city, heading toward the small airfield a few miles inland, the car had been gassed and was ready. Luccioni, out of his overalls and looking uncomfortable in an open-collared shirt and cap, was behind the wheel. To be forced to play chauffeur . . . it was too much for him, but he dared not object. Perhaps the men in the plane would take the Colonel away with them, and then all would be as it had been before.

As the plane flew high overhead, the Colonel came down the front steps of the house, dressed in an odd but dignified mixture of uniforms and wearing his anger like a decoration. He had even strapped on a gun-belt and the holster-flap was open, showing the butt of a Mauser. A creased forage cap sat uneasily on his massively maned head.

"So, are we ready?" he shouted.

"*Oui, mon général,*" Luccioni called out.

"Don't try to be amusing," the Colonel snapped back. "It doesn't suit you. You only end up being insolent, and a fool as well."

The Colonel got in, seating himself in the back, just as he would have done in a staff car. Luccioni winced; all of the old man's professed libertarian ideas had not changed one whit his idea of how a full Colonel in the Spanish Army should behave, even if he were a renegade and in France to boot.

They drove in silence up the tree-shaded road, past stands of grass taller than a man, full of russet shadows. Above, the sky was even bluer and calmer than it had been that morning.

The airfield was only a few miles away, and they reached it quickly, almost as rapidly as the plane which had had to circle and seek out the best wind for a landing. The propellers were still turning slowly as the car pulled up near the hangar which serviced the field.

The landing area was empty; the passengers had not yet alighted, and there was no one else at the field. The shades were down over the hangar windows. "Good," thought the Colonel, opening the car door and stepping out. "We don't need a welcoming committee here . . . get them in the car and back to the house . . ."

Camille Lachine and the man Portillo would be inside, the Colonel thought, trying to glimpse them through the side windows of the plane. "You may remember . . . I wrote to you about him . . ." Yes, the Colonel remembered; it was hard to forget. Raúl had written so infrequently that his father had committed almost every word of the few letters that did arrive to memory. Raúl had written: "He was an embarrassment, this Portillo. No one knew precisely why he had been jailed, and so no one was quite ready to take the risk of helping him. Exiles are strange that way but quite predictable. They seem so afraid to contaminate their own martyrdom. It was a pitiful thing to see him sitting there night after night at the Café Juliette where we all gathered . . . the outcasts of the *bieno negro*. He would protest to anyone who would listen that he'd actually done nothing at all. There's nothing, Father, that makes a man quite as suspicious as insistence on innocence, and gradually even he came to understand that. We met and became friends . . . I suppose because we were both, in our own ways, innocent but damned nevertheless. It wasn't until later that he confessed to me that he had been on the verge of changing his story and claiming that he'd committed some terrible crime, simply in the hope of achieving an audience. 'If you do nothing else for me,' he said one evening, 'at least you've saved me from becoming a liar.' But, as you see, I've done a good deal more for him. Lachine, as you can imagine, is none too happy about all of this because the one thing that Portillo does freely admit is that he was a member of the POUM. But this is the time of the Popular Front, isn't it? And, in any event, the French comrades are a little less dogmatic and a good bit more philosophical in these matters than the Russians. And we Spaniards don't understand these things at all, do we? . . . Embrace my mother and sisters for me . . . Raúl. . . ." Letter number six in twice as many months . . .

". . . Lachine isn't too happy . . ." Carvalho wondered what Lachine would say now, now that the man was traveling with him?

He wondered, too, what Lachine would look like now; four years ago Lachine had been an almost perfect specimen of that particular kind of man, small, wiry, head too large for his body, that one finds nowhere else but in France . . . adept in half a dozen languages, always ready with an amusing anecdote or a biting story . . . no wonder Raúl had taken to him so readily, no wonder they had become so quickly priest and acolyte. As for himself, the Colonel admired Lachine's intransigent Communism as little as he did the mysticism of the Spanish Anarchists. "But you're dealing with men, after all. . . ," Colonel Carvalho would protest. "Ah yes . . . men . . . ," Lachine would agree and blow on his glasses as though to clear away a fog that had gotten between him and such an obvious truth. But the man himself was admirable in every way and, most important, he could be very important now . . . all of which made the Colonel wonder just precisely why he had come. Surely not just because Raúl had asked him to; there had to be another reason.

The door on the biplane opened; sunlight glittering on the ridged aluminum fuselage made it difficult to see. A short ladder fell from the open door. Two men got out. Even from that distance the Colonel had no difficulty recognizing Lachine and at once began to cross the field to meet him.

"Camille . . . ," he called out over the dying rumble of the plane's motors.

The man stopped, then quickened his own pace. Short, perhaps a few pounds heavier than he had been when Carvalho had last seen him, the same overlarge head, eyes gray and narrow behind steel-rimmed glasses, his hair thin and carefully combed. Gray suit, neat tie; carrying a briefcase, well-oiled, he gave the impression of a banker or a successful lawyer on his way to court. The man behind him was larger, heavier, his body that of a peasant, his massive head covered by a full shock of black, bushy hair. He was darkly tanned and wore an ill-fitting suit with trousers far too large at the bottoms and a grotesquely patterned tie. He followed after Lachine at a cautious distance as though there had been no more than a truce between the two men born of nothing more than a common desire to be where they both now were.

Lachine drew closer, stopped and held out a hand. The Colonel advanced to him and, ignoring the outstretched hand, took him firmly by both shoulders.

The Frenchman smiled; "Raúl said you hadn't changed at all . . . he was right, I see." Then, with perfect dignity and attention to form, Lachine turned and gestured toward the man behind him. "Emilio Portillo . . . Colonel Enrique Carvalho . . ."

The two stared at each other in mutual distrust. It seemed to the Colonel that both the man's name and face were familiar. He recalled Raúl's garbled words: ". . . from Toledo, too . . ." Where had he known this man before? Had he passed him in the street, a face among thousands he had seen in the alleyways and narrow streets of his home city, or was there a closer connection? He could not remember. There were so many things he could no longer remember.

"I have a car," he said, "at your disposal. . . . We'll drive to my house and talk there. . . ."

"Can the plane be put in the hangar?" Lachine asked.

"I don't know . . . is the pilot staying?"

"We may want the plane later. He'll stay if I tell him to," Lachine said quietly. "It's good to see you again, Colonel . . . very good . . ."

"Shall we . . . ?"

"Wait for the pilot. Is there room for him in the car?" Lachine glanced across the field. "Of course there is," he said laconically. "Always a large car, eh, Enrique? Hard to get rid of the ways of a lifetime, isn't it?"

"I don't think it would help things for me to try to get around by mule," the Colonel replied. "In any event, then there wouldn't be room for the pilot. As it is, he can sit in front with . . ."

"The chauffeur?"

"My son-in-law, Luccioni. I believe you've met him . . ."

"No," Lachine said, a serious look passing across his face. "Your daughter, Mercedes, is married?"

"No, the other one."

"Of course." Lachine lowered his head as they walked across the field, Portillo following at some distance. The pilot had joined them by the time they reached the car. The plane remained in the center of the field, ready for takeoff.

The three sat in the back, the Colonel next to Lachine, Portillo—still silent—looking out the window, avoiding Carvalho's gaze. As the Colonel examined him in profile, he could see scars, deep marks around the man's jaw and neck. Red patches where the flesh, once, had been torn. The marks of old beatings.

The pilot got in next to Luccioni, and the car moved off. In all the time they had been there, no one else had appeared on the field. It was seldom used and then only during the brief season when the English tourists appeared, to clog the casino and the beach below. It was not yet time for them, and the city moved sluggishly to its own tempo. No one asked, no one inquired; all to the good.

The Colonel could not take his eyes from Portillo's face. He was disturbed by his inability to recall where he had seen the other man before. The few words he had spoken indicated clearly that he was Spanish; both Lachine and Raúl had said that he came from Toledo, and he bore the marks of brutal treatment and the look of a man who expects nothing more from life except, perhaps, a brief absence of pain.

Lachine caught the direction of Carvalho's gaze. "He is, as you might put it, a dead man, Enrique . . . being so close to Spain has, I think, upset him. He's been away quite a while. . . ." He paused, fumbled with the catch on his briefcase. "Would you roll the window up please . . . the wind and the dust, very disturbing . . . I have something I want you to look at. . . ."

Carvalho did as he was asked. The car turned back into the tree-lined road down which it had come. In a moment, Lachine had opened the briefcase and was fumbling among a jumble of papers and folders. "Just like the banker he is at heart . . . ," the Colonel thought. "That such a man could be a revolutionary . . . only in France . . ." and then he corrected himself. Was Lachine, the product of a wealthy family, well-educated, any more an anomaly than he himself, the lifetime military man embittered by . . . what? . . . not bloodshed but simply too much bloodshed and for reasons he could not understand . . . now allied to such men? It gnawed at him, this perpetual realization that it was not the quality of events but their oppressive quantity which had finally turned him. One less battle, one less execution and he might have remained the same. Would he ever feel that he was acting out of anything other than a desire for expiation? Or . . . was it possible that all revolutionaries became such out of a sense of guilt? Was there in the end no such thing as absolute, original dedication?

Lachine had found what he was looking for. As the car turned down a more heavily shadowed lane, nearing the house, the Frenchman pulled out a sheaf of papers and began making ticks with a red pencil in the right-hand margin of the top sheet.

"Lists," he said. "You've been wondering, of course. Raúl didn't tell you, did he? No, of course not. Not over the phone. Well then, lists. Little 'banks' we have all over. It seems that I'm to be in charge of collecting all the deposits and seeing to it that they're 'invested' in the right places. . . ."

"I don't know what you're talking about," Colonel Carvalho said gruffly, annoyed by Lachine's bantering tone.

"Of course you don't. But it's very simple. Money. If the war is going to be financed, we can't leave it to the FAI, can we? Why, they don't even believe money exists." He gave a short, unpleasant laugh. "A necessary evil and, in times like these, hardly an evil, I'd say . . ."

Carvalho shook his head and took out a cigar. Lachine winced but said nothing.

"With your permission, Camille. . . ," the Colonel said and reached across to offer one to Portillo. He accepted, silently, nodding thanks. The two men lit up, and the back seat of the car filled with blue smoke through which Portillo's voice could be heard, clearly for the first time: "Cuban?"

"Yes . . . Havana," Carvalho said.

"They don't have these in Montjuich," Portillo said and then lapsed back into silence. Lachine coughed and covered his mouth with a handkerchief.

The Colonel glanced sideways at the lists on Lachine's lap. "More about that later . . . he'll serve my purposes if I can serve his . . . a very simple rule that one shouldn't forget. But what of this Portillo? He knows a good cigar. That's something in his favor."

He puffed on his cigar and, as a concession to the Frenchman, rolled down his window and was amused to see Emilio Portillo immediately follow suit.

The car broke from the shade of high grass and trees and onto an open stretch of road at the far end of which the white Carvalho house lay. Beyond it, the incredibly blue sea sky seemed alive with dancing points of sunlight.

Lachine smiled and adjusted his glasses behind which his pale-blue eyes were magnified monstrously. He brushed back a lock of hair that had fallen over his high forehead. "We're going into the banking and investment business, Colonel, you and I. Partners. Who would ever have thought it?"

JULY 20, 4:00 P.M.: *Toledo*

BUSES WERE NOT AS COMFORTABLE as trains but were much safer. They did not enter a city at any particular point, had no stations to speak of except in places like Madrid, and would stop almost anywhere to let a passenger off. They ran infrequently and never on schedule and so were a plague to militia and police and anyone else who tried to check on their comings and goings. The psychology of the thing was important too; in this country, so Vitolyn had learned, it was inconceivable that any man possessing money, his own or stolen, would subject himself to a bus ride. Even a fleeing thief, if he had stolen sufficient funds, would at the very least take the train. Besides, it was infinitely more comfortable for the police to watch a railroad station where one could buy cigarettes, have a drink of soda or even wine, and watch the women come and go when nothing was happening, than to mount a guard on the outskirts of a city, by the highway, in the heat and exposed to the insects of the field.

The ticket seller for the bus line was located in a small shop on the west side of the Zoco, wedged between the walls of two adjacent buildings. The shop had no door; one simply walked in between the two walls and came immediately upon a counter of unfinished lumber that had been forced into the few feet separating the walls. Behind this counter sat a disconsolate little man wearing thick glasses and an official cap of some sort. He was fanning himself with the remains of a faded wrestling poster.

As soon as Vitolyn had presented himself before the counter at which so little business was obviously transacted, the man in charge assumed an entirely different attitude. Whereas when Vitolyn had first observed him, the ticket seller's eyes had been overflowing with a desire for someone to talk to, the moment Vitolyn had cleared his throat in a bid for attention, the man pretended to be occupied.

"In a moment, señor, can't you see? . . . I'm very busy."

"Of course . . ."

The fan was suddenly transformed into a counterfeit account and was now being marked with hurried pencil scrawls.

Vitolyn spoke without thinking of the words; it was good. The language came quite naturally now and without any noticeable accent. He had learned to imitate the peculiar intonation of the Catalan speaking Castillian Spanish and used it to disguise his own slight teutonic inflection. Most of the time, he noticed, no one paid it any attention at all. Sometimes someone would even say a few words in what he was sure was Catalan, and he would smile and cough as though to say, "Thank you for your consideration."

"The next bus to Ciudad Real and then to . . . Málaga, if that's possible."

The ticket seller finally squinted at a schedule, pursed his lips, and ran a damp finger up and down the line, pretending to scrutinize it with especial care though it was clear that he knew it by heart.

"What good fortune . . . are you planning to leave soon?"

"When is the next bus?" Vitolyn repeated quietly.

"Why, tomorrow . . ."

"Then I am planning to leave tomorrow."

"To Málaga? Yes, that's what you said, wasn't it?" He made a show of looking up the fare, then announced it as though delighted by an unexpected turn of good fortune. "The rates are cheaper in the summer. They only changed two weeks ago, did you know that?"

Vitolyn was absorbed in counting out the necessary money. The tin box full of schilling notes was still hidden in his room and though, by that count, he was a wealthy man, his supply of pesetas was fast dwindling. By carefully husbanding what he still had left, he figured that he could just get to Málaga and have enough left over to take passage to the African coast. It was almost impossible that the Spanish banks should have any record of the stolen money, but it was just such impossibilities that had been the ruin of many a man before him. Nothing was impossible, he had long since concluded; things were only improbable. Moneychangers were also out; they were too likely to have connections or know people who could be dangerous for him. So, despite the fortune hidden in the tin box, he continued to live like a pauper.

The ticket seller made out the tickets and passed them across the counter, taking a long time to count the change.

Vitolyn walked back into the Zocodover, leaving the ticket seller to his fanning. He had the tickets now; the bus would be at the Cambrón gate at the edge of the city at six the next day. If he went to Roig's room at about four and did not leave again until five, he would have just enough time to reach the stop before the bus came. Though the idea of spending an hour in the same room with a corpse frightened him, he could see no other way to make sure that the body was not found before he was safely on his way. If anyone came to the door, he could always answer and pretend he was Roig and sick. He had been listening to Roig's voice in El Bronco for days and had lain awake nights practicing his imitation. If he counterfeited a sore throat, he was sure that no one but a very close friend would be able to tell them apart through a closed door. And Roig seemed to have no friends at all in Toledo, which made it all the easier.

He folded the tickets into his jacket pocket and smiled with satisfaction. Although the Zocodover was full of people, not a single priest or soldier could be seen. When he had first come to Toledo, less than a week before, it had seemed as though half the population of the city was either "red" or "black" as he liked to put it, recalling Stendhal, but with rather a different meaning. After all, red and black were the colors of both the Anarchists and the Falange. What an irony! The young soldiers from the Alcázar strutted about, their white gloves immaculate in the morning sun, occupying the cafés and taverns at nightfall and remaining deep into the next morning. Daytime had formerly belonged to the priests and monks who wove a thick web of black and brown across the city, stitching church and cathedral together in a dense knot.

Now the Zoco seemed to be entirely the property of the workmen and their women. Those few churches he had passed were shuttered and the only soldiers in sight were those to be seen high up in the windows of the Alcázar, peering out and then hastily closing the shutters again.

On his way to the ticket seller's, he had passed a strange procession in the streets near what was called the *gobierno,* the military government buildings just outside the Alcázar itself. Wagons loaded with household possessions, dozens of mules and horses, men carrying pots and pans, rifles, boxes of clothing, canary cages, musical instruments, and anything else that could not be stuffed into the wagons, crowded the streets. They were not the poor of the city, however disreputable their appearance, but rather the owners of the little houses that ringed the hills on the southern banks of the Tagus. He had also seen a few soldiers or, at least, men in uniform. Most of them were well past retirement age and wore a variety of dress that was wholly unlike that he had seen earlier on the cadets of the academy.

Glimpsed from the head of the street, the *gobierno* building was a bedlam, hung with sheets, blankets, and partitions made of straw mats, piled high with boxes overflowing with clothes and furniture of every description and full of women, children, old men, and frightened shopkeepers. He did not care to approach more closely.

A few army officers could be seen striding about, trying to calm down the civilians while giving them, by their very presence all the more cause for alarm. Not a priest was in evidence.

In contrast to the confusion that had turned the *gobierno* and the streets leading to it into an overflowing thieves' market, the Zocodover seemed unusually calm. Vitolyn had skirted the edge of the plaza and turned up the street that led toward the Alcázar. As he did so, an open-backed truck carrying a dozen or more Civil Guard under its wooden hoops swung onto the street, almost running him down.

"You! Are you all right?" a nearby man in blue overalls said, extending a hand to Vitolyn. "Those bastards, they don't give a damn . . ."

"It's nothing . . . nothing . . ." He had not even fallen and wanted no help from anyone.

"*A cada puerco viene su San Martin . . .*," the man in overalls spat: "Every hog has his Saint Martin's day . . .," and walked off muttering as though it had been he rather than Vitolyn who had almost been run down.

"Saint Martin?" Vitolyn sent his mind chasing down musty tunnels of memory. It was there, stored away with every other piece of information he had ever absorbed, . . . chemical tables, languages, mathematics, bank deposits, production statistics, lists of names . . . Saint Martin, Bishop of Tours, patron saint of innkeepers. . . . He coughed in the dust churned up by the truck's wheels and moved quickly off back toward the Zoco, shorn of all desire to approach the Alcázar any closer.

"Saint Martin's day," he ruminated. "Yes, of course . . . they slaughter hogs on the feast of Saint Martin's day . . ."

AFTERNOON, JULY 20: *Biarritz*

LACHINE WAS OUT IN THE GREENHOUSE with Hector Luccioni. "Listening to his theory of 'salvation through soybeans,' no doubt," Carvalho thought. Far to the north a squall was gathering. The waves were being whipped into a gray froth by a stiff wind that had sprung up suddenly. Carvalho wished that he could feel the wind, but as yet it was something distant and quite unattainable from where he stood on the north terrace of the house. A still, motionless heat hung over the cliff on which the house had been built. Everything was silent, expectant; the only sound the Colonel could hear was the regular breathing of the man sitting behind him in one of the wicker chairs: Emilio Portillo, who had come on the plane with Lachine.

They had been standing and sitting there respectively without saying a word to each other since Lachine had left to view Luccioni's experiments. It was strange how thick the silence between them was, though they were countrymen, both exiled, both in their own ways quite alone. Sometimes common exile makes companions of strangers, sometimes it drives them further apart. Carvalho folded his hands together and thrust them over the railing.

"How differently men wait," he thought, "some with anger, some with stoicism, some with good humor. It depends entirely on what you're waiting for." Lachine's case was clear enough. He was to "collect" all the various party treasuries in central Spain and make sure that they were sent back to France where the Party would invest them with the proper firms for the purchase of arms and munitions—all for the salvation of the "Republic" of course. And, apart from Madrid, Toledo and Talavera de la Reina, some forty kilometers west were the richest of all the party treasuries in that part of Spain. That was why Lachine had come. That he might be of some incidental help to Carvalho was a fortuitous circumstance. It suited both men well but did nothing to create any feeling of warmth between them or of trust. Carvalho could not help wondering whether Lachine or any of the others would have ever left Paris if it had simply been a question of helping him personally. Raúl had often warned him that in such matters the French CP was inclined to be . . . "less . . . how can I put it, Father? . . . less understanding. . . . They are more . . . ," and he had hesitated, fumbling for the word, . . . "mechanical, abstract . . . bloodless, if you will . . ." Raúl's words: *mechanical, bloodless* . . . Carvalho could not help wondering with some amusement how Lachine was taking all of the agronomist's babbling about soybeans.

But Portillo, what of him? Since they had driven from the airfield, they had exchanged only a few words, only enough so that Carvalho knew that Portillo had a wife in Toledo, that he had been arrested during the '34 uprisings, been imprisoned, had escaped to France, and now wished to return. The man's silence was now beginning to get on his nerves. Surely, they had something to say to each other.

From within the house came the rattling of dishes, the sound of a servant's humming. Outside, on the balcony, nothing except the slow withdrawal of the heat; the sea wind was stealing toward the headlands, driving the waves before it into a lather of white foam and sharp green peaks.

Still no word of Mercedes. But now that the uprising had started in earnest, how could he possibly expect anything? They had been up most of the night, despite Amalia's constant entreaties. Paris radio had begun to detail the terrifying things that were happening all over Spain. The shortwave crackled and spit in the room just off the balcony, keeping everyone in the house from sleeping. Even Luccioni had come down to listen. At shortly after five in the morning, they had heard a rebroadcast from Radio Tenerife . . . the Generals' proclamation of war against the Republic. All through the day there had been similar messages, from Las Palmas, and a dozen other cities. The Socialist Union, the UGT, had called a general strike in Madrid.

Lachine had sat back and with his calm accountant's voice had said: "Well now, the pot is really boiling, isn't it," as though the news comforted him in some way. Why couldn't the man have common decency enough to keep his mouth closed? Carvalho was angry that the Frenchman should take satisfaction in news that not only meant disaster for Carvalho personally but for all of Spain itself. The Colonel was under no illusions; he remembered too well how the fighting had gone in '34. It all depended now on how much of the army went with the insurrectionists. It could all be over in hours or it could take years.

Portillo was sitting calmly, his hands folded in his lap, smoking a cigar. He had not stopped smoking cigars since Carvalho had given him his first "Havana" in the car on the way back from the airfield. "Like a furnace," the Colonel had thought. "He'll smoke up my entire stock in a day . . ." He wished that the man would be more open. He liked him, his solidity, his straightforwardness and, on the rare occasions when he spoke, his brevity. "Commendable . . . but for God's sake, speak, say something . . ." Two days of almost complete silence. He thought of the proverb: "Guests and fish begin to smell on the third day."

Carvalho turned suddenly away from the rail with that abruptness of motion that had always been characteristic of him.

"Do you realize, señor, that your silence is very offensive to me?"

Portillo smiled and took the cigar from his lips.

"I'm sorry, Colonel. I was thinking, just the same as you . . ."

"About what?"

"Do you really want me to answer that? Would you answer if I asked you that question?"

"No . . . you're quite right . . . it's simply that . . ."

Portillo exhaled. "We're both nervous and we're both waiting. That's what it is. But the difference is that you are a military man and are used to action. I am . . . or was, a prisoner . . . and am used to waiting. We react differently, that's all. I mean no offense. If you'd like to talk about it, about anything . . ."

Carvalho felt suddenly foolish. What Portillo was saying was quite correct. Waiting for others to do what he felt he himself should be doing, made him almost mad with frustration. Lachine, concerned only with accounts and sums, was content to bide his time until the right moment arrived. But for Carvalho every hour that passed without news of his daughter was a torment. He imagined that Portillo must feel the same way, though what, precisely, he was waiting for remained a mystery.

"Will you come with us," Portillo asked suddenly, as though he had read the Colonel's thoughts.

"To Toledo? You're going, then . . . ?"

"Yes, if we can. You know that . . ."

"I'll go only if I have to."

"I see . . ." Portillo also knew the story of the Colonel's difficulties, the strangely ambivalent position he occupied. "I might be of some help to you, you know. . . ," he added.

"How is that?" Carvalho thought back quickly, running over what little he knew of Portillo's past, realizing that he had no idea why the man had been arrested.

"I have quite a few friends in Toledo who might . . . convince your unwilling allies . . . how can I put it? . . . the FAI, to call off their private war and accept you."

"What were you, exactly? . . ."

"It doesn't matter. But I was with the POUM . . . much closer to the Anarchists than your friend, Monsieur Lachine. They won't listen to him. But we, as they, believe in meaningful revolution. They might listen to me. Lachine, of course, will do what he can, but only so long as it's in his own interest. I suppose he'll intercede with Tierres on your behalf, but Tierres and the FAI man in Toledo . . . if he's still alive . . . you remember, I'm sure . . . Manuel Torroba . . . have been feuding for years. They're both intellectuals, not men of action and, so, they'll never be reconciled. Personally, I think letting Lachine get Tierres involved would be a mistake, but that's up to you of course . . ."

"And would it be a mistake . . . letting you get involved?"

Portillo smiled. "It depends . . ."

"On what? Say what you mean . . ."

"What I mean is simply that you can't put too much trust in any man, that's all. But if it comes to a choice, choose me. Lachine, after all, has a very important matter on his mind and will probably have little time to bother with you or what to him will seem your very petty, personal concerns. I think he'll be too busy trying to stay on the good side of the Anarchists to care much about protecting you from them, that's all . . ."

"This matter of his . . ."

"If I told you how much money was involved, it probably wouldn't impress you. But for the party, it's a staggering sum, particularly in Spain."

"And they want it for arms? Not an unreasonable position . . ."

"If that were all, yes, and I would hardly have mentioned it. But getting the money back isn't Lachine's principal concern. Now, I'll deny this if you ever repeat it to him but what he's really after is to make sure that it doesn't fall into FAI hands or to the POUM either, for that matter. We all have rather different ideas about revolutions and when they should be made than do . . . certain others . . ."

"And by 'certain others,' whom do you mean?"

"Lachine and those he represents. That's all I mean and, I think, that's all I should say. Inasmuch as the FAI is dominant in Toledo and you, I understand are certainly *persona non grata* with our Anarchist friends, I don't think that getting involved with Lachine is going to help you at all. Or with Tierres either. That's all."

"You still haven't said why you are going back or what your business is . . . or why I should trust you . . ."

"As to my business . . . it's purely personal, I assure you. A family matter, just as yours is. You see, you run no risks with me that way. . . ."

"And what exactly did you do, before?" Carvalho said, running his fingers along the fringes of his beard. Underneath Portillo's calm he sensed a tension that was all the more violent for being held in check. He glanced down; Portillo's fingernails were torn and shredded. Portillo noted the direction of his gaze.

"None of us are as calm as we'd like to seem, are we? And we express our anxieties in different ways. You, for example, tug at your beard, while I . . . I tear at my nails." Portillo drew in again on his cigar. "It's very amusing, really, 'what I did' in '34 . . . my arrest. . . . Will you believe me if I tell you that I did absolutely nothing? Not that I wouldn't have if I'd had the chance but, do you remember . . . do you remember how Toledo was in '34?"

"I was at Oviedo . . . you've been told that, I'm sure. First in Morocco and then . . . ," he pronounced the word as though it were a malediction, "in Oviedo."

"Yes . . . ," Portillo said. "I know. That was stupid of me. But as you ask, there you have the answer. I did nothing. I suppose I have no right criticizing either Tierres or Torroba. I'm not a man of action either, but I was arrested nevertheless. As you will recall, they arrested a good many people who had done nothing then . . . Azaña, for instance."

"Who do you mean by 'they'?"

"Whoever was told to do the arresting, that's all. There is no malice in my 'they,' if that's what you mean. I think I understand my countrymen, and while there is this great profession of independence, I think it really covers a deep desire to be led about by the nose. And when it comes down to it, that's just what happens."

Carvalho considered for a moment, trying to decide whether he was being slyly insulted or not. Portillo went on, filling the gap: "Extreme independence is only a form of . . . how to put it? . . . a wish for discipline. The way a child acts. He can be very, very bad, to the point where he knows his father will beat him. Then he feels secure. Behaving badly is only an excuse to bring on discipline, to relieve him of a lot of worries, of decisions that he can't make. We all have that problem, don't we . . . the land, the church, the army, our politics? . . ."

"I don't like the analogy, señor . . . ," Carvalho began. He was interrupted by Lachine's metallic voice coming from the doorway to the main hall:

"I don't believe it. He's actually serious, your son-in-law, about his soybeans. Amazing, absolutely amazing."

That Lachine had come through his tour of the greenhouse without a spot of dirt on him and his neatness infuriated the Colonel who turned to glare at him with all the anger he had been about to lavish on Portillo.

Lachine stopped in the doorway, sensitive to Carvalho's stare and paused to light a cigarette, one of the long, Turkish blend that he carried about in a gold case that was too heavy and made his breast pocket bulge, the one blemish in his otherwise perfectly symmetrical appearance.

Portillo watched him with some amusement, then said, "Everyone has his own idea of the way to salvation. Why begrudge him his soybeans?"

"Why indeed," said Lachine, pocketing his lighter and coming into the room. "They're no madder than the Anarchists' notions or . . . yours for that matter."

"True enough," Portillo said, unruffled. "Mine are so mad that I managed to get myself arrested for having done absolutely nothing while the Colonel here, who seems to fall somewheres between our two stools, can't make anyone believe that he's on their side."

"I think we can end this talk . . . now," Carvalho said.

"Oh?" Lachine laughed softly. "Raúl said you were sensitive these days. I see . . ."

"You see that I'm nervous, that's what you see. Simply nervous. My daughter, in case you've forgotten, has disappeared somewhere between Toledo and the French border. In fact, I'm beginning to doubt that she ever left Toledo at all. The station in Biarritz reports no trains in from Spain in twenty-four hours . . . so . . ." He slammmed his hands together and the heavy veins on his neck began to pulse. "Here I sit . . . and wait. . . ."

Lachine was leaning against a rolltop desk and began toying with a paperweight, keeping his eyes away from Carvalho. "But not for long," he said.

"What do you mean by that?"

"Only that I intend to leave for Toledo tomorrow. If you choose, you can come along."

"I don't understand . . ."

"Your son-in-law, as you know, has a radio in the greenhouse. He may be interested in soybeans but he also keeps himself informed. While we were there we heard the latest news. Toledo appears to be safely in Republican hands, at least for the time being. The rebel drive has slowed down north of Madrid."

"In that case," Portillo began slowly, with a peculiar restraint, his voice very husky. Lachine took out a map and began marking it with a pencil. Portillo moved over to see what he was doing.

Carvalho watched the two men, barely listening to what they were saying. He kept thinking instead of his daughter and, more and more, could not understand how he could have left her where she was and trusted her to get herself out. In the first place, she might have simply refused to leave. She believed in reason too much and reason would, of course, dictate that she had nothing to fear. "That's because she doesn't understand Spain. She's been too long in Africa . . . it's my fault again. But who in this mad country *is* responsible? The Church teaches us that man is bad and, therefore, institutions must be built to restrain him; the Anarchists teach that man is good and they would destroy everything he's ever built in order to give him a chance to prove his goodness." None of it made any sense at all. It seemed to him, then, a disgraceful thing that he had not gone to Toledo himself, that he had put his own safety and his possible use to the Republic, whatever that meant, beyond the safety of his daughter. Had anyone else called him a coward, he would have struck him, but now, thinking it himself, he wondered whether it was true after all. At Oviedo, he had run too . . . yes, it was only fair to call it that: he had run. Into the thin ridge of mountains that cut off the coastal towns from the sea. He remembered it clearly. The soft fall of pine needles and the smell of apples and rushing water . . . standing knee-deep in a stream running with white trails where the water curled around boulders and outcroppings of slick, black stone. On both sides of the steep banks, thick stands of walnut and elm.

Portillo was speaking now, but Carvalho could hear only his own silence, his past. What a rush of silence surrounded him, yet it was a silence full of the drumming of artillery fire, the crack of rifles and the surprised, angry cries of dying men. He had flung his fishing pole over his shoulder time and time again, casting, watching with detached satisfaction as the line whipped out, the fly cutting a bright scarlet arc against the deep green of the trees behind it. Then, a tiny spurt of white water as it entered. He had worn his uniform though he had known that the mountains were full of fleeing miners. By keeping his eyes on the stream only, never raising them, he had thought to offer himself up to anyone who might see him from behind those trees. But no one had come, and he had been there for a day, slept on a mat of fallen boughs under a tree, gone back to his fishing the next day. Then someone had come; he had been aware only of a shape, a long, attenuated shadow that fell slightly to his left and onto the stream just ahead of him.

"Colonel." Was it Lachine's voice now or that of his aide, the young Lieutenant Mercader, then . . . two years before?

He had lowered the pole, recognizing Mercader's voice even over the sound of the water. He had not turned but simply stood there waiting. He had caught nothing. Fish were as elusive in those mountains as truth. And now Mercader had come after him; he should have known.

"Colonel . . . ," again the voice, insistent. Mercader's voice had won out.

Finally, reluctantly,—he remembered—he had turned. Lieutenant Mercader stood at the head of a line of elm trees on the bank, about eight feet above him. "I've been looking for you . . ." Mercader had said.

At that moment a mote of sunlight had passed between wind-parted branches and struck the insignia on his shoulders, a brutal reminder of what was happening, of what Carvalho had fled.

"There's trouble below, Colonel. I've done something . . ."

Carvalho clambered out of the stream bed at once, his boots glistening, his trousers black with water almost to the waist; he threw his fishing pole into the bushes.

Only when he had gotten up the embankment did he see that there were two others with Mercader—a captain and another lieutenant.

On the way back to the city, Carvalho had insisted that the others walk behind, leaving him and Mercader free to talk together. The Captain had objected but only briefly.

How well he remembered it all; he had felt the same disgrace, the same shame at having left Mercader then as he felt at having left Mercedes now.

A cough welled up in the Colonel's chest. He burst out with a loud, hawking noise as though by clearing his lungs he might clear his soul as well, turned about and faced the two men who were seated across from one another in his drawing room, both smoking his cigars, biding their time, waiting . . .

"All right . . . is there room for a fourth on the plane?" he demanded suddenly.

"Yes . . . as I said before," Lachine replied, looking up from his map. "Now let me understand all of this properly, please. . . ." He rubbed his glasses. "As Raúl explained it to me, you feel that you cannot go back to Toledo alone under the . . . present circumstances . . . because of the FAI, no? Do you think they'll trust you more now that the uprising has really begun in earnest?"

"I don't give a damn whether they do or not."

Portillo nodded slightly.

Carvalho continued: "They can shoot me if they wish, that will be their mistake, not mine. I can only forgive them in advance. But I'm going to go and it's up to you, Camille, to help me all you can. I'm certain . . ."

"I see," Lachine said and tapped his cigar into an ashtray. "It's up to us . . . so . . ."

"It is. Nothing is given free in this world. We all have our debts to pay. Perhaps you may find that you owe me something after all. . . ."

Lachine scowled. "Perhaps I may," he said. "Anything is possible."

Portillo seemed animated by Carvalho's decision. "Neither of us can be entirely sure of our own safety, you know that."

"But we both have business to attend to, and we'll take that chance," Lachine added dryly.

"So do I . . . ," Carvalho said. "There's no alternative but to help each other."

"As far as we can," Portillo said.

"Understood?"

"Understood," Lachine replied. "The plane is ready, of course. I had thought to leave tomorrow morning. . . ." "Fine then," Carvalho said. He felt suddenly at ease with himself, far more than he had any right to be. "Now . . . let's see about supper. . . ."

Outside, on the terrace, the sea wind was sweeping a broom of fallen leaves over the tiles. Darkness had fallen completely, and the stars were obscured by rushing clouds. A faint drizzle had begun to fall.

Carvalho looked over his shoulder at the dark windowpanes on the French doors and the droplets of water that were beginning to collect on their surface and hoped that the flying weather would be good in the morning.

BOOK TWO /

A Sounding

of Drums

THE CAR SHED, LIKE THE OLD FORD itself, was something of an after-thought, more a reluctant concession to convention than a necessity. Neither Francisco Mercader nor his wife knew how to drive or had ever considered learning. On the infrequent occasions when the president of "Comercio Mercader, S.A." traveled to Madrid, he would be picked up and driven by a car belonging to those with whom he had an appointment. But having a car at all meant having a driver, and so he had retained Esteban Barrera for the purpose and lodged him in a small two-room shack which, afterthought of afterthoughts, had been erected just behind the car shed. It had been so long since Francisco Mercader had driven with Barrera that he sometimes forgot why the man was there, only to be reminded at odd hours of the day, usually during the heat of early afternoon, when the driver could be heard banging away at the insides of the car and swearing angrily.

For the last two days, however, the yard had been quiet during the afternoons, and only the chickens had displayed any great energy or made the slightest noise.

That the tar-paper roof of his lodgings leaked did not bother Esteban Barrera at all; he simply moved the bed so as not to be directly under the leak, shifted his trunk and the chair over which he habitually threw his clothes at night, and made do. The room was less than ten feet across and almost the same in length. The room adjacent, the second in the shack, remained closed. It was a small, windowless chamber, more like a large closet, and he had no use for it. Besides, it reminded him of a certain shanty in the slag dumps on the outskirts of Cartenegra, where he had once waited for his cousin Infante two years before, and he did not like to think about those times at all. So he kept the other room padlocked and the cracks in the doorjamb stuffed with newspaper so that he should not even smell the musty odor that the sun generated in its airless confines.

The walls of his bedroom were hung with diagrams of automobile engines, some of them clipped from newspapers and technical magazines and others given him by his cousin's brother-in-law, Ignacio Peralta, who ran a sort of garage in Toledo. Scattered among the diagrams were a few photos of shiny new American cars, a few French models, and the latest Fiats. On the opposite wall, as far from the bed as he could get it, hung a small, brownish photograph of an elderly man who bore more than a passing resemblance to Barrera himself. A strip of black crepe given him by Sebastián Gil, who had lost his wife at about the same time, framed the picture of Barrera's father. He had to have the photo there, but he tried to avoid looking at it. The picture reminded him that . . . as much as he had loved his father . . . the man was, nevertheless, the cause of all of his troubles. Had it not been for his father's stubbornness, his pride, and above all, his overbearing stupidity, Esteban Barrera might by now have been a graduate of the University and on his way to a decent life rather than a driver for a man who did not need a driver.

The afternoon had been, as always during July, hot beyond belief. Yet Barrera tolerated it. He had learned in his thirty-two years to put up with a great deal that other men seemed to find unbearable. He had long since concluded that one had very little choice about such things. So, in a heat that others would have fled, perhaps seeking a cool wine cellar or a stone church into which the sun would not find its way, Esteban Barrera lay on his cot, his hands under his head, streaming sweat, and thinking, during the random moments when he was fully conscious, of how lucky he was that he was not freezing.

He had not taken off his soiled black suit and even still wore his jacket. It was tight on his small, light frame, as though he had been caught in a rainstorm and it had shrunken on him. His bones projected through the thin material, and the color of his once white shirt showed through at the elbows of the jacket. He himself seemed compressed by malnutrition and disease though in fact it was more disappointment than physical want that accounted for his present condition. An ill-fitting chauffeur's cap was pulled down over his face, shielding his eyes from the beams of late afternoon sunlight that poked down through the roof and dropped across the room like prison bars. His face was wedge-shaped, the hair beneath the cap thick, unkempt, and uncombed. Oil stains and grease streaked the front of his trousers. Loose ends of braided wire hung from his jacket pockets, and he gave off a strong odor of gasoline.

It was pleasant to doze in that overpowering heat. A man did not even have to concentrate on trying to sleep as he often did, overtired and too nervous simply to drop off as other men did; the heat wrapped one up in cotton, stuffed one's ears and eyes and suffocated one with a delicious torpor. He thought of nothing at all, drifted in and out of sleep unplagued by the nightmares that often came with the dark. Sleep during the day was far more reassuring and never brought dreams.

It was during one of his conscious moments, as he had pushed the peak of the cap back and was trying to use a diagram of a Renault motor as an eye chart—in the manner of Dr. Aliaga to whom the "patron" had sent him a month before—when he heard a quiet knocking at the door of his shack.

The door, six planks nailed together by cross-pieces and little protection against the wind during winter, was pushed open without invitation. Barrera raised himself a little ways up on his elbows.

"What the devil do they want of me at this hour?" he thought, adding a stream of the invective he felt compulsory under such circumstances, but said only: *"Teniente?"*

Jaime Mercader, looking less the *teniente* than a field hand, in boots, a sweat-soaked shirt, and cotton trousers covered with dust came in and shut the door behind him, letting the iron bar fall and secure the catch. Barrera thought, "Does he want me to get up or not? Why doesn't he say something. Jesus! What am I in for now? The father would never come out here."

Jaime pulled over a stool and sat down by the bed. The driver, now trapped by his own slowness in rising, could no longer get up without seeming the complete fool, so he stayed where he was, simply jacking himself up into a sitting position and throwing one leg over the edge of his cot.

"Stay," Jaime said. "Just a few words . . ."

"Whatever you say, *teniente* . . ."

"I'm not *teniente* anymore. Don't call me that."

"All right . . . 'patron' . . ."

"Nor that either."

"Jesus," the driver thought, "I suppose the next thing will be for me to call him by his Christian name. Now, there'll be peace."

"Well," Barrera said, "You came here for something, didn't you?"

Jaime looked resigned; he had hoped that perhaps he might have a few words with the man, that he could talk to him as he had been unable to talk to any of his father's friends, or the fool, Luis Pelayo. But a barrier was here too.

"All right," Jaime said. "The car. I came about the car."

"What about the car?" Barrera's tone changed from sleepy disinterest to an alert, nervous curiosity. "What have they told you about the car?"

Jaime leaned forward. Barrera, still on the bed, felt like a patient being questioned by a doctor who has found out that he has a fatal disease, but is trying not to let on.

"It wasn't my fault, 'patron,' " he said hurriedly. "There was a staff car from Toledo going to Madrid as though all the witches in La Mancha were after it, and it forced me off the road. It was the one time I took the car out this week and the one time, I think, that anyone else used that road. So, of course, we had to meet. That's just the way it is."

Jaime thought, "This man is not the fool he pretends to be. He speaks too quickly for that. Look at him, like a rooster, all stretched muscle and springs. I've never seen a man as jumpy except on the lines when there's a fight coming up."

"It wasn't serious, was it?"

"Yes and no. Serious in that the car is useless, yes? Not so serious in that it can be fixed easily enough if we can get parts. That damned General or whatever he was, he forced me right off the road and into a ditch. Something came loose in the motor. I suppose it wasn't too well fixed to start with, that a wrench like that could shake it loose, but it's an old car and . . . the 'patron,' your father, he doesn't care much for cars, as you know, so it just barely hangs together and I with it. . . ."

Barrera sat up and pushed his cap from his head. It fell to the floor by his feet. Jaime reached down and handed it back to the astonished driver.

"Why . . . thank you, 'patron' . . ."

"Please," Jaime said. "Stop that. My name . . ."

Barrera scowled. He had been afraid of this. "Yes, *teniente* . . . your name is Jaime. . . ."

"Yes. You'll call me that. We're the same age or you may be older. You look older."

"How many years have you?"

"Twenty-eight . . ."

"So you see, you were right. I'm thirty-two . . ."

"You look even older."

"So do you, *teniente* . . ."

Jaime was silent for a moment. Dust moved in the slanting sunlight that came in through the roof. A sunbeam touched his boot tip, and he felt the heat through the leather.

Barrera poured some water into a tin cup and handed it to Jaime. "How long have you been here? About three weeks, . . . isn't that it?"

"About three weeks," Jaime affirmed; he was afraid to ask more about the car. The car was too important to him now.

"I've seen you out there sometimes. You're a good rider. I wish I could ride that well. Like an Arab . . ."

"You know, my mother is a Berber . . . they're the best horsemen in the world. I learned from them . . ."

"Yes," the driver said, pouring a second cup of water and not wanting to pursue the subject further. Some people were so sensitive about African blood. Take Bartolomé Lillo who worked at the arms factory making wires for grenade springs; his mother is an African, and he'll kill anyone who mentions it to his face. Strange, in a city like Toledo where every other building was built by the Moors . . .

After a time during which they both sipped silently at their water, Jaime said: "Now tell me, how bad is it?"

"You want the car?"

"Yes."

"Well it needs a few parts. Your father, he hasn't told me to get them and money doesn't grow on trees around here the way it does in some other parts of the country and you can't dig it up out of the ground the way you can where I come from, so I'll just have to wait until he asks for the car and gives me some money to go to Peralta's and get it fixed up. Ignacio, that's Peralta, he's my cousin's brother-in-law and a genius with such things."

Jaime glanced around the room, at the diagrams and the photos. "I hear you banging away all the time and from the looks of it, you're an expert yourself. Can't you fix it up?"

"I'm a modest man and truthful, too. No, I can't do it. I know what's wrong all right, but it just isn't in these clumsy hands of mine to set things right. It calls for a real surgeon like Ignacio. And besides, I don't have the parts. Don't be mistaken, I'd love to try, but I know where it would wind up. Cars are delicate beings, don't you know that, *teniente*? They're as complex as any horse you'll ever ride and twice as temperamental. They have a soul, I swear they do. The old Ford, for instance, she cried and carried on like a woman after the accident, and she's sitting out there now, waiting for me to help her, and there's nothing I can do until your father tells me to fix her up. That could be next year for all I know. . . ."

"No, it's going to be now."

"He hasn't been in the car for four, no . . . five months. It just sits there and bakes in that oven. If I didn't take it out on the road every week, it would die, the batteries . . . you understand . . ."

"Is this enough?" Jaime dug into his pocket and pulled out a sweat-stained roll of peseta notes. Barrera leaned forward and whistled between cracked lips.

"You shouldn't carry that much around. Especially out there on the plains. Someone is going to come along and, as they say, 'share your wealth.' "

Jaime laughed. He hadn't seen a single human being on the plains in three weeks. And in Toledo even the Anarchists seemed to prefer shelter to the heat of the day. Perhaps in the winter they were more of a problem. "Is it enough, man? You know what's needed, so tell me."

"It's enough. . . ."

"You'll come with me, now?"

Barrera slapped his knee. "Shall we walk? It's a long way, *teniente*. Have you counted the kilometers? I have. I've been driving around this place for almost two years . . . almost a year before your father took me on, and I know the distance from everyplace to everywhere. It's too far to walk, especially in this heat."

"You've seen me riding, haven't you?"

"Yes . . . ," the driver looked apprehensive. Jaime laughed again, a friendly, contagious sound that surprised even him; it was the first time he had laughed like that since returning to Spain. There was something about the driver that had released that laugh, a feeling of warmth . . . yet the driver had a look about him that caused Jaime some apprehension, too, a kind of furtive, pained expression, a darting of the eyes inside that spade-shaped skull, as though he were looking for something that he was afraid to find. But he didn't let on. Time enough for that later. Jaime knew, if nothing else, that he could trust the man.

"Well then, you'll ride, too. . . ."

"I'm no cavalryman, *teniente*. You show me a horse with a gear shift, and I'll get on as fast as you like, but . . ."

The driver saw quickly enough that there was no point in arguing. Mercader would not even become angry; he simply stood there with a quiet smile on his face and opened the door, as if to say, "Come on, man. Don't be a coward or a fool or both." Barrera knew there was nothing to fear from horses, but the idea made him nervous nonetheless. He had been a city man for a long time and before that, in Cartenegra, he had walked. Horses were for heroes in paper-covered romances and Mexican movies.

Four mules stood in the dust just beyond the car shed, ignoring the flies that nipped at their shanks and watching the two men at work nearby with dumb resignation. The mules had often seen the car before, but they had never seen anyone fasten chains around the front axle or pass ropes about the bumpers, and they were justifiably puzzled. But, like so many humans, they knew that their lot was simply to be there when called upon, to do whatever they were told to do and to suffer as though they were enjoying it. So they did not protest or bray but only nibbled at the tops of what little grass they could find round where they were tethered. The sky beyond the car shed began to turn coppery as the sun lost its hold in the sky and started to slip behind the distant mountains.

Jaime, his shirt knotted around his waist, and the driver, who had retained his filthy shirt out of shame at his poor physique, strained at the chains until the front of the car was a mass of braided ropes and twisted links.

"I think it will do," Barrera said at last, giving the cables a final turn. "What d'you think?"

"The bumper won't rip off?"

"If it does, the axle will have to go too."

Jaime cast a glance across the yard toward the window from which his father often watched his comings and goings. The curtains were slack; Francisco must be in his study, going over the documents which Soler's messenger had brought earlier that afternoon—the organization of the oil subsidiary to be set up in Ceuta. Thank God, he was occupied, Jaime thought; he had no desire to repeat the afternoon's argument. Time enough once the car was repaired. By then there might be no need for argument.

Once the two double yokes had been brought from the tool shed, it was no time at all before the mules were hitched up and the car firmly anchored to the rings at the base of the shaft.

"Is the brake off?"

"Christ, yes. What kind of a fool do you think I am?" the driver shouted good-naturedly.

Jaime, without a further word, mounted his mare and sat there watching Barrera struggle into his saddle. The driver pulled himself up and grasped the reins with confidence, sure that in time he would be as fine a rider as the "Arab" sitting there, a few yards away.

"All right . . . your Ignacio is waiting for us . . . ," Jaime called.

They set off, Jaime in front, the mules and the car next, and the driver bringing up the rear. There was no choice but to take the main road. To try to drag the car overland would simply be inviting disaster.

The curtains on the upper-story windows of the Mercader house did not stir as the strange caravan passed, headed along the whitewashed wall and toward the Madrid road.

Jaime tried not to think about what it would be like when he came back and the car was repaired, but, like a remembrance of something that had already happened, he could not drive it from his mind. His father would refuse to leave, might even laugh at him in that infuriatingly gentle way of his for being so concerned. His mother, perhaps, would take his side. Yet it was absolutely necessary to go through with it and even at the risk of alienating his father still more, he would have to see to it that they left the house, got to Madrid at least where it would be safe for a time. Later, they would go back to . . . Ceuta. Yes, that seemed the only thing to do. Here, they could trust no one. Didn't his father understand that? The situation was confused, the choices so blurred. The old distinctions of party, estate, rank, even religion, had vanished. And what did it matter if Carvalho would have done the same thing; for him, it would have been a question of cowardice, while for Jaime . . .

Magpies shuttled in and out of the stunted olive trees alongside the road, making the air a vast loom for their darting bodies. The leaves of the olive trees and the pine boughs, touched in the morning with a moment's graceful silver, now glowed as though they had just been pulled from a furnace. The landscape, flat, unbroken except by the distant mountains and the few clumps of pine and olive groves, the isolated cypress standing like obelisks in some forgotten desert, appeared in the evening's dying with an angry, threatening air . . . so unlike the vast calm that settled over the desert near Ceuta, the plains below the Riff mountains and the High Atlas. Jaime, squinting into the bloody smear of sun, could not help wondering why the land should be so terrifying here when, in fact, it was really not so different at all from the Moroccan tablelands.

They passed an ancient stone well by the roadside. Next to the well lay the skeleton of a small animal. Jaime felt a suffocating pity rise; what a terrible thing to have happened. He imagined the animal, whatever it had been, sniffing the water below, on the other side of the stone circle, unable to reach it, whimpering in desperation, then dying. Because, unlike man, it had no way . . . of reaching out. It had to rely on others to help it. Was that really the difference then, that a man could help himself, while an animal had to depend on what it found, on what others had done?

The mules plodded on, dragging the car behind them, its front wheels only two or three feet from the roadbed. Once, Jaime pulled a little ahead, then stopped to look back and caught the silhouette of the mules, the car and the driver, now quite upright in the saddle, black against the forge-fire sky: the funeral cortege of some primeval beast.

Just before the land begins its downward slope toward the sunset-yellowed Tagus, they stopped and pulled the car off to the side of the road, unhitched the mules, and let them rest. The beasts were allowed to nibble grass by a stand of stunted olivars. The ravine lay just ahead, and after it the Tagus, like a moat around the high anvil of Toledo, and then the Puerta del Cambrón through which they would enter, just as Jaime had entered that morning on horseback.

They tethered their mares to the olive trees and climbed a small embankment up to a flat rock from which they could see for miles around, to where the road bent like an arrow barb toward Toledo, and north too, where it ran forlornly toward Illescas and after it Madrid.

Barrera spread a newspaper on the rock and pulled a bottle of white wine out of a bundle he had been carrying on the pommel and set beside it a loaf of crusty white bread and a wheel of cheese wrapped in a red handkerchief. He cut into the cheese with a heavy black-handled knife, slowly and deliberately, with the patience of an artisan, carving out two wedges of identical size, the first of which he handed over to Jaime. The second he placed on his side of the newspaper.

"You cut the bread now," Barrera said, passing the knife, handle first. Jaime took the knife and cut into the loaf, handing the first slice to the driver, just as the driver had given him the first cut of cheese.

Jaime looked past the driver's hunched shadow and into the flat, sun-bereft plain, now filled with shadow and a heavy, swarming red mist that had rolled down from the mountains to the west. They had gone almost a third of the distance in total silence; then only a few words. Jaime had not wanted to ask anything though he remembered the look in the driver's eyes when he had mentioned the staff car that had ridden him off the road and wanted to ask him about it, and, too, about his desolate look, his suppressed voice. The man had something sharp lodged in his chest; that he knew. Perhaps the funereally draped picture of the old man had something to do with it.

He chewed on the moist, spongy bread. He would not ask. There was no point in knowing. When you knew and tried to figure things out, nothing ever happened the way you anticipated it. Only the memory of Oviedo was a constant for him. The dreams refused to leave. Everything rekindled them and, so it seemed, everything that happened became simply an extension of those few days. No escape was possible, but into one's own silence.

At that moment, under the darkening sky, with the mules and the mares silently grazing nearby, sitting on the high rock, like an altar, he suddenly became aware again of the space around him, the piercing solidity of stone, earth, and trees and of his own being among it all, no longer isolated and sealed off but part of the amazingly immense whole, over which he himself had no control whatever.

Jaime lowered his eyes, and regarded the driver's open face. Then, he picked up the bottle, only half full, and took a long drink. He turned his head back toward the smudge of sun over the humpbacked western peaks, and stared until his vision began to fade into the light itself. Barrera saw what he was doing, reached out and touched him on the arm.

They clambered down the embankment, leaving the half-loaf of bread, the rind of cheese, and the empty wine bottle on the flat rock.

After they had hitched the mules to the car again and begun the last lap of the journey, Jaime looked back and saw the bottle still there, catching the sunlight and sending off rays of red and gold that thrust into the evening sky like heliograph signals.

The mare moved forward and Jaime could see only the road, not the car or the mules or Barrera behind him. He thought, "Everything comes full circle in the end . . . Bible or Koran . . . God knows which. Only confusion." He relaxed to the rhythm of the horse's gait, drifting into a kind of half-sleep, the reins very loose in his hands. He had learned to sleep in the saddle of a mount he knew well: it was something he could do.

Barrera began to whistle softly, and the sound was carried forward over the creak of axles and the grunt of the mules as they passed along the rock-strewn road toward Toledo.

The Puerta del Cambrón; Jaime looked up as they passed beneath the shadow of the four towers. Reading the fragments of the Moorish inscription on one of the columns gave him an unaccountable feeling of pleasure. He had discovered the inscription the day before and had resolved, without really thinking about it, always to enter the city from the west so as to receive its fierce benediction: ". . . the faithful . . . will enter no battle out of which they will not come victorious and in whatever battle they may stain their lances with Christian blood, dying that same day, they will go alive and whole with eyes open into Paradise . . ." And another, which ended: ". . . when the time of death comes, you shall be only three days ill and, dying, will go . . ." Again, like the tolling of a deep, comforting bell: ". . . with open eyes to Paradise, forgiven of all sins . . ."

"To the right, to the right," Barrera called, and his voice made a curious echo between the walls of the buildings that were fast closing in on them. A moment before, Toledo had risen against a sky almost as dark as itself, the river circling beneath it with a snake's whisper. Now it was like entering a dungeon. Another gate. Over it brooded a two-headed Hapsburg eagle, its wings like rakes, claws sunken into the stone. Ahead only the dark, indistinct outlines of roofs and towers piercing the sky like spikes, a jumble of buildings sprawling over the hill. Black streets like tunnels, so narrow that they could hardly force the old car between the walls.

"Again . . . to the right . . ."

But where, Jaime thought, where was there room to make the turn? The car would barely pass. The mules halted, perplexed, then went forward again, following the slow clip-clop of the mare's hooves on the stones. There were people in the streets now. As the cortege penetrated the city, children in rags began to follow in their wake, shouting and laughing at them. Barrera swore at them and flailed with one arm as though he could beat away the darting shadows. By the door of a *taberna,* a dozen men from the arms factory were smoking and passing around bottles of beer. The car passed close to them. They rubbed their eyes and grumbled. A few of them followed after, mingling with the band of children who had formed in the rear of the procession.

At the next crossing of streets, a few women joined the parade of the curious. "Jesus . . . did you ever see such a thing?" The mules strained as the street began the steep ascent toward the heart of the city. People in the buildings past which they moved, hearing the chatter of voices, the creak of wheels, and the echo of the mules' hooves, leaned out of their windows to see what was happening. Someone threw a pot of slop out of a second-story window. It landed with a crash on the hood of the car, spattering the mules who snorted in protest. The children began to throw small stones, then larger ones.

"Come on, what do you think this is, Corpus Christi?" Barrera shouted, turning precariously in the saddle.

"That's quite a corpse you've got there as it is," someone replied.

"Jesus Ford . . ."

"Better that than the other . . ."

A stone struck Barrera beneath the left shoulder blade, but he refused to turn again. They were almost to Ignacio's garage, and it would end there as quietly as it had begun. He was angry but not foolish, and it would do no good to make a fool of himself in the street. How Mercader managed to keep his wits was beyond him; as for himself, it was all he could do to keep his temper.

"Once more," he called over the grumbling and the clatter of pebbles. There were at least two dozen people trailing after them now. Fortunately, the roadway was too narrow or they would have been surrounded by the crowd. As it was, the close walls of the building forced the procession to string out behind him and that was that.

"Left now, this time . . ."

The mules dragged the Ford onto a slightly wider street, and at once the crowd fanned out, surrounding them. Lamps flickered in a number of open windows and a locksmith's shop, still open, cast a wide patch of light onto the dust-dry stones. A little ways farther up the street a metal sign announced "Ignacio Peralta's Automobile Workshop."

In front of the garage entrance, a squat man hopped about like an angry toad, waving his arms. As Jaime drew up to him and the mules, as if on signal, came to a halt, the man saw Barrera's distinctive triangular head outlined against an illuminated window.

He cried a greeting and at once was down the street, waving and shouting at the crowd, dispersing them with wide swipes of his hands, as though exorcising spirits. . . .

"We didn't know . . . ," someone said, defensively.

"Well then, ask . . . ," the man's voice, rough as a grate, but cheerful, appreciating the joke.

"A relative can still be a snake."

". . . no harm . . . just a little fun . . ."

"Go have fun with your wife, will you . . . leave my own people to me . . ."

"For Christ' sake, Ignacio . . ."

"Better for my sake, how's that?"

The mechanic waved Jaime down from the saddle and grinned. In a moment, the crowd was gone down the narrow, constricted alleyways and the passages that led off the *calle* now blocked entirely by the disabled Ford and the mules.

"Thanks, Ignacio," Barrera said, his feet back on the ground and his back aching from the ride. "What a pack of idiots . . ."

"Idiots are dangerous if they're not locked up; that's what we have madhouses for," Ignacio replied.

"All right, let's get it inside, and we'll talk about lunatics later. What do you say?"

What had once been a stable for the horses of Toledo's Moorish governors had, by a strange alchemy of beam, cable, steel plate, and hose, become a garage. From the outside, it seemed only another fading house of indeterminate age, crushed between two equally dilapidated buildings, its doors opening onto a street no broader than those same doors were wide. Inside, the smell of centuries-old horse urine had been replaced by the equally pungent odor of gasoline, grease, and motor fumes. There was ventilation only when the doors were open, and the doors were open only when an automobile was being carefully guided through the entrance. It was a difficult operation; there was no room in the narrow street for a car to make a full turn into the old stable. To overcome the problem, Ignacio Peralta had devised a system of platforms and wheels which could be fitted under the car body and then drawn back into the garage by a hand-cranked winch, dragging the car in sideways through the open doors. Once inside, it could be turned around again on a wooden disk, not unlike a miller's wheel, which Peralta had copied from a railroad turntable he had once seen.

Despite the evidence of cables and cranks, Jaime could not comprehend just how the stocky mechanic had ever gotten the car inside. To him the man looked more like a near imbecile mule-driver than the mechanical genius the driver proclaimed him. Peralta stood there, squat and bowlegged, spitting gobs of froth into his grease-blackened hands and grinning.

Barrera sat on an empty oil drum, a Madrid newspaper under his buttocks in a vain effort to protect the seat of his already filthy pants; he whistled encouragement now and then at a particularly forceful tap of Peralta's hammer, as though applauding a good pass at a bullfight. Ignacio Peralta was greatly pleased and after each such interruption would smile, then resume work with renewed enthusiasm.

Jaime sat on a pile of boxes near the raised car body and wondered whether, in fact, he did know what he was doing. Even then, at that moment, something could be happening . . . in Toledo, in Illescas, or Madrid . . . anywhere else in Spain or even Morocco . . . something that could turn every plan he might make on its head. Shaken by a growing doubt that everything he was doing was utterly wrong, that perhaps he had nothing to fear but his own inability to understand, he found himself locked in a kind of paralysis in which he could think but not act. Nor could he understand how it was that the Anarchist mechanic, Peralta, had consented to work on the car or, for that matter, even to allow Francisco Mercader's son in his garage. "It's all right," Barrera had assured him, "Ignacio says that even if the *Izquierda* and people . . . you'll pardon me . . . like your father are wrong-headed, nevertheless their hearts are in the right place, so it's all the same to him." Despite what Barrera had said, Jaime remained unconvinced and watched the mechanic nervously as he worked.

In his confusion, he wanted desperately to light a cigarette but did not dare. The gas fumes were too thick.

A single weak bulb cautiously installed in a wire basket furnished illumination for the entire garage. Peralta scuttled and hopped about, tapped and prodded with such assurance and dexterity that it seemed he needed no light at all.

Jaime watched, fascinated; he understood horses and artillery, but the insides of a car were a mystery to him, and he marveled at the toad-like Ignacio's silent skill and knowledge. Yet there had been so much grunting and swearing as part after part vanished under the capacious hood that he was plagued by real doubt as to whether the car would, in the end, really run again. He sat, watching Peralta's surgery with mixed emotions. He could not even recall the girl's face from their encounter that morning but rather remembered only her face as it had been at the wedding, that of a different person entirely. The reality of his present situation seemed ever just beyond grasp.

"How does it look, Ignacio?" the driver asked after a while. Jaime held his breath, not knowing which way he wanted the answer to go.

Peralta, at that moment half-hidden under the left front wheel, grunted and went on twisting wires. "You ask the same question over and over."

"Is the answer still the same?"

"Yes," Peralta said, "it goes well, brother, well. The answer is still . . . 'it goes well.' "

"Ask him how long it will be," Jaime said.

"How long, Ignacio? How long? . . . that's the question now . . ."

"Not so long as it could be," the mechanic replied, his voice echoing in the car's insides. Then he disappeared completely, trailing wires like a Portuguese man o' war.

"We tickle her belly a little, then she'll go, I promise. She's a good old woman," he said from under the car, "like my wife . . ."

"Another victory against the Fascists. We beat America's Ford," Barrera said. "Let's celebrate."

"Don't blaspheme, brother," Peralta said, his voice sepulchral. "An automobile's stubbornness is one thing, but the Fascists, they're another matter and not to laugh at . . ."

"You take yourself too seriously. A car is a car . . ."

The sound of spitting issued from under the turntable; then, "I take myself seriously because these are serious things. You don't joke about them."

"Pay no attention," Barrera said. "He's a good man, despite it all. It's because his brother-in-law is a Civil Guard that he feels he has to say such things. If your brother-in-law were an Anti-Christ, you'd be holier than the Pope yourself."

There it was again, the endless confusion, the overlapping of lives and ideas . . . Barrera about whom he knew nothing, Ignacio Peralta who was a member of the FAI, Carvalho himself who claimed that he wanted with all his heart to be on their side but could not, Barrera's cousin, a Civil Guard, the wife, Jaime Mercader who wanted only . . . what was it he wanted? To be left alone?

"As good as gold; it always is," Peralta boomed, then repeated: "As gold," emerged, rubbing his hands together. "All finished. How's that, brother? And we even have a few parts left over." He held up a length of cable, threw it into a pile in the corner. "For the next emergency. At your expense, señor, but you don't mind, do you?"

Peralta stood up, black as a swamp toad, and put his wrenches and pincers away. The wooden racks on the walls with their rows of heavy bladed tools, awls, nippers, wrenches, and spandrels made Jaime think of the torture chambers of the Inquisition; the flickering light from the unsteady bulb, acid yellow, reinforced that sinister impression. And too, there was the fact that Ignacio Peralta had not said a single word all evening about what was happening outside, about the rising, the defeats, the victories. Or about Toledo's strange silence either.

"There's a bottle of *valdepenas* here. We may as well drink it up while we can, brother," Peralta said, rubbing his palms on his overalls.

Jaime stood up; another thought stuck in his mind: Hadn't Barrera said that the Guard who was Peralta's brother-in-law, and his own cousin, was in Toledo? But the Guard, he knew, were never posted in their home districts; rather, they occupied towns at opposite ends of Spain, like a foreign army, seldom leaving their barracks, isolated from the population. Yet here it was not quite that way. Could it mean that the Guard in Toledo would go with the Government and against the rising? It had happened elsewhere, or so the reports he'd heard in the afternoon had said, and the reverse had happened too . . . *Asaltos* units had gone over to the generals. The more he thought about what was happening, the more agitated he became.

"All right . . . a drink then," he heard himself saying with abandon. "Why not . . ."

"One thing first . . ." The mechanic got into the front seat of the car and turned on the motor. It kicked over and promptly began filling the room with exhaust. Peralta got out again, wiping his face with sooty hands until he looked like a Moor.

"So, brother . . . a promise is a promise," he said. "You see? It's all fixed. Runs like an angel, if you'll pardon the saying."

They went outside into the street, taking the *valdepenas* with them. The night was hot, filled with dry, scalding winds. In the narrow street, Jaime was overcome again with a stifling sense of apprehension, as though the walls of the buildings were about to converge over his head and seal him forever to the cobbled breast of that strange, ancient city. The stars, high above, seemed a part of another world.

Peralta, having taken a long draught from the bottle, handed it to Jaime. He drank without hesitation, though he knew what the wine would do to him. Yet to admit such a weakness would make him look foolish before the mechanic, and that he would not permit. An unfathomable pride held the bottle to his lips while he drew it down in long, painful draughts.

"Deep," Barrera said. "It's a chilly night. . . ."

Jaime turned to him, puzzled; it was hot, blazing, the furnaces of Castilla were all stoked and roaring. What was he talking about?

"Not chill in the real way," Barrera said quickly. "But a chill to the bone, that's what I mean . . . A real *noche toledana*. The ghost of Amru must be out in the streets, looking for more victims. The bloodthirsty old goat."

Peralta looked worried, his eyes focused on something very distant. "The streets around the Alcázar were filled with blood that night, they say, so slippery an honest man couldn't walk upright."

Barrera went on, "There's something brewing, that's certain. You can feel it like a fever in your limbs. Maybe there's something to the old stories after all . . ."

"The old stories," Jaime thought, "of decay and misrule, of foolish men and pride and blood . . . we don't learn, we never learn, not one of us. The only thing we learn from it all is that we don't learn anything."

"You've never seen Amru, have you?" Peralta asked.

"You know that only those born in Toledo can see him. I'm from the north, but I can feel it all the same. . . . It's an odd night, all right."

Ignacio shrugged and said nothing.

The driver took a drink and pased the *valdepenas* back to Peralta. The three of them sat down on the stones while Peralta lifted the bottle again. Jaime felt the wine rushing in his head, and the stars had already begun to blur. He looked about him, regarding the street unhappily. To lose the twenty-seven mosques of Tetuán, jewels in a blue sky and forever faithful to the beholder, for what? For this? How pathetic . . .

Jaime reached out. "Where are we . . . exactly?" he said at last. The light from the garage fell into the street, but the street looked like all the others he had seen. Unless he could make out either the Tagus or the Zoco or the cathedral, he had no idea where he was.

"If I tell you the name of the street, you still won't know."

"Then tell me something I will know."

Barrera stared at him. "Man . . . don't you remember? All right . . . near the Tránsito . . . do you remember that? Four streets away, that's all. Can't you smell the old Jews?"

The bottle was suddenly back in his hands; he tried to refuse but Barrera would not let him. The wine was bitter and strong, and he was already dizzy from it.

"You wouldn't want to insult Ignacio, would you? To refuse a poor man's bottle is as much an insult as to spit on a rich man's table," the driver said.

Jaime leaned back; it was absurd, he knew, to become drunk on such a small amount of alcohol, but he had always been that way. The Koran forbade alcohol, wisely, he thought, although many of the Berbers and the other tribes drank nonetheless.

Peralta began to sing softly, wordlessly, an out-of-tune melody that Jaime did not recognize.

"A musician?" Barrera laughed. "Did you know that my cousin's brother-in-law with the dirty hands was a musician as well as all the rest?"

Peralta went on, now drumming time on his thighs with open palms. Jaime thought of the morning, as much of the salmon-colored clouds and the horizon, of the car, of the girl, and he knew what he would do.

Peralta's voice rose, a closed, nasal sound, as though the melody were being forced from his chest only with the greatest effort. No shutters opened and no lights blinked on. The mechanic then found words for his song and his harsh voice turned to a growl. He took the bottle again and emptied it to the dregs, then clasped Jaime by the shoulders.

"We will all sing," he announced. "I think we should all sing. . . ."

"And get shot in the process?" Barrera protested.

"Toledo is a city of love . . . except for certain people we don't love, but there's time for that later," Peralta said. Then to Jaime, who had been standing silently, an uncertain smile on his lips, he said, "Can you play the guitar?"

"No . . . can you?" Jaime answered.

The mechanic laughed goatishly.

"Him play a guitar," Barrera said. "Look at his hands . . . what would he do with a guitar?"

"But we have a phonograph. I must have music and, so I have a phonograph, even if it is English . . ." said Peralta. "After all, a man without music is a man without a soul."

"The FAI don't have souls," Barrera said dryly. "You're not allowed . . ."

"I spit on you," Peralta said, laughing. "Not souls in the sense your cousin Infante might understand them, but simply that we are good, that we 'feel.' That's what a soul is, feeling . . . so . . . I have a soul, and also . . . I have a phonograph."

Jaime tried to stand upright as the mechanic disappeared into the garage and emerged a moment later with an ancient crank phonograph under his arm, the end of the detachable horn thrust into his overall pocket. He looked as though he had been spiked by an enormous sunflower. The machine was made of mahogany and had a bright silver crank, carefully polished.

"Here," Peralta said, offering a phonograph record to the startled Jaime and the horn to the driver. "We'll sing to this. It's a good simple tune, though this fellow Vargas adds some decorations of his own that I don't care for . . . now . . . who do we go to serenade, eh? My wife? Make her feel like a *novia*."

"Fine . . . your wife . . . of course, your wife," Jaime replied, astonished to hear himself continuing on in such an unaccustomed way.

Barrera was startled, almost indignant, "*Teniente* . . . for God's sake. Do you understand what could happen?" he whispered. Then to Peralta he said half jokingly, half with real scorn, "What a waste, on such a cow. Are you sure it's worth it? To get killed for the sake of guarding such a cow."

Peralta refused to be angered. "Sure she's a cow. And I'm a frog. That's what they call me, *El Rana,* so what the hell! The Frog and the Cow. Let's go . . ."

Barrera shrugged and clasped his hands angrily together. He had expected Mercader to put a stop to this insanity before someone got hurt, but there was the *teniente,* allowing himself to be dragged into such a piece of stupidity and not saying a word. Was the man out of his mind, or had he simply had too much wine? Peralta moved down the street carrying the box, Jaime next, holding as the driver watched, the phonograph record. In despair, Barrera followed them. The great flared horn borne before him as though it were an offering in a Saint's Day procession.

"This is crazy," Barrera whispered, but the *teniente* seemed not to hear him at all.

The street was narrow and dark as all the others, and equally as empty. Cats squalled among the trash barrels and an incongruous scent of thyme wafted in from the hills across the nearby river. They were not far from the Tránsito, Jaime realized, not far from the Carvalho house.

A few shots, soft as the popping of champagne corks, were heard a great distance away; otherwise, the street was silent. In the hot wind, Jaime thought he could hear the chains on the front of the church of San Juan de los Reyes rattling. Surely if the ghost of Amru the Cruel, once Moorish governor of the city, walked the streets, there was ample reason for the chains of San Juan to clink.

All at once they came out on a street just off the Tránsito. Jaime could see the outlines of the buildings on Carvalho's street rising like a ragged fence against the night sky. Peralta set the phonograph on a pile of cans and took the horn from Barrera. In a moment he was cranking up the mechanism.

"You see, it's well oiled. I take care of it like a good car," he said.

Barrera said: "Let's get it over with, then. One song, just one, do you promise?"

Peralta laughed and set the machine running. The combined sound of needle-scratch and guitar broke the silence. There were lights on in a few of the windows above them, smudges of lemon-yellow behind oilcloth shades or newspapers that had been pasted over the panes to keep the sun out during the day.

Peralta began at once to sing. "If you don't know the words, listen to me and I'll teach you . . ."

> *Tres morillas me enamoran . . . en Jaen. . .*
> *Axa, y Fatima y Marien . . .*
> *Tres morillas tan garridas*
> *Iban a coger olivas, y hallabanse cogidas . . .*
> *. . . en Jaen . . .*

Jaime knew the words. It was an old song, very old, and he had heard it sung as a child by his father. It came as a surprise to hear it from the phonograph of Ignacio Peralta the mechanic. His mouth opened, and he heard himself singing, though in fact he was not. He saw himself singing before the Carvalho house to Mercedes Carvalho, not to the wife of Peralta the mechanic. To Mercedes who appeared, not as she had been on that morning, in a rough dress, her fingers discolored by the chalks she had been using, but rather dressed as he had seen her on the night of the wedding in Madrid.

Then, quite without realizing when he had begun, he was really singing, in a strong, nasal voice, in the African manner. Peralta grinned, clapped his hands and sang more loudly still while Barrera, shaking his head and totally unable to believe what was happening, pressed himself discreetly into a doorway.

The street remained dark, and but for the bray of singing and the squawk of the phonograph, still, as it had been before. A light winked on in a window directly overhead as they reached the second verse of the song, and a heavy shadow appeared behind a paper window shade.

Peralta sang louder, getting slightly ahead of the voice on the phonograph.

"For Christ' sake," Barrera hissed.

> *. . . y hallabanse cogidas*
> *y tornaban desmaidas*
> *y las colores perdidas . . . en Jaen . . .*

Far above, stars passed indifferently on their slow, unaltering courses, and the moon limped on, a fugitive in the west, bandaged by smoky clouds. Peralta wiped the sweat from his forehead, leaving streak marks, and bent to replace the needle at the beginning of the record.

"Enough, Ignacio, enough . . ."

"Don't you see, she's up there, she hears us . . ." Peralta grinned.

"So does everyone else in Toledo. Ignacio, please . . . stop this . . ."

"Shit!" exclaimed Peralta. ". . . *tres morillas* . . . ," he shouted at the top of his lungs, covering completely the sound of the phonograph.

As the opening guitar chords sounded a second time, a sudden whine cut across the street. The record jumped from the phonograph and shattered against the cobblestones.

"The bastard . . . ," Peralta swore, picking the bullet out of the mangled gears. The machine was ruined. "Look what he did. For ten years I've kept this old thing running and now look . . ."

"I warned you . . . now, you see . . . ," Barrera cried.

Jaime glanced about frantically. For a few moments he had lost track of time, of place, conveyed away by the mechanic's rough good humor. Now all he could hear was the crack of the rifle, resounding over and over again.

Whoever had fired the shot had retired immediately behind a door or a window. The smell of gunpowder hung on the air. The window above was flung open and a stocky woman with a round, glistening face appeared: Peralta's wife.

"Jesus!" she screamed. "Ignacio, are you all right? He didn't hit you did he?"

"He, he . . . who the hell is *he*? I'd like to know . . ." Ignacio held up the crank for his wife to see.

"Come inside," his wife shouted. "Who are these two . . . ?"

"It's Esteban and a friend. . . ."

That was all right, too. "Bring them all inside," Ignacio's wife called down, ". . . and quickly before someone else takes it into his head to shoot at them. And," she added, "of all the damned foolish things to do . . ."

"Eh, of course it's foolish, but you liked it, didn't you?"

"Inside, eh . . . quickly. Inside . . ."

"Have you had enough, now? . . ." Barrera whispered. His hands were shaking. The bullet had come whipping past his head and missed him only by inches.

Peralta picked up the remains of the phonograph and horn and stood there cradling them in his arms. For a second he seemed about to weep, then he stiffened and, just as incongruously, broke into a broad smile.

"Come on, we'll get something to eat. Let the woman fix us something. You don't get free serenades at her age. You have to work for them. And I'm as hungry as a wolf after that car. . . ." He turned to Jaime. "You too. Both of you. There's plenty to eat. She'll grumble a bit, but don't pay any attention to her."

Jaime barely heard him. He was still looking up the street at the spot where the shot had come from. There was nothing there, he knew, but he kept seeing vague shiftings in the shadows. And the echo of the shot. He hadn't heard a rifle go off in quite a while, and it had done something to him.

"Hey, you . . . ," Peralta was saying. "You eat too . . . come on. And you can stay the night if you want, both of you."

Jaime shook his head sharply as though trying to dislodge something: the echo of the rifle shot. He ground a piece of the record under his heel—a brittle, harsh sound. Something being destroyed.

"No. . . no. . . ," he stammered. Barrera looked at him unhappily. "Thank you, but I don't think . . ."

"Look, you can't go back tonight," Ignacio said. "So you may as well."

Peralta's wife was shouting from her window, anxious, urging them to come in before someone got killed. A few other lights had winked on down the street.

"Why not?" It had not occurred to Jaime that he could go back that night . . . the night in fact seemed to be slipping by him so rapidly that it would outstrip anything he might want to do . . . but to hear Ignacio tell him that he could not go back was a shock. "Why not, why can't we?"

"Gas, that's why. There's no gas in the tank and none in my shop. The truck comes at six in the morning. Then, there'll be gas. That's why."

"Come on," Barrera urged. "She doesn't cook badly, Ignacio's wife. I've eaten her cooking before and look, I'm still alive . . ."

Jaime tried to smile. It was too much. He had to be alone for a while, if only so that he could calm down again. He was ashamed of his nervousness, of the way the shot had affected him.

"Maybe later. I'll come up later, but for now . . . ," Jaime said. "You go up. I want to walk . . ."

"Aiee . . . lunatics are running around shooting off rifles in the streets, and he wants to walk! . . ." Peralta exclaimed.

"He goes by himself," Barrera explained. "All the time. Look, it's his way and that's all there is to it. He goes out by himself all the time. I think it drives his father crazy, but he likes it . . . to be alone. It's all right . . . but for Christ' sake, come back up here when you're through, won't you?"

Jaime nodded quickly. So the driver had been watching him too. He wondered, how many others had watched him, talked about his behavior? His riding? . . . Xaviera the cook? Lazarille the gardener? or the field hands Pascual and Rufino? How many others?

"So . . . remember the number," Ignacio said. The front door was open and his wife was standing in the hallway. "72, Calle de las Bulas . . . and there's a bed here for you, a real bed . . ."

Barrera said: "You'll come back, won't you . . . don't go far. If you want to walk, all right, but it isn't safe, believe me . . ."

"I won't go far," Jaime said. "But I may not come back tonight. I don't know . . ."

"Please," the driver said.

Peralta laughed. "Maybe he's got something else in mind . . . well, what difference does it make? You won't find much. Even the whores are out looking for rifles."

"If I don't come back" Jaime said hurriedly, "where shall I meet you . . . in the morning? . . ."

Barrera took in a deep, rasping breath. "At the Bar Goya then. You know where it is. On the Zoco? You can't miss it. Under the big white Cinzano sign."

"I know."

"All right then. At eight. But please, *teniente* . . . be careful. Don't be . . . you'll excuse my using the expression but . . . don't be a fool. . . ."

"And how do I prevent *that?*" Jaime thought. He raised his hand briefly as though in a salute and moved off down the street. Barrera stood there with part of the ruined phonograph in his arms.

JULY 20, 10:00 P.M.: *Orgaz*

SELICA PORTILLO CLOSED HER EYES and let the hum of the car motor lull her into a pleasant doze; the evening was warm, and the jogging of the car on the cratered road between Toledo and Orgaz was not unpleasant. On the seat next to her, Colonel Fernán González Venegas, commandant of the Civil Guard garrison at Toledo, was sweating, his body giving off a peculiar amalgam of odors, perspiration, pomade, and heavy cologne; he groaned slightly each time the wheels of the car caught in a pothole or an unusually deep furrow made by a wagon that had passed during the day. Dust rose, swirling in the beams of the headlights.

Venegas had difficulty seeing. Perhaps he needed new glasses; a man's eyes, as he gets older, do change, and never for the better. He knew that. He would have to see Dr. Barrio or Dr. Aliaga to get a new prescription. But for the time being, there were more important things he had to do. Yet . . . he cautioned himself, as he wrestled with the steering wheel of the unwieldly *Hispano-Suiza,* trying to avoid a deep depression ahead of him . . . "if you can't see what you're doing, what the hell's the point?"

The car lurched across the rut, sending the woman hurtling toward the dashboard. Fernán Venegas let go of the steering wheel with one hand and grabbed her by the shoulder. She murmured something and relaxed against the seat, slipping quickly back into a drowse. She was thinking of the trip they had made to Madrid the week before. She hadn't been to the films in a long while. Venegas had tried to make it seem as though he had planned the trip solely for her pleasure. She recalled the theater, dark, the buzz of fans like a swarm of insects on the ceiling, the bluish-black images on the screen. The *Cine Delicias,* what a lovely name for a theater . . . *Busco un Millionario* with Jean Harlow and *El Abuelo de la Criatura* with the two funny Americans. Laurel and . . . the other, who sounded English . . . what was it?

Venegas was speaking: "You've got to watch yourself . . ."

"What?"

"Keep your eyes open. I can't avoid these holes altogether. They've torn up the road with their damned wagons . . . it's impossible . . ."

"Oh . . . ," she said, barely listening. Her mind was still full of the blurry images, the remembered odor of the theater itself, almost spicy. She had wanted to see the new film with Imperio Argentina at the Tivoli but . . . no, Fernán had picked the *Cine Delicias* and that had been that. She never argued with him; it was pointless even to think of arguing with him. He had not even known what was playing there. Why was it so important, she had asked, trying to make it seem like a casual remark, not a question. And didn't he care for La Argentina's dancing? It made no difference; they went to the *Delicias,* and sat near the back. She had the curious feeling that then, as now, the trip was not simply for their pleasure, but for some other, more obscure purpose. At one point a man had come in and sat down in the seat next to Venegas. He had stayed only a few minutes. They had not talked, yet it seemed to her that there had been some form of contact between them. But by then she had been too involved in the action on the screen to care.

Why were they going to Orgaz . . . and at night? Venegas, she knew, enjoyed driving; it was almost a passion with him, but she could not understand how he could enjoy driving over such a road . . . and to Orgaz? One could see nothing from the castle at night. The Roman bridge might be interesting by starlight, but the sky was full of clouds which seemed to be hurrying to get away from something. The face of Gonzálo Ruiz, Conde de Orgaz, gray-brown in death in El Greco's painting replaced the blonde image of Harlow in Selica's imaginings. . . . She shuddered slightly. Angels fluttered with heavy wings through her imagination. Then the face of the Conde de Orgaz became that of her husband, and she imagined him, too, in death. How many times had she told herself that he had to be dead? There was no alternative to it. She opened her eyes a bit and glanced at Venegas. She had been the Colonel's mistress for almost two years, since the '34 uprisings and the arrests that had followed. True, he had saved her husband from immediate execution, but what had Emilio done in the first place? Nothing. Then why should he have been arrested? Venegas had always insisted that the order had come from Madrid, that he had no alternative but to follow it . . . he did what he could, he would promise . . . and things had slipped and slipped and slipped. She recalled how she had come to his office daily, how he had received her, unhappy at first to have her there at all, busy with his work, finding her only a disturbance. Months had passed, and her husband had been transferred first to Montjuich and then, to a penal colony in the Balearics. She had continued going to Venegas' office. Gradually things had changed. Venegas had begun to notice her, his impersonal correctness replaced by a more direct, almost friendly attitude. They seemed co-conspirators in a plot neither of them would discuss. Odd. Then she had become his mistress. It had seemed to her quite natural that she should have done so; he was, in a way, a link to her husband and a replacement. She was sure now, after so much time and no word at all, that Emilio must have died. There were rumors about an attempted escape, two men drowned . . . no one knew for sure. Official word never came, and everything drifted as before.

"Drifted" . . . she was drifting again. The car seemed very warm. The windows were rolled up to keep out the dust from the road. She thought she might ask Venegas to open the window on his side, just a little.

The road seemed smoother now. Perhaps . . . the faces slid, one over the other, like transparencies. She began to hum, to distract herself.

"The thirtieth marker," Fernán Venegas said. "It won't be long now . . ."

She knew better than to ask why they were going to Orgaz or why he had put on civilian clothes. In Toledo he was never seen without his uniform, always neat, starched, even in the hottest weather. "The commandant of the Civil Guard has a standard to maintain," he had patiently explained to her. "It has nothing to do with personal vanity but only with morale, with being an example to the men."

The road curved to the left. The plains and the peaks of the Montes de Toledo would soon be seen, looming up, dark as a shipwreck, into the shattered starlight. A jumble of shapes on the landscape, far in the distance, proclaimed the town. She thought that she could see the outlines of the castle, too, but might have been mistaken.

"We're going to stop outside the town," Venegas was saying, barely audible over the sound of the motor.

Was he going to have her there in the car? What a surprise, she thought . . . he'd done that at the beginning. A strange sensation at first, but she had grown used to it. But for months now, Venegas had been too preoccupied to make love properly, even in bed.

"There's a tavern . . . I have some business there," he was saying.

She let out a breath. It was the same as the trip to Madrid then. She was simply an accessory to his "business," whatever it was. But she felt no rancor; she was too tired and, at that moment, too comfortable to care. Time enough later. It was still early, barely eleven, and the drive back, after his "business," would take at most a half hour.

"Two kilometers," he announced, then, "There it is . . ."

To the right, on a slight rise alongside the road was a low building, one or perhaps two stories, it was hard to tell, sway-backed, as though it had been broken in the middle, the railing of the balcony that overhung the curved front door sagging and threatening to crack under the weight of the first man who might step out upon it. There were smudgy lights in the windows and an orange glow at the door. A few horses had been tied to a rail near the entrance and were quietly pawing at the ground. Beyond the inn, the outlines of the town could be more clearly seen; the sky had cleared momentarily and the starlight made the lime-white buildings glitter.

Venegas drew the car up along the side of the road opposite the entrance to the inn, but did not switch off the motor.

"Selica," he said. She stirred but didn't answer.

"Selica," he repeated more sharply. She sat up, opened her eyes.

"You can drive this car, can't you?" he asked, his normally high, quiet voice tinged with urgency.

"You know I can . . ."

"All right then. When I get out, you sit behind the wheel. Keep the motor running. There may be trouble. One never knows . . ."

"What are you going to do in there?" she asked, alarmed . . . not so much, she realized, for him, but for herself.

"It doesn't matter. Just do as I say, and everything will go well. I may be too nervous. I've been nervous for weeks now, and it isn't my fault. There's a lot to be nervous about, Christ knows," he said. "Dr. Barrio gave me some pills . . . would you believe it? How does he expect me to take pills? To calm me down . . . or to get me killed?" He pushed the door open, peeling off his jacket at the same time and throwing it into the back seat. He got out and stood for a moment in the road, as though waiting for something. He was a small man, perhaps five-foot-six, no more; his tenseness made him smaller, more compact. His face, which Selica had not been able to see clearly inside the car, was now brightened by the starlight that fell through the rapidly moving clouds. Selica watched him, wondering why he was standing there so hesitantly. His face was contorted by an embarrassed indecision, his eyes blinking rapidly behind the thick glasses without which he could barely see. The dome of his bald head glistened, the little hair he had along the sides of his head appearing as shadows or rather empty spaces where his skull seemed to have been carved away.

"All right," he said, to himself. He was looking over the hood of the car toward the inn doorway. "All right, now . . ." A whisper. He rubbed his hands together quickly and stepped around the front of the car. "Keep the motor running . . . don't forget . . . ," he said, watching the woman slip into the seat behind the wheel.

He walked across the road too quickly, the rapidity of his step betraying even more than the compression of his features the nervousness that gripped him.

He reached the doorway of the inn, paused again, then went inside. She watched him go without interest. It made no difference to her what he was up to. She would not ask, and he would not tell her. How many times had she been used to cover some information-gathering expedition, some meeting, some secretive contact? And before her, it had probably been someone else. For all of his lack of physical attractiveness, he had always had women enough, so much so that his reputation had been the subject of jokes at taverns and in the street in Toledo. Perhaps that had been one of the reasons she had allowed herself to be drawn in: curiosity. Perhaps.

Now she was bored. She stretched her legs under the dashboard, twisted the steering wheel to the left and the right, then tried to make out her own reflection in the rear-view mirror. She was still a handsome woman though she had let herself begin to coarsen . . . too much weight. But Fernán Venegas liked it, so what difference did it make? It was traditional and things traditional pleased him. The one time she had tried to change her hair, he had been angry for days.

Like a rooster, she thought, conjuring his just vanished image back into the road. Ridiculous compared to . . . . she stopped short, refusing to think further. She had been about to mouth her husband's name. Her dead husband. But for what purpose? It hadn't been Fernán's fault, neither the arrest nor the attempted escape. . . . but . . . her thoughts wandered . . . Orgaz, at this time of night and for what? It had not been for her after all; she was disappointed. She began to think of all the little ways she could get back at him for this imposition, the small demands she could make which he could not refuse.

She had closed her eyes again, lulled by the steady pulse of the motor. Suddenly a loud noise erupted from the inn across the road . . . the sound of men shouting, then the sharper, louder crack of pistol shots. She sat upright in the seat, gripping the wheel, her first instinct to press her foot down as far as it would go on the accelerator.

Three shots in all; then Venegas appeared in the doorway, reeling as though drunk, hands flung out and groping for support. He stumbled, as though unable to see where he was going. Yet, as he came toward the car, he kept turning half around and firing his Mauser back toward the inn entrance, toward the horses which were now rearing and neighing in terror. Bits of plaster sprang from the front wall of the inn where the bullets struck.

The door on his side of the car was open. Selica Portillo shouted at him, to guide him by the sound of her voice. She could see now why he was running in such an antic way; his glasses were broken and his face was cut. Blood blotched one cheek.

Three other men had run out of the entrance of the inn and were coming fast across the road, less than twenty meters away. Venegas, almost at the car, stopped and fired at them. His shots went wild, striking a parked car. The men scrambled for cover.

Venegas fell heavily against the side of the car, pulled himself around the door and into the front seat.

"Go, for Christ' sake . . . go! . . ." he shouted.

Selica Portillo's foot hit the accelerator before Venegas had had time to close the door and the car shot forward onto the road, the door flapping like a broken wing. He cried at her to keep going, threw the pistol onto the seat and grabbed the door handle with both hands, finally slamming it shut against the pressure of the car's motion.

"Keep going . . . I can't see a thing," he cried furiously . . . "They broke my glasses . . . the bastards . . ."

"Fernán . . ."

"Just keep going . . . go on, don't ask anything. Just go . . ."

A shot whined by. Then the car lurched around a bend in the road and out of range.

"Someone told them," Venegas muttered, half to himself, reaching up with a handkerchief to stop the flow of blood from his lacerated cheek. "They were waiting for me in there, do you know . . ." He seemed to be accusing her. She glanced sideways at him. "Keep your eyes on the road, for God's sake . . . look where you're going . . ."

When they had driven about two kilometers, he said: "They killed Soriano, did you know that? Of course not, you don't even know who Soriano was. . . . They had him all tied up in a sack in the back. It was a big joke when I walked in and asked for him. They rolled him out." He put his hands to his face; one of the lenses and the earpiece still hung from the right side of his head. He pulled the fragments loose, held the broken glasses in his hand and swore. "All right . . . that settles it. . . ."

They kept on driving until they found a side road which branched off and swung back north toward Toledo.

JULY 20, 11:00 P.M.: *Toledo*

A LIZARD OF MOTTLED GREEN and brown, its eyes like glowing nail-heads, stood rigid by the narrow, trellised balcony, staring uncompromisingly at Manuel Torroba who, far from staring back or even noticing the tiny reptile, continued to gaze fixedly into the bell of the snifter he was slowly rotating between his palms.

Sebastian Gil measured his friend's silence by the duration of each phonograph record side. He had changed the records three times since Torroba had last spoken, five times since he had poured the cognac.

Torroba sat still, hardly moving, as though to apologize, by self-abasing silence which was so unlike him, for not having come the night before. He knew that Gil had waited for him and his expression revealed all too clearly his consciousness of the betrayal his failure to appear had in fact been.

How little difference it had really made though, Gil thought; their friendship, bound up as it was by affection for Gil's dead wife, had been eroding slowly for months.

Neither of them had spoken of Torroba's failure to come the night before; when he had rung the bell in the entrance hall, Gil had come to the head of the stairs and welcomed him quietly and with a deliberate solicitude.

It struck Gil as ironic that Torroba's present silence should be caused by such a needless guilt. He would have to speak of it sooner or later but perhaps it would be better to let Torroba bring up the subject himself, as at confessional. The role of confessor, Gil thought, suited him well at that moment. He would show how well he understood and how well he could forgive. For that reason, he had been careful to arrange everything as it always was on the evenings of their meetings, the brandy bottle, the phonograph records, the chairs all in their accustomed positions.

Trying to avoid even the appearance of concern, Gil accepted Torroba's silence and absorbed himself in it. He allowed his gaze to wander about the room, devouring all its details, as though he were discovering it for the first time. Sooner or later, he knew, Torroba would speak, and then it would all be normal again.

A jungle sprouted from every wall and corner of Gil's sitting room; pots and rusty cans of all shapes and sizes, wooden boxes, troughs, urns, jugs and bottles held every variety of green, leafy plant that could be cajoled into growing in the dry air of Toledo. A tiny tiled font, decorated with blue glazed flowers, hung on the wall like a *pila* for holy water, overflowing with streamers of yellow, ocher, and green, bright against the pale white and cerulean tiles. In counterpoint to the sound of violins and cellos issuing from a phonograph hidden somewhere behind a thick palm plant, tiny insects buzzed in and out of familiar leaves and flowers.

And over it all, a gentle smile held dominion, a smile caught fast in the photograph of Gil's dead wife, Alicia, that rested on the shrouded grand piano. The fading image, already spidered with a thousand tiny cracks, was circled by a frame of silver jonquils and roses, daily polished and polished again, attended and cared for as though it were alive.

"Alicia," thought Gil, smiling back at the face in the photograph, not caring whether Torroba saw him or not, sure that if he did, Torroba too would smile. "Alicia? Yes, she would have understood all of this. She would have been such a help . . . to both of us. . . ."

The lizard scampered on its tiny pin-sharp claws down from the railing and began stalking insects by a pot of basil. Gil noticed it, nodded as though granting it permission to continue. Alicia had liked all kinds of living creatures, even lizards. Such gentleness, such concern, he mused. Poor Torroba—if Alicia were there, she would know what to say to comfort him, to quiet his nerves.

The music quickened; Torroba's expression remained unchanged. The music slowed; not a muscle moved on his face.

The lizard, glutted with flies, retreated once again to the terrace and curled up in a tangle of trailing vines.

Gil could not take his eyes off Torroba. The man seemed not to notice the intense, unwavering stare at all. "What a narrow, ascetic face; what a wild halo of gray hair; a monk's face," Gil thought, "in a Zurbarán painting." Then suddenly he found himself gazing again at the photograph. Odd that he should have chosen that particular Mozart quartet. She had often played a piano transcription of one of its melodies . . . Torroba, did he remember? Had he ever heard her play it?

He returned his gaze to Torroba's face, to that peculiar, almost religious expression combined of gentleness and ferocity that had once so attracted him, which Alicia too had found so remarkable. Was the man really listening to the music or only pretending? How sad that they could not confide in each other any longer. Whose fault? His? Torroba's? They were like two children who did not know each other playing at being friends, each wishing it, but not knowing how to make it come true.

"Don't you like the cognac?" Gil asked finally, hesitant to break the stillness between them.

"Why do you ask that?" Torroba did not look up.

"Because . . ." should he say it or not? . . . But it was already begun. ". . . Because you usually have had three by this time. And that one, that's only your first, and you've hardly touched it."

The corners of Torroba's mouth crinkled as though he were about to laugh; his eyes shone. He glanced at the photograph, then jerked his head around self-consciously.

There was the lizard, on the move again, running along the folds of Torroba's raincoat which was still on the floor where he had dropped it, where Gil, out of deference, had left it. The rapid forked tongue explored the black rosette on the lapel of the coat, found that it was not, after all, an insect, discontinued its investigation.

Torroba, watching the lizard, tipped the snifter intentionally. A little cognac spilled to the floor. The lizard came over, nosed it, licked up a few drops.

"Poor little fellow," Torroba said. "But then, he's really lucky. He can have a drink and not worry . . ."

"And you," Gil thought, "you who must worry—why do you assume such a burden? Who asks you to? Who forces you?"

"Do you want wine instead?"

"No . . . ," Torroba said.

". . . Jerez?"

"No," Torroba said again. "It's good cognac, Sebastián. It is . . . only . . ."

"Only you're nervous tonight."

"Am I?"

"Very."

"Is it only I?" Torroba asked. "What about you? I thought . . . let me speak frankly, Sebastián . . . I thought I'd find you in . . . I don't know how to put it . . . in a state, a condition . . ."

"Hysteria?" Gil smiled faintly.

"I could hardly blame you . . . don't you think it was difficult for me to turn you away as I had to yesterday? Yet here you sit, with the Gramophone on, the cognac bottle on the table, your best glasses ready . . . my favorites too, the ones with the cherubs on the stems. You remember such little things, Sebastián . . ."

"You didn't have any choice, I know that," Gil said.

"The truth is, Sebastián, we didn't have anything to do with it. I checked with Sánchez. In fact, we don't even know who the man was . . . except that Sánchez thinks . . . and this is only surmise . . . that he was a printer from Talavera. Gilberto recalls having seen him once or twice . . . or thinks he does. And this . . . also from Sánchez . . . that it may have been a fight over a woman. But who knows? There are so many factions in Toledo today, so many reasons for killing. Everyone is trying to show how strong he is: 'Look, what sharp teeth I have,' they say. So, people get killed."

"I know," Gil said in a drugged voice, gazing at the ceiling. A fly was circling there, just inches from the cracked plaster. "I didn't think it was one of your people, really . . ."

"I even spoke to Tierres," Torroba went on, driven by a compulsion to explain, to make it clear that turning Gil away in the morning had nothing to do with their friendship and that he had done whatever he could. "Tierres . . . he is, for all practical purposes, the Communist party here, as you know, I'm sure." And at that, Gil seemed to see another face, superimposed over Torroba's features, a massive, dark complexioned face with heavy, barbarous mustaches, a man of perhaps fifty, with steel teeth on the right side of his mouth, given him, it was said, by the Russians to whom he had escaped after being imprisoned in the castle Montjuich after the Barcelona risings in 1919 . . . with only half his real teeth still in his mouth.

Torroba went on: "Tierres called me the other day on some idiotic business . . . the first time he's bothered to speak to us since all that 'solidarity' talk before the elections . . . something about an Austrian 'comrade' they're looking for who absconded with a fantastic sum from the party treasury . . . they'd love to get their hands on it. . . . Of course we hadn't seen him, and if we had, I wouldn't have told Tierres about it . . . we would use the money ourselves. . . . But circumstance fortunately allowed me to tell the truth. . . ."

Gil was startled; he had always imagined Torroba's integrity to be absolute.

Torroba did not notice Gil's faintly accusing expression, continued: "So I thought I'd ask Tierres a favor in return, about the body. But he swears it wasn't his doing either. So . . . it remains a mystery . . . the chances are it was simply a personal matter . . . probably over a woman, as Sánchez suggests. Otherwise, why so brutal? A knife? The lover's weapon. We don't perform political assassinations with knives these days. No, a knife means an outraged husband or a frustrated lover. Don't worry, Sebastián . . . *not now, at least* . . . ," he concluded, emphasizing those last four words.

"A mistake? . . . By my shop rather than the bakeshop next door or Fuente's ironwares across the street, and so on? I'd like to think so. Yes, I'll decide to think so," Gil said.

"What else do I have to suggest? Who else is there? The POUM have no strength here at all, and José Antonio's people have been very, very quiet . . . smart, I'd say . . . they know what would happen if they started anything here, and besides, we're all *toledanos*, even the blue-shirts, not *pistoleros* like our friends in Madrid. We seem to have a sense of dignity here that transcends political differences. Pray that it stays that way . . ."

"Still . . . ," Gil began, listlessly.

But Torroba would not stop: "The point is," he continued, "it could have been anybody, for any reason . . . and you assume that it was a warning to you in particular . . . because you're friendly with Venegas and Reyles and Fontanals? . . . Well, what of it? For all we know, Fernán Venegas or any of the others may come over to our side tomorrow or the next day. Everybody here is waiting to see what the other fellow will do . . . everybody is hesitating. They remember '31 and '34. And when they do make up their minds, who knows what? The word is in that in Granada, the *Asaltos* . . . imagine this . . . the 'Praetorian Guard' of the Republic, have gone over to the Fascists. . . ."

"They're not Fascists . . . ," Gil said quietly. "Use another word."

"You may be right, but the label is as good as any other. It's too complex, Sebastián, so we have to simplify . . . so . . . the 'Fascists' then, and say to yourself that your friend Manuel means 'Fascists' the same way that Fernán Venegas means it when he calls everybody who disagrees with him a 'Red,' which is equally ridiculous."

Gil felt hopelessly tired. What was the point in trying to define terms as though they were having a scholastic debate? It was better to leave things unsaid; they both understood.

"And in Barcelona," Torroba was saying, "the *guardia civil* have gone over, equipment, officers and all, to the Republic. Who knows what will happen here or any place else? That's the foolishness of putting labels on everyone before . . . they choose."

Gil had never seen his friend so driven to explain, to rationalize. His very compulsion to speak betrayed a tremendous agitation. Could it be that Torroba's faith had been shaken at last, that he no longer believed in Bakunin's innate goodness of man? It was one thing, Gil knew, to speak abstractly and quite another to be faced, finally, with the necessity of putting one's ideals to the test of action. Torroba had always hung back. In '31 he had watched from the periphery. Three years later, he had cautioned his group to boycott the elections and refuse to participate in the uprisings, and they had not been touched when the Asturian miners and the Catalans had been crushed. Even now, there had been no overt action in Toledo. The news was pouring in . . . city after city fallen to the rebels. Yet Toledo, full of FAI, remained silent, waiting.

"How strange," Gil said, swirling the cognac in his own glass. "You come here expecting to calm me down . . . and you're far more upset than I am. I . . . somehow . . . I accepted what happened yesterday morning . . . you turned me away. Venegas . . . yes . . . he turned me away too, and so I said to myself . . . I said, if no one has the time to help you, Sebastián, and you can't blame them for it, then what is there to do but accept? . . . Wait, I said to myself, wait and Manuel will come, and we'll have a pleasant evening just as before . . . but you, you are more upset than I was. I ask myself why? Am I so stupid that I don't see what you see?"

"Of course," said Torroba. "You're quite right . . . what we've been waiting for all these months has actually started to happen, and now I'm as nervous as a convert at his first confessional. As if I didn't want it to happen at all . . ."

"Do you?" Gil could not help asking.

Torroba inclined his head suddenly, as though the muscles in his neck had been severed. He turned, surprised first by the question, then by his own uncertainty.

"Yes . . . yes . . . yes . . . but what I don't want is all the killing. I'm too old for the killing, Sebastián . . . Killing is for young people who don't understand yet about death." He watched the lizard trying to climb the railing. It fell back, moved in tiny circles, then gave up and returned to the raincoat. "Perhaps I shouldn't be here tonight. Perhaps that's why I'm so nervous. Guilt or something of the kind . . . but tell me, what *should* I do? We're as ready as we'll ever be. We have only to wait for the Fascists to make the next move . . . and then . . ." He halted in mid-sentence, then went on in a tone of heightened alarm. "Do you really see it? Is my nervousness so obvious to you?"

"You've been staring into that glass for ten minutes."

"Ah . . . yes . . . and what do I see there? Am I a gypsy, to divine secrets in the glass? But I can see some things clearly enough. Blood, Sebastián, such as you could never imagine . . . such as would have made even our good Goya retch. I don't want it, Sebastián, and it isn't necessary. To destroy what is rotten and corrupt doesn't mean we must kill as well."

Then, abruptly, the music stopped, and Torroba said quite matter-of-factly:

"The record is over, Sebastián. Do you want me to change it?"

Gil rose and turned the record over, just as he had been doing for the last quarter-hour.

"But . . . wait," Torroba said, "let's turn on the radio, too. For a minute. There may be news. Softly, of course, so as not to disturb the music . . ."

Gil leaned over, obediently touched the dial of the radio. A sudden rush of static, then a man speaking, absurdly distant, barely audible. Gil set the record to turning again; the needle bit down, releasing Mozart's melancholy.

"Alicia played that once," Gil thought.

The voice on the radio grew louder, more agitated, cutting in on the music.

"No," Torroba said harshly, glaring at the radio. "Turn that damned thing off. There's no news. Just some fool mouthing . . ." He got up, advanced on his crumpled raincoat as though to attack the lizard still sleeping there, withdrew, began pacing. Gil, watching him from his chair, was afraid for him, clicked the radio off again.

Torroba halted by the piano, turned back the lid over the keyboard; dust flew up in a cloud, each key visible in the light of the electric lamp.

With a look of intense concentration, he began to pick out the principal melody of the just concluded movement of the quartet. Gil could see that his hand was shaking slightly.

At the uppermost arch of the phrase, Torroba stopped suddenly and brought his fist down on the keys.

Gil felt a heat sweep through his chest and mount, unwanted, to his eyes.

"Sebastián . . ." Torroba looked up, abashed. "I don't know what's the matter with me . . . what a stupid, thoughtless thing to do."

"Gently," Gil thought, "gently as she would have said it."

"It's all right. There's no real harm. . . ."

Torroba shook his head. "I should leave, Sebastián. All I'm good for tonight is upsetting things . . . and upsetting you, my friend. If I go back, I'll find something to occupy me. It might calm me to be at work."

"I wish you wouldn't go there at night. Not now," Gil said, thinking of the deserted granary that the FAI used as a headquarters, where Torroba insisted on working late at night after the others had gone . . . the upstairs window, glowing faintly, Torroba hunched over his table, seeing only the papers before him and his own private vision of the future.

"It's not safe," Gil added uncertainly.

"If someone wants to kill me," Torroba replied, rising, "they don't have to wait until I'm alone up there. . . ."

Gil said nothing.

Torroba stood there by the window, staring at the picture on the piano. Suddenly, the frame of the picture became lambent, the wreaths of silver flowers grew golden and flickering. Light rushed in over the iron balcony railing, spread over ceiling and floor. Then the light stopped moving and flooded the room. Car headlights appeared in the street directly below.

Torroba stood there, bewildered, blinking. All at once the lights went out again and the succeeding gloom seemed twice as deep as it had been before.

"Does anyone know I'm here? You haven't told any of your *other* friends that I'd be here tonight . . . have you?"

"You know I wouldn't . . ."

"They're coming up . . . two of them."

There was a rush of footsteps on the stairs. Gil rose, supporting himself on the arms of his chair.

"Wait here. Whoever they are, I'll send them away."

Torroba moved quickly to the corner of the room, turned halfway around so that his back was to the doorway. "How odd," Gil thought, going into the front room. "Does he think that he can hide by simply turning his back . . . ?"

As he arrived at the door, the pounding started. He hesitated a second, then swung the door open. It was Fernán Venegas, dressed in civilian clothes. A dark-haired woman of about forty, attractive in a heavy, earth-bound way, waited behind him. Her eyes were red with fatigue, her manner confused. Gil recognized her at once as Venegas' mistress of two years, Selica Portillo.

Venegas stood there, squinting at Gil. The right side of his head showed an ugly cut, the blood caked his cheek, and his glasses were missing. Gil felt an urge to laugh, so grotesque did Venegas' face appear, the eyes screwed tightly together, the nose and forehead wrinkled like a raisin; the man seemed very small without his uniform.

"I have to come in," Venegas whispered urgently. "Please, quickly."

Before Gil could say anything, the Colonel and the woman were inside, and the door was shut again.

"Señora Portillo," Gil offered, nodding.

"Please forgive us . . . for this intrusion . . . ," she began. Venegas turned to her and gestured angrily.

"He doesn't want to hear apologies, Selica. Don't be a fool."

"What's the matter?" Gil asked hurriedly, trying to keep Venegas by the door. He did not want an encounter with Torroba in the next room. At the same time he felt that he could not let Venegas and the woman stand there glaring at each other; there would be a scene. Whatever it was that had agitated Venegas so, he was taking it out on the woman. She seemed on the verge of tears.

"First this," Venegas answered, producing from his pocket a broken pair of eyeglasses, the frame snapped in two. "Do you have any adhesive tape . . . some glue of any kind? I *must* get these fixed. . . . Do you realize what it is like not being able to see? Do you, Sebastián?"

"We'll find something."

"Of course, of course. I knew you would."

"Is that what brings you here, only that? Surely . . ."

"Not that," Venegas shot back. "Of course not . . . but that first, *that* first, before anything else."

The music coming from the next room caught Venegas' attention. He squinted past Gil, trying to see.

"I'm sorry to have interrupted you," he said, "but I didn't have any choice, and neither do you . . . not now." He went on speaking rapidly while the woman glanced with apprehension from side to side. Gil watched her closely, searching for some indication, however slight, of the true state of her emotions.

The mere fact that Venegas had brought her with him to Gil's home meant that something serious was in the air. "Yet," Gil thought, "what else could he have done? If his glasses have been broken for any length of time, she must have been driving for him." And it was, clearly, this unwanted dependence on her, caused by his near-blindness, that had made him so waspish.

"We haven't got much time," Venegas went on, pushing toward the other room. "I beg you, Sebastián, do not ask questions. Simply do as I say, no matter what you think. What I am doing, I am doing out of my friendship for you . . . and I ask you to believe this . . . I'm not being melodramatic when I say that what I am doing for you is at the risk of my life . . . we could have been safe already if we had not come here . . ." He paused, reaching up to probe the ugly wound on the side of his face. "Sebastián . . . can you give me a brandy? Anything strong . . . whiskey . . . I need something . . . and one for her, too. She's been through a lot already," he said, nodding at the woman, his first kind gesture toward her since he had entered. "Then I'll explain it all . . . yes, there's time for a brandy," he said, as though to himself. "She's a terrible driver, you know, Sebastián? And she's had to drive for me this last hour since they broke my glasses . . . we were in Orgaz . . . attacked . . . but that's not important now . . . I'm lucky to be alive. God watches . . ."

Before Gil could stop him, the Colonel had moved past him and entered the other room. Both Venegas and Torroba knew of his friendship with the other, but to have them confront each other, and at a time like this, was unthinkable. He stumbled forward only to feel the woman's hand on his arm, humiliating . . . she was offering her assistance, trying to help him.

The music continued, over the ever-present scratching of the phonograph's needle. "Needs to be changed . . . ruin the records that way . . . how many packs of needles left. . . . One or two? . . . order from Madrid . . . but now?"

He stopped, astounded, at the threshold. Venegas was there and he was alone. He had already collapsed heavily into the stuffed chair in which only a few moments ago Torroba had been sitting. But the Anarchist was nowhere to be seen.

"In the closet? Or the bedroom . . . where then?" Gil had a terrible premonition: "Was Torroba in hiding, about to attack the Colonel? But what could he say? . . . In my home . . . no, he wouldn't . . ."

On the table near the phonograph there was only one half-full brandy glass and the bottle. Torroba had removed all signs of his presence.

Venegas was mopping his face which had begun to bleed again and glanced gloomily at the bottle and the glass.

"Has it come to that, Sebastián?" he asked, his voice suddenly solicitous, unusually gentle. Gil and the woman came in and stood by him.

"What do you mean?"

"You can't drink it away. I would have thought you knew better."

"I?"

"Never mind," Venegas said wearily, turning away. "I shouldn't have said anything, but it pains me to see such things. You, Sebastián, with your fine intelligence and understanding of others . . . don't you understand yourself? Well, well . . . it's not important, not important now."

"Rest, Fernán . . . while we try to fix these glasses . . ." Gil said, fumbling in a table drawer for a roll of adhesive tape.

"Here, let me," Venegas' mistress said.

"Let them alone. Señor Gil is perfectly capable."

But the woman had already taken the glasses and tape.

"Please . . . I *want* to do that for you . . ."

She turned imploringly to Gil who made no move to take the glasses from her. In a moment she had clumsily taped the frames together and handed the repaired spectacles back to Venegas. He nodded brusquely, then turned at once to Gil.

"That's a relief, I don't mind telling you, Sebastián. Certainly a relief. I wonder, can you understand what it is *not to see?* No, you've got to be blind yourself and you, your eyesight is like a hawk's. . . ."

"Relax now," Gil said, trying to spot some trace of Torroba. But there was nothing. Wherever he was hidden, he had covered every sign.

"Relax?" Venegas' tone had hardened. "If only we could. Did you know, Sebastián, how little time there is? Well then, I came here to help you, to save your life if you will. There's my friendship. . . . yes, I'll have that brandy now. You see, you won't have to drink alone. Selica, do you want any?"

She shook her head, remained silent.

"Better that way," he agreed. "Do you know, if Selica hadn't been in the car waiting for me, and the engine running, we might have been killed right there on the road to Orgaz? Christ, what a night. . . ." He shook his head as though there was something he could not understand, then caught himself and checked the movement with embarrassment. "The FAI, of course . . . I was on my way to meet our informer in Orgaz . . . a foolish thing to do . . . the man who was in the office when you came in the other day, Sebastián . . . he's dead now. Someone found out and. . . ." He drew his finger across his throat. "That's that. I was a fool to have gone there myself. When I think now what might have happened. What almost *did* happen . . ."

"Be calm . . . it's all right here. . . ."

Venegas laughed. "Do you think I'm worried about my own safety? Hardly, or I'd be keeping shop as you do, my friend. No, it's hardly that."

"Then?" Gil was barely listening. He kept thinking, over and over, "Where is Torroba?" The thought that there might yet be violence in his house was growing cancerously in his mind.

Venegas broke in on his ruminations: "I want you to come with me. I've stopped here especially for you."

"Come with you? But where do you want me to go?"

"To the Alcázar. To safety."

"But why, why should I have anything to fear?"

"To answer your questions I would need exactly the time we don't have," Venegas said. "Things are happening already. Other things, I don't mind telling you . . . other things are about to happen. Granada, Segovia, Ávila, have already fallen to the revolutionaries. Burgos and Pamplona as well and Saragossa too. By an insane piece of bad luck,

General Sanjurjo was killed this afternoon. His plane crashed near Lisbon. The fool pilot couldn't even get the plane off the ground, it seems. Which leaves only Franco and Mola, and they may take their time getting here. In Madrid, the 'Reds' are already getting revenge by burning churches . . . dozens already, and the knives are being sharpened here too. Look what happened to us in Orgaz! What can we expect now in Toledo before the army reaches us? No, it is impossible just to stay where you are. You have to make your choice . . . a reluctant choice perhaps . . . but even so . . . and be ready to stand fast. But you can't even do that if you have your throat cut."

"I am no one's enemy," Gil protested.

"They will destroy anyone who does not embrace their faith, Sebastián. They have not even the little tolerance in such matters that the Holy Office once had," Venegas went on hurriedly. "The car is outside. Take some clothing, whatever else you can carry with you . . . if you have a gun, even a hunting rifle or a pistol, take that too, and any ammunition you have."

Gil picked up his brandy glass. The record was drawing to an end, and the music was scratchier than before; the inner grooves always were the first to wear out, ending any piece, however sublime, with a hiss.

"I'm not going with you, Fernán . . . really . . ."

"Reconsider. Think of what may happen. In the Alcázar, you'll be safe, until order is restored. I'll be there to help you and, Christ knows, Sebastián . . . you may not want to admit it . . . but you'll need help. Believe me you will. Down here, who knows what may happen? How long do you think you can survive, tell me that? Even your other friends . . . ," he paused, his face darkening. . . . "From the thought that I have other friends or because of who they are?" Gil wondered . . . then Venegas went on: "And if you accept their help, if you *do* become really involved with them, I may not be able to do anything for you later. I can't make any promises after tonight."

Gil's voice sounded insincere, even to himself: "You're exaggerating . . . it's one of our national characteristics . . . we exaggerate all the time, Fernán, in everything. In love, in mourning, in politics . . . look at me. I exaggerate too. I admit it. . . ."

"This isn't a case of my exaggerating, Sebastián. It's a case of your being blind. You must come."

"No. . . ."

"So . . . hopeless as always. We could continue this for hours." Venegas said phlegmatically, the excitement that had accompanied his entrance now completely dissipated, his usual manner restored. "As you know, I'm somewhat more vulnerable than you are, and time is very valuable to me, so. . . ."

"I'm sorry, Fernán. . . ."

"So am I." Venegas got up, finishing the brandy in one swallow. He took the woman by the hand. At the door he paused and looked back at Gil.

"Go on with the music, Sebastián," he said. His face seemed clouded with pain, and for the first time in memory, Gil was convinced that Fernán Venegas had really had the welfare of another man at heart and was now, in his defeat, doubly wounded. A second of hesitation; perhaps he should go. No . . . he squeezed the brandy glass in his hand, almost fracturing it. "There's one more movement, Sebastián. Play it. Think a little. Perhaps later . . . you know where to find me. . . ." He hesitated. "Perhaps I have to think a bit more myself. . . . There are things I don't understand either. . . . May God be with you," he said.

A moment later the front door at the foot of the stairs shut softly, and the cough of a motor rose in the street outside.

The door to the bedroom opened and Torroba came out, his face ashen.

"You know what that means?" he asked. His forehead was glistening with a film of sweat which had not been there before.

"That he wanted me to go with him. He's a decent man, Manuel, just as you are. . . ."

"Perhaps . . . you may be a better judge than I . . . but, do you know? Do you understand?"

"Both of you, you keep after me like hawks after a lamb," Gil said with sudden harshness.

"Because . . . and you may understand this some day too . . . we are, both of us . . . your friends. . . ."

"Then, for the love of Christ, can't you both leave me in peace?"

"If it were that simple . . ."

"Why were you hiding then, tell me that?"

Torroba looked puzzled for a second, then amused; the corners of his mouth turned up in a painful smile. "What do you think would have happened if I'd been standing here when he came in?"

"Why . . . nothing. What should have happened?" he lied, wanting to hear Torroba say what he knew perfectly well himself.

"Either," Torroba began in the tone of a schoolmaster instructing a particularly slow child, "he would have killed me or I would have killed him. . . . I think that he wouldn't have wanted that either, not in your home. But it might not have been possible to avoid it."

"This is incomprehensible," Gil burst out, then turned away, busying himself with the bottle of brandy and the roll of adhesive tape which he slipped back into the drawer. The music had long since ended, and the needle was sliding back and forth in the last groove. "Why don't you sit down," Gil said, almost pleading. It had been so peaceful before; it wasn't the way he had wanted the evening to be at all. "There's another movement to go . . . ," he added, then winced as he realized that Venegas had said almost exactly the same thing a moment before and that Torroba, no doubt, had heard him.

"You really don't understand it at all," Torroba said. "You don't. It's hard for me to accept that, do you know, Sebastián . . . but I see there's no choice. . . ." He walked over to the phonograph and reached down, lifting up the arm and setting it back on its cradle. Then he flicked the switch and turned the machine off entirely. The record continued to spin slowly on the turntable.

"It was over anyhow," Torroba said and walked out of the room.

NIGHT, JULY 20: *Toledo*

IT WAS AS IT ALWAYS HAD BEEN at Ceuta when Jaime had gone off walking by the blackened seawall at night, but there was no fresh salt breeze in the alleys of Toledo, only the smell of cooking oil and sweat and the old stones, moist with tears that would not dry out, not even in a thousand, thousand years of sun.

He had to be by himself; he had been verging on a crisis all evening and now could heal himself only with an hour's solitary wandering. None of it was turning out as he had expected it to; he should have been back at his father's house with the car, but now . . . in the morning, there would be time enough.

A hunger ache grew in his stomach, gradually becoming stronger even than the fear that had lodged in him after the shot. His head began to clear, and he found that he was also afraid of lucidity. He hurried through the cramped alleyways, under the iron lamps and the balconies. Cats skulked in the shadows, and small children who should long since have been in bed tormented one another in the hallways of the low houses. Every now and then a breath of thyme or apricot would remind him that somewhere, just beyond the walls and the buildings that hemmed him in, the river wound, a noose about the city.

Within a half hour his sense of displacement had grown too much for him, and he had found a *taberna*. Attracted by the sound of singing and the slashing strokes of a hand on a guitar, not playing the instrument so much as attacking it, he entered and sat himself down, as he always did, in a table near the corner where he would not have to talk to anyone but could watch and think.

The room was full of dirty, tired men from the nearby factories, field hands, pickers from the olive groves and the orchards in *Los Cigarrales*, all eating their rude meals, drinking their beer and their fuming wine in the dingy, barnlike room with its dirt floor.

He ordered without thinking, clams and pork, and the dish was brought and set before him along with a bottle of wine he had not asked for. "It's all too much under the surface," he thought. "It should be direct, open. Death is death. You don't sit down and eat with death . . . where's the dignity in it?" There was something different about death in Morocco. There, it came with a violence as biblical as the landscape. But here death somehow seemed tawdry, irrelevant.

He looked around the room, trying to find the guitarist. A pall hung over everything; the men in the *taberna* filled the air with the pungent blue smoke of bad cigars and latakian tobacco. A white-haired old man sat on a stool at the opposite end of the room, hunched over his guitar as though it had struck him full in the chest and he was pressing it to him to ease the pain of the blow.

Jaime could not make out the words; but the melody coiled upward in a familiar way. Not *cante hondo,* but something even more plangent, Moorish. "Why not," he thought, "in this city that the Moors built? . . ."

There was a woman too, in the shadows behind the guitarist, and her voice joined his, slipping in and out of the old man's harsh, sustained cry. It was the sound itself that struck through him, not the words. He remembered another room, full of the jangle of the *bendir,* ridden by reed flutes, other tables at which sat soldiers, a few officers, a crowd of Moorish troops in their green turbans . . . their faces tense too. The night before his *tabor* had left Ceuta for the mainland, and Oviedo.

How different were the Moors' faces, with their bright, feral eyes and white teeth, from the faces of these men, their muscles trembling with some undefined, fearfully restrained passion. Anger or fear? He felt a mingling of pity and disdain for them. It struck him . . . the same feeling that he had for Carvalho.

The old man was playing on one string, a fantastic, rapid figure that transformed the guitar into a pipe . . . the reed flute . . . it had stopped once that night, and the tambourines, issuing their call to a dance, had clouded over the echo, just as the sound of men drumming with their palms on the table now covered the silences when the old man's hand slipped down to reposition itself.

He sipped his wine; it burned. Staring down at his hands, he wondered . . . what must I do now? He had left the army, but it was not enough. To declare a vocation? To withdraw from life as Luis Pelayo had done? Perhaps to find the way to forgive Carvalho then? Nothing satisfied him, not even solitude, which he could no longer bear. He felt himself gradually receding into a mist as dense as those that had streamed up each morning from the Asturian mountains. The Spaniard, Mercader, had vanished into those mists; now only the profile of his Berber ancestry remained visible, his mother's angular shadow. He could think only of the Atlas, the high crisp peaks, snow cones, and the sparkling sun. Cold air . . . the silent hooded people, gliding among the peaks.

The old guitarist's voice rose, though his head pressed closer and closer to his chest. Some of the listeners in the *taberna* were moved to join him, and a rough choir of voices drifted into the smoke. Jaime closed his eyes. No longer Toledo, but that same black *taberna* at Ceuta, the night before . . . while the *banderas* of the Legion and the *tabors* of *Regulares* were massing at the docks, pitting the night with campfires and the sharpening of knives on flat stones, like so many teeth gnashing.

There had been a girl there too . . . wrapped in veils, only her eyebrows visible over the purple cloth. She had danced, the nasal voice of the *ammesad,* not unlike that of the old man who now sang, emerging from the dark room behind her . . . the Moorish *Regulares* swaying, rising to join the dance. A ripple of clapping hands, then as now, then a clash of palms . . . then as now . . . the soldiers stamping about the room. The universality of fear . . .

Cannon, firing from the mountain slopes outside of Oviedo, the shells crashing down about the cathedral, the Hotel Covadonga . . . all visible in a haze through his binoculars . . . the smash of aerial bombs from the flights of Berguets swarming in over the city . . .

Through the swirl of memories, Jaime forced consciousness like a spearpoint, tearing, and painful, back into the present. . . . But he did not hear the old man and the woman . . . "Concha . . ." they were shouting to her now; that was her name . . . "Concha. . . ." But rather he heard the voice of the old *ammesad* and the shouts of the men dancing, shouts of terrifying ferocity, torn from their chests like living roots. The woman's body, the undulations not of her body but of the yards of brightly dyed cloth with which she had wrapped herself . . . the light of the oil lamps and candles about the room caught by the fringe of gold metal that arced down above her thick eyebrows and by the medallions hanging from her shoulders . . .

There . . . "Concha," moving into the light, animated by the clapping of the factory workers, her body rigid, only her arms and feet moving . . . her eyes only suddenly visible as though picked out by a spotlight. He thought fleetingly of his mother, who had such eyes too. Suddenly, the old guitarist raised his head. But his face was that of the *ammesad,* yellow, lined as a date, lips stained black, his toothless mouth open in a round O from which issued an endless ululation.

The men at the tables leaned forward; the girl's motions quickened; she stamped her feet. The men strained forward, some rose, caught by the need for release. Rivers of acid in the air. The smell of fear . . . then as now . . . "the fear that loves death . . ." Who had told him that, so long ago? Fear was essential, the part of him that had been missing. Not the intellectual fears, the reasoned fears, but the dark, unexplainable fear that could rise only out of ignorance . . .

He closed his eyes, swaying in his seat. He saw the room clearly, as it had been two years before . . . the circle of Moors, the flight of lances and racing horsemen conjured out of the air by the *ammesad*'s chant . . . one single Moorish soldier had broken away from the circle of dancers and come swaying toward him, his face running with sweat, arms extended in invitation . . .

He had cried out, "No . . ." . . . the Moor had been almost on top of him when he had uttered that one sound. The Moor's sash had come undone in the dance, and suddenly the long, curved knife that had been thrust into its folds had slid down his leg and clattered to the floor. The Moor had stopped, reached down to pick up the knife, and then a strange thing had happened . . . he had taken the knife across both palms, and lifted it to his mouth and kissed the length of the blade . . . then, as abruptly as he had left the circle, he had rejoined it. . . .

Jaime's eyes snapped open . . . his hands had come up to his mouth as though he held that same remembered blade, and his hands were shaking violently . . . What had the man wanted . . . ? What did any of them there in this *taberna* in Toledo want . . . ?

". . . One man's fear requires the fear of others to keep it company. . . . A solitary fear is like a sickness, but fear shared becomes bravery."

The thought of the half-finished plate of food, the warm bottle of wine on the table nauseated him. The *taberna* was full of an incessant drumming sound. Some of the men were pounding their empty bottles against the tables . . . the sound of marching feet, of machine guns . . .

He felt dizzy. Sweat trickled along the back of his neck, and it was comforting because it told him clearly enough that his body at least was working according to its old ways. . . . He tried to stand, but it took a moment before he could get his legs under him and he would not move, make a fool of himself, until he was sure he could rise without incident. The old man was slashing violently at the guitar, and his voice pierced the smoke, the low beams of the room, like a spray of spikes. The melody had changed, the rhythm as well. . . . What was it? Every man in the room knew without even thinking, but he . . . nurtured on the *lana* and the *quasida,* the chanted epics of the mountains, of his mother's people, did not know, and it burned him, this ignorance which he now, in self-defense, had turned to pride.

The dial of his watch swam as though under a film of oil. Thrusting a few coins under his plate . . . he had no idea whether it was enough or too much . . . he got to his feet. Across the room he could make out the swaying figures, the shapes hunched over the tables and the woman's lemon-yellow face under the light, the muscles of her cheeks rigid, her head seeming to float immobile over her moving body.

He rushed out of the *taberna* and into the street. He should never have left the driver, he knew, but it was too late to do anything about that now. He had no idea where Peralta's rooms were; he had wandered too far and would never find the street again. He looked up. Above the tangle of low buildings the night sky stretched, cold, clear and ineffably distant, rich with stars. He walked quickly, listening to the sound of his own footsteps as they eclipsed the clapping and the cry of the guitar from within the *taberna*.

Confusion . . . he thought at that moment of the novel by the Frenchman Ledruc he had once read, the scene near the end where the soldier hero passes the night in the mud of his trench, waiting for the morning attack and masturbating. "Was he killed or not?" He could not remember the ending; perhaps the soldier had been maimed, not killed. It made no difference. But that one passage had remained in his mind.

The dial of his watch had stopped moving, hardened back into recognizable shape. The hour was unimportant. The face of the woman, "Concha," hung in the orbs of lamplights. And the picture he had made in his mind of Ledruc's soldier. Was he like that, waiting in his own trench? Well then . . .

He passed into a broader street not far from the cathedral and looking up over the rooftops, he could see the dark mass of the spire rimmed by its three crowns of spikes and pointing at the bone-yellow moon. Clouds drifted. People moved across the street, whispered in doorways. From somewhere he heard the static of a badly tuned radio, the jangle of another guitar and the tangled sounds of voices. Walking in those streets was like traversing the bottom of a long trench, the walls of which were impossible to scale . . . Overpowering, the urge to flee, but impossible to satisfy that urge. The paralysis of a would-be suicide who has taken drugs and has only to reach out for the telephone to call a doctor . . .

In the lamp's glow, at the turn of the alleyway, another woman, then another. A man in black, a priest, hurrying with a basket. Spurts of radio sound, electric, frenzied:

"Más vale que digan: Aquí huyó" que "Aquí murió."

But how to flee? The face, the voice of the woman, "Concha" . . . Ledruc's solution? "Possible . . . possible . . . before the sickness returns and then, maybe, it won't come and I can be free of it. . . ."

To escape the city all he had to do was turn about and walk down the streets out to the San Martín bridge and across the river, but he could no more do that than fly to the moon.

"Concha," he thought, but she had a different face, not the hard, emotionless gaze of the dancer, unwavering and scornful before the *taberna* full of men, but the softer face of another woman, hair pulled back, the eyes intense with unsatisfied curiosity, the profile thrusting forward like her father's. . . . How difficult would it be to find some one now? he wondered, and walked on, deeper into the city, climbing the uneven cobbles of the streets toward the top of the *sierra* upon which Toledo lay staked out and dead.

"Before the sickness returns . . . before . . ."

Jaime's temples throbbed, the pain in his head was fierce and unrelenting . . . still, he drove his body, and the harder he thrust, the more vivid the images became. . . .

"Dig your nails into her . . . ," he thought, ". . . to make her cry out and wake me from this . . ."

He could not detach himself. The visions came like poison gas, burning in his lungs. He saw in the folds of the sheet directly below his eyes the furrowed network of roads and alleys, the shacks and buildings that grew, almost organically, into the stone and masonry of a city . . . spots of sweat became the troop formations moving foward. Tiny, isolated dots in scattered formation, weaving in and out of the debris. Smoke, swept up in an unexpected wind, revealing a column of cavalry; a broken line of small trucks moving forward with light artillery hitched to the rear pintels . . .

He could hear himself groaning, hear the woman's stifled protest but he kept on . . . the pounding in his head grew in intensity . . . the thud of artillery and the sharp crack of dynamite, the small sticks sizzling through the air, the heavier charges set off by wires . . .

All he could feel was the sweat pouring down his back, nothing in his loins. The smell of the woman's hair suffocated him . . . the odor of cider apples. In those fields . . .

A flight of cavalry passing in a cloud of black dust, the riders grinning, lances thrust at the sky, pennants fluttering. The rumble of camions and the clank of heavy weapons being wheeled into position . . . Jaime Mercader and four other officers in a truck, driving along a rutted road abreast of a column of racing horsemen. Louder explosions from the center of the city . . . a motorcycle driving by, the man in the sidecar leaning out, handing . . . who was it? . . . the Colonel, Carvalho . . . now he could see him clearly . . . handing the Colonel a dispatch and Carvalho pushing back his sunglasses to read it. Moorish *Regulares,* wrapped in their blanketlike cloaks, advancing with elements of the *Tercio,* the Foreign Legion, all on foot, bayonets fixed. A cannonade . . . where? In his imagination? . . . in his head? His body strained to the bursting point. But he would drive to his climax; he had to.

He pressed his head against the woman's shoulder, blotting out the faint circle of light from the lamp across the room.

Darkness . . . then the road again, at the far end of the main square of the city, the Plaza Mayor. The roads cut the city into quarters, leading north and south to Gijón and León, to the east and west to Santander and Grado. Behind them, hills dark with pine, alive with the forward rush of troops sweeping over the rock-strewn ridges. The Schneiders lofting shell after shell into the railroad station and the Hotel Covadonga whose curious, minaret-shaped towers thrust up, ludicrously jaunty, above the rubble.

He tried to bring his body's motions to a halt, but could not . . . a passionless drive gripped him, would not let go. "You must, you must," he thought . . . pressed his eyes closed. "Everything must vanish . . . this too . . ." and he felt, with mounting horror that neither would he find release in this woman's body, nor in his own, nor anywhere else.

"Cry out, damn you . . . before it comes . . . ," he thought, but his muscles would not obey, and the grip remained as it was; he could not even feel her legs shifting over his back . . .

. . . the road, passed between files of desolate shops, their windows all smashed in. Broken glass lay all over the street. Humps of clothing, sometimes bodies, more often simply piles of discarded overalls, shirts, trousers, shoes, old and worn, lay everywhere. The truck passed a tangle of corpses . . . rebels, shotguns in their hands, antique rifles, sticks of dynamite uncapped, all of them dressed in brand-new clothing that had been looted from the stores, as though even at the moment of death their pride had triumphed . . . some even strung with necklaces, pendants, rings on all five bloody fingers. . . . The truck had swerved down a side street . . . there . . . The hollow clang of 75mm shells slamming into steel plate like hammers against the tocsins of Pelayo, the Goth whose capital Oviedo had once been . . . Pelayo . . .

. . . the Plaza Mayor, a no-man's land of wreckage. And a hundred yards away, the railroad station, its walls piled high with stone, plates of steel ripped from the walls of the arms factory, brick, iron bedsteads. Just ahead, an entire battery of 75s, drawn up behind a breastwork of stone, pumping shell after shell against the walls of the station, at the railroad cars drawn up on the tracks behind from which every few seconds burst clouds of bluish smoke . . . the rebels' last refuge. A sudden fusillade . . . a dozen machine guns set up on nearby rooftops opening up on the railroad cars, sweeping the armored sides. The splintering of glass and the shrieks of men within, caught unprepared by death.

The railroad cars grew larger, as though he were focusing in on them with field glasses . . . Colonel Carvalho watching, with a desperate expression on his face, one word caught between his lips, a command and a plea . . . "Surrender . . ." The shells and the machine guns raking the railroad cars, and then he saw . . . through the ripped plates at the bottoms of the railroad cars, blood leaking through the floorboards, dripping, slowly at first, then in a torrent, onto the tracks. The barricades fell under a barrage, leaving the cars completely exposed. A stick of dynamite flew forward, fell harmlessly in the center of the plaza. . . . And the cars, filling with blood, pouring it out onto the tracks . . . the black ground soaking it up . . . Jaime Mercader, watching. And the Colonel, his face now to the wall, his back exposed, saying, "Surrender . . . for Christ' sake . . . surrender" . . . over and over again . . .

Jaime felt his body stiffen, suddenly and unexpectedly. He wrenched himself away from the woman, turned over on his back.

In the dim light, he could see her on the bed, her legs drawn up, pressed against the brass bedstead, watching him as his breathing slowed. Staring at the ceiling, he saw it there, too . . . the railroad cars dripping. Somewhere, the sound as well . . . a steady, methodical dripping . . .

After a few moments, when she saw that he was not going to move again, that whatever had taken him just at his climax was gone, the woman got up and went over to the sink in the corner of the room. He did not care what she was doing, did not watch, but was aware then, only then, that the sound of dripping had come from the faucet, not from his imagination.

His head pained him, and his mouth was parched. The woman, as though she had in some way understood everything, came over to him with a wet cloth and put it on his forehead.

He looked up; it was useless to thank her. She pressed the cloth to his head, smoothed her own wrinkled slip with her free hand down over her sweating thighs and smiled.

"You gave me a workout all right," she said, trying to make him smile too. She had said next to nothing from the time he had met her on the street.

"I didn't hurt you, did I?"

She laughed, the sound at first gentle, then for a second harsh in recall of so many people who had never asked her that question.

She coughed and sat down on the bed. For a few moments she

dragged at a cigarette; acrid Turkish tobacco . . . then put it down in an ashtray by the bed, next to the packet of cigarette papers, and went to get more towels. She sponged off his body. The water was not refreshing at all, and he lay there, exhausted, letting her go on because it seemed to give her pleasure.

Then she began to hum, an odd, angular tune, not in key; almost quarter tones. She threw her head back, and her hair fell over her shoulders and then back across her face. Her hair was the most beautiful thing about her though her eyes, set in a hard, unyielding face, were fine, too.

She saw that he was staring at her. "Don't you want me to sing?"

"No . . . go ahead."

"I would anyhow. I like to sing. And you didn't pay me for silence, did you?"

She smiled and went on, pausing to take a puff on the cigarette. He lay there on his back, empty, until the blood began to flow back into his arms and legs, and the exhaustion eased. The quiet was oppressive. The end of the whore's cigarette moved in a slow arc, illuminating first one portion of her body, then another. Had he found, in his climactic hallucinations, the link he had been looking for . . . in the very thing he had fled . . . that one word, now recalled, the Colonel's anguished "Surrender . . ." flung out not as a demand but in an agony of self-reproach? He had not remembered that until just now . . .

He said quietly, "Is there anything to drink?"

"If you pay," she said and brought him a bottle of warm lemon drink. He took a sip, passed the bottle to her and she drank as well, noisily, turning away and embarrassed by the sounds she had made.

He laughed. It seemed almost clear now. In the fear that he had driven away from himself, he had found the way back, or at least the start of the way.

The woman got up and opened the window. A slight breeze entered the room. He got up and went to the ledge, looked out. Between a jumble of buildings, he could see the cliffs on the other side of the river, dotted with tiny lights . . . as though they were the lights of the sea, the ocean outside of Ceuta, glowing with the lanterns of the squid fishermen.

"Where can I stay? . . . is there a hotel near here? . . ."

"This room," she said. "Why not? For a little extra . . ."

"No . . ."

"Why pay someone else? Don't you want to pay me?"

"All right," he said, too tired to move.

"Just give me whatever you want. This room doesn't cost much. . . ."

"All right," he said again, then: "You can stay here too if you want . . ."

He reached down over the edge of the bed. His clothes were strewn on the floor. He rummaged in his pocket, pulled out a few bank notes and gave them to her. It was stupid to be carrying so much money with him, and he hoped she had not seen what he had; there was still Peralta to pay the next morning, and he did not care to be robbed while he slept.

"That's too much," she said.

"Just take it. I want you to have it."

She got up and stuffed the notes into the bodice of her slip, then put her dress on.

"You can trust me," she said. "Now go to sleep. . . ."

He rolled over on the rumpled bed and plunged at once into a dark, empty sleep.

TUESDAY, JULY 21, 6:30 A.M.: *Toledo*

VOICES OUTSIDE IN THE HALLWAY near the door, low and agitated . . .

Jaime woke suddenly. He could not remember his mouth ever having been so dry before. He looked around: a woman's robe hung on a doorknob, trailing onto the floor. On the table under the mirror were a few pots of cosmetics and an ashtray full of cigarette butts. The whore was curled up asleep in the corner on a pile of blankets. She had no pillow and was holding her hands under her head as a child does. Her breathing was deep, very heavy, and she was snoring slightly.

She did not stir as the voices in the hallway grew louder, more excited. He thought for a second of waking her, but what was the point of it? He had nothing to say to her now. He would leave without waking her if he could.

He lay there, listening, running his tongue slowly around the dry insides of his mouth.

A thought crossed his mind. Perhaps the woman had told someone about him and they had come to rob him. No, if she'd wanted to do that, there would have been time enough during the night. He could find no reason to fear, yet he was afraid. If he had been wearing his old uniform, of the army of Africa, then there might have been a reason. But there was no reason. Still, the voices were coming closer. It was light outside; the sun fell against the slats of the blinds, dropped in bars across the floor, at right angles to the planks.

He pulled himself up on his elbows. How foolish it had been for him to leave the driver. He should have gone with him to Peralta's and stayed with them for the night. Now he felt incredibly vulnerable, his defenselessness intensified by his nakedness.

He reached slowly over the edge of the bed to find his clothes, very slowly, so as not to make the springs of the bed creak and wake the woman. His clothes were still on the floor where he'd thrown them. There was an empty bottle on the floor too, the one from which they'd both had the warm lemon drink the night before. A broken bottle was a good weapon against almost anything but a pistol.

The voices slowed, became muted and indistinct.

He shifted the bottle in his hand, tried to raise himself still further but the springs under his back started to creak and he held himself rigid on his elbows.

The idea of death suddenly took hold of him again and he shuddered, not at the thought of the pain but simply at the idea of not existing anymore. He could not imagine that.

"*Fresca. . . . a . . . gua. . . . fresca . . .* for gawd's sake . . ."

"*Si . . .* of course . . ."

"Don't you understand? Not with bubbles, you bloody fool. 'Still' . . . *fres . . . ca . . . sin gas . . . sa . . . ,*" an irritated, high-pitched voice, an Englishman. Heavy accent. Jaime smiled with relief and put the bottle down again.

"Room . . . *uno . . . y . . . cinco* . . . you will remember, won't you?"

Footsteps, moving off down the hallway. A sigh. Jaime went limp, surrendering to his weakness. He felt drained, as though he had reached his climax only a moment or two before. His body was full of an odd tingling sensation as though flies were buzzing inside his bones.

He thought of the sink across the room where the woman had wet the cloth for his head. The cloth was there, hanging on the iron bed frame but it was stiff and dry. He could not bring himself to make the effort. The water, he knew, would be warm and would taste bad. He drew a breath, filling his lungs. He became aware of a stale, sour odor, like that of the body of an old man; it was his own smell and it disgusted him.

As he lay there, the silence outside gave way to a susurration of faint, unidentifiable noises. Through the blinds on the windows, he could see a tin sign hanging over what must have been the door to the hotel; "Casa de Sancho Panza." It hung silently on its iron chain, finding no breeze to rock it. Scraping noises floated up, metal on metal, then a sound like shale tumbling down a distant hillside.

The whore continued to sleep, undisturbed. She moved her knees up toward her chest, then back down again, as though she were starting to swim. He watched her, wondering if she would wake up, but her breathing became heavier still. A person slept as though drugged in such heat, he thought. The heat—that was why he felt as leaden as he did. It was only the heat.

Through the window, he could see the street, the walls of the buildings on either side, and then a brilliant patch of blue sky against which one tower of the Alcázar was clearly outlined. He had not realized that the hotel to which the woman had taken him was so close to the Zoco.

The scraping sounds again. "Shutters," Jaime thought. "They must be raising the shutters . . . but it's too . . . early for shutters." He looked at his watch; it was only six-thirty in the morning.

He got up slowly and made his way cautiously to the window. By shading his eyes and standing almost against the window frame, he could see down the street and into the square without being seen himself. The white tin Cinzano sign which hung over the Bar Goya was visible, at least part of it. No other cafe had such a sign. It was where he was to meet Barrera.

A single car, a Hispano-Suiza like the one Tomás Pelayo drove, passed along the east side of the Zoco, trailing black exhaust. He could not see whether its occupants were military or civilian. A small indistinguishable pennant fluttered from its radiator cap.

From under the steel awning frames and from behind the lampposts, a few men in their shirt-sleeves warily regarded the car, watched it disappear down the Cuesta de las Armas and shook their heads. One man spit into the street.

Metal plates and gratings had been drawn down fast over the shop windows. Doors were fastened with chains and locks. Jaime realized that what he had heard had not been the raising of shutters at all but the sound of the corrugated iron sheets being lowered at a time when the shopkeepers would normally be getting their stores ready to open.

Below, a few people walked slowly and aimlessly by. No one seemed to be going anywhere. Across the Zoco, he could see three men sitting against a wall, immobile as the carvings on the yellow stone above them. Just to their left, an archway through the building permitted a view of the ocher hills across the Tagus. Within the city, he felt suffocated. How strange it was that he should wake up and find himself suddenly hemmed in so by its medieval walls and towers, as though he were in a prison. An unreasoning dread . . . of the stone, the walls and houses themselves, seized him. He thought of Morocco, of Ceuta and Tetuán, of the Arar, the great cypress that grew on the Atlas mountains, of the Argan huddling between the Rivers Tansift and Sus, of the smell of the rich sea bathing the shore along which he loved to walk. He saw himself not naked and sweat-drenched in a stifling room but on a beach, just at nightfall, the sky red as a hearth. What a world of difference there was, he thought, between that pure and unbounded landscape and the twisted alleyways and warrens of Toledo. Perhaps it would not be such a bad thing to do as his father had asked, take up the management of the Ceuta offices, learn something about oil, about books of account and taxes. At least he would be in the open . . . he would go to see Pelayo that morning, even before returning home . . .

He glanced down the street, up to the Inn of the Three Dogs and past a sign reading "Hotel Florida." The bank had to be somewhere nearby, and Pelayo would be there finishing up his business for at least another few hours that morning.

Slowly, testing his strength, he dressed himself. Catching sight of his reflection in the cracked mirror over the woman's makeup table, he began to laugh. He could imagine walking again into the Banco Toledano, looking like that. If the guards at the door would even let him in . . . He was filthy. Stubble blackened his cheeks. Dirt, a day's growth of beard, and the sickness that had shaken him the night before had completed an impenetrable disguise.

He buttoned his shirt and pulled on his boots. Once he had been a carefully polished, erect young officer; now he looked no different from any worker at the arms factory. His face was flushed and his hollow eyes gave him a look both wasted and ferocious.

He turned his head quickly; he had had the feeling that the woman was awake, that she was watching him. But she lay as she had before, still twisted in her blankets, her knees up again. Her breathing seemed too heavy, as though she were acting. It didn't matter. He still had nothing to say to her. He put his hand on the doorknob and pushed out.

Opening the door cautiously, he slipped into the hall. No one was there. Only a small shadow, a cat sitting motionless as a lump of coal on the stairway landing. The splash of running water issued from the lavatory at the end of the hall.

He went slowly downstairs. His boots, made of good leather, began to squeak.

The clerk, asleep under his newspaper, did not look up as he passed. The newspaper over the clerk's face was upside down and Jaime could not read it, but the headlines seemed large and important. The word *Barcelona* stood out. Something had happened, but Jaime could not stop to find out.

The air outside was thick and oppressive. The sun hung heavily over the low tiled rooftops, a yellow mouth sucking up the air out of the streets. So heavy and bloated did the sun appear that it seemed impossible that it should ever ascend to its zenith that day. The sky had already filled with heat, quickly, easily, like a bowl filling with oil. If, on that airless July morning, a man could still find reason to believe in God then he could find even greater reason to fear him. As for Jaime Mercader, it was quite enough that he feared his fellow man.

He began to walk slowly down the street, away from the squalid hotel and toward the Bar Goya. An insect squashed brittlely underfoot.

Chains of black beetles scurried across his path. Ahead of him he saw the Bar Goya, unshuttered, already open. Through its greenish windows, rumpled men were visible, bent over their newspapers and glasses of thick black coffee. But no one was sitting at the tables in front of the café or at those just inside which were close to the windows.

Along the reverberant alleyways came the quick echo of rifle fire, as though to remind him that it would not pay to place too much confidence in the silence of the streets. He stopped, trying to judge the caliber of the weapon by its fading report. But the sound had vanished too quickly. Only the direction was clear. Another, louder report followed, a grenade or homemade bomb. Then, the peculiar silence fell again. The explosion had come from the other end of the city, to the southwest, near the Carvalho house. Perhaps it had only been a militiaman with an ancient rifle, practicing. Who could tell?

He hurried his pace, his strength returning. The aroma of fresh coffee grew heavier, and he could almost taste the brew, dark and bitter. He smiled; a cup of coffee first, before anything else. After all, he thought, how can a man function properly before he's fully awake?

JULY 21, 7:00 A.M.: *The Zocodover, Toledo*

IT WAS AT EXACTLY SEVEN in the morning by the expensive Swiss watch that Major Manuel Punto wore that a squad of young cadets from the Alcázar marched down the slope of the Cuesta de Carlos V and paraded into the almost deserted Zocodover. On the right flank of the column, a snare drum snapped, adding a note of unwarranted gaiety to the proceedings.

The Major, instructor in military history and geography, ambled at the side of the column, not bothering to keep in step. Gazing critically at the lines of khaki-clad cadets, he took in each detail of their irregular appearance, the exaggeration of their eager strutting, the excessive sideways tilt of the glengarry caps they wore. The polished rifles they carried at shoulder-arms were inclined at as many different angles as there were marchers. One mustachioed corporal paraded with a hand in his tunic pocket. Two cadets had rolled up the sleeves on their free, swinging arms.

The Major, already in a bad humor at having been routed out of bed at that hour for such an exercise, was both depressed and irritated. "Such innocence," he thought, surveying the rows of intense young faces. "How serious they are, and how dignified they would like to appear. And there is Anibal de Córdoba with one hand in his pocket, as though he were going for a stroll to the tavern. . . ." He shook his head sadly. "When one is annoyed to start with," he thought, "one picks on every little thing. . . ."

The squad advanced across the plaza and halted before a café barricaded by nests of upside-down chairs—the legs jutting ludicrously into the air, waiting the day's business to be set right again. A truck carrying a machine gun and a few Civil Guard, the Alcázar's one concession to caution, had been following the cadets; it halted and took up a position at the mouth of the Cuesta. Someone droned a brief command and the entire group turned left-face with a noisy shuffling of boots.

"Who's idea was this anyway?" the Major wondered. The entire business was absurd: to go marching into the Zocodover for the sole purpose of reading a "proclamation of war," to stand there while it was being read, perfect targets for anyone in the buildings all around the Zoco who cared to open fire, then—God willing they survived—to go marching back up the Cuesta.

He glanced suspiciously at his watch. Where his cap had slid to the side, the early morning sun struck his bald head as though it were a dome of mirrors. He shook his watch and addressed a lean, elegant young man with carefully waxed mustaches who bore on his uniform the insignia of a captain.

"Well, what time do you have?"

The Captain studied his own watch, held out on a wrist bent in the torturously archaic way Andalusians have of holding a horse's reins.

"Eight and one-half minutes after the hour, Major," the Captain said crisply.

"We may as well start then."

The Captain frowned. "The Colonel's orders were to begin at quarter after seven exactly."

"Yes, of course . . . the Colonel," Punto thought. "It would take someone who is still living in the nineteenth century to think of an exhibition like this . . ."

"It's somewhere near that now," Punto said aloud.

"Somewhere near, Major, is not what the Colonel said, if I may be permitted . . ."

"Let's say that my watch doesn't run on time," Major Punto replied, slapping his riding crop against his thigh. "Must it be exactly quarter past seven?"

"According to Colonel Moscardó's orders, . . ." the Captain began.

Major Punto shook his head. "I can't see why." He looked up and down the ranks. "Children playing at being soldiers, that's all," he thought. "A disgrace that we can't muster anything more impressive than . . . this."

"Such exercises," the Captain was saying, "must always be carried out properly if they are to have their effect. A show of precision is required . . . it's all a part of orderly military . . ."

"We've got to get on with this," Major Punto interrupted, his goatee thrust forward belligerently. Who was this ridiculous captain with his waxed mustaches and why was he, a major after all, standing there like a fool listening to him? The proclamation was in Captain Vela's pocket. Vela would read it, not this popinjay, and he, Punto, would tell Vela where to begin. The fact that Vela, by way of contrast, was badly in need of a shave gave him a certain satisfaction. He was sure his foppish Captain objected strenuously to Vela's ragged appearance.

The Captain, sensing defeat, shrugged. Major Punto nodded and stepped toward the lines of rigid cadets; he motioned to Vela to begin.

A whistle blew. The cadets snapped their rifles to present arms and Captain Vela drew the proclamation from his pocket; it was torn, and the red wax seal had crumbled. Major Punto wondered idly whether it was really any good without the seal. Vela, even more badly in need of a shave than the Major had thought, held the paper out before him with both hands and began to read in a flat, unemotional voice. "After all," Punto thought, "he just read the same proclamation to the magpies in the Alcázar fifteen minutes ago. And besides, there's no great need for an oratorical style here. He's only telling people what they already know. State of war doubtless, but that's been going on for days now. No wonder they're apathetic. God, we must look foolish out here . . . but when the shells start falling, it'll be quite different . . . assuming that they ever do."

From the corner of his eye, Major Punto could see a few bleary eyed civilians watching the odd little ceremony from the cafés and shops bordering the Zocodover. Some scowled with undisguised hostility; others seemed merely curious. Heads jutted from the windows above the shops. Gazing beyond the corner of the paper from which Vela was reading, Punto focused his attention on the face of a heavy-bodied workingman standing by a pile of metal chairs. "He doesn't understand a word Vela is saying. Of course he doesn't . . . well look, you fool, you lump, it's going to be a civil war this time, no doubt about it. That's what he's saying."

"Place my faith and allegiance . . . in . . . whom? . . . I never saw him in my life. General of the Army? . . . But there are some awfully stupid generals in this army . . . and colonels and majors too, I suppose. The chances are that he'll have his throat cut before the week's out, and then there'll be a new proclamation to be read. . . . Turn in weapons? . . . a fine idea that is . . . 'Here, señor policeman, here's a grenade for you, as ordered. Sorry I pulled the pin.' "

". . . in the name of our Lord, Jesus Christ, amen. God preserve us. Long live Spain . . ."

Captain Vela folded the paper and thrust it into his pocket, saluted briskly, then turned about so sharply that he almost tripped. The sergeant's whistle shrilled, the drum rolled again, and the clank of rifles went up like the footsteps of an armored giant. The cadets wheeled and marched back up the sloping Cuesta to the Alcázar.

Major Punto glanced behind him. The square was still almost empty. The few onlookers who had witnessed the ceremony remained, loitering under awnings and against pillars, silent and bitter. Heads, however, had already disappeared into open windows. A few women sat on the sills watching the receding files of cadets. Someone applauded, briefly. In the distance, from the direction of *Las Covachuelas*, the workers' quarter, and up over the tumble of chalky brown buildings, the sound of a single rifle shot was heard.

Major Punto nodded to the Captain who walked beside him.

"There will be more of that, you can be sure," he said.

The Captain seemed not to hear him. He was studying his watch. He raised his thinly mustached face and announced in a peeved tone, "It's just quarter past seven now. . . ."

MORNING, JULY 21: *Biarritz*

THE SMALL AIRFIELD BORDERED BY poplar trees had just come into view at the end of the road, but Colonel Carvalho didn't notice it; he was still thinking angrily about his son-in-law. Certainly, he hadn't wanted him to come, and there was only room for four in the plane. But Hector had known that too, and a gesture, a mere suggestion that he might be of some use, that his services were available, if required, would have cost him nothing. But he had remained on the front steps of the house, gazing silently after them as the car, now driven by the pilot, passed down the drive, not a trace of a smile, of any warmth or understanding on his face. "What a farewell," the Colonel thought. "As though the world is going to be saved by people like him, by men with artificial cow dung under their fingernails . . . by hybrids . . . that's what he is, too . . . that absurd name. I should never have allowed . . ." He lapsed into a wordless gloom which blotted out not only his own thoughts but all his fresh memories of his wife and older daughter as well.

The car jounced along, its wheels skimming the edges of potholes. It was just growing light, the sun still unseen behind the eastern ridges but just then casting a pale gilt over the tall grass. The tops of the trees stood ridged against a sky that was just then beginning to glow along the horizon. Next to Carvalho, on his right, sat Emilio Portillo, an unlit Havana between his teeth, his hair neatly oiled and combed, his head lowered slightly and inclined forward like that of an athlete ready to run. To his left, Lachine, eyes drooping, a nerve on the near side of his face twitching every once in a while . . . his fingers drumming on the top of his briefcase. From nervousness or excitement, Carvalho wondered, drawn back from his depression by the annoying sound. It had never occurred to him that the Frenchman could be excited about anything.

Now the hangar, like a great ribbed slug lying gray on the field of short yellow grass. Still no other planes, no sign of life. The field was deserted. The pilot had driven out in the evening to see to the fueling and had come back and told them that he had seen only one or two people aside from the mechanics while he was there. Most aircraft used the main field on the other side of Biarritz. Few planes ever landed here, and only a skeleton crew was kept on hand. More often than not they too disappeared, sometimes for days at a time and nothing could be done except to take off again and set down at the other, busier landing strip.

The biplane was there, visible against the sky, its wings catching the glints of the fast-rising sun. Carvalho looked away, coughing from the dust that had come in through the windows.

"So . . . Camille, now we see . . . for Raúl's sake, you'd better be of some use. Otherwise . . ." Carvalho began to revise his thoughts, realizing that he had been brought to this querulous mood by his son-in-law's quite predictable failure to volunteer. He tried to think of Mercedes but discovered to his annoyance that he could not visualize her. The idea had taken the place of the person. How long had it been since he'd seen her last? Only a few months when he had stopped at Toledo on the way through to his posting at Oviedo. They'd had dinner together in the empty house, gone for a walk in the evening by the Tagus. It was the one time he had put on civilian clothes. Even in his most relaxed moments these last five days, he had never once taken his uniform off, except to sleep.

The car had stopped. The pilot opened the door and Lachine got out on one side while Portillo, impatient and still as silent as he'd been on the day they'd driven in from the airfield, pushed open the door on his side and jumped to the ground, leaving the Colonel alone in the middle.

He sat for a moment, then with deliberate slowness clambered out, unwinding his long, angular body and stretching his muscles. The sky had a clear, glassy quality which made it, even at that hour, too bright to look at. It was just after six in the morning.

The pilot was already trotting across the field toward the plane.

Portillo had finally lit his cigar, intent on getting a few puffs before he had to extinguish it and climb on board. For a second he was caught in silhouette against the eastern horizon; Carvalho looked on, suddenly taken aback by the bull-like solidity of the man's body, his heavy shoulders, his head like a medieval iron helmet, his huge hands fanning out into open air for a brief second as though grasping at something, then falling back to his sides.

"He has his reasons," Carvalho thought, still without any idea why Portillo wanted to get back to Toledo. Lachine's reasons were clear enough from what Camille himself had said and what Portillo had added, but Lachine, in his turn, had said nothing at all about his companion.

They began walking toward the plane, distant now perhaps fifty yards. The figure of the pilot had grown small against the vast open field. The wind had quickened and was bending the tops of the tall grasses that fringed the field just before the stands of poplar.

"There I go . . . ," Carvalho thought, looking after him . . . the little, insignificant figure . . . "Am I that unimportant, too . . . ?" he wondered. It had been four days. Now, away from the house, the sight and smell and hearing of his wife and daughter and the agricultural pursuits of his fool of a son-in-law, he had become part of his own world again . . . but, it seemed, his own world wanted none of him. Since he had spoken to Raúl at the Ministry, the government had known where he was and how to reach him easily enough. Yet no call had come. No summons to the defense of the Republic. Was he to be discarded that easily then, that callously? He caught himself up short as an infuriating thought crawled across his mind; was he going back because of *that*, because of his injured pride rather than because of his daughter? Had the girl become simply an excuse?

He had no time to reflect. The pilot had come to an abrupt halt near the plane, shouting and waving his arms. Lachine suddenly rushed forward. By the time Portillo and the Colonel had arrived under the shade of the plane's four wings, the reason for the pilot's dismay was obvious.

The fabric which covered the wings had been slashed and hung in streamers from the struts and ailerons. The motor had not escaped either; someone had taken a sledge hammer to it and had staved in the nose of the plane and smashed the propeller to bits. The broken shaft lay in pieces on the stubby grass.

Lachine was trembling with anger. He had already dropped his briefcase and taken the pilot by the arm. They made a grotesque pair, for the pilot who Lachine was upbraiding was a full head taller than the Frenchman.

"How, how . . . how do you explain this . . . of all things?"

"It was all right last night, I swear it," the pilot protested. "*They* must have done it . . ."

"Who . . . just tell me . . . who?" Lachine insisted.

"How would he know?" Carvalho said quietly.

"He'd know, he'd know . . ." Lachine went on, turning toward the Colonel only for an instant. "You tell me . . . who did this?"

Carvalho allowed himself a brief smile. Though it had thrown a serious twist into his plans, he was enjoying the spectacle of the unperturbable Frenchman in a rage. Portillo stood by, a flush mounting his neck; he was controlling himself but only with great effort.

"Where are the mechanics . . . ?" Carvalho asked.

They all knew, without looking, that there was no one there, that the hangar was empty and that they were alone on the field.

"So . . .," Lachine said. "They knew the plane was here . . . anyone knew . . . anyone who came by and looked and said to himself, 'I wonder whose plane that is.' All he had to do was ask those fools and . . . so much for the plane, ah?"

"It was perfectly secure last night," the pilot insisted.

Lachine bent to retrieve his fallen briefcase. When he rose, his eyes had cleared and he had gotten hold of himself. "We should have posted a guard . . . but I didn't expect . . . anything like this." He turned back to the pilot. "It's not your fault . . . don't worry."

The pilot was busy examining the wings.

"It's hopeless," he said. "It would take days . . ."

"If we could get repair parts . . . fabric, all of it. Oh, they've done a good job," Lachine said.

A word from Portillo, dropped almost as though by accident: "Who?"

"You know, don't you?" Lachine said sharply. The implication was there. Carvalho looked on, shocked.

Lachine went on: "There won't be time now. We'll have to go overland."

"You know neither of us can do that," Carvalho said. "We're both out of Spain illegally."

"That's no problem," Lachine said. "Right here, in Biarritz . . . I can get that taken care of easily enough. You have your passport?" He was talking to Carvalho alone. The Colonel nodded. "And you? Of course not. Escaped prisoners rarely carry passports. So . . . that will take more time yet; a forged passport for you then . . . Monsieur Garnier will be busy today . . . all right, all right. Even a clumsy job will do. I'm sure the border guards have other things on their minds at the moment . . ."

"I'll need the car," Lachine announced, turned, and headed back across the field without another word.

Carvalho followed quickly; "Camille . . . you're sure you can do this?"

"Of course I'm sure . . . what fools, not to have posted a guard." He turned suddenly on the Colonel, "You, a military man, not to have thought of posting a guard. Of all people . . ."

"I?" The Colonel was taken aback. What had he to do with such things, and in France, of all places. "If you were expecting something like this, why didn't you tell me? For four days you've said nothing."

The three clambered back into the car.

"I'll drop you at the house and then go into Biarritz alone. It's better that way," Lachine said.

"And you'll return . . . when?" Carvalho asked, aware that both he and Portillo were now encumbrances rather than potential aides. Perhaps Lachine would not return. What then?

"By supper," Lachine replied. "How should I know how long it takes an . . . artist like Grainer . . . to do his work?" He sank back against the seat, closing his ringed eyes, and letting out a whistle of breath. His calm had returned completely, and his hands barely moved on the surface of the briefcase. "Or was it exhaustion?" the Colonel wondered.

"Why hasn't he said a word to Portillo? Does he really think that he had something to do with this?" Carvalho struggled to make some sense out of what had happened. Why had the plane been slashed? Had it to do with Lachine or Portillo or both? Carvalho knew that the various factions of the Marxist parties had been feuding for months and . . . that Portillo and Lachine were of different "faiths." It was possible that Portillo's warnings about the Frenchman's job held the key to the attack.

Portillo then? His reasons for returning were still obscure, the only hint had been his remark the night before: "He wants to get there for an abstraction, Colonel . . . I . . . for reasons of . . . blood. Which of the two are stronger, do you think?" But it was not clear what Portillo meant by "blood," and he had refused to say more.

By the time the tiled house came into view again around a curve in the rutted road, the blue sea spread sparkling beyond it, Carvalho had given up trying to understand what had happened. Like so much else, it was veiled in a haze of obscure political differences that he would never understand. At that moment what rankled him most was his injured pride, and even he himself was shocked by the tenacity and overpowering force of that hurt.

As the car swung into the front drive of the house, all Colonel Carvalho could think of was the fact that after five days he had still received no summons from the Republic, no cry for aid to him, personally. He tugged at the edge of his beard until a few gray hairs came loose in his fingers, then dropped his hand angrily to his lap.

All the while Portillo was watching him, a curously placid expression on his face.

But the Colonel saw neither Portillo nor Lachine, but only his own reflection staring back at him, grotesquely distorted, from the curved surface of his polished cuff button. His face was twisted to fit the frame of the button's edging, his frown drawn out into an idiot's smile. Alone, encircled, he appeared a prisoner within the button, not himself at all, but unable to change anything.

The car came to a halt at the front door, its wheels churning up a billow of fine yellow dust.

Carvalho turned his arm away sharply, and the reflection disappeared.

JULY 21, 8:00 A.M.: *Toledo*

TWO MILITIAMEN WEARING THE RED and black rosettes of the FAI were standing in the doorway of the Bar Goya, at the head of a flight of steps that led down into the low-ceilinged room. Clouds of bluish cigar and cigarette smoke floated up toward a square of sun fixed in the glass door panels. The militiamen seemed at a loss to know what to do with themselves and so, stood there like sentries, leaning against the wall and squinting at everyone, their rifles trailing at their feet.

In a corner, a group of men had surrounded an enormous radio surmounted by a phonograph horn of garnet and tarnished brass and were listening to popular songs and playing a scarifying game on the tabletop with a claspknife.

Jaime Mercader sat at a table near the rear from which he could watch the front door as well as the entrance leading back into the kitchen. There was no telling from which direction the driver might appear, if he were to appear at all, and Jaime did not want to be taken unawares. He had always had a dread of people coming up behind him.

On the table, next to his coffee, he had spread a copy of the *Heraldo de Madrid*. It was two days old. He had bought it from a shrunken wraith of a man who hung around the Zoco peddling papers and had not noticed the date. From time to time, he glanced at the columns. It gave him a strange, detached feeling to be sitting there and reading the news of two days before; it was mostly sports and foreign news. The papers hadn't yet begun to print anything about the revolt.

Out of the corner of his eye, he saw the square of sunlight below the door suddenly widen; the door had opened.

"I told you, man . . . get out of the way," one of the *milicianos* was saying, having decided to leave just at the same time as the newcomer was trying to make his way down the narrow steps to the café floor.

The second militiaman pushed past, muttering obscenities while the man who had been trying to enter stood aside and bowed his head.

"Your excellencies," he said mockingly.

"*Cabrón . . . ,*" said the second militiaman, and spat tobacco juice.

Barrera stood aside and grinned as they went out, then stepped down onto the floor and began looking about. His face, now visible in the strong morning light at the doorway, seemed even more oddly triangular than it had the day before. It was the first time that Jaime could remember seeing him wear the driver's cap, and he wondered why he had put it on.

A column of battered trucks rattled along the street outside, making the cobblestones of the Zocodover clatter. The trucks proceeded up the street, laden with women and children, brass bedsteads which caught the sun and flung its reflection hard against the walls, barrels and mounds of clothes thrown every which way into the truck beds.

Jaime watched the driver as he paused, attracted by the commotion outside. The two militiamen had stopped just past the entrance and were shouting at the occupants of the trucks. The women, some of them, shouted back. The streets seemed full of Anarchists and there was no sign at all of either the *Asaltos* or the regular government troops. The city seemed to be holding its breath, and men had probably been badly beaten or even killed for less offense than the driver's words at the doorway.

But no one at the tables nearby moved. They remained bent over their newspapers and their coffee. It was as though each man in the room was so completely unsure of his neighbor, so afraid, that he dared not do anything that might disturb the balance in any way.

Jaime caught the driver's eye and nodded toward the seat opposite him. For a second, Barrera seemed not to recognize him. Then he came over and sat down.

"Christ, you look like a corpse," he said with incongruous cheer. "What did you do to yourself? Don't answer me. Everybody's got their own way of killing themselves, and it's just as well for a man not to know too many of them." He leaned forward. "A good woman really tires you out, doesn't she, *teniente?*"

Jaime did not answer; he had no desire to talk about the night, the woman, or his dreams. He pushed a cup of steaming coffee across the table and nodded toward the empty entrance where a rectangle of sunlight now fell tranquilly across the threshold. "Forget about me. What about that? Was that *your* way of trying to kill yourself?"

"Them? Friends, that's all. As a matter of fact the big one with the equally big mouth was Eusebio Quiroga whose brother used to work for Ignacio . . . not that Eusebio wouldn't cut my heart out if he thought there was anything in it for him . . . but, then, who wouldn't these days?"

Jaime stared at him uneasily. "Of course, he knows everyone. Why shouldn't he? He lives here. Yet . . . they threw stones at him last night because he was with me . . . or the car . . . whichever it was . . . and I could see the sweat on him when we were followed. He was afraid. He couldn't hide that."

Nervously, Jaime pushed his cup of coffee across the table toward the driver.

"Take it . . . I'll get another. But watch out, it's hot as a sin . . ."

The driver blew into the cup to cool the coffee. After a moment he reached into his jacket and drew out a box of "Martel" cigarette papers. Jaime shook his head and offered in turn some Turkish cigarettes, the last he had of those he had brought from Ceuta. The driver declined: "A man could burn his tongue off with those. No thanks . . ."

"I don't smoke them very often," Jaime said.

"You couldn't," the driver replied, then started to say *teniente* but caught himself and choked off the word, continuing at once: "No, not and breathe at the same time. I always say, the Turks are still barbarians, Mustafa Kemal not withstanding. All respects to Kemal the Turk. We could use him here to civilize this country, too, I think. But look at that tobacco, will you? You could kill a mule with it . . ."

Jaime looked the man up and down quizzically. There they sat, gossiping as though it were any morning on any day in any time but the time it actually was. The driver obviously knew about the "declaration of war" on the Zoco; everyone did. There was no telling when the rebel armies or the troops of the Madrid government might appear on the hills across the river. Why couldn't they bring themselves to talk about it?

At that moment, as though Barrera had read Mercader's thoughts, the driver leaned across the table and asked cautiously: "Do you know what's going on out there? I saw it on the way over . . . they're coming in from the countryside, for the last hour or so . . . they're all over the place now, maybe two thousand, maybe three . . ."

"*They?* Who were *they?*" Jaime wondered. But he did not ask.

"Just look at this place," Barrera went on. The room was full of militia; Jaime knew that. He'd been there for almost a half hour before the driver had arrived, had seen them all, the ones with the FAI emblems around their arms or the black and red neckerchiefs knotted around their throats, the few with the Trotskyite POUM insignia. Dozens of pieces of military gear, looted, black-leather caps, pistol belts and harnesses. One man even had on a Civil Guard tricorn around which he had twisted a strip of black cloth.

"Since dawn," Barrera was saying. "I've never seen anything like this before. It looks like the fiesta of the *Virgen de la caridad.* . . ."

Jaime stared across the steam rising from the coffee cup. An image from Goya slipped through his mind, ". . . the one sane man in a madhouse . . . on a long chain, able to move about but not escape . . ."

His thoughts must have shown on his face for the driver let out a whistle and said, "Come on, come on. . ." Barrera leaned back and exhaled a long plume of smoke from the cigarette he had rolled for himself. Behind him, from the radio in the corner, a voice was urging everyone to stay tuned in, to keep their radios on at all times. There would be important news. The men looked bored. The voice had been promising important news since dawn but no news came, only the same music played over and over again. The men by the radio fidgeted with their pistols, with the rifles they had stacked by their chairs, as though they were children playing with new, unfamiliar toys.

"If only we had been able to go back last night. Ignacio and his damned gas pumps. Aie, even his wife's cooking doesn't make up for that. You know, you missed a good meal. You were entitled to some, after all. You sang louder than Ignacio. . . ."

Jaime smiled quickly. "It's all right. In fact, it's better this way. Last night I wasn't sure. Now I know . . . Listen, there's someone I want to take back with us."

"Ah? You're sure about that? We don't want to waste too much time. Last night there was no 'declaration' to contend with, but now . . ."

"The house is very near Peralta's garage. . . . There's an iron eagle on the door."

The driver whistled. "That eagle is like a plague-mark. Jesus, man, that's the Carvalho house, and we don't want to go anywhere near it, believe me. Anyhow, there's no one there, don't you know?"

"The daughter is there. She's the one I want."

"What in Christ's name for? By yourself you can make it out of here all right. All the Eusebios of this world won't bother you if you don't bother them, not now . . . but with . . . his daughter . . ."

"You know about him then?"

Barrera struck the table with the flat of his hand. "You're talking about rope in a hanged man's house . . . of course I know him. Do I know that swine General Bosch? Do I know Yagüe? The whole lot of them. Look . . . ," and he said the word now for the first time that morning . . . *"teniente* . . . ," and mouthed it with a biting scorn . . . "I was born in Cartenegra, that's only thirty miles away from Oviedo . . . we got it, too . . . my father . . ."

"Yes . . . ?" Jaime knew that he should not ask, not push the man, but he could not help himself.

But Barrera went ashen. "Nothing. It's settled. We'll get the woman, and no more talk about it. But don't say I didn't warn you. Come on then."

"You don't have to come with me."

"You think I'd stay here by myself? I'd rather gather flowers for José Antonio than hang myself here. You don't know about me, so don't try to figure things out. You can't. That's all . . ."

More trucks passed in the square outside and a few wagons jounced noisily over the stones. Through the grimy panes, the dark tricorns of the Civil Guard could now be seen, a few at a time, moving warily behind the carts. The sight of the Guard outside sent a wave of murmuring around the room.

Mercader and the driver rose, and Jaime left a few coins on the table to pay for the coffee. They went out quickly, unmolested. As they emerged on the street, a patrol of militiamen passed, moving with exaggerated caution close to the buildings on the periphery of the Zoco. They were shabby looking, uncertain men who eyed each other with as much suspicion as they had for the dark doorways and street entrances. They blinked, sweated, and shifted their weapons from hand to hand with a clumsiness that showed how unaccustomed they were to carrying them.

Jaime glanced back toward the entrance of the Goya, at the enameled "Cinzano" sign hanging over the door, at the white and pink marzipan figures in the window, then upward at the flat blue sky over the Zoco and the sun rolling heavily toward its zenith. The heat streamed down in shimmering waves that broke visibly over the tops of the buildings, spilling over the tiled roofs and down the stucco walls like a waterfall. One sensed that inside the buildings, behind each door, something was happening. But in the street . . . nothing. The Anarchist patrols moved somnambulantly as though completely unaware of the wagons bringing the Civil Guard in from the countryside. The Guard, in turn, studied the ground. Each man seemed locked inside a sphere of time, afraid to acknowledge what was going on around him. Jaime remembered how it had been at Oviedo. By the time he had gotten there, the fear had already been replaced by intense, hopeless rage. Not so in Toledo. There would be an explosion soon, and no one could tell what would set it off . . . a street brawl, a few words exchanged between the wrong people, an accident with one of the wagons, a rifle discharged without intent . . . anything.

Jaime followed the driver up the alleyway, without knowing where he was going.

"Only in Spain," he thought bitterly, "must I fear my friends more than my enemies. . . ."

What did he himself believe in now? [Did it matter? And his own father . . . the girl, Mercedes, even her father?] Did it matter what any of them believed? Would those leathery faced militiamen listen, and if they listened, would they understand? "A man must act according to his beliefs," Pelayo had once said to him, and Jaime had answered, "And what if a man finds nothing in which to believe?" Pelayo had thought for a moment, then replied, "He dies, Jaime, that's all. He dies."

Barrera stopped and leaned against the wall by a rough stone block that had once served as a horse tether. The iron ring was still there, dangling from the side of the block. [Just like the rings on the front of the San Juan de los Reyes from which the Moors had hung their Christian prisoners centuries before.]

At that moment a volley rang out from the direction of the Alcázar. The driver looked up, sniffing at the air. Thin plumes of smoke rose above the rooftops, hesitated, then swirled rapidly up into the sky. The driver replaced his cap, pulling it down firmly on his head, and lit a cigarette.

The two men glanced quickly at each other, almost furtively, neither

understanding the real source of the other's fear but nevertheless understanding that there was something unhealable there and that it had to be
respected.

"You're right, let's get on with it. We can't keep Ignacio waiting too
long, can we . . . ?" Barrera said.

"*Inch Allah . . . ,*"

"What?"

"It's nothing," Jaime said. "Nothing."

"Eh, Esteban, you've come to get your beast out of my shed?" Ignacio roared as the two men came up to the garage. The door was open.
Peralta was sitting on a barrel in the shadow, whittling. "Leave her here
a little longer and she'll have calves."

"Anxious to get rid of her now?" Barrera said warily. "What's the
matter? She's a good automobile, North American . . . a credit to any
man to have in his shop . . ."

"Nothing's the matter, to tell the truth. It's funny the way people behave though. Eusebio was nosing around with his friends an hour ago. It
isn't enough that I store his guns for him. They have to make me over in
their image too. Well, I won't put up with it, not from that shithead.
Imagine, he sees the car and . . . one, two, three . . . I've 'sold out,' he
says. I tell him, I'm a mechanic. I fix cars. What the hell do you expect
to be in here, bulls?"

Barrera glanced nervously at Jaime. "That Eusebio . . . you remember, from the Goya? No wonder he gave me such a shove, the bastard."

"So," Ignacio went on, giving the corrugated iron door a push, "So,
he says, 'well don't have rich men's cars in here, then.' And I answer him
the only way you can answer a cretan like that, and I said, 'since when
are the *campesinos* around here driving automobiles?' Well, that stopped
him all right." He kicked unhappily at a tire on the floor; it spun around
a few times and rolled against the wall into a nest of loose wires. "Still, I
don't like the way he's acting. Very mean, that Eusebio. They've got a
fever up all right. I wish we had fewer of his kind around. More like the
'patron,' Torroba . . ."

"You're a gentle man, Ignacio. That's the trouble. This isn't a gentle
time."

"It could be if it wasn't for those pigs in their stiff collars and all the
officials they send to plague us. I don't blame Eusebio, you understand.
It's the same thing when the picador sticks the bull . . . you can hardly
blame the bull for acting nasty." He went over and patted the Ford on
its hood. "Take her out of here, now, will you Esteban?"

"Sure. I don't want Eusebio to get upset."

Jaime reached into his pocket and pulled out a clip of bank notes.

"Will this be enough? With our thanks, Señor Peralta," he said,
holding out twice what the job was worth.

"Keep it. I do this one for love, not for money. Besides, we won't be needing that stuff much longer. . . ."

"Don't be so sure." Barrera said. "The generals may get themselves into the saddle yet. It wouldn't be the first time . . ."

"Oh," Ignacio replied, "I hope they give that bunch in Madrid a few good whippings so that everyone sees what a pack of sniveling fools they are and who's really got the balls in this country. Us, that's who . . . they'll see, and then it will be our turn, not like in '34 . . . this time everyone will join in. They just need a lesson, the generals and the Republicans as well. I hope it works out that way."

Barrera opened the car door and got behind the wheel. In a moment the motor was turning over nicely. Jaime stood by the wall, uncertain whether to argue with Peralta over payment or not. He didn't want to risk angering him by insisting that he take the money, yet, as Ignacio himself had just said, the man had to earn his living . . . As long as bread wasn't free to everyone the way he thought it should be . . .

Ignacio solved the problem. "Even if I didn't think that it was all over with this rottenness of laws and money and governments, I wouldn't take money from my brother-in-law's cousin in any event."

Barrera shouted over the echoing rumble of the car's engine, "You know this isn't my car. Take the money, for Christ's sake, and if you don't want to spend it, stuff it up your backside."

Ignacio broke out in a broad grin and slapped his hands together.

"That's the best use for money, Esteban, to wipe your ass just like the *señoritos* do. . . ."

Jaime, without saying anything more, pressed the bills into the mechanic's hand. Ignacio grinned.

"To make Esteban happy, only."

Then he bent his back to the turntable and brought the car entirely around so that it was parallel to the street. In a moment the mechanic began to jack the platform out on its tracks and onto the *calle*.

"Wait a minute," he called out, straightening up. "Both of you, come over here."

"What's the matter?" Barrera said, climbing out of the front seat.

"I have to stay an honest man, don't I?" Ignacio replied. "Here, here's your 'change.' " He went over to a pile of tires and empty cartons in the corner of the garage. As Jaime watched, he pulled the inner tube out of a heavy tractor tire and peeled back a strip of black adhesive tape. Then he plunged his hand inside and brought out two objects which he then held out, one in each hand. "Your 'change,' " he said. "And a little . . . what do the *madrilenos* call it? . . . they're so damned clever . . . 'insurance,' eh?"

In his right hand he held by the barrel a Mauser automatic and in his left a smaller Astra pistol.

"The Mauser for Señor Mercader. Put something that size in Esteban's pants and he'll get a swollen head. For you, Esteban, the baby, eh? To keep you humble."

"I'll take it," said Barrera, "just to pay back that bastard Eusebio for his shove this morning. But you know as well as I do, I can't shoot with one of these at all. I'm a peaceful man like you, Ignacio. . . ."

Jaime accepted the Mauser and put it in his trousers. The butt fell just below the line of the pocket. "Where did you get it?" Jaime asked. He knew that the Mausers were available only to the army and the Civil Guard. The Astras, made in the factory of Unceta y Cía at Guernica, could be purchased almost anywhere.

"We'd have to ask Eusebio. They're his . . . part of the arsenal he confides to me for safekeeping. He'll never miss them. Don't worry, the serial numbers are filed off."

"I wasn't thinking of that," Jaime said. "I was thinking of the man to whom this belonged . . . what happened to him?"

"Who knows? Perhaps he lost it at cards or on a bet or maybe left it on the floor in a brothel. In any event, whatever became of him, I had nothing to do with it." It was clear that he had been angered by Jaime's question. "I can't stop Eusebio from doing whatever he does, but I don't kill, señor, if that's what you meant, not for a lousy pistol."

"It was what I meant, I shouldn't have said it. Will you accept an apology? . . ."

"You see," Ignacio said, laughing suddenly, a harsh, mirthless sound. "The millennium, as they call it, is come. My pardon is begged by a gentleman. No offense, señor *teniente*, but as you yourself see, we are all quite equal now, aren't we?"

"It was never different as far as I was concerned," Jaime said, "nor with my father. He sold cork on the streets of Ceuta when he was a young man and . . ."

"Enough . . . ," Ignacio said. "Don't waste time with me. I gave you the guns so you'd feel safe, not so you'd use them." He went to the lever and in a moment the Ford was lowered to the ground and the turntable slid on its tracks back into the old stable.

"Tell Infante hello for me if you see him," Barrera called out of the front window of the Ford.

"That cousin of yours can go hang himself for all I care. But he'd better stay away from here. I don't want his blood on my hands."

Barrera laughed and stepped on the accelerator. The car coughed and moved slowly over the rough stones as though reluctant to leave the shelter of Peralta's garage.

JULY 21, 9:30 A.M.: *Toledo*

SEBASTIÁN GIL TOOK ANOTHER roll from his dressing gown pocket and began to chew ruefully. His eyes had the look of a man who believed in nothing that he could not touch with his own fingers and who had reached out as far as he could and found that, in fact, he could touch nothing at all.

Across the top of his newspaper, he traced a puzzled arabesque with his fingers. Burgos had fallen to the army, and Barcelona was in turmoil. What of it? Toledo was quiet and would stay that way. The city had survived Moors, Jews, and Pedro el Cruel; it would survive the generals and the Anarchists as well.

After a few moments, he pushed the newspaper aside irritably. Even "SAWA's" cartoon people with their round heads and peg noses annoyed him this morning. The aftertaste of his boiled egg revolted him and he went to the stand and rinsed his mouth with mint-flavored water and spat into a flowered bowl kept there for that sole purpose.

Then he went into the bedroom, dropping his robe on the floor and began to dress. "No one to shout at me for doing that . . . curious," he thought, then felt ashamed of himself; he was exaggerating. "She never shouted," he added. "It was I who was at fault, always so careless. No, she never shouted. . . ." It had been over a year and he still felt the loss keenly. The huge double bed had remained with him even when he had moved from the old house to the apartment on the Calle del Moro and at night he sometimes felt as if the bed would swallow him alive. The room had not been cleaned for weeks and was littered with papers, books, and phonograph records, all of which had been brought home at one time or another from his shop and never returned. Each week he would bring back an armful of records to play when Torroba or Venegas or any of the others came to visit. Yet he never seemed to find the energy to return them to his shop, and they lay there in stacks, unsold, un-dusted, ultimately to be broken during his nocturnal prowlings about the room.

The doorbell rang. Welcoming the intrusion, Gil rose and picked up his robe, put it on and went to answer the ring. The bell sounded again, insistent. Who could it be at that hour? Certainly not one of his friends who would never disturb him before ten; they all knew his habits and re-spected them. He glanced at his watch; it was only nine-thirty. Then he stepped out into the hall and made for the stairs. His head ached relent-lessly. By his best reckoning, he had not actually slept more than two or three hours, falling into a fitful doze just before dawn. After Torroba's departure, he had tossed about in the vast double bed and done battle with his relentless memories, his imagination, and his forebodings. Tor-roba, he assured himself, was not really angry with him, could not be; they knew each other too well for that. But the sudden change in his friend's attitude had frightened him and set him to doubting. He had been unable to bear even looking at the silent phonograph or touching the piano. At first, he had tried walking about, then had disconsolately swallowed two or three cognacs. But nothing had helped. He had taken down a volume of Fray Luis de León and read that sad monk's poems for over an hour but all to no avail.

The bell rang twice more as he was descending the narrow staircase, clinging to the bannisters for support. He had grown unaccountably weak in the past months, and was beginning to have spells of dizziness.

He arrived at the door in a state of indecision. Should he open it or not? But it was too late; he could tell by the coughing and the low voices outside that *they,* whoever they were, had heard him approach.

He opened the door.

Three men stood on the front step of the house. Two of them wore the blue uniforms of lieutenants in the *Asaltos.* The third, an older man with an unusual, heavy mustache, was dressed in civilian clothes, a leather jacket far too heavy for the warm weather, and a nondescript cap to which had been pinned a small metal badge of some sort. Gil could not make out the initials and neither the color nor the shape were familiar.

The younger of the two lieutenants coughed apologetically. His smooth skin twitched visibly over his cheekbones, and in his callow way he reminded Gil of Tomás Pelayo's son, Luis.

"Sebastián Gil?"

Gil nodded. "I don't know you," he said.

"We are sorry to intrude . . ."

The man in the cap cleared his throat as though about to protest over the younger man's apology but thought better of it and burrowed his fists into his pockets.

"Yes, of course," Gil said, "but, as you see . . ."

"Yes, I see," said the Lieutenant, groping for words.

"One sees many things," Gil added. The young man was obviously unused to the authority that his uniform conferred and still found himself flustered when compelled to demand things of an older man.

The man in the cap was growing agitated and was now casting angry glances at Gil, his companion, and the street.

"I am Lieutenant Fuentes . . . if you would care to see my papers."

"Please . . . if you'll pardon me. Come to the point. As you see I'm standing here in my . . . robe. What is it that you want?"

"We don't want to bother you. Nevertheless, it is . . . a matter of some importance."

"Will you come inside then?"

"Thank you, but it is not necessary. There is only one question, if you please."

"Of course," Gil said, relieved. Only a question then. A Yes or No or something in between.

"Have you seen Colonel Fernán Venegas?" the Lieutenant asked.

"He was here last night, for a few minutes, that's all," Gil answered without hesitation. "Yes . . . for a few minutes . . ."

"So . . . and what time was that, do you remember?"

"I don't see why . . . ," Gil began. Perhaps it would have been better not to have mentioned it at all.

"Do you remember?"

"Why do you come here?" Gil countered.

"You are a friend of his, aren't you?"

"A friend? Better say . . . an acquaintance. He comes here often, yes.

We listen to music . . . when he has the time. He is fond of Mozart, as I am. Last night, he did not seem to have the time."

"Ahhh . . . ," said the Lieutenant. "We had hoped . . . in any event, can you tell me when it was? How long did he stay?"

The man in the jacket looked away, annoyed and uncomfortable.

Gil was puzzled. "Has something happened to Colonel Venegas?"

"He has been missing since last night. We don't know what's happened to him. We've been instructed to find him, that's all . . . to look every place where he might be. This was the last such place." He saluted in a desultory way, brushing the visor of his cap with the tips of his fingers as though striking off an insect. "The time, please . . . When was he here?"

"About eleven, I think. Perhaps later. He only stayed five minutes."

"Did he say where he was going?"

"No," Gil lied.

"And was there anyone with him?"

"No," Gil lied again; there was no point in involving the Portillo woman if she had not already involved herself.

"If you should hear of the Colonel's whereabouts . . . anything . . . we would appreciate it . . . at the Civil Governor's office . . . ask for Major Barraca . . ."

"Of course," Gil said, wondering if the Lieutenant or the civilian really believed him, if they expected anyone to tell them the truth anymore.

The civilian cast an aggravated glance at Gil and stamped noisily down the steps. The lieutenants exchanged unhappy looks and followed the man down to where their car was waiting, blocking the narrow street.

Gil closed the door again, puzzled. Why were *Asalto* officers looking for a Civil Guard colonel? Hadn't it been *Asalto* officers who had killed Calvo Sotelo? And the civilian . . . who was he?

Gil shook his head as though to clear his thoughts. It was absurd; Venegas insisted that Venegas was right; Torroba, insisted that Torroba was right. Each insisted that the other was wrong. Yet they were both so alike, so possessed of the same arrogant assurance. Both even liked the same lustily bawling tenors. The only real difference between them was that while Venegas liked to drink sherry with his shirt-sleeves rolled up, Torroba kept his jacket on and preferred cognac. Sometimes Gil found it difficult to remember which one of them he had been talking to.

Placing one hand on the iron railing of the stairs, he began to climb back to his apartment. He had no sooner placed one foot on the first tread than a series of explosions sounded, not too far off, magnified by the acoustic of the tiled hallway so that they sounded like the strokes of a giant drum.

He stopped and listened. True, he had heard sporadic shots all morning. True, he had been awakened a number of times during the night . . . he was not sure by what. But, then, he had always been a light sleeper and even the scamper of a cat across the roof often was enough to bring him bolt upright in bed. Had the sounds at night been gunshots too? He was not sure. And the explosions now? Possibly an accident at the arms factory. There were all sorts of rumors about the new type grenades which they were manufacturing there, and some said there was a scandal brewing over faulty design.

He waited for a moment, but there was no repetition of the explosions.

He went back up the stairs, determined now to have another cup of coffee though he knew it would not be particularly good for his nerves.

The firing had started again just as Gil was nearing his shop.

Now, as he entered the curve of the Calle Zuraban that would bring him to his shop, he recalled the poems of Fray Luis he had read during the night, weighed their wisdom against the rashness of his two friends. Both Torroba and Venegas now felt that they must act, regardless of the consequences. To do nothing was a greater sin than to act in error.

What was it that De León had written? Those lines, read just before he had fallen asleep:

> Que descansada vida la del que huye el mundanal ruido
> y sigue la escondida senda por donde han ido
> los pocos sabies que en el mundo han sido.

He wondered whether it was one of the poems that the monk had written while imprisoned by the Inquisition. Certainly, it would have been apt. As he began to repeat the lines aloud, the first explosion sounded nearby.

He came to an abrupt halt and pressed himself against the nearest wall. The safety of his shop waited just at the end of the street.

The explosion had come from the direction of the Hospital de Tavera, not too far from where he stood. The initial burst was followed in a moment by a second. He realized that what he had heard had been first the sound of artillery firing at some distance, and then the sound of the shell landing nearby.

By the third report he had reached the door of his shop, unlocked the steel shutters and gone quickly inside. Someone was bombarding the hospital, that much was obvious. But for what reason? He looked out. Smoke was rising above the rooftops, going straight up, as though drawn into the sun. He could smell the reek of gunpowder even where he stood; closed doors and drawn shutters could not keep it out.

He raised the shade on the door and let a little sunlight in; it entered, murky and furtive, already poisoned by the clouds of smoke gathering above the city.

"Now," he thought, "the important thing, the most important thing . . . is to behave calmly and with dignity. . . ."

He lit a cigarette and sat down in the deep chair behind the counter, puffing rapidly, he reduced the cigarette to ash in a minute or less. The telephone sat on the counter nearby, and he eyed it nervously.

Perhaps he should try to reach the Carvalho girl. But what was the point, really? A call to the Carvalho girl could only serve to increase his own burdens, not lighten those he already had. Better to contact someone who could help him than someone he would have to help. Perhaps the best thing to do would be to phone Venegas at once. But he hesitated, fearful of another rebuff.

He tried to recall whether Venegas had really been angry. No. Even Torroba hadn't been really angry with him, only sad. He preferred anger; that at least would have been easy to take, and men get over being angry; sadness lingers. But Venegas . . . as he tried to visualize the man's face as he had stood there at the door with the Portillo woman, he recalled something else Venegas had said about the police informer and the murder at Orgaz. What if, in some absurd way, he had been implicated in the informer's death? Thank God Torroba had hidden; if Venegas had seen him, perhaps the outcome would have been entirely different. But, then, his friendship with Torroba was well known and the FAI were always shooting people, even if Torroba disapproved of such things. How can you control people once you teach them to believe that all restraint must inevitably destroy a man's spirit? Well, well . . . there was that to wrestle with . . .

He lit another cigarette, tried to smoke more slowly this time. If only he could get cigarettes with a lighter tobacco, American or even English . . . next time in Madrid, he would have to see about that . . .

He looked back and forth from the phone to the record player, could not bring himself to touch either; the one represented even further involvement, the other an all too obvious escape. So he sat there, barely hearing the distant shots, the thud of explosions, lost in his own murky indecision.

A group of men in blue "monos" rushed by outside, shouting. Gil bolted the door. More men passed, all headed in the direction of the Tavera Hospital.

Another burst of firing. Three or four salvos of artillery in rapid succession. The windows began to shake. This time, Gil could hear the whine of projectiles, clear and distinct, as they cut through the air.

The walls were vibrating in time to the rhythm of the detonations, and the long files of phonograph records trembled on the shelves. Gil watched them with horror. As the firing grew more intense, the rows of records began to inch inexorably toward the edges of the shelves. The entire wall, lined with thousands of fragile phonograph records, slithered forward at each blast.

He jumped up and ran to the wall, his arms outstretched and began to push the rows of records back. But each time he managed to force a line of them away from the edge, the distant artillery would sound again, a shell would burst nearby and another section, somewhere just out of reach, would move mockingly toward the brink. The old phonograph danced on the table behind the counter. Gil wanted to shout, to demand that they stop. What had he to do with any of it? Let them shoot at each

other to their hearts' content, but leave him alone. Didn't they realize
. . . his entire stock could be ruined?

Quite suddenly, a heavy explosion resounded only thirty meters or
so away. The windows were obscured by billows of thick black smoke
and clouds of brick and plaster dust. Fragments of stone rang from the
steel shutters. The wall split, revealing lathe and plaster beneath the flowered paper. The record shelves tipped forward, hurling their burden in
one great wave onto the floor of the shop.

Gil watched the cascade of records with disbelief. They seemed to
float, suspended, over the floor, taunting him by the slowness of their descent. The labels spun in the midst of the landslide of black shellac, a kaleidoscope of round reds, yellows, greens, and blues.

He choked, screamed, implored, but the records continued to fall.
He covered his eyes with his hands.

When he looked again, the floor was littered with heaps of broken
shellac. A thousand records, smashed to bits.

A bullet passed through the window of the door, adding a sprin-
kling of glass to the debris on the floor. The phonograph behind the
counter had not been damaged. Unaccountably, the piles of loose records
next to it had not moved at all.

In that moment, he thought of his wife, whose death had rooted him
forever to his dreams and to Toledo itself. He remembered her, slender
and dark, at the piano, playing Chopin and Brahms while he sat and listened on the terrace of what had been their house, breathing in the faint
lemon smell that rose from the nearby groves. . . . That was all gone.

Now this.

He began to weep, at first not even noticing the tears. Then, when
the tears began to roll along his cheeks, when he understood what was
happening and it was too late to stop, he gave himself over to it and
wept openly and fully.

July 21, 10 a.m.: *Toledo*

Beneath Barrera's cheerful exterior Jaime sensed a current of
fear as deep as his own. The driver seemed as apprehensive of the Anarchist militia as he was of the soldiers and Civil Guard. Certainly it was
not simply because he was in Francisco Mercader's employ. Hardly any
one in Toledo even knew that the Mercader family lived in the ravine,
let alone knew anything about them. Francisco Mercader kept to himself
and rarely ventured into the city. Even had his presence been common
knowledge, there would have been no reason for him to fear; he had always been on the side of social progress in his own gentle way, a good
and devoted member of the *Izquierda Republicana*. Why then did the
driver fear so? Nor was it the shells which had been flying overhead since
the moment they had pulled away from Ignacio's converted stable; that

was also certain. As the shells churned through the air, coming from the direction of the Hospital de Tavera and making a sound like a washing machine gone mad, the driver did not even flinch. Jaime looked up with each salvo; "Loose rotating bands. The idiots . . . they'll be lucky to come anywhere near their target. . . ." But what was their target? It was impossible to tell. Now and then a geyser of smoke would shoot up over the rooftops, fanning out like an umbrella and momentarily obscuring the sky. The driver would smile, whistle appreciatively and look totally unconcerned. Yet he was clearly afraid. The question nagged Jaime unmercifully; Esteban Barrera was afraid of his own people.

Barrera twisted in his seat as the car veered onto the peripheral road and began its circuit of Toledo. Because of the narrowness of the streets, there was only one way to get the Ford from Ignacio's shop to the Carvalho house and that was to drive completely around the bluff upon which the city was built, even though the two buildings were only a few streets apart.

"What if she doesn't want to come?" he said.

"Then, man, I'll have to take her out whether she wants to come or not."

"Well," the driver said, "just don't take too long at it. We'll be blocking the street, and I don't want any arguments with any militia, trying to get through. We're close enough to the bridge so that we might even get a Civil Guard or two coming by."

"You'll just wave at them, and they'll go away," Jaime said.

"They won't, not today, so don't count on it."

The car angled into the street on which the Carvalho house fronted, leaving behind the tree-fringed circular road and the vista of hills across the Tagus. The alleyways and rough walls closed in at once.

Barrera drove carefully up the narrow street, past the door with the Hapsburg double eagle on it and to the head of the *calle* where a wider street met it at right angles.

"Where are you going . . . ?"

"Look, *teniente* . . . if there's any . . . problem, you want to be pointed the right way, don't you?" He stopped, began to back the car into the alley they had just passed, then nosed forward again, turning so that the car was now headed back in the direction from which they had just come, toward the Cambrón gate and the road to Madrid.

"If you don't mind my saying so, let's get this over with quickly. I think we should get back to your father's place. It's not going to be so good here in a little while, not after that demonstration in the Zoco this morning. Jesus, what fools some people are. . . ."

Jaime said nothing and got out of the car. The Mauser in his pocket bumped against the car door, and he was uncomfortably aware of its weight. He did not like having a gun in his pocket.

"It would be better if she knew you were coming," the driver said.

"I know, but what can I do?"

"Why don't you leave her here? What's she to you? Xaviera told me that you wouldn't even speak to her the other night, and now?"

Jaime swore under his breath, and he could not help laughing. So it was that way at his father's house, was it? He would have to be careful if he wanted to retain any privacy at all. But servants were the same all over. The Moors in Ceuta had been just as inquisitive and just as tactless.

The front door was closed this time, and the knob would not turn. He rapped sharply on the panel just below the eagle. On the rooftops above him, he knew, men were waiting, expectant among the silent files of nodding birds. Unlike the birds, they did not sleep but listened and held their rifles close. Slivers of light sprang into the air, flung up from the polished barrels, piercing the sky. He could see the tracks of light all over the city, like an aurora borealis at midday.

Barrera had picked up a newspaper and was reading determinedly. Through the windshield, pocked with the juices of dead insects, Jaime could make out the headlines: *"El ejercito fascioso, sublevado por los jefes traidores en toda España, totalmente batido por las fuerzas leales y el pueblo . . ."*

Since leaving the Zoco, they had seen not a single regular uniform, no army, no Civil Guard, not even an Assault Officer. Only the plain people in their plain anonymous clothes and the militiamen in their overalls, waiting on the housetops under the stupefying sun, weapons held as tenderly as sacred images. They waited, those people, and their gaze had fallen heavily on anyone daring to venture out. Only the animals seemed to move without fear.

He rapped again on the door. There was a shuffling on the other side, a whisper of breath, and the rasp of the lock being unbolted.

The door opened a crack, and the old woman who had been with the girl at his father's house thrust her withered head into the sun. She blinked, trying to make out who it was.

"Let me in. Don't you know who I am?"

"Why should I let you in?" The old woman was shaking. It was his appearance, he knew, ragged, dirty, and unshaven. How different did he look from the men on the rooftops, the armed factory workers gathering in the streets?

"I am Francisco Mercader's son. And you will let me in, at once. Come now and open the door . . ."

He heard sounds coming from up the street. It was nothing, but it frightened him. He reached out and pushed open the door. As he stepped inside, he touched the old woman on the shoulder. "It's all right. You've done the right thing. There's nothing to worry about."

He went on past her and into the hall. A flight of iron-railed stairs led up to the second floor. From where he stood he could see through the open archways and into the main room and the dining hall. The portrait of the Colonel was still there and below it the draped harpsichord. Sunlight collected in slowly shifting pools on the floor. The house was as deserted as the nave of a burned-out church.

As he stood there, he could hear someone breathing above him, at the head of the landing.

"Who's there . . . Rosa? Who is it?" It was Mercedes' voice. "Rosa?"

"No," Jaime called up, trying to keep his tone light and not betray his agitation. He thought he could hear sounds out in the street again. He thought, "What if the driver leaves me here? How do I know what he'll do if there's trouble? . . ."

He could see her above him, dark against the musty light on the landing, wearing the same dress she had had on the day before at the Tránsito.

"Onésimo?" she shouted down. The unexpected sound of a man's voice had obviously shaken her.

"No . . . it's Jaime Mercader . . . your woman was good enough to let me in. . . ."

"Oh . . . ," an exhalation of relief. She gave a forced laugh. "You're much too early. We were to have lunch together, not breakfast, don't you remember? . . ."

"It's not that. Something else has happened."

She came around the landing and stood at the head of the stairs looking down at him. Behind her, on the wall, he caught sight of a Berber lance hung on brackets, probably brought back by her father, years ago after the first Riff campaign.

"I've come to take you away from here," he said, trying not to shout. "There's no time left at all now, so you've got to come. It's not safe for you here any more." He could see her staring incredulously down at him from the landing. "Listen to me . . . your father has run," he went on, trying to sound forceful and yet not betray his agitation. "Ask Onésimo when he comes back . . . if he does come back. He'll tell you. . . . Ask him who met him at the house when he drove up with all the furniture. You know yourself that your father has run from Oviedo. He's done the only thing he could do. He's run. So don't tell me that it's safe, there or here, or any place for you. . . ."

"You're crazy," she shot back, "you know it. . . . He would never do such a thing, and you . . . you . . ."

He shook his head violently. "Get some of your things together in a suitcase and come. I have a car outside, and if we're lucky we can get out of the city before something happens." He stared at her, wondering whether he had said what he had said about her father in order to convince her to leave with him or out of a need to wound the Colonel still further by destroying his daughter's faith in him just as he had destroyed Jaime's faith.

She tried to pretend she was not frightened, but he could see her backing away from the landing.

"If the Anarchists get their hands on your father, what do you think will happen to him?" he cursed, his voice rising. "Do you think it will be any different with you? They don't care, one Carvalho will be as good as another to them. . . ."

"For God's sake, what do you want of me?"

"To recognize the truth." He was no longer listening to her. He began to climb the stairs. "How can he help you? He's in France. For Christ' sake, in France. . . . He's run again, just as he did when he left me at the trials. He didn't tell you about that, did he? Well, this father of yours, he has a way of running away from things. He came back to me because of his pride or maybe because it was only a few miles, but what can he do from Biarritz?"

"He's not in Biarritz," she shouted. "You can't make me believe it. . . ."

A quick shifting of shadow below; the old woman ran across the front of the hall and through the still open door.

"Look down there," he cried, coming rapidly up the few remaining steps. "Tell me he hasn't deserted you just the way he deserted me . . ."

She let out a cry of protest and backed against the wall. A wave of dizziness passed over him as he topped the landing. As he reached out, meaning to grasp her by the arm, it passed and left him staring into her wide, angry eyes and possessed of a clarity of vision that terrified him.

Then, as he watched his own hands reaching out with a curiously archaic grace to take her arm, she half turned, and wrenched the lance from the wall. The brackets fell to the floor. The lance went back, and she held it for a second, staring at him in terrified confusion, unable to understand what was happening, how he could be acting in such a way and how she could be so suddenly alone and vulnerable.

The broken sunlight kindled the point of the spear. Her arm rose, then fell again. He was smiling; she would not actually throw it. The idea . . . he had come to help her, he had come . . . to show her what her father really was . . . no to help her . . . it made no difference . . . he wanted only to help . . .

He threw himself headlong toward her, and the lance sailed over his head, out over the railing, twisting clumsily as it fell, then dropping straight and clean down to the floor below. It hit with a solid, chunking sound, burying its weighted tip in the hallway floor. He winced from the sudden, unexpected pain as his elbows slammed against the ground. Falling against her legs, he dragged her down. She struggled for breath, making no other sound all the while. Hard, her body against him; her hair spread wide fanning over his face, cool. He pulled loose, brought himself up to his feet, pulling her up after him by the arms. How light she was, and how strong too. He held her for a moment, and they were almost as two lovers struggling against each other to die from each other's love. Then slowly, the twisting ceased, until they became very still, Jaime still holding her by the arms and she glaring back at him, tears welling in the corners of her eyes.

"He did not . . . he did not . . . desert me . . . ," she whispered.

He, at that moment, felt very calm. He had confronted her with the same anger and contempt for blindness and lies with which, now, he would have confronted her father, and had shown her what the man was. He saw in the girl not a woman named Mercedes Carvalho but her father . . . and in accusing *him* before her, he had finally, in his way, accused *him* to his face.

"Now where are your clothes. . . ?"

"I won't . . ." she stiffened, backed against the wall and began to move away from him. "I don't know . . . you . . . I won't . . ."

Over her shoulder he could see the end of the long corridor and the open door beyond which lay her room. The bed was mounded with tousled sheets, and a jar of jonquils stood on a table near the window. He took her arm and pushed her backwards down the hallway toward the door, then through it. Only when he had gotten her inside did he release her.

"Now . . . pack these," he said, swinging his arm into the closet behind him and pulling out an armful of dresses. He threw them onto the bed. She did not move as he yanked a small suitcase down from a shelf, emptied a drawer of her dresser on top of the bed. He thrust the dresses and a few other things into the suitcase, then slammed it shut and turned to face her again, the fingers of his free hand fumbling with the latch. Then she did an odd thing; without a word, she reached out with both hands and snapped the latch of the suitcase. This done, she stood there, stiff as a wooden saint, her lips trembling and tears coursing down her cheeks.

He could only think, "How unusual she looks. What a strong face despite the tears. So unlike her mother. No . . . so *like* her father." Again, that comparison . . . even to the wild explosion of her hair around her face.

"I'm sorry about your father," he said into the silence. "But it's true, every word of it, I swear it. . . ."

She shook her head but did not even try to speak.

"Hurry . . . I'll carry the suitcase. Now go . . ." he said, waving toward the door. She obeyed, covering her face with her hands but still able to see her way. He took the suitcase in one hand, his other on the Mauser in his pocket and they went along the hall and down the stairs to the front door which had been left open by the old woman.

As they emerged from the house, Barrera looked up over his newspaper and immediately brought the ancient car lurching along the narrow street. He threw open the door; the front seat was large enough for all three of them. Mercedes sat in the middle, Jaime by the door to prevent escape.

"Sweet Jesus," Barrera whistled. "What did you do to her, *teniente?*" Jaime looked again; the girl's dress was torn partly open in front, her face streaked with dirt.

"Don't stare at her, man. Just drive us out of here the fastest way you know how."

Barrera shrugged, gunned the motor and the car moved forward down the roughly cobbled street, picking up speed.

Mercedes pulled her coat around her and lowered her head. Her hair, which had come completely undone, was caught by the wind from the open side windows and billowed out, giving her a curiously carefree appearance and getting in her mouth as she tried to speak. Vainly, she attempted to brush it back out of the way.

"My father will see that you spend the rest of your life in prison for this," she said in a low, tensely controlled voice.

Jaime didn't answer her; there was no point in it. He felt peculiarly at peace with himself, and that calm communicated to the driver.

"And you," the girl was saying, "whatever your name is . . . you'll be with him, for this idiotic thing. . . ." Barrera nodded, as though agreeing with her.

"We all do idiotic things in our lifetime," he said, wrenching at the wheel as the car jounced over the stones in the direction of the Bisagra gate. The sun seemed to have withdrawn unusually high into the cloudless and glassy sky, as though trying to put as much distance between itself and Toledo as possible.

"Ignacio did a good job, no?" Barrera said. The whine of the motor rose higher and higher, very smooth. "If we get out of here, I may see about his sister again . . . who knows? It wouldn't be such a bad thing to have a mechanic like that as a brother-in-law. . . ."

"And you may run into a wall the way you drive. Slow down, man," Jaime said. Mercedes, meanwhile, had lowered her head still further and closed her eyes.

"We'll try for the Madrid road. We can't get over the bridges anymore. They're blocked off," Barrera said.

"When did that happen?"

Barrera didn't answer, only glanced disgustedly out of the corner of his eye. Jaime was shaken; again, the driver had known something that he hadn't known.

At that moment the sound of machine-gun fire exploded not far ahead, and the sudden, outraged shouts of wounded men filled the morning air. It was, unmistakably, the sound of an ambush.

"Listen to that . . . they're really serious about it this time."

"Go left, toward the arms factory," Jaime shouted. There was a second road there which might be less dangerous. The firing was directly in front of them now. Down the street he could see the figures of crouching men stumbling and running awkwardly about, trying to get out of the way of a steady spray of machine-gun fire that sent cottony little puffs of smoke spurting from the roadway wherever it touched.

The car plunged into a side street. A few men, caught unawares, scurried out of the way. There was barely enough room for the car to pass, so narrow was the street and so wide the ancient vehicle. The motor had begun to trail bluish vapor and to make ominous knocking sounds again, but Barrera seemed completely unconcerned.

The car spun around the next bend, narrowly missing the wall of a building, and lurched up another narrow street.

"Try for the road by the bullring."

"You don't have to tell me . . ."

A great rack of pots and pans which had been set up before the door of a small café went flying with a tremendous clatter, caught by the bumper of the car as it passed. Chickens raced for safety in the doorways, and a frightened mule brayed and stamped.

The firing seemed to grow more furious. It was coming from someplace directly ahead of them rather than from behind, as it had before.

The car at last broke out of the constricted Calle Real and entered a slightly wider road which pointed toward the bullring on the northern edge of the city and, eventually, toward Madrid. Ahead of them, through the spattered windshield, they could see more men, hundreds of them, spread out across the roadside, all running for cover around the low buildings near the bullring. Some of the men wore blue overalls. A black and red Anarchist flag jutted incongruously from the middle of the street where it had become wedged between some torn-up cobblestones. Next to it, a man lay face down, streaming blood.

Barrera swore in Galician dialect: incomprehensible.

A bullet passed through the upper part of the windshield. Glass sprayed around the inside of the car. Mercedes, whose head was still down, was not touched but a sliver lodged in Jaime's cheek, drawing an involuntary shout from his lips and an instant stream of blood.

Ahead of them, the road had suddenly become full of trucks, all coming from the direction of the arms factory. Most of the drivers seemed to be naked to the waist. Men, in what was left of officers' uniforms clung to the running boards of some of the trucks, waving pistols and shouting obscenities which could be heard even over the tumult of firing and the grinding of the Ford's old engine.

The trucks were headed directly toward them, a heavy file of a dozen or more, all traveling at a good speed.

Barrera tugged frantically at the wheel, and the car lurched around, almost tipping over. "This is impossible," he shouted. "There's no place to go now . . . Christ . . . the only road out of here and this has to happen . . ."

"The bridge . . ."

"It's blocked, I told you . . ."

Mercedes lifted her head; "You see . . ."

Behind the trucks, all over the wrinkled yellow countryside to the north, tiny dots could be seen; fragile threads of smoke rose only to lose themselves in a dirty gray pall hovering over the hills near the arms factory. Shafts of sunlight, reflected from the windows of the speeding lorries, speared at the sky, giving the scene a hallucinatory, carnival atmosphere.

The trucks bore down on them, pecked by random rifle fire which now seemed to be coming from the rooftops rather than from the militia deployed near the bullring. Civil Guard with smoking Mausers dashed for shelter behind piles of stone. A few uniformed soldiers bunched up behind low walls and behind trees, firing wildly. And, visible again, the wave of blue "monos" advancing across the northern fields, pressing toward the Bisagra gate.

An officer tumbled from the running board of the lead truck, screaming, and fell onto the roadway, his body rolling head over heels. The rest of the trucks sped by headed up the hill toward the Alcázar, one of them passing directly over the still twisting body.

Jaime caught a glimpse of the area around the bullring, now swarming with men. A makeshift armored car lumbered angrily across the field, looking like a giant flatiron, its plates flapping, its passage accompanied by puffs of greasy black smoke and a great churning of dirt. Then Barrera's car screeched around another corner, and the bullring and the trucks were lost to sight.

Jaime wrenched the Mauser out of his pocket and rested his arm on the edge of the open window. Not that he would be able to hit anything moving at that speed, but the posture reassured him.

"God's balls, what a mess," Barrera shouted. "What's going on here?"

"I thought you knew . . ."

"How the hell could I know . . . look at this . . ."

"It must be militia from Madrid," Jaime answered, barely able to hear his own voice over the tumult.

"There's no other way," the driver cried. "The only way out now is by the river and this damned car won't swim . . ."

As if by way of comment, there was a rumble of artillery in the southeast, and the whine of more shells with loose rotating bands cut across the sky over the city. The chunking of the explosions was lost in the general din.

The trucks were suddenly all around them again. Barrera had been traveling for a distance of more than a hundred meters along a street parallel to that on which the convoy had been moving. Now, as he brought the car once more into an eastbound street, heading back into the jumble of Toledo and away from the bullring, the trucks had reappeared.

This time there was nothing they could do. The car slid unceremoniously and helplessly into their ranks; they were boxed in, trucks in front and trucks to the rear.

"*Ca!*" Barrera breathed, almost in relief.

"Follow the trucks," Jaime said, feeling foolish even as the words left his lips.

"Wise, . . . as we haven't any other choice."

"Follow . . . ," Jaime said again. He wanted to follow because he had willed it, not because they had no other choice. Everything had ended in failure. Mercedes was staring at the bullethole at the top of the windshield. She had not noticed it before when the car had been hit.

"We're going to wind up in the Alcázar," Barrera said. "Jesus . . ."

Jaime stared at him. The caravan was rumbling up the winding street known as the Cuesta de las Armas, headed for the Zocodover, right back where they had come from earlier that morning.

"The Alcázar then," he said hopelessly.

JULY 21, 10:30 A.M.: *The Alcázar*

THE ALCÁZAR, LIKE SO MANY OTHER imposing symbols, was hollow. The walls which appeared so massive from the outside were but one corridor's width thick and gave way at once to a columned arcade which opened in turn onto a large, sun-dried courtyard, big enough to hold a troop of infantry in review. At the center of the courtyard, gazing sternly about from atop a pedestal of five concentric steps, Carlos V stood in stone effigy, clutching a spear.

"And what good, just exactly what good is that spear going to be if they drop a bomb on his head?" Major Punto thought, mopping the sweat from his forehead. He knew that he should have worn a hat, but he was too tired to go back inside the building and fetch it. If his brains curdled in the heat, what difference would it make? As he saw it, every man in the city had apparently had his brains curdled some time before.

He had set his table up just inside the gate which led to the north terrace. Having debated for a time on the choice of tables, he had finally settled on a wide trestle which had stood in the library for as long as he could remember, buried under a pile of moldering old maps tied with ribbons and three boxes of diplomas which had never been made out. Just after dawn, he and Remedio had dragged the table into the yard and set it up. Ever since the declaration of war, Remedio had stuck to him like a second skin. The boy's face, broad and unaccountably cheerful, gave him some comfort, and he could not bring himself to chase him away though he knew that Remedio should have been with the other privates helping build fortifications on the upper walls. Instead, Major Punto had allowed the boy to attach himself as a sort of unofficial aide. He thought, sometimes, that Remedio was the only person in the Alcázar smiling.

Perched on the edge of an ornately carved armchair, Punto shuffled his lists around the tabletop and jabbed now and then at a bottle of ink. For three hours he had been carefully listing the names of all those who had come to seek sanctuary within the Alcázar. No one had told him to make lists, but he had done so all his life and had come to believe in them as effective insurers of order. "Things recorded, are not forgotten, and things not forgotten are things in their proper place." Colonel Moscardó, the commandant, had passed by a half hour before, wrinkled his nose as if to say, "Well, what can we expect of old majors who teach geography . . . ," and gone on his way. So Punto had continued in his methodical way, cataloguing, ordering, and arranging.

He looked out at the crowd which filled the yard. The fortress was going to overflow with useless civilians, all of whom would have to be fed and looked after. Groups of soldiers, their leaves interrupted, stood about conversing with forced animation to hide their nervousness, some of them only partially in uniform. Civil Guard and their families had come in from the outlying districts the previous day and hung together now in tight bunches as though consoled and encouraged by the sight of each other's uniforms. A few retired officers with absurd whiskers looked about the courtyard, expectantly searching for old acquaintances behind the pillars of the arcades. Townspeople who had not known what to do when the firing had started the day before and to whom the walls of the Alcázar offered the only logical security threaded their way about the crowded yard, adding splashes of red, saffron, and grass-green to the monotony of earth-colored tunics. Of all the people in the Alcázar, only the few cadets who had been there when the trouble had started, seemed at ease. One could even detect a faint holiday spirit, the expectation of great adventure.

The odor in the yard was already too strong; the men who had come in the day before, after long and grueling rides from Oliás, Mocejón, and Torrijos, had not been able to wash, nor had their families. The smell of sweat and gunpowder mixed with the scent of cheap perfumes and toilet water, cigars and brilliantine. Many of the women from Toledo had come in their best clothes, as though going to the theater. Food turning rotten in the sun lent a sweet pungency to the air. There was no telling how much food was going to waste, jealously wrapped in fragments of cloth, bandanas, and old shirts, putrefying before it could be taken to the cool cellars and vaults below. Flies had already begun to investigate noisily.

Punto pulled at his collar and rolled up the sleeves of his tunic. The heat had made him slightly dizzy. All he could think of was the awful odor that dead bodies would make in such a heat; there would be no place to bury them. The Alcázar and the surrounding buildings were built on foundations of solid rock.

An elderly man dressed in a moth-eaten uniform of a cavalry captain presented himself at the desk, his eyes red from lack of sleep. He began to recite his military qualifications in a deep, sacerdotal voice.

"Yes . . . what year? . . . will you repeat that again, please . . . yes . . ."

Punto's pen moved mechanically over the paper. Did the old man realize how foolish he looked? Did he think, honestly, that he had had to come, that anyone outside gave a damn whether he lived or died? How many such people had come to the Alcázar, Punto wondered. "If they didn't come here in the first place, nobody would bother them. By running, they *become* guilty . . . it's because they *think* something will happen . . . why, then it does. No other reason . . ." Perhaps he should urge the old man to leave now while he could.

But he said nothing, went on taking down the dates and regiments that the old man was carefully cataloguing.

He looked over the moving end of his pen. Near the wall was a woman who had come to his table brandishing a huge horse pistol. She wore a red neckerchief around her throat; a Carlist. They took themselves seriously, too. She had come with her husband, a major with only one arm who had been mutilated twenty years before in the Riff. Now they were both Carlists. Why? The pretender was dead without heir, wasn't he? She was sitting on a stone, cleaning her pistol with a rag. A few feet away an unusually tall, flaccid man sat slumped against the wall in despair. A heavy canvas satchel bound with leather straps lay on the ground by his right foot, and in his lap he held an old-fashioned crank phonograph with a large flared horn, gilded and decorated with violet flowers. He had come in an hour before, asking for the Colonel of the Civil Guard whom no one had seen in days, then gone walking aimlessly around the yard until his strength had given out. He had been sitting there for at least half an hour, not moving except to wipe the sweat from his bald head. People, even people like the man with the phonograph, always seemed familiar to him if he looked at them long enough. Inevitably, he found in each new face something that spoke to him confidentially and demanded special attention which he was loathe to give.

He thought he heard a noise, the sound of motors, but there was so much shouting and talking in the courtyard, he could not really hear. Perhaps it was the sun. He should have worn a cap. Foolish thing to sit for hours under the sun with no hat on.

"We will advise you . . . when you're needed, Captain Suarez."

Remedio stifled a laugh. The ancient Captain gave a rickety salute and went off. Overhead the sun glowed fiercely. Sweat trickled down Punto's ears, making him irritable.

"Do that once again," Punto said to Remedio when the old Captain had gone off, "and I'll see that you're . . . just don't do it again, do you understand?"

Remedio nodded in a distracted sort of way. He, too, seemed to hear something.

The rumbling on the other side of the wall had in fact become louder. A shout rose from the esplanade. The Major craned his neck to see what was going on.

"It's the trucks from the *fábrica*, Major," Remedio said, grinning as though his cheeks would split, as though he himself had caused the convoy to appear.

"So . . . trucks? Food or ammunition? Can you tell?"

"Ammunition from the arms factory, Major. Lots of ammunition."

"So," Punto thought, "now it will last for a long time. Plenty of ammunition. Enough to kill everyone five times over."

The trucks had rolled up the ramplike road called the "zigzag" and halted on the broad terrace just below the north wall. Officers without their tunics jumped from the running boards of the trucks, brandishing pistols and shouting for assistance. One man fell forward onto the terrace, a great red splotch under his shoulder where he had just been hit by sniper fire from the opposite roofs. He was immediately lifted up and carried away. A few men kneeled behind the trucks and returned the fire that seemed to be coming from the belfry of the church of La Sangre, a hundred yards away. Punto stood up, shading his eyes; the scene behind the arch was a blur of light and indistinct shapes. The Carlist woman had gone running toward the archway too, but her husband, his empty sleeve flapping, had appeared and was holding her back; the two of them were shouting at each other angrily.

As Punto watched, he sensed an animal uneasiness among those who were still waiting around his table; they seemed disturbed by the fact that he had stopped writing in his ledgers.

"In a moment, in a moment," he said, waving back the dozens of men and women pressing in on him.

"Moment . . . ," echoed Remedio.

Outside the walls, cadets and guards surrounded the truck and began unloading boxes of ammunition. There were ten trucks in all, and in the middle, almost lost amid the cluster of heavy vehicles, was a large, dusty black car, its windshield smashed, the engine hood and the doors pocked with bulletholes.

As the boxes of ammunition were lowered from the truck backs, the occupants of the car, a young man, the driver in a chauffeur's cap, and a woman got out. The woman began to shout at the two men who appeared embarrassed and were trying to quiet her. Rifle bullets splashed about on the esplanade, but they did not seem to notice. The young man was bleeding freely from the face, long red streaks reaching down over the breast of his shirt, like fingers. He had one arm around the woman but was having difficulty holding her.

Three Civil Guard assisted the car's occupants into the courtyard. The woman stopped shouting as soon as they entered the courtyard and began whispering to the young man. She seemed, now, more confused than angry.

"Do . . . you understand . . . what you've . . . done? . . ."

"I know, I know . . . I didn't intend . . . ," the young man said.

A louder, "chunking" noise near the esplanade. Someone was firing a mortar, but the shells were falling into the gorge beyond and going off a hundred meters below.

Punto watched the woman, fascinated by the play of conflicting emotions on her face.

"Here . . . for God's sake . . . of all places . . ."

". . . quiet . . . don't shout . . ."

The man in the chauffeur's cap shook his head. Suddenly, he seemed to see someone and let out a shout which could be heard even over the din of small-arms fire coming from the esplanade.

"Infante . . ."

A stocky Civil Guard, with a broad, intelligent face and a proud Roman nose came running across the yard, his tricorn in his right hand, a sack of cheese in the other.

While the driver and the Guard threw their arms around each other the young man and the woman went on arguing. Punto could see their lips moving but could make out nothing of what was being said.

She, too, looked familiar. The Major struck his forehead in annoyance. Out of the corner of his eye, he saw that the people around his table had begun to draw closer. In a moment, they had blocked his view. Remedio circulated among them, trying to move them away, but no sooner had he convinced one to step back than another saw his opportunity to get closer.

The woman and the young man were now making their way across the courtyard toward the east arcade where the man with the phonograph was sitting. They seemed to know each other and for the first time in an hour, the man with the phonograph looked up, and a hint of animation brightened his face.

Then a woman stepped up to the table, blocking Major Punto's view again.

"I want to get downstairs with my son . . . you see, he's downstairs, my son . . . ," the woman said.

"Then go, you don't have to wait here. You can come back."

"Yes?"

Punto shifted to the side, caught sight of the young man again. He was gazing up into the sky, shielding his eyes with his hand.

Punto hadn't heard it but the others had. Through the babble of voices and the constant clatter of boxes being unloaded on the terrace, the pulse of distant motors suddenly asserted itself.

The noise grew louder, and three planes came in low over the hills south of the Tagus. All movement in the courtyard ceased instantly, the milling crowds transformed into a yellow frieze of uniforms and drawn faces.

Slowly, the aircraft floated into view, black-winged and fat, like airborne slugs. They wheeled and came in straight toward the Alcázar.

As the wing racks opened and the bombs came loose, the young man with the cut cheek shouted and threw himself against the girl, rolling them both between the columns of a doorway by the wall. The man with the phonograph stood where he was, watching the slowly descending bombs.

It had not occurred to Punto to rise or run. He looked down, saw Remedio flat on the ground, his arms folded over his head, digging at the stones with the toes of his boots in curious little circular motions.

All at once a part of the west wall and a corner of the courtyard seemed to rise gently on the crest of a giant wave. Showers of concrete and stone rushed into the air and a shaft of smoke sprang hungrily at the cloudless sky. A tremendous roar filled the air.

Then the sound was gone and only the hailstone rattle of falling rock and plaster remained. The three aircraft banked and swung back high over the esplanade and away across the Tagus.

The stone shower trickled away into silence. Punto had felt nothing, only a kind of "push" of air as the blast rolled across the yard. He had remained sitting right where he was, his right hand splayed on his ledger sheets, holding them down.

The anonymous whimpering of the frightened and the injured trembled through the courtyard. People got to their feet and brushed the dust from their clothes, astounded, unable to believe they had survived.

"Jesus," said Remedio, his head still down.

"It's over. You can get up. . . ."

"Jesus," Remedio said again.

The young man was holding the girl by the shoulders and was shaking her. Nearby, the man with the phonograph was searching the rubble-strewn yard. The satchel lay where he had put it, covered with shale and dust. From a mound of stones, the horn of his phonograph jutted like a flower.

The smoke gradually dissipated, carried off by the rising heat. Flames sputtered in the piles of rubble. Dozens of men moved about the yard, poking in the debris.

The tall man had squatted next to the pile of stones and had begun to clear them away from his phonograph. His fingers touched the crank. It moved, labored against the springs. He glanced up at the sky but there was no sign of the aircraft.

They had gone back to Madrid for another load of bombs.

JULY 21, 11:00 A.M.: *The Alcázar*

THEY HAD FOUND EACH OTHER almost at once, Esteban Barrera and his cousin Infante Delgado, the Civil Guard. It had been a week since they had seen each other, and they sat down together on a slab of dusty stone to smoke and talk while the dust of the bombing settled. For a moment each looked at the other and remembered a day when they had sat on just such a pile of slag inside a shack on the outskirts of Cartenegra, and for a moment neither of them spoke.

Above them, the hot sun seemed to buzz in the sky, beating down and cooking the blood in a man's head.

"So, cousin, what the hell are you doing in this filthy pen?" said Infante, at last.

"The same as you, cousin."

"Not the same, I don't think . . . nobody wants to cut your scrawny throat for you."

Barrera laughed but in a frightening way, remembering a time when that was not true. But now it was true, and he nodded and showed his teeth.

"How come you're not with your 'patron'? Doesn't he feed you enough anymore?"

"He feeds me all right. I don't eat, that's all." Barrera shrugged. "That was the son I came in with. We got caught in the middle of the trucks while we were trying to get out of the city."

"Bad luck. Now you're stuck here the same as me."

"Here or there, what difference does it make?"

"Don't let Ignacio hear you talk like that. He thinks there's a difference." Infante stuck a knife into the wheel of cheese on his lap.

"Poor Ignacio."

"Poor Ignacio. If my sister doesn't finish him, we will, I'm afraid."

"Why . . . 'afraid'?"

"I really like the bastard, that's why I'm . . . afraid. If he wasn't so stupid, he'd be a good brother-in-law."

"He's not so stupid, believe me," Barrera said. "You should have seen the job he did on the car. With only a few parts . . ."

"Monkey-work. That doesn't take intelligence," Infante snorted. "You just have to know where the wires go, that's all."

"That's something."

Delgado took off his tricorn and polished it on his sleeve until it shone; then he held it up as a mirror, inspecting his square, flat-featured face. Looking at them, no one would ever have guessed that he and the driver were related.

"No," Infante went on. "That's not what I mean . . . take Ignacio for example . . . why not? That's who we're talking about anyhow. Now Ignacio doesn't read books. He doesn't think for himself. He just listens to people, and he soaks up ideas like a sponge. And who's to say who's right . . . I mean, whose ideas are right . . . his or mine . . . or yours, whatever *they* are? They're all someone else's property, so it depends on who you listen to, that's all. At least *I* can see that."

"Ignacio doesn't?"

"No, the thickhead. Not at all."

"Did you ever stop to think why Ignacio wants to listen to all those second-hand ideas in the first place? Do I have to take you by the throat and shake you so you remember what it was like in Cartenegra? Don't you remember your own father's funeral?"

"Listen, a man hears what he hears. It all depends on where he is. If he's in church, he listens to a priest; if he's in a factory, he listens to the organizers. It's all the same crap . . . ," Infante spat between his boots. "Paradise in the sky or paradise on earth. We'll never see either."

"That's garbage, and you know it. Besides, it's probably all your sister's fault."

"How's that?"

"If she didn't drive poor Ignacio out of the house all the time, he wouldn't do what he does. A man who's happy in bed doesn't waste his time at CNT meetings."

Infante slapped his leg; the idea appealed to him. "Poor Ignacio, the little frog . . . I bet my sister is just like that, too. She never did know how to behave."

Barrera thought of Peralta, and it hurt him; there he was, between Infante Delgado, to whom the disorder was simply another police obligation and Peralta, who had the fire of revolution in his eyes. How odd that they should all have come together in one family. Yet it was a pattern being repeated in every town and city of the country. Fathers with knives to their sons' throats, brothers against brothers, cousins against cousins. The boundaries of each man's ideology were established by the distance he could gaze. He neither saw nor thought farther.

In the north, Barrera knew, the Carlist *Requetes* were polishing their ancient rifles, putting on the red berets, the color of which meant something so different from the red of the Communists in the cities. The Anarchists raised their eyes and saw their old tattered dreams still drifting in the Catalonian skies and the *Izquierda Republicana* Socialists rumbled on in their own uniquely phlegmatic way, trying to accommodate everyone. Old men dreamed of Alfonso XIII while their impatient sons sharpened the arrows of the Falange and waited their moment. The army, accustomed to having its way and embarrassed by the disorder which its own failures had caused, looked heavenward as well but saw too often the ghost of the church, not God, lurking in the clouds.

Delgado broke open the chamber of his revolver and squinted down the barrel.

"I just hope I don't run into Ignacio," he said.

"Why should you?"

"Who knows?" He snapped the pistol shut. "I'd hate to get into a fight with him. I'd never hear the end of it from my sister if I shot him."

"Well, if Ignacio has the good sense to stay away from the Alcázar you won't have any problems. . . ." He wondered if he should tell Infante about the guns that Ignacio had hidden in his garage. It could only make trouble, he thought, so he remained silent.

"We've got orders to go out and collect some hostages this afternoon. Someone drew up a list of people who'd be better for us inside . . . you never know what for . . . I tell you, I don't like it, I mean the idea of going out there again . . . mostly because of Ignacio. God's truth, that would be terrible. . . ."

"Hostages?" Barrera said, wrinkling his forehead. "What the devil do they want hostages for? That's a stupid idea . . ."

"Why do you say that, cousin?"

"Because it's stupid . . . just look at it this way . . . suppose you pick up a couple of Anarchists. Are the Reds going to stop doing whatever it is they're doing because you threaten to shoot a few FAI people? Christ, they'll cheer, that's what they'll do. And do you think the Anarchists will give a damn if you put a dozen Reds up against the wall? Why there's nothing they'd like better. And if we get some UGT people, everyone will cheer . . ." He stopped short; up until then he had been saying "you," but all of a sudden he had said "we." It had slipped out.

Delgado seemed not to have noticed. "There's something to that," he agreed reluctantly. "Yes, there . . . is . . ."

"Because that's the way it is, and you know it."

Infante nodded. It was the same, he thought, as with a bottle of bad wine. If it was paid for, you drank it all the same, and that was that.

"What the hell," he said. "It doesn't make any difference. We've got to do it, no matter what."

He loaded each chamber of his revolver carefully, rubbing the bullets one by one on his sleeve. Barrera noticed that the slugs were notched at the tip so that they would spread on impact and tear a hole the size of a melon in anything they hit. The Guard caught his cousin's glance and winked.

"My *banderillas negras*," he said. "They'll slow down anyone who gets too frisky."

Barrera said nothing. The Astra that Ignacio had given him weighed more than its weight in his trouser pocket.

"Do you want to come, cousin? We can use an extra hand."

"Me? What the devil for?"

"Because you know the streets around here as well as I do and most of the rest that'll be with us will be from Talavera or Illescas. Green as new grass. I could use you, believe me. Here . . . ," he said, digging up a folded piece of paper from his pocket. "These are the ones we're supposed to fish for."

Barrera studied the list. One or two of the names were familiar. "Paco López . . . wasn't he from Madrid . . . ?" Perhaps he had driven him once or twice in the days before he'd gone with Mercader . . . Permanyer . . . Ramalle . . . León Penagos and César Roig, the Communist liaison between Toledo and Talavera whom Barrera dimly remembered driving once or twice.

"Sure," he said at last. "Why shouldn't I?" And, once outside, if he decided to remain, that would be easy too. For a second he thought of Mercader, but the *teniente* had disappeared with the girl. "It's his lookout now," Barrera thought, but felt a creeping guilt all the same.

Delgado finished loading his revolver. "Seriously, what do I do if we run into that *cabrón* of a brother-in-law of mine?"

Barrera thought, "It was probably true . . . he's more afraid of his sister than of the bullets."

Another Civil Guard was waiting for them in the shade of the east arcade. His name was Damaso Vargas, and he had a bottle of *magnol* stuck into his tunic. He uncapped it and passed it around, but it was warm and Barrera could barely swallow his share.

Noon, July 21: *The Alcázar*

"Don't you understand, Major? It was an accident. The trucks forced us . . ."

"I know that," Major Punto said, trying to remain calm. He had been standing there in the corner of the courtyard listening to the young man for a number of minutes and was close to losing his patience.

"Then, let us leave . . ."

"That's impossible. Look around you. How many times do I have to tell you? You saw . . ."

"Just open the gates and let us out. You have no responsibility."

"You'd be shot down before you even reached your motor . . ."

"Then it would be our choice. This way . . . ," Jaime's face was twisted with anger, and he was barely able to control his hands. He knew that the Major was right, and that made it even worse.

The courtyard was full of activity. Guards were clearing up the debris left by the bombing raid, and a fire had been lit in the center of the yard to drive out the clouds of dust that still hung over the balconies and arcades. Rifle fire could be heard from the direction of the military government building to the north where the Alcázar garrison still had an outpost.

"I can't stand here arguing with you forever," Punto said in exasperation.

Gil, who had attached himself at once to the girl, hung back, a disconsolate look on his face. He had not been able to find Venegas, and though he had no desire to leave the Alcázar, he was becoming more and more concerned every moment.

"And what do you say, señorita?"

Mercedes didn't answer.

At that moment, there was a clatter outside the heavy doors leading to the north terrace. Someone in an upper window began to shout and suddenly there was a burst of rifle fire from the direction of the Santa Cruz, across from the northern approach road.

"Lorry . . ." a soldier in the tower shouted. More rifle fire, most of it splattering harmlessly against the outer walls. The sound of a wheezing motor and a squeal of brakes. A half a dozen Guard ran past and threw themselves at the doors, forcing them open. Fortunately, the barricades had only just been begun.

The double doors were only part-way open when the truck crashed through, the wobbling hoops slamming against the upper arch and splintering as it passed. It was a small truck, about one and one-half ton, painted gray, with a canvas cover halfway rolled up in the back. The Guards who had forced open the doors jumped back out of the way, and as the truck lurched into the courtyard, it struck a pile of timber which had been intended for the barricade. The driver, streaming blood from a gash in his scalp, lost control and for a second, the lorry swerved, careened and then came to a shuddering stop against a heap of trunks and household goods. Pots fell, and some glassware shattered. A chicken squawked in alarm inside a willow cage.

The truck was a Civil Guard vehicle and had a number and a name stenciled on the hood. It was from the outpost near Bargas, not far from the San Pedro Monastery. As soon as the lorry had stopped shaking from the impact, men began to climb down from the back; they had been lying flat in the truck-bed, trying to shelter themselves from the bullets with steel boiler plates and a few wide-bladed shovels which they still held over their heads even as they came down from the back of the truck.

"There's one wounded. He needs help . . ."

"Get a litter . . ."

Before Jaime could make a move forward to help, the doors had been swung shut again and the Guards began piling logs and trunks across the entrance. They helped the driver down and led him to the east arcade where a woman was ready with a bowl of water to bathe his head wound. All the men were Civil Guard. There were two women—their wives or daughters—and they were unwounded. One of the women was crying hysterically. The other seemed dazed, unable to realize that she was safe.

Two men came up, bearing a litter, and a nun brought a roll of bandages. She went around the back of the truck and gave a cry as she saw the wounded man being lowered from the truck-bed. His chest was crushed, and his bones stuck out through the flesh. He was still conscious, and his lips were moving as they lowered him onto the litter.

It all happened so fast that afterward Jaime could not place the exact moment he had seen the man's face for the first time; it was as though he had known all along that the man with the crushed chest was Tomás Pelayo.

One of the Civil Guard who had been in the back of the truck was explaining what had happened. They had been on their way in from Bargas when they had run into an Anarchist column just north of the San Pedro Monastery.

"Thanks to their rotten aim . . . what cretins they are . . . we got through. I'll tell you, we never would have made it if they'd been regular army or our own men. Point-blank and they still managed to miss us. Look at that, hardly a hole in the canvas. . . ."

They had found the civilian along the roadside a half mile farther up and had stopped for him even though they were still under fire. "We couldn't just leave him lying there, d'you know?" It seemed that he had just come from the San Pedro Monastery.

Jaime moved up and asked: "Did he tell you what happened? He was unconscious, wasn't he? He couldn't tell you . . ."

"No," the Guard said, wiping his face. "He told us all right. He's an ox, that scrawny little rooster . . . his chest caved in like that, but he told us. His son; he'd gone there for his son . . . at the monastery, well, I'll tell you, then we were thankful to God we'd stopped and taken him and not one of us hurt either . . . he was there when the 'anars,' came. The monks had brought in rifles and started shooting as soon as they saw the militia column. But they didn't plan on the 'anars' having artillery. There's nothing left of San Pedro now except a heap of rocks. That one . . . ," he gestured at Tomás Pelayo who was just then being carried into the building on the litter, "he was crushed by falling stone. I don't know how, but he crawled out onto the road. It must be a half mile from there to where we found him. . . ."

Out of the corner of his eye, Jaime saw that Gil had followed the litter down into the building. He hadn't said a word, had just turned and gone down, and the girl with him.

The Major was staring at him, a worried expression on his face. Jaime turned and walked across the yard to the door through which Pelayo, Gil, and the girl had only just then disappeared.

He went down the short flight of steps to the first level of underground rooms. Hearing the clink of bottles and the moaning of wounded men, he needed no other guide to the hospital room. Down the corridor he could see a square of smoky orange light. The sounds grew stronger, and the smell of disinfectant deepened.

It took a moment for his eyes to get used to the gloom; figures emerged like images slowly appearing on a photographic plate. The wounded—lying on cots, some on piles of blankets—and the white of their fresh bandages; that was all he could see for a moment, only their bandages, not their faces.

Tomás Pelayo y de Suelves was lying in a corner on a pile of old mattresses. A nun had just left him and Gil and the Carvalho girl were standing at a respectful distance. Pelayo's face was stiff and already turning grayish, and the blood was soaking through the bandages the nun had wrapped around his chest. Jaime could see her murmuring to herself. She was making little signs of the cross all over the front of her dress. It was obvious that Pelayo would be dead in a very little while.

Seeing Pelayo made it clear to him; it was as if a seal had been set on everything, as if someone had said, "This is final; this is the way it is going to be, so you'd better accept it." Jaime cast a quick, resentful glance toward Gil who was now bending over Pelayo. Gil's hands were trembling, and it had obviously cost him a great effort to bring himself that close to the dying man, to look into his eyes, to recognize him as a human being who was suffering what he himself might suffer in a matter of hours or even of minutes.

Jaime looked away, saying to himself, "Watching another man's death creates a gulf. He's not human anymore. He can't touch us anymore. His experience is something we can't possibly understand."

Pelayo had always seemed a small man. Now, he was even smaller, a figure carved out of ash, rigid, clumsily hewn. His life was the merest bubbling at the corners of his mouth, only a faint palpitation of his bluish nostrils. Yet he was conscious, and Jaime felt that he was staring at him even though he could not engage his glance directly.

Behind him, he could hear the sounds made by the nuns who were acting as nurses, as they moved about with tin trays of medicine and antiseptic. The room smelled of blood and camphor. There was a Persian rug on the floor already soggy with blood. An oil lamp burned on a table, casting fantastic shadows.

Pelayo's lips parted. ". . . it's all burned down now . . . if they hadn't tried to . . . poor Luis . . . poor Luis . . . poor Luis . . ."

Jaime resented the guilt that he felt being forced on him, but it was there, and he could not avoid it. If he had cared more, had been more persuasive with Luis, Tomás Pelayo would not be lying here now. Jaime could not help wondering what he would say to his own father . . . how he would tell him. Whatever else, he knew he could not lie about it.

"Will you . . . help Luis . . . my son . . . ?" Pelayo whispered.

"My son?" Jaime was not sure whether Pelayo meant Luis or was addressing him, in his delirium as . . . "my son" . . .

Gil coughed. It was the first time since his wife's death that he had watched someone he knew die.

A nurse was passing behind him with a length of rubber tubing and some bandages; Jaime caught at her sleeve.

"Can't you do something for him?" He heard a strident note in his own voice. "Why . . . ?"

She looked quickly down; now, there was a froth of blood on Pelayo's small mouth.

"We haven't got any equipment here. His lungs are full of blood."

"If you don't have what you need, then he should be taken to the hospital outside. . . . Can't you take him . . . ?"

The nurse looked puzzled, unsympathetic. "The gates are shut. I'm sorry . . ."

"The gates are shut," Mercedes repeated dully. Gil looked at her, then glanced about the room. There were a dozen or more wounded lying on cots and mattresses stretched out on the floor. In the far corner of the room, partially hidden by a pile of boxes, two bodies were laid out under tarpaulin covers. No one seemed to notice them except Gil.

He plucked at the nun's arm: "They shouldn't be lying like that . . . it isn't right."

". . . no other place . . ."

"All the same. A man has his dignity . . ."

"They don't care . . ."

The nun left the room quickly.

Jaime went down on his knees, leaning over Pelayo. He was angry with himself; he had no idea what he was waiting for; yet, it seemed to him that he had to wait there until the man died. He kept wondering if Mercedes would say something to him, but she kept silent.

Gil was circling about the two corpses under the tarpaulins. Perhaps it was easier for him to be near the truly dead than near Pelayo who, for all his waxen immobility and the hideousness of his wound, was still recognizably human and, so, much more frightening. Pelayo's pain demanded compassion in full measure and that was difficult for Gil to give; he had grown so used to thinking only of himself.

The girl saw him and went over, gently drawing him back. Gil seemed reluctant to follow but offered no resistance.

Jaime lost track of time; it was perhaps another half hour before Pelayo died. At one point, Pelayo's eyes opened wide, and he seemed to be staring through Jaime, trying to see something on the wall beyond. His breathing simply diminished until it ceased entirely. It was impossible to tell the exact moment when he died. There was no spasm, no final wrench. He slipped into death without seeming to notice.

It was chilly in the underground room, but Jaime had been sweating profusely. He was wholly unmoved by what he had seen and felt only anger at Pelayo's pointless death. What had he accomplished by going to the monastery? Only to die at the same time as Luis. Jaime knew what Luis thought of his father, that he would never have come back unless it suited him and that Tomás' going there made the boy's refusal even more certain. "To do a stupid thing like that, just because you think you have to . . ." The thought licked across his mind but not in his own voice, as his thoughts usually came but in an older, deeper voice as though he were hearing someone else say the words. Colonel Carvalho's voice? He turned away from the corpse, found himself facing the girl who had been waiting silently all the time by the wall.

"He was at your father's house the other night, wasn't he?" she finally said.

"Yes. I knew him . . . for a long time . . . since I was a child."

Gil was edging toward the doorway, a low arch which led onto a corridor and thence to a stairway that ran up to the ground floor and the courtyard. He was muttering to himself and shaking his head: "It took . . . so long . . ."

Jaime followed Gil toward the arch, taking the girl by the arm. This time, she did not shake him off.

Near the doorway there was a pile of blood-soaked clothing which had been cut from the wounded as they were brought in for treatment and had been simply thrown on the ground in a heap. On the top of the pile lay a pair of binoculars with a long leather strap. One lens was smashed, and the fragments stuck out like frozen petals from the rim on the glass.

Jaime reached down and picked them up; the glasses were a military model and had belonged to a soldier or a Civil Guard. He slung the strap over his shoulder and went out behind Gil and Mercedes Carvalho. The strap was damp with blood and slid about his shoulder.

By the foot of the stairs, Gil had stopped and was making weak signals with his right hand as though for help. His chest was heaving and he began to shudder every few seconds.

"Let me . . . a moment . . . just a moment . . ." He sagged down onto the bottom steps, his long, fleshless legs splaying out, his arms hanging down between his knees, rubbing his hands together the way a man who has lost feeling in a part of his body will do to see if the sensitivity has returned. "You see . . . I knew him, Mercedes. . . . It isn't just that he died . . . I knew him quite well. And I didn't like him . . . is that why it upsets me so?" He looked up with wide, liquid eyes toward Jaime. "You . . . you were his friend, weren't you . . . as your father's son . . . what did you . . . ?"

Jaime spoke to the girl: "I think we'd better help him get upstairs; it isn't good for him to stay down here . . ."

"No, leave him alone . . ."

"Yes, yes . . . leave me alone for a minute . . . I'll be all right," Gil said. There were tears in his eyes and a look of utter confusion on his face. "I don't know why . . . I really didn't care for him at all . . . you've seen men die before, haven't you? Does it do this to you to watch it?"

Jaime thought, "I've never seen a man's face at the moment of death before. I've fired artillery into cities miles away, I've heard men die, invisible behind the walls of railroad cars, I've seen figures, no bigger to me than children's puppets, crumple up in the distance, but you can't call that watching a man die. I don't know . . . I haven't had time to think about it. . . ."

"This was the first time," he heard himself saying, adding in a whisper, ". . . so close . . ." Then why were the memories of Oviedo, filled with those impersonal deaths he had just distinguished, so vivid, so terrifying while this death, Pelayo's, moved him not at all?

"You're lying," Gil hissed, suddenly angered. "Don't mock me . . ."

"I'm not mocking you. You can go to the devil."

Mercedes turned on him, her face flushed, moving at the same time protectively toward Gil.

"Don't . . ."

"What's the use . . . ?" Jaime shouted. "Look at him, look at him . . ."

Gil mumbled into his hands; "Venegas . . . yes, Fernán will understand . . ."

Mercedes sat down on the step with Gil and touched his arm, looking up at the same time at Jaime. She seemed to understand them both, had neither anger for Mercader nor disdain for Gil. It was this understanding, this refusal to . . . give in, that infuriated Jaime so.

"Christ," Jaime said and stepped past them on the stairs. "I'm going up to see what's happening . . . I'll find you later. . . ." He started to stammer something else, realized that he was forming an apology and then rushed up the stairs.

"It's all right," he heard her say. "Go . . . I'll look after him. . . ."

As he climbed the stairs, he could look down through a window cut into the stone at each landing and see into the courtyard. It was swarming with people, some helping to clear the debris left by the bombing attack, others carrying boxes about, still others waiting under the arches of the arcades. No one tried to stop him. Below, a thick pall of masonry dust floated in the air, gradually rising with the smoke and heated air from the bonfire.

He thought once, "I should go back . . . what a fool I am to be acting this way. . . ." But even as he thought it, he began to climb more resolutely, until he had reached the tower room, and there was no point in going back before he had had a look. He could not get Pelayo's face out of his mind, but worse still he seemed to see, superimposed over it, a mirror-image of his own face, impassive, motionless. Wasn't it bad enough to feel as he did . . . ? did he have to see it visualized in his flesh, too? But he knew that that image would now take its place beside those of Oviedo, of the Colonel fishing in the woods in the Asturian mountains and all those other images which he could not exorcise and which were unwilling talismans of an even more unwilling guilt. Yet . . . he would ask himself: "Guilt for what . . . ? what in Christ's name have *I* ever done. . . ?"

The tower room was small and empty. A table stood in one corner and a chair lay on the floor, overturned by the blast, one of its legs snapped off.

He crouched before a slit in the stone like a medieval bowman. The sunlight struck the pendant binoculars and sent ripples of light dancing off the walls of the San Servando church a hundred yards away.

Even with his naked eye he could see the tiny figures moving southward across the smoky, dun-colored landscape, from the direction of the Tavera Hospital; they crawled with infuriating slowness, like flies over the wrinkled hide of some great dead and desiccated beast. The rout had begun, and from that moment on everything would move inward upon the Alcázar, not outward from it.

He could see a pillar of smoke rising from beyond a fold in the hills. The San Pedro Monastery, still smoldering.

He put the glasses to his eyes. The binoculars gave him a sense of reassurance; he was able now to relate objects hitherto blurred and unreal, not only to each other but to himself as well. He could now at least fix his position in that landscape of unfamiliar, threatening shapes.

He scanned the horizon, searching for the lumpy shadows of armoured cars, for tanks, for the tiny beadwork of dots that signaled the approach of yet another column of troops from Madrid.

The hills in the direction of Illescas and north to Torrijos were smoking as though a fire had only recently blazed across their breast. Ragged, coal-black streamers which Jaime knew were only clouds rode continuously above the plains like an exhalation of the ground itself. The mountain ranges far to the east brooded black and somber, defying approach.

He tried to pick out the ravine where his father's house lay, but the whole area was blanketed by a thick pall of smoke. The house itself, which he had expected to be able to see, which, in fact, he was afraid he would see, was hidden behind a rise in the land and further screened by the impenetrable smoke.

From the plain beyond came the faint ping of rifle fire and now and then the rumble of artillery. Jaime wondered how far off the heavy pieces were and whether they were converging on Toledo or perhaps were headed elsewhere.

He looked down toward the terrace. It was pitted with dozens of holes full of shadow, like tiny cups, running the full length of the esplanade . . . teethmarks left by rifle- and machine-gun fire . . . clear even from that height.

In the distance he could see where barricades had been thrown up, looking like smashed buildings which had collapsed full length into the streets.

He could see into the Zoco and also part of the way down the Cuesta de las Armas. That curious foreshortening that always occurs when distant objects on a plane are seen through field glasses amplified his sense of unreality. Everything seemed disconnected. Sights, sounds, even smells. Where the odor of cordite, burning rubber, and gunpowder should have been, there was only the delicate scent of thyme from the hills and the fresh damp smell of the river.

He could not help himself; he turned the binoculars again toward the northern plains.

"Christ, how different it all is from . . . home," he thought. The hills before him did not even share with the Moroccan mountains the same range of earth colors. Here, everything was raw and red, like hacked flesh. In Morocco, he had always felt the comforting presence of the sea, felt time suspended over everything. Here all was harsh, forbidding, insistent. Things happened, demands were made. Men had no choice. Even the few trees he could see seemed to rise up from the stony soil more in protest than in natural growth. Towns erupted occasionally on the crests of low hills along broken-backed roads, all white as bones and sucked dry of any life.

"Gabriel . . . ," he said aloud . . . his great-grandfather, the first of the Mercaders to contract that dread infection *Morocco* . . . "Gabriel . . . the fool, the saint . . ." and he could see him there before him on the plain, his reeking musket over his shoulder, head bent under the wind-whipped red banners of the Pretender Don Carlos, the red mark of Cain of all Spain. "There was a picture done by a gypsy in Cádiz, a drawing on yellow paper. . . ." He remembered it from an album in his father's study . . . crumbling, the ink turning dust brown. . . . "A huge man with a head like an iron stove," and his eyes full of shame, fixed on the paper in a moment of glaring rage. "Vergara . . . the battle at Vergara," which drove him from the land. Gabriel had been able to accept it all but when the generals embraced in the midst of a field planted with the corpses of his friends, his great-grandfather could no longer stand it and he ran . . .

"So . . . the Mercaders have learned to live with defeat, but not with reconciliation. . . ." The stain in his blood that made him search so hard for a way to forgive and at the same time precluded his ever finding it. . . . How far back it went, to the day Gabriel Mercader fled the land itself, crossed the straits pursued by those Eumenides' voices, cursing the land and the lies, and shaking his fists at Algeciras while the spray foamed in his beard and the seeds of his bitter loneliness took unseen root. A bleached coastline, a white house, a wife, a child, chaining him to the white earth and Ceuta.

Now, against the bleached plain below, Jaime could see his grandfather Narcisco, growing wild while his father, Gabriel, brooded, his eyes on the invisible orange groves of Valencia, peered at the cicatrix of his own soul. Narcisco, not a gypsy's dim ink-faded drawing but a real face in a photograph, the face the same as Jaime's when he was a child, strange because there was no Berber blood in Narcisco. But their eyes were identical and the hook of their noses almost the same. Jaime thought of his own father, and of how he would have felt . . . if Narcisco had gone, as Gabriel had gone, storming off into the Riff, in search of some private vengeance, his rifle on his shoulder and a scrap of red cloth dangling from the barrel . . . never to return.

He thought, looking at the Sierra de Gredos, but seeing instead the Riff mountains with their white escarpments and heraldry of flying opal clouds, ". . . the mountains will eat us all alive . . . and the cities are mountains too, of men." Narcisco had hated the mountains as fiercely as Jaime loved them. He had blamed the land for the absurdities men perpetrated on its crust. Francisco had told how his father had taken his moment of vengeance when General O'Donnell had swarmed ashore from Spain with troop and neighing horses . . . vengeance for having been left alone, fatherless, for having been cheated by those mountains of the man he feared and loved. Of how that vengeance had led him to a cot in a hospital in Melilla, betrayed in the end by General O'Donnell's dreams and taught a lesson in reality by the sultan at the battle of Tetuán. Had he even known what had happened? A stretcher, borne from the field, a rolling, pitching boat carrying him grudgingly back to the arid land his father had fled . . . months in another hospital. A memory of alcohol and pus. Crutches . . . he had taken to the road . . . Jaime remembered his father's words, "Better to die on the road than in that pesthole." . . . And Narcisco had hobbled across the prostrate body of Spain, north to south, east to west, from job to job, until he had come to Barcelona. Marred, shrunken into himself, guarding his limp as a prize, the knife scar on his hip an emblem. A shopkeeper, tending accounts, his only concession to his history a fondness for iron objects . . . Francisco remembered that, spoke of it even now with a faint quiver as though he were about to cross himself . . . "iron objects with points, hooks, gaffs, pokers with spears like lances, hanging from the walls of the shop . . . oh, yes, I can see it very clearly . . . spikes and edges . . . like a medieval armory." How they would have loved each other, Jaime thought, he and that tortured and desperate man, his grandfather, but they had never known one another. "We could have comforted each other in this damned ignorance. . . ." The infant Francisco squalling in the upstairs room over the shop, above the raised pikes and ax heads. Narcisco brooded. Narcisco made bombs. At night, so the stories went, Narcisco would disappear into the coal-dusted, smoky streets. Barcelona heaved and gasped, trying to expel its poisons. Blood in the streets, and that blood awakening dim memories of Melilla and Tetuán. . . . Francisco had told him how his father had grown dark with the blood, "like a slug, before God . . . it was like watching a slug suck it all in. . . ." Francisco would shake his head: "In the end no one knew . . . I never knew and perhaps my mother did, but she wouldn't say. It might have been one of his own bombs that killed him. But he had a talent for vanishing, just like his father. He'd leave us alone for weeks at a time, and no one knew where he was off to . . . some say that he died in prison. It was after that that my mother packed up and came back to the land. . . ." He always called Morocco . . . "the land" . . . as though it had some mystical significance that he dared not even try to explain. "She sold all of those thorny implements of his as fast as she could and took me back to Tetuán. We had a shop there . . . you remember, where the two blue mosques are? I took you there when you were seven, don't you remember?" And, recalling the words, Jaime recalled, too, the smell of cork, hemp, hot stone and dust and heat, and saw the pools of violet shade and felt the constant breezes from the nearby sea. He remembered the loft . . . Francisco had pointed it out to him, taken him up there, and they had sat in the swollen heat for a while. It was there that Jaime had been conceived during the siege of the city. Jugs of cool water, dates and oils, cheeses, all of it. Time . . . weeks . . .

Nothing cool anymore. He looked up, shaking away the memory of that airless room. Heat was heat; the heat was his link. He looked out of the window again. The remembered heat of Tetuán from the fire trapped on the flanks of the Castillian hills. Heat, heat, and more heat. The Riffs, he remembered, would gently cut open a man's belly and place hot coals in his stomach and then sew him up again. It took hours to die that way. The flesh of Spain, he thought, held that same ravaging fire.

Jaime brought the glasses up to his eyes and turned the focusing screw furiously. The peaks swam closer and the face vanished. Only clouds. When he looked down along the plains, he could see an eruption of dots . . . men, trucks, moving in toward Toledo.

He thought that he would probably kill some of those dots or be killed by them and that it was absurd because he did not know them, nor did they know him and yet, without knowing why, they would kill each other.

A burst of rifle fire sent dust spurting from the walls and the street. The sound ripped through the membrane of his imaginings. He blinked, dropped the binoculars on their strap, and they slammed against his chest.

He knew he would have to go back down, find the girl and find something to say to her. A fear had begun to grow in him, a fear that he would never escape the fortress, that every rifle shot that fell from the walls below was a rivet fastening him more firmly to the Alcázar. He could see the old Ford, its hood smashed in by bullets, not too far away on the esplanade. Possibly he might reach it at night . . . but there was the fear again. Did he want to reach it? Would he be any better off out there or would it simply be a mirror-image of his present predicament?

A dot moving slowly, drifting through the shimmering sky to the north, caught his eye. He lifted the glass, trying to bring it into focus. The shape grew more distinct, a bird, gliding high, its wings perfectly still. Then, as it grew larger, blacker against the reticle pattern of the binoculars, he saw that it was no bird at all but an aircraft, its wings loaded with bombs, coming in from Madrid.

The tower was no place to be if the plane dropped more bombs. Nor the courtyard where the girl might be waiting . . .

As the sound of the motors reached him across the plains from Illescas, he dropped the glasses again and left the room.

BOOK THREE /

Mad Horse,

Wild Horse

JULY 21, 5:00 P.M.: *Toledo*

As THE LATE AFTERNOON SHADOWS thickened in the alleyways, Civil
Guard patrols spread quietly through the city, seeking hostages. Birds
winged up from the cobblestones, frightened by the sound of boots on
the stones, as though they understood the meaning of the footsteps. No
one else had noticed, so silently and quickly did the Guards move.

"Get it open. Kick the damned thing in if you have to," Infante Delgado whispered.

Barrera, standing behind them, nodded, then threw his weight
against the door. Delgado grinned; he was twice as heavy as his cousin.
Barrera, his shoulder painfully bruised by the impact, paused to catch his
breath, thought fleetingly of what Peralta would say if he could have seen
them at that moment.

The door groaned and opened. The three men went quickly into an
empty hallway which smelled of rancid oil and sweat. Sheets of brittle
newspaper lifted from the stairway on the sudden draft. The interior of
the building was dark; the shutters had been drawn to guard against the
afternoon sun.

The other Guard, a private named Torres, hesitated, as though the
revolver in his hand had suddenly become too heavy for him.

"Upstairs . . . it should be the first landing," Delgado said. "Look
for the name on the door . . . César Roig. . . ."

The guards went up the stairs with pistols held out like divining
rods. There was a clatter just past the landing. Barrera remained below,
watching the front door. He did not want to be there when they broke
in, and if the guards shot the man, Roig, he did not want to witness it.

Anton Vitolyn had just placed the passport and wallet of César Roig
in his own jacket pocket when he first became aware of noises in the
stairwell. He paid no attention; no one, as far as he knew, had any idea
that there was such a man as Anton Vitolyn in Toledo.

It was surprising how much like Roig he looked, particularly with
the dead man's eyeglasses on his nose and his hair parted in the middle
and brushed to either side just the way Roig's hair had been combed. A
change of clothes and glasses, and the transformation was complete.

He regarded himself contentedly in the mirror. For a second his face
assumed the same expression of apprehensive curiosity that Roig had
worn at the moment Vitolyn had reached into his pocket for his pistol.

As the noises continued downstairs, Vitolyn moved quickly about
the cluttered room, cramming his pockets with anything he could find
that might serve to confirm his new identity—jewelry, photographs,

scraps of paper of any kind. As he looted the drawers, rifled the pockets of the clothing hanging on the back of the chair near the window, he wondered what it was that Roig did and why he had found no clue at all to the man's occupation. One would have expected some kind of commercial cards, perhaps a sample case or a brochure or at least a few price lists, old bus tickets or a notebook. It didn't matter; he would make something up. He glanced at his watch. He had exactly a half hour to get to the bus stop outside the city gate. The fighting had died down, and now all of the trouble seemed to be centered on the Alcázar. Just as well. That would leave the north side of the city quiet and unguarded. All the troops that had come in that morning were concentrated near the Zocodover, firing away at the fortress from behind barricades of old beds and torn-up paving.

He glanced for a second at the still open closet into which he had jammed the body. Roig, his eyes wide open, the small hole between them hardly bloody yet, seemed to be protesting the theft of his glasses which now perched unsteadily on the bridge of Vitolyn's nose. Through the glasses, the shadowed sun-hazy room seemed blurred and unreal, but Vitolyn could see well enough to distinguish objects and distances and to move about without fear of collision.

"But what does he do for a living . . . ? It's weird, absolutely weird. A salesman, or . . . what? A good suit, shabby but well-made. And why did he pick this place to stay . . . a filthy hole . . . ?"

Before closing the closet door, Vitolyn bent over and removed Roig's wristwatch. The inside of the band had been inscribed with a short personal message: "Eternal love, Consuelo . . ." He slipped the watch on at once, shoving his own watch down into his inside jacket pocket where he had put Roig's papers. Next to the passport and the wallet was a fat envelope into which he had crammed a fortune in high-denomination schilling notes. The tin box was still under his mattress in Florez's house, empty.

The closet door was still open a crack, and he could see Roig's face. He could not keep from looking back, yet when he did so, he was unmoved. He felt no revulsion, no guilt. The man was dead but it made no difference that he, Anton Vitolyn, had killed him. Would it have made a difference if it had been someone he knew? It would have been comforting to think so, but he knew it was not true. It would have been the same whether it had been Stoplinsky, whom he had admired, Zipser whom, in his way, he had loved, or Baumgartner whom he had hated. He shivered at the thought.

He had never killed before, except in his dreams and then had always awakened just at the moment of death. His refusal to kill Stoplinsky had, after all, been the cause of all his difficulties, but now he felt none of the violent emotions he had always expected. Perhaps it was because Roig had died so easily . . . a single shot, no louder than a popping cork, directly between the eyes. A slump, a look of surprise, almost of chagrin, nothing more, not even blood until minutes later. The fact was that he had killed without compunction and now felt nothing. Had he been wrong then to have refused Baumgartner? Had he betrayed himself in the end and was all his suffering the result of a mistaken belief? He knew that he must not dwell on it too deeply. In that one question was the seed of madness.

As the noises downstairs grew disconcertingly louder and nearer, Vitolyn closed the closet door on the corpse and prepared to leave. He patted his pocket where the bus tickets were folded and pushed the eyeglasses up on the bridge of his nose.

His hand was on the knob of the door when Delgado and Torres kicked in the panels, sending Vitolyn sprawling back across the narrow room, his borrowed glasses flying and the gun sliding from his pocket across the floor.

Before he could get to his feet, the Civil Guard had planted one boot on his groping hand and was pointing the nose of a Mauser directly at his heart.

"Surprised, Señor Roig?" Infante asked, smiling a toothy smile.

Above him, Barrera heard a scuffle, muffled cries of protest. He did not look up; the front door was open a crack, a lemon-yellow line of sun running along its right edge. Should he slip out quietly, disappear into the alley? Perhaps Ignacio had some answers, knew what a man should do in such times as these. What business did he have staying in the Alcázar? Damn, Infante . . . if it hadn't been for him, he would have slipped away long ago, but now he couldn't bring himself to leave. "If a man helps to save your life," he thought, "you owe him something, that's certain, but what's the best way to pay off such a debt?" If it hadn't been for Infante, he would probably have been killed that morning in Cartenegra after the stupidity with Jeronimo Modreno, shot in the back of the neck, and shoved into a zinc pit. Hadn't Infante gotten him out of the town, set things up for him to come to Madrid, then to Toledo? "Sure," he thought, "that's all true, but what good does it do Infante for me to get myself killed with him?"

Why then? Was it because the people outside the walls were stronger, that the Alcázar was . . . resisting . . . just as he himself had wanted to resist all his life? How childish, he thought, reproaching himself. Yet, it seemed to be the answer. Resist for the sake of resistance. His whole life had been spent on that.

A loud shuffling of feet on the stairs interrupted his thoughts. He turned, bringing up the pistol Ignacio had given him. He wondered if he would be any good with it; it had been a long time since he had fired a pistol.

The Guards were pushing a small, ugly and emaciated man down the stairs, pistols jammed into his right and left sides. His face was flushed with pain.

"For God's sake!" Vitolyn shouted.

"You people don't believe in God," said Infante. "So don't give me that shit . . ."

"Why are you doing this to me? What do you want?" Vitolyn cried out. Perhaps it would be better to admit having killed Roig if it was Roig they really wanted. He could see himself outside in the alley, up against the wall. Such things happened often now.

"My name is not . . . not . . . Roig . . . I . . . am not César Roig. . . ."

"You're Roig all right," Infante said. "I remember you from the last time you were here. We should have picked up you then. Now you'll wish you'd stayed in Talavera all right. . . ."

"Let's go," Torres said. "Kick him downstairs if he doesn't want to go. . . ."

"Please . . . my name is Anton Vitolyn . . . I'm an Austrian citizen . . . for God's sake, I beg of you . . . ," he reached for his wallet, then stopped short. Torres caught his motion, pulled the passport out of his pocket and grinned.

"Listen to him. That's very funny," he said. "Look at this."

"Believe me, it's not mine," Vitolyn went on, but he was unable to bring himself to speak of the body in the closet.

Infante Delgado glanced at the picture on the passport, then thrust the papers back without a word.

Vitolyn hesitated, licked dry lips. How could he tell them? It would be bad either way, telling them or not.

Barrera nudged the front door open again. The street was clear, and they hurried out.

"One word out of you and your head is all over the street. Come on now, let's run a little," said Torres, ramming his pistol into the man's back. The prisoner wheezed with pain.

"Don't do that . . . please, my back . . ."

"My back," Infante mimicked, laughing. One Civil Guard on each side, Barrera behind, they made their way through the alleys and back streets toward the Cuesta and the Alcázar. The streets steepened, the shadows thinning to needle points. Overhead, the sun still bubbled in a sliver of blue sky.

The towers of the Alcázar appeared over the tiled rooftops. The group turned a corner behind a stable. At the head of the alley, another Guard patrol passed, returning with two bloodied prisoners. Barrera and the other three rounded the stable wall. A curtain of buzzing flies confronted them . . . a huge pile of horse manure by the back door of the stable . . . and the smell of rotting hay. Face down in the manure pile was a corpse in civilian clothes. The back of the man's head had been blown in, and an officer's baton was jammed into his anus. There was blood; it was obvious that it had been done while he was still alive. A suitcase lay broken on the stones at the foot of the heap, clothing flung in all directions. On the pile, some feet away, lay a pair of eyeglasses, taped with adhesive.

The guards stopped for a moment. Barrera covered the prisoner with his Astra, forced him against the wall, hands over his head.

Infante turned the body over with his foot; the officer's baton snapped off.

Barrera saw the man's face, a bloodied hole, open-mouthed, as if caught by surprise in some embarrassing act.

"Christ, that's the Colonel . . . Venegas," Infante said. "Look what the bastards did to him . . . Jesus . . ."

"Ahhh," Torres breathed, feeling it himself.

"We'll do the same to them . . ."

"I know him," Barrera said. "I drove him around a few times, with a woman. He was all right to me. . . ."

Torres crossed himself. "Come on, we've got to let him lie . . ."

"You can't leave him. He'll rot out here before they give him decent burial," Infante protested.

"A lot it matters to him," Torres said.

Barrera thrust the pistol into his belt. He felt, somehow, that the corpse's squinting eyes were accusing him. He knew that they must have knocked the man's glasses off before he was shot.

Barrera bent and pulled the body upright, heaved it around to his back, locking the arms about his neck.

"Sweet mother of God . . . look at him," Infante said, marveling. He hadn't thought Barrera had that kind of strength.

"He was decent to me," Barrera explained. "It's the least I can do."

As Barrera lifted the body, the two guards turned briefly to watch, leaving Vitolyn for the moment unobserved. In those few seconds, he dropped one hand to his chest, slipped the envelope of money out of his pocket and let it fall between his body and the wall. It landed unnoticed in a mound of garbage next to his left leg.

Another patrol passed at the end of the street; one of the men whistled urgently.

"All right, we're coming," Infante said.

JULY 21: *The Alcázar*

"IF YOU DON'T MIND, SEÑOR . . . *por favor,* get your ass inside," the Civil Guard corporal said, giving Vitolyn a shove.

Vitolyn could hear a low murmur coming from the interior of the chamber but saw no light at all as the door was opened.

"Is there any . . . air . . . ?"

"Plenty. Fill your nostrils. A lovely stink, no?"

The door closed behind him.

He rubbed his fingers ruefully in the dark . . . "that swine who knocked me down and stepped on my hand . . ." His mind filled with thoughts: Why had the Guard kidnaped Roig? For what purpose? And what was that about "Talavera"? The Guard had said, . . . "We should have picked you up then. . . ." When was "then"? It began to dawn on Anton Vitolyn that perhaps he had made a terrible mistake, that he had taken on the identity of someone even worse off than he was . . . and now, a prisoner, a hostage. . . . What if one of the other hostages were a friend of Roig's? What if Roig were really someone important? He began to shake. It was one thing to be penned up as a prisoner, quite another to be locked up with one's potential murderers.

How many others were there in that lightless cell? No, not completely lightless. His eyes became used to the dark, little by little. A tiny trickle of sun entered through a crack between the sand bags which had been piled high up over the window near the top of the wall. The light was caught and reflected in a dozen or more pairs of eyes around the edge of the room. The chamber appeared full of monstrous crouching cats. The prisoners' exchanges quickened, grew louder, as the iron bar slid solidly down into the lock-slot on the outside of the door.

"Who is it now?"

"Light a match."

"There are no matches, you fool. They took them away when they threw us in here, don't you remember, or has the heat got you already?"

"Can't someone reach the window? A little light . . ."

"*Cabrónes* . . ."

Vitolyn reached hopefully into his pocket; no one had taken away his matches—he still had a box. Better not to waste any, he thought—but one match, what harm could that do? They might appreciate it; perhaps he could get on their good side. He struck a light. The glow spread about the room. A humped, spindly-legged man rushed over with a candle, thrust the wick into the flame and set the taper on a now visible barrel.

Vitolyn could see that there were twenty or more people in the room, all men, some of them obviously workmen from the arms factory or the steel shops, others dressed a little better in the inevitable black jackets and dark ties, looking for all the world like mourners just returned from some shabby funeral. Vitolyn stared at them, at their seamed, hard faces. How fierce they were, and how much like the faces he remembered from Baumgartner's cellar. He felt at once reassured and terrified.

The hump-backed man lowered himself heavily onto a barreltop, careful not to upset the guttering candle.

He said, in an amiable way: "Who the hell are you?"

Vitolyn pressed against the wall and coughed.

"I know everyone else here, but I don't know you." The hunchback prodded a fiber from between his teeth. "Who are you?"

Vitolyn scarcely had time even to attempt a reply when the door behind him opened abruptly. It was the Guard who had brought him.

"Who's got the matches in here?" the Guard shouted.

The candle continued to sizzle. The hostages remained silent. Only the hiss and pop of hot wax answered the Corporal's question.

"It's dark in the hall outside, and the damned light shows under the door. It's lucky for you I'm the one who saw it, not Augustin." He advanced cautiously into the room, his hand resting on the butt of his Mauser.

"You know you're not supposed to have any candles in here. Are you trying to make trouble for me?" He took out a list from his pocket and held it next to the offending candle and, without taking his eyes entirely off the retreating prisoners, consulted it and then began squinting about the room.

"Give me the matches. Don't make trouble," the Corporal said, as if he knew who the guilty man was.

No one moved. The Corporal looked about unhappily, then glanced at his list again.

"I won't look. Just put them on the floor there. I don't even want to know who's got them . . ."

Still no one moved.

"Damn you all . . . all right, all right . . . if that's the way it's going to be . . . what's the use trying to be decent, if a man gets treated this way?" He looked quickly at the list once more. "You . . . Roig . . . it was you, wasn't it?" he said vengefully.

Vitolyn pretended that he had not heard, hoping that the Guard would not remember his face.

But the Corporal was looking right at him and cried in an offended voice: "You . . . shithead, yes, you. You did it, didn't you? . . . You, Roig, come over here."

Vitolyn did not move. He groped hastily in his pockets for the matches, trying to force them with his fingers up to the top of the pocket and out onto the floor without being seen.

"There's no 'Roig' here," said the hunchback. "You're crazy," and he spit on the floor.

"Go ahead, spit . . . shit on the floor, too, if you want. You'll have to live in it." The Corporal unholstered his revolver and pointed it at Vitolyn. "All right, you . . . come over here. Don't make me . . ."

Vitolyn, helpless, moved forward and stopped a few feet from the gesturing Guard. The others watched from the walls.

"Drop your pants and kick them over here," the Corporal said.

Vitolyn did as he was told.

"The jacket next, and the shirt too . . ."

Someone laughed.

"All of it. Right down to your bare arse. Now kick it over here."

Vitolyn's skin ran with perspiration, from fear as much as from heat. He shivered, the hair on his body bristling. He could feel dozens of eyes on him and was overcome by an absurd sense of mortification. Now he stood naked; his hands unconsciously dropped to his groin.

The Corporal prodded the clothes one by one, lifting first the jacket, next the shirt, shaking them out over the stones. The two boxes of matches fell from the trouser pocket and clicked on the floor. The Corporal picked them up and kicked the clothes back toward the prisoner. "Now blow out the candle."

Vitolyn again did as he was told.

The Corporal backed to the door. "It's a good thing for you I'm a charitable man. All I care about is the matches, so I'm going to leave you alone." He closed the door. The throw of the outside latch sounded like a hammer stroke.

Vitolyn, still naked, stood in the center of the circle, near the dead candle and the barrel. He bent to fetch his clothes but stopped short. The hunchback again . . . whistling. Vitolyn realized that the whistle was coming with his breath, asthmatically, not through his teeth.

"You're not Roig . . . why did he call you Roig?"

"It's a mistake . . . ," Vitolyn began. "Really . . ."

"They don't make mistakes like that."

"Ah . . . but . . . ," Vitolyn stammered, trying to think of an explanation. Before he could say anything more, a harsh voice interrupted him from only a few feet away. Someone down on his knees. "Here, Paco . . . these fell out. Take a look."

Vitolyn saw with horror that the crouching man was handing up the packet of identification papers. It was all happening, just as he had imagined it minutes earlier.

"Somebody get me up to the slit so I can see," Paco said.

A man moved to the wall, and the hunchback was hoisted to his shoulders. When he had been lowered again to the floor, he said in a loud voice, "This bastard has César's papers. What do you think of that?"

Vitolyn tried again to retrieve the remainder of his clothing, but someone he could not see reached out and snatched the shirt and trousers away. All he had left were his shoes and socks which he had not taken off. Standing there naked, he felt not only desperately afraid, but utterly foolish as well.

"Where did you get these?" the hunchback said. "You better tell us . . ."

Vitolyn backed toward the door. It was hopeless to try to explain; it had been hopeless with Baumgartner.

"Where?" screamed the hunchback. "Where, you pig?"

The door felt cold against Vitolyn's back, the iron strappings, like pikes, jammed into his spine. A dozen men began shuffling across the room toward him. Vitolyn had seen this sort of thing often enough in Austria to know what the outcome would be. Hadn't Baumgartner himself, an educated man of high principle, almost shot him down once right in the cellar? These men, he knew, would not even listen to the few words Baumgartner had allowed him. All the hopes he had built up in the past few days disappeared. The hostages closed in on him, pinning him bodily against the door. Hands pulled at him, fists pummeled the side of his head.

He felt blood in his mouth and the breath of twenty men on him, but could barely hear their shouting. He sucked air into his lungs as he slid down to the floor along the door, the iron strappings ripping the skin from his back in long strips. He screamed as loudly as he could. A hand clamped down over his mouth; he sank his teeth into the fingers and screamed again.

Someone was kicking at his legs, just below the knee. A shoe crunched down on the toes of his right foot and fists thudded against his ribs. His head was under someone's arm; he could no longer see anything, could hear only the sound of blows against his own flesh and bone. Then, over the grunting and the disembodied sound of his own scream-ing came a gabble of excited voices.

He felt the door again press inward behind him, this time blocked by the weight of his own body, heard shouting out in the hallway and the sound of boot-soles slamming the stone corridors. Something struck the door behind him and it was forced inward.

A square of light fell into the room and a pistol shot cracked across the ceiling. The sudden smell of powder in his nostrils told him—though he still could not see—that the shot had only narrowly missed his own head.

Vitolyn opened his eyes and wiped the blood from his lips. Two Civil Guard were standing in the doorway. The hostages had retreated immediately to the far walls at the sound of the shot and waited against the sandbags and barrels. Only Vitolyn, naked, his feet tangled in his clothing, remained in the center of the room, quite alone. His back pained him terribly and the side of his face felt as though the cheek bones had been broken.

"God's teeth, look at this," one of the Guards said, flashing a search light.

The Corporal who had come in before appraised the scene. "It's the one with the matches," he commented. "What a mess . . ."

"You'd better take him out of there, that's clear enough," the other Guard said, "or we'll have a corpse on our hands by nightfall."

Vitolyn did not move until the Corporal pointed his pistol at him. "Come on, out you go again, and take your clothes with you . . ."

". . . put them on first. You don't want the women seeing something like *that,* do you?"

Vitolyn pulled on his trousers and put on his jacket, stuffing his shirt into the jacket pocket; it hung out like a tail.

The Corporal turned to the men waiting by the wall. "What was it all about? Somebody better tell me. For Christ's sake . . . do you all want to get shot?" He turned abruptly on Vitolyn as though he had caused it all. "You, again . . . it was you, wasn't it? You can't leave things alone, can you . . . ?"

The other Guard waved his pistol at the hostages, and they pressed still farther back.

"You'd better take him to the Major," the Guard said.

The Corporal snapped back, "I know what to do, don't tell me. I'm in charge here . . . ," and then to Vitolyn, "you heard me, come on now, before I change my mind and leave you here. . . ."

"What . . . are you going to . . . ?"

"Never mind, just get moving."

Vitolyn blinked in the half-light of the corridor. The sun, setting over the cathedral spire, had turned the sky to a heavy, medicinal red, and the light that filled the arched corridor seemed to him simply a visualization of the blood that filled his mouth. Though the sky still bore testimony to the ever-present heat, he seemed to feel a chill sweep through his body. Once again he was walking down a corridor flanked by guards, now trapped between the equally disastrous consequences of admitting how he had come by Roig's papers and of continuing to conceal it.

"If you cause any more trouble, I'll personally see to it that they shoot you," the Corporal said and then in a more confidential tone, "The Major's a good man. You just tell him the truth, and you don't have a thing to worry about. Maybe you'll tell me, why did they beat you up like that?"

Vitolyn put his hand to his mouth and took it away, full of blood. He shook it off against the wall, and the red droplets stood out dark against the white stucco.

"All right . . . you'll have enough time to talk . . ." He prodded Vitolyn in the ribs with the muzzle of his Mauser, annoyed that the man wouldn't tell him what it was all about. He felt like a fool; something was going on, and it didn't seem right that he should not know what it was.

As they moved off down the corridor, Vitolyn's trousers began to slip and in a second they were down around his knees. He tripped and went tumbling forward onto the stones.

The other Guard laughed and prodded him in the buttocks with his foot.

"None of that, Miguel," the Corporal said, helping Vitolyn up, "none of that around here . . ." Then he whispered angrily to Vitolyn, "Once more, and I'll kick your ass all the way to the Major's office, do you understand? Now get moving . . . Are you trying to make a fool out of me . . . ?"

JULY 21: *The Pyrenees*

THERE WAS NO POINT IN TRYING to get over the frontier in the north. The rebels were in control of everything but a long, narrow wedge of territory shaped like a croissant and stretching from Vivero on the west to

Hendaye on the French border. The only way to reach Toledo from Biarritz would be to drive along the western flank of the Pyrenees, perhaps even as far as Andorra, and try to make a crossing somewhere east of Gerona.

The villages through which they passed were tranquil and neat, inhabited mostly by pipe-smoking old men and cows who paraded each morning through the streets making a tremendous clatter with their hollow bells. An occasional gendarme could be seen lazing at the roadside guard-box, reading a newspaper and nibbling at a loaf of bread or a chocolate bar. Bottles of wine and beer were in plentiful supply. The color of the wine itself pleased Colonel Carvalho, and on their frequent stops he would hold the bottles up to the window and let the tinted light fall on the tablecloth or the wall of the inn. The colors always seemed gentle, muted, as though Spanish wine were blood but French wine . . . only wine after all.

The roads were no better than they should have been. Few people drove in that area, and one could continue on for hours and never see another car. As they left the Basse-Pyrenees and entered the higher, rougher southeastern region, villagers who had heard the sound of the car motor in the distance would come out and stand by the side of the road to watch them go by. But they did not smile. Rather, they stood silently and watched with ill-concealed envy. Some even shook their fists. Colonel Carvalho thought it an odd thing for them to do, as though anger were the exclusive prerogative of the Spanish nation.

Camille Lachine had become the reluctant navigator, his tools a piece of cardboard, a Michelin road map, and a child's compass purchased in Cauterets; the compass had a red needle, which for some reason annoyed him. "Compass needles should be black or silver . . ." From time to time he would protest and threaten to take over the driving instead. Colonel Carvalho insisted that he remain "navigator": "Because you know the roads, Camille, that's why." He was unable to understand why Lachine found it so difficult to cooperate. After all, wasn't he, a full Colonel in the Spanish Army, acting the role of chauffeur without complaint? The real reason for the Frenchman's distemper was so obvious. Since they had left Biarritz, the Colonel had more or less naturally assumed command of the party, distributing tasks, giving directions. Lachine's immediate usefulness had ended once he had secured from Monsieur Garnier the forged passports for Emilio Portillo and for the Colonel, and he knew it. He was just a passenger until they reached Spain. The Colonel understood that it was dangerous to allow Lachine to smolder so, that he would sooner or later have to rely on his good offices but, nevertheless, he could not help but relish the Frenchman's discomfort and be amused by the waspish ways in which he manifested his annoyance.

Emilio Portillo slept in the back seat, snoring now and then in a resonant bass, waking up every hour or so to inquire as to their position and to smoke another of the Cuban cigars the Colonel had given him at Biarritz. Carvalho was more than ever convinced that if anything had

brought about the Republic's present plight it had been too much attention to the import of Cuban cigars and not enough to controlling people's emotions.

"Why can't we try to cross at Arinsal? The way you're driving, we'll
be all the way to Port Bou before you make up your mind," Lachine
complained. This remark set off another argument. It was plain from
what they had heard on the radio in the French village inns and from
what little they had been able to gather from the newspapers en route
that the military situation in Spain was changing rapidly and constantly.
The rebel forces had already taken Huesca, and only God knew where
they would be in twenty-four hours' time. They were moving too fast for
anyone to take chances. Town after town was falling to its Civil Guard
garrison or to the trickery of a few army officers. Even Oviedo, of all
places, was in rebel hands, the sole island of military dominance in the
northern "croissant."

"If you're that anxious to get yourself shot . . ."

"It would be worse than that," Lachine said, "a lot worse. You don't
even understand your own people, do you? '*Viva Criste el Rey,*' they'll
shout, and then they'll crucify you with real nails. All right, drive on. Do
it your way. You're probably right . . ."

"I'm glad that you're listening to reason," Colonel Carvalho said.
"Now . . . how far are we from St. Girons?"

Lachine looked at his map, then at his fingers. A cousin of his had
been an observer with Budënny's cavalry in 1920 and had fallen into the
hands of Baron Wrangel's army; he knew what "White" officers were capable of, and he had no doubt that the Spanish variety was every bit as
brutal as their Russian counterparts. Or even more so because of their
Latin temperament and their peculiar mystique about death: "All that
coagulated blood on the plaster Jesuses . . . it makes you gag."

Another thing that annoyed Lachine was Carvalho's habit of driving
with the window open. But the feeling of the wind in his beard reminded the Colonel of the days he had led his cavalry units pell-mell
across the Moroccan desert in pursuit of the Beni Bou-Ilfrur or El Raisuni. He knew it was foolish to allow himself such vanity, but there was
more to it than that: it helped him forget how complicated things had
become and how difficult it was not only to know right from wrong but
to have even a vague idea of the direction in which one should start looking for answers. The oddest thing was that at times he felt himself transformed into his son, Raúl, though he knew perfectly well that Raúl
would never have behaved as he was behaving, that Raúl unfortunately
had neither the strength of will nor even the desire to undertake decisive
actions, however ill-advised.

Nevertheless he felt, at times, what was almost a transmigration of
souls, as though he were offering his body to his son in penance for having ruined the boy's promising career. "It wasn't my fault, but . . .
nevertheless . . ."

The wind rushing about the inside of the car seemed not to bother

Emilio Portillo at all. He slept on, storing strength within his massive body.

They passed through fertile valleys, tinted in a dozen shades of green, and just now were passing from the promise of spring to the oppressive fulfillment of mid-summer. Chestnut and oak trees rose in thick stands between outcroppings of brown rock. The mountains, vast in the purple distance, breathed a deceptive peace and reassurance over everything. The road passed through valleys heavy with cherry trees, their scent making the air almost unbreathable with its sweetness. Arched stone bridges that vaulted effortlessly over foaming cataracts carried them farther and farther into the mountains. Carvalho, giddy from the lush greenery, could hardly believe that they were headed for Puigcerdá and the barren country between Lérida and Castellón.

They turned south into the broad valley of the Cerdagne and passed for a time along the banks of the Ariège.

By the time they stopped again to eat, it was mid-afternoon and Portillo had awakened. Like the great bear he so resembled, he was complaining of an enormous hunger. It was the first indication of really human reactions in the man Carvalho had yet noted, apart from his craving for cigars. At lunch, the Colonel ate almost as much as Emilio Portillo; both of them were amazed at the rejuvenation of the Colonel's appetite and scornful of the way Lachine pecked nervously at his food.

The proprietor brought them a copy of the only available newspaper, *Le Matin,* a daily from Toulouse. The headlines were taken up by an account of a croupier at the casino who had committed suicide by jumping from a balcony right onto a roulette table at the height of the evening's games; he had been caught by the management embezzling a small sum from each evening's house winnings. Beneath his picture was another story, this one concerning a woman who had murdered her six-month-old son and tried to dispose of the body by flushing the parts down the lavatory drain.

Colonel Carvalho angrily turned back the first page. There, next to an advertisement for a Czech traveling circus, was a column headed by boldface type; a few words struck him with the force of a blow: *Huesca, Jaca . . . Madrid.* But he could not read French well enough.

"Here . . . what does it say?" He thrust the paper across the table at Lachine. The Frenchman smiled thinly at this tiny triumph and began to scan the column.

"Read it, at once . . ."

Lachine looked up and stared at the Colonel, then nodded with mock obsequiousness. "The situation at a glance is this," he read. "In Madrid, all resistance at the Montaña barracks has come to an end, and it is reported that General Fanjul has been incarcerated in the Modelo prison. Also, attempted risings at Getafe and Carabanchel have been suppressed by loyal officers together with units of militia. In Barcelona the Civil Guard has joined forces with Anarchist militiamen and units of the *mozos de escuadra,* the special police of the Catalan Generalitat, and have thus far succeeded in storming the Atanzares barracks and holding the city for the Government. Our correspondent, M. Juyel, reports that a declaration of Catalan independence, as in 1934, is expected momentarily. Elsewhere . . . ," Lachine paused and his forehead became a sea of wrinkles. ". . . elsewhere," he said again, ". . . the military insurgents . . ."

"Go on," Colonel Carvalho said impatiently. "What is it . . . elsewhere?"

"The following are reported to be in the hands of rebel units: Sevilla, La Coruña, Oviedo, Granada, Cádiz, and Córdoba. In the north all major cities appear to be under the control of the military, from Vitoria, Burgos, and Pamplona to Zaragoza and Huesca. Teruel and Jaca have fallen without resistance." At this, Lachine crumpled the page angrily in his fist and hurled it to the floor.

"So, I'm not such a fool after all, am I?" was all Colonel Carvalho said. He gazed triumphantly at the crumpled wad of newsprint.

Portillo asked slowly; "Is there anything there about help? Are the French going to do anything at all?"

Lachine shook his head. "Nothing yet, and I assure you, there will be nothing. They'll pretend that none of this is happening, and when someone asks them to help, they'll deny they know anything about it. That's Blum for you. Oh, he'll make a gesture or two, but in the end he'll let himself be talked out of it by the English . . ."

The way Lachine used words like *they* and *we* amazed Carvalho. He never quite understood whom it was Lachine was identifying with at any given moment or why, and by the time he had sorted out what the Frenchman had said, Lachine had inevitably passed onto another topic.

But why couldn't Lachine forget about Léon Blum? It seemed an obsession with him; everything that occurred seemed solely to provide him with an opportunity to complain about the "little Jew" who was "ruining France in the name of Socialism and ruining Socialism in the name of France."

Portillo spooned quantities of spiced sausage and mushrooms into his mouth and remained quiet.

Outside the inn the sunlight tumbled through the leaves of a clump of oak trees, dappling the dirt road along which they had come with cottony yellow spots. A child pedaled by on a yellow bicycle, his hair and skin the color of a gold *duro*. Somewhere a phonograph was playing a tinny *cerdane*, not so passionate as those to be found on the other side of the border, Colonel Carvalho thought, though there was certainly good reason here for a lack of obvious passion: in the village everything was tranquil, golden, and calm. It was so hard to believe that beyond the frontier a nation was about to devour itself. For a fleeting moment, Colonel Carvalho found himself hoping that the army might prove overwhelming, sweeping everything away before it in a few days' time. There would be so much less bloodshed that way, so much less time in which hates could grow.

Outside the inn Lachine stopped for a moment, gazed off into the mountains to the northwest of the Cerdagne valley, and said something which, to Colonel Carvalho, seemed most curious.

"Some day," Lachine breathed, barely audible, "I should like to visit Roncevaux . . ."

As they got into the car again, Colonel Carvalho could not help wondering what the ascetic little Communist could possibly find to stir him in so foolish a legend as that of Roland. Certainly he would never dream of behaving himself in so impractical a way. . . .

Portillo volunteered to drive, and for a while Carvalho took over the map-board and the child's compass while Lachine sorted his papers in the back seat. Perhaps it was true that money would be needed to buy arms. Perhaps France would not help the Republic, as Lachine had warned, and it would be left to those like himself to organize the financing of the resistance. Certainly the Anarchists could not be counted on for anything.

He reflected bitterly on the probable truth of Lachine's predictions and this intensified his growing dislike of the man even more. It was not only that he resented the superiority of the Frenchman's attitude, his almost priestly infallibility, but also that he disliked being in someone else's debt, especially in the debt of a foreigner in his own country, and that was precisely what it would come to, sooner or later.

By mid-afternoon they had arrived in the little town of Bourg-Madame, just across the Sèvre River from Puigcerdá. The bridge over the stream, for that was all it was, was no longer than a carpenter's plank, and it was absurd to think that such a narrow band of water separated peace from war. Once a year the villagers would hold a festival to commemorate the signing of the trans-Pyrenean railway pact in 1904. After singing the *Marseillaise* on one side of the river, they would march across the little bridge into Spain and join in lustily bawling whatever song seemed appropriate to the Spanish authorities at the time.

The Guard Mobile at the border station at which Carvalho halted the car barely glanced at their passports. The man could not believe that they actually wanted to cross and stared at them with an irritating intensity, as though he were studying the faces of a group of would-be suicides. He kept glancing toward Puigcerdá and shrugging his shoulders while he affixed the necessary stamps.

"If you ask me, you're making a mistake, gentlemen . . . of course, I won't do a thing to stop you from going over. But coming back, that's another story. You may find me a different man when you decide you've had enough."

The control station on the Spanish side was deserted. A pile of ashes lay on the ground outside the sentry box, and the banks of the Sèvre River were littered with papers. Carvalho stopped the car abreast of the deserted shed and blew his horn. No one appeared except the Guard Mobile on the other side of the river who walked to the edge of the stream and shouted: "It won't do any good. They're gone for keeps, can't you see . . . ?"

Lachine leaned forward—he was still in the back seat—and urged Carvalho to drive on. The ashes in front of the sentry box were still smoldering. They passed along the road and into the town. All at once, the mountains appeared more forbidding, harsher in their sundering of light and shadow. The stones of the town seemed washed with acid.

There were very few people in the streets of the town. Once the car passed out of sight of the frontier station, the mounds of ashes and the litter they had noticed about the guard's post increased noticeably. Thin trickles of smoke were visible over the rooftops. The air was sharp, even a bit chill and hard to breathe, something Carvalho had not noticed while they were on the French side.

A few people turned to look at the car as it passed. A few carts and many mules, most of them standing about, going nowhere, with mournful expressions on their faces. A smell of rotting vegetables. And above it all, the sharp smell of smoke . . . paper burning.

The town flattened out and the road tipped downward through steep embankments of evergreens and cypress.

"Do·you know," Portillo said, "I didn't see a single uniform on the streets . . ."

"I don't know how good that is," Lachine replied. "I really don't."

Carvalho cast him a glance, then returned his gaze to the rough road that lay before him. Lachine was thinking the same thing. The smoke, the empty frontier station, the absence of any uniforms, even those of the local police, clearly meant that something had happened. It was not simply that the military rising had not reached Puigcerdá but that something else quite specific had occurred.

"Look there, I told you . . . ," Lachine said suddenly.

A hundred yards or more away down the road a group of men were driving an immense herd of cattle toward the town. Some of the animals were trotting on the road; Carvalho blew his horn again.

"No, no . . . don't you see . . . ?"

"I see cows on the road. How the devil are we going to get past?"

Hundreds of cows. The sound of his horn only seemed to draw more of them onto the road. The drovers were carrying shotguns and looked angry, all the more so when the horn honked again.

"You fool . . . ," Lachine whispered.

The cows moved off onto the shoulders of the road, and the car passed slowly through the herd. The drovers made no move to unlimber their shotguns which they carried slung over their shoulders.

"So . . . you see . . . ," Lachine said as they drew away from the fly-swarming mass of animals.

"What do I see?" Portillo asked. "A few cows and a shotgun or two?"

". . . and the ashes . . . the fires . . . the papers burning. You smelled it. That's not our work," Lachine shot back. "Who is it who goes about burning all the land records the first minute they can? Who attacks town halls and registers' offices instead of barracks and police stations? Who are the ones who are addicted to these ridiculous bonfires?"

Even as Lachine was flinging his questions angrily at the roof of the car, Colonel Carvalho was recalling similar scenes in Oviedo, in Casas Viejas, in a hundred places where the Anarchists had tried to destroy everything that stood in the way of man's finding himself. With a mystical fury, they would fling themselves on birth registers, land records, tax rolls, anything that bespoke of property, of the system. Burn the records and you destroy the thing they record. Without deeds there are no landowners. Without marriage registers there is true, free love. In its own way, it made a certain savage sense. They destroyed not through love of destruction but to purify. Carvalho often asked himself, how can you hate men like that? Pity them, yes, but hate them? And then he would stop and ask himself if the priests who had tortured adolescent girls and burned old men at *autos-de-fé* had not been of the same stamp. Where was the real difference? He would be damned if he could see any.

"But there were no banners," Portillo was saying. He and Lachine were deep in argument while Carvalho pursued his reminiscences. "The first thing they do is run up the banners."

"Maybe there's a shortage of cloth here. The Falangists use the same colors, don't they, red and black . . . maybe they've used up all the cloth. How should I know . . . ?"

Colonel Carvalho was hardly listening. The way lay straight ahead of him, the oaks and pine thicker along the steep sides of the road; a donkey stood forlornly chewing on a stand of purple flowers, untended. What had become of the people in the hotel at Puigcerdá, the ones who played on the golf course in their white shirts and trousers? A few birdcages lay in the tall grass, their doors sprung, their occupants fled. That was a bad sign. There had been birdcages on the road into Oviedo, too. Empty birdcages meant only one thing. Would he see eucalyptus trees such as had grown in the garden of the Bishop's Palace, too? No, it was summer; somehow that made a difference. There would be no smell of apples and no wild geese overhead. His hands were trembling slightly on the wheel. Those damned birdcages . . .

"Look, I told you . . . ," Lachine cried in alarm.

The wind was stirring a cyclone of ashes along the road ahead of them which made it hard to see. White scraps of paper whirled like snow. Then the wind blew it all to one side and revealed a roadblock that had been set up a hundred yards or more ahead. Bed frames and wardrobes had been piled on each other, along with old mattresses covered with blue and white ticking. There were at least a dozen men behind the barricade.

"There's your banner for you. Look at the damned fools," Lachine added. And he was right: a red and black flag fluttered from a pole stuck into the barricade.

Two men carrying shotguns stepped out from behind the pile of furniture and waved the car to a halt. Carvalho could not help wondering why they had gone to the trouble of hauling such a collection of junk out of the city . . . why not use trees or a truck set across the road?

The men were wearing bandoleers of ammunition and workmen's caps. All ages were represented: a grizzled old man with a beard like fleece brandished a knobbed club, and a young boy who could not have been over fifteen was shifting a butcher's cleaver from hand to hand.

Without thinking, Carvalho pulled on the brake and got out.

A man wearing a rumpled corduroy jacket, a sweater and a beret dogtrotted over to meet him. He carried a heavy-gauge shotgun which he pointed at the car rather than at its occupants. The man was about fifty, with the sun-seamed face of a shepherd. He seemed pleased with himself. Three others came close behind him, similarly armed. One of them wore a thick woolen scarf around his neck even though the weather was mild.

The man with the shotgun began shouting at them in a dialect that Carvalho at first did not understand. Then he thought, "Catalan . . . ? Why not? Of course. He probably doesn't even speak Spanish?" The idea sent a tremor of anger through his body. If it hadn't been for the Catalan separatists in 1934, and their "President" Companys, the situation wouldn't have been half so bad nor the repression that followed half so severe. Azaña would never have been arrested, and the resentments that followed would never have been so violent. There might even have been a chance for accord after the last elections. But as it was, all the bile that had been collecting for almost two years had broken loose: riot, disorder, murder, looting. And now the uprising, to put an end to that. "But what's the point in aiming a finger and saying, 'You're to blame for it all?' There's always something or someone else just behind the one you blame who's to blame for what the other one does. Things happen, that's all. And one thing leads to another."

The shepherd was still shouting in Catalan, angry that he was not being understood. One of his companions began to speak in Spanish.

"Don't you know that automobiles have been abolished?"

"That's better," Carvalho said. "Speak so we can understand you."

"Don't you know . . . ," the shepherd repeated. So he did speak Spanish after all. Now, he seemed irritated. . . .

"I know that we are on the way to Toledo, and we have important business . . ."

"If you say . . . if you say . . . ," the shepherd answered, stopping a few feet away and shifting his feet in the dirt of the road.

It was an FAI barricade, there was no question about that. The shepherd was eager to explain it all: The Anarchists had taken over the entire town. In fact, the mayor himself had been an Anarchist and no coup had been necessary. A delegation had simply been let into the town hall, and the record-burning had begun without any opposition at all. The mayor, one Pérez Lasauga, who was watching the operation of the barricade from a position in the woods not far off, had even supervised the destruction of the tax rolls himself. Now the shepherd seemed puzzled. People who drove automobiles were automatically suspect. And to top it off, the driver was wearing an army uniform. He consulted quickly with his companions. One of them suggested an immediate execution, but the shepherd, who seemed to be in charge, was not convinced.

Carvalho said: "Not everyone with a uniform on is against you, remember that. What about the Civil Guard in Barcelona? Didn't they stand with you?" The one item in the Toulouse newspaper that had interested him concerned Companys' speech of thanks to the FAI after the military rising in that city had been subdued. Surely these men had heard what had happened.

"I don't know anything about Civil Guard or Barcelona," was the abrupt reply. "This is Puigcerdá."

"Well then, it's time you did hear. Go call up Durruti and ask him, if you don't believe me. Without the Civil Guard they would have been mincemeat, and that's the truth." He pulled the Toulouse newspaper from his pocket and thrust it toward the shepherd who stared uncomprehendingly at the French headlines and shook his head.

The mayor, Pérez Lasauga, a chunky man who walked with a precarious forward thrust, scrambled down the embankment and came over.

"Who are these three?" he demanded.

Lachine and Portillo identified themselves. Portillo's papers were handed back to him at once without comment, but the mayor squinted at Lachine's passport with a great show of concern. "What's this? . . . What's this?"

In a second, Lachine had handed him another set of documents identifying him as an important member of the French Communist party.

"That's all very well, but it doesn't mean anything here," said Pérez Lasauga, handing them back. "All these names . . . who knows whether they're real or not? I could sit down and fill a paper with names too. . . ."

"They're real enough," Lachine said, trying to keep his temper.

The shepherd was staring at Carvalho's papers. "There's something about this . . . ," he kept muttering. Carvalho sensed what was coming and anticipated the man.

"You've heard of my cousin, that's what there is . . . about that . . ."

"Your cousin?"

"Enrique Carvalho," the Colonel went on while Portillo looked on, an appreciative smile crinkling his mouth. "An officer at Oviedo, two years ago. Certainly you remember . . ."

"I had a . . . cousin . . . at Mieres," the shepherd said. "Yes . . . you're right. Your cousin . . ." He rubbed at his chin, as though trying to force something out from under his skin. "Damn it, here. That, for your cousin." And he thrust the papers back into Colonel Carvalho's hands.

"So you're . . . the cousin of the 'butcher,' " Mayor Lasauga said suddenly.

"As you see."

"We should shoot you right now."

"For what? . . . for being born to his mother's sister? You're not that stupid . . ."

The mayor turned away and shook his head. "No, I'm not. But we'll see just how smart you are. . . ."

Lachine looked stricken. Yet what was there to do? Their papers were plain enough. The Anarchists had surrounded the car. One of them had opened the hood and was examining the motor.

"The car belongs to the town of Puigcerdá," the mayor declared abruptly, turning away. "That's all there is to it, and if you don't like it, you can find a ditch to lie down in right now." He signaled to the others. "Put them in the 'birdcage' for a while. We'll see . . ."

"I have important business . . . you've seen my papers . . . ," Lachine protested.

"I don't read French, so what do they mean to me? You're not back on the other side of the Sèvre, just remember that."

"That car belongs to . . ."

"The town of Puigcerdá," the mayor snapped. "Everything belongs to the town, to everybody else. Don't you understand that? Well, I'll give you some time to think about it and be happy we don't shoot you right off. . . ."

Portillo put a restraining hand on Lachine's arm.

The mayor walked back into the forest followed by a group of his lieutenants and a shaggy black dog who had come yapping from out behind the barricades. Butterflies rose in a yellow cloud from the grass.

Portillo, for some reason, was smiling. Perhaps, thought Colonel Carvalho, he's only doing it to make Lachine angry.

The shepherd lowered his shotgun and marched the three of them into the woods. They followed a path through a grove of chestnut trees and then through a stand of sweet-smelling pine that grew so high that they blotted out the sun overhead. Were it not for Mercedes, he would have been content to let things take their course then and there, and if the Anarchists meant to shoot them, as they had no doubt shot the guests at the Puigcerdá Grand Hotel, well then, let them . . . if they were that stupid.

Lachine kept fumbling in his pockets for something. None of them were armed, so Carvalho could not understand what he was doing. Two men with rifles walked along behind them, whistling, while the shepherd walked a little to one side, with his shotgun hanging on its leather strap and looking as though he would much rather have been out hunting partridge.

After a few minutes they came to a small clearing where a high stand of evergreen enclosed a small yellow-walled house and a shed. They were ushered into the shed, once a chicken house, hence the name "birdcage," and the door was closed behind them.

Lachine had found what he was looking for, a wad of French bank notes. Carvalho understood at once what he had in mind.

"Don't you think that's dangerous . . . they don't believe in money, remember?"

"Do you believe in getting killed for nothing? And that's just what they'll do, don't worry," Lachine said. "They don't understand discipline. . . . They're savages, that's all."

The chicken house was rank with droppings and wet straw. One of its tenants was still in residence. Portillo coaxed the old hen over and began to stroke its head.

"You seem remarkably unconcerned," Lachine said, turning on him.

Portillo went on stroking the hen's head and didn't answer.

Lachine's face took on an expression Carvalho had never seen before: a tension bordering on despair. "You don't think that they'll actually shoot us . . . for nothing? Do you? We're on their side, don't they understand that?"

Carvalho shrugged. "I warned you," he said. "Up here they don't understand or care about Communists. You're a Frenchman, that's all, and they don't know who you are or why we were driving in such a fine car. I suppose they've decided that we're tainted, corrupted by it . . ."

"But they'll drive off in it themselves . . . you heard him . . ."

Carvalho allowed himself a short laugh. "That's precisely the joke of it. It's a little like blessing the battle standard, isn't it? The right incantations, and it becomes purified. 'This car belongs to the town of Puigcerdá' and . . . voilá, if you'll excuse me, it becomes a vehicle of the people's wrath rather than . . . if you'll pardon me again . . . a symbol of bourgeois decadence. . . ."

"I don't find that amusing, Enrique . . . ," Lachine said.

Just then the boy who had been playing with the cleaver came to the door of the chicken house and brought in a bottle of beer. He wrinkled his nose at the smell and wrinkled it even more when Lachine exhibited the roll of bank notes. Without a word, the boy slammed the door again.

Carvalho was almost pleased.

A moment later the shepherd reappeared, together with three other men. Lachine was taken, protesting, out of the chicken house and led across the clearing. The sound of argument was plainly audible. Apparently they had all stopped just short of the woods and were talking loudly; a few new voices joined the conversation, among them that of the mayor who had come to see what was happening with his new prisoners.

A moment later, Portillo was led outside and the door shut again. Carvalho remained in the "birdcage" alone, sitting on a pile of straw by the far wall. A small window allowed a shaft of sunlight to enter obliquely. It fell in a square on the floor at his feet. The hen got up and came scrabbling over, set herself down in the patch of warm light and closed her eyes. Carvalho fell to stroking the bird's head while he waited.

The next thing would be the sound of shots, he thought. He could not repress a smile. The Anarchists had been carrying Mausers, no doubt taken from the gun racks at the frontier station. The rifles, however, were of the type that had been made for use in Paraguay, in the "Chaco" war, but never sent. They took 7.4 ammunition and the bandoleers that the Anarchists had been wearing were full of regular 7.0 cartridges. What a surprise they would have some day.

After a while, he looked at his watch. A half hour had passed. Still no shots. The sound of argument had faded off into the woods, and everything was still. He could hear the insects chirping in the trees outside. Tiny ticking noises; fleas leaping about in the straw. One landed on the back of his hand. He brushed it off. It fell on the hen's head, and the bird shook it away. He reached down and petted the hen again, pleased that the two of them had reacted in precisely the same way.

He had never been a religious man; he had been too close to death all his life to believe that corpses would ever be received in heaven. Yet he contemplated the idea of death without resentment. Everything which occurred in life had its foolish side, birth as well as death. It was all a matter of accident. A man could never count on dying without regrets of some sort; his own regret would be that he had not reached his daughter or done something more useful to help her. But in the end, what had he lost? Only the chance to help her stave off death for a few more years. Left her to die in childbirth or in a car accident or some other absurdity.

Everything was so peaceful; he began to doze, was awakened abruptly by the "birdcage" door being flung open. It struck the slated walls with a bang, and his head jerked forward. The sun had shifted position in the sky so that now, as the door was flung open, a flood of sunlight entered the chicken house. Only with difficulty could he make out the three figures in the doorway. It was amazing how his eyes stubbornly refused to focus, how the sudden light had almost blinded him. At that second the thought snapped through his mind: "You are an old man, Enrique. Things aren't as they once were."

He got to his feet, still finding it difficult to see, and convinced that he was going to be taken into the copse and shot. All because of a new automobile . . .

"You see, I told you . . . ," Lachine's voice, very self-satisfied.

Next to Lachine stood Portillo and behind him another man whom Carvalho didn't recognize.

Once he was outside and his eyes had begun to function again, Carvalho stared at the third man, waiting for someone to tell him what was happening. He noticed that the mayor of Puigcerdá and a dozen or more of his "militia" were waiting some twenty yards away.

The newcomer was a thick-set man with a deformed arm that seemed permanently crooked. But his face was open, his eyes bright and precise under a tousled mane of hair. He smiled as Lachine introduced him.

"Comrade Renom . . ."

The tousle-headed man nodded perfunctorily, obviously uneasy at the sight of the Colonel's uniform. "You didn't tell me . . . ," he began.

"I vouch for him," Lachine said quickly. "His son has been very helpful to us in Paris, as I told you . . ."

"Helpful to whom in Paris?" Colonel Carvalho could not help thinking. He knew nothing about Raúl being "helpful" to Lachine in the manner implied by the Frenchman's tone of voice. Sympathetic, a good debating partner, capable of spending long hours over an aperitif, playing devil's advocate on every subject imaginable. But "helpful?" The word had an ominous ring.

"It's lucky," Comrade Renom went on. "For you and for all of us, that you were able to get to me. You should have stopped on the way through the town and gotten a safe-conduct. Everyone is issuing them. They would have respected a safe-conduct. But now . . . I'm afraid, the car is gone. They've already smeared it up with paint and driven it off to the town hall."

"CNT and FAI, in the biggest letters you ever saw, all over that nice polished hood," Portillo volunteered, chewing on a cigar stub. "Well, thanks to this señor, we're at least free to go."

As they walked back across the clearing and entered the line of trees, watched all the while by the shotgun-toting Anarchists, Renom told them how things were; that the Communists were less than a dozen in Puigcerdá and that it was only thanks to the deals made in Barcelona with Durruti that they hadn't been wiped out by the FAI along with the guests at the Puigcerdá Hotel. Six men had been shot down on the golf course on the first day, and the corpses were still there, between the seventh and twelfth holes. But the Anarchists were at least reticent about quarreling openly with Renom's group. It was time for common effort; later, Renom observed, things would have to be sorted out but for the moment, the *mozos de escuadra,* the FAI, and the Communist militia would either have to make common cause or else go down one by one.

"But how are we going to get to Toledo?" Lachine interjected. It was an impossible situation, he went on. Without the car, what would they do? Puigcerdá was not exactly a center of commerce, a crossroads. All he could see was one dirt road heading south—which might end anywhere, he was not sure—and the highroad to Barcelona. He could not even recall having passed a railroad spur.

"I'm not insulted," Renom laughed. They had passed into the woods and were on the path back to the main road, the mayor and his group following resentfully at a distance. "Places such as this are important too. Granted, there's not much in the way of industry here, few people . . . a hotel, a church. That's all. But think of the position the city occupies! If arms are to be brought across . . . why we can outfit all of Cataluña from here, with a little help. . . ."

Lachine disagreed. As they walked, he repeated his dour predictions. France would wring its hands but do nothing. A few rifles, a few volunteers, but nothing more. Just enough to get the Republic in even deeper trouble. "There's nothing like giving a man a rifle with only six cartridges . . ."

There was a battered Chevrolet truck waiting on the road near the barricade.

"I can take you as far as Seo de Urgel," Renom said. He laughed: "There are *two* dozen of us there and we get a little better treatment."

"Do you know," Lachine said to Carvalho, "that they were actually planning on shooting you?"

"I thought they might."

"For being your own cousin . . . ," Portillo added.

Carvalho glanced back over his shoulder at the ragged band of Anarchists who were padding through the forest at the road's edge, headed back to their solitary barricade. He could hear someone singing "*Hijos del Pueblo*," but the man stopped in mid-verse, having lost the tune.

From Seo de Urgel, Renom explained as they climbed aboard the truck, they could get a ride to either Lérida or Barcelona. Barcelona was a better idea as it was safely in the hands of the Generalitat, "Or so we allow them to say," Renom added meaningfully, "and you can get a train from there to Madrid. You shouldn't have too much trouble. If you go to see Draz Oliver in Urgel, he'll stamp your papers with the necessary safe-conducts. From there on it will be easy, at least through Barcelona. Look, I'm sorry about the car, but you see, there is not much I can do about that."

The truck rattled down the road. On either side, in the purple distance, the mountains rose like walls, shutting in the valley. The earth smell was serene, fruitful. The air was full of tiny winged creatures.

Carvalho looked back along the road, just before the truck rounded a bend taking them out of sight of the barricade. The Anarchists were still standing there by the roadside, holding their shotguns. The mayor was up in front, his hands clasped before him as though he were a mourner visiting a cemetery.

"Do you know," Carvalho said, lighting one of his own cigars which Portillo had just handed him, "what offends me most about those people?"

"No . . ."

"They almost make me lose my sense of humor," the Colonel said. "That's what offends me most."

JULY 21: *The Alcázar*

VITOLYN WAS WALKING DOWN a long uneven corridor and at the same time he was standing absolutely still. It was precisely this absolute contradiction that confirmed the reality of the experience. Behind him he sensed the presence of a man whose hair gave off a distinct odor of pomade. Yet he knew that actually the man smelled of soil and had dirt under his fingernails and shreds of mushroom fiber caught in the weave of his jacket.

He knew that his own eyes were closed, and yet it seemed perfectly natural, in fact inevitable, that he should be able to see. Someone was pushing at his back and sniffing intermittently as though he had a bad cold. But he didn't care; the snorting went either with the man with pomade in his hair . . . or was it some kind of oil? . . . a green oil or brilliantine in liquid form that he'd seen in a window full of bottles on the Gran Via . . . or was it the Kohlmarktstrasse? . . . he couldn't recall which . . . either with that man or the one with dirt under his fingernails. It didn't matter. The light was bad but better than one could expect when one's eyes were closed. He had always suspected that it was possible to see through one's own eyelids, and that certain people had secretly developed this trick. He had that feeling about people in hotel lobbies and restaurants especially. Never trust a man who appears to be sleeping; you can't tell what he's up to or what he wants.

There was a silence, too, which was cluttered with the after-echoes of his shoes hitting the stones underfoot hard and making clicking noises with the nails driven into the heels. But while he heard the clicking plainly enough, it seemed to be part of the idea of motion, a product of his walking, which was impossible, as it was perfectly obvious that he was standing still.

Baumgartner was there, rising up behind the table with his broad, flat head and drooping mustaches and his jacket, which he somehow had gotten padded in the shoulders so that he looked as though he were a carpenter's plumb bob stood up on end. Bork and Stillman were there, too. He knew they were hiding from him and that in their own way they were jealous of what he'd done, that it had had, at least, a kind of style that they knew, with their mean, cramped lives, they would never achieve.

He could hear Baumgartner shouting at him.

"Stoplinsky has to go, that's all there is to it. Don't you see?"

"I don't see. And besides, even if I saw, I wouldn't do it. You know he's a friend of mine. Well, not precisely a friend, but . . . damn all of us . . . I do admire the man. . . ."

"So . . . there . . . precisely. Precisely why it has to be you. Don't you see it? A 'friend.' Whatever you want to call it. To get inside his guard. Someone he won't suspect. Admire him? So much the better. We never suspect a man who fawns on us. Disgusting . . ." he licked the ends of his mustache in that annoying way he had. "Already he's suspicious and he sets himself apart. He's a wary one, I'll tell you . . . you're the only one he'll let get near him."

"No . . . I won't do it."

"He's impossibly dangerous to us. You know that."

"But he *believes* . . ."

"But what does he believe *in*? Not the same thing as you and I. Not any more. And what will he do? This is no time to attract attention by rash acts. Caution is the word."

"He burns . . . he's . . . like a flame . . ." What an absurd figure of speech, yet it seemed apt enough at that moment; Stoplinsky himself was absurd, with his pockmarked face, his predilection for old marine pea jackets and knit caps, his fuming meerschaum pipe. Revolution was his oxygen, and without it he would be snuffed out like a flame . . . yes; it was apt after all.

"More like a flame on the end of a fuse, I'd say. Step on him or we all get blown up. Besides, it isn't a matter for decision. The orders are plain enough; there isn't to be any trouble and that's it whether you or I like it or not."

"For fifteen years he's been loyal," Vitolyn protested.

"It's *now* that counts. So, what's your answer . . . ?"

"I won't do it. Get someone else."

"Shithead . . . no . . . there's no point in blaming you." He said it very slowly; "You're afraid, that's all."

They weren't going to catch him so easily, not with something as transparent as that. Let them think what they want and say what they want. He knew the truth of it. "I won't play Trotsky to your Kronstadt . . . if he's wrong, convince him that he's wrong."

"With a bullet, we'll convince him. If not yours, then someone else's. It will be harder for us, but we'll do it all the same."

"Convince him, for God's sake. Talk to him . . ."

Baumgartner cracked his knuckles so loudly that Vitolyn thought he had broken his fingers. "If you feel that way you should have joined a monk's order. . . ."

He could still hear those words, feel the scorn pouring from them; "join an order . . . you're afraid, that's all . . ."

"I don't see what this is for . . . all these questions of yours . . . what right have you got to conduct an inquiry, to frighten me this way? You haven't even got any legal training, not a bit . . ."

That voice didn't belong with the others; whose voice was it? The words were loud, blotting out Baumgartner's voice. It wasn't Bork or Stillman or even Zipser, and the language was wrong, too, even though he'd understood it as quickly and automatically as though it had been German.

He opened his eyes.

His first thought was how amazing it was that he had managed to walk the entire length of the corridor with his eyes closed, and yet not have collided with a wall or so much as stumbled over a loose stone.

He had come to a halt opposite the entrance to a small room that opened just off the corridor. A young man in a filthy uniform leaned against a rifle and watched with listless eyes the back of a larger, older man who was just then coming out of the room, still facing toward it and waving his hands.

It was that man who had been speaking.

"Hold it," the Civil Guard who had accompanied him said. Vitolyn, who had not been moving, angled his head back and for some reason smiled. The Guard's immediate reaction was to scowl and shove Vitolyn in the ribs with the muzzle of his gun. "As though I were a desperate criminal," Vitolyn thought, then realized that in fact he was, that he had killed a man only a few hours before and that the Guard had every reason in the world, if only he had known about it, to be even more careful than he was.

"I demand to know . . . ," the man who had just been leaving went on, addressing himself to the occupants of the room whom Vitolyn could not quite see. "You forget, I have friends. You know of Pascual Soler? Well . . . ask him about me . . . and your foolish questions. Ask Francisco Mercader, ask . . ."

"That's really enough, Señor Gil," came a voice from within the room. "There's no need for this . . . at all . . ."

"Then why . . . ?"

"You've answered our questions, and we're satisfied with your answers. Doesn't that please you?"

At that moment Gil became aware for the first time that there was someone behind him. He turned clumsily, bracing himself against the wall with one arm. There was no equaling the man's expression, Vitolyn thought; surely it was the most desolate, woebegone, and at the same time the most repulsive, look in the world. A look of plain, unashamed fear, precisely what Vitolyn had been trying so unsuccessfully to feel. It did exist after all. "Use that man's face as a mirror; force *your* image to conform. Find your way back to *that* face. Use it as a map. . . ."

Gil began murmuring apologies and moved to get out of Vitolyn's way. The Guard was pushing Vitolyn again, and the soldier by the door shifted his Mauser from one hand to the other. Vitolyn was vaguely aware that his trousers were beginning to slip again.

Gil whispered: ". . . what do they want from *you?*" in such a tone as to sound as though he had known Vitolyn all his life.

"Corporal Moya, do you have someone or not?" came the voice from inside the room. An impatient sound, the tone of a man who wants to get home to his dinner. All his life Vitolyn had prided himself on being able to tell what a man was thinking by the tone of voice he used to say the most commonplace things.

"Moya . . . ," more sharply this time. The Guard pushed with the muzzle of his pistol. Vitolyn saw no need to resist. The only thing that disturbed him was that he felt quite calm. It was wrong, and he knew it. He had become so used to suppressing his own panic that in its absence he had no real idea how to behave.

The room was small, little more than a large closet. One light bulb hung from the ceiling in a frosted green-glass shade. A table and a few cane-back chairs. A crate of papers, files of some sort, lay on the floor. Sandbags were piled waist-high across the window opening, and a blanket was pinned to the upper part of the frame, keeping the light in. Broken glass lay on the floor, and there was a litter of newspaper in one corner and ashes all over the boards.

An officer, a major of about fifty, sat behind the table. He wore a rumpled tunic, a Sam Browne belt, and a huge pistol in a holster made of an old shoe cut and held together by wire. His bored face was creased by a disdainful curiosity. He had a bald head and a straggly "Chinese" goatee, the tip of which he was just then winding about a yellow pencil. An untended cigarette was turning to a long white ash in a dish bordered with blue flowers.

By the window, another officer stood, this one a captain, younger, with the regular, even features of a film actor, small mustache, and large, almost too-large, brown eyes. He was looking over his shoulder at Vitolyn; his body was still turned toward the window, though he could clearly see nothing from it because of the blanket.

"So, so, so . . . ," Vitolyn thought, hesitating at the threshold, "it's the 'set-up' . . . one of them will threaten me, brutalize me, and then the other will intervene, make him stop, be my 'friend' . . . he'll stop the first one from crushing me, and then I'm supposed to confide in him . . . the 'brute' will leave, of course, and then I'll tell the other one what he wants to know . . ." He paused, surveying his position more objectively. "What do they want to know, after all? What possible interest can they have in any of this? It's the old story: fart quietly, and everyone pretends they don't smell a thing, but make a loud noise and they all have to investigate, so no one will think it was them. . . ."

The Guard shoved him again, and Vitolyn stumbled.

He took a few steps forward, put his hands on the back of one of the chairs.

The Major examined him critically. "You can sit down if you like. There's no sense standing. . . ."

"The hostages tried to kill him, and he won't tell us why," Corporal Moya said indignantly.

"I know all about it," the Major replied, reclaiming his cigarette and taking a deep draw. "Captain Escobar gave me a report, though I don't see why we should concern ourselves . . ."

He pushed aside a large green book which lay on the table, the place where he had been reading carefully marked with a folded newspaper: Casteljon's *A Short History of the Peninsular War*. The Major glanced quizzically at Vitolyn again.

"Come now, sit down as I asked you to. I don't like talking to people who are standing over me. . . ." The Major began describing circles in the air with his index finger.

"Thank you . . . you . . . excellency. I'd rather stand." Vitolyn had a dread of being beaten while seated. He had seen Baumgartner do that to a man once; you could not even spare yourself for a second by falling, and you never knew when the blows would land or where. They did it from behind.

"Look here . . . I asked you to sit down. . . ."

"He'll be the one, the 'brute' . . . he's working himself up to it, latching on to little things so that when the time comes, he can make it seem as though it were my own fault that I'm being treated so badly. But

. . . it's frightening . . . he looks so bored. . . ." Pray, let him not brutalize out of sheer boredom. They were the worst, the ones who inflicted
pain without any passion of their own.

The Major turned his head toward his companion: "How many
more after this one . . . ?"

The Captain shrugged and ran his hand across his forehead in a gesture of irritation. "They haven't told me either. We'll sit here all
night. . . ."

That was not meant for Vitolyn, he knew, and he pretended—
circumspectly—not to have heard.

"Look here," the Major said, turning back to Vitolyn. "Didn't I ask
you to sit down? Now, sit down. . . ."

The Guard behind Vitolyn blew his nose loudly.

"Do you understand why you're here? . . . what this is?" the Captain said from the window. It was all beginning to upset Vitolyn.
Both were behaving in too pleasant a fashion. It had him off balance.

Vitolyn shook his head.

"Just a few questions, that's all."

The Major gestured peremptorily with his pencil. "Sit down. . . ."

Vitolyn lowered himself into the chair. He caught a glimpse of his
own face reflected in a patch of glass showing under the blanket . . . a
face caked with blood, covered with scratches and purple bruises. Yet he
hardly felt it. Out of the corner of his eye he could see Corporal Moya
standing in the doorway; he felt better being able to see him.

"Moya . . . get some water if you can find any. Bandages or at least
some cloth so we can clean this man up before he gets infected." He lowered his eyes. "Now . . . no one is going to hurt you if . . ."

"Of course . . . ," Vitolyn thought. "There's always an *if*, and what
will it be this time? What will he ask me to do, and who will I have to
betray to save myself? . . . who, in fact *is* there left for me to betray except . . . myself?"

"Your name?"

Vitolyn drew in a breath. It always began that way. Perfunctory
questions, one after the other, tempo increasing. Age, birthday, place of
birth, and so on and so on. Then, the meaningful questions. He would
refuse. Then, they would begin again, another delicate dance and, finally,
the beatings. He wondered when he would give in?

"Anton Vitolyn," he heard himself say. It made no difference.

"Yes," Punto said, "but that isn't the name on the passport . . .
what was it?" He stirred anxiously in the porridge of papers before him,
found what he was looking for. "Yes . . . this . . . César Roig . . . ," he
held up the passport, a vaguely conciliatory look fluttering across his
face. "Now we know that you're not César Roig . . ."

"I told them that when they kidnaped me. . . ."

"Yes, but they didn't listen. None of these people listen . . . Moya,
didn't I tell you to go and get some water?"

"I can make him talk," Moya volunteered, fingering his belt. "This one, he won't last long. You can tell by looking . . ."

"Moya, get out of here at once," the Captain said.

"Lock him in the closet and forget about him. Two or three days . . ."

"Are they doing this for my benefit?" Vitolyn wondered. "How transparent, if they are . . . if not . . . then . . ."

The Major started to rise angrily behind his table. The Corporal slammed the door.

"Insufferable . . ." the Major muttered to himself and then said to Vitolyn in the same flat, expressionless tone: "Now your nationality . . ."

"Austrian. I told them that too when they . . ."

"Kidnaped you. Yes, I'm sure you did. So . . . ," he wrote something down, pausing to inscribe the initial *A* in a florid hand wholly unlike his usual script. Pleased, he smiled encouragingly. "Now, you will tell me . . . there's no point in wasting time with preliminaries . . . we understand all about that . . . just what was the fighting about. Just why did they want to kill you?"

"I don't know . . . they attacked me, that's all. How should I know why? This city . . . full of madmen. Ever since I came here . . ."

"Yes . . . how would you know? Well then . . . if you're not Roig, then perhaps you can tell me . . . what you were doing in Roig's room when our . . . fishing party . . . threw its line in . . . ?"

"I? . . . his room? . . ."

"Yes, what were you doing there?"

Vitolyn shrank back into his chair, felt an overwhelming urge to urinate. He was positive that the Major had sniffed the truth. But he could not bring himself to confess. What if he were wrong and the Major knew nothing? He was like a man convinced that he has cancer who contemplates suicide before he goes to the doctor to find out whether he is right or not.

"You . . . an Austrian national, in the room of this . . . César Roig who is . . . if you didn't know . . . a courier for the Communists in Talavera . . ."

Vitolyn let out a long breath. In a second it had all become clear. Of course, he should have realized that it was something like that; it had to be. It seemed to him then that he had known it all along, that he had even done it deliberately, picked out a man who had to . . . involve him still further. It was the way things were for Anton Vitolyn. Always.

"What were you doing there . . . ?" the Major insisted.

Vitolyn began to shiver. This bored man was driving him almost mad. It occurred to him that he actually felt better, that he was reacting in the familiar ways. He stared at the Major, scrutinizing him; long ago he had convinced himself that the men who seemed the most considerate were in fact the most dangerous. Better to face an acknowledged sadist than a disinterested, seemingly amiable fellow like this goateed major. From his well of memories, the figure of Inspector Porfyri Petrovich emerged, just as he had first imagined him, genial, grinning. Vitolyn had no desire to play Raskolnikov.

When were they going to start on him? Maybe he had been wrong all along. Maybe it was the Captain who would play the sadist . . . the Major would ply him with questions, get no responses . . . just as it was going now . . . and then he would turn around and say, "Captain, he's all yours. Do what you have to . . ." and then he would leave. There was always that possibility. Nothing was going quite the way it should, and Vitolyn was beginning to be worried.

"You're silent. Does that mean . . . ?"

"It means," Vitolyn said suddenly, "that I am trying to think how I can say this to you so you'll understand it. I said to myself, 'What can I possibly tell this man that he would believe? Certainly not the truth which is too absurd . . .'"

"Let's try the truth first. Then, you can go on to something less fantastic if you like. . . ."

"I could make up any story at all and be just as unable to prove it as I'm unable to prove the truth . . . ," Vitolyn went on, trying to stall while he thought of something.

"If you must invent, please invent a story that at least has the . . . ring of truth . . . something utterly unbelievable. . . . I think I like you, man . . . go ahead . . . why were you there . . . ?"

"Look at the picture in the passport."

"This?" Punto flipped it open. "Yes . . . I see. Are you related?"

"No . . . we simply met . . . fantastic, yes? So . . . you believe that or you don't, what can I say? The resemblance was extraordinary. We both thought so. It was very amusing. So . . . I was traveling to Madrid, on my way to Tetuán for a tractor-parts firm, Hirsch and Felbermayer, of Vienna, number 64 Parkring, that's their address . . . ," he lied, inventing with a flourish, the words tumbling out with remarkable ease.

"Of . . . Vienna . . . yes. Go on." Punto thumbed the photo of Roig.

"It's as simple as that. We got to talking . . . as you see, I speak your language fairly well . . . that's why they have me travel for them here . . . language, that's all . . . no particular knowledge of tractors, I assure you . . . so, we talked. We thought the resemblance was very amusing. . . . He invited me to his apartment for a drink. Perhaps I shouldn't have gone . . . but who would have suspected such a thing? . . . in my country . . ."

"His papers . . . you haven't told me how . . ."

"I'm coming to it . . . in a moment. . . ." He drew himself together. It was a gamble, but he had no other choice. He was aware that he had been licking his lips and crossing and uncrossing his legs. The urge to urinate was becoming an agony.

"So . . . ," he continued, trying to slow himself down a bit, just to sound convincing. "I went with him, for a drink, that was all. It seemed a unique thing, just stumbling across such a man. . . . I mean, one who looks like you so that you could be a brother. I suppose I thought that we'd sit there and find that we had a common ancestor somewhere . . . I suppose. . . . What else can I say? Once we were in his room, having that brandy he'd promised, he attacked me. It's all . . . ," he paused, trying to gauge the effect his words were having and for a second the absolutely blank expressions on the officers' faces almost completely unnerved him, ". . . all so stupid . . . I should never . . . I know . . . but it's clear now where it wasn't before. You say he was a political person? A Communist? Well then, isn't it obvious? *He* wanted *my* papers. He must have known that someone was after him, and he thought he could get away if he took my papers. I must have been heaven-sent. . . ." He paused and laughed, "Yes, absolutely heaven-sent for him. . . . Well, it didn't turn out that way. He came at me, but I struck him with a lamp and . . . and . . . ," he paused, his gaze flickering back and forth over the officers' faces, still trying to gauge the effect. "I think I killed him . . . it all was a muddle, and I was terribly frightened, you understand . . . I tried to take my papers back from him and . . . I took his instead . . . I would have noticed but it was just then that your policemen broke in on me . . . I was frightened, you understand, I thought, 'They know I've killed a man, and they're going to kill *me* now. . . .'"

The Major laughed quietly. "Very good, very good. . . . here, do you want a cigarette? Of course, I suppose you do . . ."

Vitolyn sat back, limp, yet tingling. Was it possible, that they didn't believe him? And he had told it so close to the truth that he had frightened himself terribly. Why then was the Major smiling? And the Captain seemed completely unmoved, as though he didn't care at all.

"No, thank you . . . ," he heard himself saying, choking back his desire, ". . . your excellency . . ." He had not had a smoke since an hour before he had killed Roig. He was ravenous for tobacco but was afraid that he might give himself away. Nervous people often did. When a man thinks that he is thinking clearly, he's often at his most confused. And he was growing hungry, too. Whenever he became tense, his hunger magnified enormously. But it wasn't right. He wasn't tense, and yet he was ferociously hungry.

"You don't have to be concerned. This isn't . . . Germany or Austria. . . . There will be no drugs or poison in the cigarettes."

Vitolyn's bladder began to throb. The way the man went on and on. If he didn't believe, then let him say so. Suddenly Vitolyn was exhausted, had no desire to protect himself anymore. It occurred to him, dimly, that the truth stood as little a chance of being believed as his most elaborate fabrications; what he had said before about the truth being too fantastic was . . . true itself . . .

"The answer, for now . . . ," Major Punto went on, opening his book and lowering his head, as though he were already reading, "is that . . . frankly, I don't care *what* the answer is . . . you've told me enough . . . you're either an artful liar or a very unhappy man . . . and it doesn't matter much which. If you're lying to me, you're careful enough, and I don't think you'll do anything stupid. You know the situation here, I'm sure . . . we're besieged . . . trapped in this place, with Anarchists, Communists, Socialists, this 'ist' and that 'ist' all around . . . can't get out . . . so, and you're trapped in the middle, Austrian national Anton Vitolyn . . . make the best of it. Don't cause trouble. I don't believe in shooting people for nothing, so I'm letting you go for now . . . you will go downstairs and stay with the old men and the children, and you will be watched. You will only go where you are allowed to go and only after you have asked permission to go there. No one will bother you if you behave yourself but if you don't . . ." He flipped a page, then another. "And when you're ready to tell me the . . . truth . . ."

"What do you mean . . . the truth?" Vitolyn croaked out, appalled.

"Don't be an ass," the Captain said, leaving his meaning quite unclear. He spoke to the Major: ". . . a little sleep now, before they bring someone else up?"

"You go ahead. I'll write this up. . . ." He opened a thick ledger book of the kind accountants and bank examiners use, and began to scribble something in a tight, even hand; his arm hardly moved as he wrote.

Corporal Moya entered abruptly with a basin of water and a wad of cloth stuck under his belt. Vitolyn started to turn, then brought his head around; his body thrummed with pressures, as though every organ was ready to burst.

"Please . . . ," he cried out suddenly. "For the love of God . . . !"

The Major inclined his head and rocked back in his chair. "Yes? There is something?"

Vitolyn licked his lips, uttered a grating, unhappy rasp.

"Please . . . let me go outside. Now . . . I have . . ."

"Yes? Something to tell us?"

Vitolyn drew a breath, more angry than embarrassed at having to so demean himself.

". . . I have to . . . pass . . . water . . . ," he said.

JULY 22

The Government has organized the necessary means to clean out the last revolutionary "pockets."

Madrid returns to normal.

Measures are being taken by the Presidency of the Council and the Ministry of Finance relating to public officials who participated or collaborated in any way in the insurrection.

General Riquelme subdues the cadets in Toledo.

Government congratulated.

Rebels take refuge in the Infantry Academy.

It will be attacked today.

El Sol

JULY 22: *The Alcázar*

JAIME LOOKED AWAY, TOWARD THE DARK ceiling of the riding hall, to where the candlelight did not reach, and the shadows clung like risen smoke among the beams. Only the grave was lit and the faces of the dozen people gathered around it. Not a grave really but a shallow trough scooped out of the earth beneath the stones of the riding-hall floor, the only place in which the ground was soft enough to bury a man.

He tried to see the dial of his watch so as to know how long it had been that he had been waiting there in the hall for the rest of them to come. No one had told him that there would be a burial party that evening or that it would be in the riding hall, and he had no real understanding of why it was that he had come there. Except that it seemed to him that it was the only place he could come and that it was the only place where the bodies could be buried. Almost nine o'clock; he had been there a little more than two hours, ever since he had finished with the sandbags on the upper floors and had begun to think about Pelayo again. For a moment, when he had crossed the esplanade, just after sunset, he had looked up to where the points of the stars were just beginning to pierce the hide of the half-dark sky, and all at once he had thought himself free of it; he had only to walk down the embankment to the river and follow the river along until it shook loose of the city, and no one would stop him or even call after him. But he could not do it. In full view of the snipers who had been firing all day from the belfry of the Santo Cruz, he stood like a child, looking innocently at the sky as though he could even begin to count the stars.

Then he crossed to the riding hall and sat down inside in the dark to wait.

Now it was not the corpses that troubled him but the presence of the others, the mourners, and the soldiers with their shovels and iron bars for prying up the stones. It was between himself and Pelayo alone, and the others should not have been there, not even Mercedes or Gil. Jaime looked across the hall, puzzled by the ugly, theatrical expression of grief that distorted Sebastián Gil's face. He had not been nearly so upset watching Pelayo die. Gil had known the banker only slightly, certainly neither so long nor so well as Jaime who could remember Tomás Pelayo walking with Francisco along the Royal Wall in Ceuta when Jaime himself was only a child . . . why then such a display now? Jaime resented it, especially as he could not find any such sorrow within himself now but only a gnawing sense of obligation and a fine, unfocused guilt that eluded his grasp like a handful of smoke. A round-faced, handsome woman whom Jaime had never seen before was standing next to Gil, one hand resting lightly on his arm as though to comfort him. For a second, she caught Jaime's eye and returned his glance with a level, emotionless stare. That stare seemed to mirror Jaime's own coldness perfectly, and he felt an immediate empathy.

The bodies had been carried out on wooden stretchers covered with canvas sacking. Over the head of one of the corpses the sacking had turned brown with blood.

Jaime's hands trembled and he caught at them, one with the other, trying to hold still. He thought that he might move closer to the graveside, let Mercedes see him, if she hadn't seen him already, but not until he stopped shaking. The dead had never disturbed him that much; he'd seen burials so many times before. Why, then, was he shaking so?

A short young man in an ill-fitting uniform stepped out in front of the group and began to read from a list the names of the dead. There could be no mistake; everything had to be done properly, even here.

". . . Teodoro Vargas . . . ," the soldier's voice was like that of a choirboy whose voice is changing. Absurd . . .

A woman moaned.

". . . Julio Pacheco . . ."

It was all Pelayo's fault for dying and thus for making him come here . . . his father's fault too, for involving him with Pelayo, just as he had apprenticed him to Colonel Carvalho. . . . For a second he had a terrible vision of himself lurching across the floor of the riding hall and seizing the corpse of Tomás Pelayo y de Suelves by the shoulders, shaking it and shouting in its face that it was not his fault and that no one had any right to accuse him.

". . . Colonel Fernán Venegas . . ."

The name caught Jaime by surprise, and his head snapped around in time to catch Gil's choked expression, a look not so much of grief but of fear and disbelief. Jaime's resentment drained from him in an instant, replaced by a horrifying urge to laugh. It had not been Pelayo's death that had brought the shopkeeper there at all but that of the Civil Guard colonel he had been so sure would protect him. Jaime recalled the name from his father's table; Dr. Aliaga taunting Gil about his dangerous friendships, Ruperto Barcenas laughing caustically, and Gil defending himself in such a pitifully clumsy way. Jaime had felt compassion for the man then but now, it seemed, the shopkeeper had determined to fatten on his own misery. Pity was a waste of time.

And the girl, why was she there? Because of Gil or because she knew that he would be there? She could have guessed it, if only from the way he had acted that afternoon.

". . . Gonzalo Rodriguez . . ."

Gil was rubbing at his eyes, and the girl was staring at him with a look of veiled disgust on her face. Gil took a few steps away, toward the bodies. No one moved to stop him. He looked down at the stretcher on which Venegas' corpse had been laid, the muddy shoes still sticking out from under the canvas, a bit of bright orange peel stuck to the left sole.

Which one was Pelayo? . . . Jaime's eye settled on a small figure, completely covered, and he decided that that one would be the banker, whether it was or not. The smallest of them except for the children's bodies.

The bodies seemed to have no weight at all, no mass, as though they might rise from the stretchers and float away at any second.

The first deaths, the first burials . . . why did he persist in thinking in such terms? . . . *the first* . . . there would be no more. Pelayo and Venegas, their deaths linking them all, the four of them, joining them together. The Berbers believed in such omens; it would have meant something to his mother, he knew . . .

The others looked on, an already ragged group of men and women who seemed confused more than anything else and kept looking around the huge, bare room as though they could not understand why they were there or what was expected of them . . .

". . . Tomás Pelayo y de Suelves . . ."

A cavalry captain, tall, painfully thin and trying with some difficulty to remain erect, went over to the graveside and began to intone the ritual with the slow ease of a man unpracticed but compellingly sincere. Each error of liturgy was transformed by the force of his belief into something incontestably correct. The others stood with bent necks, hands clasped before them, breathing slowly. No one moved. All Jaime could hear was the shopkeeper rubbing his head and the muted running of the Tagus over its weirs.

The first of the bodies was hoisted and lowered into the hastily prepared grave. It was dark, the only light coming from a rank of candles that had been placed on a low table near the trough they had dug as a common grave. The stones that had been torn up were piled neatly to one side and there was a faint smell of earth in the air, moist and, in its way, inviting.

The Captain continued to read, his voice never changing pitch.

Two more bodies to go. There had been six. Seven had died that day but the seventh was a Falangist, and his body had been given over to his own people, to inter according to their own ceremony. Sixty of them were still locked up in a storeroom somewhere because the colonel in command didn't trust them. "Why should he trust anyone?" Jaime reflected. "Or himself for that matter?" A tremor of unexpected self-reproach took him like a chill. Why had he come? Pelayo had brought it on himself. How could you feel sorry for such a man? You had to *do* something, not just allow yourself to be borne along, thrown against events like a piece of driftwood. He stopped himself; had he done any better? He had rebelled at Oviedo, done what he thought was right, and where had it gotten him? The men had been executed anyway, and he himself had almost been shot. Only Carvalho, who had betrayed him, had come away unscarred. And now, hadn't it happened all over again? He'd acted positively only in that he had tried to avoid positive action. With the same result. A real prison this time, and worse because in a way he was still free inside it.

Gil had gotten control of himself and was standing there as though in a trance, his eyes wide open. The woman next to him still held his arm. It was ludicrous, Jaime thought. He should be helping her. How brutally selfish. It made him feel better to turn his anger outward.

Suddenly a woman began to wail. Jaime saw that the sack they were lowering was smaller than the others. It was one of the children who had been killed in the air raid that morning. The woman kept wailing as the earth and pebbles fell over the body, the dirt striking the canvas like rain. The woman who had been holding Gil's arm looked around for the source of the sound, her face waxy and immobile. The pupils of her eyes seemed even from that distance like nailheads, devoid of any expression whatever.

The cavalry Captain hesitated for a second, then went on reading.

Another body was lowered into the grave. Then more earth fell. Jaime's gaze passed over the faces of the mourners, seeking in each pair of eyes some clue as to the reason that six men . . . no, seven . . . were already dead or why any more should die. But the expressions he saw were impenetrable as they always are when men come to contemplate, ritually, something they cannot understand in any other way.

Venegas' body was lowered into the grave. The woman standing by Gil seemed to tremble for the briefest moment; then her face became rigid again, and a stony look came into her eyes. "Venegas' wife or his mistress?" Jaime wondered. She followed the descent of the corpse with her eyes. Gil stood there, his hands touching only at the fingertips like a Buddha figure made out of cracked yellow clay. His face was creased by confusion as though it had crossed his mind that he ought to make some gesture at the graveside but he did not know what to do without looking ridiculous.

The last dry clods hailed down over the sacking. The mourners stood silently for a moment, embarrassed by their composure. Then, quite stiffly, the woman who had been at Gil's side went over to the open trench. She held a bunch of dried yellow flowers out over the grave and dropped them in quickly, pulling her hand away as though she had touched something unpleasant.

The cavalry Captain laid aside his book and stood at attention, his arm raised in a salute. The others followed his example, except for Gil who had hidden his face in his hands, Jaime stepped back into the shadow of the wall. He could not bring himself to salute.

It was finished. The group filed out of the squat building and onto the southernmost portion of the esplanade. The terrace faced the river, and there was no fear of sniper fire. The *milicianos* in the belfry of the Santo Cruz were too far away to see anything at night, even though the starlight was vivid and clear.

It was a violent change from the oppressive dark of the riding hall. Jaime had a feeling of pressure relieved, as though the walls had fallen away and all the graves in the world blown triumphantly open. Constellations spread a foaming wake across the sky all the way to the eastern horizon, and the rumble of the Tagus directly below in the gorge seemed to imitate the roar of the heavens. Above the esplanade the glow of searchlights had spread into the sky, faint and milky, like anisette poured into a bowl of water. The contrast between that blurred, opalescent zone and the farther, northernmost corner of the night sky where the searchlights could not reach was staggering.

The members of the burial party had reached the wall where a doorway opened into the Alcázar. They bunched up as though waiting for someone to tell them that the ritual was really over and that their obligations to the dead were at an end.

Jaime felt dislocated, as though his feet were no longer in contact with the ground and his bones were turned around inside of him. He had the sensation of a man present at a theatrical performance who has somehow managed to wander on stage and get mixed up with the actors. Just as he had had to remain with Pelayo until he died, he had had to come to the burial. For no reason other than that he felt it was expected, as though his father were watching over his shoulder. . . . His father; he didn't even want to think about that and had somehow succeeded in forcing all thoughts of the house in the ravine out of his mind.

The door into the wall stood open. A pool of light fell onto the esplanade. The searchlights flickered out above the Zoco. Darkness. No firing at all. For the moment, the air had a crystalline purity, softened by a touch of breeze from the west. Far to the north a blazing house smudged the sky.

Mercedes was still standing just outside the entrance.

He wondered, can she be waiting for me? Did she even see me? He went over to her. He could see that her face was set in hard, compressed lines, and her hands were twisted together. He stood by her, a few feet away, waiting for her to speak. She looked up at him without surprise, and he realized that she had known all along that he was there.

She let out a breath. "Sometimes . . . the hardest thing to do of all is to find the strength to be charitable . . ."

He knew what she meant, without her telling him.

"That man," she went on. "I've known him all my life. He was a friend of my father's and a friend to me . . . I thought . . ." She stopped. "He kept saying . . . , 'He's deserted me. He's left me alone . . .' as though his friend had died simply to spite him. How do you deal with such a person? I try to forgive . . ."

It struck Jaime that he had thought of the girl's father in precisely that way, said precisely the same thing about him. ". . . try to forgive . . ." Was that the most important thing, or was it more important to understand why a man acted the way he did? Didn't compassion, in the last analysis, consist simply of really understanding what moved a man?

He touched her on the arm, and she did not shake him off as he had expected her to do.

"Mercedes . . . ?"

She nodded.

"I expected more of him," she said quietly. "That's all."

"Sometimes people surprise us . . . we think we know them . . ."

"Don't," she said. "I know what you're going to say, but not now. . . ." Her tone was restrained, accepting, and it caught him by surprise. It was almost as if she had given up a pretense, was willing to admit . . .

"Let's go inside. . . ."

Through the door they could see the cavalry Captain moving about in the corridor. Over his arm he carried the cloths he had used, and in one hand he held the long candles like a bunch of twigs.

Mercedes stood just by the doorway. "You don't have to wait here with me. I just want to watch the river for a while. Do you know, I never saw it from here, not in all the years I've lived in Toledo?"

For a moment they stood watching the pale, flickering fires light up the rooftops, making ragged cutouts against the naked child-moon. Only six days old.

"He wants to stay," she said after a time. "Gil . . . I don't understand it at all . . . how can he?"

Jaime remained silent, thought, "What difference does it make, really? Stay or go? Inside or outside? My father for instance . . . what is he doing now? Does it make any difference that he's outside and I'm here? Will it clarify anything? . . . make dying any easier? Or Pelayo . . . why did he die? Because the monks fired before they knew what was happening, and the troops fired back not knowing who was shooting at them? And to have been there in the first place because of that fool Luis . . ." He gradually became aware that he was speaking, not merely thinking, that his thought were taking shape on his lips. How long had he been doing that? A look a chagrin spread across his face.

"It's all right," she said.

"Don't understand me when I can't understand myself. . . ."

She smiled briefly.

"Let's go inside. It's a foolish thing to stand here where they can shoot at us. . . ."

They went in.

JULY 23

Yesterday's victory was decisive.

The Loyalist Forces completely defeated the rebels of Toledo and Guadalajara.

The rebel "pockets" still active are about to be defeated.

Soldiers rise in revolt against their superiors and rebel officers.

El Sol (Madrid)

JULY 23: *Barcelona*

BARCELONA. ANOTHER STORY ENTIRELY. From the moment the three men had clambered down from the back of the truck that had driven them in from Seo de Urgel, they had entered a world so completely different from the solitary forests of the Cerdagne that it took their breath away. Even Colonel Carvalho had never seen anything quite like it before. Barcelona was alive to a degree that made it almost impossible to focus for more than a second on any single thing and, in the end, could not help but make a man dizzy.

Trucks daubed with the initials of a dozen political organizations careened up and down the streets carrying men waving rifles. The Civil Guard, their Mausers strapped stiffly to their backs, stood on corners and under the awnings of cafés, observing everything with wooden smiles, as though they were faintly amused but determined to remain tolerant. The initials UGT and POUM were as much in evidence as those of the FAI and the CNT, and there was no shortage of hammer and sickles painted on walls and the sides of cars. Captured artillery pieces were everywhere, and the horses of the mounted police cantered elegantly along the main streets. Machine guns with huge metal shields on either side had been set up at the street corners and were watched over by helmeted members of the *mozos de escuadra*.

Barricades formed of the bodies of horses who had been killed during the early hours of fighting were to be found in front of many buildings and, inevitably, there would be a few children standing there sniffling. Everyone, it seemed, was sorry for the horses.

Cannon went by drawn by wagons which in turn were pulled by horses, the whole looking like ghosts out of the Peninsular War. A few bodies still lay under lampposts, unmoved but covered with Catalan flags held down at the corners by rocks.

To Colonel Carvalho it was all bewildering, as was the ubiquity of the initials UHP: "Unite, Proletarian Brothers," just as in Oviedo in 1934. History seemed to be playing a cruel trick on him, reversing itself, doubling back. He had often wondered what he would have done two years before if he had found himself on the other side. Now, he realized, he might well find out.

Portillo, however, was neither bewildered nor ill at ease. His face remained solemn, his expression slightly ironic and lightening only when a group of good-looking militia-women would go past, carrying rifles clearly too heavy for them, sometimes with bouquets of flowers thrust into the muzzles.

Comrade Renom had succeeded in getting them all the documents they needed at Seo de Urgel. The FAI chief there had been a relative of the Communist leader Díaz Oliver, and it was simple to get the necessary stamps and cards. Permits to ride vehicles, permits to drive a car—an irony, if there ever was one, after their experience with the mayor of Puigcerdá—even permits to bear arms. All stamped with the requisite FAI–CNT stamps.

But, as they had boarded the truck that was to take them into Barcelona, Draz Oliver had told them they would have to see about a train ticket to Madrid by themselves. "There's nothing I can do about that.

The train doesn't even run up here. It never has and probably never will."

The truck had left them off on the Calle de las Cortes, a few blocks from the Plaza de Cataluña. Stone barricades reinforced with sandbags and dead horses were everywhere, but there were few people on the street. Those who passed were either wearing the dark-blue uniforms of the militia, with their multicolored party badges, or else appeared in a peculiarly altered kind of civilian clothing. Almost no one had a hat on.

Trams and buses were running; a few passed, so crowded with people that it was hopeless even to try to board them. But there were no taxis to be seen on the streets.

"A little walk will do us all good," Colonel Carvalho said, stretching his long legs. Lachine was not so sure, and kept shifting his briefcase from hand to hand and examining his palms and fingers for the red lines caused by the weight of the case.

The thing to do was to find the PSUC headquarters, Oliver had said. Carvalho had almost laughed; "The United Socialist-Communist Party of Cataluña." Such a thing could never be. "Sooner the Federation of Lions and Lambs," he muttered. Draz Oliver, who had heard him, smiled and said nothing.

They continued their walk toward the Plaza de Cataluña. Smoke rose in thick black columns above the waterfront, like the ropes of Indian fakirs climbing into the air and ending nowhere. The building that had belonged to the Italian Steamship company, the Cosulich line, was on fire. A battle had taken place there a day or two before, and the building was still burning.

Lachine stopped for a moment and sat on a stoop under a huge poster that warned that looters would be executed on the spot if caught.

"That's a little foolish, isn't it," Portillo said. "I mean, if they're *not* caught, well obviously no one is going to . . ." He lit another cigar as a finish to his sentence and blew the smoke skyward in imitation of the burning steamship building. Colonel Carvalho glanced about; the harbor was only a few streets away, and he would have liked to have stood there for a few minutes and watched the boats coming and going.

Lachine got to his feet again, and they proceeded along the Calle Pelayo until they entered the Plaza de Cataluña and found themselves directly opposite the Hotel Colón. The Rambla, Barcelona's main street, was emptying hundreds of people into the plaza every minute. Soldiers, Civil Guard, some on horseback, others on foot, Assault Guards, civilians carrying arms of all sorts, militiamen in their blue overalls, women, even children carrying sticks and wooden rifles. Dogs ran about everywhere, adding their frustrated protests to the general din. No one, it seemed, had bothered to feed the dogs of Barcelona for some time. There had been too much other business, such as the storming of the Atanzares barracks, the attack on the old Captaincy General building where General Goded had barricaded himself, and not least of all, the burning of every church in the city.

Over the entrance to the Hotel Colón someone had hung a huge banner on which the initials PSUC had been painted in whitewash.

The guards at the entrance checked all the papers and passes which Diaz Oliver had obtained for them in Urgel and seemed satisfied.

The ground floor of the hotel was swarming with men and women. A babble of voices and languages: Catalan and Spanish, French, German, English. Newsmen with their credentials pinned to their lapels passed carrying huge cameras. Soldiers milled about. Names were being called out repeatedly over the loudspeaker system and, somewhere, a radio was playing loudly the inevitable "Riego's Hymn."

"The train tickets," Lachine kept repeating. "That's the thing." "Now who . . . ?"

The trains, Oliver had told them, were no longer running normally. Everything was under the control of the Generalitat which in turn, so he had warned them, ". . . is completely out of control itself."

"You'd better let me do the asking," Colonel Carvalho said. "Your Spanish is good, but I don't think it's up to this babble. . . ."

Lachine refused: "No one has ever had to speak for me before. . . ."

"Don't be a fool, Camille . . ."

"We'll see who's a fool," Lachine snapped back. Why was he so edgy? Perhaps he always acted that way in crowds. Some people could not stand being surrounded; a form of claustrophobia. Others couldn't stand open spaces.

Lachine went from table to table, trying to read the signs, talking to people. Where was the Committee for Transportation? Whom did one see to secure a place on the Barcelona-Madrid express? It was very important. Here were his cards, his special passes. And these two men with him . . .

They would have to see the officer in charge at the Generalitat on the Rambla, an exhausted captain of the Assault Guard tried to explain while writing so rapidly across a sheaf of papers on the table before him that it seemed impossible that he could be putting down anything intelligible. A telephone at his elbow kept ringing, and the radio had been turned up louder and was now flooding the room with dance music.

"Where is Javier Verdaguer?" Lachine insisted. Verdaguer was the man to whom Oliver had directed them. Lachine kept shouting the word *Donde* . . . over and over again, trying to make himself heard. Portillo nodded and nudged the Colonel on the arm: "He sounds like a bell gone mad, doesn't he . . . ?"

The three men felt uncomfortable in each other's company. It was as though they had been fused together and now weighed so much that it was impossible for any one of them to move.

Lachine was irritable, and it was clear that this was the cause, not simply his inability to find the missing Javier Verdaguer.

"You have to go to the Generalitat," the Captain at the table insisted, "That's all there is to it. Really, I can't help you. . . ."

Lachine threw up his hands. "And there they will tell me to go to the Captaincy General building, I'm sure, and from there to the University, and from there . . . let me tell you something, what you people do not have, no indeed, what you definitely do not have, is any sense of organization. Passion, art, character, integrity, yes . . . all of those things, but absolutely no organization. How infuriating it all is. . . ."

With everyone's consent, Lachine decided to go alone to the Generalitat to see if he could find someone who would at least admit to knowing something about the railroad system.

"We'll meet at the Café Horno . . . you know where that is, don't you?"

Carvalho had never been in Barcelona before; no, he did not know where the Café Horno was. Portillo, looking off through the walls in the direction of Montjuich prison, said that he knew. If it was not open, they would meet in the street outside. Lachine left at once, the briefcase banging against his leg.

Carvalho tried to imagine how he would have felt in Lachine's position, burdened with two men he neither needed nor wanted, alone in a foreign country in the middle of a civil war. Not an enviable position. Yet, because of the Frenchman's manner, Colonel Carvalho could not summon up any sympathy for him.

"I'll admit it," Carvalho said, answering Portillo's brusque question. "I don't like it . . . I don't like him. I suppose it shows. . . ."

"It does . . . but don't worry. I think you'd be mistaken if you put too much faith in what he can do for you. . . ."

"You understand my situation. . . ."

"Yes. Exactly. And I don't envy you."

"Here, it doesn't matter. The Government seems to have things under control but in Toledo . . ."

"I wouldn't be too sure, even here," Portillo said. "Look at the flags. Red and Black. Everywhere. How many Catalan flags have you seen? How many UGT badges on the militia? It's all very well and good to paint initials on walls, but look and see who's carrying the rifles and who's behind the machine guns on the Rambla."

"Are you trying to frighten me?"

"No . . . just 'wiping your windshield' for you . . . ," Portillo replied. "I'm too fond of those Havana cigars of yours to risk losing the source of supply so easily. . . ."

Just then, a group of officers came by, flanked by Civil Guard wearing little tricolor flags on their tricorns. The loudspeaker in the lobby was blaring; a list of names was being read, the men all instructed to report to the second floor to a Major Peñas for further orders.

"It's pointless to stay here . . . ," Carvalho said.

The voice on the loudspeaker was calling, in an irritated tone: "Major Serrano-Guridi, to the third floor . . . Serrano-Guridi . . ."

As they left the Hotel, Colonel Carvalho remarked: "I once knew a man by that name, in Melilla . . . don't you think that's rather remarkable?" He was surprised at the sound of his own voice—calm, with even a trace of his old bluff good humor. What was there about crowds, disorder, that made him affable? A fault or a quality? He wondered . . .

Open trucks were cruising the Rambla, filled with militiamen and workers in their shirt-sleeves, all with rifles.

A flight of planes, three in all, droned by overhead. The sky above the harbor was intensely blue, much brighter than the overalls of the militiamen.

As they passed the Hotel Falcón, halfway to the Generalitat, Portillo stopped. An armed guard stood by the entrance instead of the usual liveried attendants, and a banner with the initials POUM spanned six windows on the fourth floor.

"I wonder if any of my old cell mates are in there . . . ?"

"From Montjuich?"

"From Montjuich and before and after that too. . . ."

"The way you say it . . ." The Colonel had noticed a certain sarcasm in Portillo's voice that matched perfectly the ironic expression that passed across his own face everytime someone said something complimentary about either the Trotskyites or the Communists. . . .

"I'm through with them all, of course. You know that."

"I know it, but I don't understand . . ."

"My business in Toledo. I've told you, it's purely personal. I've said that to so many people so many times, and still no one believes me. Well, so much the worse for them. Still, I'd like to see . . . would you mind?"

"The Café Horno?"

"Just down the block. I'll join you," Portillo said and went inside, passing the armed guard in an instant.

Colonel Carvalho continued on alone along the crowded street.

The Café Horno was so named because of a huge open fireplace in the back. Built of brick, it sported an immense iron spit upon which whole lambs could be roasted. Now there was no fire and the bricks were dull with unwashed soot. Chairs had been set upside down on some tables, and there were only a few customers around, no more than a dozen. The only sign of life was in the kitchen behind the huge brick fireplace. Through the circle of glass on the door, a bustle of activity could be seen.

Colonel Carvalho went in and stood for a moment, trying to adjust his eyes to the gloom. A few globes mounted on iron brackets gave off little light. The windows, of a dark greenish glass, allowed almost none to enter from the street.

Not a single table held more than one man. No "conversation groups," no gatherings of friends, no domino games—just a dozen or more solitary figures sitting there reading newspapers and sipping drinks, trying to make believe that everything was just as it had been.

One man caught his eye. He was astonished. It was the Major whose name had been called with such irritation over the loudspeaker: Serrano-Guridi. Colonel Carvalho went over at once and without a word sat down opposite him.

Major Serrano-Guridi was a slender, almost boyish-looking man with still-black hair and a narrow, almost accidental mustache which had earned him the nickname *El Cepillo*, the "whiskbroom." A supply officer at the Melilla garrison, he had devoted his spare time, in fact his passion —for he was a singularly ascetic bachelor—to collecting inlaid Moroccan daggers which he had kept in a huge glass case in his apartment.

"Guridi?"

"Ah . . . Carvalho . . . ," the Major said. "Yes . . . Carvalho . . ."

"I didn't know you were here," the Colonel said brusquely.

Major Serrano-Guridi looked up and, without registering the slightest surprise at the appearance of a man he had not seen for at least five years and, then, in a city which might as well have been at the opposite end of the world, said: "I hardly understand it myself, Colonel. . . ."

There were six tiny glasses lined up in a neat row next to a bottle of anisette. Major Serrano-Guridi was toying with a seventh. His little mustache was damp, and he had a habit of blowing into his glass as if to cool the liquer. There was no question, from his expression, let alone the six glasses, that he was deeply depressed.

"Take an anisette, Colonel . . . and tell me how you happen to be in this place."

Carvalho reached for the bottle and poured a tiny bit of anisette into one of the three empty glasses that stood, unused, on the other side of the bottle. "You're not surprised to see me, Major?"

"Of course, of course. But then I'm really no more surprised to see you than to be here myself." He lifted his glass and sipped without interest.

Carvalho nodded. He recalled how often he had talked with Major Serrano-Guridi before and how seldom it had been necessary to explain things. The man had a way of knowing . . . "Do you know that they're calling for you over the loudspeaker at the Hotel Colón," he asked.

"It doesn't surprise me. But I refuse to let them upset me. No, I'm past the point where I get excited about such things." He leaned forward, confidentially, an amused look suddenly in his eyes. "Do you know, I'm not in the army anymore. . . ."

"But the uniform?" The Major was wearing a uniform with all his insignia in place; very neat, as always.

"Three days before our . . . 'associates' decided to get nasty," he began, "my request for discharge was accepted. Look, I have the papers right here in my pocket. Foolish man, I thought I would relax for the first time in my life. Plenty of time to buy a new set of clothes. I went to a shop on the Via Layetana. Very fine goods, mostly English. There I ordered five new suits and all the trimmings. When the Anarchists stormed the offices of the Fomento del Trabajo Nacional, right next door, that was the end of my suits. So here I sit, in uniform but not in the army. Now tell me, what are you doing here, and is your uniform still the real thing or a sham the way mine is?"

The anisette sent a shudder through Colonel Carvalho's body. He had forgotten that he hadn't eaten since morning. He cast a longing glance toward the oval of glass in the kitchen door. A waiter caught his eye and came over. There was little to be had; a dish of *pulpitos,* baby octopus, was brought at once—grayish and overcooked. But Carvalho ate with relish while Major Serrano-Guridi looked on. Between mouthfuls, Carvalho explained what had brought him to Barcelona.

"Yes, yes, yes . . ." the Major kept saying, breathing into his glass.

"So there you have it. Do you remember Mercedes at all?"

"She was a child. But, yes, I remember her and your wife, Doña Amalia, as well. . . ." He poured out an eighth glass of anisette.

"Why do you do that?" Colonel Carvalho said sharply. "You never did that before."

"Were the times and circumstances ever like this before? I've had to sell my collection of Moroccan daggers. Would you believe it? . . . to an Englishman . . . and for very little at that. But the money wasn't important. I didn't sell them for that . . . I sold them because I couldn't bear looking at them any longer. . . ."

Major Serrano-Guridi talked on; it had been very hard for him to understand what was happening. Every time he thought he had sunk anchor, the bottom turned out to be muddy. Nothing would stick. He'd convinced himself, after reading in the papers about the way the insurgents had been executing their opponents that he'd found a center of reference, a focus. "But then I went out to Tibidado. As you know, that's not far from here. A pleasant suburban resort where people go on Sundays to walk about and enjoy themselves. And so they do. You can go out there tomorrow and see them. All enjoying themselves. But at night they drive trucks out there from the prison and execute hundreds at a time. I was there. I saw it. Now what do you make of that . . . ?"

"Nothing," Colonel Carvalho said at once; he fought back an impulse to take the man's hand. Suddenly, his temper hardened. "It's always been that way. It proves nothing at all . . . I myself . . ."

"I know . . . I know . . . and I'm sure you did what you could to stop it."

"Yes," Colonel Carvalho said, not sure whether he was telling the truth or not. At least it was as he liked to remember it.

"So you see . . . it doesn't help to be a man of good will, not at all. It's enough to drive a man mad, isn't it? But do you know what the worst of it is?"

Carvalho leaned across the table; why was it that the man seemed to be talking perpetually in questions? Had he uttered one single affirmative sentence in the last five minutes?

"The worst of it is that because of all of this . . . this killing, which is becoming a kind of contagion which won't be stopped by compresses or sulfa, you can be sure, that this 'war' of ours is turning into a revolution. You should be as afraid of those cars with skulls and crossbones and 'FAIs' and 'CNTs' on them as I am . . . but not for the reason you think. They won't ever win; you can't win by destroying everything.

After all, aren't they the best refutation of their own arguments? Man is perfectable, a pure being. He is corrupted only by the artifices of society. Nonsense. Look at them. No, you don't have to worry about that. But because of them, we're going to get a boot clamped down on our necks all the same. . . ."

Colonel Carvalho was aware of an uncomfortable tingling along the back of his neck. The anisette? No, impossible. Serrano-Guridi was still talking, looking more depressed than ever.

"What I'm afraid of is this, my friend . . . that the Government, you and I, the people who abhor this 'sacred' killing for causes and think that there ought to be some other way to convince a man than by shooting him, we, the *Izquierda Republicana,* the Centrists, whatever you want to call us, are going to make a deal with the generals. Because all of these allies of ours are going to make a revolution right under our noses and once the tumbrels start rolling . . . and if you go and snoop about Tibidado at night as I've done . . . you'll see that they've started rolling already . . . the rest of us, I think, are going to take another look at our friends the rebel generals, and they won't look so bad after all. At least with them, a few things might remain in place. And then Madrid is going to think twice about all of this. Do we want to knock out Mola, really? Is Franco so bad? You wait and see. You can hear it already at the Generalitat. The Catalans are no fools, and they're terrified." He put his glass down with a sudden thump, and stared wide-eyed at the Colonel whom he had not seen for so many years. "And so am I, my friend. Believe it. I am . . ."

Carvalho remained silent, thoughtful. If that were true, and it was frighteningly logical, then it would all be for nothing. What could a man say to the orphan of a man killed for nothing, to his widow, to his mother? Hadn't he sniffed some of the same stink at Oviedo? But whose fault was it, after all? The fault of the very people who would sell themselves into bondage now . . . again, out of fear.

"Don't feel sorry for me," Serrano-Guridi said. "I'm no longer in the army, and no one can give me orders, no matter how loudly they shout into the loudspeaker at the Hotel Colón. Here, have another drink. It's excellent anisette . . . French, prime grade."

Emilio Portillo had come in and was standing unnoticed behind Colonel Carvalho. Serrano-Guridi looked up and gestured; it was the first Carvalho knew that someone was standing behind him, and he turned his head nervously. An ash from Portillo's cigar floated down and fell on the tip of his beard. Portillo reached out and flicked it away. Carvalho withdrew, angry at the presumption—he disliked being touched, by anyone, even by his wife, unless he himself invited it—and at the same time relieved to see Portillo. He had been at a complete loss for words with the Major, so often his problem when faced with an undeniable truth.

Portillo introduced himself and sat down. A few more people were entering the Café Horno, and there was increased activity in the kitchen beyond the little oval window.

"I've gotten rooms for us at the Falcón," he said. "Two rooms and a bath . . . a miracle, under the circumstances."

Serrano-Guridi smiled a cynical smile. "It would take Leon Trotsky himself to find rooms at the Falcón today. . . ."

"There, you see our Spanish tendency to exaggerate in everything, even the smallest detail of life," Portillo said with a flourish, handing Carvalho, unbidden, one of his own cigars. "No, it's not that bad. Certainly they've taken over quite a few rooms, but I think if you took all the POUM people in the city and put them in the Hotel Falcón, there would still be a hundred rooms left over."

"I wish . . . ," Serrano-Guridi began but drowned his sentence in anisette.

A cook in a filthy apron came out of the kitchen with a scuttle of charcoal which he dumped into the silent brick hearth. In a moment flames were crackling and sparks leaped high, giving the room an air both festive and diabolical.

Portillo asked for some bread and a bottle of wine. The two men ate silently while Serrano-Guridi poured himself an eighth anisette, then a ninth, and then a tenth. But so deep was his depression that the alcohol barely seemed to have any effect.

A troop of mounted Civil Guard went by on the Rambla outside, their arms raised in revolutionary salute. All that could be seen through the dark glass of the windows was a file of blurred, gray-green shadows gliding past. The sound of their horses' iron-shod hooves rang in the air.

When Lachine finally entered the café, he wore an unusually self-satisfied expression.

"There is, at last, some organization," he announced, sitting down. "And from those from whom we might expect it. Naturally."

He had gotten rail tickets for the three of them. The train would leave the following afternoon and make its way to Madrid via Valencia. It was necessary to follow the coast that far in order to avoid territory held by the rebels who had already dipped as far south as Teruel.

"Second class, but with all the necessary passes and stamps," Lachine said proudly.

Now, Serrano-Guridi addressed himself to the newcomer. "I thought we'd abolished classes," he remarked with a bemused expression.

Lachine did not know what to say. Was the man being facetious, or was he simply a fool, or worse—drunk? He raised his head with an expression of Olympian disdain. After all, he had located Javier Verdaguer. Everything was in order, his credentials were recognized, and Verdaguer had even given him a few words of encouragement, of envy. Lachine's mission was certainly important. How long could the arms and munitions they had seized from the military barracks and storehouses last them? Supplies would either have to be manufactured, which was unlikely, given the state of Spanish industry, or be purchased from countries willing to sell. And for that, money would be needed—in huge quantities. And for money in huge quantities, Verdaguer had gone on, approvingly, filling out the vouchers for rail transportation, a mind such as Lachine's was required. A shame that he was not a Spaniard, but in time he would teach Spaniards. Even the Anarchists would ultimately have to learn, whether they liked it or not.

Lachine was very hungry, but he could not stomach the *pulpitos* that Carvalho was eating and, so, contented himself with a bowl of beans and sausage. The fire in the brick hearth was only for show; nothing was being roasted, nothing at all.

After a while, the party left the café and went back into the Rambla. Major Serrano-Guridi stayed behind. He gave his best wishes for a safe journey. "I'd like to make the trip myself, Colonel. If I could only get a ticket for the train. But that's as impossible as finding my five suits, isn't it? I'd like to go back to Alcalá de Henares where I was born. It's not much of a place but a man could raise chickens there and be happy." Perhaps they would all see each other some time soon. If the Colonel went back to live in Toledo, he could drive by Alcalá de Henares someday and see if the Major was there. "Just ask anyone. They all know the name. In any case, my best regards to Doña Amalia and to your daughters."

"That man is a dangerous fool," Lachine said once they were outside. Another troop of Civil Guard was passing, no longer gray-green shadows but sharp, precise figures of patent leather and steel; Carvalho thought of Lorca's lines: "Skulls of lead . . . patent-leather souls. Wherever they stir, they command silences of dark rubber and fears of fine sand . . ." Not these men; yet there was something about them that set them apart from all the rest, even though they had thrown their lot in with the government. They still seemed . . . outside of it all. A nocturnal patrol of invaders from another planet.

"A good night's sleep," Portillo suggested. Lachine walked ahead a little, as though afraid to be part of the group. He was not pleased with the idea of staying at the Hotel Falcón, but he had been unable to get rooms at the Colón or the Continental, which the FAI had taken over.

"Do you know," Portillo said quietly to Carvalho as Lachine made a show of reading a wall poster a few yards ahead of them, "I tried to get through to Toledo before . . . ?"

"Ah . . . ," Carvalho felt his chest tighten. There was that curious tingling at the back of his neck again and a surprising stab of pain in his left shoulder blade. He grimaced and waited. It subsided. Portillo was chewing on a dead cigar.

"The telephone exchange is working. The Americans are running it, as always. For both sides, it seems. It's probably the only thing in Spain that's succeeded in maintaining its neutrality. . . ."

"And? Go on, man. Did you get through?"

"Yes, but it wasn't any good. All lines seem to end in FAI headquarters, and nobody knew anything about . . . our business . . . yours and mine."

Carvalho let out a breath he had been holding. Of course. No one would stop to look into something so insubstantial as the whereabouts of a man's daughter. Not with a war going on, and that's what it was. Wasn't that why he had decided to go to Toledo himself, regardless of the consequences?

"Perhaps it won't be so bad for you," Portillo said quietly. "In Toledo . . . one thing I did find out. Manuel Torroba seems to be in charge of the FAI there. He's an unusual sort. There aren't many like him around now."

"How do you mean?"

"He believes in men," Portillo said. "He honestly believes in men."

They passed a shop with a smashed window; pieces of glass lay in the street and little blue and pink bottles were scattered everywhere. It had been a perfumery. The scent of lavender and artificial lilac hung over everything.

JULY 23: *The Alcázar*

THE COURTYARD WAS FULL OF PEOPLE. Civil Guard, soldiers, men, women, even children. They had come streaming up from the underground rooms in answer to a summons carried to them by ashen-faced cadets who ran through the corridors, up and down the stairways, shouting for everyone to come up at once and assemble in the courtyard. There was news.

"Did they say? Did anyone say why?"

"Not a word. Just 'come up, there's news.' "

"That's just like them. 'Go here, go there. Do this, do that.' "

"As if it mattered."

"Well, if you don't like it, you can always go outside. There's the door."

Nervous laughter. The courtyard was blazing hot, the sun buzzing overhead. The rustle of clothing, of leather belts creaking in the heat, ungreased rifle belts sliding stiffly up and down, men spitting thick gobs of sputum.

Jaime saw Mercedes. He went over to her and took her by the arm. She turned her head as though to ask him something. Her lips moved but she said nothing. He shook his head. Her face was caked with dust and powder, her hair grimy. None of them had been able to wash.

There was a shuffle of boots on the balcony at the south end of the courtyard, a creak of door hinges. Then a door slammed heavily.

Captain Blancaflor, Captain Isla, Majors Montalve, Punto, Cirujano, and Baroja and three lieutenants came out onto the balcony and lined up by the railing, looking down at the crowd.

Mercedes shivered; "Something terrible has happened. Look at Major Montalvo's face. . . ."

It was true; Major Montalvo was weeping. Long tear tracks ran down his face, and he was biting his lip. A trickle of blood stained the stubble on his chin. The lieutenants exchanged anxious looks and did not know what to do with their hands. Each of the officers seemed to be waiting for the others to speak first.

"I don't know. I don't know . . . listen . . . ," Jaime whispered.

"If they'll only say something . . ."

"Spit it out, man," someone shouted from below . . . an old man's voice.

"Yes, out with it . . . ," this time a woman. "We have children . . ."

Major Cirujano raised his head. For a second, his eyes narrowed with anger, and then he raised his hand, palm down, as though giving a benediction.

"It is all right," he said. "You're forgiven, all of you. You couldn't know. No one could know what a terrible thing has just happened . . ."

The rustle of clothing froze in the air, hung suspended.

"I will tell it as simply as it happened." The Major began, "Ten minutes ago, Colonel Moscardó received a telephone call from the *Diputación* where the Reds have set up their headquarters. Colonel Moscardó was told that his son Luis has been captured and that if he did not surrender the Alcázar at once then his son would be shot."

Jaime's fingers drove into Mercedes' arm. She flinched with pain, turned her face toward him.

He ground his teeth together. "Do you understand . . . what this means . . . ?"

Major Cirujano went on. "Colonel Moscardó asked to speak to his son. There was no doubt about it. Luis Moscardó was there. We, all of us, heard his voice. Colonel Moscardó said to him, 'My son, commend your soul to God, shout *Viva España* and die like a hero,' and to the Reds he said, 'The Alcázar will never surrender. You may as well shoot my son at once. . . .'"

"Where is he now . . . ?" a woman's voice from somewhere in the crowd, anxious as a mother for her son. "The Colonel . . . ?"

"The Colonel has gone to his room. To pray. As should we all. For the soul of Luis Moscardó, whose life has been sacrificed by his father for the sake of the New Spain . . ."

The officers lowered their heads and two of them crossed themselves. The others followed suit. Not a man or woman of the crowd moved but to cross himself. A murmuring of prayers filled the air for a moment. Then a thick, impenetrable silence fell. Men and women glanced hastily at each other; they were all implicated now. On each hand there was a drop of the blood of Luis Moscardó. Surrender now would be unthinkable.

Jaime drew Mercedes to a corner of the courtyard.

"That madman, whoever he is out there, has just sentenced us both to death," Jaime whispered.

Mercedes did not understand. What was he saying? Sentenced them to death? What had they to do with Moscardó and his son?

"Don't you see, girl . . . once they start killing hostages, once they start shooting people who are the sons and daughters and wives of other people . . ."

"You mean . . . my father?"

"Yes."

"But no one knows where he is . . . you said so yourself. You said that he had run away from Oviedo . . . if that's true . . ."

"And if he has reached France safely, what will he do? Can you tell me what he'll do?" He held his head in his hands, shutting out the light. Everything he said was a contradiction; his fear was itself a contradiction.

Mercedes thought for a moment, then turned her head, avoiding his stare. The officers were still on the balcony, looking down at them all. The crowd had started to drift toward the doorways and the arcades.

"One of two things," she said slowly and with certainty. "He will either come back for me or he will place himself at the disposal of the Republic . . . or both."

"And in either case . . ."

Her face suddenly became mobile, animated by protest. It was not right. She would not believe that men could behave in such a fashion. She was one person, her father someone else, acting according to his own beliefs.

"And Colonel Moscardó's son?" Jaime said slowly. "What about him? Do you think he was asked what his beliefs were, or was it enough that his name was Luis Moscardó?"

She shook her head stubbornly.

"Because of his name alone, he's dead now. They shot him because his name was Moscardó, don't you understand?" He took her arm. "As hard as you can, pray . . . pray, Mercedes Carvalho, that your father doesn't come anywhere near Toledo, that if he is alive that he is what I thought him to be . . ."

"Jaime . . ."

"That he is as false to himself as he was to me. That he stays in France and . . . washes his hands of it all as he did once before. Pray that your father doesn't change now, of all times . . ."

She turned away from him and began to walk toward a high stone door that led into the east corridor.

"Don't," he called after her. "It's the truth, isn't it?"

"I don't know. I don't think it's the truth, no . . ."

"What are you going to do?"

"If I went to Moscardó himself and told him all of it . . ."

"No . . . ," the word emerged like a flung knife. How could she even suggest such a thing? Yet, he knew, she was perfectly capable of doing it.

Two of the officers who had been on the balcony passed, a Captain and a Lieutenant, neither of whom Jaime knew. The Captain nodded as he went by. His face was gray, his eyes fixed at some point, movable itself, just ahead of him. The Lieutenant was muttering; he was younger than Jaime and tried to walk with military bearing. He was obviously shaken.

When they had passed, Jaime said: "You see? Go ahead, explain it to Moscardó. Explain it to these men. How long do you think it will be before everyone with a suspicious name is down there in the hole with those poor wretches they yanked out of their beds the other day?"

"But what good would it do them? Why? For what reason? Did Moscardó surrender? There are too many involved for single lives to matter."

Jaime looked after the figure of the Captain and the Lieutenant and for a moment seemed to be listening to the heartbeat of the Alcázar itself.

"Vengeance. Have you forgotten about that? Believe me, I know . . . there's a point when nothing else matters. And who can tell how far away that point is for these people."

At that moment Mercedes' face was ugly, the slightly oversized features craggy and swollen, her hair, which was already becoming matted with dirt, reminding him of the witches in Goya's fantasies. "These people," she said with open sarcasm. "*These* people . . . Jaime, for God's sake, realize . . . *we* are 'these people.' We . . . and no others . . ."

He did not answer her for a long while. Then, when he spoke, it was in a far-off, impersonal tone, as though he had just encountered a stranger on the street who had asked him the time or the way to the nearest railway station.

"I'll go to the radio room and see if there's anything . . . they may have repaired the radio by now. . . ."

He walked away, leaving her standing there alone.

JULY 24
Toward the eradication of the rebellion.
Progress of the victory of the Republic.
A new and indisputable victory in the Sierra paves the way for the Loyalist columns on their way to Segovia.

JULY 25
Nothing will stop the sweeping push of popular heroism in the noble defense of freedom.
Yesterday our heroic air force bombarded rebel "pockets" throughout Spain.
FORWARD! FOR SPAIN! FOR THE REPUBLIC!

El Sol

JULY 26: *The Train from Barcelona*

EACH TIME THE TRAIN ROUNDED A BEND it was possible to look back and see not only the remaining twenty cars gliding slightly on the curve of track but also the long stream of curled black smoke that hung in the air over the entire length of the train. The smoke trailed back for miles, getting fainter and fainter, pointing to the north, toward Barcelona. The sky itself was brilliant and blue, absolutely cloudless, as though it had been recently washed and polished.

Then the train would straighten out, and the world became the one compartment in which they were traveling, the wooden benches, the bulging baggage racks overhead.

A half dozen more people had been crammed into the compartment. A young soldier sat by the window, eating a chocolate bar and fingering a harmonica. Two anxious-looking women, sisters, one with a small child, sat like Siamese twins near the corridor door. Camille Lachine, discomforted by the presence of so many people, tried to sleep. Portillo had already succeeded. Carvalho alone was awake, and he found it difficult to concentrate. His head kept filling with thoughts of his daughter, then of Major Serrano-Guridi; an odd combination certainly. "Watch the landscape," he kept telling himself. "You've never been through this part of the country before, and you should take care to see whatever there is to see. . . ."

And there was a good bit to be seen, even from a rattling train. While the high arch of sky itself was blue and clear, the ground often breathed fire. Puffy columns of black smoke rose from villages like piles of white blocks thrown on the landscape by a careless child. In the larger towns they passed, the spire of the church was always the first thing to be seen clearly, and it was inevitably smoking, often broken and leaning tipsily. Once or twice the church would be hung with a banner; red and black or simply red. Where roads could be seen, they were almost inevitably blocked by barricades such as the one they had encountered outside Puigcerdá. Often, the railroad tracks came close to an adjoining road, and groups of men became visible behind the barricades. If the train slowed down for a curve at such a time, it was possible to make out the arms they were carrying—ancient shotguns, rifles that must have dated back to the Carlist wars, even pitchforks. Occasionally a machine gun of the kind with huge side shields. At one village near Castellón, a huge cannon had been drawn up on the road. Someone had had the idea to polish the tube, and it shone like a heliograph mirror in the sun, announcing its presence for miles around.

The soldier by the window was trying to play his harmonica but clearly did not know how. Even so, Carvalho thought he recognized the tune: *"Donde vas con manton de Manila . . ."* He had taken Mercedes to see the *Zarzuela* from which it came, once, at the theater behind the Cortes in Madrid. Everything now reminded him of his family. Even the young soldier, when he turned his head in a certain way, looked like Raúl when he had been that age. A certain thrust of the upper lip; prideful, a trifle overbearing. What was Raúl doing now? Most likely taking an aperitif on the Champs Élysées or going to one of those films which showed naked women. . . .

He glanced back at Portillo who seemed to be sleeping the sleep of the just, even in the midst of such confusion. Though he had no specific reason to complain, there was something about Portillo's ever-present calm that upset him immensely. It was, in its way, the rare calm of the condemned man who knows that nothing in this world can touch him anymore.

Or was Portillo calm simply because the closer he got to Toledo the more things were coming under his control? From the few words he had spoken about the FAI leaders in Toledo, it was clear that he knew them, was confident that they would help him. Carvalho felt no such confidence. The way things were going, it seemed that Lachine and all his friends in the Communist cells would be of little assistance. The FAI were the real masters, at least for the moment. But he was committed and could not turn back. He thought with disgust of Luccioni, no doubt puttering in the greenhouse, and of Inés. Even his wife Doña Amalia seemed to have become less than flesh and blood to him. Only Mercedes mattered. It had occurred to him that he might be deluding himself, that his concern for the girl might be a way of avoiding impossible decisions: "See to her safety first, *then* we'll talk about what's to be done by way of the army . . . where I'll go, what I'll do . . ."

The ironic thing was that while he had deserted from Oviedo as much out of fear of what would happen to him when the city fell to the Anarchists as out of opposition to the officers' plotting, the army garrison at Oviedo had held out, and the Anarchists had not taken the city. If he had known, would he have stayed? He was no longer sure. A day before, even six hours earlier, he would have had no trouble answering. But each trail of smoke that rose over each village that they passed diminished his certainty even more.

The sisters in the corner were trying to buoy their spirits by talking loudly, and one of the children was crying. A man sitting next to the child reached into his pocket and gave the boy an orange which the child ate, skin and all.

The train swayed crazily from side to side. The baggage in the overhead racks bulged against the straps, threatening to fall. The wheels struck up a regular dance rhythm on the rails, and the boy seemed delighted by the soldier's attempts to play the harmonica.

More soldiers passed in the narrow corridor outside the compartment, shouting and laughing. A few officers went by, identifiable by the outline of their stiff peaked caps against the frosted glass.

Somewhere outside of Cuenca, the train suddenly began to shudder. A squalling noise issued from under the floorboards and great shoots of steam jetted up outside, obscuring the windows. The baggage lurched forward in the racks, then back. A suitcase fell, disgorging its contents on the floor; the man who had given the boy an orange cursed and began to pick up his shirts and socks.

The train came to a halt. More steam rose from the wheels and a long whistle pierced the air. Outside, the landscape was cracked and harsh. Limestone bluffs and broad stretches of arid plain, the color of dead skin.

A conductor came running along the corridor, rapping on the compartment windows: "Everyone out. As quickly as you can. Everyone. Don't cause trouble."

Cries of protest and confusion arose. The young soldier gave up trying to play *"Donde vas . . ."* and put his harmonica in his pocket. He was suddenly greenish and sweating. Lachine struggled out of the half-sleep he had only recently found and began licking his lips; he had been dreaming of deserts and was momentarily horrified to see his nightmare materialized in the landscape outside the train window. While the train had been in motion, the countryside had seemed beautiful as it fled past but now that the train had come to a stop, the plains and blistered yellow hills looked desolate and hot as the walls of a blast furnace.

Portillo shrugged and opened one eye, got to his feet and hoisted the little boy to his broad shoulders without even asking the women whether it was all right or not. The boy laughed delightedly: to him it was a game.

Already dozens of passengers had clambered down from the train, some through the windows and the compartment doors, others from the ladders at the ends of the cars. They stood about on the rock-strewn embankment along the tracks looking puzzled and frightened. Some had taken their baggage with them, and the area around the tracks now had the appearance of a sort of thieves' market, a grand scattering of suitcases, pots and pans tied together with ropes, baskets, bundles of blankets and even a few birdcages filled with canaries and parrakeets. Colonel Carvalho tried to look out of the window to see what was happening but a voice called insistently "All out . . . everyone. At once . . ." Portillo was tugging at his sleeve.

"Better do as they say. We'll see what it is soon enough."

They had to help Camille Lachine down. The siding sloped away from the tracks at a steep angle and Lachine, always afraid of heights however insignificant they might seem to others, refused to jump. It was only four feet. Carvalho and Portillo brought him down like a cripple. The little boy from their compartment was already busy looking at the train's wheels and the couplings.

Down the tracks they could see a troop of armed men standing on a rise just parallel with the locomotive. A tree trunk, partly charred and partly green with leaves, had been thrown across the tracks. Nearby on a knoll stood two tractors and a truck, all three machines grotesquely caparisoned with armor plate. The letters FAI–CNT were painted on their sides and hoods. A machine gun had been mounted on a crude contraption made of iron pipes just behind the driver's seat on the first tractor.

"Is this some kind of a game they like to play? Barricades, those ridiculous tanks . . . whatever . . . what children they are . . . ," Lachine protested. The sun was in his eyes, and he was squinting badly. It was clear that the heat was a terrible shock to his system. He seemed to be wilting before their eyes.

An army officer wearing a leather jacket and carrying an enormous pair of binoculars was pacing the line of track, followed by a dozen militiamen brandishing shotguns and rifles. Another man, in a military tunic and blue trousers, bareheaded in the sun, his bald scalp already flaming red, was carrying a large notebook of the kind schoolchildren use and had a pencil stuck behind his ear like a bank clerk. The militiamen were trying to separate the male passengers from the women and children.

There were hundreds of people now standing about along the tracks from one end of the train to the other. Some of the officers who had been riding aboard were complaining angrily and trying to talk to the man in the leather jacket who seemed to be in charge.

Abruptly, the machine gun on the tractor fired a burst into the air. Tracer bullets, bright red, floated gracefully across the blue sky. Dozens of people flattened themselves on the ground. Women screamed and dogs barked. The man on the tractor who had fired the burst began to laugh.

Carvalho could see that they were checking papers. The group would stop before each man and demand his documents, then check his name against the lists in the book that the bank clerk carried. Other militiamen were herding groups of male passengers away from the train, separating them into twos and threes, never more than six at a time, and questioning them. It was astonishing the different ways in which the passengers responded. Some cursed and shook their fists at the men who had stopped the train. Others drew themselves up with dignity and made their interrogators feel foolish, while still others behaved as if their last minutes on earth had come.

Every so often, a man would be yanked away from the others and shoved across the embankment to the knoll where the armored truck and the tractors stood. There they were made to sit with their arms around their legs. A few of them were civilians and a few were soldiers, mostly officers.

Some women nearby were screaming, and a baby had begun to cry somewhere. It had been left inside the train by accident and was hungry.

"Just do as they ask, Camille," the Colonel said hurriedly. "Don't cause trouble."

"I? What do you take me for? But . . . who are these people? Who . . . ?"

The officer in the leather jacket came up to them and held out his hand without even asking for their papers. He was looking particularly hard at Carvalho. The Colonel returned his gaze, trying to discover on the man's polyglot uniform some trace of insignia by which to identify him. The man's face was sallow, as though he had been out of the sun for a long time, or in prison, and his eyes watered in the strong light.

"Carvalho, Enrique. Colonel . . . ," the man read aloud. The bank clerk ran his finger down a page of his notebook and shook his head. The Colonel took back his papers; his name had made no impression.

But then they were much farther south now, in a part of the country that had only read about the risings in '34.

The Colonel could not restrain himself; the man in the leather jacket looked so little like an officer, despite his cap and binoculars. "What do you think you're doing . . . the least you can do is explain this . . ."

Leather-jacket looked surprised, then laughed. "Looking for deserters, Colonel, that's all. You wouldn't be one, would you? That's funny, isn't it? Sorry, but you're not on Sancho's list, are you?" He laughed again, a pale, unpleasant laugh.

"Deserters from what army? Not yours, certainly," the Colonel said.

"For God's sake . . . ," Lachine hissed. His papers were still being examined.

"Oh, that's a good question, isn't it? What army? Yes, ours, don't you know? Ours, not yours anymore. You officers give me a pain in the ass. . . ."

"And you?"

"I'm a general, can't you see? I promoted myself yesterday."

Lachine retrieved his papers as did Portillo, both without incident.

Leather-jacket scowled, uncertain what he should do about this tall arrogant Colonel who looked like a biblical prophet.

"I should send you to sit . . . over there . . ." he said, waving toward the prisoners with their arms around their knees. "It would teach you a lesson. You think we're fools, don't you," he exploded suddenly, his eyes darkening. "Well, we've found all of those so far. Deserters, every one of them. Maybe they were on their way to join the Fascists, who knows?"

"Who gives you the authority?" Carvalho asked.

"That . . . ," the man pointed back toward the armored trucks and the tractor with its clumsy machine-gun mount. "And that's all we need. . . ." He walked away, kicking up dust with his heels. The bank clerk cast an angry look at the Colonel and followed. One of the militiamen whispered as he passed: "Good for you. The bastard deserved it. He thinks he's God himself. . . ."

The questioning went on down the line. No one seemed to be in any hurry. On the rise opposite the tracks, the militiamen were prodding their prisoners to their feet with the butts of their rifles and marching them along the rise to a gully about a hundred yards distant. Carvalho watched, fascinated. He could hardly believe that such a thing was happening.

"Isn't that the man . . . ?" Lachine said suddenly, pointing to a group of three prisoners who were passing along the ridge less than twenty yards away.

And it was. His head tilted back at a sharp angle so that it looked as though he was searching for something in the sky, Major Serrano-Guridi was being pushed along by a short militiaman in blue coveralls. Serrano-Guridi's eyes were closed, and he kept stumbling, thrusting out his arms to balance himself. He was still wearing the same uniform he had worn in the Café Horno.

"He was on the train all the time, and I didn't know it. . . . He said he wanted to go to Madrid . . . ," Carvalho muttered. He started forward but Portillo grabbed him by the arm, and he offered no resistance. It was pointless, he knew, and all he would do would be to get himself shot as well.

Though it was impossible that Major Serrano-Guridi had heard the Colonel's voice clearly at that distance, he suddenly turned his head and opened his eyes. For a second his gaze met Carvalho's, and the Colonel felt a suffocating heat in his lungs. What could he say or do? If only the tailor on the Rambla had finished the five suits in time . . .

A militiaman standing between them had seen Carvalho's involuntary gesture and was pointing a rifle at him.

"He knows one of them," he shouted. "This one here. . . . I saw it." The man in the leather jacket turned and came back at a trot.

Two of the Anarchists had pushed Serrano-Guridi out of the line and forced him back down the embankment, a pistol at his head.

Leather-jacket was grinning. "So . . . after all," he said. He swung about, his binoculars slamming against his chest. He stared at Serrano-Guridi whose face was, if anything, even whiter than it had been the night before.

"You know him? Tell me who he is and you're free. What's he done? You're only a lousy major. I'll exchange you for a colonel any day. Come on . . ."

The Colonel felt somehow relieved; it was the same feeling he had experienced in the "birdcage" near Puigcerdá, only many times stronger. He felt like smiling at his old friend. One word, that was all that was needed. Who could blame him? After all, what had Serrano-Guridi done? Nothing at all; while he himself . . .

"Come on, out with it," the "bank clerk" said.

Serrano-Guridi shook his head. His eyes were wide open but the pupils had contracted to pinpoints.

"I stumbled, that's all," he said in a voice barely audible.

Carvalho's lungs were bursting. He knew what he should say: that Serrano-Guridi had been discharged the week before, that he could vouch for him, that he, Colonel Enrique Carvalho, was a deserter, from the army, from himself . . . that there was never a greater deserter in this world . . . and if anyone should be taken over the knoll to be shot, it was he. . . .

But he kept silent.

Leather-jacket spat. "All right, get him back. You know what to do. He says he stumbled. That's all. . . ." He walked away angrily. It seemed absurd to Carvalho that the man should have needed an excuse to shoot him, that for some reason, unless he could find a reason, however flimsy, the man in the leather jacket, could not bring himself to send him over the hill to be shot.

"We won't waste our time now," leather-jacket shouted back. "But next time . . ."

Lachine was puffing as though he'd been running. "I would never have believed it," he said. "Do you know what you almost did? And I thought for a moment there you were actually going to . . ."

Carvalho's hand shot out and clamped down on Lachine's shoulder. For a second Lachine's face clouded with pain as the Colonel's massive fingers dug deep into his flesh. "No, it just isn't worth it," Carvalho said. Portillo remained silent; he seemed to understand.

The prisoners disappeared over the rise opposite the tracks, followed by leather-jacket and the bank clerk. The passengers from the train were left to stand there in the sun, waiting for someone to tell them it was all right to get back on board and continue on to Madrid.

The armored tractor gave a rumble and began to move off, pulling the tree to which it was attached by a length of chain clear of the tracks.

There was a burst of machine-gun fire from beyond the rise and almost at the same time one long shriek rose skyward, like a nail driven into the sun. It lasted only a second, and it was the only one. The other seven died without a sound.

Lachine brushed his ever-damp forelock back over his head and adjusted his glasses. As they climbed back on board of the train, he said: "You were lucky. Do you realize just how lucky?"

They found their way back into the same compartment they had occupied before the train had been stopped. The little boy was already there with the two sisters who refused to look up as the men entered. Their faces were rigid and dark.

The young soldier who had been trying to play the harmonica did not return to his seat. As the train moved off, Carvalho wondered whether he had been shot or whether he was trying to play *"Donde vas* . . ."* in some other part of the train. Anything was possible, he thought. Anything at all.

July 26: *The Alcázar*

EACH MORNING JAIME MERCADER awoke with a new plan for escape, and by the evening of each day he had given up in despair, not so much because of the impracticality of his ideas but rather because of his inability to take even the first step toward putting them into effect. Watching the daily life within the besieged fortress churn on with such an appalling semblance of normality was bound, sooner or later, to rob a man of his strength and will to resist. From sunrise to sunset they were subjected to a continual barrage of badly aimed rifle fire. They watched for aircraft and hid in the subcellars when the planes came over, took their meals in the deepest underground shelters and buried their dead under piles of stones rather than in decent graves of soft earth. They grew weaker and weaker from lack of proper food but learned to regard 150 grams of bread or a three-inch strip of horseflesh as an incredible luxury. They got so used to the smell of excrement and unwashed skin that they no longer noticed it. All of this they ceased to regard as anything in any way out of the ordinary.

Yet, as Jaime recognized, he had never adjusted easily, had always resisted changes and even when at last he had had to accept them, he had tried to preserve that identity, that "shape" of self which had been formed during his previous period of life.

His life, it seemed to him, had been simply a series of unnecessary dislocations: no sooner had he begun to acclimate himself than he was wrenched away and plunged into a new situation. It was this change from his accustomed, clearly perceived pattern of behavior that disturbed him most now. He should have been struggling even more violently than ever to extricate himself, yet he seemed overcome by an insidious, unshakable lethargy. He moved like a sleepwalker through the fortress, unable to translate thought into act. There was a time which came often enough, when he would be asleep and dreaming and would know, somehow, that he *was* dreaming. Sometimes he would dream that he was drowning or falling over a cliff's edge or in the path of an oncoming railroad train with a cyclops headlight five stories tall, and he would know that if he did not wake up at once he would be killed in his dream, and afterward he would not know how to wake up. So he would struggle to move an arm or a leg, even to open his eyes, to force himself into a safe consciousness, but he could never do it. Something would always intervene, or the dream would simply stop. He would not die after all, but the feeling of paralysis would linger for an hour or more after he woke, terrifying him.

That was the closest thing to what he felt now.

Even when the officers in command of the fortress began to send out sorties into the city, he was still unable to move. Whether Mercedes was watching him or not made no difference. What she expected of him was irrelevant. What right did she have to expect anything of him? None, of course, nor did he really think that simply for the sake of demonstrating his manhood was he expected to shoulder a rifle and risk getting killed for nothing—or, what was worse, for something he could not understand at all and which he doubted was understood by anyone either inside or outside the Alcázar. It would have been absurd to risk his life for a sack of rice or a few cans of beans. It was one thing to sacrifice one's self for something one believed in—if such a thing existed that could legitimately call for the sacrifice of one's life beyond which nothing at all mattered—and quite another to do so where the end to be achieved was not only not of one's own choosing but absurd as well.

So he waited as the sorties went out, first at night, then during the day, and even once during the afternoon meal hour when the command hoped to catch the *milicianos* by surprise. The nominal purpose of each of these missions was to get food, to add a few cans of fruit or milk, a sack or two of dried beans, rice, even coffee to the store of provisions.

The garrison was holding its own, and life inside the Alcázar seemed to be closer to normal than that in the rest of the city. Jaime went time and again into the northeast tower to observe what was going on through the one-lensed binoculars he had picked up the day Pelayo had died. It was his only way of even guessing what was happening outside, and it was infuriating to him that the glasses were not powerful enough for him to read the newspapers that fluttered by outside.

And each morning he would go to see how Amado Leorza was coming with the radio.

Leorza was a shy little white-haired man. Until the preceding month he had been a clerk at the telegraph exchange. As he knew something about electrical equipment and wiring, he had been put in charge of the wreck of a radio which was the Alcázar's only hope of communication with the outside.

"A few hours and a piece or wire, that's all that's needed. Just so . . . long, a piece of wire, just so . . . long . . . ," Leorza would say, but the hours turned into days and still the radio sat there, obdurate and voiceless. It had been ruined in the very first bombing raid. Leorza kept at it day after day, promising each evening that he would have the radio working by morning.

Jaime regarded Leorza's enterprise with concern. Each time he went to the little room where the old man was working, he wondered what would happen if the set was finally put into operation and something should be heard concerning Colonel Carvalho. Everyone in the Alcázar knew who Mercedes was, that she was Enrique Carvalho's daughter, but thus far she had been protected by her father's reputation as the accomplice of Generals Bosch and Yagüe in the Oviedo affair. How ironic. No one even suspected the truth. But, Jaime agonized . . . what was the truth, really? Carvalho had, after all, betrayed him at Oviedo; what was to stop him now from betraying himself, and his daughter as well? He might just as easily have gone with the rebels as stayed with the Government, depending on his situation at the moment he had to choose.

It occurred to him that in the almost two weeks that had passed, many things could have happened and that he did not really know who those people outside were or why it was, now, at that very moment, they were so intent on destroying him. No one, after all, had even so much as asked him what *he*, Jaime Mercader, wanted to do, whose side *he* was on, or if he wanted to be on anyone's side.

These thoughts so preoccupied him that he forgot almost entirely about his father and mother and the house just beyond the farthest curve in the north plain, where he could not quite see.

It would have been simple enough to steal a radio tube while Leorza wasn't looking or to pull out some wires, but he could not bring himself to do it. It seemed so pointless, a temporary reprieve only; whatever would happen, would happen. That was all.

If the radio were suddenly to recover its voice and blurt out that Carvalho was in command of a column of government troops or had denounced the rebel generals, Jaime wanted to be the first to know about it, just as a man on trial for his life prefers to hear the verdict read to him in private before it is read in open court—no matter what the verdict is.

JULY 27: *The Alcázar*

BARRERA'S LEGS FELT HEAVY. He mounted the steps only with great difficulty. Above, up the stairwell, he could hear a buzz of activity, garbled voices, and the clank of rifles and ammunition boxes. Somewhere, someone was whimpering. Another patrol was returning. There had been some fighting in the outposts in the buildings directly around the Alcázar, the Capuchinos and the old dining hall south of the Riding School. Why hadn't they heard the firing? Perhaps the flares they had seen, the machine-gun fire, had been meant for someone else: the other patrol.

The voices grew louder at the head of the stairs. A light pulsed, at the landing. As Barrera topped the stairs, he saw that the corridor was full of men, all coming from the west end of the building. About two dozen, mostly Guard, a few soldiers, all with blackened faces. Three men were dragging a machine gun. Some of the soldiers were bleeding but, oddly, seemed not to notice their wounds. One man walked stiffly along the wall, groping for support and hissing a continuous stream of obscenities through clenched teeth.

A litter, borne by two civilians approached, the wounded man on it looking at his hand which was covered with blood. He was trying to clench and unclench his fingers but could not. As the litter passed, the wounded man caught sight of Barrera. "Stop a minute," he called out.

The civilians pulled the litter to the side. Barrera recognized the man: it was Torres, the private who had gone with him and his cousin the afternoon they had taken hostages.

"Is that you, Esteban?"

"Yes . . ."

"Then you better get back there and look after Infante. He's in a bad way."

Barrera went rigid. "Was he hit?"

"No, but it's worse, and there's nobody to take care of him. I've got it easy . . . blood gets everyone excited, and they look after you. Infante, he's not bleeding, so they don't care, but . . . man, you better go look after him."

"Come on," said an officer passing by. "Get that man down to the hospital."

The bearers carried Torres off. Torres tried to turn his head again but could not manage. *"Adios . . ."* There was a puddle on the ground where his hand had dripped blood onto the stones.

What the devil did Torres mean, "He's not bleeding"? If you're shot up, you bleed. But sometimes, he knew . . . he remembered from the days at Cartenegra . . . the miners got concussions and died, and there wasn't a mark on them . . . or gassed . . . or their lungs went black. . . . What the devil did Torres mean?

He stayed close to the corridor wall so as not to interfere with the soldiers still coming the other way. At the end of the corridor, he turned and found Infante Delgado sitting on a block of stone by the wall, his Mauser on the ground between his feet. The rifle was smashed and the rock that had done it was still in his hand. He was looking down and cursing quietly, almost sadly, to himself. Tears rolled down his sooty cheeks. He looked up and saw Barrera.

"Oh Jesus . . . you . . . get out of here, cousin . . ." He began to moan.

"What is it, Infante? I just saw Torres and he said . . ."

"Ai . . . this for Torres . . ." He made an obscene gesture. "And you, you leave me alone, do you hear?" He shivered and his teeth began to click absurdly. He stilled them with a grimace, drawing blood from his lip.

Barrera went on his knees before his cousin. Delgado's face was swollen and blackish. He went on cursing.

"Infante, for the love of Christ," Barrera shouted, "tell me what it is."

"Get the hell away from me. You don't want to come near me. What he said, Torres, it's true. I swear, it's true. That Torres . . ."

"I don't understand. Torres didn't say anything . . ."

"I didn't mean to do it, I swear to you." Infante's face twisted in an agony of contrition. So exaggerated that it was almost comical and, therefore, twice as frightening. "Oh, Mother . . . I . . . did . . . not mean to do it to him. It was his fault for being there, I swear it. Why wasn't he home in bed with his wife? Why wasn't he . . . ? my sister . . ." He suddenly looked down into Barrera's face. "Get away from me. Leave me alone . . ."

"Didn't do what? For Christ' sake . . ."

"You mean? . . . Torres didn't tell you?"

"No."

Infante gathered a deep breath, then spoke in a very low, harsh voice, trying hard to keep calm.

"I killed Ignacio. . . . Do you understand that? He was out there and I shot him right in the chest. I swear to God, I didn't know it was him until after, when the searchlight fell on him . . ."

Barrera put an arm around his cousin's shoulder and eased him to his feet. Infante let himself be guided along without resisting. They walked slowly down the corridor. The soldiers had dispersed into the side tunnels and the barricaded rooms. Two more litters were borne by, headed toward the infirmary.

They drew abreast of one of the hollow-rock rooms where the Civil Guard and the soldiers had spread their blankets, then went inside.

"I don't want to go to sleep. How can you think I could sleep? He

. . . he won't let me, even if I . . . ," Infante's voice trailed off. He sat down on a pile of filthy blankets. "Don't push me . . ."

The room was almost empty. There were only a few other men there, sleeping or collapsed from exhaustion. A single light burned.

Delgado let himself be stretched out on the floor, a blanket pulled up over his chest. Then, suddenly, his body contracted and he sat bolt upright; then he jumped up, the blanket tangled in his feet.

"Get away from me, Esteban. I can't stand to have you near me. I can't stand to have anyone near me. . . ."

Delgado had pulled his bayonet from its scabbard. "I'll cut you up, cousin," he shouted . . . "I'll kill you the way . . . I killed . . . ," and here his voice ascended almost to a scream . . . "Ignacio! . . ." He lurched back against the wall, waving the bayonet before him, shouting at Barrera to get out.

"All right," Barrera said. "If you'll just sit down . . ." He put his hands on his cousin's shoulders and forced him down to the bench. Infante sank back, rigidly, but offering no resistance.

"Look, man . . . how was it your fault?" Barrera said. "Who told the frog to be out there shooting at you . . . ?"

Infante held out his right hand. "I pulled the trigger, that's how it was my fault. It's that simple."

"But he was there . . ."

"And I was there . . ." Infante turned a tear-stained face toward his cousin. Barrera shivered; he had never seen Infante cry in all his life, not even at his father's own funeral when poor Joaquín Delgado's body lay in the shed for two days, and Infante had sat beside it all that time, as though trying to memorize every broken bone, every inch of crushed muscle and flesh, all that was left of his father after the mine accident.

"It was my fault, that's all," Infante said. "Don't try to tell me anything else." He looked down at his feet. "Look, I know you want to help me . . . but can't you see? . . . I want to be left alone. Go away, cousin, and don't come back . . . just leave me. Forget about me . . ."

"Forget about the man who has saved my life maybe two times . . . my father . . ."

"Shit on your father, and shit on you," Infante shouted, suddenly getting to his feet. "Listen, man . . . I don't want you here . . . do you understand? Get out . . . if you come back . . . if you watch me . . . I warn you . . ."

"I won't," Barrera said, backing away. He had caught the glint of a small knife in Infante's hand. He was crazy; no, maybe he wasn't so crazy after all. How would he have felt if it had been he who had pulled the trigger on Ignacio? It was all very well and good to talk, to say, "Don't worry, it wasn't your fault" . . . but if you knew . . . if you really knew . . .

He went out quickly. As he left, he turned his head, not wanting to look even one more time at Infante, not for that moment anyhow. And so he did not see his cousin drive the point of the knife into his own palm. The blood spurted, mixed with the dirt, but Infante only grunted and pushed the point in still further.

JULY 28
Yesterday our glorious fleet heavily shelled the African coast.

The Alcázar of Toledo evacuated by the remaining rebels.

Official news, later confirmed by the Dirección General de Seguridad, reports that rebels entrenched in the Alcázar have finally surrendered at two o'clock in the afternoon and that the building has been evacuated.

The news has been received with indescribable joy in Toledo.

JULY 30
Rebel "pockets" immobilized by the pressure of the severe siege of the Loyalist troops and the armed militia.

Decisive victorious action on the fronts in behalf of the Republican cause.

El Sol (Madrid)

JULY 31 TO AUGUST 3: *The Alcázar*

AT THE BEGINNING HE HAD BEEN alone most of the time. During the first few days he had seen the driver, Barrera, in the yard a few times but the man had seemed to prefer the company of his cousin, the Civil Guard, Delgado. Jaime watched with amazement as Barrera went out, day after day, with the raiding parties and actually came back again each time. "When he could just as easily have escaped, walked away from it all, just like that."

Jaime, too, had had his chance, that night when the first burial party had gone into the Riding Hall, when he had been alone on the esplanade with no one around to stop him from doing whatever he wanted to do. There *had* been a choice then, just as there had been a choice before. "A man is always able to choose, no matter what he tells himself; it may be easier to accept things as they are, to excuse what one does by saying that to do anything else would be futile." But wasn't that precisely what he had condemned Carvalho for doing?

On the ninth day, Barrera had come up to him in the courtyard, his eyes sunken, his face dark with unhappiness. In a moment, he had blurted it all out: "He insists that he shot Ignacio, can you believe it? Torres swears it isn't true, that it wasn't Ignacio at all . . . but, Christ, it's destroyed him . . . such a fine man . . . he just sits there now, like a statue . . . looking at his feet. I don't know what to say to him."

From then on, Barrera had followed Jaime about just as before. They sat and talked. Nothing made any difference. Together they went down to where Infante Delgado still sat, alone, on a stone bench like a penitent, just outside the room they were using as a hospital station. "Why shouldn't I be close to the dead and the dying," Delgado said slowly when Infante tried to get him to leave. "To remind me of what I've done, no? It's my penance." There was no moving him and no arguing with him. He sat there and banged his forehead with his blackened knuckles until there was a series of red lumps all over his skull between brow and hairline.

For Barrera it was as though he had been suddenly cut loose from an anchor and was floating away against his will. In the midst of some pointless task, building more barricades, shoring up walls, smashing furniture to fuel the stoves that baked the bread with which they were fed, he would turn to Jaime and say, "Let's go down and see how he's doing, *teniente* . . ." And they would go and nothing would have changed at all. Barrera would stay and curse at his cousin, and that would be that.

When Jaime was not building barricades or cutting wood . . . he had not refused thus far to arm himself or take part in the fighting though it seemed to him that it was inevitable that he should do so . . . he would try to see Mercedes. The women had been quartered in a large chamber on the second level below the surface, and another room had been set aside for those who had children.

In the childless women's room, a single candle burned, day and night, the light broken into a webbed pattern by sackcloth hung from a rope across the chamber. Sometimes Jaime would stand outside in the corridor—men were not allowed into the room—while someone went in to get Mercedes for him, and he would hear the murmuring voices inside. It seemed to him that he had listened to the same stories over and over a hundred times, but the voices were always eager, persistent. Each woman had her small store of tales, and she clung to them as though they were her only possessions. And each time the story was told a new strand was woven in, a detail changed, a personage added.

". . . made him piss into the chalice, and then he had to drink it, with bird droppings for a wafer . . ."

"And afterwards?"

"What d'you think? They shot him of course, like all the others, when . . . he wouldn't . . ."

"Wouldn't what . . ."

"You know . . . with the statue of the Virgin . . ."

"What a foolish thing . . . why not?"

"Ah . . ."

"That's not true. What about Padre Marin?"

"But he was . . . one of theirs, so that doesn't count. They wouldn't kill one of their own, would they?"

"Well, someone will . . . the Judas."

The women were not allowed to help in the defense but only to aid the wounded and prepare food. No one prevented their coming up to the surface, and Mercedes was able to get away without difficulty. Most often, they would meet in the evening and take their meals together in another chamber where a large series of tables had been set up. He would explain his latest plans, and she would approve them, always, and then they would sit on the steps outside of the room and talk about what they would do once they were outside the Alcázar. He had not yet had the strength to talk to her about her father again, though he could see well enough that she expected him to, that she had prepared herself and was ready for him.

On the evening of the eleventh day, Jaime saw by his watch, which was still running perfectly, that it was time to go down to the subcellar.

Jaime descended the stairs to the dining hall; he had found a piece of bread and was taking it to Mercedes. He had not sunken quite so far into an acceptance of things as they were that he could not appreciate the humor of what he was doing, and he permitted himself an infrequent smile as he went down the stairs. How nice it would have been to have been taking the girl flowers or candy outside . . . at her home, at his home . . . anywhere but there. But a piece of bread? . . . a single piece of bread?

Below, the light cast by the resin torches which had been thrust into the wall at each landing eddied like liquid, and the smell of pine filled the stairwell. Pine and smoke . . .

The same smell, he thought, recalling it as he descended, the same smell as then . . . when the night had come down like an iron lid on the cinders of the Hotel Covadonga and the University . . . skeletons of twisted beams and steel. The Moors had sung around their campfires in the ruins, and oil lamps had glowed in the windows of many of the buildings, casting onto the stones of the streets outside the shadows of the captured and the condemned as they passed the courts-martial tables.

The officers presiding had rarely looked up.

"Munguia . . . guilty . . ."

"Patricio Cuevas . . . guilty as charged . . ."

"Gregorio Aznar . . . guilty . . ."

Names, floating about like lost spirits, threading their way into the refrains of the Moors' songs . . . volleys of rifle fire and the startled cries of men caught unprepared for death . . . not really believing it was there.

"Fernandez . . . guilty . . ."

Jaime had passed a house, come out onto an open clearing. A table had been set up there under the stars. Only a single paraffin lamp on the table and a weary captain in a leather coat, hunched up and chilled, shivering. A shadowy group of prisoners had drawn themselves into a congealed mass of filthy flesh, ringed by soldiers with bayonets. Weariness on their faces too. "Get it over with. We don't want to listen anymore."

One man had been pushed from the group . . . his name read out, the sentence pronounced. He had begun to protest and struggle. The captain behind the table had lifted his pistol and shot him on the spot. The body had been left on the ground where it had fallen while the next man was brought up. He had stood looking at the corpse at his feet, not once lifting his eyes to confront the captain behind the table. No name was read. The man would not answer, seemed to have been struck dumb by the sight of the body at his feet.

"I saw him myself. He threw dynamite. I would never forget his face . . . ," said a soldier hidden in the dark, outer ring.

"So . . . then . . . without a name . . . you. Guilty . . ."

Jaime had walked on . . . nearby a volley of rifle shots rang out. Every wall in the city ran with blood. The Moors had hunted through the ruins, killing indiscriminately. Their officers, having given up trying to control them, had let them run loose and pretended not to see what was happening. There had been no point in trying to stop them.

A man had run down a nearby street, crossing almost directly in front of Jaime. He had stopped, his face twisted not so much with fear as with confusion. He had been filthy, black with smoke, and burned.

Then he had begun to run again. A dozen Moors had passed a few seconds later, laughing, running like cats that would never tire. Jaime had stopped where he was. A second later there had been a short barking cry. The Moors had caught the man. The bark had dissolved into a liquid sound . . . the knives . . . no waste of cartridges . . . the knives at night . . .

Now he was almost to the bottom of the stairs. It wasn't the shots he had been hearing after all but the clatter of pannikins and the clank of a spoon against a kettle, and the voices had been simply those of the people gathered there to eat, calling each other's names. A man's name is important at such times; saying it aloud relieves him of his anonymity if only for a split second, and creates an illusion of identity . . but an illusion only.

"It doesn't exist," Jaime thought . . . "none of it does, none of us do. Is there a Patricio Cuevas down there? Such a fine name. It probably belonged to a clod of a man who never even had a chance to know how fine a name it was before . . . we shot him . . ."

He unwrapped the lump of bread and tossed it from hand to hand.

A piece of bread. A single piece of bread.

AUGUST 1

A rebel column annihilated by the forces of Lieutenant Colonel Mangada in Navalperal de Piñares.

The Government is clearly optimistic about yesterday's military action.

AUGUST 2

Forces from the Levante and Ciudad Real arrive in Madrid.

The Mangada column continues its victorious advance.

The military situation is clearly favorable to the Republican regime.

El Sol (Madrid)

VITOLYN WAS IRRITATED; wasn't it bad enough that there was almost nothing to eat? He shifted nervously on the long wooden bench, casting angry glances out of the corner of his eye at the man who had sat down next to him. It was the man who had been coming out of the Major's office the day they'd brought him there for questioning. What did he want: Vitolyn didn't like it at all. It could be a trick and even if it wasn't, it was hardly a good idea to be around someone who was so obviously frightened. Fear has a way of communicating itself whether you want it to or not, and he knew that if the man didn't leave him alone, he'd begin to fear himself . . . It crossed his mind that that might not be so bad after all . . . he'd been disturbed that he hadn't felt as frightened as he should have.

The man was speaking to him again; he hadn't answered him the last time they'd met but that hadn't made any difference. The man was still asking questions.

Vitolyn was thinking, "I've told them the truth, almost, and they don't believe it because they expected me to lie. What a situation . . ."

"What did they ask you," Gil was saying, trying to speak in a low but friendly voice. It was most unconvincing.

Vitolyn didn't answer him but went on trying to scrape up the little remaining fat that had adhered to his tin plate.

"Don't you hear me?" Gil said, leaning closer. He smelled of an odd mixture of pomade and sweat which Vitolyn found particularly offensive. "I hear you. It's simply that I have nothing to say to you, that's all."

The rough wooden trestle table at which they sat was over thirty feet long. It had been set up in the middle of a narrow underground chamber that had once served as a dungeon for the prisoners of the Moorish governor of Toledo, Amru. At the end of the room farthest from the stairway that led up to the surface, a small fire had been kindled within a circle of bricks and loose stone. A soot-black kettle swung slowly over the sputtering flames, giving off a rancid odor: grease and horseflesh simmering. There were some women seated not far off and Gil kept glancing at them, then looking away.

Why had Vitolyn allowed the man to sit next to him in the first place? Of all people . . . but then, how could he have stopped him? The bench was free and no one had any particular seat. Perhaps it would have been better to have had seats assigned, as at a theater or on board ship. If anyone would listen to him, he would make a suggestion. . . .

He was aware that his companion was still waiting for him to speak.

"Questions, that's all. Lots of foolish questions," Vitolyn said at last.

"About what?"

"That's my business, don't you think? Look here . . ." Vitolyn banged his fork against the edge of his plate.

"They asked me questions, too," Gil said. "I don't know why. What were they after, I want to know . . . ?"

A constant dry shuffling of tin plates along the trestle and a scraping of spoons. The slither of tongues licking dry lips, trying to lap up the last drops of fat, to consume the tiniest fibers left clinging to the teeth. There was an obvious art to extracting nourishment from horseflesh, strips, two inches long . . . the simplest of rules: don't waste anything.

The soldier by the kettle went on turning the spoon around the inside, scraping the bottom.

"Look here, you have to trust somebody, don't you?"

"Please . . . ," Vitolyn protested. What was he going to do? So far no one was looking. What if this man had actually done something? It wouldn't be good to remain in his company, to be seen talking to him, would it?

"I'll trust you, I've decided that . . . ," Gil said, leaning closer. The smell of pomade and sweat grew stronger. Gil went on: "They were asking you questions, too, weren't they? . . . trying to get something against you? It isn't fair. That's why I trust you . . . listen . . . you have to talk to somebody. Do you want to know what they were after . . . with me, I mean? I think I understand . . . it's unbelievable but I do understand it."

"No, I don't want to hear. I'm going to go now, so . . ."

"No . . . ," Gil gave a gasp and took hold of Vitolyn's arm. "Please don't . . ."

"Listen, they think I killed . . . a man . . . I'm sure of it . . . there, now you know."

"So?"

"Do you understand what that means? To be accused of . . . he was a friend. I had nothing to do with it, but it looks . . . yes, I can see it their way, and it looks as though . . . but how do you explain? That's why I thought that you . . . you . . ."

"No," Vitolyn shot back, trying to turn his back but unable to do so because of the narrowness of the bench.

"I saw you, don't you understand? And you . . . you . . ."

"What?"

"You were . . . afraid too. . . ."

Vitolyn's elbow struck the edge of the table. He winced, turned, and stared full at Gil. Afraid? Had he seemed afraid, and all the time felt nothing himself? There was no telling then what mistakes he could have made about himself, about others. "I was afraid?" he whispered. "You saw that?"

"Yes. Why would I say such a thing if it wasn't so?"

Vitolyn's hand was trembling, and he could barely keep the last scrap of meat on the spoon. It kept sliding off. His face took on an oddly plaintive expression.

". . . Venegas, Fernán Venegas, that was his name . . . ," Gil was saying. "He's only been buried, a week or so now, and you'd think they'd be decent enough to wait a while . . ."

"They never do . . . they can't wait, ever . . . ," Vitolyn said vaguely.

"Can you imagine, the two of them sitting there. . . . Of course, they did it to you as well . . . imagine . . . like judges, smoking and not even offering me a cigarette. If they had known how much I . . ."

"I don't have one either," Vitolyn said quickly.

"Oh . . . ," Gil tried not to sound disappointed, went on, "about the *Asalto* officers visiting my house the morning I came here. They seem to think that was quite significant. Someone saw it, you see. You have to be careful about people who see things . . . they fit them together, those things, and they make a false picture. . . ."

Vitolyn's stomach tightened; was the fear really returning? No, it was only the hunger, but it made him feel as though he were terribly afraid. That's what Gil had noticed before . . . only the hunger. He hadn't really been afraid. It was just that he hadn't eaten.

The only way he could keep Gil away, keep him from digging into his own secrets, was to express an interest in what was bothering the man. That was clear enough. All right. He'd do it. It was a small enough price to pay.

"Assault Guards," Gil went on hurriedly. "*Asaltos* . . . you're a foreigner, I can tell by the way you speak, of course. You can't be expected to understand these differences. The *Asaltos* are the ones, so they say, who murdered Calvo Sotelo. So you can imagine . . ."

How ironic it was, Vitolyn thought; everything here was upside down from the way it had been in Vienna. Upside down, but with no real difference at all.

"And you?" Gil asked. "Haven't they accused you of something, too?"

What was the man getting at? It was like the interminable prelude to one of those operas by Pfitzner or Wagner that his father had taken him to as a child, making him stand all the while. Would Gil never get to the point?

"You have no right to talk to me that way," Vitolyn said. "Oh, I know what they were hinting at, but it's all . . ." He turned his head away; enough was enough. ". . . a lie," he concluded.

Gil smiled knowingly, but said nothing.

On both sides, men dipped and bobbed over their tin plates like Moslems at evening prayer. A ways farther down, some of the women sat, and among them the Carvalho girl and Venegas' mistress, Selica Portillo. Gil cast a glance in their direction and thanked God that they were no closer and that he would not have to talk to them. A while earlier he had been afraid of Selica Portillo. She had been watching him, but he thought it best to stay away from her. He remembered that the Major had asked him how long Venegas had stayed at his apartment that night and whether anyone else had been there at the time. He'd told the truth, partially. He knew the exact length of time, because the record had just been put on when the doorbell had rung and just finished when Venegas left: a total of not more than three minutes. He could hear the melody clearly enough and recalled it now at the oddest moments. Alicia had told him that the composer, Smetana, had spent the last years of his life hearing a high E which he could not get out of his ear . . . But he hadn't told them about Torroba at all. What if someone had seen Torroba there, perhaps even the same person who had informed about the *Asaltos* on the following morning? It made him dizzy; his head was shot through with sharp, migraine-like pains. He cast another glance at Vitolyn who turned away, refusing to speak to him any further. Perhaps, Gil thought, he had been too incautious. After all, the man was a foreigner. He was frightened, alone, in a strange, hostile place. Of course he would be on his guard, would not want to talk to strangers. But yet, of all of them, the Austrian was the one man Gil had felt at ease in approaching. The others terrified him: how was he to know when one of them would turn and accuse him? Twice now, in the past week he had seen Venegas' friend Umberto Reyles in the Alcázar and each time the man had avoided him; wasn't Reyles supposed to be his friend as well? Yet Gil was positive that it was Reyles who was egging on the Major and the others. Perhaps that was why he felt comfortable with the Austrian, because the Austrian could have no part in any of it. He was a complete outsider and, so, completely safe.

Time enough later. Even in the Austrian's reproaches he found reassurance. Eat, and forget it for the moment. Stay away from the others, the Carvalho girl who can only bring trouble with her unpredictable father and the young Mercader who will one day bring ruin on himself and anyone who is too close to him. Stay away from them all and concentrate on this man . . . but for now, concentrate on . . . food. To live one must eat. To eat . . . must have . . . food.

He slid his plate about on the trestle. He had but to think the word *food* and everything else vanished. He began to mumble to himself as he stared at his plate.

"There *must* be . . . more . . ."

He said it again, louder this time, so that everyone around him heard it. But they all looked away, embarrassed, so that in the end, instead of attracting attention, he had forced it away.

Vitolyn watched, fascinated. He had always thought that his own hunger was the one uncontrollable, terrible driving force in his life. He dreamed at night of being locked up in a cell and slowly starved to death. He knew that they did that in Germany: put a man into something no bigger than a closet and just let him die there, without food or water. But here he was, watching with clinical detachment as someone else gave in to a hunger that was even more uncontrollable than his own and, by simply watching, he had managed to master himself. It was true then, that the sight of another's suffering somehow fortifies us. We forget our own pain when we became absorbed with the pain of others. Vitolyn was chilled by the thought; what if it ever turns inward, this exultation in another man's anguish?

Gil's hands suddenly went scrabbling in the pannikin; he had dropped his spoon. He was trying to grab something, chasing it about the slippery plate and clawing at it with fingers that had only the stubs of nails left and so could not seize on something so tiny.

With two hands he succeeded in capturing the scrap, lifted it to his mouth. His hands were trembling and for a second Vitolyn saw a hideous vision of what he himself could so easily become. His own hunger was so terrible, rooted in every part of his body. It was the one clear emotion he had experienced all day, and it consumed everything else. Yet to become like this man . . .

Suddenly Gil lost hold of the scrap; it slipped away between his fingers and fell to the trestle, a tiny gobbet with strings of flesh hanging from it like threads.

Vitolyn had not noticed; there was an elderly man wrapped in a tattered blanket, his face the color of charred wood, sitting on the other side of Gil. The man had been bent silently, bleakly over his own pannikin.

A hand flew suddenly from the mound of blanket and snatched up the sliver of meat from the board. Gil turned on the man.

The old man stared at him and chewed with wrenching, circular motions of his jaw until he had extracted every last drop of nourishment from the scrap. Then he spit it out.

"You let it drop," he said.

Gil seemed to be suffocating.

"Leave him alone . . . it's all right," Vitolyn said quickly.

"No . . ." Gil was trying desperately to keep control of himself. Other people were watching him now. "He had no right . . ."

At the far end of the trestle, on the women's side, Venegas' mistress, Selica Portillo rose, pannikin in hand. Gil watched her with a horrified understanding of what she was about to do. She was coming over to him. Quite slowly, as though it were the most natural thing in the world to do, she laid her plate in front of him, nesting it in his own empty pannikin. There was a small lump of meat on it.

"This is for you. I'm not hungry any more. . . ."

"Señora . . . ," Gil protested. "Please . . . don't do this to me. . . ." How could he take food from a woman, and in front of everyone else? They had turned their heads away, all of them, as though by some common, instantaneous communication they had determined to leave him to his shame in peace.

"Fernán would have done no less for you," she said and walked back to her seat.

In the one second that their eyes met, he saw materialize in the air before him the ghost of Venegas, ruined now by bullets, fouled and wrapped in canvas, saw him slip by with incredible rapidity yet saw him clearly . . . a dumb show of the scene in his room two weeks before. "Life, mocking man's intentions, plays jokes of its own devising and forces us to laugh or be destroyed . . . ," the words of Madriaga that he had read afterward while trying to read himself to sleep. What could he say to her? The way she looked at him, with such sorrow. Was he deserving of such pity? Was it he himself or something that she knew was going to happen to him, that she could read on his face like a gypsy telling fortunes from the creases in a man's hand?

He glanced back at Vitolyn. What did he know? What did they all know?

He picked up the piece of meat, guarding himself with a crooked elbow from the old man on his left.

No need . . . the old man had fallen asleep over his plate.

AUGUST 5
San Rafael is recovered.
    The Loyalist forces completely surround the rebels in the Sierra.
The [military] operations have reached a decisive phase.

El Sol

AUGUST 5: *Aranjuez to Toledo*

NOT FAR FROM ARANJUEZ, the locomotive broke down. For hours an army of trainmen sweated and cursed over the engine in the broiling sun, but nothing could be done. Passengers, among them women with umbrellas and men with folded newspapers over their heads, once again descended from the train and stood alongside the tracks watching the fruitless labors of the engineer and his crew. One family made an outing of it; the father drove poles into the ground and then strung a sheet over them, creating a sort of Arab tent under which his wife and two children sat eating cheese and oranges. The trainmen, stripped to the waist and glistening with oil, looked leprous, their torsos splotched with black soot, their hands darkened by coal dust.

Lachine at first thought that they had encountered another barricade. This time he rummaged quickly in his briefcase and took out a little Beretta pistol which he had put in his trouser pocket. His face had acquired a strained, nervous look, and the lock of damp hair that habitually hung down over his high-domed forehead was unusually limp.

Carvalho, for his part, could not forget the face of Major Serrano-Guridi nor the sound of the shots over the rise. All the way from Cuenca he had argued with himself that there was nothing he could have done about it. He had been a fool to antagonize the "general" in the leather jacket. And it was only by a miracle that he had not been shot himself: a quirk in the "general's" character and the lack of an ultimate justification. He had talked about the incident with some of the other officers who were traveling on the train.

"There was an officer named Huerta who was in charge of the firing squad at Nebrija prison," one of the lieutenants who had been listening said. "Whenever a man was condemned to death, this Captain Huerta used to visit him the night before he was executed and sit in his cell, insulting the condemned man, arguing with him, saying whatever he could to arouse him, until finally the condemned man would strike him. Then Captain Huerta would get up and leave. Without that blow, he could never bring himself to give the order to fire the next morning. He was well known for it. . . ."

"And the 'general'?"

"The same," the Lieutenant said. "The same, I suppose."

Once the train had gotten underway again, they had elbowed their way through the narrow corridors to the first-class section. There they had found still more officers, a dozen or so, all over the rank of captain. Most were moderate Republicans as he was, a few of them Freemasons as well, though one major and two captains in the Assault Guard tried stridently to justify what the Anarchists had done on the ground that it was essential to maintain a strict discipline in what remained of the army. Deserters, traitors, and spies could not be tolerated.

"They took off two priests who were traveling in disguise," a captain by the name of Jaca told Colonel Carvalho. "They were gentle men. I don't see why . . ."

All of them sat about looking at each other, trying to understand why they had done nothing to intervene, each one sure that there was nothing he could have done. Carvalho had gone back to his own compartment, more convinced than ever that he was worthless.

After four hours, the trainmen gave up and went back inside the cab to rest and drink warm soda. The passengers, hundreds of them, began the trek to the nearest town, Aranjuez, which was less than three miles away. A strange procession indeed, Carvalho thought, strung out as they were along the tracks like the Hebrews fleeing the pharaoh. The officers drew together until they formed a skeleton company. Many were from the Basque provinces and the north coast and were not used to the shattering heat.

"It's not so bad," one of them, a Major Compredon who sported a huge and bristling gray mustache, shouted encouragingly. "It was lots worse at Melilla." He set an example for the rest of them, striding on ahead with his shoulders thrown back. He was the only man among them who seemed even older than Colonel Carvalho and, given his forceful conduct and his martial behavior, it was impossible to understand why he was still a major at his age.

The sun descended grudgingly over the Sierra de Gredos to the west, streaking the landscape with long tracks of red and saffron. The train grew small behind them, alone and desolate on the tracks, something prehistoric, lying there in the desert.

Tall feathery grass, yellow and withered, grew in sparse clumps on the rises. Overhead, puffy white clouds fled the advance of night, accelerating their escape to the east, as the sun sank down to graze the tops of the western sierra.

The squat outlines of the Mudéjar church at Ocaña came into view.

The line of train passengers now extended for a good half mile, like a column of ants crawling toward an unseen hill. Even Portillo was showing signs of fatigue. He had not lit a cigar since Cuenca. He seemed to be struggling with some particularly agonizing problem though. Colonel Carvalho thought: "It's possible that what disturbs him so much is that we're so close to Toledo now." Portillo turned every so often and gave Carvalho an ambiguous glance which made the Colonel nervous; it was a look such as he might have given himself directly after Serrano-Guridi had been shot. It said: "I know that there was nothing you could have done, but you could have done something."

Near Ocaña, the file passed by a military encampment in the fields. A dozen or more tents had been set up, and a cluster of lorries and cars had been drawn about in a circle near a group of whitewashed farm buildings and an old well. The vehicles cast long shadows over the ground, fingers of dark which seemed to reach out toward the line of passengers as though to draw them in. A pennant fluttered over the farmhouse; the tricolor of the Republic. A few small field pieces stood near horse-drawn wagons, their muzzles pointed at the setting sun. Wires had been strung from the vehicles and thence to a series of telegraph poles that marched down the road toward Ocaña.

Carvalho drew his companions away from the line of passengers and toward the camp. Most of the other officers followed. They had no idea what to expect in Ocaña but at least in the encampment there was some hope of order, of things being the way they should be.

Portillo agreed; it would be better to stop at the encampment, even if it meant a delay. They could hardly afford another encounter with an undisciplined band of Anarchists. Lachine was uncertain but allowed himself to be persuaded; he had seen how little his credentials meant once outside of a decent sized city. There were two worlds, one where slips of paper and stamps had an almost mystical significance and another where they meant nothing at all. Though at first Lachine had been contemptuous of Carvalho's fear of the Anarchists, now he was beginning to see what the Colonel meant. As a result, he became more convinced by the hour of the importance of his own mission, to ensure the collection of enough funds to purchase arms and to seat his own people firmly in power. Otherwise the war would be a disaster. What would the Anarchists do the first time they came up against disciplined troops? It would be a slaughter. No, something had to be done to ensure that control passed to those most fit to exercise it.

They entered the encampment surrounded by suspicious sentries who could not believe their eyes when they saw the long time of passengers come trudging across the low rises that formed the camp's defilade.

The soldiers were mostly recruits who had simply been there when the rising had started, on field maneuvers outside Aranjuez, and whose officers had remained loyal. There was a captain named Segurra, who was senior officer, and a number of lieutenants who had set up the camp's signal system. The group consisted of a survey party, two light artillery pieces—75 mm Schneiders—and a signal detachment. Outside of the two field pieces, their only arms were a dozen machine guns and the usual complement of pistols and rifles.

"We have radio contact with Madrid," Captain Segurra explained, welcoming the party of officers from the train, "and plenty to eat, so why should we worry? Besides, don't you think the countryside is beautiful at this time of day?" He lit a pipe and invited everyone into the whitewashed farmhouse where he had made his quarters.

The evening meal was simple but more than ample, and there were even enough chairs for all the newcomers to seat themselves. The owner of the house had been a carpenter and had supplied a number of shops in Ocaña and Aranjuez with chairs and tables. An entire shed full of chairs had been found behind the house.

There was a bottle of cognac after the meal, a bit incongruous considering the simplicity of the food, but welcome nonetheless. As senior officer among the fugitives from the train, Carvalho found himself explaining, painfully—and quite reluctantly—what had happened to them near Cuenca.

"Ah, it's the same story every place," Captain Segurra observed, blowing smoke toward the beamed ceiling of the house. "We've got to pull together, don't you know, or we're all going to find ourselves in a ditch with Fascist bullets in our necks. Now, take Lieutenant Orillas over there. . . . He's as much a believer in social progress as I am or as those fools with their black and red flags are . . . but you can't win a war by destroying everything in sight, can you?" He poured himself a little more cognac. "Well, what am I talking about? It's not a war at all. And it's going to be done with in a week or two, and then we can all go back home, wherever that may be."

The Captain and all four of his lieutenants were members of the *Izquierda Republicana*. None of them could understand how the government could have permitted the arming of the people and the raising of the Anarchist and Communist militias, not to mention the POUM troops, and why, now—at least—they did nothing to restrain them.

"Because they can't," Lachine observed laconically. Some of his usual sang-froid had returned. With him it seemed to be simply a case of getting used to a situation, any situation. "You're too late to stop them now, that's the trouble," he went on while Captain Segurra gazed at him in astonishment, not so much because of what he was saying, for they all knew it to be true, but for his bad manners in violating their hospitality by saying it openly.

A pot of coffee was passed around. Lachine declined, waving the cup away as though he perceived that it was meant to silence him. "One of my hobbies," he said, "is collecting other people's legends. . . . It helps to understand them, I've always thought. Now, if I remember, you have a tale about a young man who was given exactly six years to the day to make his fortune and claim his beloved as his bride. The day after the sixth year she was to be married to another if he hadn't returned."

"Yes . . . ," Captain Segurra said. "Don Diego de Marcilla . . . yes."

"And as I remember it, the young man didn't quite get back in time. He was one day late and found the girl was indeed married to another. And, if I'm not mistaken, the lover appeared at her window and asked for one last kiss, knowing he had lost her forever, and she, out of that curious honor you people have, refused him and he died on the spot. . . ."

"Yes, yes, and what does all this mean?" Captain Segurra said, a trace of irritation in his voice.

"Consider that the Republic is now . . . six years old, almost to the day, and that it has, like your Don Diego, failed to make its fortune. Consider that it is asking Spain, its beloved, for a last kiss and consider, too, that Spain has its honor as well and will refuse." He sat back on his rude peasant chair and ran a finger around the rim of his glass. "Simply consider that, perhaps, your country has taken its vows already and now has another master. What will the Republic do, I wonder? Die on the spot?"

Carvalho was astonished. Certainly he could understand Lachine's thinking that way, but to give voice to his thoughts in such a gathering, that was incredible. Of course, the French—whatever their politics—were accustomed to insulting each other at random and seemed to take a delight in irony at the expense of others. Witness Raúl and his impossible remarks concerning his brother-in-law, Hector.

Captain Segurra's face darkened, and Lieutenant Orillas began to drum on the tabletop with his fingers. Carvalho looked around; the security he had felt on seeing so many uniforms, the equipment, the tents, all vanished at once. What were they, after all, but fifty men alone in the middle of the plains of La Mancha with their absurd little Schneiders and their spools of signal cable?

"I'm sorry that you think that way, señor," Captain Segurra was saying. "Perhaps you're right. Who can tell? But remember this, too, that though our Don Diego died . . . on the spot, as you say . . . , he has been remembered with reverence for seven centuries. If the Republic can say as much for itself after all that time, perhaps it will not be so bad after all. . . ."

Lieutenant Orillas started to interrupt, his sharp young face compressed and visibly angry. At that moment there was a knock on the door of the room.

"Come in. Come in . . ."

A corporal with his cap thrust into his belt came into the room carrying a sheaf of yellow paper.

"This message just arrived, Captain. On the telegraph . . ."

Carvalho was surprised, so surprised in fact that he neglected to whisper to Lachine to curb his tongue.

The Captain smiled as he read the telegraph transcription, and then announced in a satisfied voice: "We're to displace at dawn and join the

Republican column at Toledo. It seems they think our two Schneiders can be of some help and perhaps our rifles as well. It's signed by General Riquelme himself, gentlemen."

The news was greeted with mixed emotions. Clearly, some of the younger officers would just as soon have stayed put. The farmhouse, with its comfortable rooms and its well in the back, was almost like a summer resort, and at least there they were in charge of their own destinies.

"What guarantees do we have once we reach Toledo?" Lieutenant Orillas interrupted. "You know what we've been hearing . . ."

Captain Segurra shook his head. "That will be enough. At dawn, and no questions. What do you think this is, an Anarchist militia where we take a vote to see if we should attack or not?"

One more glass of cognac around the table and a toast to the morning. The junior officers went out in a group, leaving Colonel Carvalho, Captain Segurra, and the two civilians alone in the room. A spirit lamp on a nearby table sputtered, giving off a pungent odor.

"I can't say that I blame them entirely," Captain Segurra remarked when the door had closed again. "What with the situation in Toledo the way it is . . ."

"And what is the situation?" Carvalho asked nervously. All his fears had been rekindled by those few words, by the look on Lieutenant Orillas' face: the young man had been genuinely distressed, and not by the prospect of battle either. Something else entirely. "I think that I should explain to you just precisely what my situation is, and then you may understand . . . ," Carvalho said.

He began to speak in a stifled voice, acutely aware that he was having difficulty talking. Yet despite his fears, he felt that he could confide in a fellow officer. He had met the man only a few hours before; yet there were some men whose faces were so transparent that they could be read at a glance. Captain Segurra seemed to him such a person. As Colonel Carvalho completed his narrative, he placed his hands palms down on the table, then turned them as though to show that nothing more was hidden.

"What can I say to you?" Captain Segurra began . . . "I only know what I've heard. The academy garrison, as you know, has fortified itself in the Alcázar after reading a 'declaration of war' in the main square of the city at an hour when no one was even awake to hear them. This has been going on for almost two weeks now, and it's turned into a kind of fiesta. First three thousand men go marching up the road from Madrid and invest the fortress. One building, mind you, and three thousand men can't take it. But, do they attack? Do they storm the walls? No, they do not. They errect barricades all around and hide behind them and spend their time taking shots at the walls with their rifles. A very useful occupation, as you can guess. Oh, yes, and I shouldn't forget, there's a good bit of killing going on, too. That's what Lieutenant Orillas doesn't care for. "Why we're no better than the Fascists," he says, and maybe he's right.

But can we help the company we're forced to keep? I told him, just as long as you yourself don't cut the balls off any priests, you'll be all right. But I don't know if I believe that myself. In any event, there it is. General Riquelme has emplaced artillery on the other side of the river, and they've even sent planes over to bomb the place, but I understand that most of the bombs have either fallen into the water or on the Zocodover . . . which isn't much help, you'll have to admit. They say that last Sunday there were twenty busloads of people out from Madrid for the day, and the people all wanted to take shots at the Alcázar. It's beyond belief."

Carvalho sat back; General Riquelme—the name was familiar. Perhaps he could be counted on to maintain order. Perhaps he would not even need Lachine and his friends to serve as a buffer between himself and the Anarchists. It had occurred to him that it would be ironic, indeed, if things worked out just the other way around—if Lachine were the one to need protection and he were the one to furnish it. . . . But the girl, what about her? Nothing he had heard about the situation in Toledo gave cause for immediate concern. To be sure, the Anarchists were killing priests. That was to be expected. And he had grave doubts about the safety of Don Aurelio Aguilera de Tella and his apricot orchards. But as for the rest of them, perhaps he had been too fearful all along . . . perhaps . . .

Captain Segurra rose and showed them to an empty room next to the kitchen. There were blankets piled on the floor and even a few worn mattresses, torn, with the stuffing leaking out, but usable nonetheless.

"I suppose you think I should apologize for my behavior," Lachine said just before pulling a blanket up over his head. "Well, the truth is the truth, and the sooner you people learn to see it, the better for you."

"At dawn," Colonel Carvalho thought, paying no attention to the Frenchman, "at dawn we will be on the road . . . and then, an hour or two later, Toledo." He glanced at Portillo to see whether the man showed any signs of sharing his excitement, but Portillo was already asleep, an unlit cigar lying on the floor next to him, one hand flung out, palm up, on the boards. An ant was crawling across his index finger.

There were no shades on the windows of the room, and the moment the sky began to lighten, Colonel Carvalho awoke. He was stiff and felt damp, as though he had been sleeping in the open without any covering at all. A bitter taste filled his mouth. He got up and went quietly outside. The room where they had eaten the night before was empty. Captain Segurra had already risen and was outside issuing orders to his men, getting the column ready to move out. The wires leading to the distant telegraph poles had already been taken down and spooled.

Colonel Carvalho walked around to the back of the house and stood by the well looking east, toward Cuenca and the rising sun. The sky was swimming with whorls of repellent pink which reminded him of blood spit into a dentist's bowl. A grayish nimbus hovered about the horizon.

The uncertain light made the low clouds that had come in during the night from the north tremble and seem to slice through the sky with alarming speed. As he watched, a spot like a forge fire began to grow, starting as a hot shadow and swelling until he could no longer look at it. The sun sent up fiery grappling hooks and pulled at the clouds.

The plains of La Mancha shuddered, and the night shadows drew together. From horizon to horizon, the vast spread of emptiness took on a terrible, frightened quality that Carvalho could not comprehend. It was only a sunrise, just as on any other day. Yet . . .

He became aware of someone breathing close behind him. He turned his head slightly. Lachine was standing there, staring at the sunrise, the blanket draped over his shoulder like a cloak and falling almost to the ground.

"Looking at this," he said, as though taking up in the midst of a conversation, "I think I can understand why your Don Quixote hallucinated so often. In such a place, why shouldn't windmills look like giants and hovels like castles?" He paused, as though considering what he would say next, then added: "And perhaps in this country, they are . . ."

Carvalho looked at him in astonishment. All thoughts of what Lachine had said the night before vanished. For those few words spoken now, as the two men watched the sky fill with blistering light, Carvalho could have forgiven him almost anything.

Then, unexpectedly, Lachine said: "Don't worry. We'll get your daughter out safely enough. I promise you . . ."

If only such a simple thing as dawn could touch all men so, Colonel Carvalho thought, how much easier things could be. But the moments of dawn passed quickly, and the bright light of day cut through so many shadows that were better left untouched. Shadows softened things, made other things possible. . . . "The light of day shows us that we really are."

The column was forming up on the road. Captain Segurra was to ride ahead in the lead truck and the others would follow, some in the open-backed military cars, and the rest crammed into the trucks along with their equipment.

Captain Segurra waved at them. The tents had already been broken down and folded and all the wire that had crisscrossed the landscape like a giant cat's cradle was rolled on drums and hooked to the sides of the trucks.

Soldiers were moving about, picking up everything in sight. Lieutenant Orillas passed on his way to the rear truck and shook his head with a vehemence that left little doubt as to his disposition.

Portillo came out of the house, the last man to join the column. He rubbed his eyes with his fists and moved with obvious reluctance. "Is he still asleep?" Carvalho wondered, "or is it something else? Why doesn't he talk about his wife? I wonder. I've told him so much about Amalia . . ."

One of the open-backed cars was put at their disposal and they were given second place in the line, right behind Captain Segurra's truck. Engines turned over, and the air shimmered with exhaust fumes. The sun had mounted a little higher above the horizon; the vehicles of the column cast long, distorted shadows over the rocky ground.

Following the road to the west, the column soon passed into the town of Ocaña. In this gray-and-white village, pale as its own ghost, the only color visible was the green of an occasional tree and some pale sienna brickwork breaking out in leprous splotches on the walls of the Mudejar church. Ocaña, where once two kings of Spain had convened their *Cortes,* seemed as deserted now as though it had never been built at all but was only the bare bones of the desert thrust up among the sullen rocks. There was not a trace of the hundreds of people who had passed through its dusty streets the day before, fugitives from the disabled train. A donkey stood silently, tethered to a post, and newspapers blew under the wheels of the passing trucks.

One of the soldiers at the rear of the column was singing, and the wind, heading from east to west, carried his voice over the canvas hoods and the steel hoops and sent it flying along the road ahead of Captain Segurra's truck, aimed like an arrow at Toledo; a *saeta* . . .

The sky behind them suddenly lightened, taking on the color of the dust churned up by their wheels, then asserted itself in a burst of brilliant blue that broke like a hundred mirrors from the upper arch of the sky.

The column headed north, swinging up along a dirt road toward the main Madrid–Toledo axis so that they would make their approach from the north of the city on a paved highway along which the Schneiders could pass without fear of turning over.

The landscape began to change almost imperceptibly. The ground rose up in massive humps of rock that became, farther on, stands of dark green cypress. Long yellow grass, sharp as needles, stood straight up from the ground. A white stone, tipped like a grave-marker that had sunk into the earth, sprang up suddenly from the parched grass at the bend in the road. The column turned onto the Madrid road just north of Illescas and headed south between flatlands of yellow grass which seemed walled in, as far as one could see, by low mountain ranges. Illescas passed by as though the town were moving and the trucks standing still; houses, white and whiter still, of brittle clay . . . an inn, farther down the road with a few wire chairs standing in front of it . . .

All this time the three men had ridden in silence. Portillo's manner had changed markedly; he seemed, upon awakening, a different man from before—now sullen and thick with concern. He kept staring at his hands and had not lit a single cigar since leaving the camp in the fields outside Ocaña. Lachine, on the other hand, was highly animated.

The clouds were very low on the hills, so thick and dark in some spots, Carvalho thought, that they seemed to be smoke rising from the ground rather than anything born of the sky itself. He kept glancing about, trying to see just beyond the limits of his vision. The road was beginning to look familiar. There was a low rise on which he had once stood with Mercedes. You could see the first coil of the Tagus from there as it wound its way about Toledo. And there was a cluster of pine where, he was sure, he had once walked with Amalia after having taken a picnic lunch under the mid-afternoon sun. How she had complained of the heat and how he had scolded her for it until she had admitted that it had been so much worse in Tetuán. . . .

He had grown used to the sound of stones clanking against the underside of the car, but now he heard sharp popping noises that sounded like caricatures of gunshots, a puppet theater rendition of the sounds of warfare. He leaned from the side of the car, as though a few inches more to the right might enable him to identify the sounds. The road was very familiar now: the side road to Francisco Mercader's house lay less than half of a kilometer ahead. He could already see the tops of the tall cypress that flanked the road and led to the white stone fence that he recalled so vividly. He had not stopped there when he had last come to Toledo, on his way to the garrison in Oviedo, nor had he even phoned. He had been afraid that Francisco's son might answer. It was possible that he had returned to his father's house. The Colonel had lost all track of him since the day he had taken his discharge papers and boarded a morning packet at Ceuta without so much as a word of good-bye.

The tops of the cypress seemed wreathed in smoke. Not clouds, but smoke from a dying fire, thin and acrid. He could smell the odor of charred wood. He strained to see more; the vehicular column mounted a rise in the road and he saw the stone fence, the file of cypress, and one corner of the white house, far distant in the hollow between the hills. That was where the smoke was coming from, from the house. And the trees beyond it were on fire too. He could see a number of trucks outlined against the glow. A greasy rope of smoke began to uncoil toward the sky, even as he watched. The distant side of the hill, low and gently sloping toward the house, was swarming with tiny figures. He could see dots of blue and of brown; men moving about. Some in the yard of the house, some at the shed behind it.

"Make a turn . . . here . . . break out of line," Colonel Carvalho shouted.

The corporal turned and gaped. What was he to do? He could not break out of the column, but the Colonel was waving his fists and his face was dark against his white beard.

"Turn, damn you . . . !" The Colonel groped for his revolver.

The driver wrenched at the wheel, and the car plummeted onto the side road. Behind them, the column came to a halt; then the truck carrying Captain Segurra turned into the road after them.

The house was as he remembered it, low, white, distinctly Moorish in design, just as Mercader had wanted it, to remind him of what he had left for the sake of cork and fuel oil. Memories flashed through Carvalho's mind as the car careened into the gravel driveway before the house, narrowly missing a parked truck. Recollections of the night Francisco had first shown him his sketches for the house and asked him if he knew of an architect, perhaps even an army engineer, who might be willing to do the design work for him. Someone with Moorish blood if possible. And Carvalho had found such a man for him . . . and the house had come into being, suddenly there, like a caïque that had somehow lost its way in the sea off Ceuta, had been blown inland and become hopelessly stranded on the arid desert of La Mancha.

But the windows were smashed and a pale smoke, almost a haze, was drifting past the shards of broken glass. From a breach in the east wall, more smoke issued, and through the shattered masonry, the interior of the dining room could be seen; the long trestle table at which he had sat so often was overturned, the chairs in splinters around it.

Twenty or thirty armed men were milling about the yard. All of them wore the rope-soled sandals and blue coveralls of the militia, and among them were numerous uniforms of both the regular army and what looked like a fantastic conglomeration of Civil Guard and Mexican bandit.

A machine gun spread its side shields across a bank of shrubs. Tracks ran every which way across the grass; runnels of black dirt had been turned in the sod.

There was firing just beyond the hill to the rear of the house; the echoes rose from the flatlands beyond and made the reports themselves seem insignificant.

Colonel Carvalho got down from the car and stood staring with unbelieving eyes at the wreckage around him. It was impossible to tell what had happened. The house had been almost completely gutted. Flames still crackled intermittently through the broken windows. The roof had caved in at one point.

The truck carrying Captain Segurra pulled up behind them, and the Captain jumped down. One of the militia men came running over to meet them, gesturing at the Colonel who was advancing, completely indifferent, into the boiling smoke, toward the front door of the house.

"Get that fool out of there," the man was shouting. "Can't you see . . ." The rattle of rifle fire from beyond the wall to the rear of the house suddenly ceased.

No one made a move to stop Carvalho. Captain Segurra shouted something, but his words were lost in the smoke. Neither Lachine nor Portillo had gotten out of the car, but the driver was standing up on the seat, with a rifle in his hands.

Carvalho took in a deep breath and plunged through the front door. The panels of the door were smashed, and splinters of wood lay about like huge matchsticks on the floor of the hall just below the stairway. He turned, as if by habit, toward the dining room. The lower parts of the walls below the shattered windows were spattered with blood, now turning brown and crusty. Fragments of steel jutted out of the plaster and left gaping holes in the blue-flowered tiles. The floor was littered with pieces of wall, wood, furniture, and bright little pieces of glass. But the room was empty. A small fire was spitting in the corner by the east window, eating up the paint on the door to the kitchen.

Colonel Carvalho could hear the sound of boots and the slither of es-
padrilles behind him. Others had come into the house behind him. It
made no difference; he stalked ahead, back through the empty dining
room and across the front hall. A picture had fallen from the wall and
lay tipped against the wainscot, upside down; a portrait of Francisco
Mercader.

He could hear a few words: "What does he want here? . . . Does
he . . . ? Why . . . ? get him . . . dangerous . . . may collapse . . ."

The main room, the "living" room as Francisco had called it after
the English manner, was in similar disarray. One wall had cracked completely open. A grenade of some kind or a bomb had been thrown into
the room. Again the telltale streaks of blood. Brass cartridge cases lay in
profusion all over the floor, making the footing insecure. A crumpled
civil-guard tricorn sat on the one chair that had not been overturned,
and the fireplace was stuffed with gray cardboard, the remains of ammunition boxes.

Carvalho stopped, his breath caught in his throat; and again that curious tingling sensation on the back of his neck. From behind the overturned sofa, a foot projected, so clotted with blood that it was hard to
tell even whether it wore a boot or shoe. He went over to the couch. Just
then Captain Segurra and two *milicianos* came into the room, followed
by Portillo and Lachine. Segurra shouted something, but Carvalho did
not hear him.

The corpse of the middle-aged man in a Civil Guard uniform lay on
its back behind the sofa. The chest had been blown away but for some
reason the face bore only an expression of surprise, as though death had
come too quickly for pain to register. The hands were flung out the way
an infant flings out his arms when startled, and near to his splayed fingers lay the twisted remains of a rifle.

The face was unmarred, but it was no one the Colonel knew.

"We don't know if we got them all . . .," the *miliciano* said. He was
speaking to Captain Segurra. "Bastards . . . it took us two days . . ."

"Where is the owner of this house?" Carvalho shouted. "Where is
he?"

The *miliciano* regarded him suspiciously. Carvalho saw that the man
had the star of a lieutenant pinned on his blue coveralls. Another group
of men entered the room, three *milicianos* and a half-dozen soldiers wearing regular army uniforms.

Carvalho could not take his eyes off the ruined walls, the fireplace,
and the shattered windows. He was only half-listening as the "lieutenant"
explained what had happened: two, perhaps three days before, no one
was sure, a group of Civil Guard had been belatedly trying to make their
way to the Alcázar from the town of Maqueda. At the same time a group
of reinforcements for General Riquelme's column, which was already in
Toledo, had been coming up the Madrid road, and the two groups had
walked right into each other. The Guard had taken refuge in the house,
and a sort of miniature siege had begun. The militia, supplemented by

three squads of regulars from the Carabanchel barracks, had had nothing but small arms and a few grenades; they had come up the road singing, totally unprepared to meet any resistance. The fighting, ". . . as you can see . . . ," had been fierce, and only when two small boys from the *Coralillo* quarter of Toledo, both sons of workers in the steel factory, had crept up under cover of dark and managed to throw grenades in through the windows, had the militia been able to take the house. As the final attack had occurred less than five hours before, while it was still dark, the "lieutenant's" men were scouring the nearby hills and the plain beyond, looking for survivors. "You can't tell who got away. It was too dark . . . and we didn't know how many of them there were to start with."

"The dead? . . ." Carvalho said, "where are the bodies? I want to see them."

The *miliciano* shrugged. "Whatever you wish. It makes no difference to me."

Captain Segurra touched the Colonel on the arm. "You know these people?"

"Yes . . ."

They went outside again. Some of the regulars from Carabanchel were sitting on the whitewashed wall that ran behind the car shed.

"In there . . ."

The old Ford was gone; Carvalho remembered the car, how proud Francisco had been when he had purchased it, how stubbornly he had refused to learn to drive it. The shed smelled of ashes and gasoline. Empty cans had been flung against the walls, and the planks were stained, black with the gas someone had poured along the bottoms of the walls.

A row of bodies lay on the ground, covered by blankets. Seven in all. But for a protruding foot, a hand jutting from under the edge of a blanket, there was nothing to indicate that those seven mounds had ever been human beings. In the gas-reeking shadow they appeared simply deformities of the ground, humps of soil with a curious covering of gray-green moss.

"Turn the blankets over. I want to see them. . . ."

"Listen, now wait a minute . . ."

"Do as he says," Captain Segurra said quietly. "Remember, you are a lieutenant. This man is a full colonel. Now . . ."

"All right." The *miliciano* gestured to the men who had come into the shed with him. A little light fell through a window which had been covered over with pages clipped from a newspaper. The morning light made the diagram of a car body stand out in bold relief and cast a curious geometrical shadow across the room.

The soldiers went along the line, pulling back the blankets from the faces of the dead men.

It was as Carvalho expected; the fifth body was that of Francisco Mercader. There was a neat wound in his forehead, a small purplish puncture that looked like an Indian caste mark. Nothing more. His face, however, was twisted in fright. Clearly, death had not come as a surprise.

Who had shot him then, the attackers or the attacked? It could have been either, Carvalho reflected, just as it might be some day with himself. The Civil Guard might have shot him because he was a Republican. The attackers might have shot him because he was rich. Or it might have been an accident; but such a neat wound, so exactly centered, does not happen by accident except once in a hundred thousand times . . .

"You can cover them again," Carvalho said. The tingling had increased to a steady pulse along the back of his neck, and his right arm felt leaden. He went out of the shed and found Portillo and Lachine waiting for him by the whitewashed wall.

The *miliciano* followed after him. When everyone was clear of the shed, someone set a match to it and it exploded in a rush of flames. Carvalho turned, outraged.

"He was a Catholic . . . you can't . . ."

The *miliciano* lieutenant shrugged. "He was dead. That's all. If you have time to bury them, here, I give you a shovel. Next time, it's all up to you. But these we burn. We don't want disease and rotting bodies, particularly those kind. . . ." He ground his teeth and then passed his hand through his hair. "Such corruption . . ."

There was no point in asking the man how it had happened, or why. The chances were that no one knew and it did not matter anyway.

"The woman? Did you find her too?"

"There were three still alive when the attack was over. A woman, yes . . . we found her in a closet. The cook tried to attack one of our men with a cleaver. She was shot, just a nick in the arm. Nothing much. It's not good to shoot women, but sometimes it can't be helped. And one of the Civil Guard, too . . ."

"What did you do with them?"

"With the Guard? What do you think? The women we sent back to Madrid. Let them figure out what to do with her. She was his wife, the owner of the house. And the cook. Her arm will heal in a day or two, the bitch. The Modelo prison is full of that kind now . . ." He walked away and gave an order to fold up the machine gun and load it onto one of his trucks. His men were coming back in from the rise beyond the house. There was nothing there, they reported. One *miliciano* appeared carrying a bag of hazel nuts he had picked, and another man, a regular soldier, had a huge and bloody rabbit tied to his belt. It had been shot at least a dozen times. There was no shortage of ammunition, so they had been told. The munitions factory at Toledo had been taken during General Riquelme's first advance and truckloads of rifle and machine-gun ammunition now passed every hour along the road to Madrid.

"I'm sorry," Captain Segurra said when they had returned to their own vehicles. "What can I say? What can I say, my friend, the Colonel?"

Carvalho stood still for a moment, trying to feel the emotion that he knew he should feel. The pain in his arm seemed of more immediate concern to him than the fleeting vision of Francisco Mercader's white face above the army blanket. So Señora Mercader was in Madrid . . . well

. . . what did it matter? Would he confront the body of his daughter with the same lack of passion? He recalled how even the thought of his own death had failed to stir him . . . twice now within the last few days. If a man doesn't fear his own death, how can he fear the dying of others?

The car shed was crackling like a bonfire, sending up a ribbon of thick smoke. An unpleasant smell was beginning to rise from the burning building. Carvalho turned away and got back into the car.

"Don't talk to me," he said, "not a word, for God's sake."

But neither Lachine nor Emilio Portillo had any intention of saying anything to him. Tragedies, they knew, came in all sizes, and the most immediate were not necessarily the most important.

The car moved jerkily down the road along the white stone wall. Behind it, the vehicles of the militia column were starting up. Smoke hung over everything. Someone had fired the main house as well. The shallow valley was filling up like a bowl with smoke. The cypress strained to keep their heads above it, to keep the blue sky and the blinding disk of the sun in view.

It was all anyone could do . . .

AUGUST 10

The decisive victory of the Republic and freedom is near.

Ibiza and Adamuz have been occupied.

The provinces of Huelva, Cádiz, Baleares, Lugo, La Coruña and Pontevedra have been declared military zones.

"With each day's passing, I am more and more optimistic," says the Head of State.

Sunday marked by absolute calm, especially in Madrid.

Juan José Manso, Communist deputy, who arrived recently from Oviedo, reports on the situation in that capital.

The court is to judge Generals Goded and Burriel.

Death penalty asked for both. Court-martial to be held on board the *Uruguay*.

El Sol (Madrid)

AUGUST 10: *The Alcázar*

A SINGLE VALENCIA ORANGE, neatly peeled, the segments lined up on the window ledge. The skin, slit, opening like a flower, held in the cup of Jaime's hand.

He watched her as she bent over the tiny segments, smiling. No matter how happily she smiled, it still frightened him; her skin was waxy now, drawn tight over her cheekbones, the blue veins beneath all too visible. Her dress hung loosely on her, and her breasts were shrinking. As she reached out to count the tiny pieces of orange, her hand trembled slightly. It was what hunger did, and he was helpless. Except for the orange.

"It's lovely," she said. "Where did you get it? There can't be many in here now."

"The driver, Barrera, he got it for me. He's been going on raids. He keeps coming back, and the last time he brought this. He said it was for you."

"You're making that up."

"All right," Jaime said. "But he would have wanted you to have it if . . ." He stopped, brushed her arm with his fingertips. She didn't seem to notice.

"Are there always the same number of segments?"

"Why do you ask that? Come on now, eat them . . ."

"Not all of it. You have some, too."

"I'm not hungry," he lied. There had been almost no food at all for a week; only strips of horseflesh and the tiny, rock-hard rolls.

"One piece," she said and took a segment and forced it between his lips. The pulp was fresh, the juice strong, and he could not help but smile, then smile again as he watched her eat first one, then another and another.

They had come up to the north tower to eat their orange in private, ". . . no," he thought, "in secrecy." It was a rare treasure. How wonderful that such a simple thing as an orange could bring so much delight. Yet he felt guilty in a way and knew that she did too; one of the children should have had the orange. But she was only a child herself . . .

He could hear the sound of the military band, the tubas and the trumpets guffawing in the inner courtyard. And the low buzz of voices, the few shouts of encouragement. The concert had been in progress for some time. They would go to the inner balcony and watch. But first the orange.

He looked out of the window, away from Mercedes who was now sitting in the corner, her skirts pulled down over her knees. He leaned on his elbows, thrust his head out of the glassless window. If there had been any light, he would have been a target for the snipers in the belfry, but it was dark except for the upper reaches of the sky where the searchlights lurched stiffly back and forth, shedding light down into the streets like milk poured carelessly over the edge of a bowl. He raised the binoculars with one hand, still cupping the orange peel in the other, careful not to injure it, not to waste . . .

There was enough light spilled down from the searchlight beams into the streets so that he could see. Alleyways, gates, lattices, and barred windows; the circle of vision climbed with a cat's quickness across mounds of barrels and trash cans. Lingering on a window, he pretended to decipher moving shadows, invented whispers and conversations, conspiracies. The air smelled . . . heavy. The clouds shifted over the spires and rooftops, swollen with rain.

"Have you finished?" he asked.

She had, but she had put away three pieces for him.

"Then come look, look at this . . ."

He handed her the glasses. "Look there, just beyond the end of the street . . ."

She took the glasses but did not raise them to her eyes at once. Rather, she turned the binoculars over in her hands pensively.

"Could I . . . borrow these for a few hours?"

"Of course. But why? . . . what do you want to see?"

"Not for myself. For Selica Portillo. You remember her?"

"Yes . . . ," and for a moment his mind filled with remembrances of the funeral, its lights and sounds. The woman who had thrown the flowers into the grave. The Civil Guard colonel's mistress . . .

"She wants to look for her husband . . . outside. She's sure, now, that he's alive and will come. Don't ask me why. Women are sure of things like that sometimes. Isn't it strange? For two years she was positive he was dead, but now, because Colonel Venegas is really dead and she's seen him dead . . ."

"I understand," Jaime nodded. "She can have the glasses. Of course. But now, you look, just the way I did. . . ."

With the glasses she could actually see faces in the street, and when the light fell on them it was possible to make out every line, every furrow and stain. She smiled, laughed lightly. It was like being in a theater, in the last row in the balcony, and watching the tiny figures moving far below.

She handed the glasses back to him. He raised them to his eyes for one more look at the world outside the Alcázar. While he was thus absorbed, she wrapped the orange segments in a piece of tissue she had been saving and slipped them into his pocket.

Mercedes' fingers dug into his arm, and he lost his grip on the binoculars. They fell against his chest. The music from the military band playing in the courtyard seemed to quicken, become more jaunty, more defiant. Touching her arm was like touching something cut out of wood. . . . It was rigid, cold, and lifeless.

"What are you thinking?" she said. They were by the door, at the head of the stairs and had started down without really being aware, either of them, of moving—drawn by the music.

"Of my father . . . ," he said dreamily. "I wonder if he's still alive."

"You say it so simply."

"It's a simple thing. I know, I can't see over the hills. It's maddening . . . just out of sight. But there's been so much smoke coming from there . . . artillery fire and troops along the road. They must have burned the house."

"What reason would they have to do that?"

"They don't need a reason. In fact these things are done without a reason, always. That's the way they're done. The people who kill each other never have a reason to do it. They'd be much more comfortable sitting down with each other over a bowl of olives and some wine. But they kill each other nevertheless."

She was silent for a moment, paused a few steps farther down and waited for him.

Then she said, "Were you thinking about . . . my father too?"

He shouldn't have been surprised, he knew. He'd been waiting for her to say something for a long while now. Weeks.

The band in the courtyard was playing the *"Marcia Real"* now. The tubas were out of tune.

"Do you hate me?" she asked, not really a question but almost a statement of fact uttered in a tone of voice that showed no rancor, only a distant hope of contradiction.

"Why should I? That's a strange thing for you to say. . . ."

"I don't hate you. . . ."

"You should . . . for what I've done to you. I brought you here. It wasn't right, I think I know that now. But how do you know, at the time, what's right and what isn't? You do what you think you have to do. . . ."

"Did you come for me because of . . . that . . . or because of my father . . . ?"

He gripped his right wrist with his left hand and leaned against the wall. She went on.

". . . I mean, have you thought about it at all, Jaime? I have . . ."

"I don't understand you. . . ." But he did, more than he wanted to admit. He could see that she was about to say what he himself had been thinking for days, to put together into a whole all the little pieces, the contradictory things he himself had done.

"My father once said to me . . . I can remember it very clearly . . . I was a very young girl then, and I think that he said it to me only because he thought I couldn't understand . . . it was when we were still in Morocco. He had been out in the mountains for weeks, chasing the last of Abd-el-Krim's men . . . and he came home suddenly one night, after midnight, and rushed into the house. My mother tried to find out what had happened, and all he would say was that the expedition had been a success. Then he started to shout at her, and she went upstairs, crying. I came down, and I watched my father for a long time. He was sitting in a big chair in front of the window. He didn't move for the longest time, and I began to think that he was dead. . . . I couldn't have been more than eight or nine at the time. Then I went downstairs and stood next to him for a while, but he didn't see me, and he didn't move either. Then when he noticed me, he gave me a look I will never forget and he took me by the shoulders and pulled me to him in a very rough way.

"I didn't cry out because I think I understood that he couldn't do anything else, that he hadn't the strength then to control himself. And when he let go of me, he said . . . I remember the exact words . . . I think I knew that it was important even though I didn't understand them. . . . I wrote them down in a little diary that I kept, you know what little girls do . . . diaries and things like that, but they prove useful sometimes . . . as though I could understand him: 'Sometimes a man simply cannot live according to his faith, Mercedes. So, isn't it better to go on living than to offer yourself up as a sacrifice?' I began to cry and so did he, something I'd never seen him do before. Much later I found out what had happened. The expedition hadn't been chasing Abd-el-Krim's men at all, but had gone out after the Beni Bou-Ilfrur instead . . . you remember, I'm sure, you were older then . . . the atrocities at Monte Arruit that the Beni Bou-Ilfrur had committed and how furious everyone was . . . well, it was a punitive expedition. My father hadn't wanted to go, but they'd made him. In fact they'd put him in command. . . . They'd gone to Usian, in the mountains, and in the week they were away, they'd wiped out the entire tribe . . . men, women, and children. They'd even used the artillery on them, and when they were done there was nothing at all left. It brought peace for a while, but it almost killed my father . . ."

Jaime's voice broke in, and he was aware that Mercedes had been speaking more and more softly until her voice was almost a whisper. He could see Colonel Carvalho . . . only ten years older than he was at that moment . . . sitting there with his child. . . . Beni Bou-Ilfrur, that was in 1922 . . . the Colonel would have been about forty-five then, certainly not more. . . . He wondered, had Carvalho really wept or was Mercedes wrong in remembering that? But how different was it from the moment when Carvalho had uttered that strangled "Surrender, damn them . . . surrender . . ." at Oviedo. No, she was probably right.

"It's not enough," he said. "I've thought of that, all of what you've just said. But it isn't enough. . . ."

"You loved him, didn't you . . . my father?" she said suddenly.

"I . . . ?"

"Yes . . ."

He nodded. It was true, of course.

"I know. Otherwise why would all of what happened to you cause you such pain?"

". . . more, I think, than even my own father . . . ," Jaime said, barely aware that he was speaking. "He seemed to me the one man I'd ever met who lived by what he believed in, and then . . ."

"And then what?" She had been waiting for such an opening. Her voice took on a brightness, a hard edge, not unkind, but probing. The music lumbered on, sometimes louder, sometimes softer. An incessant, pounding rhythm.

"And then what? You tried to force him to prove his ideals for you, to test him . . . is that it? Or was it that you were trying to force him to prove something else, Jaime? A love for you which would be even greater . . . than his ideals? Could that have been it? Don't be surprised that I ask that. It's a natural thing for a woman to see . . . sometimes we can look through the screens you men set up and know what's really behind them . . . so . . . could it have been that?"

"No . . .," he shot back. "How can you say that? Look at what he's done to you."

"What *has* he done to me? What could he have done for me? You've said it yourself, they would have killed him if he had stayed in Oviedo. Oh yes, I'm quite ready to believe he ran from Oviedo, I think I believed it all the time, that I knew it from the moment, the day he went there. So he only did . . . what you yourself thought he had to do. What's wrong with that?"

"But he left you . . ."

"How could he have helped me here? Even now, if he were to show up, it would only be to get himself killed and probably me as well. Outside, the Anarchists would cut him up, And in here . . . as soon as they found out whose side he had tried to be on, that would be the end of me and you, too, probably. . . . There have been two already or didn't you know? You were right about it, Jaime. I should have known. One of the raiding parties brought back a copy of the *Heraldo,* and there they read that General Alvarez had stayed with the Republic. Well, it happens that his cousin Damaso Turq is here. They put him in custody at once. And in the same paper there was a line about the hero of some skirmish around Huesca, who turned out to be the brother of a baker from Toledo who was here also. He hanged himself after they'd put him in with the hostages . . . or haven't you heard about it at all? I suppose not or you would have said something. Well, then . . . how could my father help me, here? Either way? He's more important, after all. He can do something to change all of this, perhaps . . . and if he's willing to sacrifice me to save himself, well, he's more valuable than I am. That's the truth and admitting it doesn't mean he loves me the less. Do you remember the story in the Bible about Abraham and Isaac? Abraham loved his son more than anything else in the world, except God. . . ." She looked down, and for a second seemed to be struggling to compose herself. He had not noticed how agitated she had become in the last few moments. "It depends on a man's gods, doesn't it?"

"Would Abraham actually have killed Isaac?" Jaime heard himself ask. "I never thought so. It would have been too cruel."

"But if it had been necessary? . . . if God had demanded it?"

"Don't . . .," he said and took her arm brutally. "I'm not Isaac and your father is not Abraham. And there is no equating God with his catechism of political ideas. . . ."

"They're yours as well, aren't they?"

He was silent, found himself not so much thinking as listening to the music that seemed to well up even louder from below, trapped and amplified in the stairwell.

The march grew louder, more discordant, lost shape. A burst of distant rifle fire, then tubas and trombones. He pulled her along after him down the stairs. As they descended they saw, through fractured walls and ogival windows, the flying dumbbells of a juggler. The march had stopped suddenly. Solitary figures hurtled through the air, men on each others' shoulders. Applause, laughter. A man walking on a tightrope in midair glided past a green-glass window, unshattered, on the second floor landing. The man turned and stared in their direction, grinned.

He only spoke once between the tower and the second landing.

"I will not be his Isaac . . . ," he said.

She was panting from the exertion of the climb. It pained him to see and hear it, but his concern for her was submerged then under alternating waves of confusion and self-reproach. The things that she had said to him—about the Colonel, about herself and about him—all made a kind of sense that he could not, for the sake of his own sanity, acknowledge. If *that* was the real truth, then he had been betrayed again, but this time by himself.

They came out onto the balcony which ran along the second floor and looked over the inner courtyard. There were two levels of balconies and theirs was the uppermost. Below them, on the first floor tier, there were many people watching the concert.

Crumpled programs littered the balcony: The "Alcázar Circus". . . The conjurer Trapellini and his sister . . . Exhibition of tightrope-walking by Chu-Ling the Fabulous. . . . The humorist Mr. Zaka. . . . Fandango in carioca style . . . Songs and selection of marches.

Just then the band resumed playing; the overture to *El Tambor de Granaderos*. Through the gaps in the balcony railing, he could look down into the courtyard where the band, surrounded by hundreds of spectators, was playing as merrily as though on the Zoco on a festival day. The firing had died down; those few shots that still bounced futilely from the outside walls of the fortress seemed to come in time to the music.

"Let's not talk," Mercedes said, "let's just listen to the music. . . ."

He gazed down. It made him dizzy. Young guards and soldiers squatted on the rocks and leaned over the lower balcony railing. Civilians had drawn up wire chairs, taken from the cafés along the Zoco. Some of them had wooden deck chairs of the kind seen on shipboard. As the band played, two young men were busy taking down the tightrope wire on which the daring Chu-Ling had just performed . . . the Fabulous.

At the far end of the courtyard from where they stood, Jaime could see a tightly grouped bunch of men. In the flickering light from the resin torches he could see that they were roped together. On either side of them there were a few Civil Guard with rifles. The hostages, Jaime thought. They had actually brought the hostages up from the cellar to see the show too.

He swayed slightly, as though the music itself were a hurricane wind and was threatening to tear him from the balcony. There they all were, the soldiers, the Guard, even the hostages, gathered to listen to a concert, to watch a juggler and a tightrope-walker perform, as though nothing were happening. While outside there were thousands of men who wanted, for whatever reason, to kill them. But worse, he thought, and the thought made him tremble with anger, those people below, placidly listening in the gentle torchlight, they were killing people, imprisoning people themselves, for what reason? For no reason. And one had hanged himself. Why? Had he that much to fear, the baker whose name he didn't know? So much to fear that he preferred to die by his own hand? A mortal sin, if he believed. Jaime was not sure whether he believed or not, but it seemed to him that it was not a question of whether one believed or not, but that to kill one's self was the worst possible sin because of its absurdity, total surrender . . . a sin against the man himself, not God.

So they had made the baker hang himself. And below, there was another man, a cousin of General Alvarez, who was in chains. Had they brought him up to listen too, and then would they take him back down below and kill him? What was the reason? Because he was there, because of his cousin? None of it made any sense: for a few moments he had been able to avoid thinking directly about Carvalho, but he knew that thinking about the baker and Damaso Turq was only another way of thinking about the Colonel and what any word of him might mean.

If he were dead, then they would be safe . . . but he would not be dead. He had such a talent for survival, that man . . .

She was there, but she was not looking at him. One of his hands was shaking, and he thrust it into his trouser pocket to hide it. His hand pressed against the orange segments which Mercedes had put into his pocket.

Had she said, "Sometimes, to attempt to do good, to oppose evil is simply self-destructive . . . it can be not only futile but can end forever your capacity to do good of any kind"? But it hadn't been Mercedes speaking at all, but, rather, her father, with his gruff, unmistakable voice, tinged with perpetual sadness. Dry as his brush-fire beard . . . he was standing there, or rather sitting, behind a table, just as the judge had sat behind the table at Oviedo when they had brought Jaime before the court-martial, after he had freed the dozen men, and there were two candles, one at each elbow. Colonel Carvalho looked straight at him and shook his head. "In short," he was saying, "is a man obliged to be a martyr and lose all chance of accomplishing any good at all in the future, however small, rather than become an accomplice, however unwilling, in the smallest evil? I really don't think so, do you, Jaime? Can you be that harsh with me . . . or with yourself . . . ?"

The music stopped suddenly; the final cadence. Applause drifted up. Through the latticework, Jaime saw the players salute with their instruments, then retire to make way for a small group of men with violins tucked under their arms. . . .

"I don't believe it," Mercedes whispered, touching his arm in excitement, "a string quartet . . . where did they ever find the instruments?"

The applause subsided, and the four men sat down on wire chairs and began tuning their instruments.

Far to the east, an aircraft passed, warming the night with the whir of its motors.

"Do you know what that is?" she whispered. The quartet had begun to play. No, he didn't know what it was. What difference did it make? They had made a man hang himself down there, and now they were listening to a string quartet. And if the Colonel appeared, if there were any word of him . . . , he thought, suddenly terrified, will we hang ourselves too? Will there be any choice at all in what we do . . . ?

". . . an accomplice, however unwilling, in the smallest evil . . . ," He was not sure that the Colonel had ever said that, but it was possible. The afternoon he had gone up into the mountains, under guard, to find Carvalho and had discovered him at the bottom of a little ravine, knee-deep in a stream, fishing. . . . They had walked back through the forest, with the guards trailing behind, nervously shifting their weapons, but not daring to interfere as the Colonel, with his fishing rod over his shoulder, had argued with him until . . . yes, he remembered it now, there had been tears in the Colonel's eyes.

"Surrender . . . ," or was that what he had said at the railroad station when they were bombarding the miners who had barricaded themselves in the railroad cars? "Admit you were wrong . . . then I can patch things up. There will be no hearings . . . admit, admit . . . even if it's not true . . ."

He had refused, and then the Colonel had said: "Jaime, even if it is not true, admit it. You may come to realize that it is true later . . . later . . . later . . . ," the words trailed off like an echo.

Music drifted up. The mood was changed, the brassy clangor gone, melted into the soft melody of strings, a whisper like the wind in the forest trees that day. The sun coming down in slanting ladders through the tall trees, kindling the autumn leaves on the forest floor. The Colonel's boots squeaking because of the water in them.

He hadn't admitted anything; he'd defended himself and shouted insults at the other officers, called them criminals, murderers, and fools. But there had never been a verdict. His judges had retired, and they'd put him in an old storehouse, under guard for the night. He'd lain there all night, listening to the Moors singing at their campfires, and it had made him so homesick that he had almost wept. It was beautiful, even though those same men had spent their day killing, for no reason other than that it was their way and someone had said, "Go, do things in your way," and they had not even hated those they killed. Which was perhaps the worst of it. In the morning one guard had come for him and had taken him to a truck and then they had driven off to the south. Two days later at Burgos where they had taken him, he had received word that he was to join the Colonel in Madrid the following week. He had never found out what had happened or why they had let him go. But he had been bitterly proud that he had not "admitted" anything and that, still, they had let him go. No, that . . . still . . . Carvalho had had to intervene, despite himself. Or hadn't he known all along that he would?

"Don't you know," the girl's voice, teasing, "what they're playing?"

How could she pass from one mood to the next with such ease? Ten minutes before she had been cutting him deeply, as a surgeon, now she was behaving like a schoolchild.

"Schubert . . . it's 'Death and the Maiden,' " she whispered. Then, suddenly, as she said those words, her voice thickened and her hands clasped convulsively together over the railing. "A child died in the women's quarter this morning, a little girl . . . did you know about that?"

He shook his head. It was impossible for him to think straight now, and he barely heard what she was saying. He kept thinking about something else Carvalho had once said, rather a word that he had used, so often. . . . "You have to salvage as much as you can. . . . *salvage* . . ." What a strange word for a military man to use . . . more fitting for a naval officer. *Salvage?* What a puzzling word . . .

"A little girl, about nine," Mercedes said.

And Damaso Turq was made to hang himself, Jaime thought. Or was it the other man, the baker?

Why would he do that, the baker? Hadn't he something left to *salvage?* Could it ever come to that, that a man had so little control over what was happening to him that it was better to kill himself?

His hand was still in his pocket. One of the orange segments broke beneath his fingers, and the juice flowed out, cool and sticky. He took it out of his pocket and put it on the ledge. The skin was still there too, and he held it out to Mercedes. She shook her head and put it to his lips.

"You . . . ," she said.

He opened his mouth and took it, not knowing why, except that he could not refuse her.

He wished that she would have smiled at that moment, but she did not.

The music continued below, and now there was no firing outside at all.

AUGUST 12.

Death sentences for ex-Generals Goded and Burriel.

The Fascists responsible for the Fascist military coup in Cataluña face the inexorable severity of the law.

AUGUST 18.

The rebels of the Trench Diggers' barracks surrendered in Gijón last Sunday.

The sentence delivered against ex-General Fanjul Goñi and ex-Colonel Fernandez Quinto was carried out yesterday.

El Sol

August 18: *Toledo*

How MUCH BETTER IT WAS than he had expected it to be and yet how much worse. There was much less destruction and turmoil in the city than he had feared, but over the whole of what there was hung a festival gaiety infinitely more frightening than any amount of pure destruction could have been.

Colonel Carvalho hated bullfighting and any mention of it, but he could not help drawing a comparison between the atmosphere he found in the heart of Toledo and that which filled the bullring, a kind of heightened intoxication with death that transformed all who had survived from simple human beings who were thankful for life into creatures who exalted their own survival into a feat of will which proved their superiority to the dead.

In many places, nevertheless, the city was in terrifying disorder. Churches as yet unburned pulled their still cold walls tight about them, clasping purple memories of Mass and gazing helplessly at the prophecy of their own destruction made corporeal in the nails of smoke that rose all over the city. Only the cathedral itself, posted with a guard of armed Republican officers, had thus far kept sacrilege at bay. The Zocodover, pleasant and basking in its desert charm the last time he had seen it, now presented to Colonel Carvalho the aspect of a volcanic ruin. Houses had cast themselves headlong into the plaza; naked skeletons of buildings once proudly armored with rich stone carvings rose mournfully against a background of perpetually hissing fires. Barricades were everywhere: chairs, dressers, beds—curiously, the artifacts of peace turned grotesquely to the service of war's madness.

Yet it was not war at all. The faces of the men he passed in the street displayed only a holiday drunkenness or, at best, a blankness and absence of understanding which made men who were in their ordinary lives as clever as the next seem irretrievably dull and stupid.

He recalled paintings he had seen of revelers during time of the plague; the faces around him were like that.

Captain Segurra's column had entered the city by the Bisagra gate and started at once up the steep street leading to the hilltop heart of the city. The presence of large numbers of regular troops in addition to the FAI militiamen made an optimistic note resonate in Carvalho's heart. The disorder he saw was somehow tempered by the presence of uniformed soldiers and officers with regular insignia on their tunics.

Destruction, certainly: walls had fallen, buildings had been burned, and streets torn up for no apparent reason. Armored cars, crude as those he had seen at Mercader's house or by the railroad tracks near Cuenca, lurked in alleys barely wide enough to accommodate them. But what he feared most, a general massacre, he saw no sign of. Here, perhaps, the representatives of the *Izquierda Republicana* held the reins firmly enough to prevent precisely those excesses which had led to the generals' uprising in the first place. What an irony. And in an Anarchist center at that.

How difficult it was, he thought, for men of good will to make their way in this world. But it was not wholly impossible.

Captain Segurra was ordered to emplace his two Schneiders at the north end of the Zoco where they could fire directly on the walls of the Alcázar. "We might as well throw pelota balls at it. Just look at that stone. . . ." But he did as he was told and soon the field pieces were emplaced behind barricades and all but the gun crews had dispersed for a few hours relaxation in the cafés and taverns nearby.

Lachine had taken both Colonel Carvalho and Portillo with him to Communist party headquarters which was located in what had once been a rare bookshop on the narrow Calle Izcaza, not far from the cathedral. The businesslike atmosphere of the rooms, all still walled with books, the cigarette smoke and the smell of coffee stale in iron pots, and most of all the continual clatter of a typewriter somewhere in the back, had had an unexpected effect on Carvalho. Instead of being a relief after the turmoil of the streets, an island of seeming sanity which he could find at least congenial, it had caused him to sink at once into a deep depression.

An enormous man with one shoulder noticeably lower than the other conveyed them to a back room. There, they obtained the necessary documents, the passes, the identification cards which would ensure their free passage about the city: "Under the Protection of the Communist party of Toledo." Carvalho maintained a stony silence and put the papers in his pocket without comment. Edmundo Tierres, the local leader, passed in the narrow corridor outside the room, and, as he thrust his head inside to see what was going on and who the newcomers were, he seemed to recognize Lachine. Not that he had ever met him before but the description which had been sent was, as he said, ". . . better than the police could do . . . I could have picked you out of a crowd anytime . . ." Lachine grew voluble but Tierres had little time. He was a large man with a pair of deep-set, penetrating eyes of a disturbing violet color. He gave the impression of being carved out of wood: everything about him seemed slightly rigid, even his sparse hair which was combed flat over a high forehead and oiled. He wore heavy mustaches and what could be seen of his upper lip was covered with tiny red heat dots. A glint of metal flashed from his mouth when he spoke: steel teeth.

Lachine remained behind to discuss matters with Tierres' lieutenants. Rooms had been arranged for all three of them at the Hotel Maravilla. Portillo walked with the Colonel to the end of the Calle Izcaza and then excused himself. "What I came to do is better done alone. I'm sure you understand." He walked away, his shoulders thrust forward, his head tilted to the side in a curious, uncertain way, as though he were forcing himself against a resistant wall of air.

Not once had he even hinted at what it was he had come to do, though it was clear from what Lachine had said that it had something to do with the man's wife. "Why think complicated thoughts?" the Colonel warned himself. "He wants to see his wife just as I want my daughter. Why does there have to be anything more to it than that?"

Colonel Carvalho avoided the Alcázar, even the Zoco, now that he had seen what it had become. There was no reason for him to go there; the way to his own house lay through a tangle of cramped and twisting streets that angled so steeply in places that steps of flat stones had been laid in place of the regular cobbles. The thought of the men trapped in the fortress, starving but as prideful and stubborn as his aide Mercader had been once, as he knew he himself could be, given the provocation, pained him, especially as it contrasted with the holiday atmosphere of those who, between bottles of cold beer and Italian ices sold from push-carts, sent their bullets cracking against the Alcázar's flanks.

He looked at his watch: it was almost noon. How strange it was to be so close to the end of his journey. What had seemed in Biarritz like an almost impossible task had not been so difficult after all. It had required of him only that he do whatever was necessary at the moment. No, not quite, he thought, turning up an alleyway filled with a burnished gold reflected from the upper windows of the houses on either side of him. There was Serrano-Guridi. He could have done something there, but he did not. The man had not wanted him to do anything; he had said as much. What more exoneration could he ask? Was it possible that the Major had remembered what Carvalho had told him about Mercedes? . . . perhaps even had remembered the girl as he knew her in Morocco and have made a conscious choice . . . ? Best to put the matter out of mind if he could.

Waves of heat rose from the stones underfoot. A dead mongrel lay a few feet ahead of him, covered with flies, a bullethole in his side. The corpse was not the first he had seen since entering the city. A plague of bullets seemed to have stricken the dogs and cats of the city.

He shuddered as he passed the crumpled animal. The flies rose up for a second, then settled back again onto the sticky hide.

Pistol shots in the distance; the sound of breaking glass and a curious noise, as though someone had brought his fist down on a piano keyboard. Then the resounding twang of strings amid a clatter of metal and the groan of splintering wood. Without doubt, a piano had been pushed out of a window somewhere nearby.

A window slammed shut overhead and a pot of pink flowers quivered on an iron rail. He turned into a familiar street, his own, and saw the doorway to his home, the iron eagle with its wings embracing all the shadows that had ever settled in the narrow street. The nailheads in the door were bright with captured sunlight.

Perhaps he should go first to the Tránsito. He recalled that Mercedes had been making drawings of the old carvings. When he had asked her why, she had simply smiled, and she had said something that had unintentionally wounded him: "I feel sorry for anything old." She hadn't meant to offend him, hadn't meant anything by it, he knew. But all the same . . . yes . . . she would probably be there. Surely not in the house at such an hour. She always had to be doing something. God protect a father from busy children . . .

He was only a few feet from his own front door and gazing down the street toward the Tránsito and the paseo with its peaceful lines of trees bright emerald in the mid-day sun. No trace of killing there. Perhaps the militia had not known quite what to do with a building that was at once Jewish and Catholic. Perhaps they were so overwhelmed with their hate of priests as to finally forgive the Jews for the death of a Christ in whose existence they professed not to believe.

He knocked on the door. The blows resounded like drumbeats. Of course, the house was empty, all the furniture had been trucked away by Onésimo Ramos and César of the "strong-back." Patience. Why become nervous, now, of all times? The street was empty, no one was about. The Zoco and the barricades, the absurd Schneiders of Captain Segurra, and the militia in their rope-soled sandals seemed a million miles away.

He struck more forcefully at the panels; his hand glanced off the iron eagle, and the flesh was torn. A trace of blood, sudden and very bright, stained the bird's rigid wing.

"Mercedes . . ."

His voice rang out in the street, echoed as though in a canyon.

"Mercedes . . . open the door." Was that his voice, harsh, rough with barely restrained panic? Two knocks on a door and this?

"Mercedes . . . Rosa . . . open the door . . ." He had almost called out to Raúl as well. What was happening to him? In a moment's time, he had lost all self-control.

He threw his shoulder against the door; the iron eagle bit into his arm. Then he began to kick at it with his boots. The clamor attracted the attention of two men who were passing below near the Tránsito. They were young, perhaps twenty. One was carrying an iron bar. The other had a scapular tied around his head as a sweatband. They were laughing.

"Hey, old man. You need some help?"

In a moment they had stepped up to the door and were taking turns slamming at the panels with the iron bar and shouting obscenities at the eagle. Carvalho stepped back, watching them and feeling mortified. What a spectacle he must have made, kicking at the door that way.

The boy with the bar shouted in triumph as the panel holding the Hapsburg eagle splintered, leaving a gaping hole in the door. Two more blows and the door was demolished down to the height of a man's waist.

They stood back, proud of their accomplishment. The iron eagle had come loose from the door and lay on the street. One of the boys picked it up and slammed it with the iron bar. It went hurtling out into the street and clanged against the wall of the house opposite.

"Thank you . . . you've done very well . . . I thank you . . . ," Carvalho said with a curious formality that seemed to him necessary at the moment. The two looked at each other, puzzled.

"Who lives in there? Who are you after?"

"I lived in there . . . once," Carvalho said.

The boy with the bar scratched his head; the old man had lived there once, had been put out and was now about to even the score.

"Fine. If you need us to help, old man . . ."

"No."

"Luck then. *Salud.*"

Carvalho reached in through the ruined door, threw the bolt, and went inside. The noonday sun was warm and thick as a carpet in the downstairs rooms. The dust stirred on the floors, reluctant to rise. The house had a peculiar, stifled smell; the windows had been closed and the air trapped within, subject to a slow process of dessication, until it had become almost dust itself. The Colonel moved from room to room, holding his nose and mouth with a handkerchief. He called out over and over again. There was no response.

The house was as he expected it to be, empty, sepulchrally calm. In the main downstairs room he came suddenly upon the harpsichord standing in a corner under a light square on the wall where his portrait had been. The portrait itself had fallen from the wall and lay, face down, on the floor; the frame was broken. The shroud that covered the harpsichord caused him an uneasy moment, recalling the blanket over Francisco Mercader's body and so many others like it. He went over to the harpsichord and flung the drapery back, struck the keys with his splayed fingers. A strident jangle issued from the strings. One of the plectra snapped. He struck the keys angrily, producing, completely by chance, a full minor chord.

Upstairs he found nothing except a scattering of clothes near his daughter's room. He looked at them—a blouse, a few stockings, and a bracelet—with growing concern. In her room he found a basketful of colored chalks and a packet of drawings. He spread them out on the bed: a full set of renderings of the Hebraic carvings on the upper walls of the Tránsito. He remembered them himself and how fascinated by them she had always been. Yet they were there . . . she was not.

He went back downstairs. Through the window, he could see the two boys still in the street, shying stones at a dog. He went to the window, flung it open; the sound of distant rifle fire drifted in like tiny electrical pops. Somewhere high in the sky a single aircraft droned like a great bee, unseen.

No one in the servant's room. Disarray there too, even greater than that in his daughter's room. But all the essential possessions seemed to be missing. The clothes were gone except for those obviously intended for winter—a coat, a heavy shawl. Rosa's comb and brush were gone, too, and her bottles of scent which had always struck the Colonel as so amusingly presumptuous.

He stood again for a moment near the harpsichord, trying to get hold of himself. Had he really expected to find her there at midday? She had no idea that he was coming. If she had been forced to remain in Toledo—and it was clear from what had happened that she had had no choice—she might be anywhere in the city. With friends or anyplace she thought it safe. She was no fool, and she knew what could happen to her if she stayed alone.

He went out into the street again and hurried toward the Tránsito. There was an old man, a caretaker, who often helped her with her drawings. Perhaps he knew.

Acosta Matteu was not there. The Tránsito was locked, and two guards stood in the shade near the doorway, cleaning their rifles.

"There's no one in there, Colonel. It's locked up so tight even a Jew couldn't get in."

His companion laughed. Carvalho went to the side wall, peered in through a dust-filmed window.

"Don't you believe us?" the second guard shouted belligerently. "You think I'm lying to you, Colonel . . . ?"

Carvalho stalked away, paying no attention. He could hear the iron eagle clattering against the stones; the boys were kicking it back and forth.

Where could she be? He had been so confident of finding her at home that it had not occurred to him to think of where else she might be until that moment. He glanced about; there were guards in front of El Greco's house across the street, and he could see guards behind him, hidden in the shadows of the Santa Maria la Blanca, also once a synagogue. Ahead rose the crenelated tower of San Juan de los Reyes.

He walked down the path, slowly, to give himself time to gather his thoughts. It was possible that Pascual Soler was in the city, or even Tomás Pelayo. Of Don Aurelio Aguilera de Tella he had not a thought; if the man hadn't been prudent enough to flee at the beginning of the rising, he was either dead or in a prison somewhere. What a pity; though the man was a fool, he had never done anything to harm anyone. "But," he thought, "so many of us harm people precisely by . . . doing nothing to harm them. . . ."

Soler. Where would he find him? He recalled dimly an office somewhere near the Zocodover which the lawyer used when he was not in Madrid. The Banco Toledano would be closed, if not destroyed, and he would have to look for Pelayo elsewhere. There was no telling where Sebastián Gil might be. Was the phone service working? It might be prudent to go back to the bookseller's shop and ask Tierres for help. Or Portillo, if he could find him.

He discovered that he was in front of the San Juan. The sun was directly overhead, and his hair felt as though it might ignite at any second. The stones sizzled. A few magpies winged by, like flung stones, their tiny bodies fierce in flight.

He circled the city on foot, stopping in any shop that seemed familiar and was still open to ask after his daughter. Lucas the butcher had not seen her, nor López Mona who sold coffee and tea from huge barrels which were normally always full but were now almost empty. José Fuentes shook his head and found it difficult to answer; his cousin, a seminarian, had been shot the day before, and his hands were white and bloodless from being clenched for the last twenty hours.

The nearer Carvalho came to the center of the city, the steeper the streets' ascent; his shoulder began to pain him again, and he thought of Dr. Blas Aliaga who also had a small office in Toledo. If he got a chance, he would have to see him or someone else about the pain in his shoulder. It was too recurrent to be shrugged off.

He passed one of the churches which had been unguarded and, hence, was burned out. It was a pitiful building of no importance, no beauty, its only purpose to incense the poor. And so it had been gutted. Wooden polychrome images of Christ and the Virgin, too poorly done to warrant anything more destructive than laughter, had been hacked to pieces, the brightly painted splinters scattered around the streets. A dog was urinating on Jesus' left arm as the Colonel passed. Another figure which Carvalho at first took for a large wooden image such as are carried in religious processions lay stiffly by the corner of the building. But it was human, not wood; a priest who had foolishly kept on his soutane.

By late afternoon, Carvalho had spoken to over two dozen shopkeepers, Pablo Rubio at the telegraph office which was still functioning, Manolo González at the postal building, three female assistants who were still sorting mail, and over a half-dozen proprietors of cafés where he knew Mercedes would sometimes go with Rosa for a lemon ice.

No one had seen her.

Late in the afternoon, he even located the man who used to sell bus tickets in a booth on the Zoco. The man was so frightened by the Colonel's uniform that he could do nothing but shake his head; some of the militiamen had threatened him. "I'm not an exploiter," he protested. "How can they say that? I only sell tickets for bus trips. Why don't they shoot the people who make the buses? Or the drivers? If they don't like bus trips . . . why don't they walk?"

Carvalho had not eaten at all since the early morning; his hunger had given way to a brooding, empty sensation. The face of Serrano-Guridi kept returning, the wide eyes, the placid look of acceptance.

He sat down on a low stone wall near the Zoco and tried to light a cigarette. His hands had begun to tremble so that it was very difficult for him.

He sat and smoked for a few minutes, but had no patience and flung the still burning cigarette into the gutter. Through a gap between the building he was afforded a view of the Alcázar. The building was still smoking from fires set by a bombing run made by three Government trimotors that afternoon.

He could hear the cough of Captain Segurra's Schneiders. How long had they been firing? He could imagine the Captain's exasperation as shell after shell bounced off the fortress' walls, and Madrid kept sending instructions to continue the bombardment.

Nightfall; the Tagus seemed to swell, to empty its deep blues and greens into the sky. Livid pink smears ran from the horizon high into the arch of the sky. The clouds that had spent the day trying to climb into the sun lay exhausted on the ridges of the Sierra de Gredos.

The building where Soler's office had been was gutted. Only the interior stairway remained, standing alone in the rubble, like an accusing finger pointed at God. Many of the bombs aimed at the Alcázar had fallen in odd places around the city, destroying a house here, a church there, a workingman's hovel there. Whole streets had been set on fire accidentally.

As the color of the sky deepened, the streets emptied. People retired to their houses, leaving the alleyways to the militia. A busload of men carrying rifles chugged down the Cuesta, heading back to Madrid. It was a yellow bus and carried a dozen flags which had been stuck into the radiator cap, the windshield, and the windows.

Carvalho passed Tierres' headquarters, the bookshop, which still bore the words: "Gómez y Martín, Rare Books and Incunabula" in gilt letters over the doorway. Lights were burning, and a haze of blue cigarette smoke obscured the front windows.

Carvalho went on past, suddenly afraid of talking to anyone. He could not bear the thought of sitting down and telling anyone what had happened. One had to bear one's fears, one's private catastrophes, with dignity. But what else was there to do? He had to have help.

An armored car was parked near a café on the Calle de la Trinidad. The sounds of music issued from inside the cafe, and much laughter. He thought for a moment of returning to the Hotel Maravilla but that would mean, ultimately, facing Lachine with his failure and of having, finally, to ask the man for help. He could not bear that.

Inside the café, he found a table near the door where he could sit alone. Copies of *Claridad* and *El Socialista* lay crumpled in balls on the floor, and the walls of the room were covered with photographs of battles and men in uniform giving the clenched-fist salute. Oddly, there was one huge picture of General Mola clipped from the Monarchist daily *ABC* which seemed to dominate the room. It had been hung up as a target, and a few men were throwing things at it. A phonograph was grinding out mournful Murcian folk songs, but instead of inducing sobriety, they seemed to encourage only more and more laughter.

The room, partially walled with mirrors, was filled with over a hundred men, most of them in uniform. Their reflections multiplied and multiplied again in the glass panels until it seemed to Carvalho that he was lost in the midst of a huge army. Smoke hung over the tables, thick as the music. The smell of beer predominated. Men were coming and going constantly, and the door was hardly ever closed. A spice of wine-soaked wood sharpened the air.

He had often read that men can be overcome by an overwhelming sense of isolation in the midst of tumultuous crowds but had never experienced the sensation before. Now, he felt not only a sense of isolation but the even more frightening sensation of being completely outside . . . of everything, as though he were watching it all through a thick pane of one-way glass. How many nights had he lain awake imagining what would happen to him if he dared return to Toledo once the Anarchists had risen? Yet now he walked the streets of the city, and no one paid any attention to him, no one even asked to see the card that he carried, signed by Edmundo Tierres. No one cared. The Republic had not summoned him, nor had the Anarchists demanded his head. He seemed to be, in the phrase that the Soviets had made current, an "un-person." He had no existence and related to no one, to nothing. Only to ruins.

At that moment, a short, thick-bodied man, dark as an oak, entered the room. His shirt was open, and he wore a gray suit jacket and neatly pressed trousers. No hat. He should have been wearing a tie, and there should have been a handkerchief in his pocket, or at least a flower in his lapel, but there was not. His few strands of hair were combed over an almost square skull. Broad mouth, wide mustache, and deep circles under his eyes. For a second, neither man recognized the other.

Then the man who had just entered blinked and cried: "Enrique!"

Carvalho half stood up from the table.

"Pascual . . ." It was Soler, the lawyer whose bombed-out office he had just passed.

"I would never have thought . . . you . . . here, at . . . this . . . time?" Soler hesitated, trying to find the right word. He sat down at Carvalho's table at once.

The Colonel pulled his documents from his pocket. "Does this explain it?—'Under the Protection of the Communist party of Toledo, signed, E. Tierres.' Thanks to my son and his friends . . ."

Soler took a moment to digest what he was being told. He was used to absorbing the most astonishing information without batting an eye. In that respect, he had always thought, a lawyer was much like a confessor: it was his duty to listen and not to betray his own moral judgments.

"So . . . I see . . . it makes things easier, doesn't it? But what are you doing here . . . ?" He began to speak more rapidly, as though by accelerating the tempo of his speech he could put more words between an unpleasant subject and the necessity to comment on it. "I could weep for joy to see you. We all thought you were still in Oviedo. Dead by now, to guess at it . . ."

"And you," Carvalho said with genuine warmth, for he had always liked the lawyer though it disturbed him now to see the man without a tie, without a hat, without his flower; it signaled a capitulation to absurd attitudes the Colonel thought he himself might have resisted. "Your office is nothing but a ruin . . ."

"An accident. Remember, war is 99 percent accident. The side that is spared that final 1 percent is the side that wins, that's my theory. Come, tell me how you've gotten back. . . ."

For a few moments they exchanged stories in anxious, overjoyed voices as though rapid, unrelenting speech was the only way to confirm their discovery of each other and keep it alive, as though if they fell silent for a second, one or the other of them would vanish. The story of Carvalho's escape from Oviedo caused Soler to laugh in his barrel-deep, faintly nasal voice, honed as it was to its cutting sharpness by so many years of courtroom orations.

"So . . . do you think he's found his trousers yet, that driver of yours? Or is he still in the bushes, playing his own flute, no doubt, to keep himself occupied."

"That was weeks ago," Carvalho said, surprised that he had never given a thought to the driver's predicament; the driver had been no more than a boy, and he had left him almost naked by the roadside ten miles out of Oviedo. Now it seemed to him to have been a necessary but nevertheless cruel thing to have done.

Soler told him what had occurred in Toledo since the rising had begun. There was nothing that Carvalho did not know already, except that De Tella had gotten away just in time, "Though I doubt he understands yet why he had to leave his apricots." Dr. Aliaga was tending the wounded in a military hospital set up by the militia just the other side of the Tagus. "Mostly those who have shot themselves by accident trying to blow down the walls of the Alcázar. . . ."

Then, suddenly, as the Murcian reapers' song repeated for the fifth time its odd, medieval refrain, the two men found themselves staring at each other through a fragile pane of silence.

"Your daughter . . . ," Soler said.

"Yes."

"You came for her, of course. . . . Is she well?"

"I don't know . . ." Carvalho said after a pause. "I've looked everywhere for her, but there isn't a trace. Only this . . . ," he put the filagreed bracelet he had picked up outside her room down on the table between them.

Soler shook his massive head. "The last time I saw her . . . ," he began, finding it difficult to force out the words, "she was at a dinner given by Mercader. I don't suppose you know . . ." He looked down at his ringed fingers. "I heard this afternoon, from Blas Aliaga that . . ."

"I was at the house. I saw it, Pascual . . ."

"What can one say?"

"Nothing." He shook his head. The air filled with Murcian folk song.

"So . . . that was the last time then, Enrique. I wish I could tell you something, or be of some help, but the simple truth is. . . ." He forced a smile, "We'll find her, I'm sure. The dawn patrols have been too busy with priests to worry about women. . . . We may be able to control those savages yet. Certainly, General Riquelme doesn't like them at all . . . even so . . . God, I'm rambling, I know, but that's the way it is . . . even so . . . they haven't taken to shooting people just because of their relatives . . . yet . . . why, even Moscardó's son is still alive. They phoned Moscardó up there, did you know? . . . and told him that they'd blow out his son's brains if he didn't surrender. Of course the old man had no choice; he told them to go ahead and shoot, he wouldn't give up. That fool of a fat man, Candido Cabello . . . one of my colleagues at the bar, if anyone would believe it . . . he thought up the stunt. What did he imagine, that the other thousand or so up there in the fortress would give up and march like lambs to the firing wall just for the sake of Luis Moscardó? Even Cabello couldn't have been that stupid. Well, in any event, they haven't shot Luis yet . . . though Colonel Moscardó probably thinks they have . . ."

Carvalho chewed on a tough silence for a moment. How fragile must be the lives of the hostages inside the Alcázar, and those of anyone who had a father or a son on the Republican side. He expressed his fears at once. "Did Señor Cabello think of that?"

"I doubt Cabello thought much at all. He simply saw a chance to become a hero without moving that unimaginable bulk of his out of his chair, that's all." Soler wagged his head from side to side, his equivalent of shaking it. "And a lawyer too . . . that's what happens to us when we can no longer practice our profession as we're accustomed to doing. We succumb to the temptation to become God."

It amazed Carvalho that he could sit there conversing with Soler in such a way; he should be out in the street again, looking for some sign of his daughter. Yet he was so weighted down by the enormity of his task, the sheer impossibility of it, that he could not even bring himself to ask Soler anything about her.

Soler went on, trying to seem matter of fact. The room was filled with militia, and the regular army men had withdrawn to one corner as though guarding themselves, as ill at ease with their strange alliance as General Franco's *Tercio* must have been with their Moors.

"I'm a man without a profession now," Soler said. "It seems that we are in the midst of a time when abstract notions of justice are simply irrelevant. What was just and what was not will be determined by the ultimate conclusion of this affair, rather than the other way around, I'm afraid."

The two men went out into the Calle de la Trinidad. Searchlight beams could be seen swinging back and forth over the Alcázar, and the crackle of rifle fire seemed as unreal as the noise made by the slapstick of puppets in Retiro Park in Madrid.

"Where are you staying?" Soler asked.

"At the Hotel Maravilla."

"I'm not far from there. Blas Aliaga's given me the loan of a couch in his office while he's off patching up the wounded and sleeping on his feet." Soler took Carvalho's arm in a sudden, powerful grip. His broad, stolid face broke into a smile that seemed an expression not so much of pleasure but of a pain so impossible to bear that there was nothing left to do but smile at it.

"If I can be of any help . . ."

"How?"

"I don't know," Soler admitted.

The lawyer turned down a narrow street and waved once in his own individual way, with three fingers joined together, a sharp stroking of the air.

"*Salud,*" Soler called. The Colonel replied softly, "*Salud.*"

Carvalho continued on. He passed the bookshop: "Gómez y Martín, Rare Books and Incunabula." A light was on. Two men and a woman in a blue print dress were posting photographs on the wall. The pictures seemed to have been culled from a thousand different sources. Some had been clipped from newspapers, others taken from family albums, still others were from passports or other official documents and were pocked with stamps and raised punch-holes.

"They're the hostages the Fascists are holding up there," one of the men explained. "We don't want to kill them by accident when we take the place, so we're putting their pictures up for everyone to memorize."

Carvalho stood just inside the doorway, examining the pictures by the sulfury light of an unshaded bulb. When he had done, he realized that he had been looking for Mercedes' picture. She was not there.

Next to the wall of pictures was a typewritten list of names, the people known to have gone into the Alcázar on their own volition.

Mercedes' name was not on the list.

"I've seen you before, no?" the woman said.

The Colonel turned, and the light made his beard seem as though it were on fire. He lit a cigar.

"Yes, you have. I was here before . . . today . . ."

"With the Frenchman . . . I remember." The woman was not attractive at all, thick limbed, but she had a pleasant robustness about her. "In that case, would you like some coffee? Ramón always has a pot going."

"Thank you, but no . . ." The Colonel went out. He was far more tired than he had realized. It was late, and he had not realized it; the siege of the Alcázar with its lights and noises had managed to freeze night in its early hours, where it would hold it until dawn came.

"*Salud,*" said the woman from the doorway.

The Colonel walked with his eyes closed for a few yards. "*Salud,*" he thought he heard himself answer.

AUGUST 20

The Sierra de Guadarrama is the tomb of the Praetorian Fascism.

The fall of Granada believed imminent.

The great offensive underway.

Córdoba and Huesca under heavy combat action of the Loyalist forces.

Gijón cleaned of rebels after the surrender of the Simancas barracks.

El Sol

328

VITOLYN HAD INTENDED to listen to the music for a short while simply to calm his nerves. He did not really care for music, certainly not the crude braying that was going on in the courtyard below, brassy marches fit only for . . . bulls . . . and people stupid enough to go into a ring with them . . . that was all . . . but music, any kind of music had the power to soothe him, even to anesthetize. There had been a street fight once, right after a party meeting; the police had ridden in, and two of his friends had been arrested. He'd gotten away and wandered over to the *Kursalon,* the casino, in the woods where the Schubert-Ring and the Park-Ring join, and they'd been playing stupid little waltzes by Leo Fall and Stolz. He'd forgotten all about the meeting and the police, and had just stood there, as he was doing now, swaying in time to the music. A child had pointed to him and asked his father why the man was bleeding. He hadn't noticed the blood himself. When the father hurried the child away, he'd left the Park. It took something like that to wake him up, the power of the music over him was so strong.

Below, in the vaults, he'd been able to think of nothing else but Roig and the sly Major. He was convinced that he was being followed. How similar Spanish faces all seemed now—the faces of the hostages, of Roig, of the Major, and the Captain. They repeated themselves everywhere he looked. It was Gil's fault, this fear he had developed of being followed.

"I tell you, he follows me wherever I go. Look, you can see him. His name, I even know his name. It's Ortiz. Call after him and see if he doesn't answer. That Captain Herrera has put him up to it. I'm frantic, but I don't know what to do. Even at night. Even when I go to the lavatory, he's there on the other side of the partition. I know it . . . I know his boots. . . ." Vitolyn would look when Gil would suddenly point into the shadows. Sometimes he thought he actually saw someone there. The Guard Ortiz? He could never tell for sure.

They had been together a great deal since that evening in the underground dining hall, each man finding in the other an unexpected source of comfort. A kind of symbiosis had developed; Vitolyn drew from Gil's fears some stimulus for his own and thus began to break out of the anesthetized emotional state that he had been in for weeks. Gil, in his turn, found in Vitolyn's seeming placidity a source of reassurance.

Gil coughed by the doorway. Vitolyn did not look back, tried to make believe he hadn't heard. Why wouldn't Gil listen to the music too? If he didn't want to listen, why had he come?

Gazing down at the crowd gathered in the yard below, at the warm, hypnotic lights pooling on the stones and the comfortable, geometric arrangements of figures on wire chairs, Vitolyn experienced a growing feeling of calm. The music was taking hold, like a shot of morphine . . .

slowly, insinuating its way into his bloodstream. Even the fact that the hostages had been brought up to listen to the concert did not disturb him. They were manacled and could do no harm.

If only Gil would stop making those odd noises in his throat. Yet Vitolyn realized that it was precisely Gil's deplorable state that so attracted him, that in its way redeemed him. . . .

"Why doesn't he blow his nose . . . or cough or do something?" It was getting difficult even to hear the music, loud as it was. Gil continued sniffling.

"Can't you stop that?"

"But . . . it's so hard . . . there's so much dust, all the time . . . of course, I'll try. . . ."

Why can't he even argue with me? . . . Then at least I could be angry with him, Vitolyn thought. But what do you do with a man who admits everything and keeps on doing it nevertheless? He shook his head and looked back toward the window. His fingers ceased their nervous exploration of the ledge. A piece of pale white fungus came loose under his fingernail. Zipser, he thought . . . Zipser's mushrooms.

From behind him came a soft, tentative sound: Gil was trying to clear his throat, very quietly. So as not to disturb . . .

They weren't playing marches anymore.

The music had changed so suddenly . . . or was it that he had been so preoccupied with Gil's noises that he hadn't heard? . . . yet, there it was, a march no longer, but a sighing of strings. The melody was disturbingly familiar. He began to mouth words that seemed to fit the rhythm, annoyed by his inability to remember where he'd heard them before:

"Gib deine Hand . . . du schön und zart gebild . . . bin Freund und komme nicht zu strafen . . ."

Gil was quiet, tense in his silence as though he were holding his breath. A little light came in through the window, and Vitolyn could see Gil's face, cut by a slight, but broadly curving smile as he sat on a block of granite with his back to the door.

Vitolyn's gaze wandered without direction from the wall to the man's face, then to the wall again. He found himself staring at the door, at its frame, ridged by elaborate wooden carvings, the wooden lintel inscribed with some indistinguishable poem in four lines and interwoven with raised wooden flowers. The sighing music blended with the neutral images, produced a hazy half-sleep. He barely heard Gil's breathing now.

Gradually, he became conscious of a shapeless stirring in the darkness by the edge of the door. The movement seemed to stretch both forward and backward in time; he had the feeling of having noticed it long before it had actually entered the periphery of his field of vision and, so, was not disturbed by it. . . .

As he watched, still seeing the oddly beatific smile on Gil's face more than anything else, something swung slowly out from the half-shaped darkness beyond the door, from the corridor outside, and hung poised over Gil's head. The club, a piece of beam, splintered at one end, began to descend . . . very slowly. It was too late, even ridiculous to cry out. But he choked out a sound nevertheless, obliged . . .

"Noooo . . . ," a token protest only, sure proof of his own paralysis.

The club completed its descent, striking Gil sharply across the back of the head. Gil slumped forward without uttering a sound. He pitched forward and sprawled face down on the floor, a thin jet of blood flowing instantly from behind his ear.

Vitolyn, terrified, flattened himself against the window frame, his head far back, for a moment catching a dizzying, inverted glimpse of the courtyard.

"Get over here," said the man with the club. A lumpy piece of shadow detached itself from the doorway, grotesquely small, twisted, became the hunchbacked hostage Paco. He held a pistol in his hand; it was much too large for him. A thought passed through Vitolyn's mind: "How can he get his finger around the trigger?"

"If you shout," the hunchback said, "it will be the end of you right there where you stand . . . if you make one single noise . . ."

The hunchback approached only close enough for the powdery moonlight to brighten his features, not to clarify them.

"Listen to me, you—there isn't any need for . . ."

"Shut your mouth," the hunchback Paco Orsuña said. "I don't want to talk to you, so just keep your mouth shut." He gestured with the pistol; it was ludicrously large in his small, childlike hand, a Civil Guard Mauser with a wooden handle. Vitolyn obeyed at once and flung his hands up over his head. Odd, but he could still hear the words rattling around inside his head, though he was no longer speaking.

"This way, man . . . whatever your name is. Put your hands behind your neck. . . ."

It was dark in the corridor, and no one was about. They were all below in the courtyard, at the "Circus." The corridors were long funnels of shadow, so crisscrossed with distant reflections of the candlelight leaping in the yard below that the walls seemed alive, almost fluid. Vitolyn looked frantically about. If only a soldier, even a woman or a child would pass and see him. All at once a vision of the room in which the hostages had been kept came back to him, perfect in every detail. He could even recall the odor.

In a moment they were on their way down to the basement. Vitolyn stumbled and cut his face against the wall, drawing a mouthful of blood. He spat it out at once. The hunchbacked Paco Orsuña mistook the sound.

"No talking, I said. Not now. You'll have plenty of time for that when we get outside."

"What?" Outside? What did he mean by that? They were going down into the depths of the Alcázar's cellars and this shrunken little man was talking about *outside*.

"Just what I said. We're going out. Over the wall. Or under it if the *señorito* prefers . . ."

Vitolyn was dumbstruck. Then there was a way out after all. How had all of this come about? And what did they want with him? It was all Roig's fault: that they had almost killed him that day in the prisoners' room . . . that this was happening now.

"We want to know what you did with the lists, comrade," the hunchback said. "Did you ever take a trip on the 'airplane,' comrade? The soldiers taught us that one. You hang a man up by his hands and feet and . . ."

"What lists?" Vitolyn felt as though he were being enveloped by a huge, soaking wet blanket that followed every contour of his body and which he could not throw off no matter how hard he struggled. "What lists, for God's sake?"

"Keep your voice down," the hunchback said. "And don't play that game with me. Why else would you have . . . you did kill him, didn't you? How else could you have gotten his papers?"

"Please . . . what lists . . . I'll tell you if I know . . ."

"The lists of our people inside the POUM. Come on now, don't be a fool. He had them all. Every name. The agents in the FAI too."

"I don't know what you're talking about," Vitolyn stammered, feeling the full weight of his disaster clamping down on him. He could not believe what was happening. Roig was, after all, taking his revenge.

"I never saw them . . . I don't know anything about . . . lists . . ." They were descending deeper and deeper. How much farther could they possibly go? The air had grown moist and foul smelling, heavy, like the air in catacombs or an abandoned mine.

"He had them on him, so don't expect me to believe that shit . . . Christ's balls, man . . . just get moving . . ."

"This is ridiculous. You must . . . I don't . . ."

"There are ten little bullets in this gun. You'll feel each one of them in a different place before I kill you . . . now, move . . ."

The blood continued to ooze in his mouth. Lists of Communist "plants" in the Anarchist and Trotskyist organizations. What a ghastly tangle he'd gotten himself into and what way out was there? He didn't know where any "lists" were. For all he knew, Roig had committed them to memory; the lists might only be found inside a shattered skull in a closet in a room opposite Florez's house. He shuddered. What a terrible thing it was to contemplate the possibility of dying for something one did not understand at all, simply because one had gotten caught in the middle of someone else's fight. . . .

"Move . . . ," Paco Orsuña said again.

Vitolyn shuddered; he knew that voice. It was Baumgartner all over again . . . the same flat, toneless quality.

They passed below ground level, and the air at once became damp with the Tagus' dark breath. Vitolyn felt a chill, felt rather than heard the hunchback's steps at his back, expected any second the thud of a bullet in the back of his neck.

He remembered. The voice, the cold. The same dreadful sensation at the base of his neck. A table in the cellar. The smell of mushrooms raised in flat wooden trays by comrade Zipser. Near the boiler, a stronger smell of mushrooms and oil from the sputtering lamp. Baumgartner, seated, with a revolver on the table in front of him. "Ludicrous," he remembered thinking. "Ludicrous. . . . Where is the flag? . . . the music?"

"Stealing, Comrade Vitolyn . . . of all things . . . *stealing*. What an incredibly bourgeois thing to do . . ."

He was standing in the cellar, seeing not Baumgartner or the others, but only Stoplinsky, who was not there at all, a thin, almost emaciated figure in a sailor's blue sweater, a knitted watch-cap above his pockmarked face, a cigar thrust, dead center, in his mouth. But in the midst of all that ugliness, Stoplinsky's eyes had shone with a terrifying luminosity. Vitolyn had often wondered what Stoplinsky saw that the rest of them couldn't see. To Baumgartner, Stoplinsky's vision was a mad hallucination, and to follow it meant ruin. Hadn't Stalin himself hounded Trotsky all the way to Alma Ata for the same heresy? But even more disturbing to Vitolyn was the nagging doubt that he had refused to obey Baumgartner's orders not because he had believed Stoplinsky was right or because he could not bring himself to kill for a faith which held, as he saw it, that every man, no matter how wretched, had a right to live . . . but simply because he was afraid. Street brawls were one thing, but to put a revolver bullet into a friend's skull was quite something else.

"Afraid." That word consumed his thoughts, his night's rest, and even the food he took into his stomach. It left him drained and empty, a withered, sleepless shell. And yet . . . how ironic . . . he could not now feel fear at all.

For weeks after his refusal, he had avoided them, spoken to them only when it was absolutely necessary, tried as much as possible to remain apart from them, to go his own way alone and unobserved. He grew resentful, imagining their reproaches, turning over and over in his mind Baumgartner's bitter attack. The deeper his distrust of his own motives became, the more he turned against the others. They were morally bankrupt, liars, hypocrites. No better themselves than the Fascists. He argued, debated with himself. "Fear," his nights whispered seductively. "Moral degeneracy," his mornings shouted over the gothic rooftops of Vienna. "Bankrupts . . . you are all moral bankrupts."

On the morning that Stoplinsky's body was found floating in the Donau canal, Vitolyn had rushed wildly to Baumgartner's glass shop and pried up the floorboards in the cellar under which, in a clay flower pot, the party treasury had been secreted. Wads and wads of high denomination schilling notes. "That will teach them. When they feel *this* loss, they'll understand just how rotten they've become. . . ."

His mistake was in not leaving immediately. Two days later, when he finally made his way to the railroad depot with the intention of taking the next train to Hamburg, Zipser, and three others were there waiting for him. All Zipser could say as they hustled him back to Baumgartner's cellar was, "Shame . . . shame . . ."

"Stealing . . . ," Baumgartner had shouted, in that same cellar.

"I stole to show you how corrupt you have become."

"Stealing," Baumgartner had shouted again in a voice doubly betrayed.

"Josip Djugashvili robs a bank and that becomes a great revolutionary deed, and forget that he may buy himself some new suits and a few tins of herring. I, however, steal from *you,* for your own good, to show you how dependent on money you've become, how corrupted, to save you, in a word . . . and that becomes a terrible crime. Where has your sense of justice gone? Look how purple in the face you are. Look at yourself. Does money mean so much to you, Helmut? Ah . . . yes . . ."

"You stole out of greed . . ."

"Out of dedication. To you and to my ideals. Our ideals."

"Shit," Baumgartner shouted, placing a long sheet of paper on the table. "We shall see. So . . . a new car, four dinners of disgusting extravagance at The Sacher . . . so . . . out of dedication you spend like a drunken soldier at Frau Wessl's brothel. Not once, but three times. Out of this same dedication you purchase three suits of clothes, one of Chinese silk, two woolen overcoats, two hats, four pairs of shoes, nine shirts . . . shall I go on?"

"You left out the brandy, Helmut. Four bottles, please."

"So . . . four bottles of brandy," Baumgartner said through his teeth, scratching at the list, adding numbers and words. "What kind? Tell me, what kind was it?"

"It doesn't make any difference. I didn't drink it. I poured it down the toilet."

"So much the worse for you."

And afterward, a pounding of revolver butts on the table. Then silence. Only the sound of Zipser's mushrooms growing in pans near the boiler.

"You're not serious," Vitolyn had blurted out.

"We'll see, Anton. You can't say you weren't warned."

"But a death sentence? It's ludicrous."

"You leave us no alternative."

"Helmut, for God's sake . . ." Vitolyn had begun, almost laughing, a peculiar vibration taking hold of his limbs, as though his entire body had gone to sleep and was just waking. "You're trying to frighten me . . . a joke is a joke, but . . ."

"A joke is a joke," he heard himself saying to the hunchback. "But now that you've scared me . . . well, what's the point of it?"

"You'll see that soon enough."

"How did you get away . . . ?" Vitolyn asked in a weak voice.

"Why?"

"I don't know . . ."

"I'm small, you see? I hide in a barrel, no one sees me. The others go out. . . . It's very simple. Now don't ask so many questions. We have work to do."

A dank, river-rotten smell, the sweet odor of putrefying flesh. No light at all. Then the hunchback struck a match.

Vitolyn drew in a breath. They were coming to the baths, a long, sinister-looking room where the cadets had gone swimming before the siege. The water had been drained off day by day for drinking purposes, leaving the pool only partly filled. Along the walls, niches had already been dug for burial purposes against the time when the Picadero would no longer be available. The dead could wait but only so long. Then they would begin to protest in the only way they could.

Long rows of curved shower heads jutted down like pincers from the ceiling over the narrow pool . . . a spindly railing along the edge . . . an arched ceiling full of shifting shadows; reflections of torchlight flung from the surface of the water and from the glistening backs of the water, bugs that skimmed across the pool. The electric lights hung overhead, dead and useless. Vitolyn looked down from the pool's edge into the water. He reached out for the railing, felt it vibrate in his trembling hand.

"Get down there," the hunchback ordered.

Vitolyn began to descend; the ladder steps were slimy. He almost lost his balance. Footsteps resounded, loud and hollow, in the empty chamber. He half turned, tried to make out the man's face, to determine, from his eyes, whether he intended to shoot him there or whether it would be later.

"Why are you doing this to me?"

"You ask that? The lists, man, the lists. You knew when you killed Roig, didn't you? Well, we're going to find out how much you know and where the lists are. It would have been easier if you'd told me up there. Then I would simply have shot you and gone out myself. But if you won't tell me, you'll tell Tierres and the others, that's all. It's your choice."

"My God . . ."

Vitolyn was in the water up to his knees, then up to his waist. Surprisingly, it reached no farther. He began to push toward the end of the pool. The hunchback had not followed him down, but padded along the pool's edge, holding onto the hollow metal railing. If he had descended, the water would have been up to his chest.

Orsuña gestured with his pistol. "There is a loose stone at the end there, just below the marker," he said, indicating a tile on which the depth had been written. "It pulls up and out, and there is a passageway behind it. Now get to work."

Vitolyn bent and his elbows broke the surface of the water. He could barely control his hands and they splashed helplessly, foaming the slimy surface. The hunchback leaned against the railing, pointing the pistol directly at him. "I was one of the work gang that built this pool for the *señoritos* to paddle in. I sweated my balls black so they could wash themselves twice a day. We found the tunnel while we were building the pool. It used to be a conduit for water, but it's wide enough for a man to get through . . . Come on now. Get to work, pig."

The first stone slipped out easily, then a larger one. Four tiles dropped with a quiet bubbling sound to the bottom of the pool. A passageway, barely large enough for a man to crawl into opened in the wall just above the level of the water.

"I'm not going in there . . . ," Vitolyn said, his voice choked with panic. A terrible fear of enclosed spaces suffocated him; better to be shot dead at once. Nothing in the world could make him crawl into that black hole.

"You'll get in there or I'll blow your head off. We're going out of here . . . now."

"I will not . . ." He bent his head in protest.

The hunchback spit and leaned farther over the railing as though to take more careful aim. The gob of sputum dropped to the surface of the pool and fizzed in the water. At the same time, Vitolyn heard a thin, creaking sound, little more than a vibration at first, then a sudden, precipitous shriek of metal. Startled, he looked up, saw the railing over which the hunchback was leaning, slowly bend under his weight into the pool. With a shudder, the railing gave way completely and Paco Orsuña plummeted headfirst into the water, his right arm flailing wildly, one end of the railing still held fast in his left hand. The pistol clattered against the tile somewhere.

A whirl of froth erupted next to Vitolyn as the hunchback splashed into the water, his arms and head going down smoothly as a diver's. Vitolyn, without thinking at all of what he was doing, reached out, his hands passing over the spot below which the hunchback could now be seen struggling up toward the surface. As though it were the most natural thing to do, he intercepted the surfacing shoulders and pressed down as hard as he could. For a moment, there was a terrible thrashing. He watched, fascinated, as bubbles spurted first in two jets from the sides of the man's mouth, then diminished to a jerky, infrequent stream.

The water refracted the drowning man's image, making it fluid, deceptively beautiful.

Vitolyn raised one knee and pressed it down on the hump. A few bubbles circled in fragile chains about his legs. Then nothing, only the gentle side-to-side slide of the water, slower and slower until the surface of the pool was once again motionless. The hunchback went limp under the water, but Vitolyn continued to hold him fast. Vitolyn stood there, one leg drawn up, his knee on the man's back, his hands twined in the material of his shirt, rocking slowly back and forth. Then, very cautiously, he shifted his weight, loosed his hands and slipped back a few feet toward the ladder.

The body floated languidly to the surface and hung there, face down, the shirt still full of air.

Vitolyn could barely comprehend what had happened. Shaking, he pushed the body across the surface of the water to the edge of the pool; it turned lazily, the head bumping against the tiles. Vitolyn fastened the corpse to the ladder with the hunchback's belt and went about replacing the stones so that the passageway was once again hidden. He shuddered to think of it, but at some time in the future, the passage might be his salvation; it was good to know about such things.

When he had finished with the stones and the tiles, he hauled the body back out of the pool, dragged it over to the crypts which had already been dug into the wall.

Into one of these hollows he crammed the body, then covered it over with brick and loose mortar. With the last brick in place, he paused to consider how like the situation was to the scene in Roig's room. But what he had done then had been deliberate; here it had been the result of impulse, of automatic, unthinking reaction. "I am a man who hates killing and pain . . . how can I do such things?" The real reason Baumgartner had hated him so fiercely, and persecuted him so uncompromisingly, was because he had refused to kill. Why *now,* after all these months did it come so easily?

His trousers were plastered against his legs, black with water, and he began to tremble with cold. He left quickly, mounting the same stairs he had descended only minutes before. He would have to find Gil. Perhaps he had been killed too. The hunchback had struck him hard, directly on the head. Men did not often get up after blows like that. Life was not as it was shown in the films where every man had a head of iron. Skulls actually fractured when struck.

He climbed the steps from the basement. No one was about in the corridors. The music still hummed in the courtyard. "My God! Still Schubert, the third movement? . . . or was it the fourth?" A tarantella rhythm, as though the gentle Austrian had finally been shamed by his Spanish surroundings into some vaguely Latin expression. Had it all been that fast? Only one movement's worth?

Sebastián Gil had never been able to bear pain well, neither his own nor that of others. He admitted it, made no secret of it, even laughed at it. "Call Dr. Miranda. I've stuck my finger with the phonograph needle again," he would shout to Alicia.

Now it was a good deal more than that. His head throbbed furiously. There was blood on the back of his neck, and he was afraid to even touch the spot for fear of finding the back of his head laid open. His whole head felt stiff, swollen and the feeling communicated itself to his body as far down as his waist.

How long had he been lying there? He could still hear the music in the courtyard. Distant, strangely distorted, as though every instrument was out of tune. He got to his feet. The room was empty. The Austrian had gone. Of course. Why should the Austrian involve himself in his troubles?

Suddenly, it struck him; he had been attacked. It had gone beyond insinuations, sly accusations, questions, dark looks, and muttered threats. Now they were really going to kill him. But if that were so, why not just put him up against the wall and shoot him? Did they think they could terrorize him into confessing? What? He had nothing to confess. Didn't they understand that Venegas had been his friend too?

Gil trembled. Suddenly, he remembered the trips to Paris with Alicia, the concerts she had given in the Bois de Boulogne. Two deputy ministers had attended and Alfred Cortot himself had been there and smiled once after Alicia had played the D minor prelude of Chopin. What an honor. A smile from Cortot. Why should he remember that now? His glance fell on his wristwatch; on the rear of the case was an inscription from her, a chain of little notes that traced the melody to the words *Il mio tesoro*. What had all that to do with this place, this insanity? The notes, the concerts, his wife—that had been his real life, and the Alcázar and Toledo were only figments of his imagination. But it was not so; the Alcázar was real enough. Real as the little room where they had taken him three? . . . was it four? . . . times. Real as the table, the muddied boots, muddied although it hadn't rained in weeks. Major Punto's endless questioning, his voice jovial, faintly ironic; "You really don't mind all of this, do you? Just a little talk. We never know what we'll turn up that might be interesting, do we?"

He grew angry. It was all because of Torroba. Who had asked him to be a friend? If it hadn't been for Torroba, they would have no reason to suspect him of anything. But what difference did it really make? Fathers were set against sons, daughters against fathers, men against brothers, as it always was. Hadn't even General Franco's brother, Ramón, been a rabid Republican, at least in 1930? But a man's relatives were his curse. "You can choose your friends. You can't choose your brother." There was enough truth to that. Had he chosen Torroba? But, then, Fernán Venegas had chosen him. He had come to the Alcázar only in desperation, not out of choice, propelled there by the explosion that had destroyed his shop. Now he had trapped himself. Four stone walls surrounded him; above, only a glimpse of sun tightly imprisoned by the upper walls, pinned in place by the four towers or what was left of them. Surely if he were on the outside he might have found other alternatives.

Gil's own weakness terrified him. He heard sloshing sounds, the labored pumping noises of organs swollen with fluids, congested lungs straining for oxygen, all magnified, incredibly. Exaggerated heart sounds such as one might hear through a monstrous stethoscope. Such sounds had always terrified him, and now they brought him back to precisely that time in his life he wished most to forget, when his wife had lain in coma, and he had waited night after night for death to slip into the room.

"You keep this my friend." Dr. Miranda had handed him a stethoscope. "Every half hour, mind you . . . listen. If you hear anything that alarms you, call me right away. You know, anything that sounds . . . well, to be blunt, like a broken pump . . . eh, eh . . . of course . . ."

For days he had listened, not moving from the wicker chair by the bedside, until he thought he would go out of his mind with fatigue. Every whisper, every pulse beat, exhalation, tremor of that heart he knew until the body in which it lay grew for him transparent and there was only the heart and his wife was no longer there. Overwhelmed by his exhaustion, he had in one unguarded second wished that there would be an end to it at last, and as if in answer to that wish, the liquid sounds had come. By the time Dr. Miranda had arrived, she was dead. And it was Gil's own fault for wishing. He knew that.

Now he squinted down the corridor—coal dust darkness, granulated, each particle of air thick and impenetrable. The corridor was empty. Everyone was at the concert, and no one had bothered to light a torch in the niches along the wall. He felt his way along, impelled to move forward but without any idea of where he was going or why.

At the end of the hall near the chapel he caught sight of a thick, heavy figure. A gleam of light darted for a second from an oiled leather tricorn, then blinked out. Another spark of light followed, gold, flashing, "Do you have a cigarette?"

It was the Guard, Ortiz, suddenly there in front of him. He could not make out his features but the width of the man's shoulders, the primitive thrust of his trunk, these were unmistakable. And the flash of steel from his mouth. Gil pressed against the wall, and without speaking took a single cigarette out of his pocket and handed it over to him. The gray-green uniform blended with the shadows, making the guard look like some kind of mossy growth on a tree trunk.

"Obliged," said the Guard, kindling a light.

Gil blinked at the sudden flame, kept his eyes closed as he sniffed the sharp smoke. "He's going to hit me again. With a club or his pistol or a bottle. Oh, Christ! Don't let it be a broken bottle. . . ."

Nothing.

When Gil opened his eyes again, the Guard was gone. In his place hung a column of bluish smoke transfixed by a single shaft of errant torchlight.

He could no longer trust his senses. He hadn't seen the Guard, Ortiz, at all. It had been a hallucination. He had slipped and fallen: that's how the gash on his head had gotten there. It was just that he couldn't remember. Vitolyn had gone for help and he, like a fool, had wandered off.

The band in the courtyard was playing a march again, something he did not recognize at all. It was said that the bandmaster had written an anthem especially for the Alcázar. . . .

"What ugly music." Somewhere, beyond the walls, Torroba was having his evening cognac. . . . "What kind does he prefer?" It frightened him that he had forgotten so soon. Not once in all the years Gil had known him had Torroba missed his evening cognac. Evenings of music, wine in pitchers filled with spiced fruits. And, so long ago, his wife at the piano, spinning a web of Chopin and Brahms for them both across the latticed moon. Sometimes Albeniz or the latest piece by De Falla . . . *"Pour le Tombeau de Paul Dukas . . ."* Her face, so like the Carvalho girl's face.

He passed a window, looked out and up. The sky was dark, the stars simmering above the towers; the moon, he knew, was hidden somewhere beyond the Tagus. Perhaps it would pass over the fortress. He would have to watch for it.

He went into the old map room. One of the tables was piled high with books, some of them open. A few maps had been laid out on the floor. He wondered why he had come into the room, bent to examine one of the open maps, attracted by the snaking lines.

When he straightened up, he thought he saw Ortiz, "steel teeth," in the doorway. He started to shout, but the shadow, the glint of steel had disappeared again . . . only an old bookcase, a glistening knob, nothing more.

He sat down in an ancient high-backed chair. The window of the room opened out over the Tagus to the east and was not barricaded. He could see the hills across the river, now dark, seeming to move as though slowly breathing in the hot night, their flanks shifting, dotted with trees that shone eerily in the starlight. Then he realized that the glow was not starlight at all but a searchlight's beam, now swinging lazily back and forth over the Alcázar. The moon was nowhere to be seen.

He became aware of a clangorous, regular beat, as of an enormously enlarged heart. Listening, he began to identify the form, the shape of the sound; it seemed to come not from the whitened hills but from inside the fortress itself:

"Ba-roomp-oomp-oomp . . ."

"Ba-roomp-oomp-oomp."

He moved away from the window; the sound became louder.

A march . . . a royal march . . .

"I am going mad," he thought, hunting in the doorway shadows for "steel teeth," finding nothing. The march grew louder, more discordant, lost shape again. A burst of rifle fire, then tubas and trombones.

"Ba-roomp-oomp-oomp . . ."

Gil clutched his temples and rushed from the room.

". . . omp . . . oom . . ."

He ran toward the sound, not away from it. The noise made his head ache terribly, the pain seated now more in his temples than in the back. Without quite knowing how he had gotten there, he came out onto the east arcade.

The courtyard was full of moving lights. Candles, naphtha lamps, mule-fat drips, a red hurricane lamp with a long glass bell, the shape of a distorted tulip, metal lamps that sputtered and cast a greenish glow. Candles in racks or stuck on nails. The transition between light and dark was too violent. He stopped short, rubbing his eyes.

Under the arcade, figures leaned one against the other like discarded statues, and in the yard itself sat stiffly in wire chairs or on boxes or pieces of formless debris, all drawn up in a circle. No one was moving; it looked like a tableau in a waxworks.

A string quartet had taken the place of the military band. What were they playing? It was familiar, but he could not place it. He moved cautiously out of the cover of the arcade. He and the wicks of two dozen candles, the only things moving besides the bows of the string quartet.

Ranks of wire chairs drawn up in a circle, chairs that had once been used by the students of the academy as they dozed through lessons in cartography and geo-politics. Gil saw a familiar head directly in front of him; Vitolyn. What was he doing out there? Hadn't he been in the room upstairs . . . how long had it been? He looked at his watch; the second hand remained frozen. It must have stopped when he had fallen, struck his head. *Il mio tesoro* was the only thing the watch said now.

There was an empty box next to the chair where Vitolyn was sitting. Trying to control his trembling hands without success, Gil sat down on the box, caught his neighbor's face in profile. An elderly man with a stubbly gray beard turned his head and glared at him reproachfully. Gil was sorry; he would try not to make so much noise.

Vitolyn seemed to sense Gil's presence, but Gil was sure that the Austrian's eyes had not moved, that Vitolyn had not actually seen him. The music sighed on. One of the violins was slightly out of tune, and the sour notes tore painfully at Gil's ears. No one else seemed to notice.

The quartet stopped between movements to tune their instruments.

Gil leaned over; he had seen something which fascinated him and at the same time sent an unexplainable wave of foreboding through his body.

"Your trousers are wet to the waist," Gil whispered.

Vitolyn turned slightly. "So?"

"Your trousers are wet," Gil repeated, fascinated by the dark splotches that ran from the tips of the Austrian's shoes to his trouser belt.

Vitolyn looked away, irritated.

Gil said, "It hasn't rained at all tonight. . . ."

"Don't be a fool."

A man's trousers don't get wet like that from a few spilled drops of water or even pissing in his pants, Gil thought. Could it be that the Austrian had been down the embankment and got as far as the river? The thought that Vitolyn might actually have gotten out of the Alcázar and even as far as the banks of the Tagus, only to start across and then come back, made Gil's whole body ache. "Maybe he doesn't know how to swim? . . . What else could it have been?"

"Your trousers are wet to the waist," Gil said a third time.

The muscles in Vitolyn's face had contracted, giving him a nasty, knotted appearance that accentuated the vicious thrust of his nose. His eyes flashed.

At that second, the man on Gil's other side, the aristocrat with the wire-sharp, bristly beard, coughed in annoyance and gestured with his hand as though he were at a concert in the Teatro Liceo. His wife, a gaunt-faced woman wrapped in the remains of a silk shawl, smiled with satisfaction. If one forgets one's manners, one should be reminded.

The quartet began the second movement.

"Arriaga," Gil thought suddenly, forgetting Vitolyn and his water-stained trousers, forgetting Ortiz, forgetting Major Punto and Captain Herrera, even forgetting for a moment the ghosts of his wife and Manuel Torroba.

"It's Arriaga's A Major," he thought, supremely pleased that at such a time he could remember a thing like that.

August 20: *Toledo*

IT WAS NOT THE NOISE that woke him, for that had been going on all night, and he had slept through it. The mattress was too soft and his back had begun to ache; he sat up and swung his legs over the edge of the bed. The sky outside the hotel room window was just begging to lighten, though it was still predominantly a tremulous, inky color, livened only by the swinging searchlights over the Alcázar. The curtains over the window did little to keep out either the light or the heat. Colonel Carvalho was soaked through with sweat, and he could hardly bear the smell of himself.

He had the sensation of a weight swinging back and forth inside his head like the clapper of a bell, unbalancing him. He swayed back against the wall, caught himself, sat upright again. His hands felt clammy. Across the room, he could see Emilio Portillo, asleep on his back, his arms straight at his sides, looking like a corpse laid out for burial. The only difference was that Portillo's chest moved ever so slightly up and down.

Enrique Carvalho rubbed his eyes with the back of his hand. Disconnected thoughts wandered about in his mind, the last echoes of whatever he had been dreaming. It was impossible for him to sort them out.

Lachine was asleep in the next room, alone, on a cot. He had come in much later and thrown himself headlong onto the bed as though he were casting himself, a suicide, from a rooftop or into a river. Rumpled clothing, almost steaming from the heat, his glasses on the floor next to him, one hand trailing on the ground. Most of this in silhouette. Faint whistling noises that counterfeited breathing.

How could a man feel so incredibly distant from two human beings who lay only within a few feet of him? Carvalho could not understand what had happened to him. He got to his feet and began to pad silently about the shabby motel room. He realized that none of them had spoken to each other in days, that each of them was hermetically sealed within the sphere of his own problems, and he most tightly insulated of all.

He could not even remember what he had been dreaming, only that the dream had contained the sound of weeping. As he stood there, the lines of one of Lorca's poems came to him, quite unbidden: "I have shut the window of my balcony because I do not want to hear the weeping, but from behind the gray walls nothing else is heard but the weeping . . ."

His tunic was lying across a chair; he picked it up, put it on and walked out of the room in his stocking feet. Outside, in the hallway, he put on his boots. A glance in a mirror hung near the landing confirmed his worst expectations; there stood a lean, angular, wrathful man, his white beard tangled and spiky as a bramble, his eyes sunken and ringed. An old man, a decayed prophet, almost dead from the desert heat and absurd in a military uniform that became him no more than it would have become a wooden image of a saint or a plaster Jesus.

There were a few men awake in the dingy lobby, a French reporter who could not sleep and was trying to cure his insomnia by doing Spanish crossword puzzles, and a few bored soldiers. The night clerk was asleep under a tent of newspapers.

The air outside was unexpectedly chill and damp.

Fumes of gasoline, naphtha and cordite poisoned the air in the streets, drugging the cats and dogs and even stilling the swift, glass-green lizards to a crawl on the cobblestones.

Carvalho walked quickly, his joints paining him and the pain giving him a curious exhilaration as though with each step he was conquering something hateful within himself. The outlines of the buildings on either side of the narrow, medieval street through which he passed faded at their upper edges into the flinty sky. Every sound which rang through those streets seemed a plea for affirmation of some lost identity; the wind-whirled spirits of the Second Circle trying to convince the passing Dante that they had once really existed.

Suddenly, he understood where he was going. Of all of the people he had known in Toledo, he had thus far forgotten only one. Should he go to Sebastián Gil's shop first? Absurd at such an hour; it was just a little after four in the morning. His apartment? If he could only remember. The direction in which he was walking yielded the answer. He had been going the right way without realizing it. A plaque on the wall of a building, half-covered over with dirt flung up by passing wagon wheels: Calle del Moro.

He could smell the damp breath of the river, the night spume, mixed with the scent of thyme, the reek of wooden floors soaked for centuries in raw wine. Cats scavenged vengefully amid dank piles of refuse. Beyond the end of the street the alley opened into a slightly wider passage. A car passed, and he stopped to watch it go; in it were five men in blue boiler-suits carrying shotguns and rifles. Their faces were white as carnations, and they leaned forward with an odd, predatory tension. Then the car disappeared, shrouding its passage in exhaust smoke.

Enrique Carvalho shook his head. He could not even force himself to think what that apparition meant, or to wonder how many others like it were abroad in the city of Toledo that inky morning.

Calle del Moro; he could not remember the number, but he knew the house well enough—the balcony, the pinkish stucco on the walls.

It was not long before he reached the doorway. Sheets of paper had been tacked to the door and pasted onto the walls. It was too dark to read them and no *sereno* with a lantern was likely to pass. Chalk marks ran up the walls like wounds.

Carvalho stood below the familiar balcony. There was a faint light showing in one of the windows. Gil, who filled up the empty bottle of his own life with borrowed wine, was awake. Or else he had fallen asleep with the light on. How like him, Carvalho thought scornfully. "Perhaps he is afraid of the dark now. . . ."

He went into the unlit hallway and up the stairs. Without a thought to the hour, he began to pound on the door.

There was a clatter within, the sound of a man grunting his way up out of sleep. Then Carvalho noticed that the heavy door was not locked. It had in fact given slightly under his pounding. A crescent of light fell in the hallway.

He pushed it open still farther, and walked in. An electric lamp was burning in one corner of the front room. It was the only unbroken piece of furniture in the apartment. Tables had been smashed. The book and record shelves had been overturned, and fragments of shellac mixed with loose pages from volumes of poetry and the nineteenth-century novels that Alicia Sandoval had so loved to read when she was alive. The large gilt mirror that used to throw back any visitor's reflection in his face was cracked in a hundred places. And beyond, in the sitting room, Carvalho could see the wreckage of Alicia's piano. It had been hacked to bits with an ax and was nothing more than a jumble of wires and splintered boards. Alicia Sandoval's picture lay in its silver frame amid a tangle of strings that reminded the Colonel of barbed wire. . . .

He heard someone in the next room stepping over what sounded like broken glass.

"What the devil are you doing here . . . ?" the man said. Not Gil at all: a *miliciano,* about thirty, in his undershirt, two holsters strapped to his waist after the manner of an American cowboy. His hair was rumpled and kept getting in his eyes. "You better explain yourself, man. . . ."

"After you explain yourself. What's happened here?" Carvalho demanded imperiously. He was unarmed but, somehow, the two huge pistols in their ludicrous holsters, the belt bunching the man's undershirt, seemed no threat.

The man turned: "José," he shouted into the room containing the ruin of Alicia's piano. "José . . . get your ass out here . . ."

Another man struggled out, cursing, wearing boots and little else. A blanket was draped over his shoulder.

"Where is the man who should be here . . . ?" Carvalho insisted, holding his ground. The scene was too grotesque to be frightening.

"We are the ones who should be here."

"The man who owns all of this, where is he?"

"No one owns anything anymore, don't you know?" the man with the pistols said. "Don't use that word . . . *owns*. It doesn't mean . . . damn, what are you doing here anyway? Who sent you up?"

"Sebastián Gil, where is he?" Carvalho shouted.

José's head snapped up, the sleep fleeing his eyes. His face was suddenly alert, wide awake. "Listen you," he said. "You catch a man asleep, and he looks ridiculous, don't think I don't know that, but we've got a right to be here, that's all. Who knows where the other one is? I don't even know his name. He's gone, that's all, and what business is it of yours or ours?"

"Did you two do that? Answer me at once," Carvalho said, staring at the wreckage of the piano. A half-dozen bottles of cognac had been smashed against the wall leaving great, coppery blotches on the wallpaper.

"And if we did?" said the man with the pistols. Carvalho's manner, if not his uniform, had put the militiaman on the defensive.

The one who had answered to "José," spoke, much more quietly, as though returning a challenge. "We did, whatever business it is of yours."

"Why?" Somehow, the reason for smashing those bottles seemed at that second even more important than discovering what had happened to Gil.

"We haven't touched a drop of it, if that's what you're thinking," the man called José said. "We smashed it because it's degrading and someone else might drink it and do something to betray himself. That's the reason, and it's good enough, as I see it."

Carvalho was speechless. He had once heard Gil's friend, Alicia's one-time suitor, Torroba, talk that way, but even Torroba drank. Had he actually encountered Bakunin's purified man in the midst of such a mess? And what had happened to Gil?

"Excuse me, señor . . . ," Carvalho began.

"Don't call me that," José said. "You make it sound even more disgusting a word than it is. . . ."

Carvalho shook his head as though he had been trying to converse with someone in another language and was giving up in despair. "All right, whatever you like . . . but now, you will tell me what happened to the owner of all of this . . ."

"Dead. Who knows? At any rate, he's not here. So we're in the apartment. There's room for a few families in here, don't you see, and they say one man had it all. . . ."

José stepped forward, trying to adjust the blanket. Finally he threw it off, stood there in his underclothes. "This apartment is FAI property."

Carvalho could not resist; "Your friend says there's no such thing as 'property.' So you'd better make up your mind . . ."

"Listen," José said. "I don't know who you are, with your uniform and all that, but I don't care either. Just get out of here or lie down and go to sleep. There's plenty of room, and it makes no difference to me. If you're a friend of the one who lived here, then you'd better watch it. Wherever he is, if he hasn't been paid properly yet, he will be. His name's on our list. We were told to do this. It had to be destroyed, just as all the rest of this kind of crap has to be destroyed . . . and now, as you see, we . . . live here . . . until it's time to die somewhere else."

"I see," Carvalho said. Without another word, he turned and walked back to the stairway. The door slammed behind him. Again, everything had been turned upside down. He was shaken and that new barometer of his agitation, the back of his neck, had begun to tingle again, and the pains to well up under his left shoulder blade. For a moment he had to stop, half-way down, to catch his breath. Clasping his chest, he bent forward and gulped in the damp, chill air. It caught in his lungs; then everything passed, and he could breath again. The pain vanished.

Was there no end to the shape the Anarchists could assume to haunt him? Oviedo, the shepherd of Puigcerdá, the mock-general at the train, God knew how many others . . . now these two, walking over Sebastián Gil's shattered cognac bottles.

He reached the front door. Everything inside him was turmoil. At times he would forget entirely about his daughter and this—when he remembered again, pained him the most—that considerations of ego, of his own admittedly narrow moral judgments, should take precedence over Mercedes, even for a minute . . . and then there was his growing suspicion that something was wrong somewhere inside his body.

There was no sound on the stairs behind him. The two Anarchists who had taken over Gil's apartment had apparently gone back to sleep.

Down the street a group of men were gathered around an open-backed touring car, the canvas top of which had been torn almost from its frame and was trailing behind the vehicle like a muleta. Six or seven men; he could not tell in the oyster-gray light. They were all carrying rifles or pistols. One had an engraved shot gun with a silver stock. In the back of the car sat two other men, one in his shirt-sleeves with his eyes closed, a gaunt, elderly man with an almost shaven head from which the hair sprouted in frozen tufts. He wore an expression of resignation and had his hands folded together in his lap. Not so the man next to him, a stocky person of about fifty, wearing a black cotton jacket. He kept saying over and over again, like a litany, "I'm a shoemaker, can't you see? I'm a shoemaker, can't you see? . . ." and holding up hands horned with calluses.

As Carvalho watched, one of the armed men went over and slapped the self-proclaimed shoemaker on the side of the head with his pistol. The shoemaker grunted, turned an accusing look on his tormentor and said again, "I'm a shoemaker, can't you see that? . . ."

One of the men, in a blue boiler-suit, noticed Carvalho standing in the doorway.

"You, what're you doing? Hey, come over here . . ."

Carvalho walked over. There was a hammer and sickle painted on the hood of the car. But that meant nothing. There was such a confusion of emblems and insignia in the city. One of the "dawn patrols," he had been told, had insisted on painting a swastika on their car; their leader had read somewhere that it was an American Indian good-luck sign, and he was adamant: "Just because the Germans stole it, that doesn't change things. It's primitive, so they say, and that's good enough for me."

He saw that the elderly man was in his undershirt. The scooped neck revealed his collarbones and gave him a faintly ridiculous look that warred with the pained, determinedly noble expression on his face. The "shoemaker" saw Carvalho, his uniform, and began to scream: "Officer, you're an officer . . . you can see . . . look at these hands . . ."

The man in the blue "mono" came up to Carvalho and inspected his papers. He bit his lip. "Tierres signed this for you?"

"Yes, you can check it if you like."

"That's good enough for me. I know his signature," he remarked proudly. Carvalho looked at the card in his hand: the signature was a scrawl that anyone could have imitated.

"Still," the man said, "what're you doing out at this hour? It's dangerous, don't you know? The 'anars' are out, too, and I don't know whether they'd respect this or not."

"Tierres seems to think they will."

"He's not always right, you know. Nobody's infallible except the pope, or haven't you heard?" He laughed. "Ask that one there, if you can get him to open his eyes. He thinks we won't shoot him as long as he's got his eyes closed. He's right; we'll just wait until he opens them, no matter how long it takes."

The other men were getting restless. The shoemaker had started in again, his voice rising and falling in a mechanical way.

The man in the "mono" said: "Do you want to come with us? It might be safer."

Carvalho turned back and glanced at the apartment; the light had gone off.

"We're taking these two out to the bullring. There's a nice wall there."

"Who are they?"

"One's a priest and the other's his friend. We found the priest hiding in our shoemaker's bedroom closet. I don't know why they do it. Nobody makes them, but they do it all the same, and they all get caught sooner or later. He's the sixth one tonight. . . ."

Carvalho looked at the stocky little man whose face was almost entirely hidden by his outstretched hands. Why did he do it? The old priest sitting next to him in his underwear was lost in himself and did not even move when the "shoemaker" turned to him and extended his hands: "Father, look at my hands. Tell them . . ."

The other men got back into the car.

"There's plenty of room," the man in the mono said. "We'll drive you back afterward, wherever you want to go."

Carvalho shook his head. He went over to the car and rested his arms on the rear door, his face inches away from that of the shoemaker.

"Tell me. Why did you hide him?"

The shoemaker lowered his hands and stared at the Colonel as though he had not understood the question. It struck Carvalho that more than anything else, the man seemed ashamed.

"Tell me," Carvalho said quietly. "Why? . . ." He noticed, looking past, that the old priest was biting his lip; a trickle of blood flowed down the stubble on his chin.

The shoemaker could not speak.

"All right, that's enough of that," the man in the blue "mono" said, climbing in behind the wheel. The car was barely big enough to hold them all. The motor turned over, and exhaust jetted from the rear of the car, making the torn canvas top billow out for a second.

"*Salud,*" the driver waved. The car moved off down the street, its occupants sitting with their rifles pointing up into the sky.

"I'm a shoemaker . . . ," a voice called.

Carvalho stood there, barely moving. He put Tierres' card back in his pocket with the other permits. He thought of how revolutions always were . . . they went up like a tremendous wave at first, all forward movement, power, very glorious to see . . . and then . . . splash. Nothing but foam and scum lying on the sand.

He looked at his watch. It had stopped. But he knew it was some time past five o'clock. The sky was dusty with dawn, a curious, uncertain color, half-gray, half-sand.

He thought he would go down to the Zoco and see if he could find Captain Segurra. It would be nice to have a cup of coffee with him if he could.

AUGUST 26

The Loyalist forces in Estremadura inflict severe punishment on the rebel factions.

The Moors from the Protectorate Zone against the rebels.

The United Socialist Youth volunteer to work, for the Government, two extra hours in the war industries.

AUGUST 27

The Loyalist forces annihilate enemy column after heavy fighting. The rebels leave behind 300 bodies and a large quantity of arms.

Ceuta, Granada, Sevilla, Córdoba, and Cádiz heavily bombed by the Republican Air Force.

Special tribunals created throughout Spain to try cases of rebellion and sedition and others offenses against the security of the State.

El Sol

UP THERE? YOU'RE NOT SERIOUS . . . ," Jaime protested.

"I swear it, he went up there about a half hour ago. With his cousin. He's up there now. . . ."

"It's impossible."

"See for yourself. I told him, don't go up there, you can get yourself killed. I told him, look, they've hit that tower twice already in the last two days, but he went up anyhow, and the cousin, he didn't seem to hear anything at all."

Jaime looked up. It seemed insane that anyone should want to go up there. Most of the pyramid-shaped roof had been knocked away by the shell blasts and the spire itself now lay under a pile of stones outside the walls. The tower chamber, once an enclosed space, ventilated only by four small windows, was now open to the sky. It had become a sort of ruined watch platform, the wreckage forming a natural crenelation which served as shelter for anyone who might find reason to mount.

The Guard Corporal shrugged and went on puffing his eucalyptus-leaf cigarette, making sour faces and trying to clean his rifle. Jaime began to climb. The stairwell was still intact though there were places where the debris was piled so thickly that it was almost impossible to pass by.

He kept thinking of the baker who had hanged himself and of Barrera who might, of all people, explain to him why. The wall that existed around Jaime, that kept him from any real contact with the other people in the Alcázar, did not exist for the driver. He heard things, saw things, knew things.

Every so often the wall gaped open and Jaime could see the night sky through the broken stone. The searchlights were on, and the air had a kind of intense purity that made Jaime think of snow though it was hot and the breeze from the north plain was no relief at all. Small points of fire glowed within the buildings across the Cuesta, as though gypsies were camping there.

He kept climbing. The air smelled from burned things, buzzed with odors that made him think of many times and places, but nothing so much as the baker who had hung himself. Since the concert had ended and he had taken Mercedes down to the women's quarters, he had thought of nothing else.

He reached the step of the stairwell, climbed over a fallen beam, and at last entered what used to be the tower room. There was nothing there now but a shell of crushed masonry. He came suddenly out into the open air, and for a second he shivered, not so much from a chill as from the immensity of the sky that rushed over him, the stars with their brutal majesty, and the fresh wind that lashed unexpectedly at his face.

There were two men sitting there under the ruin of the northern-most wall, not three meters away.

"Esteban Barrera?"

"Shhhh," came the reply.

The other man didn't move. He was asleep, huddled in a dark green horse blanket.

Jaime took a step onto the platform and Barrera came up onto his knees, then approached him in a kind of crouch. "Get your head down. . . . They can see from over there. . . ."

Jaime sank to his knees and the two men faced each other like two squatting frogs.

"*Teniente* . . . you. Well, that's nice. You've come up for some air?"

How was one to answer the man when he spoke like that? His bantering tone tore at Jaime, and he felt himself flush briefly with anger.

"Some air . . . yes . . . do you mind?"

"You've been hiding . . . ?"

"And you?"

Barrera put a finger to his lips. "Try to speak softly. . . . I've finally gotten him asleep. It wasn't easy, and I don't want to wake him. . . ."

The position on his knees was uncomfortable and his joints had begun to ache. Jaime sat down against the wall and Barrera joined him.

"That's better."

"Yes . . ."

A star shell burst high over the courtyard, sending down a graceful shower of greenish-white phosphorus. Then it went out. An acrid smell remained, lingering in the air. Far off, they could hear a brief clanging as the burned-out shell-casing fell into the street.

Barrera went on; "He's been like that for more than a week now. He hardly talks, and he hasn't been able to sleep at all. I think this is the first time. I told him, 'Infante, you come out into the air, the way we used to do, sleep under the stars, then you'll be able to sleep.' And I was right . . ."

Jaime thought back: hadn't it been something about Peralta, the mechanic? The Guard had shot the garage-keeper. He was astounded. He had had no idea that the man would have been affected so. But, there it was. Annoyed, he waited for Barrera to finish; he hadn't come up to talk about Infante. He had things he wanted to ask. About the baker.

"Can you imagine anything more senseless than to kill a man simply because he has blue overalls on?" the driver whispered. "And you can't convince him that it could have been anybody else. Maybe it wasn't Ignacio after all? Who the hell knows? He can't see in the dark, but he's driving himself crazy about it . . . well . . . we're all crazy, so what's the difference, eh, *teniente?*"

Jaime still had one piece of orange in his pocket. He took it out and gave it to Barrera who took it without a word. Only when he was licking the juice from his lips did he offer thanks.

"That was a bribe, even if it was from the orange you gave me," Jaime said, trying to lighten his tone so as not to betray his agitation. "I want some information. . . ."

"What do I know that you don't know? We're all locked up in here the same way. We all know the same things, which is to say . . . nothing."

"No . . . Esteban . . . ," he stopped short. It was curious. He could not recall having addressed the driver by his first name before. ". . . Esteban . . . I've heard of something, and I want to know whether it's true or not. You go out on the raids, you mix with them all, and your cousin there . . . he tells you things. What I want to know is . . . is it true about the arrests, that they've been arresting people in here and that one of them . . . ," he paused again, finding it difficult to get the words out. ". . . has hanged himself?"

Barrera took a deep breath, let it out in a whistle. Infante, still wrapped in his blanket, groaned and shifted his body against the wall.

"It's true. The man's name was Pío Blanco. He was a baker, I think . . . from the city. He did it yesterday. They don't want anyone to know about it though, so don't talk too much. . . ."

"Why? Why would such a thing happen?"

"You know or you wouldn't ask. You're afraid of the same thing for Señorita Carvalho, aren't you?"

He didn't answer.

"And yourself, too. It could happen. Only you wouldn't kill yourself."

They remained silent for a moment.

"This baker, Blanco . . . was it so bad that he had to do that, hang himself?"

"I think it was because of his brother. Damn the newspapers. What do they know about bakers and the people who get hurt by what they print? And who would have thought that it would get in here. It's our own fault. We brought back the paper four days ago. Used it to wrap up some vegetables we got on one of the raids. And there it was, big as you please, on the front page." Barrera licked his lips. There was still a little juice from the orange there. "He had nothing to do with it, the man Blanco. He wasn't very strong. Maybe they gave him a hard time down there, I don't know. But maybe it was because he had nothing to do with any of this that he hanged himself. That would make sense."

"I don't understand you. Christ, man, I don't understand you at all."

"Sure you do. Think about it. Here's this fellow that they lock up, and he doesn't know why. Then when he figures it out, he knows that there's absolutely nothing he can do about it. It's all because his brother or some relative was a Fascist hero, two hundred miles away. What the hell has he got to do with that, with what his brother does? So he sits there, and he figures he's done for anyway. He hasn't got anything to say about it. He can't confess or make up for it or anything because he hasn't done anything at all. Isn't that a good reason to hang yourself . . . ?"

"If it is,' Jaime said, "we'd all be swinging."

"You know, *teniente,* you're right. That's true enough, it is . . ."

Infante groaned again but did not wake.

"Is that why you go out on the raids?" Jaime asked suddenly.

"Is that why you stay in and don't go?"

"I can't answer that. I don't know. Do you believe that? I don't know why . . ."

"I know about it," Barrera said. "Christ, I know why I go out, but it's no real answer. I'm just as bad as you . . ."

"No," Jaime said, and he thought, "How can any man be worse off than I am at this moment? I understand it all now, and yet I don't. I still don't know what I should do. . . ."

"I go out because it doesn't matter whether I do or not. Does that make sense to you?"

Jaime shook his head; he was barely listening. He was watching Infante as he twisted under his blanket, dreaming. Jaime wondered, is he dreaming about Ignacio Peralta in his blue overalls whom he has shot or about the baker . . . or any of those things?

"Do you want to know about it, *teniente?*" Barrera said suddenly. "Christ, it's all bottled up, and I may as well tell you as anybody. I can't talk to him, that lump over there, though God knows he's the reason for it all. . . . At least the reason for my being here. God, I love him, that lump over there, but what can I do . . . ah, I'm not making sense, am I?"

"None of us makes sense," Jaime said. "Who can make sense? . . . yes, tell me, whatever you want to tell me. I'll listen, but don't ask me to understand anything. I'm so confused now, I don't know what to think."

"That's it . . . that's it. It's better to be confused than to see it clearly because you can't bear it when you see it too clearly, that's what I think. . . ." He drew his knees up and folded his arms around them so that he became a small compact bundle, seeming to shrink into himself. The searchlights scythed the air above them, casting shadows and bands of light like flames.

"It was almost three years ago. I was in Madrid," he said, "when I got Infante's letter telling me that something was going on. It was my father, you see. He worked in the mines at Cartenegra. Whatever he made, somehow he made it be enough, and after a while he had a little house to live in out on the edge of town. That's where I grew up and it wasn't bad at all. In '32 he didn't get himself mixed up with the rising. Every few years there was trouble, but he always stayed clear, because of my mother and us children. I was one of five, so I guess he didn't think it would be too good to make a widow out of my mother. Not that she lived so long, and then he was left with us. He was sixty by the time I went to Madrid, and then Infante sent the letter. Jesus, look at him over there, finally asleep it looks like, well, it's a good thing for him. . . . He's my cousin, but you know that, don't you? His father and my father were brothers and his father was killed in the mines when we were young. After that and as soon as he was old enough, he joined the Civil Guard and went away for a long time, but then after the risings in '32 he got himself transferred back to Cartenegra. They almost never do that, and I think he bribed someone to let him go back to his own town, and everyone had to make believe they didn't know him. That was about the time

I went to Madrid to find some work because I was damned if I was going to go into the mines the way my father did.

"I didn't hear from my father in all the time I was there. He couldn't write, so I really didn't expect anything.

"So when the letter came, I was really worried. It seemed that he'd gotten fired from the mine because he was too old. They had rules about that, the English owners, they'd only keep a miner on until fifty, and my father had lied and lied and for a long while, because he was strong as a young man and they'd pretended not to notice, but I suppose he got into a fight with one of the overseers who knew and that was that. Infante had been looking after my father, taking him food while he was out of work, taking it over there on the sly and my father accepting it, but hating Infante for bringing it just like he hated him for becoming a Guard. . . . He could never understand that, but I could, because it was a way to get out of that place and become something . . . but anyhow, I hitched a ride on a truck that was headed for Santander . . . we'd come up from León, and he hadn't been so bad really, the driver, because the company rules said no riders and he'd taken me anyhow. He let me off just on the outskirts. That was in the fall of '34, you remember how it was then . . . and I was really scared. I got the rest of the way into town on foot, and the first thing I saw were all the railroad lines and the trestles and the mining pits, just as they were before. You had to be careful about the trains, because they came rushing out of the dark with no lights on, and plenty of people had gotten killed. The shacks were there and the pits and the slag heaps.

"I almost didn't remember my own father's house . . . all right, it was a shack, not much more . . . two rooms and a fireplace and that was that. He wasn't very happy to see me, my father, and he sniffed out why I'd come back right away. At first he didn't want to tell me, but then he spilled it all. He'd gotten mixed up with the FAI, and he had guns and dynamite under the damned floorboards, right under his feet where he sat chewing an onion and smoking his pipe. And it was none of my business, he said. He could do what he wanted to do. . . . There wasn't any arguing with him so I let it go at that, and we sat there staring at each other. *Teniente,* I'll tell you, I felt like an old man myself then, all weak and almost dead.

"It was cold and all the houses around had fires going except my father who didn't have any wood. Infante came in just then. My father was like an animal with him. But Infante just laughed and gave him a bundle of food he'd brought and some sticks of wood for the fire. He hated Infante, and he swore that Infante had been involved in the riots in '30, but Infante swore he'd never even taken out his pistol. But my father ate the sausage Infante had brought and the cheese, too. Well, we talked, and for days it went on that way . . . my father snarling at Infante and me and telling us to mind our own business and we trying to talk him out of his rifles and his dynamite before something serious happened and it was too late. Infante said that the Anarchists had only taken him on because he was good at least to blow up one armored car or maybe a machine gun. . . . He's seen things like that before, where old men who didn't have anything else going for them tied dynamite around their waists and blew up things with their own bodies. Well, my father must have known that that was all they wanted him for, but he didn't care. He kept saying that this time they'd win. We never saw any of them around the house. The mineowners knew about it too, and the Guard. Infante always kept us warned, but it was getting pretty bad. There were fights, and a couple of men got killed. That was in September of '34.

"I suppose it was to keep my mind off how futile it all was that I started seeing Angelica Dominguez. . . . I'd known her before, you see, and Infante had mentioned that she still wasn't married so I thought, why not? . . . All this time, then, I was seeing the girl and arguing with my father. She was living with her mother and father. Their house wasn't much better than my father's but it was a lot cleaner and closer into town. All this time I was picking up a little work, whatever I could find and taking the strain off Infante. After all, it was my own father . . . but the business with the girl started getting out of hand and . . . would you believe it? . . . in the middle of all of this arguing and the rifles and the dynamite, I decided maybe it was time that I got married. That wasn't so easy because there was this cousin of Angelica's who was much older. His name was Jeronimo Modreno, and he was an official in the tax collector's office in Cartenegra. The Dominguezes had it all figured out that he'd marry Angelica, and that was that. So they tried to get rid of me, but I kept coming back. I suppose I thought that as long as I was there and went on talking nothing much would happen.

"One night I went over to the Dominguez house, and there was a light on, so I went up to the door. I knocked but nobody answered, and then I pushed the door open. The room was empty, but there was a fire in the fireplace. I heard a noise in the other room, like someone struggling but not wanting to scream. Angelica was in there . . . with her cousin Jeronimo. God, what a mess it was, crockery broken, pots and pans all over the place, and jugs smashed on the floor. He had his hand up her skirts, and I couldn't tell whether she was really trying to get away or not. I just went for him and we started to fight. I was shouting at him, and he didn't know what to do because his trousers were coming down and he couldn't move his legs too well. I got him by the back of the neck and started pounding him with my fist until he had a bloody nose and God knows what else. I let go for a second. I shouldn't have let go because he jumped away and tried to get over to the wall where there was a pile of old junk, andirons, an ax with a broken handle, some wood, and things like that. I think it was the ax he was after. But he lost his balance and he fell and hit his head right on the blade of the ax. Angelica started to shriek as soon as she saw the blood and went running out of the house. All I'd wanted to do was smash his face in for him, and there he'd killed himself.

"Well, I went out to the slag pits where Infante and I had always gone when we were kids, and I went to this tar-paper tool shack, and I waited there all night. In the morning I found a boy, and I gave him a few coins to go in and tell Infante that I wanted to see him. I sat there all day in that shack, waiting. I couldn't even think about my father but only Modreno there on the floor with his head split open. Just after sunset, Infante came out with a horse and a rifle for me. It was all over town, what had happened. Only no one knew it the way it had really been. According to the stories, I had been mixed up with the FAI too, and I'd killed Modreno because of politics. They were looking for me and there was only one thing to do and that was get out if I could. I didn't dare ask what had happened to my father. I was afraid they'd arrested him already, but Infante said no, they hadn't but that they were watching him. I knew that they'd find the rifles and the dynamite sooner or later, but there wasn't anything I could do about it, so I took the horse and the rifle and I rode out of there at night.

"I got as far as León where I traded the horse for some clothes and a little money and then got on a truck headed for Madrid. The whole thing was idiotic . . . I saw an item in the newspaper about it. They'd made the thing into a real political assassination and me into some kind of hero. I have a hunch it was my father's friends who spread the rumors, but everyone believed them, and that was that. I got back to Madrid, and by that time the story had really gotten around. That was the beginning of October, and you remember what happened . . . the revolt in Barcelona and the Asturian mess. I sat it out in Madrid while the army was up there in Mieres and Oviedo, and all the time I was frantic, wondering what was happening to my father and what the hell I was going to do. When it was all over, I got word from Infante that my father had disappeared during the fighting. Cartenegra hadn't been too badly hit. No bombing planes or anything like that, but there was a pitched battle at one of the mines and a whole section of the town near where we lived got blown up. Well, the police weren't looking for me anymore, at least not very hard, but there was still the problem of papers.

"Then I got word to go to the shop of a forger Infante knew of . . . maybe through my father's friends or my father, . . . because I think the forger was an Anarchist too. I went there all right, and he was expecting me, a little goatish man named Sousa with a pointy beard and yellow eyes, but he was a good forger all right, and he had a shop very near the Raspro so it would have been easy to get away if I had to. They had my picture taken, right there in the back of the shop, and there was a bunk in the upstairs for me to sleep in while he was getting the documents ready. I stretched out. Jesus, it was good to just lie down for a while, you have no idea. I closed my eyes, but I wasn't even asleep before some men came into the shop. He was expecting them, too, and he sent them right on back to see me. Well, it seemed that they were from the FAI, and one was a CNT delegate, and they'd heard all about what was supposed to have happened at Cartenegra. When I tried to tell them the truth, they just laughed. They weren't interested at all. They had their own truth, and that was good enough for them. Well, why had they come? I'll tell you . . . to get me to join up with them. The risings were over, and it was a terrible mess, as you remember, and they needed some heroes, I guess . . . and I was one of them. I laughed at that, and they got very angry. They said I had to do it for my father's memory which meant to me that they were pretty sure he was dead. I told them I'd have to think it over, and they left. I think they knew pretty well I wasn't going to do it because I'd said some pretty harsh things about the whole business and how stupid I thought it was.

"When they were gone, the forger told me to go back to sleep, that the documents wouldn't be done until morning and that he would have to go out at night to get some special paper to print up the identity papers. I tried to sleep, but I didn't do too well. I woke up in the middle of the night and started to walk around the room. It was full of old boxes and drums of ink and it stank to high heaven, so I went out into the front of the shop, meaning to go into the street and get some air. For some reason . . . I don't know exactly why . . . I thought to open the drawers of the old man's desk and sure enough, I found the papers he was supposed to be finishing for me, only they were all done . . . the photograph and everything. Well, that gave me a start. There were the papers, all done, and the old man out of the shop for the night and just me, alone, supposed to be sleeping away up there. I took the papers all right and stuck them in my pocket, and went out of the shop by the back way. I wanted to see what was going to happen, so I went up onto the roof of the house across the street where I could see the front of the shop.

"Around five in the morning, it was just beginning to get light, and two cars drove up in front of the shop. A dozen Civil Guard and police got out and went inside. They came out quick enough. I couldn't hear anything from up where I was, but it was clear enough what had happened. Someone had tipped them off, and they'd gone to collect me. I was supposed to be sleeping, you see, and they knew right where to find me. The FAI had given me up as a loss, and better a good martyr than a hero who doesn't want to be a hero. I guess they thought I'd be more useful to them that way. Well, I had my papers now so I just stayed up there for a while. Maybe I would have gone down and settled things with the old man but I figured he only did what they told him to do, and he was going to give me the papers. There they were, in my pocket anyhow, so I came down when it was safe and hid in the Raspro for a while. Then I got in touch with Infante again, the way we'd arranged it, and after a while I got to Toledo where he thought it would be better for me. That was about the time they were throwing Azaña in jail. The revolution had been broken up, and all the Socialists and Communists were in jail. Infante managed to get me a job as a driver at one of the hotels and even got a car for me after a while . . . Jesus, what I don't owe that man. I love him. So you understand why I have to look after him now, don't you? He fixed it all for me, and he could have gotten his own neck in a noose for doing it if they'd ever found out about it. Well, I drove around Toledo for a while and then your father hired me and that's that. You know the whole thing now. . . ."

"Your father and the baker's brother," Jaime said thickly . . .

"What's that?"

"It's nothing," Jaime said. He looked straight at Barrera. "I didn't know . . ."

"Of course you didn't, but now I've told you, and you know. It feels good to have told you . . . you'll have to tell me about yourself sometime, too. . . ."

"Sometime . . . ," Jaime could barely speak. All the while Barrera had been talking, he'd been thinking about the baker, about fathers and brothers and cousins and friends and the way things happened not because a man wanted them to happen that way but because of other people doing other, stupid things that you couldn't control. . . .

"Why did you ask me about the baker," Barrera said.

"I just wanted to find out if they were really doing things like that, here, inside . . . just the same as outside."

"Ah . . . the girl's father?" Barrera guessed softly.

"Yes, he. I suppose it will be the same thing if they hear about him."

"Maybe he's dead."

"It's possible . . ."

Another star-shell went off over the Santo Cruz, and for a second the platform was bathed with a wavering, greenish light. Infante stirred and groaned, and pulled his blanket more tightly about him.

"You could try to get away, you know."

"I've thought about it, but how . . . how do you do it?"

"Just walk out. Go out on a raid and walk away when the firing starts. That's all. Go out the way I've been going out."

"Is that why?"

"Maybe it is. But I can't ever make up my mind to do it, not with Infante here. You see . . ."

"It would be the same with me," Jaime said hopelessly.

"The girl?"

"Yes . . ."

Barrera didn't say anything more. He appeared to be thinking, struggling hard to clear up something; his face knotted with concentration, but nothing came of it, and in the end he simply smiled and put a hand on Jaime's shoulder.

"It wouldn't matter anyhow. You can try, but it won't make any difference. . . ."

"I know," Jaime said. "It won't . . . I know."

SEPTEMBER 6

The enemy, in disorder, retreats twenty kilometers in the Talavera sector.

The frantic defense of the Alcázar is coming to an end.

357

Some of the rebels barricaded in the Alcázar of Toledo attempt to flee.

In Toledo, the incessant bombing of our artillery has demoralized the rebels in the Alcázar, some of whom tried to escape.

The situation of the rebels barricaded in the Alcázar becomes more tragic each day.

A belt, bristling with rifles and machine guns, surrounds the Alcázar. The building, in ruins, is about to collapse.

El Sol

SEPTEMBER 6: *Toledo*

CARVALHO HAD SPENT THE DAY with Captain Segurra's two Schneiders which were now emplaced on a bluff above the Alcantara bridge from which they had a direct line of fire for their low trajectory projectiles. Portillo had come with him, for the first time. The day had been so hot that the brass shell casings neatly stacked behind the field pieces, were sizzling to the touch.

"Why doesn't the powder go off?" Portillo had asked, genuinely puzzled.

"Actually," the Colonel observed, "they should spread a cover over them. But in this heat, it makes little difference." He wrung the sweat from his beard; it came to a point, damp and matted. The clear blue sky seemed to him melancholy beyond anything that could have been produced by dark, low clouds, lack of sunlight or even rain—which, to him, was normally the most desolate of all natural phenomena. Now everything seemed inverted; this as well.

If one stood directly behind one of the Schneiders and knew just where and how to look, one could follow the trajectory of the shells, see them flip through the air like heavy, death-sworn birds, only to blink out in a flash of orange against walls which took no note of their arrival but for a spasm of dust.

Segurra shook his head. Did they realize how many shells he had thrown against that wall and how many times he had told headquarters what a waste it was? And yet they insisted. "If this business were left to the military instead of all these political personages . . ." He was fond of that phrase. To him, a "personage" was the worst thing you could call someone; the term embraced arrogance, presumption, and incompetence, all in equal degrees.

"The 155s make a dent, that's true, but they've got them emplaced too far away for maximum effectiveness. Though you'd think, with all the maps the general staff has at its disposal, they ought to be able to get the coordinates right and hit it every time." About a hundred yards away a battery of 105mm howitzers was firing salvo after salvo. "Those things are just as foolish as mine. We might as well throw rocks . . . It makes you wonder, doesn't it, whether someone . . . the architect who built that monstrosity perhaps, had a sixth sense . . . I, for one, believe in witchcraft and fortunetelling. An Andalusian gypsy once told me precisely the kind of woman I would marry, and there she was, years later."

The Colonel and Portillo walked back over the Alcantara bridge just before evening. The sky was murky with rain, and it was hard to tell the billows of smoke above the Alcázar from the clouds that came scudding in over the ragged landscape from the northwest. Far away, sheets of greenish rain fell somewhere on the plains beyond Aranjuez.

"Have you found something to do," Carvalho asked, "or are you still playing the tourist?"

Portillo walked with his hands thrust into his pockets, an unusual thing for him to do. It was plain that his fists were clenched and that he was hiding them. The man still slept deeply in the hotel room, falling onto his bed more often than not fully clothed, his face sleek with perspiration; he would never talk before falling asleep, and the times when Carvalho could exchange even a few words with him were becoming rarer and rarer, which was a shame, for the Colonel, who was almost old enough to be his father, had taken a liking to the man, for all his bull-like stolidity and intransigence.

"Well, have you found something to do . . . or not?" Carvalho repeated hesitantly. Portillo still had not said a word about his real reason for returning to Toledo.

"You know I haven't," Portillo said. They were almost over the bridge.

"Lachine tells me you haven't even contacted your old . . . how shall I put it? . . . your old . . . organization. . . ."

"There was no organization. Then or now . . ."

"The police thought otherwise in '34, didn't they?"

"They were fools then as they are now. I'm not responsible for that."

"What then?"

"There's no one, believe me. Two men, that's all, two men and myself who believed in real revolution, and three boys who put up posters. This isn't Madrid or Barcelona, remember. That's what made the whole thing so ironic. The Anarchists here didn't budge in '34, and the Communists . . . your 'friend' Tierres . . . had powerful friends of his own in Madrid, so they left him alone. Me, however, they sent to Montjuich."

"And you had actually done nothing?"

"No . . . to my eternal regret, I had done absolutely nothing. And what's worse, I hadn't even thought of doing anything . . ."

Carvalho remained silent. He knew that the POUM now had a membership of over two hundred in Toledo alone and that Portillo was lying. At least about that. But he was telling the truth about having avoided all his old acquaintances. He had even left the Café Obisba once when someone he had known came in.

As they began to climb the hill toward the Zoco, he said: "You wonder what I want here, why I came back, don't you?"

"Yes, but it's none of my affair. Let me be truthful, Emilio, I feel . . . how can I say it . . . very fond of you, as though I'd like to help you if I could . . . the same way I felt about a young man who was my aide once. But I think I'm not good at helping others and not very good at helping myself either. My failures are enormous. So I don't ask anymore. I leave things as they are. I have a feeling that any interference by me would just make matters worse. Can you understand that feeling? It's not indifference, believe me. It's caution . . . and self-knowledge."

Portillo smiled, his face taking on a vaguely oriental caste as his eyes narrowed in folds of sleepless skin. "When Captain Segurra said that about the fortuneteller . . ."

"His wife?"

"Yes. Do you believe in such things?"

"Sometimes. My friend Francisco Mercader . . . may he rest in peace . . . had a Berber wife who believed in such things. Some swore she was a sorceress . . . a very amiable sorceress and an excellent cook but . . ."

Portillo held out his hand. "What do these lines say, I wonder?"

Carvalho shrugged. "If you believe in such things, they mean whatever you want them to mean."

"Long life?" He smiled bitterly. "Under the circumstances, I'm not sure whether that would be a blessing." He held up his hand as if to catch the rays of the setting sun in his fingers. "A short life then. An end to all of this . . ."

"What is . . . 'all of this'?"

"My foolishness, I suppose. Pride . . . or whatever you want to call it. That self-hate that makes me stay here instead of leaving and trying to get on with things as best as I can. I wear Toledo around me like a hair shirt now. . . ."

"I don't know why you came, Emilio . . . you've hinted but you've never told me and I haven't asked you. I won't now."

"No . . ." That crooked smile again, distorting the dark face. "The strange thing is that I'm not much different from you. I've come back here to pick up where I left off, to gather the loose ends and pull them tight. In one word, my friend, I came back for my wife."

"And? . . ." Carvalho halted by the edge of the bridge. The Tagus was rushing far below them in the murky gorge.

"And I've found her, of course." His chin sank onto his chest, and he buried his clenched fists in his pockets again. "Do you know where she is? . . ."

"Man, if you've found her, why this? I don't understand it at all. If I had found my daughter, why I'd . . ."

One hand ripped from his pocket and went rigid in the air, a finger pointing up the hill toward the Alcázar. "She's in there. Can you realize what that means to me? In there, and she went of her own free will."

Carvalho thought he understood, and nodded. "A person loses perspective, particularly a woman . . . after your arrest it must have been hard . . . for her. . . ."

Portillo smiled again in a way that chilled the Colonel through: "Let me make it even more simple. She was the mistress of the Colonel of the Civil Guard, a certain Fernán Venegas. Oh, yes, I knew him . . . that's the irony of it. And to make matters worse, he had nothing to do with my arrest and in fact was a pretty decent person, considering the job he had to do."

"Is he up there too?"

"According to Alvarez Sánchez, whom you don't know . . . one of Torroba's men . . . he was killed the very first day, though no one can find the body." He leaned on the railing and gazed down into the waters. "So, there it is. Why do I stay, I ask myself, and . . . damn it . . . I have no answer. Everyone knows and no one will say anything to me. You're probably the only person in the city who knows me and didn't know the story. I can't stand being around these people, but I can't bring myself to leave either, knowing that she's up there and may still be alive."

"And if she were to be released . . ."

"Don't say 'released.' Didn't you hear me? I said she went up there of her own free will."

"Like Gil," the Colonel thought. "Who is to say what is free will and what is not in times like these. We're not built for meeting crises of such magnitude, for making these kinds of choices, and when we do and it comes out right . . . or whatever seems right when it's all over . . . it's almost always been by pure accident." He felt an overwhelming pity for the man, all the stronger because Emilio Portillo seemed such a massive, indestructible person.

"All right then," Carvalho conceded. "If she were to desert . . . escape . . . change her mind . . . be freed . . . whatever . . . man, what would you do?"

Portillo turned from the railing and faced Carvalho with a terrible expression on his face.

"I don't know . . . ," he whispered. "That's what's so frightening to me, Colonel. I simply have no idea . . ."

BOOK FOUR /

The Mine

SEPTEMBER 8
Señor Largo Caballero was in Toledo yesterday where he was acclaimed by the fighting men and the people.

Our artillery continues with the destruction of the Academy whose surrender is imminent.

SEPTEMBER 10
Siege of Oviedo continues under heavy fire from air and artillery forces.

SEPTEMBER 11
Shelling of Oviedo continues without interruption.

El Sol

MORNING, SEPTEMBER 12: *The Alcázar*

FOR A WEEK NOW, THE LOUDSPEAKERS had begun blaring just after sunrise.

The trucks were moving closer all the time as the outer buildings in the Alcázar's defense ring were taken one by one by the advancing *milicianos*. The worst of it was that the noise continued into the small hours of the night. The speakers were turned off only between three and six.

"The bastards, three hours sleep . . . better if they didn't let us get any at all," a tar-faced Civil Guard standing nearby said. "It's like letting you get into a woman and then . . ." He stopped short, cast a glance at Mercedes Carvalho and the Portillo woman who were not so far off, sitting on a pile of rocks, then shrugged and moved off. Jaime hadn't even noticed. Well, what difference did it make, now, of all times?

"You know what I mean," the Guard concluded, turning a corner.

Jaime didn't answer. He had been watching Mercedes and Selica Portillo and wondering whether Mercedes would change her mind. Ever since they had gotten word that a priest would be allowed into the Alcázar under a flag of truce, she had been sitting there watching the main gate, as though simply to see the priest enter would satisfy her needs. But it wasn't for herself; he knew that. It was for the Portillo woman. It amazed him how she found the strength to worry about others when she was so near starvation herself.

Selica Portillo's head was bowed. She was making small, twining motions with her fingers as though she were telling a rosary. It was simply nervousness. She was sure that she'd seen her husband outside, across the Zoco. She'd borrowed his one-lensed binoculars twice. The last time just the day before.

"Of course it's he. How could I not know him, even after all this time? . . ."

"Men change in prison," Mercedes had cautioned gently.

"Emilio was never *out* of prison. All his life, he said, he was in prison . . . real prison wouldn't change him."

She wouldn't let any one else look and refused to point him out. What was the point? No one else knew him, not even Mercedes.

Mercedes lifted her head and gestured to Jaime. Just as he was about to speak, a burst of raucous music exploded from the loudspeaker trucks outside.

Then, a second later, a metallic voice cut in over the music. People looked at each other; it was as if God's voice had sounded, and they were frightened even though they'd heard that same voice with its flat Catalan accent every morning for two weeks.

"You hear us in there? Do you hear? Want to know what it feels like to sleep in a real bed? Do pigs sleep in a bed? Why do you let pigs sleep in your beds, soldiers? We've got nothing against you, soldiers. We don't blame you for anything that's happened. We were like you until we killed our officers and showed them what an honest Spaniard is . . ."

"What kind of . . . animals . . . are they?" Mercedes said. It was strange to hear her speak that way, about those outside. Her father might be among them. The radio still hadn't been fixed, but Jaime was becoming convinced that if they lived long enough themselves, they would find her father out there one morning. And his own too, probably. That would be the crowning irony. Both of their fathers on the outside.

"Animals like . . . you and me," he whispered, sure that he was not heard. "Human animals, I suppose . . ."

"Why don't you come out and join us for something to eat? We've got plenty out here to spare. Hams and suckling pigs, nice and roasted. Wine? Do you want some wine? . . . or a nice cold beer?"

"If they start on the cigarettes again, I'm going to make it a point to kill one of them myself, the next time I go out . . ." the Guard said, shoving his fist. "I don't smoke myself, but, the bastards . . . oh, those bastards . . ."

Jaime thought, "The next time they go out, maybe it will be the time I'll go too." Every time he looked at Mercedes, his whole body ached. She had to have some food, even if it meant his going out and getting it for her himself. What did any of it matter if he could get her something to eat? He knew that to refuse to go, to refuse to do anything but wander around the corridors and the underground rooms, or the north tower where he still went to gaze longingly at the battered hulk of his father's automobile lying on the esplanade, all of this was simply to torture himself. What good would it do him to preserve his . . . his "purity" . . . if he died in the process and if Mercedes died with him or, even worse, before him?

The voice on the loudspeaker was promising clean clothes, amnesty and cigarettes too. Then the music returned, a scratchy record of the "Ride of the Valkyries," played by a military brass band.

Just then there was a stir at the main gate. But it didn't open. Someone had heard something outside and, thinking that the priest was coming through that way, a few dozen of the people who had been waiting under the ruins of the arcades moved out into the blinding sunlight of the courtyard so as to be the first to see him.

The music grew louder outside but the door didn't open, and the crowd fell back to the colonnades, mumbling. Some of the women began to cry. That was something he hadn't seen yet, Jaime thought. People had cursed and screamed, threatened and howled like animals but no one, no one he'd seen had wept. Not until now.

"What if he doesn't come?" Jaime heard himself say. He was talking to Selica Portillo who had not moved at all.

"It won't make any difference," she said, still not looking up, "but if he does . . ."

"Then . . ."

"He'll hear confession . . . that's what he's coming for, to take confession." She spoke with such a tone of finality that he could not think to question her further. What was to be between her and the priest was not his business.

The music was even louder now. They could see each other's lips moving and make out the sounds of each other's voices only because they could see the words forming.

There was a stir under the colonnades to the left of where they were sitting; three women and a ragged schoolteacher who was wearing the remains of an old brown coat and carrying, of all things, a walking stick. The women were pointing toward the door. Jaime turned to look at them and at the moment he did so, the women saw him and looked away as though they had been caught at some shameful act.

Inside the building, the hallway was suddenly filling up with a mass of struggling people. A murmur swept across the courtyard, pushing aside the thick fall of the sun, audible even over the insistent thump of the "Valkyrie" tubas.

"It must be . . ." Jaime said wearily. "They've brought the priest in from the other side, by the Riding School . . ."

Selica jumped up and Mercedes rose, too, with a look of resignation, as though she knew what was going to happen and was not anxious to face it.

They were engulfed. Dozens of men and women, soldiers and Guard, pressed on by them, finally hemming them in so tightly that they were borne along whether they wished to go or not, under the arcade, through the door and into the dim, undersea corridor. The faces of those who passed them were graven with the most frightening expressions Jaime had ever seen, looks which said, "This is the last chance for me, and if I don't snatch at it now, there will be an eternity of damnation." How can it make such a difference to them? he thought. It was not that he did not believe himself; he did. But only that God, in such a setting, and a priest even more, seemed simply irrelevant. If God had shown any concern at all for their situation, he would never have allowed it to degenerate into such an absurdity where heroism and bravery became laughable, and every human virtue except man's instinct for survival became blurred and indistinct.

Mercedes held on to his arm. He felt her weight dragging him down. She was heavier than he would have thought, or he was weaker.

The sudden transition between blinding sunlight and the shadow of the corridor had made him dizzy and he, in turn, took her arm for support, trying to disguise the gesture as affection. She looked at him hard and could he have seen her clearly he would have known how miserably he had failed.

It was not far from the courtyard to the crypt to which the priest had been escorted. They had only to descend a few short steps, to an intermediate level and then pass under a carved stone archway which had remained miraculously unharmed by the bombardment. They had no choice; they could not have turned around even if they had wished to, so closely were the men and women packed together.

His eyes pained continually now. He could hear, almost feel on his skin, the massed, heavy breathing of the men, women, and children, the words of the Guards and soldiers, some already beginning to mutter prayers in stiffled, private voices. They were on their knees in the cellar chamber. The long, loaf-shaped room was crowded and more people were entering all the time. Smoky lamps sputtered along the walls, giving off a spasmodic, sulfurous light that made the upturned faces of the worshipers look as though they had been cut from yellow clay.

At the far end of the room, behind a make-shift altar over which a splendid carpet bearing the coat of arms of Alfonso XIII had been thrown stood a tall, stoop-shouldered man in a rumpled suit of civilian clothes. No collar, no soutane; only a threadbare black jacket and a yellowing shirt with frayed cuffs. He was sallow, of indeterminate age, with a large head and the expression of a discontented civil servant.

The priest was arguing with a bald-headed officer who seemed to have been frozen in the act of climbing part-way onto the altar. The two men hissed angrily at each other but only a few words came through clearly over the rumble and murmur of the crowd. It was as if the crowd was not there at all and the two men were disputing in complete privacy. It struck Jaime as degrading, that they could ignore so many other people in such a contemptuous way.

A word or two: the priest's cheeks grinding, his teeth aggressively bright in the lamplight. Badly in need of a shave, he scratched at his stubbly cheeks with a crumpled handkerchief, wiping away the sweat. The chamber was hot, made even hotter by the candles and the tightly packed bodies.

The officer flung up his hands in a threatening gesture.

The priest glared at him, mopped his neck; "No . . . I will speak . . ."

"This is outrageous . . . Major Roja didn't . . ."

"I'll speak, and you'll let me, or I'll leave at once . . ."

A frightened movement from those closest by . . . were they to be deprived? The priest could not be allowed to leave. He'd only just come.

"I won't be . . . responsible . . . ," the Major said harshly.

The priest would not answer but smiled in an infuriatingly patronizing way. The officer's right hand dropped suddenly and brushed the butt of a pistol protruding from his holster.

"Now . . . or I leave . . . ," the priest insisted.

"Not as before . . . ," the officer said. "You will change your tone . . ."

"Now . . . or I leave. My way, or none at all."

Hands reached out; a shifting of bodies on the front benches, men rising from their knees to pull the officer down from the altar. It was as though he saw it even though he was turned away. He threw up his hands in a gesture of futility and shouted in a loud voice, "I'm absolved of this, I'm absolved . . ."

He fell back and was at once swallowed by the crowd.

The priest wiped his neck once again and gazed out into the room with an expression that passed at once from anger and fear to one of defensive superiority.

"He's saying to himself, I'll get out of here, but you . . . ah, that's a different story . . . ," Jaime whispered.

"No . . . let him," Mercedes said. "Please . . . for her . . ."

He'd almost forgotten about Selica Portillo. She was there, right next to them, but not there at all. Her eyes betrayed her absence. She was staring at the priest as though he had but to open his mouth and her trials would be at an end.

The priest coughed, lowered the handkerchief from his cheek and blew his nose, then looked up commandingly at the smoke-stained ceiling.

"Down," he seemed to be saying. "Become as all the others . . . down on your knees." Reluctantly, Jaime knelt, and Mercedes with him. A hush fell over the crowd. Even the children stopped their whimpering, and the young soldiers ceased murmuring their prayers. There was an odor of fear in the room, of blood and stale dressing, antiseptic, a stench like a hospital.

What was the priest saying? No confession? "There isn't time for that, of course. We should have known. Well, what have we to confess, after all? But, God, look at their faces, as though to spit it out cures everything. I'd tell him something if he'd listen, but that wouldn't help at all, unless he's got a few answers . . ." Jaime looked out of the corner of his eye at Selica Portillo. She remained impassive. What had she come for then if not to confess, to gain absolution . . . but for what? Better God himself should confess and explain why he had done this to her. But she remained there, unflinching, a faint, satisfied smile on her lips.

The news was greeted by the sound of labored breathing, of stifled weeping. From relief? If there are no sins to confess, how can there be absolution? Jaime struggled to keep himself on his knees. He should not have come, he knew. But for Mercedes, but for the woman whom she had promised . . .

"Look up here, all of you," the priest was saying, his voice surprisingly rich, deep as a drum. Transfigured by the sound of his own voice, he raised his arms in an ambiguous gesture. Jaime glared at him as though the command had been directed at him alone. Where was the officer? . . . and why had they been arguing so? What had the priest already said before they had arrived? Clearly, the service had already commenced. There was no wasting time here . . . the Republican artillery outside was waiting to start up again. And the loudspeaker trucks hadn't even switched off; through the walls, could be heard the distant lumbering of the brass "Valkyries," mounting toward the clouds over the cathedral spire for the tenth time that morning.

All about the room, faces, dimly illumined by the candlelight, suspended in a tormented expression halfway between thankfulness and disbelief. There had been no priest since the siege had begun. Now one had appeared, marched in under a flag of truce, blindfolded. For a single hour. One act of charity committed by those outside who, it seemed, believed neither in charity nor even in God. It was clear from the expression of those in the room that they had been caught off-guard by what the priest had already said. An aura of distrust hung over them; but also of hopelessness. The voice of the heretic on the pyre echoed faintly: "If God permits this, how can I hope?"

The officer, a major, stood up again suddenly, snatching at the priest's sleeve. His dark hand with its white nails flared on the threadbare cloth. Livid knuckles like a row of punctures.

"No, not again," he shouted. "You don't dare."

A burst of angry voices. The Major was pulled down, and the priest smiled. He coughed once more, a dry, painful cough. His eyes were round with fatigue masquerading as compassion.

"What do you see?" he went on, his voice very sure and gathering resonance and momentum. "What do you see? Do you see a shabby priest who needs a shave, whose clothing is torn and dirty? Certainly, certainly you do. Oh, you say, yes, that's him . . . he's the best we can do. He's all they'd send us, so let's listen to him and see what he has to say? What harm can it do? Oh, not all of you, I see that. That man, he tried to stop me, but you wouldn't let him. He didn't have the right to take away from you what I've come into this charnel house to tell you . . . what you *have* to hear. And you knew that. You wouldn't let him stop me. All right . . . now you'll listen. He's a priest, in spite of his clothes, and that's what counts. It's his being here, not what he says. That's it, isn't it?

That's what you'd like to say to yourselves. Well . . . if it is, then you're blind, and you don't see what's in front of your eyes. This is not a church, not a house of God this is . . . a crypt. And this . . ." He paused, waved his hand about him, describing a circle. "This, behind which I stand, this is not an altar to God but a tombstone on which . . . all your names are inscribed."

The priest's voice rose. "Look at each other. Look with your eyes and see what's there. See what you are. What you have become. Yes . . . at yourselves . . . you are dead, all of you, corpses waiting for a judgment which none of you can escape. How do you like that?" His eyes narrowed, and he blew his nose loudly. Somehow, the sound did not fracture the tension, rather . . . intensified it . . . He remained silent for a moment, taking the measure of the crowd, then began again.

"Judged for what you are, not what you think you are. Look here . . . this poor candle is not a candle at all, don't you see? Try to understand it for what it really is . . . in this poor candle is the first flicker of the fires of damnation. The fires are already all around you. Have you the courage to look and admit that it is the fire, that you are all damned?

" 'Why,' you ask each other, 'why does he talk to us this way? Haven't we suffered enough? Why does he add to our misery, this shabby man who says he is a priest but has no collar to prove it?' Well, why don't you ask me? Ask me, if you dare. I've come from the outside . . . yes, out there, that place . . . I know. I know the truth of it. From a shabby priest who comes to you with a Judas mark on his brow. Oh, yes, all the real priests have been slaughtered, you're saying. They've all been killed, or they've run off to France. Only the Judases, the renegades, are left. Ah, but we, the Judases, are the ones who can make our peace with any man, because we know . . . *I* know . . . that even those poor creatures out there who machine-gun the images of our Lord, the Christ, even they still have their souls even if they deny them. I tell them the truth without fear, and I'll tell you the truth, too, whether you want to hear it or not. You, who are damned . . . you pray for absolution, do you? When you're in the midst of mortal sin? Then stay your hand first and afterward pray for help . . . Then He'll listen to you. Afterward, not before. Stay your hand . . . ? From what? You there, Colonel . . . and you, young Captain . . . and you, soldiers, and Guards . . . isn't it bad enough that you yourselves are suicides? Yes, suicides . . . that's the truth of it. . . . What you are doing can only lead to your own deaths and the deaths of all around you. You know that and I know that. And that is suicide and suicide is mortal sin . . . for which you will never be forgiven. Believe me, there will be no forgiveness. But that isn't the worst of it. What about the women and the children? Your wives and sons and daughters who are trapped here with you? Who asks them what they want, the children? Who asks the children? Are they to be suicides too or is it that you are all murderers? Do you take such a terrible double sin on yourselves? Murder *and* suicide? Have you asked them whether they wish to live or die, the children? Do any of you understand what you are doing well enough to explain it to the children? Can you explain to them why you are sacrificing their lives as well as your own?"

"For Spain . . . for Spain . . . ," a cracked voice cried out.

"No . . . for pride, for pride," the priest shouted back. "Only for pride." He paused, looked about as though he expected to be attacked. "I can't explain why those outside these walls should want you dead . . . it's incomprehensible to me. And they don't understand it themselves either. They are as mad as you are. But let me tell you, mad or not, they have no wish to kill your wives and your children. Even they know that children and women among you do not mean them any harm." Sweat was running down the priest's neck like oil from a lamp. A moaning had gone up in the room, not only from the women but from some of the men as well. Curious mixture of treble and faltering tenor; dry, wretched, desiccated voices.

"Shame," cried an old man in a tattered uniform.

"Shame," the priest cried back. Shame on all of us that we are here . . . that we have done this thing to ourselves, that I have to come here to tell you what should be so obvious to all of you . . ."

"For Spain . . ."

"For God himself," the priest shouted, leaning far out over the embroidered carpet. "For God and your immortal soul." His voice suddenly conspiratorial and urgent; "Listen, quickly, listen . . . from Major Roja who is in command outside . . . any women and children who want to leave can leave with me. He has your Colonel's word on it. There, now you know . . . Leave now, with me, before it is too late for you . . ."

There was turmoil in the room. Selica Portillo sank forward on her knees, covering her face with her hands. The candle flames and blurry lamp light danced on the walls, fragmented by the shifting of massed shadows, a frieze of gold and coal black shapes. Men struggled to their feet, fighting against their instinct for survival. They flung up their arms, beseeching each other to silence. Women wept loudly and the priest, eyes closed, stood silently between the two candelabra and droned over and over again, "You will all be damned . . . leave with me . . . or you will all be damned . . . leave with me . . . or you will all be damned . . ."

An officer pushed by. Jaime curved one arm protectively over Mercedes' shoulders. The officer's face was swollen, his eyes running, and inflamed. He seemed to be fighting back a flood of tears.

"We'll send that pig back to the Reds in a basket . . ."

The turmoil in the chamber grew. The priest's eyes were closed, his fingers laced across his chest, and he was still murmuring, "Damned . . . damned . . ." Already, three or four officers had clambered onto the rostrum and were pulling the carpet with the royal crest from the altar. First one, then the other of the gold candelabra spun into the air and clattered to the floor. Someone had hold of the priest from behind. He did not protest or try to fight back; he could no longer be heard. His voice had sunk to a low, inaudible moan.

Then, someone fired a revolver into the ground behind the altar.

"Everyone get out! . . ." This cry more desperate than any before it.

It was hard for Jaime to see what was happening. The crowd began to push its way toward the arched opening and the corridor beyond. He began to pull Mercedes to him. They had become separated from Selica Portillo but he could still see her, a few feet away, on her knees, her head covered by her arms.

"What in Christ's name is the matter with her?" Jaime said.

"I don't know, I don't know."

The priest was shouting again: "You can leave, all of you. Anyone who wants to can leave." And every few seconds he would lower his eyes and shout at one of the officers, his mouth gaping wide so that it looked as if he were trying to bite rather than to speak. "You, you'll all be damned, all of you . . ."

Men and women stumbled over one another. Old men brandished canes and shouted back at the priest by the altar . . . imprecations . . . unintelligible protests . . . obscenities. Some were sobbing, others crossed themselves. Passing bodies slammed against the kneeling Selica and she rocked back and forth, refusing to rise.

"You can't leave her here . . . Jaime, help me . . ."

Jaime cried out. It was almost impossible for him to hold his ground as the crowd swept by him. They were forced back, pressed to the wall.

The bald Major and the other officers were shouting at the priest but their words could not be heard, only the priest's piercing voice, keening over and over that those who wanted to could leave with him. . . .

Though Jaime was barely aware of it, the room had all but emptied. Suddenly, the last of them had gone, and the mass of worshipers were now only an echo of boots and angry voices, fading away into the endless underground chambers of the fortress.

Selica was still on her knees. The skin of her shoulders and her back showed through where the material of her dress had torn. Her head was still covered.

The Major, seeing her, jumped down from the altar where the other officers were still holding the priest. One of them had clamped his hand over the man's mouth though it seemed absurd now for there was no one in the room any longer, and he had shouted his lungs out already.

"What's the matter with her? Get her out of here, out . . . for God's sake . . . ," Major Punto shouted.

"I don't know . . . ," Jaime said. He moved toward the woman. Her entire body was now as immobile as her face alone had been before.

"Is she hurt?" the Major asked, then turned back to the priest. "I want him bound . . . yes, and if he causes any trouble, I don't care what he is or who promised what, you're to shoot him, do you understand? Now . . . ," turning again, "what's the trouble here . . . ?"

Selica dropped her arms from her head and stared at the Major, at the priest behind him. She said. "I want to go with him. . . ."

The Major stopped in his tracks, his hands flung out to grasp empty air.

". . . with the priest. He said we could leave if we wanted to. I want to."

"Señora . . . do you know . . . ?"

"I know."

Punto snorted. "She doesn't know what she's saying. You," he was talking to Jaime, "do you know what's the matter with her? Is she yours?"

Jaime shook his head. "No, to both questions . . ."

They had the priest down on a bench below the altar now and had tied his hands loosely together.

"I want a blindfold," he said.

A captain shouted an obscenity at him.

"A blindfold," the priest repeated.

"Does she understand what she's saying?" the Major went on. "Is she all right?"

"Is it so impossible that someone should want to get out of this place?" Jaime replied with sudden resentment.

Major Punto frowned. "Of course . . . no, you're right . . . the Colonel promised him. I had no right . . . but for God's sake, can't you see?"

"I can see . . . ," Jaime said. "I can see it, but she wants to leave, that's all. Let her . . ."

"I have to," the Major replied. "All right . . . you'll stay here, too. You know her?"

"Her name is Portillo," Mercedes said. Selica was still on the floor. Her eyes were now on the priest, but they could tell she was listening to them and every so often her mouth would wrinkle a little as though to smile and then relax away into a blank, emotionless expression that told no one anything.

"All right, all right. Moscardó promised. Damn these people, damn all of them. . . ." He turned away, shaking his head as though it were too much for him to understand, but in reality he knew that it was too easy to understand, and he simply could not bear it.

One of the officers was tying a blindfold around the priest's eyes. Two others had sat down on the nearby bench. One held a Mauser with its muzzle pointed toward the ceiling, and the other had picked up one of the candelabra and was turning it in his hands.

"Why the blindfold?" Punto said, seeing it for the first time. "What is this?"

"He insisted, Major . . ."

"Well then, he insisted, ah?"

The priest raised his bound hands; "I don't want to see any more of this . . . ," he said. "I've seen enough of it."

Punto looked around the room. There were four officers left—and Jaime. One of them was already by the door.

"I'll go for the Colonel," he said.

"It's not necessary," Punto shot back. "He doesn't have to be involved in this. We'll take the priest out of here, just as we promised. And that woman with him, if she still wants to go . . . just as we promised . . . so . . . go, go and tell them at the gate. Send word we're coming out."

He turned to Jaime. "Who is she, for God's sake?"

Jaime and Mercedes exchanged glances; then Jaime explained it all to the Major, about Venegas and about the husband outside. Punto put his hand to his bald head and began to rub until his temples were red. Finally he shook his head and stood there repeating the name "Venegas" over three times, each time with a different emphasis. At last he dropped his hand. "Well, what can we do about that? If it's what she wants . . . all right. At least she has someone out there. Maybe it will work out for her . . ."

Jaime knew he had been watching something extraordinary; an intelligent man being forced to understand something he does not want to understand and yet maintain control of himself. Jaime knew very little about the Major, but he could not help wondering whether the Major, too, was there by accident, not choice.

Major Punto touched him on the arm with a surprising gentleness. "You'll go with her, won't you. To make sure?"

"Outside?"

"Yes. As part of the escort. It will be better that way."

He hesitated. It wasn't possible for him to go. In going out with the escort he would be irrevocably committing himself. They'd see him outside. He would be recognized and they would know that Jaime Mercader was alive, was in . . . there. No matter what he did, he knew that he would condemn himself, but it no longer seemed possible for him to remain aloof. The blood of those who had been dying around him in the fortress for the last two months commanded that he declare himself.

"I'll go," he said. "All right . . ."

"What's your name?" the Major asked. "I don't know you."

Jaime told him. The name made no impression. It was as Jaime had known all along: his father's name meant nothing at all in Toledo.

Major Punto nodded and walked out of the room. One of the officers followed him.

Selica remained on the ground, Mercedes stood nearby. She had only to say to the Major that she, too, wanted to leave. Hadn't the Government promised freedom to any of the women who left with the priest? But if her father were really out there, if he had escaped from Oviedo in time and managed to convince the Leftists that he was genuinely on their side, wouldn't the sudden appearance of his daughter from within the Alcázar compromise him all over again? Who would believe that she had been there by accident, not choice? And what if her father had not succeeded in washing away the blood stains of 1934? What if he had been killed the moment he offered himself to the Government? What then could she expect—outside? And then there was Jaime. She knew, without understanding why, really, that he would not abandon her. How then could she even think of leaving him?

It was impossible. The only thing she could do was to do nothing.

She stood there, leaning weakly against the wall, trying to keep her fear and confusion from showing. But Jaime could see it. He was frightened too. They were alone in the room with the blindfolded priest and the guards. The room was still and there was no sound from the outside, no murmur of voices, no music from the loudspeakers.

Jaime looked at Selica Portillo, then at Mercedes. She nodded and went over to the woman, knelt herself and touched her on the shoulder. Jaime felt helpless . . .

He tried to imagine what it would be like outside, in the sun, without the walls around him.

"Don't you understand . . . ?" The voice took him by surprise. He had forgotten what the Portillo woman's voice sounded like. She was speaking not to Mercedes who had already stepped away but to the priest.

"Father, *don't you* understand it?"

"Please," the priest said. "I can't see you."

"You can't see in the confessional either. That's how it should be." Selica started to move toward him on her knees. "Listen to me. Before we go, I want you to listen to me."

"I won't," the priest said. "I can't. Not here . . ."

"You must," Selica Portillo said very softly.

The priest suddenly sat back with a shudder of resignation, his blindfolded eyes turned toward the ceiling. The officer who had been holding the Mauser turned toward the wall.

"I couldn't mourn for him," she said. "If you can understand what happened, you will be able to forgive me, I know. It was a terrible thing not to be able to mourn for him, but that's how it was. I can't help it . . . I didn't care. It was worse than that. I didn't care, and it gave me satisfaction to see it, Father. Is that the worst thing that a person can do, be satisfied with someone's death? Please . . ."

The priest said nothing; was he trying not to listen?

"We were driving around, do you know?" she went on, in a calm, almost conversational tone as though she were relating to the priest something he already knew. "After we'd gone to see Señor Gil, we drove around the countryside. Can you imagine him wanting to do that, after what had happened, instead of coming right up here?"

The priest's mouth opened slightly; "Who . . . who are you talking about?"

"At dawn, we came back into the city and we ran out of gasoline near the San Juan de los Reyes. How stupid it was, to run out of gasoline. He was always so careful about things like that, but he was upset, not so much about what was happening but because of . . . his friend Gil . . . the sun was up already. We weren't more than a hundred yards away from the Alcázar, in an alley. There were two *Asaltos* standing there, one of them was almost asleep, and they saw him. Not me, just him. He left me standing there when they saw him. They recognized him, so he ran. He used to be proud that people in Toledo recognized him wherever he went, but not this time. He didn't care about me at all then. He tried to make me think . . . he said . . . I'll never forget what he said . . . he said to me, 'They don't know you, you can get away.' Just like that . . . I stood there and watched them up the street when they caught him. I think I wanted to see what they would do to him," she stopped, trying to remember something. "They never came back for me. That was odd. They didn't come back . . ."

Mercedes whispered; "Maybe he really meant it . . . maybe he did want to save you . . ."

Selica hadn't heard. She went on; "He was like a mole without his glasses. He couldn't see a thing. And he'd broken them again. I think he dropped them when he started to run . . . there were fishbones all over the alley, I remember that, white as chalk . . . and manure in little piles, and everything smelled of garbage. It wasn't a good place to be . . . but. . . . He never even saw the man who shot him . . . and I . . . there . . . that's what happened," she said. "I couldn't mourn for him. I don't ask forgiveness. I just want you to understand. Father, why should I feel guilty? I didn't love him . . ."

"Now, I want to go," Selica said.

Jaime nodded and the priest turned his head toward her.

"I am a priest. I have to listen . . . ," he said, as if to himself, vaguely.

Major Punto came back into the chamber with another officer. He went up to Jaime. "All I ask is that you get her out as fast as you can. Obviously . . . I won't lie to you . . . I don't want the others to see this. I've spoken to the Colonel. He'll honor his promise, of course, but we don't want the others to know about it. Do you understand?"

"Why? What difference would it make?" Jaime said; it was the old difference, he knew, the inevitable difference, between doing something because someone told you to do it and doing it because it was the right thing. Even when the two were the same, the difference was there. But the Major's eyes told him more than his words. Jaime had seen the man around a great deal, hurrying to and fro, taking charge, making notes, very efficient. But now the Major was afraid. That, at least, he could understand and forgive. "If only we could all be afraid," Jaime thought, "but to be afraid, you've got to understand things first. . . ."

Major Punto took Jaime's silence for assent, and said to him and the officers, "You'll go out through the north wall. Then straight down the Cuesta to the Plaza. We've sent word so they won't fire. They're expecting you to come out within the next ten minutes so you'd better get started now."

The officer who had been sitting on the altar holstered his Mauser and looked about nervously. He was shaking his head. It seemed to him that it could all be avoided by simply shooting the priest, and he said so. No one replied.

The priest in the meantime had risen and was holding out his loosely bound hands.

"Don't you want to tie me tighter?"

"Go to hell." The Major turned away from him.

SEPTEMBER 12, 11:00 A.M.: *Toledo*

"CARVALHO?"

"Yes . . ."

"Colonel Enrique Carvalho?" the *miliciano* asked slowly as though he could not believe that anyone would admit to such an identity.

The Colonel extended his papers automatically. He was used to being stopped, questioned, to having to show the passes signed by Tierres. At first he had thought it demeaning, but no longer; it was simply an annoyance.

The *miliciano* turned the papers in his hand. It was obvious that he could not read. His companions, three of them, shifted their rifles awkwardly. One of them was a miner with blue dynamite caps thrust into his belt.

"You're to come with us then, if you're Enrique Carvalho," one of the *milicianos* said.

Carvalho looked down the sun-scorched street toward the Alcázar. A *campanile* was drumming the hour of eleven into the blast furnace morning sky. He shook his head. "I'm going to the Zocodover."

"To see the fun?"

"To be there when the priest comes out," Carvalho corrected him sternly. Lachine had told him all about the priest and about General Riquelme's promise to let the priest bring out any of the women who wanted to come. Portillo was waiting there to see if there was any news of his wife and Carvalho had promised to wait with his friend.

"You can go afterward," the miner with the dynamite caps in his belt said. "Come on, don't make trouble."

Down the street, Carvalho could see a constant flow of people going in the direction of the Zoco. He had seen the newsmen setting up their cameras a few hours before; if any of the women came out, they wanted to be sure to record the event so that it could be shown all over the world. The women, deserting their men.

"Come on," the *miliciano* said again. "It's not far."

Carvalho looked around. He was alone. The nearest man was thirty meters away down the street. He could tell from the look in the miner's eyes that the man knew who he was and would have no hesitation in shooting him down right there if he gave him the opportunity. It would be better to go with them, to get it over with and then get back to the Zocodover. Somehow, there would be time. The priest would be late.

Or perhaps no one would come out with the priest after all.

They walked down the street and turned into a narrow alleyway. For a few minutes they walked in silence, and then the *miliciano* who was walking behind the Colonel started to whistle.

"Stop that," Carvalho said, at once ashamed that he had reacted so strongly to such a stupid thing.

"You don't like it? All right. We're almost there anyhow."

They came out onto a small plaza, facing a blackened Visgoth church. A few men were standing by. A man in a neat black jacket and tie leaned against a wall, watching two men in blue monos roll drums of gasoline toward the entrance of the church.

"Torroba?"

"Over there," someone called.

The *miliciano* waved. "We've brought him his company. . . ."

They stopped for a moment near a truck which had been squeezed into the mouth of an adjoining alley. Carvalho could see into the interior of the church. Wires from a detonator box ran down the center aisle, disappeared under a pile of smashed wooden objects. Hieratic figures, tables, benches, were splintered over the nave like fagots. Only a large stone crucifix suspended over the altar remained untouched.

At the corner of the street a water truck waited. A small crowd had gathered silently at the far side of the plaza to watch the burning.

"Bring more gasoline," someone shouted. "There are five more drums in the truck."

"How many do we need?"

"Two should be enough. We've got at least three hundred liters in there already. . . ."

"Are Blanco and Madrero out? They were setting the charge."

The man in the black jacket came over to where Carvalho and the two men in monos were standing. Carvalho stared directly at him; the man had a bushy head of thick, silvery hair, full eyebrows, and the expression of a wild, desert saint on his face.

"I'm Manuel Torroba," he said. "And you are Colonel Carvalho?"

"Yes," the Colonel replied. Automatically, he extended his hand and, to his surprise, Torroba took it.

Two more men in overalls came up from the truck, rolling barrels of gasoline, each of them with zebra-like red and black stripes.

"Punch holes and spread it around, up in front." It was Torroba who had turned his head slightly and shouted. Then he was facing Carvalho again. He nodded to the three men before speaking to the Colonel again and they moved off at once.

"You see," Torroba said, "I wanted to speak to you in private."

"Did it have to be now?" Carvalho asked, thinking of what might be happening on the Zoco.

"I won't keep you long, Colonel," Torroba said. "Please . . . bear with me for just a few moments." The intensity of his expression shocked the Colonel into silence. He nodded. A few minutes more or less would make no difference and, besides, what choice did he really have?

Torroba smiled briefly. "Come, let's get back. There's going to be a lot of fire, and we're too close." The two men moved back across the tiny plaza. Just then Carvalho could see again into the interior of the church. Rows of smashed wooden benches shimmered with a film of gasoline. A *miliciano* with a black and red rosette on his collar went over to a detonator box. Inside the church nothing recognizable remained. All the usable furniture had been torn out, the rest destroyed by axes.

Torroba turned his head and gazed at the entrance to the church, a look of calm spreading on his face. "Good, good," he said to himself in a low murmur. "It all must be as a ritual sacrifice. Calmly and with dignity. No one must think that we lash out in blind rage. . . ."

Smoke, black as ink, rolled suddenly from the church's interior. A wave of heat shimmered down the steps. The stink of burning gasoline rushed out like a breath. "Look," Torroba said. "Look at how beautiful it is. . . ."

Carvalho was growing agitated. He shook his head. "Say to me what you have to say or let me go. My friend is waiting . . ."

"Your friend . . . ," Torroba murmured. "Yes, it's about one of your friends that I want to speak to you. . . ." He caught the direction of the Colonel's gaze now fastened on the crackling frames within the blackened stone shell of the church. "Don't misunderstand," he said quickly, "I can appreciate the beauty of these places as much as any man. I understand them, I know what went into their making. But they have to be destroyed, don't you see? Gently, perhaps regretfully. But they must be destroyed. Many of our people don't understand that. In kindness and respect for a great thought, a magnificent idea, gone cancerous."

The flames were now thrusting like pikes through the upper windows of the building. The water truck moved a little nearer, in case the flames should jump the gap to the nearby houses.

Torroba touched Carvalho on the arm, a firm, friendly gesture quite unlike the hesitant proddings of Lachine. Carvalho detested it when a man laid hands on him, but he tolerated the Anarchist's touch.

"Please," he said quietly. "I know what you're going to say."

They began to walk away from the plaza, leaving the *milicianos* standing in front of the burning church. Torroba said, "I've heard all about you . . . from . . . it doesn't matter. Friends. And people who are not your friends. Your name isn't well known here, but I know you. There are others of us who know you, too, and don't wish you well. You've got to be careful."

"I do what I have to do, that's all."

"Do you? Do any of us? At least not until it's too late? I don't think that ever in my life I've done 'what I had to do' when I should have done it. But only when someone else forced me. Isn't that the way it is?"

Carvalho scrutinized the man, growing slowly aware that Torroba was deliberately trying to avoid something, talking in circles so as to keep away from whatever it was that had made him summon the Colonel in the first place. It was so transparent, so obvious. The Colonel didn't reply and after a second, Torroba, realizing that he was understood and that there was no point in delaying anymore lit another cigarette, without offering one to Carvalho, and began to speak in a wholly different voice:

"A few weeks ago . . . two or three, I think . . ."

"Yes . . . ?"

"You went to a certain apartment, entered, left again . . ."

"Yes."

"The man whose apartment you entered . . . did you . . . ?"

"I knew him, that must be obvious," Carvalho said guardedly. So this was why Torroba had summoned him. Something to do with Gil.

"You were reported, you know. By the two men who were in the place. You were fortunate not to have been shot right there. One of them knew who you were . . . he recognized your face. . . ."

Carvalho, remembering, shook his head. "Neither of them would have shot me."

"Are you such a good judge of human character?"

"I wasn't always, but I think I am now. . . ."

"Ah, I wish I were. . . . What a wonderful facility, Colonel, to be able to judge men accurately in matters of life and death. I've failed, you know, so many times . . ." He became silent, his face disappearing for a moment behind the dark bluish cigarette smoke. "This person," he went on, "this Sebastián Gil . . . do you know what's become of him?"

"No, not really. Some say that he's up in the Alcázar. I've seen his name on the wall in Tierres' headquarters. They have two lists, one of the hostages and one for . . ."

"The others . . . yes, I know." Torroba became quiet again, his fingers knit. He seemed to be searching for words.

"What did you want of me, can you tell me now . . . ?"

Torroba looked up, suddenly, with an expression of surprise on his face; surprise that he was thus surprised. "I can't say . . . it is about Sebastián Gil and, then, it isn't . . . I say it isn't because . . ."

"He was a friend of yours, wasn't he?"

Torroba nodded slowly. "You know that? Yes, I suppose that's it. And I assumed that because you went to his apartment, that you were a friend of his, in some way, too, that perhaps you could tell me something. . . ."

"About what? You know as much as I do . . . that he is in the Alcázar?"

"No, I know more than you do. I know why he's there. I know how it happened which is what, I suppose, made me want to speak to you."

Carvalho waited for him to continue, puzzled.

"We are alike in many ways, Colonel. Believe me when I say that. Similar in that we like to think that we do things because it is our duty to do them. But so often we disguise moral cowardice as 'duty,' don't you think, Colonel? We try to excuse indefensible acts by saying that it was our obligation to do them . . . When can you ever be sure, can you tell me . . . ?"

"I don't understand you at all . . . ," Carvallo replied. "Not at all."

"Ah, perhaps I don't understand myself, well, let it be. . . . I have failed a friend . . . our friend. A man who was helpless when left by himself. A good man, nevertheless, but unable to do anything for himself in this world of ours. He is too good, perhaps; that's his trouble. And I, not good enough. Listen . . . I drove him up there. I. Because of me and me alone he is up there. . . ." He pulled the cigarette angrily away from his lips. "Listen . . . how is it that we so easily confuse murder with saintliness, can you tell me? You're a man who understands what it is to have death on his conscience. . . ."

"It's something I never have understood. I think that if I did, I would not be able to go on living myself. In short, I fear the answer."

"I fear it too and that, perhaps, is why I've got to search for it. As for Sebastián . . . there's my special regret, the specific that makes the general insignificant." He drew heavily on his cigarette. "Could I have done otherwise, that's the question that bothers me. . . ."

"Otherwise than what?"

"It was I who ordered his name onto the list . . . who took his belongings . . . who had his piano smashed . . . I've buried him before he was dead. Because he was too weak . . . you see, I know he didn't go up there by choice . . . not choice as you or I would conceive it, Colonel. Sánchez and some of the others saw him stumbling through the street with his pitiful phonograph and his suitcase right after . . . by accident . . . believe me . . . a shell landed near his shop. They say, and I have no reason to disbelieve it, that he was out of his mind. . . . Poor Sebastián . . . how often we murder those we wish to save. Isn't that so? The weak don't survive our ministrations . . . and yet, it's that very weakness of his that made him my friend in the first place. . . ."

"And now you regret what you did . . . ?"

"No, but at the same time . . . yes. Just as I regret all the failures of human acts to make the sense they should. My failure was in not guarding the man against his own humanity, his weakness. Once I'd failed in that, the rest was inevitable, wasn't it? Yet, I could have prevented it . . . ," Torroba's voice trailed off.

Rather than exciting compassion, the Anarchist's pained confusion simply angered Carvalho. Had the man had him brought there simply to act as unwilling confessor? Torroba was searching for a justification he could not invent for himself, but Carvalho was the last man on earth who could find it for him.

"May I go now?" the Colonel said tersely, glancing at his watch.

"You took me from something I wanted very much to do. . . ."

"What was that?"

"We both have . . . friends. My friend will be at the Zoco just now, I think, waiting to see who comes out of the Alcázar with the priest they've sent in . . . I wanted to be with him . . . to . . ."

"So that if the person whom he is waiting for does not come out . . . as, of course, none of them will . . ."

"Yes . . ."

"Ah . . . I'm sorry then, Colonel, to have kept you . . let us both walk back . . . yes, I'm sorry . . ."

Torroba stopped for a moment to stub out his cigarette. "You see," he said, "I thought I could speak freely to you . . . for some reason . . . and I see that I could . . ."

"Only enemies can speak freely to each other."

"Must we be that? I don't think so . . ."

They passed by a gutted church, rich with the smell of cold ashes. Behind them the fresh fires were turning the bellies of the low hanging clouds a seared, poisonous red. "Can you understand, Colonel . . . that I have doubts? Because of what I see here in the streets. I see too many men killing not because they find it necessary but simply because they enjoy it."

"That's not a sickness unique to your people."

"When we kill, we must kill with understanding . . . with compassion." Torroba struck his palms together. "How long can I hold these people together, Colonel? You, you're used to command. You must understand such problems and their answers. How do I hold these people together?"

Just then a group of FAI militia went by at the head of the *calle,* some carrying rifles, others with pitchforks, even scythes. Torroba stared after them, searing their features in the flat, strident sunlight. There was nothing in their eyes he could recognize. "Sometimes," he said, "I think Kropotkin was a fool after all, perhaps worse, a madman. Look at those faces and tell me, are those the men whose love will be our salvation? They need me, Colonel . . . to teach them that love . . ."

Abruptly, Torroba glanced at his own wristwatch. He looked up, troubled. "I'm sorry . . . look at the time . . . it's over now, isn't it? The priest was to come out at eleven. . . . If your friend's . . . woman . . . it must be a woman, isn't it . . . or his son, whatever . . . well then, she's out by now. Or not. Whatever has happened, you've been spared at least a little . . ."

"I didn't want to . . ."

"I know," Torroba interrupted. His voice dissolved into silence.

The two men stared at each other for a moment. Then Carvalho nodded and walked off by himself toward the Zocodover from which, at that moment, the sound of excited voices was coming, breaking the unusual stillness of the morning and reminding them all of what an ephemeral thing silence is.

THE FOUR OF THEM FORMED UP around the priest like an execution squad, the Captain and the two Lieutenants in front, the priest in the middle and then Jaime, with the woman by his side. Mercedes looked on.

Major Punto passed along the line, ignoring the priest. When he came to Jaime he said, "Maybe you don't want to go out there? I understand. But if I let her go with these . . . they might . . ." There was a confidential note in the Major's voice, almost one of trust.

"It's all right. I understand . . . perfectly."

"Do you?"

"Yes."

Jaime grew angry again. Those irrepressible waves of anger were coming more and more frequently now, and he could barely control himself. Did the Major really mean that the others might kill the woman rather than let her go? Or, perhaps, the Major was simply seeking to compromise him . . . ?

Punto smiled sadly. "See if you can bring back some cigarettes, will you?"

Jaime was taken aback. Why was the Major talking to him this way, as though he were an old friend?

"Why don't you go yourself, then?"

"I know all of them out there, and they know me. I don't want to see their faces, and they don't want to see mine. If I were to see them, I might think . . ." He stopped short, his face darkening.

"Yes?"

"How idiotic this all is, that's all. Now go on . . . you've used up two minutes already. I don't want any of you shot by accident."

They moved obediently out of the room, behind the captain. As Jaime passed Mercedes he said under his breath, "It's all right. . . ."

She looked surprised. What was all right? What a meaningless thing to say. Yet his tone kindled a certain calm. Why? she wondered. What reason for calm had he suddenly found?

"I'll come back," he whispered. "I won't . . . go over . . ."

"Come on," said the Captain with the bandaged arm.

They went quickly along the corridor until they came to a large, bolted door. The sounds of the crowd were all around them, rushing through the thin brick walls that separated the courtyard from the corridor as though it didn't exist at all. A ragged aperture let in a harsh slice of sunlight. Then the door opened onto a dark hole. Steps leading downward were barely visible. The Captain stepped hesitantly into the blackness, and Jaime pushed the priest, who could not see anyhow, ahead of him. The priest stumbled. No one moved to catch him and he recovered himself against the wall, bruising his forehead.

Going out, Jaime realized, was the first really positive thing he had done in weeks, and it surprised him that it was no more difficult than simply remaining inactive as he had done. So many commitments are made simply by silence, he thought. He took Selica's arm, thinking that it would reassure her, but it was he himself who needed reassurance.

There was only one sputtering torch in the corridor. Its light fell on the individual stones, seeped into cracks deep as volcanic fissures. The smell of gunpowder and the pungent odor of damp ashes engulfed them. Somewhere a fire was smoldering; Jaime could hear the sparks popping with an arrogant gaiety . . . echoes. The three-headed dog, Cerberus, would be there at the end of the corridor, guarding the gates. Which was it? He tried to remember, as though there had ever been a question: did the monster guard hell from humans or guard humans from hell? Most likely the first, he thought. Those already in hell had at least given up all aspiration. What a tranquil place hell must be then.

The priest was mumbling to himself. One of the officers turned and told him to be quiet in a surprisingly gentle voice. Selica reached out and brushed his back with her hand. Jaime moved along in the dark as though he could see clearly. From above came the sound of other people's feet, people running in the corridors, running off their fear like animals before a thunderstorm.

How calm here; he could walk forever in that silence and that dark.

The Captain halted, asked who had the flag of truce. Someone fumbled along the wall. The dim light of a single torch, lost around the last bend, was enough for Jaime to see by; a crooked pole with a rag on it.

The door opened . . . furnace-hot white light scoring the wall.

The flag of truce was pushed through. The light fell on the Lieutenant's face, the wrinkled face of an old man, haunted by the imminence of death. His arms moved. The flag waved.

"Come on. We won't fire. Don't you trust us?"

The door was flung open, and the sunlight rushed in. Even the priest, who still wore his blindfold, was struck back by it.

Without waiting for permission, the priest reached up with his bound hands and tore away the blindfold, stood there between the four men, blinking. For the moment he was as blind as he had been before.

It took Jaime's breath away; he had forgotten how brilliant the sun could be or what it felt like to be in the open with no walls around him. Once, in the mountains outside Ceuta, he had come to the conclusion that the ancient Egyptians had been right after all: the only real God was the sun and all the rest was nonsense. It was that way now.

They had come out below the north terrace, at the head of the Cuesta del Alcázar. The street sloped down, a slide of torn-up cobblestones, each one circled by deep shadow. Beyond were tumbled walls of the buildings, only a few still upright and those seamed with machine-gun fire. The rest had fallen against each other at various angles or were altogether in heaps. At the bottom of it all he could see the Zoco. There it was, as though a hand had brushed aside the fallen buildings, the alleys, widened the mouth of the street, piled brick and stone to one side until the way was clear. The tile roofs sheltered rows of windows gaping like confused eyes on streets they would never have seen if the shells from the Dehesa de Pineda hadn't knocked down the walls.

At the foot of the Cuesta there was a sound truck, a Renault with a gray, corrugated tin back. A huge, flared speaker-horn painted orange sat on top of the cab, and the wires trailed off into the Zoco. Beyond it, in the plaza itself, Jaime could see a group of men waiting, more than two dozen of them, and behind, crowds of people in the alleyways and doors, watching as at a soccer game or a bicycle race. Sunlight glittered from military buttons though most of the men were in civilian clothes or blue boiler-suits. Some of them had hand-held movie cameras, others had cameras on tripods.

Through a gap in the broken buildings on the other side of the Zoco, he could see a corner of the granary where the Anarchists made their offices. A strip of red and black cloth, a pennant, hung limply from a pole over the lintel.

The men who were waiting for them at the mouth of the Zoco seemed to draw together, not into one mass but into tiny, hard groups. He wondered which was which. In Toledo it was not easy to tell the factions apart. In the north, where the Anarchists were factory workers, bootblacks, miners, and day laborers, they all wore the same black badge of grime on their skin. But not here. The sun of La Mancha bleached and burned until those distinguishing features were gone, and they all looked the same—the FAI, the Communists, the confused Republicans whose inaction had led to all of this horror, the Socialists, the Trotskyites, if there were any still left in the city . . .

He looked again, hearing his own footfalls and those of the men around him like the beat of a metronome. The woman was breathing rapidly; wet, small sounds.

Closer now . . . the jagged tower of the cathedral caught his attention. There were more banners fluttering from its spiked shaft . . . a multitude of colors clamoring at the sun.

The men below drew together, the groups converging as though circled around with a herdsman's noose. Presenting themselves conveniently as a better target for guns that would not fire because, only because of the absurd strip of white cloth hanging from a stick. The frightened young lieutenant who was carrying the flag of truce tried to mask his fear by chewing on his upper lip.

Jaime seemed to be walking above the stones. He had lost contact with them, felt nothing solid under his feet. The figures at the other end of the Zoco seemed to tilt and slide as they came nearer. The uneven descent, strewn with rubble, walls of houses collapsed into the street, constantly caused his angle of vision to shift, so that everything was viewed as tipsy as though it were a picture projected onto a screen caught in a windstorm.

Their faces were flat, unmoving. He was close enough to see them now. A bald-headed man in an officer's tunic. A man with a head of shaggy, almost gray hair with his hands thrust into his pockets, two men in undershirts . . . one who looked like an assistant manager at a bank, men in blue overalls, a man wearing a bloodstained apron and carrying both a cleaver and a rifle, his expression not half so fierce as his clothing . . . small, dark men with movie cameras on tripods, filming everything . . . but their faces, that was what bothered him. From the neck down they were all different, but above there was a blank, frightening similarity that transcended differences of nose, the shape of a mouth, the length or color of hair.

The faces of Oviedo . . . of the dead. But were those dead entirely guiltless themselves? Hadn't they, too, killed and, by killing, brought themselves to their own deaths? And had he, Jaime Mercader, by protesting and refusing to condone, been any the less a part of their deaths? To free men's consciences for a slaughter, isn't it always necessary first that one man shout "no"? If the one man remains silent, the others remain unsure. Perhaps they hesitate. But let him shout that one "no," and he unites the others. What a fool; isn't he then as much a party to what he opposes as if he'd pulled a trigger himself? By taking on himself the secret guilt that they all feel, he has freed their consciences at least long enough for them to kill.

"It was a lie then, . . . even that," Jaime thought. "You knew nothing would happen to you, that Carvalho couldn't let it . . . so you too were a fraud. . . ."

And the complicity of the others, the dead. They were no more innocent than he.

Dizzied by the heat, he searched among that crazily tilting frieze of faces. The sun descended, flat, crushing out shadows, making everything incandescent . . . skulls about to ignite, hair on fire . . . the butcher's face . . . the bank manager's eyes. He looked about, into the alleyways, into the smoldering pits above the iron railings of the buildings along the plaza. Was Carvalho himself there?

Carvalho must be there. With his fraudulent lesson of man's capacity for self-redemption. "Even he couldn't live with his damned half-truths. He won't have the nerve to come here . . . those half-truths were his scapegoat. . . ." Yet it would be just like him to be there now, among those sweaty, ugly men who fear as much what they themselves may do as what others may do to them."

There was less than fifty yards between them. He thought he felt the stones underfoot again. Selica Portillo was saying something to him, but he could not hear her clearly and did not turn his head. Out of the corner of his eye he saw the priest who was standing more erect now. Blindfold him again, Jaime thought. He shouldn't see any of this. His tongue should be torn out.

It made no sense. It was upside down. The priest was on the wrong side. Carvalho was . . . wherever he was . . . himself, his father. Which side? Were there sides at all? Beyond the rim of buildings, out over the flat plains there were armies massing. Whose, and with what purpose?

Made up of as many immiscible elements as those who crowded the Zoco now? He shuddered at what it portended for the future.

Now the faces were entirely clear. He saw, mostly, their white teeth, and in some faces, black holes where teeth should have been. How like the hooded figures in the Good Friday processions of his youth. The orders and the brotherhoods, their faces hidden under their conical hoods, only the eyes peering out of the ragged cutouts. The faces of the men waiting for them by the barricades were the same, blank, as though they all wore hoods. . . . The eyes the same too, riveted and mesmerized by the candles the hooded penitents would carry before them.

He was slowing down without noticing it. Wasn't it he himself who was now marching in such a procession? He had never marched before, but rather watched from the balcony of their home with a curious mixture of guilt and revulsion. Open fright at what he saw and a greater, more secret fright that he was not part of it. His father had hung back, as uncertain as himself, and his mother had touched his arm. She understood him. The real thing to be frightened of, she had said to him once, was that such things as that should be at all. They were produced not at God's bidding but out of man's impulse to hide, as the brotherhoods and the orders hid inside their habits, to hide their distrust, even their secret hatred, of God.

"That's far enough," a voice said. Jaime shook his head sharply.

The lenses of four movie cameras were pointed at them like the muzzles of artillery pieces.

The Lieutenant with the shaggy mustache forced himself to step forward. The flag of truce hung limply. There was no breeze in the Zoco at all, not for the flag of truce nor for the Anarchist banner on the granary.

He felt Selica Portillo's fingers dig into his arm.

"He's there. Mother of God, he's there . . . look . . ."

What was there to look at? Did the woman expect him to recognize a man he'd never seen? She had gotten him out there. It was because of her that they were all looking at him, that they recognized him and knew where he was and what he was doing.

The Lieutenant was conferring with a large man with thick mustaches and the glint of steel teeth in his mouth who seemed to be in charge. The others remained drawn off a ways. Weapons were nowhere in evidence, but it was an insulting gesture, almost ludicrous. Did anyone doubt that behind each railing, in each alley, on every roof there were not a hundred rifles . . . ?

"You had Colonel Moscardó's promise," the Lieutenant was saying. "And so, here he is, back again. As for myself, I would have given him to you in a basket . . . piece by piece. . . ."

The man with the steel teeth didn't answer. Jaime looked past him, still searching. His heart was still hammering in his chest. Underfoot, clamped down by his boot-heel, there was a torn fragment of newspaper. The front page, or part of it, of *Claridad* from Madrid. In one column, he saw the letters ". . . v-a-l-h-o . . ." His boot had torn the rest and he could not read it. Besides, it could be someone else. How many hundred names ended in those letters?

"You are, señor? To whom do I have the pleasure . . . ?" the Lieutenant said to the man with the steel teeth.

"Listen to him," said a man standing behind the one in charge. "As if he was at a ball. Well, we've finished with that kind. . . ."

The man with the steel teeth ignored his companion. "Tierres. You know the name?"

"Yes," the Lieutenant said. "And now that you have your garbage back again . . ."

The priest stepped past him with a look of deep resentment. Hadn't he risked his life for these people, hadn't he done what he could to save them?

The newsmen's cameras were boring in. Jaime shifted uneasily. Then he saw a familiar face: Ruperto Barcenas. The man was dressed in a freshly pressed suit and still had that absurd rosette in his buttonhole. Next to him . . . how strange that he should not have noticed before . . . was Pascual Soler.

The priest was talking rapidly to the newsmen who had already begun to question him.

A few words floated clear, ". . . the children? . . . women . . . none?"

"Only one." The priest turned and pointed. Jaime thought for a second that the man was pointing at him. He had forgotten all about Selica Portillo who was still standing next to him.

The woman let out a cry.

"Emilio . . ."

A thick-set, dark man, his face flushed, stepped forward just one pace and waited.

"Her husband," Tierres said, watching. "Well, that's something . . ."

"What was she doing there in the first place . . . ?" someone said.

"It doesn't matter."

"We'll see . . ."

Selica Portillo had thrown her arms about the man's neck and was weeping into his shoulder. He held her, very rigid and without visible emotion, looking out over her shoulder toward the smoking Alcázar at the top of the Cuesta.

The truce party had broken up and was spread out in the Zoco. Someone had offered the Lieutenant a cigarette. He refused.

"Don't be such an arrogant pig. We won't poison you. Besides, you must by dying for a smoke and you know it. . . ."

Suddenly, the men were talking to each other, but instead of easing the tension, the conversation seemed to heighten it. Cigarettes were passed around. Razor blades and a few newspapers changed hands. Jaime looked around desperately. Was someone going to offer him some food, something he could take back to Mercedes? He could ask for a cigarette, he knew, and it would be given to him, but his pride prevented him from begging for food, even for someone else. It was maddening; if only someone would offer. . . .

A dozen men stood between Jaime and Pascual Soler. Barcenas had actually stepped back; it was clear that he did not want to be seen talking to anyone who had just come out of the Alcázar. That sort of thing was all right for people like Tierres and his friends. But a man like Barcenas had to be careful. Jaime understood it all at once. Things had been happening out there. Everything was polarizing. How long would they allow a Ruperto Barcenas to wear the FAI emblem?

Why was Soler also looking away? He had made no move to come toward Jaime though the young man knew he had been recognized. Soler's expression was one almost of embarrassment. Children looked that way when caught at something dirty. But why? It was certainly no surprise to find Soler on that side of the barricades. Soler had even almost been elected a deputy once.

The lawyer slowly raised his head and stared full into Jaime's eyes. Even in the blinding sunlight, Jaime could see Pascual Soler's face etched deep by grief. A sudden grief moreover. The harder he stared at Jaime, the more swollen his eyes became. Barcenas, now directly behind him, took the lawyer by the shoulder and tried to pull him away.

Soler swallowed hard, his shoulders hunching together, and nodded. At that instant, a militiaman stepped up to Jaime, cutting off his view of Soler.

"Come on, have a smoke before you go back in there. Look, I know what it's like. I was at Alto de León last week . . ."

Alto de León? What was he talking about? Had there been a battle at Alto de León? Jaime was only dimly aware of taking the cigarette. He said in a hushed voice, so soft he could barely hear himself, "Do you have . . . something to eat?"

The militiaman did not hear him. He was busy striking a match. He reached over, smiling, to light the cigarette.

"To . . . eat . . . " Jaime mumbled, holding out his hand.

The militiaman still did not hear him; his mind was on other things. "At Alto de León," he said with a curious masculine pleasure, "we had some time there, not like the picnic you're having up there. Look, it's all there . . ." He stopped short. Jaime was staring over his shoulder, trying to find Soler. A picture of the man's stricken face remained on the surface of his eyes like the sun after one has stared at it for too long. It could mean only one thing: his father, his mother—something had happened to them. What else could have made Soler pull back so? Everyone was milling about aimlessly. The officer who had carried the flag of truce had sat down on a pile of empty food cases and was twisting the flag between his hands.

Selica Portillo and her husband were walking toward the mouth of the Calle de Comercio.

"Pascual Soler," Jaime shouted.

One of the newsmen turned, swung his camera, smiling, straight at him and said something in French.

The paper under Jaime's boot tore, dividing the letters "v-a-l . . ." from those of "h-o . . ."

Just at that moment there was a cry from the direction of the Calle de Comercio and then a single shot. Jaime looked around. There was no place to take shelter. The officer with the flag had rolled over behind the packing cases. People were running about. The Anarchists, the Communist militiamen and the Republican officers were looking wildly at the rooftops. Jaime caught sight of Soler and three other men in a doorway just beyond the near barricade.

"You can't trust them, I told you . . . ," someone shouted.

"Who fired? There were strict orders . . . ," Tierres' voice.

"I assure you . . ." One of the officers was pointing toward the Calle de Comercio. Two Assault Guard ran toward the mouth of the street. In the midst of all the confusion, the newsmen had kept their cameras pointed toward the Alcázar.

Jaime struggled up from his knees, surprised that he dropped at the sound of the shot. The militiaman who had given him a cigarette was on the ground too, staring at him with a puzzled, a hurt look on his broad face.

At that moment the two Assault Guards and a few *milicianos* came back around the corner, pushing Selica Portillo's husband. He was wounded; blood streamed from his side and flowed down his trouser leg. Ashen-faced, even in that milling crowd of sun-bleached skulls, he seemed, for all that he could hardly walk, was more stumbling, first against one of the Guards then against the other, seemed . . . peaceful . . . content.

Then Portillo dropped to his knees where he swayed for a few seconds while the Guards stood back, watching him with the scowls of their profession glazed by expressions of genuine compassion, watching him rock back and forth like a penitent on his way on his knees to the cathedral. His arms flung wide, he pitched forward on his face. Quickly, the Assault Guards turned him over. There was a splotch of blood on his forehead. The Anarchists and a half-dozen men in uniforms formed a circle around him while the men of the truce party picked themselves up off the ground, swearing and brushing off their trousers.

Jaime stood up, so close to the militiaman from Alto de León that he could smell garlic on his breath. How simple it would be just to walk over to the barricades, lose oneself in the crowd. Now that this had happened, whatever it was, and it was all confusion, what better time could there be? Soler would help him. His father would help him, if he were still alive . . . that look on Soler's face. . . . And Barcenas pulling away like that . . . how could he trust them now? Wouldn't they be as likely to turn on him as the others, simply because he'd been . . . there? To his shame, he had to concede that it was not the thought of leaving the girl alone in the Alcázar that prevented him from crossing the invisible line that separated him from those across the Zoco, but simply his fear.

He heard himself say: "You're hurt." It was the militiaman, "Alto de León." In falling when the first shot was fired, he had opened a gash in his hand. Without thinking further, Jaime took a crumpled handkerchief from his pocket and tied it around the man's hand.

"Alto de León" mumbled thanks, and together the two of them went to where the two Assault Guard were standing over Selica Portillo's husband. Tierres was kneeling by the wounded man, with a distant, puzzled look on his face. A faint red foam speckled Portillo's lips. He seemed so strong, his muscles so thick and powerful that it struck Jaime as simply impossible that such a man could actually be dying. The bullet had left a ragged hole in his back where it had come out. The shot had been fired from a Mauser, and the bullet had probably been filed. But as each man had his weapon out, and there were at least five Mausers among the group it was impossible to tell who had shot him.

"What happened to the woman?"

One of the Assault Guard pointed back toward the Calle de Comercio and muttered something that was lost in the grinding of the cameras. The newsmen had recovered their wits and were filming the whole thing. The men from the truce party stood about, at a loss what to do, while the priest they had brought out made his way in the company of a half-dozen militiamen in overalls toward the place where the Portillos had gone a moment earlier.

". . . with a knife," Jaime heard someone say. "He just stood there and did it, as calm as you please. And she knew he was going to do it, and didn't make a move."

"It wasn't until he got the blade in her that she even cried out."

Jaime looked down at Portillo. The man's eyes had opened for a second, and then closed again. His face was bluish in the sun and already a few flies were investigating the pool of blood under his back. On his face there was, if not exactly a smile, a look of peace.

". . . couldn't he have waited until he got home? Here, in front of everyone . . . the fool . . ." It was one of Tierres' men.

The officers had remembered the men from the Alcázar and were gesturing at them to reform their group. "There's nothing for you to see here. Stop gaping, damn you."

"Alto de León" looked at Jaime and shook his head. It was clear that he had no idea what had happened, yet he sensed the contours of the event, and it was enough. There was, after all, something permanently above the secular hates that flared there on the Zoco, a common denominator of passion which still had the power to obliterate all political distinctions and push aside all barriers erected by the intellect.

Jaime said, "She was the Colonel's mistress, that's why. He must have known it."

"The Colonel?"

"Venegas, the Civil Guard . . ."

"Alto de León" was silent. The newsmen were taking pictures of the dead man and asking questions in a babble of French, English, and Portuguese.

"It's all over. Go on home, all of you," a Republican captain shouted. "You've got four minutes."

"Four minutes," Jaime thought; he wanted to laugh. "Why four? Why not five or three?"

"Alto de León" gave him three more cigarettes.

"They say he came all the way from France." The militiaman shook his head. "Even so, to come all that way? Why didn't he just stay where he was?"

Jaime thanked him for the cigarettes.

"Your handkerchief was worth more. It's all right. We'll be killing each other in an hour. That's funny, isn't it?"

Jaime didn't answer. The party was forming up again, the four officers forming a rank of sorts. They intended to march back in formation. "Let those disorganized bastards, who can't even keep their people from killing their wives, let them watch and see how it's done."

Jaime fell into place without thinking of it. It seemed absurd to march back. Perhaps it would be better if they simply ran. He had the feeling that the moment their backs were turned, the men at the barricades would open fire. The moment they realized what had happened between the Portillos, they had turned angrily on the escort party. There was only one explanation: they were humiliated by it. Yet there, in the very fact of it having happened, was the way they could have understood each other.

"Four minutes."

They began to walk. The Zoco was absolutely silent. The Lieutenant with the ragged mustache scuttled sideways, keeping an eye on the barricades, as though by watching them he could shame the *milicianos* out of shooting at him. Then, all at once, he changed his mind and turned his back, taking up his place at the rear of the group.

Jaime kept his eyes forward. There was no point in looking back. Soler and Barcenas had disappeared. For a moment he had felt the tug of a reality he had lost in the weeks he had been in the Alcázar . . . the outside. But it was just as false as that within the walls. None of it seemed to have anything to do with him any more. The man at his right coughed. Their feet were kicking up clouds of yellowish dust that was getting all over their clothes, their faces, and into their lungs.

He knew that it had all happened too quickly and that a full understanding of it would only come later. Somehow, the moment Mercedes had told him that Selica Portillo had seen her husband outside, he had known what would happen. Looking back at it, it seemed the only thing that could have happened.

Now, he wondered, what was he going to say to Mercedes?

NOON, SEPTEMBER 12: *Toledo*

BY THE TIME CARVALHO had reached the lobby of the Hotel Maravilla the body of Emilio Portillo had been carried in on a stretcher and laid on the floor by the front desk. The manager was talking to a young lieutenant of the Toledo police while trying at the same time not to look at the uncovered face of the corpse which was smeared with blood and, unaccountably, smiling. Half a dozen militiamen in blue "monos" stood around, smoking, not knowing what to do. A few of them had been on the Zoco when Portillo had died and were talking about it. Someone made a joke and another silenced him; it was nothing to joke about. In the back, a radio was playing a Gardel tango.

Carvalho was out of breath; he had come close to running the last few hundred meters. As he entered the lobby, he at once caught sight of Lachine who was standing near the stairway, shaking his head and looking around. It was the first time in his life that Carvalho had even seen the Frenchman look so upset. Surely it was not because of Portillo's death.

"They've gone up to our rooms," Lachine protested. "Six of them."

"Who? What are you talking about?"

"Police, politicals, *Asaltos* . . . how should I know? They're tearing our rooms apart." He stopped for a second to catch his breath, then pointed to the corner. "What in God's name happened to him? No one will tell me."

Carvalho glanced hurriedly at Portillo's corpse. There was blood spreading on the floor under it, slipping across the tiles in neat little rivulets. What a lot of blood the man had in him. The Colonel felt nothing but a whirling emptiness; Portillo's death was both an insufferable loss and an insufferable insult. At that moment he wanted to kill Torroba for having kept him away from the Zoco. He had arrived minutes after Portillo had died; one of Tierres' men had told him what had happened.

"What are we going to do?" Lachine said.

"Go up, what else? . . . they'll have to explain to me . . ."

"Wait, you can't . . . ," the young police Lieutenant shouted as Carvalho drew Lachine after him, up the stairs.

"Pay no attention to him. You don't have to listen . . . ," Carvalho said.

The police officer shouted again and started after them, a nonplussed expression on his face. The *milicianos* did not move. Then the manager came out from behind the desk and said something to the policeman, and he shook his head. By then, Carvalho and Lachine had disappeared up the stairway.

They climbed quickly. No one in the lobby moved to follow them. A murmur of voices, an agitated pounding below. The manager explaining loudly that they were the men who had been living with the murdered man.

"Why did they bring the body here?" Lachine asked, out of breath again. "And what do they want with us . . . ? My papers . . . if they've touched my papers . . ."

"It's only the stupid police," Carvalho said angrily. "Forget about them. Forget about your papers. Emilio is dead, don't you realize that?" He was incoherent with anger, stammering. The sight of the police, the *milicianos* in the lobby had infuriated him. It was probably one of those same men who had shot Portillo down. Damn Torroba . . . if he had only been there, perhaps he could have stopped it.

"The lists, they mustn't get into the wrong hands . . . How do I know who these people are? . . . They . . ."

"One more word out of you, Camille, about your papers, and I swear, I'll throw you down the stairs. . . ."

There was a crowd on the landing, and a little ways down the hall Carvalho could see that the door to their rooms was open and that there were men milling around inside. A soldier tried briefly to stop them, but when he saw the insignia of rank on Carvalho's uniform, he stepped mutely aside.

The small rooms were full of people. Three men in civilian clothes were engaged in sorting through the contents of the dresser drawers, all of which had been pulled out and emptied on the floor. Another man, in the uniform of the Assault Guard, was rifling through Portillo's card-board suitcase which he had opened on the couch. A fourth man, a plainclothes police officer, was standing near the window writing something in a small brown notebook.

"You have your nerve! . . ." Carvalho shouted from the doorway. "All of you . . ."

"What's that? What's that?"

Lachine hissed at him, genuinely frightened; "Be quiet, Enrique . . . these men . . ."

"I don't give a damn who these people are . . . ," he said quite loudly. Then, to the man with the notebook, he said, "Now get out of here, all of you . . . what right do you have in here? . . . to break in like this . . . ?"

The man pocketed his notebook and gave the Colonel a look of un-concealed sarcasm, one eyebrow raised, a patronizing smile on his lips. "You, and who are you . . . ?"

"These are my rooms . . ."

"Also the rooms of the man who was killed, aren't they?" He held out his papers, returned them to his pocket without giving Carvalho a chance to read them. He could make out only the name "Ibáñez" and the official identification: political police.

"There's no reason for this . . . ," Carvalho said. The turmoil in the room, the mess the police agents were making, infuriated him. He would not tolerate such treatment, not from the "political police" or any-one else. Lachine was searching about the room, trying to locate his brief-case in the hope that the plainclothesmen had not found it yet and pulled out his bank lists.

"We want to know why this happened," the policeman said quickly "and we shall find out, of course. . . ."

The Colonel stood there, strangling with anger. Why had it hap-pened? Was that what they wanted to know? It was so perfectly clear that even a child could see it. He began to shout: "You mean to tell me that you must pull drawers apart, empty suitcases on the bed, rifle through my belongings . . . mine . . . to know why a husband kills an unfaithful wife?" Even as he was saying this, he added mentally "whom he still loved."

"It was that simple, was it?" the police officer said, fingering his notebook. "The man was a Trotskyite, a POUM leader, don't you know that? Of course you know it, living here with him. Well, we'll find out all about you, too . . . don't worry. . . ."

Lachine, meanwhile, had crossed the room and recovered his brief-case.

"Here, you . . ." one of the police cried at him. The Assault Guard wrenched the briefcase from his hand and, in an instant, had broken the lock and spilled the papers out onto the floor.

"Here . . ."

"You bastard," Lachine shouted. "Tierres will . . ."

"We don't have to answer to Tierres or anyone else . . . ," the As-sault Guard said, pushing Lachine back against the wall.

Carvalho moved to help him. The police officer raised his arm to stop him. The Colonel struck at him and the man winced with pain, caught by surprise.

The Assault Guard had drawn his pistol and was about to bring it around when Carvalho struck him sharply on the arm. In that instant, the Colonel had drawn his own pistol and was pointing it at the police officer.

"Now, all of you . . . you will get out of here. You will, first of all, pick up everything and put it back where you found it."

"You're out of your mind," the police officer said. "Do you realize . . ."

"I realize that I am a Colonel of the Spanish Army and that this is my room. I realize that a friend of mine has been killed by your men and that it is a lucky thing for you that I don't know which one of you ac-tually shot him. I realize that you have dragged his body in here like a sack of grain and thrown it on the ground. . . . That man, a man who spent years in Montjuich prison . . . he deserved more respect than that, no matter what he'd done. I realize that you cannot be expected to un-derstand such things . . . yes, I realize . . . I realize a great deal. . . ."

He leveled the pistol at the police officer. "Now pick it all up. You, you start. Everything . . ."

Lachine was on his knees, sorting his papers, stuffing them back into the briefcase.

"Camille, get up. I don't want you doing that . . ."

"It's all right . . ."

"No it isn't . . . get up. Let *that* man do it. . . ." He gestured at the Assault Guard who had emptied the suitcase. The man got at once to his knees and finished what Lachine had begun.

"As you wish," said the police officer. He got down and began to scoop up the clothes that had been dumped out of the dresser drawers.

"And when you are finished, I want Señor Portillo's body taken for a proper burial, do you understand, not just dumped someplace like garbage. I expect to be advised of the time and the place . . . you, Inspector Ibánez, that's your name, isn't it? I hold you responsible . . ."

"You hold *me* responsible?"

"For a great many things . . . yes, you . . ."

The police officer didn't respond. He had finished with the clothes and stood up, dusting the knees of his trousers.

When the room had been restored to order, Carvalho ordered the six men out. The police officer nodded and smiled again, his irritating, condescending smile. "We shall see about all of this . . ."

"We certainly shall . . . ," Carvalho said. "About all of it . . ."

When they had gone and the door was closed again, Lachine fell into a chair, the briefcase on his lap. He was sweating profusely, the beads running down his broad forehead like oil.

He let out a long, pent-up breath, like a whistle. "You don't understand what that was all about, do you? . . . my God . . ."

Carvalho reholstered his pistol.

"I understand insolence when I see it. . . ."

"Insolence? What has insolence got to do with any of this? . . . respect, rank, propriety? Don't you understand what is happening here? What these people are? What you are? What I am . . . ? Any of this?"

Carvalho shook his head. "Not any more, Camille. Once, not so long ago, I would have answered you by pretending I understood it all because, otherwise, I could not have understood myself . . . but now? It's all changed . . . poor Emilio . . ."

"Forget Emilio . . . he's dead. And that's all. But what about you . . . ?"

"What about me, Camille?"

"They'll crucify you for this. . . ."

"If not for this then for something else . . . have you any doubt?"

Lachine did not answer. Carvalho sat down on the edge of the sofa, his long legs thrust out, his hands clasped between his knees. Under his right foot there was a torn brown sock, one of Portillo's, which the police had failed to replace in the dresser drawer.

Carvalho leaned over and picked it up, shifted it for a moment from hand to hand and then wadded it into a ball.

He threw it into the corner next to where Lachine was sitting.

By NOON ALMOST EVERYONE in the Alcázar had heard what had happened to the woman who had gone out with the priest. It was impossible to keep it a secret; too many people had been watching from the walls and a few, like Jaime, had field glasses and had observed everything quite clearly. The only person who seemed to have missed out was Amado Leorza. As always, he had remained bent over his table, poking wires into the back of the radio, jiggling tubes, and muttering prayers for divine intervention. Neither of the two cadets who had been helping him were in the room that morning. They were too busy elsewhere, one of them was with a small force of Civil Guard and civilians who were trying to defend the perimeter buildings, the *gobierno,* while the other, León Espargo, a boy of eighteen who had dreamed of being an electrical engineer, was trying to help fix the motorcycle engine which was used to grind the garrison's ever-diminishing supply of wheat.

Leorza's room, on most days, seemed to have taken the place of the local café. People gathered there while Leorza worked on, methodically and unperturbedly. He had become, for many of them, the one constant point of focus in the Alcázar. From time to time, someone would turn toward Amado Leorza and his two apprentices and say: "It's just that there aren't any broadcasts, that's all. Isn't that it?" Sometimes Leorza would ignore them completely, and sometimes he would say, very precisely, "It won't be long now, you'll see, you'll see," while León Espargo cast withering glances around the room. He had noticed that almost all those who gathered there were "older" men. None of the young men ever appeared with the sole exception of the long-faced Mercader, "the Berber," as everyone had taken to calling him. He would simply stand there in a corner and now and then ask if the radio was working. When he was told that it wasn't, he would linger for a while as though to make sure, and then leave only to return an hour later with the same quiet question.

But on this morning the radio repair room was almost empty. On two occasions, someone had come to the doorway with the intention of telling Amado Leorza what had happened, but he seemed so busy, so magisterially indifferent to everything but the jumble of wires and parts in front of him that his visitors simply bowed their heads out of respect for his diligence and went on their way.

Major Punto, who was exhausted from his experience with the priest, had already made a trip to the office where the daily news sheet, *El Alcázar,* was run off on an old mimeograph machine. Something told him that the printer, Jiménez, who had taken over production of the paper, would not let well enough alone, and he was right. On entering the room, he found Jiménez in the process of cutting a stencil. Jiménez not only wanted to print the whole story but to embellish it with some details of his own invention.

"But there are people here who know what happened," Major Punto protested. "You'll look like a fool."

"Well, in that case," Jiménez conceded grudgingly and tore the stencil from his Remington, crumpling the waxed paper into a ball. He hurled it against the wall like Luther exorcising the devil with his inkwell. "In that case . . ."

Punto was relieved not to have further complications. Of course he could have ordered Jiménez to delete the story, but it was much better to have him do it voluntarily. "Amazing," he thought, walking back up the stairs. "Amazing how a man's fear of looking foolish will make him do things that all the logic and common sense in the world won't. . . ." He glanced at his watch and noted with annoyance that it was getting close to one in the afternoon. He had promised himself to question Sebastián Gil again before the noon mealtime. It was odd, because there was no lunch to be eaten in the Alcázar, the total ration for the day consisting of one roll and strip of horseflesh eaten in the early evening. But so many, including Sebastián Gil, continued to behave as though the old schedules and procedures still governed. For Sebastián Gil to be standing in Major Punto's office answering questions when he felt that he should be eating, made him just that much more nervous and that much more prone to tell the truth. In the five sessions that they had had over the past weeks, Major Punto had learned nothing at all of value. Gil, however, had grown more and more nervous each time. If he persisted, Punto had concluded, he might just ask the right question, perhaps even by accident, and then the doors to the truth would open wide. What he might see on the other side, he was not at all sure, nor was he sure that he really wanted to look further. Yet once having committed himself to such a course, he had no alternative but to continue.

"They're killing people outside for no better reason than that they've looked the wrong way at some Communist or other or gone to Mass too frequently and you, Manuel Punto, keep looking for hidden reasons why the commandant of the entire Civil Guard garrison in Toledo should be assassinated. Jesus, man . . ."

But there was something else that disturbed Major Punto far more. He realized that he was beginning to derive a certain pleasure from the inquistorial process itself. It was, he assured himself, simply the pleasure of a craftsman in a job that is going along well. Though why he, an instructor in geography and history, should have come to regard himself as a "craftsman" in a field usually associated with policemen and members of the Holy Office, he could not really explain.

From the total experience, from all his doubts and the counterarguments they raised, he was beginning to distill a faint understanding of what made men do the things they did . . . kill, maime and torture, seemingly without reason, without any relation between professed goals and the acts done purportedly to achieve these goals. For this, he was deeply ashamed. How easy it was to abuse power; no matter how little power one held, it was always possible to find someone less powerful than oneself. It would have been easy, attractive, to blame Umberto Reyles for what he, Punto, was doing, but he could not bring himself to such an easy escape. Umberto Reyles, a sour-faced little vintner who had been regional secretary for the CEDA, had been a good friend of Venegas and had gotten it into his head that Gil had told the *Asaltos* something that morning. Reyles was bitter and not without cause: he had lost his son Jorge when a gunfight had broken out during a military parade on the Paseo de la Castellana in Madrid three months before. He had never ceased blaming the Assault Guards for his loss and the fact that Gil had talked with two of them just before Venegas' death served to transfer that hatred from the *Asaltos,* whom he could not reach, to Gil who at least was close at hand.

"Did you see the crocodile tears the man shed at Fernán's funeral? Make him drown in those tears, Major, make him drown."

Punto had at first argued against the idea vehemently, even to the point of insulting Reyles.

"No matter," Reyles replied. "The guilty man has to be found."

"And if we can't get at the ones who really did it, because they're outside," Punto had replied, "then we'll find ourselves a substitute, is that it?"

Reyles had not replied.

Punto's anger spilled over. "Get someone else to do this," he shouted.

Reyles, bearing himself with stern dignity despite his filth and emaciation, smiled grimly. "No, Major. You do this so well. In fact, you seem to enjoy it. A man does well what he enjoys, wouldn't you say?" Then he had turned and walked stiffly out of Punto's office.

There . . . Reyles had put his finger on it, and that was precisely what made Punto so deeply ashamed of himself. He was taking out his own frustration at his helplessness on Gil.

The sessions with the little Austrian were another thing entirely, a skillful match which would end eventually in the scoring of points which would mean nothing at all. Gil's case was another thing entirely.

He walked out of the sun and under the east arcade, thinking, in spite of himself, "It might be a better idea, after all, to wait until it gets dark. Then I could point a strong light at him." It would be interesting, among other things, to know how he has reacted to the Portillo woman's death. It would all tie in, he was sure.

As he passed into the cooler shadows of the corridor, Major Punto made a mental note to call the young man who had escorted Selica Portillo across the Zoco up to his room for a few questions. It occurred to him that he had seen him talking to Gil a number of times. The very first day, in the courtyard, now that he thought about it.

Jaime Mercader, however, had no thought that by having gone with Selica Portillo he might somehow have involved himself with Sebastián

Gil. Ever since his return that morning he had been able to think of nothing but how Mercedes would react to the news.

When he had told her what had happened, Mercedes had at first let out a low, anguished cry. Then a dark, and to Jaime, an obscure look had passed over her face. Her jaw had tightened, and she had corrected herself sternly.

"No, she must have wanted it this way."

He recalled how he had felt, standing there near the *Asaltos* and Emilio Portillo's body, and that he had thought the same thing. But he had also felt he was being illogical even though it was the first, natural thought that came to him, and it annoyed him now that Mercedes should say the same thing.

"I don't understand it. She must have considered the possibility that he was still alive when she became Venegas' mistress. And she must have known that her husband would find out all about it. . . ."

"If she was weak and did it because she was weak . . . or if she was strong and was doing it for her husband all along, would it have made any difference?" Jaime felt his chest tighten; that "dark" look, the furrowing of her brow and the clenching of her teeth that always accompanied it accented her emaciation so that he could hardly bear to look at her. If only there were more oranges. More food of any kind. He would give her anything he could, do anything for her, if only she would not continue to waste away. Her breasts had already shrunken and her skin was waxy and yellowing. The women, as a rule, got even less fresh air than the men. The rule was that they were to remain below in the deepest, safest chambers. Only when they went to the bakeshop or the surgical rooms or the chambers where the wounded were kept did they get a chance to see daylight.

"It's possible, isn't it, that she could have really loved Venegas? Isn't it?" Mercedes asked.

"She said . . . ," Jaime began, recalling her confession.

"That was at the end. What about the beginning?"

After a while, she left him to help in the bakeshop. Selica Portillo had worked there too, and it would seem strange being there without her.

Jaime went immediately to look for the driver, Barrera, stopping off at Leorza's room to see if anything had happened.

"Only static," Amado Leorza said. "But it won't be long now, you'll see."

When Jaime repeated what Mercedes had said to the driver, Barrera's only reaction was to chew more rapidly on the stem of the acacia leaf that hung from his mouth.

"How should I know about such things?" And then, after another moment's reflection, he added: "That's the trouble. It seems that almost everything is beyond me. I've come to the conclusion that either I'm a very stupid man or that no one else is acting in a very sensible way at all."

Jaime thought about that for a moment. In a way, the driver was right. No one was acting rationally, least of all himself. Something on his face must have betrayed his thoughts, for the driver cocked his head to the side and asked suddenly, "When you were out there, you wanted to get over the barricades, didn't you?"

"And you?" Jaime heard himself say.

"I'm happy where I am."

"Why? You, of all people . . ."

"Because I understand that nobody understands it all. Answer me truthfully, *teniente*. Who are *my* people? Infante or Ignacio? Which one is mine? Where am I supposed to be? They can both make good arguments. But I'll tell you what I think. I think that if you left it to either side, they'd chew me up and spit out my bones into the gutter. Nobody gives a damn for me, so I better make myself useful. That way I stay alive. An uncle of mine used to say, 'Your side is the side you're on when the fighting starts.' Now, that's true, as long as they'll have you . . ."

Jaime had not heard the last few words. He was looking past Barrera and up over the north wall. As Barrera caught the direction of his astonished gaze and turned to follow it, he became aware that others were looking up as well. From an interior window in what was left of the west tower, a man leaned out and began frantically waving a long blue scarf. Sun sparkled from the lenses of the binoculars he had slung around his neck.

A few shots crackled from the streets outside, like a string of Chinese firecrackers.

From where Jaime stood, all he could see was the sun and a small patch of sky. It was like looking up from the bottom of a cistern. But he could hear something, and the sound was coming directly from the heart of that very patch of sky.

The aircraft slowly lofted into view as though being pulled by invisible wires up and over the parapet of the northwest walls. It was flying not more than a hundred feet off the ground. A biplane, wobbling and dipping its wire-strung wings. Jaime recalled the Beringuets and the Vickers seaplanes over Oviedo, but it wasn't one of them. He couldn't make out the design at all. Nor was any insignia visible on either wing or on the fuselage or tail. He felt a curious exhilaration.

The plane passed between the fortress and the sun. There was no point in trying to take cover for there was simply no time to reach shelter. If the plane was on a bombing run, they had less than five seconds left.

Jaime stood there, with his head thrown back, gazing into a sky now latticed by wing and strut.

The plane dove down over the courtyard, so close that it was possible to see the circles struck by the sun from the pilot's goggles. Two pincerlike clasps situated between the clumsy, jutting wheels, began to open with infuriating slowness. A square, black object, like a chest or a steamer trunk fell from the belly of the plane and began to tumble end over end toward the yard. The plane swooped effortlessly up and vanished over the southeast tower. The sound of the engines seemed no part of the plane's motion at all and Jaime was so absorbed in watching the hurtling aircraft that the tumbling box was almost forgotten. He could not help thinking at that moment of the similar grace of the huge carrion birds that hugged the air currents in the high Atlas, gliding soundlessly, without moving a wing, for hours on end. It seemed to him somehow improper, against God's will, that a plane should be able to fly in the same way.

There was the box again, floating into the periphery of his vision. It was clear that the box would land only a few yards from where he was standing. "If it's a bomb, then these are my last thoughts. . . ." Yet he made no attempt to move, though, from a very great distance, he could hear the driver shouting at him.

The box struck the courtyard almost at its exact geometric center with a great clang. The lid sprang open from the impact and objects sprayed out as though from the kind of children's toy that sends up a geyser of candies and little figures when the lid is opened and the spring released. Metal cannisters, black cardboard containers and a whirlwind of leaflets shot into the air. The chest rattled for a moment and then fell over on its side.

There was no explosion. The black cannisters which looked so much like grenades did not burst. The boxes failed to detonate. Only the leaflets moved, now settling slowly down over the stones of the courtyard like a coarse snow.

The aircraft wheeled about again at the far end of its arc and swung around over the Tagus. Jaime followed the sound with his eyes. The plane seemed to be heading directly toward the castle of San Servando on the opposite bank of the river. A scattered web of rifle fire was flung up from the streets and from the Dehesa de Pineda some fool was trying to shoot the plane down with a howitzer. Then, as Jaime stood there, he heard the unmistakable sound of an aerial bomb exploding near the castle.

The aircraft had carried bombs after all, but it had only dropped a tin chest on the Alcázar.

Jaime lowered his eyes; gold and orange circles alternated with purple orbs, sliding across each other, obscuring everything. He had been gazing toward the sun too long. As his eyes began to focus again, he saw that he was surrounded by a crowd of people who had spilled almost soundlessly from the arcades and ruined entranceways of the building.

Soldiers, a few cadets, Civil Guard in what was left of their gray-green uniforms. Some still had their patent-leather tricorns. Even now, most had their pillbox hats. Civilians in all sorts of absurd costumes. One of the raids had netted a trunk full of theatrical disguises. There was a harlequin and a conquistador, a red Indian, and two French policemen.

"*Teniente,* you didn't get killed. . . ." A voice, Barrera's, somewhere nearby. The crowd had almost smothered Jaime. He realized that he was standing very near the tin chest, very near the spot where most of the cannisters and boxes had come to rest.

He saw someone appear at the door in the south arcade. He seemed to be able to see over the heads of most of the people around; had they shrunken or was he taller? Major Punto, shouldering his way through the crowd, and close behind him, as though being dragged by an unseen chain, Sebastián Gil. Gil dogged the Major's footsteps, a frightened look on his face, as Punto pushed his way through the milling crowd, shouting things that Jaime could not hear clearly.

Then Punto's voice came through clearly: "Don't go near it . . . it might explode . . ."

"Let's see what it is," someone said. "It hasn't exploded, you can see that . . ."

Punto shouted sternly: "Wait at least one hundred and twenty seconds, then look for wires. Menéndez, Corporal Serna, and you, García . . . someone get a probe . . . a wire, anything like that. Damn it, man, get away from that thing. Stand clear."

The soldiers permitted Major Punto to approach unhindered. Jaime thought, "So they allow him this prerogative at least, to be the first to be blown apart if it explodes. Well . . ." As the Major straddled the empty chest, Jaime was pushed back. The crowd formed a wavering circle around the chest and the scattered containers.

Punto nudged one of the black cans with his toe. Nothing happened. No one spoke. He looked up, surprised. He was walled in by a mass of tattered uniforms, anonymous faces out of which shone the same identical bloodshot eyes. All of them reduced to a skeletal common denominator.

For a second Punto felt a twinge of panic, as though something he did not know or understand was expected of him, and if he failed in this uncomprehended duty, they would all fall on him, this army of corpses, and tear him to bits.

Nearby a man with a crutch under one arm bent to pick up a leaflet, almost losing his balance. Another man reached out to keep him from falling and almost fell himself, a victim of his own weakness.

" 'Greetings, Brothers in Christ,' " a man read. " 'Greetings from the Army of Africa and the Army of the South, to the brave defenders of the Alcázar . . .' "

Punto listened, astounded. To his right stood Gil. He had only been questioned for fifteen minutes before the plane came over. Why was he so frightened? Nothing had happened; it had been as harmless as though they had been talking about the weather.

" '. . . Your hour of victory is approaching,' " the man went on reading. " 'We shall relieve you soon. In the meantime, resist as you have been doing. Resist . . .' "

" 'The Army of Africa,' " someone shouted from the edge of the crowd. "What have I got to do with the 'Army of Africa'. . . ?"

"They're going to save us, you cretin. Don't you see?"

"And who's going to save us from them? The 'Army of Africa', that means the Moors, man . . . Moors, do you understand?"

Everyone was shouting, pushing to get at the leaflets. Punto looked about, trying to find some way to restore order. Was he the only officer in the yard? Where had all the rest of them gone?

". . . . time comes . . . little help. We are advancing . . ."

"*Viva España* . . ."

"*Arriba España*," someone shouted; it was one of the young Falangists who had been found hiding the first few days of the siege.

"Cut out that shit, you . . ."

"*Arriba España*," the young man shouted again; he had somehow managed to hang on to his blue shirt. Old men turned and glared at him with unconcealed suspicion, and the air was rent with the clashing of Monarchist *vivas* and the *arribas* of the Falange . . .

Punto stood there, rooted to the ground, amazed. "So that's it now," he thought. "We shall all shout *Arriba España* . . . until we're blue in the face and shoot anyone who doesn't do likewise. Well, what do the Anarchists yell? . . . and the Reds . . . and the *Izquierda?* And what would the leaflet have said if the Leftists had picked up the old cries first? They're as much entitled, I suppose." What strange new form of words would have to have been invented. In the beginning, hadn't Christians taken off their hats in church only because the Jews kept them on? "God in heaven, what asses . . ."

Nearby Jaime, two men were arguing, each hanging on to one side of the same leaflet.

"The army is one thing, but those people . . ."

"If we all get killed, it won't matter much, will it Grandpa?"

"In Primo's time . . ."

"But that's all done with now."

"All right, but what about the milk. Is there any milk for the children? We can't eat paper. We're not goats . . ."

"It's food," someone shouted. "Real food . . . look . . ."

The word passed suddenly like a wind-borne seed. Everywhere it touched it left an animal nervousness. The crowd stilled, stuffed the leaflets into their pockets, and stood eyeing the heap of cans by Major Punto's feet. They wiped their palms on their trousers and glared at each other with unconcealed suspicion.

Major Punto's fingers fell on the flap of his holster, and he found himself, without willing it, clasping the butt of his Mauser, then drawing it from its holster and waving it over his head.

He began to shout, pleading with them to stand back. It might be a trap. How did anyone know? His voice echoed in the courtyard. Near him stood Rubén Góngora, the barber, who had run a shop near the cathedral. The barber was staring at him. Then the Major realized that he, Manuel Punto alone, was shouting. In fact, no one else was saying a word. He was trying to overcome nonexistent opposition. He lowered his voice at once. Rubén Góngora smiled sheepishly and stepped back.

But the Major still kept the Mauser over his head, pointed straight at the sky.

"But the plane, it dropped a bomb on the San Servando castle," someone shouted.

"It *must* have been one of ours."

"Did they hit it? No, they did not. At least you don't know that they did," Punto shouted. Where was someone to help him? Had they left him all alone to cope with the rest of the mob? "Rest . . ." then he was part of it too . . . curious distinction to make. The crowd was closing in and there he was, holding discourses with himself.

"No! . . ." Everyone was shouting at once.

"It doesn't prove anything. It could have been a trick. Drop a bomb on the castle, and everyone thinks they're on our side. Then we gorge ourselves on poisoned food and . . . ffft . . ."

"Milk. There's powdered milk there, I know it."

"And tinned meat."

Slowly the ring of red-eyed men drew even tighter about the chest. Around the periphery of the courtyard, the rustle of women's voices could be heard as though they had been called up by some magic, soundless summons to claim what belonged to their children.

"No one is to touch anything . . . ," the Major insisted. He was looking about frantically. He could expect no help from Gil, of course. There was Rubén Góngora again, looking away, and the Austrian standing by the edge of the mob. "God, what he must think of us. They call us a primitive people, they have such scorn . . . well, perhaps . . ." He caught sight of the young man he had sent out that morning, the one who had gone with the woman who had been killed, but he too seemed to be looking away, or rather almost through him. It was as though he could not see at all. Blinded.

"There will be order here. No one is to touch anything." He was still the only officer in the yard as far as he could see. He tightened his finger on the trigger and was about to fire once into the air when the absurdity of the gesture struck him with shattering force. Whatever he did now he would probably start a riot. Everything had been so well controlled up until then, but hadn't that been because there was nothing anyone could do anyhow, no reason to bolt, to protest, no hope that protest might yield anything? Now, there was food. A few lucky ones might get something to eat. But then they might be killed by the others. Hunger makes a man capable of almost anything, and women trying to feed their children, well, that was worse yet.

Major Punto was sweating profusely, his bald head shining. As usual, he was not wearing a cap.

"Did anyone recognize the make of the plane?" He was trying a different tack. So little time left; the edge of the crowd was only a few yards away. "Did you? Did anyone?"

No one answered. Someone waved a leaflet.

"What's the difference?"

"What's the difference? You imbecile . . ." The man cringed. Punto began to shout, not at the crowd but at the one man who had cried, "What's the difference?" It was amazing how, in the instant he had directed himself at that one man, the others all seemed to draw back and to re-establish, by that withdrawal, the line of authority that he had been unable to draw before by himself. Now, it seemed, he was in confrontation with one single man, and all the rest of them could focus on that conflict and safely await the outcome without taking part themselves.

"What's your name?"

"What d'you mean? Who wants my name? What for?"

"You heard me."

The man paused, looked about for help. "Why should my name matter? I mean, it's not your business to ask people's names, is it?" No one spoke up in his defense. Forced by their silence to reply he stammered "Well . . . if you must. Ciro Salas. So, there. What of it . . . ?"

"Ciro Salas . . . then tell me, Ciro Salas . . . it could be poisoned, couldn't it?"

"How should I know those things . . . that's your . . ."

"Exactly so . . . well, answer. You don't know, do you . . . ?"

"Poisoned?" said the man who had been singled out.

"Wouldn't that be a fine way to do it, Ciro Salas? Why not? Why not, I ask you. So why shouldn't we find out first? Why shouldn't we test them to see if they're safe?"

Ciro Salas was muttering to himself.

Major Punto bent over and picked up one of the cans and held it out. Salas stepped back involuntarily.

"You wanted it. Go ahead. Have some. We'll watch . . ."

"What d'you mean. Me?"

"Yes. Go ahead. I'm ordering you to eat . . ."

A whispered hush. The others drew back. Punto cast his eyes around the edge of the crowd. The young man of the morning was there, no longer blind. He was smiling in an ironic way. He understood what the Major was doing. Punto flushed with pleasure. And it was working, too.

"No, not me . . . ," Salas said.

"Ciro, for the love of God . . ." It was his wife who had pushed her way through the crowd. She took his arm, imploring him to come away.

"You see, my wife, she insists . . ."

"Eat," Major Punto said once more, his voice very tight and level. Salas pushed his way back into the crowd. Someone said, "Fool."

"So . . . ," Punto lowered his outstretched arm and dropped the can back onto the pile. It rolled back and forth, then came to rest.

"So . . . ," he repeated. "No one is to touch any of this until we have it tested. Someone, find me a dog or a cat."

A voice cried out, "We've eaten them all, Major. . . ."

"No, there's Pluto who belongs to the little Oñas boy . . ."

"Yes, Pluto . . ."

Major Punto pointed sharply, once, twice, three times, with an index finger and gestured at the cannisters. The men he had indicated began gathering everything up and stacking it back in the tin chest. An angry buzzing went up. The sight of those three men with their arms full of food parcels while the rest of them stood by empty-handed raised immediate, blind resentment.

"The officers are going to take it all for themselves . . . ," someone said.

"Who was that?" Major Punto barked out, raising the pistol again. "There are fools and there are fools . . ."

No one answered. Major Punto smiled and holstered his Mauser. The crowd was still. Of course the food was probably all right. The whole thing was too absurd to be a hoax. "More than fifteen hundred people in this place and they drop two-dozen cans of tinned meats, a few packets of powdered milk and a hundred leaflets which, as the señor correctly observes, we can't eat because, after all, we're not goats. No, the thing is too stupid to be a hoax. . . ."

One of the soldiers kicked the lid of the chest closed and stared down at it angrily. Major Punto wondered whether he was thinking the same thoughts as he was. He looked about. All the familiar faces had disappeared and the crowd was thinning out. It was as if they had all realized at once what fools they had almost been and how the only real food that had been dropped that would matter to any of them was a little hope, and not too much of that either.

SEPTEMBER 13

Victory, Victory, Victory

Energetic action by Republican forces continues in the Talavera sector.

The sound of cannon thunders over the Alcázar again.

In opposition to the humanitarian efforts of the Government, that has tried to save women, children, and the deluded soldiers, Moscardó and his henchmen persist in their cowardly behavior.

SEPTEMBER 13: *Toledo*

YOU CAN PUT ON YOUR SHIRT NOW if you want to," Dr. Blas Aliaga said. "There's nothing more I can do for you, not here. . . ."

Colonel Carvalho sat on the edge of the examining table and stared after the doctor as he turned his back and bent over the squat, German-made refrigerator in which he kept his medicines. On the wall above the refrigerator were two objects which caused Enrique Carvalho an immediate and intense despair: a mirror in which his partially naked body seemed frozen in all its bony gracelessness and, next to it, a map of the southwestern quarter of Spain up which the Fascist armies had been crawling the entire month of August. It was impossible to look at the mirror without seeing the map, or at the map without seeing the mirror. Perhaps the doctor, with his taste for irony and his disdain for human pretensions, had done it deliberately.

The small room was stifling hot. No breeze entered through the window even though the panes had been flung wide open to receive it at the risk of an invasion by the flies which had begun to infest Toledo in the past weeks. A fan in the ceiling tried vainly to cope with the oppressive heat. The office bore a look of improvisation, in fact it was really a case of deliberate inpoverishment. Dr. Aliaga had donated much of his equipment to the military hospital across the river and all that remained were the most elementary examining instruments. If he should have had to do so much as set a fracture, he would have had to requisition regimental command for the necessary equipment.

Carvalho sat still, watching the sweat trickle down among the whorls of white hair that covered his chest.

"What can you tell me?" he asked. Dr. Aliaga's back was still turned, and he was hunting for something in the refrigerator. A wisp of vapor curled up over his head giving him the aspect of a haloed saint.

"Do you want the truth?"

"Of course."

Dr. Aliaga turned. He was holding a flask of pale yellowish liquid and two glasses which he had kept in the refrigerator. "Lemonade? My wife made it herself. She's good for a few things . . ."

He poured out two glasses. The Colonel drank his slowly.

"That's it. Not too fast . . ."

"So I won't shock my system?" Colonel Carvalho suggested.

"So many people do. It's not good, for you or for me. But don't worry, it has nothing to do with your condition."

Carvalho winced at the way Dr. Aliaga had used the word *condition*. So effortlessly, as a matter of course. Then there was something the matter with him. Why hadn't he come sooner? But there had been so much to do, so many places to look. Nothing had helped. There was not a sign of his daughter. And all the while the pain under his shoulder blade had gotten worse, then had extended to his arm . . .

"The truth?" Dr. Aliaga suggested again. "Well, the truth is that I'm not sure."

"And if you were to . . . lie to me? What would you have said then?"

"I'd say I'd found nothing. Which is true, but it isn't the entire story. To find nothing means, too often, that you simply haven't looked hard enough or with sufficient care. Some people prefer that. Particularly when they suspect something serious . . . like cancer, say . . ."

"It's not that, is it?"

"Of course not." He sipped his lemonade and smiled with pleasure. Little droplets of liquid ran down his chin and into his pointed goatee.

His glasses, which he had put on in lieu of his usual pince-nez, began to fog up. "I'd say . . . if you insist on 'something' . . . that you've got the beginnings of angina . . . angina pectoris . . . don't frown like that. Not fatal in most cases. Certainly quite painful sometimes, but we can cope with that. . . ."

But could he? Carvalho wondered. He had never really had to cope with pain before, not in all of his life. Privation, thirst, exhaustion, starvation even—all the normal by-products of a military career. Being wounded had always been so abrupt that he never counted it as painful in the way a constant, degenerative disease could be.

"The function of pain," Dr. Aliaga was saying, "is to serve as a warning to us that something is wrong with the mechanism." He nodded his head backward toward the map. "Thus, it's actually very useful, like that, the map, for instance. Painful, isn't it, but useful as a warning."

Carvalho rubbed at the sweat that was trickling down his chest. "General Yagüe's been lucky, that's all." A curved red line, like the blade of an Arabic sword, ran from Sevilla to Navalmoral de la Mata, only about ninety kilometers due east of Toledo. First it had been Mérida on August tenth, then Badajoz on the fourteenth, and finally Navalmoral on the twenty-third; the *banderas* of the Legion and the *tabors* of the *Regulares* advancing, flank to flank, under General Yagüe.

"Perhaps," Dr. Aliaga said. "If you look at it the right way, then I suppose you can call it 'luck' . . . the same way you could call saying that I'd found nothing 'the truth' . . . a certain kind of clouding of fact. A question of emphasis only. Yes, he's been lucky. The Anarchists deserting, refusing to follow orders, attacking when and where they like, refusing to dig trenches, to get their hands dirty . . . yes that's General Yagüe's luck. But it's our responsibility too . . . we should never have let things like that happen."

Since Carvalho had been in Toledo, he had been asked many times to take up staff work. Captain Segurra had asked him and so had a representative from General Riquelme's headquarters, but he had refused and they, with a rare delicacy and respect, had let him alone. "When I've found her or I know she's dead," he would say. Captain Segurra shrugged and did not argue. In the weeks since he had been there, Colonel Carvalho had become a familiar figure in his shabby uniform, asking questions, wandering like a lost spirit about the narrow streets of the city, as likely to be seen at three in the morning as at three in the afternoon. He had begun to acquire nicknames among the *milicianos* and the soldiers who mounted nervous watch at night: "the Phantom," "the one who never sleeps," "the crooked ghost," and so on. When he had discovered, through an idle remark dropped by Lachine, that General Riquelme had been ordered to tunnel a mine under the Alcázar for the purpose of blowing the entire building up should continued efforts to take it by assault prove fruitless, Carvalho's nocturnal wanderings had increased. At first he had not believed the rumors, but when truckloads of Asturian miners had appeared one morning and, the next evening, a section of narrow streets near the Alcázar had been roped off and guards posted, he had been forced to admit to himself that it was all true.

"How can they do such a thing?" he had demanded of Lachine.

"There is nothing more inhuman," the Frenchman had replied, "than a beleaguered humanitarian. It may seem odd to you that our friends believe . . . and they truly do believe it . . . that they can make a better world for us all by blowing up women and children but . . . there it is. It's your country, Enrique. Don't accuse me . . ."

There the conversation had ended.

In the nights that followed, Carvalho had begun to wander nearer and nearer to the roped-off area where the mine was being sunk. He could hear the clank of tools, the hum of motors. It had driven him mad. His body had begun to ache, the circles under his eyes thickened to the point where Lachine and Portillo, each a prey to their own secret griefs, had frequently tried to put him to bed and make him stay there, even resorting to putting powders in his evening coffee. Hence, finally his visit to Dr. Aliaga. . . .

The doctor was speaking again: "I have to admit it . . . I'm a little shaken by all of this. I'd be a fool if I pretended otherwise. Enrique, how the devil is a man to stay afloat . . . ?"

"To tell the truth, I was surprised when Soler told me you were still here."

"Why? You know my sympathies. They're not so different from yours."

"I wonder, Blas . . . are they? And I wonder also because I'm not sure what my own feelings are at this moment. . . ." He had already forgotten about his sickness. His eyes were on the map. Dr. Aliaga seemed content to go along with him. He knew that there was nothing he could do there. They would have to go to Madrid where electrocardiographic equipment was available. With the crude tools he now had at his disposal, everything was guesswork.

"I didn't believe that the Left would ever force a showdown," said Aliaga, "but now, I'm not so sure. Certainly it wasn't the Communists who had Calvo Sotelo shot. They wouldn't have been so foolish. Oh, I know that 'La Pasionaria' is supposed to have threatened his life in the Cortes, but find me one man who will swear to having heard it. Doesn't it make more sense to believe that the POUM or even the 'anars' did it as a deliberate provocation? I wouldn't put anything past them . . . that's why I still lean toward the Communists. . . ."

"Lean? . . ." Carvalho smiled. "I thought you believed in always taking a definite stand, no matter what, in defining your position. . . ."

"Ah, Enrique," he sighed, pouring another glass of lemonade. "My profession interferes. I'm convinced that no doctor can ever be a conscientious Communist. To do so, you have to first believe in the innate dignity of man, even of the humblest peasant, the most ill-tempered factory worker. But how can I, who spends my life looking at men's stomachs, open on an operating table, believe in such a thing? Put a scalpel up a man's rectum or a catheter up his penis and see how much dignity he has. Illness reduces us to our essentials. And there's the simple truth of it. . . . Look at yourself, for instance. There, in the mirror. Look . . ."

Carvalho lowered his eyes. He knew all too well what the mirror showed. Did he feel a faint pain in his arm, a tightening of his chest at that second or was it his imagination? He put his shirt back on.

"No, I'm sympathetic, but I can't really be a 'believer.' As long as they're for science, for organizing things and trying to do them in a planned, orderly way, I'm for them . . . that's precisely the lack that's estranged me from the *Izquierda Republicana* and all the well-meaning people who have allowed this situation to develop by doing nothing about it."

"But look what's happening," Carvalho protested, trying to get his thoughts away from his own body. "Everything is even more disorganized than it was before."

"True enough, but they're trying and, perhaps, in the end they'll succeed in stopping this insanely destructive revolution the Anarchists are trying to foist on us."

"Do you mean," Carvalho said with sudden astonishment, "that you believe that your Communist friends are . . . against . . . the revolution?"

"It's the last thing in the world they want. Does it take two sets of eyes to see what will happen if things get out of hand? Already we've had German Junkers ferrying Franco's men from Africa and Italian fighter planes over Madrid. A real revolution, one that showed signs of winning, would have every nation in Europe marching across Spain. . . ."

"Didn't they try that in Russia? And look what happened."

Dr. Aliaga smiled and jerked a thumb at his map. "My dear friend, the distance from Hendaye to Cádiz is approximately that from Minsk to Moscow, while from Barcelona to La Coruña, clear across the width of Spain, is not even equal to the distance from Moscow to Odessa. In short, you could tuck Spain away in one corner of Russia and not even know it was there. That's the key . . . distances and, of course, weather. No. The British and French and the Americans and all the rest failed in 1917 for the same reason Napoleon failed in 1812, but the Germans and Italians won't fail if they come trooping in here to save us from the 'Reds.' It's not the same thing at all . . ."

A phone began to jangle in the corner of the room. Dr. Aliaga gave it a withering look. "It seems I have to answer it myself. . . ." He was thinking of his office in Madrid, his two assistants and the nurses who helped him with his patients and his appointments. All of that was put by for the time being, and when he thought of it he could not, for the life of him, understand why he had done it.

He picked up the receiver, an incredibly ornate piece of black metal with a bulbous mouthpiece. "Yes . . . yes . . . of course, he's here. . . ." It was obvious that the call was for Carvalho. Dr. Aliaga put the receiver back on the cradle. Carvalho was surprised.

"It was for me, wasn't it?"

"Yes. Tierres' headquarters. They're coming for you with a car, in ten minutes. That was all. I suppose you'd better get dressed. Do you want another lemonade?"

"No, but regards to your wife all the same. . . ."

Dr. Aliaga's eyebrows went up in an arch, something that happened often when his wife was mentioned. A born womanizer, he had, ironically enough, made an alliance with one of the least attractive women Carvalho had ever seen, a masculine, rugged-looking female who would have looked much more at home, so his own wife, Amalia, had often said, ". . . in English tweeds, with those horrible walking shoes they wear on her feet and a knobbed stick in her hand . . ."

He smiled. "Do you really think she made this? I was only joking. A lovely little nurse at the dispensary, who doesn't know POUM from piff-paff or a Fascist from a mountain goat . . . a genuine blonde, too, which is rather unusual in this area . . ."

The doctor helped him on with his tunic. He had heard from the lawyer, Soler, how fruitless Carvalho's search had been up to then. He now observed in the Colonel a kind of suffering which he simply could not deal with, perhaps the only kind over which he was absolutely powerless. Some men who suffered so withdrew, became madmen or priests; in any case, a refusal to recognize reality was bound to have evil consequences. In the midst of a war, the siege of the Alcázar, with General Yagüe's troops less than a hundred kilometers away, the man persisted in looking for a woman he should have given up as dead weeks before. How many people had vanished throughout Spain in those first few weeks? How many lay in unmarked graves or had been disfigured beyond recognition? Yet a man like Carvalho could continue to hope. It was among such types, the doctor concluded, that Cervantes must have found his models. Did they exist in any other country under God's eye?

"Don't take my arm like that, Blas," Carvalho complained as they went down the stairs to the street.

"I'm sorry. It's habit . . . and the past few weeks . . ."

"Is there anything I should do . . . to be on the safe side?"

"Do? Of course there is. Live somewhere else, in a peaceful country where you'll have no worries, no strains. Get rid of that uniform. If you can find a monastery, go there. Above all, get some sleep. Try to relax. That's all a horrible joke, isn't it? But what else can I say? It's true . . . the 'real' truth you asked for. . . ."

The car was already waiting in the street below. It belonged to the Communists and had the usual decorations in place. Its driver, however, was a regular army corporal, and he saluted without embarrassment.

"So, you see? . . . What confusion," Dr. Aliaga said, shaking Carvalho's hand as the latter got into the back seat. "Remember, rest. Above all, rest . . . or it may get very painful . . ."

"Will I die of it?"

"Not if it's what I think it is, no . . ."

The car moved away from the two-story building. Dr. Aliaga remained standing there in his white smock, his hands in his pockets, looking more downcast than the Colonel could remember that cynic ever having permitted himself to look. Obviously his condition was more serious than Dr. Aliaga was letting on. The absurd part of it was that Aliaga must have known that his friend would read his expression accurately. "How the world moves about in a series of pantomimes: we see what we want to see, we hear what pleases us, and all along, none of it really exists. . . ."

"Where are we going?" he asked. The driver looked back; he had instructions to take the Colonel to a militia headquarters near the Puerta del Sol. No, he did not know what it was about; he'd been sent to pick the Colonel up. That was all.

Carvalho sat back; it was stifling in the back seat, and he kept recalling the driver who had taken him out of Oviedo; the boy in the front seat looked much like him. One thing led to another, and he found himself thinking for the first time in weeks of Jaime Mercader. How pleased the boy must be to see the disorder into which the Government had fallen, so obviously a victim of just these vices that Mercader had decried so loudly, of that demon of compromise which had trapped the Colonel himself at Oviedo. "If he's still alive, he must feel vindicated by all this, and, damn him, he's entitled to it, I suppose. . . ."

The car turned down a street of pale tan stones and under a jumble of hastily strung phone wires, stopping at last in front of a brick building which had once been a storehouse for olive oil. Barrels of it still stood about, some open and going rancid.

He was directed inside to a small room at the back of the building. Inside were two officers he had never seen before and Lachine and Edmundo Tierres himself. On a bench in a corner, near the desk behind which Tierres was sitting, was an old woman, her head bent, clasped in open hands in the classic attitude of despair.

"Colonel . . . ," Tierres rose in a peculiarly official way. "I think we have something for you. . . ."

Lachine looked apprehensive. Whatever it was, he was clearly unsure himself. Carvalho glanced at the woman. She seemed familiar, but the Colonel could not see her face.

Tierres was speaking: the woman had been picked up by the militia while trying to get across the San Martín bridge, "with a suitcase full of . . . all sorts of things. These, for example . . ." He reached into a drawer, took out a bag, and emptied it on the tabletop: silverware, a Moorish goblet, and some jewelry. In the center of the pile was the mate to the bracelet Carvalho had picked up outside his daughter's bedroom. He reached for it, turned it over in his fingers as though it were burning.

He did not look at the woman. He was afraid of what he might see.

Lachine broke in: "She told the militiamen that she hadn't done anything wrong. She'd only taken these things from an enemy of the people, 'the man who had killed all the Anarchists in the north two years before.' She mentioned your name, and so . . ."

Carvalho got up and went over to the woman. He pushed her hands aside, brought her face up with a sharp jerk. The corners of her mouth were drawn down, her eyes bulging. It was Rosa, the housekeeper.

"You . . ."

She began to weep, her whole body shaking.

Tierres got up. "She'll tell you whatever you want to know. It may be something. Now, if you'll excuse me . . ."

Carvalho hardly knew what to say. Try as he might, he could not bring himself to be genuinely grateful to the man. He distrusted him, distrusted even this seeming generosity. How difficult it is, he thought, to keep one's instinctive, superficial judgments of people from preventing a comprehension of their real value.

"I have two daughters myself," Tierres said. "Believe me, I understand all of this. Good luck." He took the Colonel's hand. "I hope she knows something . . ."

Lachine sat on a wire chair and watched Tierres leave. One of the officers followed him.

Carvalho turned back to Rosa. She was staring at him, certain she was about to be shot.

"I didn't mean what I said. I had to say that or they would have . . ." She began to babble, yet under it all he sensed a cutting hatred he never had realized the woman harbored. She was lying to him just as she had lied to the *milicianos*. He wondered what her own "truth" really was.

"Pour her a glass of water," Carvalho said to the Lieutenant who had remained.

Once the woman had had a drink, she began to breathe in deep, lunging gasps, then slower, until she seemed to have gotten hold of herself.

"Now . . . nothing is going to happen to you," Carvalho said. "As long as you tell the truth. . . ."

"I would have given all of these things back, señor Colonel . . . I didn't understand about you. . . ."

"Forget about that; it's not important. It's Mercedes I want to know about. . . ."

She let go a long, stifled whine and covered her face again. The Colonel felt his chest tighten and Lachine, in turn, looked stricken. For a fleeting second, Carvalho had the impression that despite his impossible manner, his waspish tongue, and his fanatic politics, the Frenchman really cared . . . of all things, about a girl he had never even met . . . but the daughter of his friend, the Colonel thought . . .

He braced himself, asked once more, trying to sound calm.

She lowered her hands again and told him. In less than a minute, it was all there. She had seen almost all of it from the house across the street where she had run after Jaime Mercader had first entered the house.

Suddenly, he thought, there was something else, something he had seen on one of those mornings he had gone by to pass a few minutes with Captain Segurra at his emplacement of 75s . . . something he had seen through the field glasses Segurra had given him. He wracked his brain but could not think what it was.

"What's the matter with you, señor . . . ?" The woman made a rapid sign of the cross.

Lachine was halfway across the room with the water pitcher when Carvalho suddenly shook as though an electric current was ripping through his body. Of course . . . the north terrace. One bright, sparkling morning. There had been a clear view, before the bombardment had started. And he had noticed a wreck of a car on the terrace, the only vehicle out there besides a truck which had been disabled the very first day by the bombers from Madrid.

A Ford. The black Ford that Francisco Mercader had never learned to drive.

"Camille . . . come outside with me . . . please . . ." It was the first time that Carvalho had ever let his weakness show. He felt unable to keep control any longer. His mind was full of Blas Aliaga's warnings. Lachine took his arm, a puzzled look clouding his glasses, his damp forelock swinging like a pendulum over his forehead.

"Colonel . . . a moment. . . ." It was the Lieutenant. "What shall we do with the woman?"

"Let her go."

"Colonel?"

He turned. Lachine stepped away. "I said, let her go." A glint of light caught his eye; the bracelet on the table and the silverware and the chalice. He picked them up and threw them in the astonished Rosa's lap, all but the bracelet which he thrust onto her right arm.

"Tell your men, Lieutenant . . . tell them that she is not to leave this city. And tell them also that if they ever catch her without that bracelet on her arm, they are to shoot her on the spot. I want everyone to know . . . do you understand?"

Outside, Carvalho stood for a minute by the doorway of the house, his fists clenched, and his nails digging into his palms until the blood spurted. The pain, for some reason, made him feel better.

Lachine stared at him; "The Greeks, you remember, killed messengers who brought bad news. Such a thing I can understand . . . but why that?"

"I don't know myself," Carvalho said. "But just then, when we were inside, I hated her. It's such a strange sensation, Camille. I think that from this day on, I'm going to be more charitable toward men who do things out of blind hate. I'm going to pity them, Camille. . . ."

"Does that mean that you think that you yourself should be pitied now?"

"Perhaps," Colonel Carvalho said, but what he meant was, "Yes, before God, yes." For there was nothing else of value left but pity now.

The two men walked in silence past the car that had brought the Colonel from Dr. Aliaga's office. They had no need of it.

They walked up the Calle del Arrabal and toward the winding hill that led up to the Zoco and to the Alcázar itself.

AFTERNOON, SEPTEMBER 13: *The Alcázar*

IT WAS SETTLED: JAIME WOULD GO out that night with one of the raiding parties. They were to attempt a sortie in the direction of the old granary building and then pull back as soon as they had engaged the militia and drawn as many as they could into the fight. Meanwhile, a second party made up of the smallest men who could be found would crawl across the Riding School terrace and make their way down into the Calle de Carmen. There, insisted a Frenchman, one Isidore Clamagiraud, who had owned a bakery in Toledo, was a small building in which the Bank of Bilbao had stored tons of wheat which had been collected in repayment of loans. If the baker's story proved true, there would be sufficient there to feed the garrison for a month or more.

It seemed logical enough to Jaime. The only important thing was that Mercedes did not starve. He had come to the conclusion that it was better to do something, even if he was sure of failure, than to sit by passively, waiting for someone else to decide the hour of his death. A single thought had taken possession of him, that Mercedes would die first and that he would have to watch her die. He had envisioned the scene over and over again, in a thousand painful variations. If he let her die, he would be guilty of almost the same crime her father had committed, and he would live the rest of his life strangled by the same guilt. It was the exercise of will in the service of his beliefs that made a man, that was plain enough, not simply the formulation of his ideas. Wasn't Spain's agony entirely the fault of men like Colonel Carvalho, who had sat back and simply let things happen? Full of good ideas and good will, those men; but when it came to implementing those ideas, ah, that was another story. Did the Solers and the Barcenases honestly think that there would have been a revolt at all if the fat bottoms in Madrid had been able to maintain order? He'd been thinking about that too for a long time, ever since he had watched Selica Portillo's husband die on his knees in the Zocodover. It was strange that such a small, almost insignificant incident could serve so to marshal his thoughts.

He looked out over the courtyard, lifted his one-lensed binoculars, and scanned the upper edges of the dark walls, knowing he could see nothing but doing it just the same. It was already past sunset though he had no idea of the actual time. A few long red clouds floated across the deep sky catching the last rays of a sun already well below the horizon. Under the arcades, clusters of bearded, grimy men waited, slouching as though from an intolerable weariness. Their rifles stood at careless angles beside them. Some of the men wore the pillbox cap of the Civil Guard, others the torn glengarries of the *Regulares*. Still others were civilians, dressed in a combination of street clothes and military gear that made them look like South American guerrillas. One man even wore a conquistador's helmet taken from the military museum. There was Corporal Santiago with he jet-black hair and his incongruous red beard, and old Mununga, called *El Chino* because of his sallow complexion, who had no business going on raiding parties in the first place but whose heart would have been broken if he had been refused permission.

Without thinking, Jaime leaned his Mauser against the wall at an angle exactly like that of the man next to him and assumed the man's same slouch as well. There were a few fuming torches in the yard and a mule-fat lamp cast an orange light in one corner where a few boxes of ammunition had been broken open for distribution. Jaime had taken all the ammunition he could carry, and his pockets were stuffed with 7mm cartridges for his rifle. He was glad not to be touching the rifle for a while; it held, for him, a frightening fascination. On the butt was stamped the model number: "1893" and the place of origin: "*fábrica,* Oviedo."

A cadet walked by, trying to saunter, but it was obvious that he was afraid. Jaime thought, "It's his first time out at night," then realized that it was his first time out at night as well. But, then, he thought bitterly, *he* was a veteran. He'd shot at men in the railroad cars, watched men die before firing squads. That was what separated him from the cadet who was now eyeing him warily as though he had been caught in some embarrassing act. The boy's name was Oswaldo Perez, and Jaime could see the shiny gold *duro* that he kept tucked in his left ear. Oswaldo Perez kept it there, so he said, "In case there's something I want to buy on the outside." He had a terrible hunger for chocolate, and the first thing he was going to do when he got out of the Alcázar was go to the café on the north side of the Zoco, if it was still there, and buy a huge cup of chocolate. He didn't want to be caught without money, and so he carried the *duro* in his ear to make sure.

Perez had gotten hold of a pistol and had thrust it through his belt, pirate style. He went on by, heading toward a small group of boys, what was left of the formation of cadets who had marched down the Cuesta on July twenty-first. They had been so sure of themselves that morning. Would anyone ever be so sure of himself again?

Jaime had lost a great deal of the faith he had had in most things; it had drained out of him like water from a leaky barrel over the last few years. "The only thing we can be certain of is that we can be certain of nothing." His father had called him a cynic for saying that but, after all, wasn't it true?

Actually, there were only three things he was still sure of. First, that his father was dead; Soler's expression had told him that more clearly than any words could have expressed it. He did not want to know how Francisco had died. If it had been in some brutal, senseless way, for no reason or by accident, then it would be unbearable. Thus, it was just as well that Soler had not spoken to him. Secondly, and just as surely, he was certain that his mother had somehow survived. How he knew this, he could not say, but he would have wagered his life on it and that of Mercedes besides. Xaviera, the cook, had always sworn that Jaime's mother could divine the future, cast spells, tell fortunes. Perhaps some of that primitive sorcery had been passed on to him along with his mother's dark color and hawk's nose. Finally, he also knew that if he lived long enough, he would find Enrique Carvalho again, on the "outside" and that they would confront each other once and for all, false priest and novice betrayed, and he would demand the answers that were his right. That they would both most likely die before any answers were given, that he knew as well; the thought comforted him. He could die far more easily without having gotten his answers than he could without having asked the questions that plagued him.

He thought of Mercedes and the few words they'd had an hour before when he'd told her that he was going out on the raid. For a while she'd tried to dissuade him. He had answered quietly but with determination, always saying the same thing. "Don't you see, it's for you," and then he would look her up and down, and she could read in his eyes the pain that seeing her wasted body caused him.

"No, it's just the opposite," she said after a long while, allowing herself a smile of resignation and a tenderness that he did not quite understand. "It's for you, and that's why I'll let you do it."

Even though she knew it was true, she was sorry that she had said it. If he thought that it was for her, then anything that he might suffer because of what he was doing would be more bearable, but if he was risking his life only to satisfy himself, what then?

He had thought about what she had said a great deal; he was still thinking about it now, the idea mixed up in his head with blurred visions of the Zoco and of a nightmare figure with a bristling beard who might have been her father but somehow was not. "Is it really for myself then? She's right . . . in so many things." He shifted the cartridges in his pocket but could not come to a conclusion. Then he started to laugh, his predicament reminded him of that of Sergeant Gaiferos who turned up two or three times a day at the "radio room" to ask Amado Leorza if he had heard any news about the lottery. Gaiferos had four tickets which he'd bought just before the uprising. "One of them's bound to be a winner, you'll see," he kept saying, but he always seemed relieved when Amado Leorza shook his head and delivered his usual speech about the radio being in order "soon, but not now." Jaime would ask him what he would do if one of his tickets was a winner, and Sergeant Gaiferos would turn red in the face. "Well, it would be quite a thing to win, wouldn't it? I'll bet you never had a winner."

Sometimes it was better not to know anything for certain, Jaime thought. But sometimes they wouldn't let a man do that; they forced him, insisted . . .

It had been more than two weeks since Anton Vitolyn had last been summoned to Major Punto's office. They had left him alone and he had survived, just as he knew he would.

Now this.

"That's him, all right," Sergeant Ortiz had said. Vitolyn stared at the man, trying to remember his face. "I've never seen him before in my life." Yet there was something familiar about his silhouette, his bulk, even his broad hands with their stubby black fingernails which he trimmed with a rock he kept in his trouser pocket. Vitolyn was sure that it was the man Sebastián Gil had been complaining about, the one who had been following him.

The Major blew a smoke ring. Where had he gotten a cigarette? Vitolyn was in mortal agony at the sight of the smoldering ash. The cigarette, though, was not real at all but only a "Martel" paper wrapped around crushed acacia leaves which the Major pretended to smoke for the precise purpose of upsetting men he was questioning who had been without a cigarette for a month.

The Major seemed interested not at all in the fact that Vitolyn had stolen a can of meat, despite Sergeant Ortiz' constant interruptions and mutterings about "food for the children." It was as if the Major discounted the possibility that the Sergeant could possibly be interested in little children and was using the incident merely as an excuse to take out his frustration with Gil on someone more immediately available. "So be it." Major Punto would use the matter as an excuse too, a reason to reopen the whole subject of Vitolyn's identity and his reason for being in Roig's room.

The session lasted over an hour. Vitolyn was forced to stand the whole time, trying to be afraid and thereby to activate his defenses but achieving only a cold, unproductive emptiness. He looked about the room to find a mirror in which he could study his face. Finding no such mirror he began studying Ortiz' face, Major Punto, and the lean, handsome Captain who came into the room now and then to see how things were progressing and to look at his wristwatch and announce the time. Finally, the Major pushed aside the third of the fake cigarettes he had lit since beginning the interview. Vitolyn was no longer fooled; he had noticed that the Major never inhaled, only blew the smoke out of his mouth and even then did so with a faint, barely disguised grimace.

Punto looked at his watch.

"If it wasn't that I have more important things to do," he said enigmatically, bringing the interview to a close, "we could keep at this for a long time, don't you think? Well, you must be tired, so . . ."

"We're finished?" Vitolyn could not understand, just as he could not understand why, in the midst of a siege at the end of which they were all surely to be killed, the Major persisted in his stately game of inquisition.

Ortiz spoke up. "I could keep him occupied while you're gone, Major. Who knows, maybe he plays cards, or dominoes. . . ."

"You're going with Lieutenant Tamayo's group, or did you forget?"

Then Vitolyn was out in the corridor again, quite free, watching the Major, the Sergeant, and the Captain, who had come in one more time to announce the hour, as they walked away down the hall.

Vitolyn found that he was hardly disturbed at all by the rekindling of Punto's interest in the Roig affair. The outbuildings had fallen, and the Alcázar was being more and more tightly ringed by government militia each day. Two or three attacks between sunrise and sunset were not uncommon. The tempo was picking up and sooner or later, Vitolyn was positive, one of the assaults would penetrate the walls. Then none of this would make any difference. It was, in a way, comforting to know that.

No, what did disturb him was precisely that lack of feeling he had noticed the day he had permitted Zipser to let him escape and which had grown, swollen in him until it had pre-empted all normal human emotion. After all, he was an intelligent man and knew well enough when he should feel guilty. With mounting horror, he saw himself more and more as a "specimen," an experimental animal. "You put a mouse in a maze, thusly, watch him run about. Can't get out, poor creature, but he doesn't realize it." He was the mouse, but he was also the psychology professor standing there and stroking his goatee, breathing on his pince-nez, and wiping the fog off the glass on his smock. The terror he felt was precisely from not feeling frightened. A curious reaction. He began mentally to compose a book on the subject as he descended the stairs. He could see the title page: *Absence of Emotion Seen as a Positive Emotion in Itself*, by Anton Vitolyn. But he could not get past the first line: "One must be careful not to mistake the anesthesia produced by an excess of true fear for the numbness which comes from the realization that the strongest stimuli, such as extreme fright, overwhelming guilt, etc., actually produce *no reaction at all*."

The only thing he felt was hunger. It was odd how the smell of boiling mule-flesh could cause his salivary glands to function now, where only six weeks before, he would have retched at the thought of eating such food.

He reached the foot of the stairs and entered the dining chamber. It was as it had always been before. The room was filled with whispers. Heads were bent in monkish solemnity over empty plates. No one looked up.

Through the penumbra of lamplight, the trestle extended, thirty feet of rough boards laid on sawhorses, fading into the shadows at the end of the room. Tin plates slithered and clanked; the teeth-shattering scrape of spoon against pannikin. A corporal of the Guard in an apron who stood partly wreathed in smoke eddying from beneath a slowly swinging kettle seemed to care enough to look about, as though he were measuring the hunger of the people in the room against the remains of the "Alcázar stew" in his kettle. He rocked the kettle with the end of a long iron spoon to keep it on its slow, pendulous course and tried not to look inside too often.

Vitolyn picked up a pannikin and went over to the kettle. It seemed as though nothing more could be extracted from the iron pot but, somehow, a strip of meat no longer and no wider than his finger was found and laid in his kit. Vitolyn went back to the trestle, found a place and sat down. He had forgotten about the roll entirely. No one had offered it to him, and he had been too preoccupied even to think about it.

His stomach throbbed, and yet he could not bring himself to eat the strip of meat on his plate; he knew that to eat it would simply be to intensify his hunger.

Without thinking, he popped the meat into his mouth, first wadding it into a ball. He chewed slowly, grinding the fibers.

Thank God, Gil was not there, he thought. He could not shake off the idea that, somehow, Gil knew about the tunnel. The subject of escape had been creeping with increasing frequency into their conversations during the past week. Gil was prodding, testing, trying to find out something. Vitolyn reacted angrily; if Gil wanted to get out so badly, why had he come in the first place? Gil smiled gently; how was he to have known that things would turn out this way, that Umberto Reyles would go mad, that the Major would persecute him so? "Then desert, leave, there's no one stopping you," Vitolyn had shot back. "But how?" Gil shrugged as though the answer was obvious and the question meant merely to annoy. "Why," Vitolyn answered, "every day someone deserts, the soldiers desert, the cadets desert, even the Guards desert . . . Two yesterday . . . six last week . . . five today. If you're so set on escaping, why don't you do as they do . . . simply leave?"

"The opportunity, Anton, where is the opportunity to be found? Oh, believe me, I've studied all of this very carefully. What you don't realize, my friend, is that every man who has escaped this place has had the opportunity to do so."

"They made their opportunities because they wanted to go." Vitolyn sensed that he was being led into a trap.

"No, in each case," Gil corrected him, "and you can check this easily, as I have . . . the man escaped while on a patrol or in the midst of a skirmish outside the walls. It's that simple, Anton. To *get* out, you've got to *be* out already. And I'll never have that chance. Who would put a rifle in these hands . . . these . . . and send me out to kill someone? No, I'm too old and helpless and, besides . . . you know . . . the one with the steel teeth, Ortiz, my watchdog . . . so, you see, even if it weren't for him, how would I ever get out? I'm no soldier and it's only soldiers who have escaped. The rest of us are prisoners . . ."

Vitolyn had reflected; it was true. He had long since come to the same conclusion. Thus the tunnel was the only way out. All the more reason for keeping it secret. "Then we must stay put, mustn't we?" Vitolyn had said.

"Unless . . ."

"Unless what?"

"Nothing," Gil had replied lapsing into a watchful silence.

Vitolyn looked about him, to make sure Gil was not, after all, somewhere close by. "What a dangerous man. Why can't I rid myself of him? Because I need him, someone weaker than myself, that's why. Oh, what a miserable person you are, Anton. . . ." Gil no longer spoke to anyone else. He kept to himself, emerging only to follow Vitolyn, to trail him into the dining chamber, to accost him in the hallways when he was alone. They were so alike, and Vitolyn understood this clearly enough. After a time, a grudging, secret respect had begun to emerge; perhaps the man was guilty after all, perhaps he had killed the Guard Colonel. Else how could he have survived such repeated questioning? Gil had been in the Major's office five or six times now. Only the truly guilty have the strength to resist so; the innocent quickly find hidden, surrogate guilts and will confess to anything because they know that, no matter what, they are really guilty. That, Vitolyn had discovered a long time before, in Austria.

He tried to put such thoughts out of his head. Gil was not there. A blessed relief. And his hunger was ferocious.

The man opposite him on the other side of the table had unwittingly dropped a thumb-sized strip of meat. Vitolyn's eyes narrowed. He began to reach out again. His fingers moved only slightly along the dry boards, though it seemed to him that each finger had puffed up ten times its size. What a disgrace to see himself behaving in such a way, but what could he do? No one was watching him. Silence, only heavy breathing, a clink of tin forks and pannikins.

Finally, painfully, he succeeded in arresting the movement of his fingers. The slimy morsel was still inches away. His fingernails seemed to glow a bright pink . . . strange . . . his fingernails. He'd hardly noticed them in weeks. The lamplight danced on the white half-moons.

Everyone could see his fingers, he thought.

As he watched, puzzled, the muscles of his arm began to tighten, and his fingers moved closer and closer to the fragment of meat.

At that moment the man who had dropped the scrap opened his eyes, looked down and saw what had happened. His mouth twisted in a half-smile: regret, polite embarrassment as though he was sorry for the trouble, the temptation his carelessness had caused. He reached out at once to reclaim his food, at once lifting the tiny brown strip to his mouth. As it vanished between the man's jaws, Vitolyn stiffened and he rocked back on the bench.

He rose suddenly and stumbled out of the room. No one but the man across the table had taken any notice of him.

A little way up the stairwell, he stopped and held himself against the wall. The air was damp, and he kept seeing the body of the hunchback under the stones and kept smelling the faintly chemical odor of the water in the swimming bath. The idea of the tunnel, barely wide enough for a man to crawl through still terrified him. His fear of closed-in spaces, of closets and barrels, of hollow walls and stand-up cells made him dizzy. Yet it was a way out. "Apply some of your professorial detachment," he told himself. "Look at this as an experiment. Yes, we understand all that about claustrophobia, but here *is a way out,* and you won't take it. A way to get out, to escape the Major Puntos and the Sebastián Gils and the comrades in their room below, to make a new start for yourself. More cautiously this time. No false 'identification papers.' It's wartime now. A man's papers get lost. A bombing raid, that's all. Lucky to have escaped with your life. 'Papers? Well, yes, I had them, but that was before the planes came over.' " He was just an Austrian tourist caught in someone else's war, that was all. "I want to go . . . where? . . . to Portugal. Yes, there I can pick up a boat to Bremen or well, it doesn't matter, just a boat to take me home."

He began to visualize Cabo da Roca again and to feel the salt spray of the Atlantic. But the odor that had thus kindled his imagination was simply the damp of the lowest cellar of the Alcázar. Without knowing quite how he had done it, he had been going down rather than up and now stood at the bottom landing, near the entrance to the swimming baths.

Night, September 13: *The Alcázar*

Major Punto leaned against the balcony railing, his clasped hands extending over the edge, his eyes fastened not on the men gathering in the courtyard below but on the unscarred night sky above him. A net full of stars hung between the four ruined towers of the Alcázar, and he himself, conceit of conceits, the astonished fisherman, overwhelmed and grateful to the point of weeping over the richness of his catch.

He had been angry but that anger was now spent. A deep, drugged composure had taken hold of him, his mood touched with self-reproach. He had had no right to feel so impatient with the other officers. It was necessary, of course, to plan everything carefully, to balance exactly and time the two raids that were to go out that night, the one across the Riding School terrace and the other, as a diversionary tactic, down the Calle de Comercio to the edge of the Zoco. In the distance he could hear the sound of phonographs playing everything from Catalan songs sung in Vendrell's unmistakable, nasal voice, and Andalusian guitar music to North American dance tunes and Carlos Gardel's tangos; a strange cacophony, but somehow comforting to the Major, a mirror to his own confusion, confirming and excusing it at the same time.

Maps, charts, pointers moving over walls, the endless drone of instructions. Watches synchronized as best they could synchronize them, sweep second hands; all very precise. A sudden darkening of temper. Why? He had no idea. At least he had been able to control himself; no one had noticed. "A little dizziness, Carlos, it'll pass . . . thanks. All I need is some air." Attacks of dizziness were quite common now. Sometimes it was hunger, sometimes the chemical fumes that kept leaking up into the tunnels below ground, or the constant smoke from the fires that surrounded the fortress.

Behind him, from the doorway which opened onto the corridor down which he had just come, issued a low murmur of voices. He tried to project a vision of the scene against the night sky; a dozen officers, gathered together in the Colonel's office: Captain Herrera with his newly acquired facial tic; Major Ollivara with a shoulder wound that caused him to grimace every so often with an unexpected pain; Lieutenant Tamayo, stiff as wax with the effort that it cost him to stay on his feet; Rincón, also a Lieutenant, with his maps and a pointed divider thrust perilously in his breast pocket, one prong searching for his heart. Wan-faced, all of them, pacing behind the oak-ribbed door, their faces runneled with shadows, their eyes reflecting the orb of the single hurricane lamp that spread its cheerless apricot glow about the room. Suddenly, he had felt as though he were being asphyxiated, not by the atmosphere, but by their talk, the empty expressions, the vacant eyes. "It's not their fault," he thought, but could not help himself and succumbed at once to a sense of estrangement which angered him in a way he had never experienced before.

A phrase passed through his mind, though he could not remember its source: "Communing as conspirators with their dreams of history . . ." He smiled at his own pomposity. "They're treating this as though it were a formal military exercise, not the insanity that it is . . . they poke about their maps, draw lines, discuss barriers and counterattacks as if they were students in my tactics classes. . . ." There was nothing more frightening to Major Punto than to see men conducting themselves in complete disregard for the absurdity of their situation.

He had looked about, desperate to discover one man among them all whose eyes betrayed any real understanding. "Not a one," he thought, resentfully. . . . "We've become so *used* to things. . . . Man's most inescapable curse . . . that he can become *used* to anything." He paused. "I should write that down . . . somewhere . . . ," and he smiled at himself again.

But now, all the anger had flowed out of him, leaving him filled only with an exhausted self-reproach. He was no better than they were and perhaps much, much worse. Just an hour or so before hadn't he been on the point of brutalizing the foolish Austrian? And before that, during the afternoon, he had done the same thing to Gil, a man, moreoever, whom he had known ever since he had come to Toledo. To make matters worse, he had not the slightest belief that Gil had had anything to do with the death of Colonel Venegas.

So . . . then, what excuse was there for him, Manuel Punto, to be acting in such a way? He had questioned Gil four . . . or was it five? . . . perhaps six times now and taken pleasure too in Gil's continuing deterioration. And to make matters worse, he knew that if Gil gave him the slightest justification, he would turn him over to Reyles and there would be a trial and then . . .

No, there was no reason for him to feel superior to the other officers and to scorn their refusal to acknowledge his reality. He was, if anything, worse than they and a hundred times more to blame for what he did because of the very acuity of his self-knowledge.

He looked down over the balustrade, into the debris-littered yard. Steel and shattered stone lay everywhere. In his mind, Punto tried to turn the looming shape of a twisted beam into a tree, a dark configuration of rubble into a hillock of flowers. "No poplars or plane trees, no fern, not a whiff of orange . . . only this. . . ." For a second, he read in the curled outlines of a fallen girder the profile of a thickly burdened olive tree; then the charred steel reasserted itself, driving into his imagination an awesome presentiment of destruction. He passed his hand across his forehead, was surprised to find that he was not wearing a cap. His head felt cold although the air had not yet turned chill.

High above, the beam of a searchlight scythed through the sky, gathering momentum as it curved past the mid-September moon, then slowing again as though reluctant to return to earth. He followed the beam with his eyes; the light seemed to smother and disappear as it fell somewhere in the direction of the Sierra de Gredos. "Perhaps," he thought, "it has even touched my 'refuge,' " and he wrinkled his lips in a thin, counterfeit smile, recalling the tiny shack he had glimpsed so often through his binoculars. It lay in a sea of parched, yellow grasses at the foot of a low black mountain whose name he did not know and which he could not identify on the map in Colonel Moscardó's office. A thin trickle of smoke rose high each morning into the lambent air. He had carried on imaginary dialogues with the unknown occupant, thanking him for keeping the shack in good repair, for filling it with stores and provisions, for looking after the well and the garden patch. It would be waiting for him, a week, a month from now, when he walked out of the Alcázar and out of Toledo forever.

In the shifting white light, the broken towers and walls of the Alcázar seemed as dreamlike as a lunar landscape. Thin knives of stone rose, silver and indistinct. Walls dissolved into the lowering sky and over the whole now hung a fine, opalescent haze which cut off from clear view the redeeming sight of the stars. Major Punto shook his head and glanced at his watch; it was almost time. The silence was filled with a hundred furtive sounds: the click of a rifle belt, a sneeze, a cough, a cat's dismal complaint. He listened, surprised. In that elegiac calm, the simple act of buckling on his holster seemed a sacrilege. Gently as though stealing out of a sleeping child's room, he abandoned the balcony and descended again to the courtyard.

If he survived it all, what then? Jaime thought. What was the next impossible choice that awaited him? The easiest way was to die and be spared the consequences of any choice at all. But God constantly threatened a man with survival and, with survival, came the worst punishment of all, the continuance of conscience. Sooner or later, he too would have to decide whose throat to go for. Worse than the wild animals of the forests: "Even the wolves know better. The loser always offers up his throat, but the victor never kills."

A soft whistle interrupted his thoughts. Two Civil Guard in shredded uniforms, one with a bandaged arm, went by carrying a Hotchkiss machine gun between them; the sight struck a painful echo. Two men had run just that way with just such a weapon across the street in front of the Oviedo railroad station.

Two more men followed them, weighed down to the ground by a dozen bandoleers of ammunition. Everything was ready. The patrol formed up rapidly. There was no reluctance, yet no enthusiasm either. Suddenly, all Jaime could think of was the fact that they were only a decoy, that the driver Barrera was even then preparing to crawl across the esplanade and bring back sacks of wheat while he, Jaime Mercader, was simply offering his body to be shot at. He had seen a film once, a short subject at the *Cine Delicias* in Madrid; it showed how ranchers in Brazil drove their cattle across a river infested with piranha. One old cow would be driven upstream and its flanks slashed; then the drovers would force it into the water. In a moment, the smell of blood would attract thousands of the razor-toothed little fish and, wild-eyed, not understanding what was happening to it, the cow would be eaten alive, stripped of its flesh in minutes while it sank in a frothing whirlpool of its own blood. Jaime would never forget the cow's eyes, which stared pitifully about, hurt and full beyond comprehension with unjustly suffered pain. The only difference between himself and that poor dumb beast would be that he would know why, when the bullets ate him alive on the Calle de Comercio. Yet he had volunteered to go. He could just as easily have asked to go with the other group but for some reason he did not. No, that wasn't true; the other group was made up only of small men. He was too large. They would not have allowed him to go.

Another whistle and the men moved forward.

A door under the arcade opened, and the men of the patrol entered the building as cautiously and as noiselessly as though they were already outside. Passing down a long corridor, they came first to a short flight of stairs, descended, then stood facing a thick door which led through the outer wall to the north esplanade. They regrouped in silence before the door, stood about, barely visible one to the other although they were separated only by inches. A man could tell how close he was to the next in line only by the sound of his breathing.

Then the door began to open, slowly, on hinges greased with precious mule-fat. A narrow opening appeared, just wide enough to allow a single man to pass through—a line the height of a man, spattered with stars almost blinding in their brilliance. At the head of the line, Major Punto tapped the first man on the shoulder and guided him out, then another and another. They went out automatically, each in an identical crouch, with the weary precision of men who have gone into death's presence with exactly those same motions so often that they have become immune to their implications.

The men were all there, and each man was looking up, amazed, into the star-bright sky. All at once, men who had for weeks seen nothing but the shattered walls of the Alcázar and the dark curves of its countless tunnels, found themselves beneath an open, overwhelming sky, the whole vault of it coruscating with stars as far in any direction as they could see. The young blinked at it, the older men shut their eyes and averted their heads; it was not for them. It reminded them too keenly of their own mortality.

In the lower dark, pierced only by the light of the stars and the wavering glow of secret, buried fires, Jaime could see nothing clearly. The guards appeared as one long row of indistinguishable shapes, swaddled in their coats, their flat caps, like rows of squat bottles.

Jaime heard a distant whisper: "Remember, the streets are mined now. Be careful . . . pass it down the line. If the paving looks like it's been torn up . . ."

The men moved forward. Jaime dropped against the wall, pressed himself next to the last man in the file. He could feel the heat of the man's body. Pistol unholstered, Major Punto skittered by on half-folded legs, graceful, almost elegant, like some strange species of giant insect.

"Remember . . . the streets are mined now . . ."

At a half crouch, the file moved down along the road. The street ran downhill, narrow walls leaning in over the cobbles, each window a sandbagged eye, black and soulless. Still no firing, not even the muted pop of a pistol shot.

At the end of the street, the Arca de la Sangre hulked like a guillotine, opening onto the Zoco.

Below him, a torch cast rippling orange figures on the walls. Vitolyn closed his eyes, felt the nausea surge up. He flung his hands to his mouth, fought it, found that he had nothing to vomit. In the black circle of his shuttered vision, he saw many things, processions, candles, sheets of white linen waving like sails, the faces of Paco the hunchback, old August Zipser with his crumpled leather cap, Helmut Baumgartner's mustache, floating like a pair of wings, even the face of Sebastián Gil, all green and overgrown with moss.

He wavered on the steps, hands still at his mouth, gagging.

Gobs of damp plaster came loose from the walls under his nails. The thrum of distant shellfire was audible through the walls, through earth rich with the pulverized bones of countless Moorish governors and Arab nobles.

He passed through a low-arched doorway. Beyond it lay the swimming baths, the pool and the shower-heads, like pincers, in a line above it. The stench was heavy, almost unbearable. His eyes passed along the flat stones piled about the edge of the pool. The hunchback was under one of those piles. The pistol was . . . where? Somewhere along the edge of the pool? . . . or at the bottom? He could not remember. Hadn't the hunchback dropped it when he had fallen into the water? Vitolyn searched for a few moments, on his knees, until his hands were bleeding from the sharp stones, but he could not find the pistol. He rose, knowing that his searching for the pistol was only an excuse, a reason to put off opening the tunnel-mouth and crawling in.

The long chamber was lit by a torch rammed into a pile of rocks at the far end, just above the pool's edge. The burial party had left it there.

The water had now been entirely replaced by slabs of rock which were almost up to the four-foot marker at the shallow end. Dozens of corpses had been interred under the slabs during the previous weeks. The *picadero*, too vulnerable to the flame-throwers and grenades of the *milicianos*, had closed its gates to the dead. The courtyard was too hard; digging graves there had proven impossible. Here, at least, a few feet of privacy remained to each man who rested beneath the slabs. The pool was already half full, the most recent bodies deposited so hastily that arms and legs and patches of clothing were still visible between the stones covering them, like torn gray blankets stiff with cold.

Vitolyn swayed dizzily as he tried to support himself on the unsteady railing. It moved with his body, and he thought again of the hunchback Orsuña who was watching him from behind a pile of rocks. The dead could see through stone. Zipser could see through mountains, through the fabric of whole countries. César Roig had only to pierce a wooden closet door and a few walls to make out his murderer. The hunchback had no more than a few feet of shale through which to see.

Some tools had been left in a corner by the gravediggers; a pickax and a few shovels, three crowbars and a paraffin lantern. Vitolyn chose the crowbar, hooked it onto his belt and lowered himself into the pool. He tried to keep from looking toward the depth marker below which the tunnel was hidden; he could not bear to look at it and he knew that if he did finally enter the tunnel, he would only do so with his eyes closed.

He wrapped a rag around his face, trying to close out the smell but succeeded only in giving himself the appearance of a bandit in a North American Western film.

The slabs rocked and tipped underfoot as he advanced toward the shallow end of the pool. He had a horror of tipping up a slab too far and revealing the face of a dead soldier below it. If the eyes were open, were looking at him. . . . He walked more carefully, like an acrobat on a wire.

The depth marker. How deep did the tunnel beyond it go? What if it ended somewhere in a destroyed building, a pile of rubble, in an inferno? Bombers had been over Toledo almost every day and the artillery had been blasting the surrounding streets and dependent buildings for weeks. A million fires smouldered beneath the debris. Once in the tunnel, he might be baked alive, suffocated, smoked like a sausage.

Good . . . he was feeling fear, the precursor of guilt. He shook so that he could barely hold on to the crowbar. His hands were bleeding.

"Good," he thought again, his mind's voice screaming, "good . . . good . . . you *feel* something now, Anton. Feel it, *feel* it, strong . . ."

The torchlight paled, grew feeble from lack of air. The smell was almost solid within the chamber, as he tore at the tiles below the depth marker, pried the stones back with the iron bar. He was, in his own way, preparing to bury himself, with the same tools that the soldiers had used to bury their own dead. It seemed right; he was as dead as the corpses under the stones.

"Is this yours? Do you want it?" A voice . . . his own, he thought . . . and paid no attention to it . . . went on pulling at the stones.

Again: "Do you want this?"

He turned. Sebastián Gil was standing there at the opposite end of the pool, near the archway, holding the hunchback's pistol in his hand, the butt toward Vitolyn, the barrel pointed at his own chest.

"Good, I'm glad you heard me. I was afraid . . . ," Gil said.

Vitolyn tore at the mask over his face as though he would be unable to speak with it in place. Even in the quavery light, he could see how pained Gil seemed to be. Almost embarrassed.

"I don't want you here. Go away . . ." he cried.

"Is it a tunnel?" Gil asked, ignoring his protest, still holding the pistol out, pointed at his own chest. It was the hunchback's pistol, no question about it. Yet Gil seemed to be offering it to him, not threatening him with it.

"What are you doing . . . Anton . . . ?" Gil asked hesitantly.

Vitolyn shifted the crowbar in his left hand, expecting to see the shadow of Ortiz, the Civil Guard, slide through the archway at any moment. In a way, he was quite relieved. Of course Ortiz would be there, and it would be unnecessary even to decide whether to crawl into the tunnel at all.

"It's a way out, a tunnel. That's what it is."

"Why didn't you tell me before?" Gil asked reproachfully. He was halfway down the pool now, still holding the pistol in that impossible way, as though about to commit suicide. His voice was full of reproach. Why hadn't Vitolyn told him before? Didn't they share each other's suffering? Didn't that sharing entitle each of them to whatever good the other might find as well?

"It's no use," Vitolyn said suddenly. "I'm not going. I can't."

"Don't say that. It isn't really a tunnel, is it?"

"How should I know? I haven't been through it, you fool, can't you see? Maybe it's a tunnel and maybe it isn't."

"Then we should find out, shouldn't we?"

"You go." Vitolyn had a strange feeling of *déjà vu*. It was almost the same scene as the day before on the parapet. Was he to go first and see that the way was clear, Gil to follow after? "No," Vitolyn said again. Loosened stones suddenly fell away behind him, and the tunnel mouth gaped open, just wide enough for a man to crawl into. Acrid gray fumes escaped the opening and curled slowly toward the ceiling.

"I don't understand you," Gil was saying. "You weren't going to share this with me either, were you?" The pistol had gotten turned around in his hand. "I wanted to give you this, you see . . . but . . . if you won't share with me . . . please, I don't know what to do with this . . . I might hurt you . . ."

The pistol was pointed directly at him; Vitolyn raised the crowbar.

"Please," Gil said again, very softly.

Ortiz did not materialize; the torchlight wavered. It would be hours before they came down to bury the day's dead.

"Please?"

Gil clambered down over the pool's edge, still pointing the pistol at him. The first stone upon which he trod tipped up revealing a gray face covered with the wild, frizzy beard that grows on corpses after death. Vitolyn gasped.

Vitolyn could not look at the dead man, nor at Gil. He turned his back, threw the crowbar away, drew in a breath, and forced his head and shoulders into the tunnel opening.

As he began to pull himself forward on his elbows, trying at the same time to breath very slowly so as not to choke on the fumes, he heard Gil's voice very close behind him: "I'll help you when we get to the other side, you'll see. I'll help you."

NIGHT, SEPTEMBER 13: *Toledo*

ACROSS THE MOONLIT TERRACE of the Riding School, the men of the sortie crawled, silent as caterpillars under the clouds. They moved slowly, one after the other, climbing up the embankment at the north end of the terrace and passing with a ritual grace across the blackened ground that opened between the embankment and the ruins of the Riding School. Each man was pulling a sack of wheat alongside of him. The last man had just emerged from the roof of the house where they had found the wheat stores, exactly where the baker Isidore Clamagiraud had said they would be.

Barrera paused as a burst of machine-gun fire resounded somewhere beyond the west wall, followed by the chunk of a grenade. Then a clatter of rifles and pistols. He pressed himself into the ground. The sack of wheat weighed heavily against the muscles of his arms. Letting go of the rope for a second, he dug instinctively at the flinty ground. Never before had he been so conscious of the expanse of stars.

More grenades. A Very light soared into the sky, exploding pink against the clouds. Then silence.

4 3 1

Barrera worked his legs slowly and painfully back into a crouching position and began to move forward again. How difficult it was to move so slowly . . . he had never realized.

Twenty yards ahead of him, the next man in the chain had reached the foot of the ramp leading up to the esplanade. Twenty yards behind him, another man struggled along with two sacks. "Hey . . . don't you drop anything and make a noise," Barrera thought. He pulled the sack into his arms, half-carried, half-dragged it. "Please, man . . ."

The house had been empty, forgotten. Against the walls, sacks of wheat were stacked. Threshed wheat. Neatly bagged and marked with red tags bearing the name of the debtor and the number of his loan. In front of the house, the Calle de Carmen shambled past on its way to the Tagus; across the street, dozens of *milicianos* lay asleep, dreaming of places more pleasant than Toledo, completely oblivious to what was happening right under their noses.

Barrera turned his head. Very far off he could see the last man silently slide the tiles back over the hole they had made in the white roof, then start up the embankment.

Another flare arched overhead, spraying streamers of phosphorus into the sky. The men pressed against the ground behind their sacks. A line of machine-gun fire from the Santo Cruz swung lazily over the terrace like a sudden summer rain, kicking up tiny puffs of dirt. It lingered among the twisted acacia trees which dangled, uprooted by the railing, then suddenly passed, rattling away into the quiet night.

The men began to drag their sacks forward again until they had reached the charred skeleton of the *picadero*. Others were waiting for them there, the riflemen who had covered the sortie.

Hands lifted the sack from Barrera's shoulders. He shrugged and rubbed his nose with his knuckle. Looking back, he saw that there were only three more men on the terrace. Everyone else had reached the Alcázar safely. He tried to straighten up, but could not; striking at his knees he forced himself into an upright posture and shuffled painfully into the building.

He brushed the door with his shoulders, sidled by a barrier, found himself back in the dimly lit room in which the sortie had first gathered. Men stood about, hovering protectively over the lines of sacks they had just brought back. Nearby, a mule-fat drip sputtered on a table. Through the door came other hunched figures, bringing the last of the booty.

The Captain with the name almost like his own was there, marking down figures on a pad of paper, his handsome face black with cork all except for his forehead which glistened in the lamplight. He seemed sad, pensive. Barrera went up to him.

"Ah, it's you," said Cristóbal Herrera. "Were you out there?" He knew Barrera, just as the driver knew him, because of his name. Once he had said, "We could make a good juggling act for the Circo Price, don't you think? Herrera and Barrera?"

Barrera nodded in response. "Were you out too, Captain?"

"Yes, but I found I couldn't carry one of the sacks. It seems I'm weaker than I thought I was."

Esteban Barrera shook his head. "The smaller ones like me last longer, that's all."

Captain Herrera made another entry as a sack was deposited at the end of the line. "I don't like being weak," he said.

"Don't worry about it."

Another sack of grain was brought in. Herrera made his entry. "Do you know," he said, "all of this makes me a little sad."

"Oh?"

"Now, we won't starve. Do you know what that means? We'll be able to hold out indefinitely."

The room filled with the smell of wheat. One of the sacks was open at the top and Barrera plunged his hand in. The wheat trickled over his fingers, cool and reassuring. He crunched a few grains between his teeth. A good, clean taste. He spit out the husks and leaned against the edge of the table trying to ease his cramped legs.

A few officers came in and exchanged words with Herrera who handed them the list he had made. The last of the men on the sortie arrived, the thick-necked Guard who had carried the crowbar they had used to pry the tiles from the roof. His pockets were bulging with wheat he had scooped up from the floor of the storehouse.

As Barrera lazed against the wall, the smell of the wheat in his nostrils, the taste of it sweet on his tongue, the door was closed, the night shut out again. A heavy bar clanked into place; a chain was fastened across the barrier.

One by one, reluctant to leave, jealous of their treasure, the men went out. There was no joking, little conversation; they departed as silently as they had entered.

The tunnel had opened only a few streets away from the granary where Manuel Torroba, the Anarchist, had his headquarters. By the time Sebastián Gil had struggled out of the tunnel, the Austrian had disappeared. For a moment Gil was stunned; where would Vitolyn go, what could he possibly do by himself? He would probably get lost within minutes.

Suddenly he became angry: "Let him fend for himself," he thought. He owed Vitolyn nothing.

Gil made his way through the deserted streets, staying close to the walls, and heading in the direction of the Zoco. His heart hammered anxiously as he catalogued the passing buildings, delighting in each familiar detail, each balcony, each roof, each latticed bell tower. All the time he had been inching through the tunnel, he had thought only that Torroba could not refuse to help him now. Hadn't he risked his life to escape? Wasn't that proof enough of where his loyalties really lay? His "loyalties"? He had never thought in such terms before; the potentials were staggering.

Motionless against the wall, he surveyed his position; two dozen meters to the north the *calle* opened onto the Zocodover, and Gil could hear the brassy sounds of phonograph music, flamenco mixed incongruously with tinny American jazz, of men's rough singing, a jumble of many tunes bawled against each other. Somewhere, someone was rapidly firing a pistol trying to imitate the rhythm of castanets, a *jota*.

To the south, at the summit of the Cuesta, the ruin of the Alcázar blew dense columns of smoke into the night air, the breath of a dying giant. Landslides of rubble surrounded it; small pits of fire flickered in the debris. To the west and east, the bullet-scarred walls brooded silent and blank. There was no sign of life whatever.

Rubble all over. Gil had to step gingerly to avoid tripping. It looked as though the street had been deliberately torn up. Chunks of twisted metal lay about in profusion. A brass bedstead jutted out horizontally from the wall of a house the side of which had fallen away.

Directly in front of him stood the old granary, still redolent of wheat and mouse droppings; a single dim light wavered in a second-story window. A few broken tables and chairs lay about in the street near the door amid piles of damp, sweet-smelling refuse. The front door was open. A chain with a broken lock dangled loosely from the handle. The red and black banner over the door hung limp and without a breeze to prod it open. The light was still burning in the upper window; someone was there. Why, thought Gil, why could it not be Torroba? It had to be.

Gil went in, stood just over the threshold, peering about in the musty dark. The ground floor was an immense, open room, some twenty meters across and as deserted as the street outside. At the rear a dozen rows of tables and chairs barred the way to the stairs, giving the granary the look of an abandoned schoolroom. A few empty ammunition boxes stood in the corners and, nearby, Gil saw a pile of Mils bombs and jam-tin grenades piled carelessly on the floor.

He climbed quickly to the second floor, trying to move as quietly as he could. "Yet," he thought, "perhaps I shouldn't move *too* quietly . . . what if it isn't Manuel at all . . . I could be shot. . . ."

From the landing, he could see through the doorless archway and into the room beyond, dark but for the flickering of a candle. There was only one man in the room and he was bent over a table, absorbed in his writing. An outsized pistol lay before him. Gil recognized him at once by the wide, spreading mane of silver-gray hair. Only Torroba had hair like that. What a chance he had taken, that Torroba would still come there, to work alone at night. . . .

A board creaked underfoot, and Torroba turned around slowly, an anxious look on his face. He squinted into the darkness at the doorway, could not see clearly because the candle was in his way. He moved it aside slowly, groping with his other hand for the pistol.

"Manuel . . ."

"Who's that? What . . . don't come any closer . . . let me see . . ."

Torroba half rose from his chair. "You," he cried suddenly. "Sebastián . . . how can this be . . . ?"

"Manuel . . . oh, God. . . . I'm here, I'm here. . . . I got away from them."

Torroba hesitated, checked the start of an involuntary embrace. The skin of his forehead, now almost as pale as his prematurely gray hair, was beaded with perspiration. Rubbing one hand against the other as though washing, he shook his head and mumbled, "No . . . Sebastián, you must let me think . . . I must have a moment to think about this. . . . All right . . . sit down . . . there . . ." Then, even as Gil watched, the lines of Torroba's face recomposed, hardened, muscles regained their firmness. The bright, inflamed quality left his eyes.

"How did you get here, Sebastián? How?"

"The streets were deserted. It was so easy. There wasn't a person out there to stop me."

"That's not what I meant . . ."

"Yes, yes, of course . . . you just don't understand, I'm so happy, so confused by all of this. There was a tunnel, the Austrian found it, and we came out together . . . My God . . . if you want to know, I'll tell you all about it later, but I can hardly speak now, Manuel, I'm so happy, I'm overcome with joy, I'm . . ."

Torroba flushed, embarrassed, even angered by Gil's outburst. Would the man never cease looking at things so simply?

Gil was weeping now; "I found you here, too . . . it's a sign, that's what it is. It's all going to be fine now. You being here, the streets all empty . . ."

"Don't you know what's happened?" Torroba burst out. "The streets have been mined. We're expecting a counterattack from the Alcázar. Nobody goes into those streets now. This building, this place, is the farthest limit. We don't even use it as our headquarters any more. We've moved into the cathedral . . . isn't that a joke . . . ? Only a few of us come here at all. Me, Sánchez, a few others, for the records. I come here . . . to think . . . do you know what we do here, Sebastián? We draw up lists for executions . . ."

"Please . . . please . . . don't talk about such things. Shake my hand, Manuel, embrace me . . . I have gotten away from them, just as you said to do. . . ."

"I said nothing like that. What I said was that you should have come with us in the first place."

"But that's all past now, isn't it? It was an accident that I went up there, believe me . . . I can explain it all." Gil moved toward his friend, his arms out as though to clasp him by the shoulders. At the last moment he fell to his knees and flung his arms around Torroba's legs. "My shop was destroyed. You do understand that, don't you? They shelled me. For what? I didn't do anything to them but they almost blew up my shop. They drove me up there, you can see that, can't you? I don't even know

. . . oh God, it's so confused . . ." He pressed his head against Torroba's knees.

"Don't . . . don't do that . . . it's . . ."

"It's disgusting? . . . all right. That's what you were going to say . . ."

"No. It's demeaning. That's the word, Sebastián . . . demeaning, for both of us."

Torroba put a hand on Gil's shoulder and stared off toward the window as though to look into Gil's eyes were more than he could bear. "You simply can't do this, not now, my friend. No, not now."

"They were willing to let the women out, weren't they? The priest said so. Then why not me? If a person wanted to come out . . ."

"You're a man, that's why. Men are supposed to be able to choose for themselves—and to answer for their choices."

"Manuel . . ."

"I know," Torroba said. "It doesn't always work that way. But what can we do, my friend? What can we do about it? . . . tell me." It was as though he were addressing a dream. Through the window, Torroba could see the ruddy glow of flames rising in the street nearby. "My poor, poor friend." The expression on Torroba's face had now become one of awesome tranquillity.

Gil kept his head, childlike, against Torroba's knees.

"You will help me, won't you, Manuel? I have such a fear now, of dying a meaningless death."

"We talked, Sebastián, do you remember? We talked and talked again, and to you it was only talk and, perhaps, to me . . . it was . . . a little . . . only talk, too. But that won't do now. You're on the list of men who went up there, don't you understand that? This list . . . right here." He dug among his papers. "A list I have signed myself. You made a choice, and the execution squads, my execution squads, they have those lists. I know about it. Perez knows. Manolo knows. Sánchez knows. They won't forgive you even if I could. How long do you think you can last out there?"

"For Jesus' sake, Manuel, . . . you can't mean what you're saying . . ."

"What was left of your shop . . . was taken. All the radios, the parts, the motors, the wires and the tubes. Everything. We took them, Sebastián, do you understand that? We took them. A squad was up to your apartment. I sent them there myself. Yes . . . they found your books and the crystal cognac glasses and your wife's piano, all just as they had to. There's nothing left. Two Murcians are living there now."

Gil shook his head in disbelief: the piano . . . Alicia's piano . . . her picture lying smashed in a tangle of twisted piano strings and shattered keys . . . and Torroba had allowed it all to happen. He had ordered it.

"We've burned the churches too, Sebastián . . . for the same reason, I suppose . . . the same reason as those poor wretches with their axes and revolvers destroyed your fine crystal and your piano . . . because even real beauty, if it turns a man's eyes away from his own suffering and from the indignities he has borne, if it makes him forget for one minute or softens his vengeance for one second, then all of it has to be destroyed. Man has to be cleansed, do you understand that, Sebastián? You've read Bakunin, haven't you? If he was wrong, then we're all doomed."

"What has this got to do with me, Manuel? The devil with Bakunin. I'm asking you . . . begging you . . . as a friend . . ."

"I can't be your friend, not any more. Your friendship . . . contaminates me, Sebastián . . . at least in their eyes. And they need me too much for me to let them lose me that way. There are so many of them and in such need . . ."

"All I asked was to be left in peace."

"There's no peace anymore," Torroba said. "I told you that once." Torroba lifted his hand from Gil's shoulder. He began to rummage among the papers before him on the table and upset an inkpot. A blue-black stain spread over the wood. With extreme care, Torroba raised the long barreled revolver from the table and pointed it at Gil's forehead.

"You must leave here at once before anyone comes and finds you . . . with me." His face was creased with pain, his voice full of compassion. "I can do nothing for you."

Gil drew in a breath that threatened to choke him.

". . . and if you don't go, I swear it, Sebastián . . . I'll kill you right here."

Gil fell back on the floor, his hands behind him, his legs twisted clumsily one over the other, feet touching the rungs of Torroba's chair. "Then kill me . . . ," he cried. "You do it. My friend. Better you than anyone else."

Torroba raised the revolver, his own hand shaking so violently that it seemed that he would not be able to hold the weapon up at all.

"For God's sake," Gil said, waving the muzzle away, "where will I go?"

"You can't ask me that. You lost the right to ask me that when you went up to the Alcázar." Torroba's eyes closed for a second; the revolver wavered.

Gil remained where he was, an expression of horrified disbelief spreading over his face.

"Please . . . don't force me . . . I *will* do it, Sebastián . . . if I have to . . . to save myself . . . for . . . them."

Gil struggled to his feet, began backing away from the table. Torroba remained where he was, his lips pressed tightly together, his feet hooked around the legs of the chair.

As Gil backed through the doorway, Torroba said in a low, tremulous voice: "Sebastián . . . the streets . . . be careful. There are mines all over the place . . . remember . . ."

Gil stumbled back along the landing, slamming into the door frame and making the candlelight jump on the walls. He rushed down the stairs. Across the empty granary he ran, colliding with chairs and tables.

Dry grains of wheat crunched loudly underfoot. The front door was open, just as he had left it. He paused. Torroba would come after him. He hadn't really meant what he'd said. But there was nothing, only the distant cacophony of music from the Zocodover.

Alone in the street, he saw his shadow thrown suddenly two stories high by the flames that crackled at the south end of the street. It seemed to him that his shadow was no longer a part of him but was possessed of a life of its own . . . about to devour him.

"And what will I do?" he thought, groping up the street toward the fires.

"What will I do . . . ?"

The file crept down through an alley which had not been there the day before, an "alley" which was a passageway through the heart of a building which had been split in two by an aerial bomb or a shell. The men passed through what had once been inhabited rooms, and the walls were not stone or concrete or blank stucco as were the walls of other alleys in Toledo, but rather painted plaster still decorated with many pictures, some in frames, some without, curled remains of photos clipped from newspapers, pictures of saints and cyclists from the weekly magazines. Curtains hung in charred shreds, and tangles of electric wires spilled down the shattered walls.

Jaime kept thinking, "What if they've finished or if they've found no wheat at all and have gone back? We'll be killed here, and it will have been for nothing." He looked around him, trying to make out the pictures on the walls but even in the fierce starlight, he could not see the faces clearly. The faces on the newspaper clippings were watching him. Was one of those faces that of Colonel Carvalho, he wondered? "Watch me. It's because of you that I'm doing this."

In the street again, the real street; steel shutters hung like flaps of skin from the flanks of buildings. The men were down low, even the spidery Major. Jaime's back was against the wall, his legs hooked out under him, and he edged along, certain that at any moment the wall against which he was thrusting his weight would give way and he would plummet backwards. The ache in his fingers grew stronger; the rifle seemed incredibly heavy. Yet there was a youngster not far ahead of him easily carrying part of a dismantled machine gun that must have weighed almost as much as he did.

Yellow cartridge cases swinging on the chests of the Civil Guard. Two men wearing formal black hats, as though intent on facing death with a manic and defiant dignity; yet their trousers were torn and ragged and strips of cloth were wrapped around their legs like puttees. He could see another boy carrying the ammunition drums that belonged to the machine gun; the boy stopped to examine a crumpled newspaper that had drifted across his feet. His expression was visible—intense concentration, as though by force he could make the letters on the dark, burned paper come to life and tell him what he was doing, who the people on the other side of the walls were and what they wanted from him. The boy was nicknamed "Sparrow" because of his weight and his huge beak-like nose now profiled against the darker, high shadow of the cathedral spires.

A whistle blew a few hundred yards away, followed by an eruption of machine-gun fire. Jaime tensed. He could not raise his rifle. Not fear, for he had never been afraid, not in the mountains of the Atlas nor the streets of Oviedo. Not fear but puzzlement. The sound had not come from the surrounding buildings but much farther away, toward the Zocodover. Now, suddenly, music. A reedy tenor from the horn of a phonograph, singing in Catalan: *"La Balenguera . . ."*

The patrol moved out slowly, away from the walls and the doorways in which it had been sheltering and toward that sound. Then they fell into a slow run, a sort of jog trot which made the bandoleers and ammunition boxes swing and clank noisily.

"Why *toward* the firing?" Jaime wondered, running too. "Why toward it?"

The sound of singing stopped, then began again. Another shot, then laughter, heavy and slightly drunken.

Dogs suddenly began to bark somewhere nearby. Others joined in. Bright lights lanced, ferocious as lightning, through the dark, became tracer bullets weaving a cat's cradle of phosphorous over the face of the moon. The dogs stopped barking.

As they reached the bend of the street where the walls swung left at the convergence of the Calle de Comercio and the Calle Cadenas, a huge ball of flame suddenly mushroomed up just ahead of them. A wall of hot air rushed through the street, forcing the windows of the flanking buildings in on themselves with a shattering crack. The explosion slapped hard at the men of the patrol, forcing them back against the stones. Then the roar of the blast rolled over them, enveloping the tiny plaza.

Caught in the forward rush of men, Jaime stumbled around the edge of a wall and into an open space between buildings which was now boiling with flames. Everything smelled of gasoline. Geysers of thick black smoke jetted up, and a rain of debris fell through the air.

"A mine," he thought . . . "they've got the place mined . . . yes. . . ." Without thinking, he raised his rifle, searching for a target, blindly waving the muzzle toward the smoke as though the flame itself was alive and his enemy.

Flashes of light traversed the street as an undirected crossfire began. It was obvious that no one could see. At first there had been no light at all, and now the light was blinding; every man, whether of the patrol or from the surrounding forces, had been reduced in a flash to nothing more than a flat shadow dimly perceived through smoke and soaring flame.

The force of the exploding mine had disembowled the street, ripping up the paving stones. Bricks and splintered wooden beams from the stores that had been caught in the blast fell everywhere. The dogs began to howl again. A cur darted across the plaza, his pelt burning from the phosphorus. Everything was on fire; even the air seemed on fire.

The voice, still singing in Catalan, was even louder. Someone had turned up the volume just after the explosion.

It was impossible for anyone to have seen them. Why then had the mine gone off? Who had set it off? It could not have been one of them, Jaime knew. Not a single man of the patrol, not even the Major, had reached the plaza at the V of the Comercio and the Cadenas when the mine had gone off.

And no one in the Zoco was paying any attention. The shouting went on, clearly audible above the crackle of the flames.

Jaime tried feverishly to orient himself. Somewhere not too far off, was the Banco Toledano and to the left, he thought, the building where Soler had his office. But nothing was in the same place anymore, nothing the same shape. The buildings had been mangled beyond all possibility of identification.

His attention was caught by a blur of movement on the opposite side of the plaza. Their own men? No, they had fallen at once into the remaining doorways or behind piles of rubble, and he could see no one, not even "Sparrow" who had been right in front of him.

Who then? Militia or Assault Guard? Regulars? Only one vague shadow screened by a shooting wall of fire. He squinted hard; shapes began to emerge. One man scuttling along the far wall on the opposite side of the plaza. A second shape, higher, seemingly poised at the very apex of the flames, at the top of the pile of rubble thrown up by the blast. Jaime gagged, felt his stomach roll and his lungs contract forcibly.

A heap of stones and beams just beyond the pit ten meters away; one long, ragged beam thrusting up from the pile and at the end of it, a man, impaled, the sharp end of the beam through the lower part of his body. He was still alive, screaming weakly, his legs pedaling as though he were on a bicycle, desperately trying to find something solid in the air against which to push, to free himself.

Jaime pressed his face against the ground but could not hold it there, found himself staring against his will again at the struggling figure, fascinated by its agony. He could see the man clearly in the light from the flames. It was the man who had brought Mercedes to his father's house, Sebastián Gil.

Even as Jaime watched, Gil's hands found the stake beneath him. He wrenched once at it, succeeded only in forcing his body still more firmly down on it; his eyes rolled in his head, gleaming with pain.

Everything in Jaime began to shriek at once; Gil had to stop, he had to die, at once. You could not inflict a sight like that on men and expect them to remain sane. An echo resounded in Jaime's brain, the voice of Carvalho crying to himself, "Surrender, damn you, surrender," as he turned away from the riddled boxcars.

Jaime slid his rifle along his forearm, found himself raising it, sight-ing down the barrel, bringing Gil's head to balance on the forward notch sight. Vomit had begun to trickle out of his mouth; he pressed his lips together to hold it back and fired.

Gil jerked once, his arms shooting straight out to his sides like the wings of a bird trying to gain the air. Then his body seemed to collapse, shrinking instantly to half its volume, and hung like a rag on the stake. A second later he was engulfed by a rush of smoke issuing from the wall directly behind him.

Jaime remembered the Goya drawing, the figure of the impaled man, ". . . it wasn't only the Turks that did it then . . . the French, too. Now, Spaniard to Spaniard." The legend beneath the drawing, "This is worse." What could be worse? Nothing.

He fell against the barrel of his rifle, scorching his cheek. A gush of tears exploded in his eyes. He felt as though his feet had lifted from the ground, that he was floating dizzily just over the cobblestones, trying desperately to keep from falling.

The roar of gunfire and explosions was now so loud that all distinction between thought and speech was extinguished. He no longer knew when he was thinking and when he was shouting.

Across the plaza the other figure was jumping about in a bizarre, spasmodic way against the wall. The flames were closing in on the man, and he flung his arms up over his face to shield himself. He was the only man visible in the plaza; all the men of the patrol were back in the doorways and behind piles of rubble.

The man ran forward through the thin wall of flame and up the Calle de Comercio, waving his arms as though trying to signal someone.

Then Jaime saw what it was.

Hidden behind a pile of sandbags and splintered furniture above which a dresser mirror on pivots thrust at an angle, askew, like an emblem or a medallion, there was a gun position. The snout of a Lewis gun caught the firelight and sent off darting reflections. One of the gunners wore a round English-style helmet while the other had on a wide-brimmed straw hat from which dangled a cluster of black and red ribbons after the fashion of a Venetian gondolier.

The man kept running, directly toward the startled militiamen.

A few words floated back; he was shouting: *"Brudern* . . . don't shoot . . . *bin von euch* . . ."*

In German. Why in God's holy name would any one be shouting to Spanish militiamen in German? Jaime strained to see, rolled out from behind his barricade which had once been part of a storefront; as he twisted into a position from which he could see, the remains of a wall poster which had been on the storefront passed almost directly in front of his face:

¡Cuando precise hacer super-alimentación; recuerde! ¡
"El super-alimento. Cerebrino MANDRI!

The gunner in the straw hat rose slightly as though to get a better look. The men of the patrol, hidden and unseen because of the smoke, held their fire.

The man, still shouting a grotesque mixture of Spanish and German kept running, now a bit slower, toward the machine-gun nest.

"Help me . . . *Brudern* . . . *ich komme* . . . I'm coming over . . ."

The Lewis gun began to sputter, the bullets careening off the stones some twenty feet from where the man was standing. He stopped short, hypnotized by the spurts of stone dust in front of him.

As the militiamen raised the snout of the machine gun and the pattern of bullets moved up along the street, the man gestured frantically, then turned about and ran zigzag back toward the plaza where the men of the raiding party still crouched, unseen, in the doorways.

The bullets followed after him like the clumsy drops of a spring rainstorm.

The arc of fire swung slowly around the plaza, showering bullets indiscriminately over the stones, the walls, and the men of the raiding party who, though still unseen by the gunners, were now caught in the direct line of fire.

Half a dozen men pitched forward, one after the other, from the doorways and fell into the street. The rake of bullets passed, gathering in every living thing in its path except the man at whom they were aimed.

"They can't see them," Jaime screamed. "They don't even know we're here!"

A few feet to his left a soldier gave a hoarse cry, startled and indignant, and twisted out of a doorway amid a hail of bullets, his mouth partly torn away and his chest stitched from one side to the other. As he struck the ground, a gold *duro* fell from his ear and rolled away into the gutter.

The man who had been shouting German tripped over a tin Cinzano sign which had fallen into the street. His clothing was blackened by smoke, his face and hands dark as a Moor's.

The men of the patrol, what was left of it, were scrambling to their feet, trying to break from their suicidal positions in the doorways to take cover beyond the bend of the street. Two Guards jumped from behind a barricade of stones and fell upon the man who had been shouting in German. In a second, the man had been dragged back across the street toward the Alcázar.

Major Punto was in full view, waving his arms as if urging his men to attack. But he was pointing back toward the Alcázar. A green star-flare had just exploded in the air above the gutted west tower, the signal to return.

Another machine gun suddenly opened up from a roof across the street. The Major's whistle shrilled, two short blasts. Major Punto was running along the street now, blindly firing at windows. The high pitched ring of glass hitting the street mixed incongruously with the crack of small-arms fire.

"He's gone mad . . . Jesus, look at him," Jaime thought, going forward as low as he could manage without losing his balance. The Major had shot out four shop windows already.

It was impossible to tell who was shooting at whom. For all Jaime knew, they were firing at each other. Smoke billowed across the streets, and the thrusting flames produced shadows which could not be distinguished from the men who cast them.

The patrol fell back in disorder from the plaza. The two civilians in their black hats were standing at the mouth of the street rigid as statues, firing away with their rifles and smoking cigarettes.

Flames from the mine explosion lit up everything, turned the men into black paper cutouts. More machine guns hidden in the upper stories of the buildings across the Calle de Comercio opened fire. Four more men fell into the gutters. One of the men, who had been wearing his hat and smoking a cigarette, lay writhing with his left foot almost shot away.

Jaime found himself bumping along the wall, carried along by his own momentum. He had no sense of direction or of what he was doing. Somewhere nearby, he thought he could still hear the voice that had been shouting in German, high, shrill, almost hysterical.

The firing from the upper windows had become erratic. The smoke made it impossible to aim at all. Even those few militiamen who were high enough so that they could still see what was going on in the street were too far away for their rifle fire to be accurate. Bullets splattered harmlessly high from the alley walls. A cat, shot through the body, tumbled from a balcony, mewing in pain.

Over the continued slamming of the Lewis gun, he could still hear the screams of the man with the wounded foot.

"Sparrow" ran by, still carrying his half of the Hotchkiss: "What good's half a machine gun?" he shouted. His face was smeared with blood from the cuts inflicted by flying rock chips.

The wounded man began to shout even louder: "You bastards . . ."

"They must be going down to get him," Jaime thought. He turned to see if he could do anything. He had to help somebody. . . .

Then something hot tore across his forehead. He felt a tremendous shudder sweep his body. It was as though his head had simply exploded from within. Red disks swirled in over his eyes, grew enormous, began to blink like traffic signals. In the instant before he lost consciousness he could think only of the boy with the lottery ticket . . .

"What if he wins . . . ?"

September 14
Oviedo, Córdoba, Granada, and Teruel under constant bombardment

In Galicia, groups of armed peasants severely harass the rebels.

El Sol

He had been wandering around the streets on the western flank of the Zoco for hours. He glanced at his watch; it was after eleven. Above, the searchlights swung through the sky, catching the towers of the Alcázar briefly, then passing indifferently by. A portion of the west wall and one tower was framed for a second between two buildings at the end of the street; it was all he could see of the fortress, and it appeared to be moving in a kaleidoscopic pattern of light and shadow as the beams passed back and forth over its walls. As though the Alcázar were trying to shake off the light.

Carvalho shivered. The night was unexpectedly cool and damp. He was wearing a loose coat which he had hung over his shoulders like a cloak. In his pocket he carried a pair of wire cutters.

Portillo's death had both shaken and inspired him. How he had come to depend on the man's massive silence, his seeming solidity, and how he had been betrayed in his trust.

"The more rational the man, the more likely he is, in a moment of extreme stress, to commit a wholly irrational act. That," Lachine had once said, "is what I think we are pleased to call humanity."

Carvalho could hardly accept the fact that Portillo was dead. The suddenness of his death, the brutality of the murder, the shooting, the squalor of the body dragged back up to the hotel room and thrown into the corner by the window while the police agents rummaged through his paltry belongings, all of it was too unlike the man himself to be believed. Yet the sum of it all was above all to confirm Carvalho in a sudden, unexpected urge to violence. However futile the gesture might be, he had to do something. He could no longer simply stand by and wait.

When he had left the Hotel Maravilla earlier that evening, he had had it in mind that he might cut the wires leading from the mine itself to the detonating device. But what good would that do? It might postpone the firing of the mine a day or so, that was all. Yet, he kept the cutters in his pocket. For a long while, his left hand had remained jammed into his pocket, his fingers clenched around the handle of the cutters. Now, he withdrew his hand slowly, unbent the fingers with effort and examined them as an infant does who has never noticed his hand before.

"What an amazing thing . . . one's own hand . . ."

There were many soldiers and militiamen in the streets. As he drew closer to the buildings where the mine shafts had been sunk, the visible guard doubled, then tripled. There seemed to be an armed man in every doorway. The mine shafts had been driven from the patios of two houses on the Calle de Juan Labradors, just twenty meters west of the Cuesta but completely out of sight of the Alcázar watchtowers.

"Hold it, stop . . . right there . . ."

The voice was not directed at him but at another man some yards ahead of him. Captain Segurra had told him that no one was allowed near the mine tunnels unless he knew the countersign that was being changed constantly. "My countersign is this . . . ," Carvalho had said, tapping his insignia of rank. "You'll see," Segurra had replied. "It's not so easy. And remember, my friend, you'll be dealing with the Asturians . . . our 'special imports'. . . ."

The man ahead stopped. A flashlight beam swung over his face. A shop window with a translucent green shade in it threw its glow over the Cuesta, making everything look greenish, as though it were the bottom of a pond.

"Phosphorous matches," the man said quickly.

"All right . . ."

The guard disappeared back into his doorway. Odd, misshappen shadows filled the streets. A donkey was tethered to a ground floor iron railing. Nearby a few men were playing cards, their rifles stacked against a wall. Someone had pulled a mattress out of a building and had lain it right in the middle of the street and was fast asleep on it in his underwear.

The perpetual rattle of rifle fire; no one paid any attention to it, not even when a stray bullet passed close by.

Carvalho moved ahead, not as sure as he had been of himself, of his "insignia." The guard stepped out of the doorway again. He was an Asturian miner. His belt was stuffed with blue-paper dynamite cartridges. If one of them were hit, he would explode like a fireworks. Perhaps that was the way he wanted it. He was a youngish looking man and held his rifle awkwardly. As he challenged the Colonel, others looked on from doorways not too distant.

"Phosphorous matches."

The guard looked at him suspiciously, eyeing the insignia, the uniform.

"What do you want there?" he said.

Carvalho didn't answer but simply stared at him wrathfully.

The man hesitated, then stepped back. "Go on, you bastard . . . ," he said.

Someone laughed across the street.

Carvalho pulled his coat around his shoulders and shivered again. He went up the street, angled to the right and found himself on the Calle de Juan Labradors. The two houses from which the mine shafts were being sunk were not far apart, and he could hear the muted ringing of tools on rock far below. He stood still. For a moment he thought he could feel the ground vibrate under his feet.

This was the closest he had come to the houses all week. How many times had he gone out at night, wandered around the Zoco, sat talking to the lonely nighttime pickets, the few *milicianos* who were still awake and who sat at their posts, now and then firing a few shots at the north wall of the fortress, sometimes—for no reason at all—jumping to their feet and pumping bullets into the wall, then just as abruptly, sitting down again to read a magazine or take a drink of beer or soda. Men on the rooftops, so he had been told, fornicated between volleys. The *milicianos* would look at him strangely when he began to talk, to ask them what they would do if they had a daughter or a son up there, or a wife or sister.

What was he trying to do? What difference would it make if he talked a few men out of firing their insignificant rifles at the walls? It could only lead to disaster, this constant badgering of his. Already he was beginning to get a reputation, and some of the other officers were grumbling about his nightly forays.

When he had asked Segurra if he would fire high deliberately, the Captain had simply turned away. "I understand why you asked that, Colonel, don't think I don't . . . but . . . let's have no more, please . . ."

Lachine too was adamant; "You'll only end up getting yourself shot. This isn't the way . . . don't you realize it? A few riflemen, a cannon or two . . . stop it, or you'll compromise all of us."

Only Portillo had understood, and he had died before he had even known. "What else can you do?" Portillo had said once, about something else entirely, but it seemed now as if he had known all along, "A man must at least try, even if he knows he can't possibly succeed." How prophetic those words had been. "Poor Emilio," the Colonel thought, "but he was right, and so am I."

The ring of tools became louder still. Suddenly the ground began to shake beneath him; an abrupt "chunk," as a small charge went off. The miners had reached solid rock. For days it had been easy going, following the old drainage systems the Moors had dug, but now they were up to the outer edge of the foundations.

A trickle of bluish smoke, lighter than the sky, wisped up over one of the houses. Carvalho passed the guards at the door with a gesture at his insignia and the countersign rapidly thrown out. The men looked sleepy and paid little attention to him.

In the patio of the house, dirt and fragments of rock were piled up everywhere. The entrance to the shaft looked like a bombcrater. Wires and conduit poured into the hole. The miners were using pneumatic drills and electric shovels now. A few of the Asturians sat around the edge of the hole, smoking and mopping their bodies. It was hot underground, and they glistened like olives.

There was a ladder leading down into the shaft.

"*Salud,*" one of the miners said.

"*Salud,*" the Colonel answered listlessly. He realized that he was gripping the wire cutters so hard that his hand was trembling inside his pocket. Wire cutters; how foolish. Yet . . .

"What do you want, Colonel?"

"To see the pit."

"No one is supposed to go down there. There's not so much room," the man said. "People go down, and the work stops. We don't want that."

Carvalho took out the card signed by Tierres and held it out. Apparently the man recognized the configuration on the pass, perhaps even the wild scrawl, without reading it. He seemed at once surprised, even disturbed.

"All right. There's room enough for you, I suppose. But you're a big one. You'll have to bend your head . . ."

"Then I'll bend my head. It won't be the first time."

The miners laughed.

"I don't know what *you people* . . . ," the miner said, emphasizing those last two words ". . . what *you people* get out of seeing a hole in the ground. Every few hours, someone comes poking around. All right, go ahead."

"The Ministry is interested . . . ," Carvalho was surprised at himself; why had he said that? The Ministry? What about the Ministry? He thought of Ramón Linares and his friend López Sotomayer who was with General Miaja's staff . . . yes, the Ministry. Why not?

"What do they know?" The miner spat onto the ground. "Did one of them ever lift a pick in his life? They're just like all the rest of them. You'll see . . . in time there won't be any ministries either . . . but I suppose we have to put up with them for now . . . all right . . . eh . . . Morales, you want to go down with him? Show him the sights?"

The other miner shrugged, swung his legs over the lip of the pit and onto the ladder.

"Come on."

Someone had hung a sign over the tunnel entrance; it consisted of a drawing of a hand raised in an obscene gesture.

The climb down was difficult, the descent much deeper than the Colonel had expected. He grew dizzy, had to rest for a moment, clinging to the ladder and swaying back and forth precariously while Morales whistled below him.

"What d'you want down here anyhow?"

"I want to see it. Enough . . . I'm coming . . ."

"Whatever you say, Colonel," the miner replied, continuing the descent. The miners had no love for officers, no matter whose side they were on.

Carvalho wondered what the man would do if he knew who he was leading down into the shaft . . . or if he remembered the name Carvalho at all.

At the foot of the ladder, the pit broadened. A tunnel slightly higher than a man had been carved out. Broken lengths of ancient ceramic pipe lay about where the miners' picks had smashed into the Moor's centuries-old water system. Lanterns hung from wires affixed to crossbeams. The whole tunnel had been shored up with care and precision. The miner Morales went ahead. He was short, thick-bodied and moved effortlessly in the confined space. The Colonel, however, had to stoop.

Ahead, Carvalho could see a group of men working with a pneumatic drill and another man swinging a pickax into the wall, trying to chop out a mooring for a beam that lay by his feet. The blows of the electric hammer made the lanterns vibrate and released clouds of pale white dust into the air. Carvalho felt as though he would choke, but fought to keep it back. For some reason it seemed to him that it would be shameful to cough . . . these men worked underground for hours, for days, barely seeming to draw a breath. While he . . . after a minute . . .

"So, there it is," the miner Morales was saying. "What d'you think of it?"

Carvalho tilted back his head, gazed at the roof of the tunnel which was, at that point, only a few feet above him. If he could reach through the rock himself . . .

"If we had another couple of drills, a little more room . . . we're doing fine. Another day, that's all. Only about ten yards. Then we're under. Oh, we'll burrow a bit more, just to make sure . . ."

In the corner, near the man who was swinging the pickax, lay an open box of dynamite sticks. Dozens of them. He could see that they were already fused.

Carvalho looked up at the roof of the tunnel again, the crisscross of beams. The cutters of his pocket felt very clumsy, useless. There wasn't a wire in sight. Only the box of explosives for enlarging the shaft. He could not take his eyes off the dynamite sticks.

"Come on . . . there isn't that much room here, and the air's precious. You've seen it all, Colonel, so let's go now . . ."

"A moment," Carvalho waved peremptorily, as though studying something.

"Damn it . . . ," the miner Morales moved off, turned his back.

The Colonel fumbled for his cigarette lighter. It was in his pocket, next to the wire cutters. Carefully, he eased it out. He was having audible difficulty breathing now. Morales turned.

"Take it easy," he said, suddenly thoughtful. "All right, rest a minute. Then up we go. I told you, it isn't so easy to breath down here unless you're used to it."

Carvalho leaned against the tunnel wall, angling toward the box of dynamite. A few of the fiber-cord fuses trailed over the edge of the box. They were short; five seconds' burning time. He had only to get the lighter out, fire one of them . . . hide the sputter with his back . . . who would notice in that swirl of dust? The swinging lanterns made it difficult to see even the largest object.

The idea of such a sacrifice had never occurred to him before. He acted automatically, without any attempt at moral justification, as though he knew that any attempt to justify what he was about to do would have to take into account not only himself but the six miners there in the tunnel with him. If only he could send them all to the surface . . .

The miners' sweat-polished backs vibrated before him; he tried not to look toward the hand which had already come clear of his pocket with the lighter enclosed tightly in his fist. One finger was over the flint wheel.

"Christ, man . . . ," the miner Jorge shouted, dropping his pick. He lunged across the few yards that separated them and flung himself at the Colonel. Carvalho, caught unaware, fell full-length on his back. The lighter rolled out of his hand. Jorge had pinned his arms to the ground.

"Look at this." Morales had the lighter now.

"What the hell were you going to do . . . ?"

"What was he going to do? Look here, I told you. Look at this . . ."

Jorge let go of the Colonel's shoulders and sprang up to a crouch, the pickax in his hand again.

"Now you tell us . . ."

Carvalho lay there. The lanterns had been set to swinging wildly, and the rolling beams of light made the tunnel seem fluid and unreal.

Jorge fingered the end of the pick and stared at Carvalho. "Did you see what he was up to? One spark . . ."

"I saw it . . ." the other said. The four miners had gathered around him in a tight circle. One of them had dragged over the drill.

Morales held the lighter between thumb and index finger as though it were something incredibly filthy.

"You, what have you got to say . . . Colonel . . . ?"

Carvalho took a deep breath; his eye kept darting back and forth between the lighter in Morales' hand and the tip of the electric drill. "You saw . . . don't ask me."

"I'm asking you, man, and you better say . . ." Jorge shouted. He jerked a thumb at one of the other men. "Get Lieutenant Somora down here . . . See if you can find him. Let the pigs take care of their own . . ."

"No . . . ," Carvalho said. He raised himself on his elbows.

"What'd you say? 'No'?" Morales spun the lighter, tossed it up and caught at it. "You said, 'no'?"

"You don't have to get anyone . . ." Carvalho knew what was happening now; it was the same as it had been in the "chicken house," and at the railroad embankment near Aranjuez. He wished that he was up on the surface, but perhaps it was more fitting that it be there, underground, in a mine shaft. Where no one could see.

"Look, man . . . I want to know . . . ," the man named Jorge said. He was kneeling, a look of real concern on his face; he seemed to be pleading for an answer that could explain why the old man had been ready to blow them all up. For what? Jorge was sweating, his face as gray as the Colonel's beard.

Had he himself looked that way, Carvalho wondered, there in the railroad plaza at Oviedo, in front of the bleeding boxcars?

The Colonel pointed up to the roof of the shaft. "My daughter," he said, ". . . my daughter is in the Alcázar . . ."

"A hostage?" one of the men asked quietly.

"She was taken up there against her will," Carvalho said; there was no doubt in his mind. He could say it without wondering whether it was true or not.

"Jorge . . . ," the man who had just spoken said. "My brother's wife is up there, too."

"Christ, man . . . but you don't try to blow us up."

"I know, but . . . his daughter . . ." the man said. "A daughter is . . . different . . ."

The miners were silent for a moment. The lanterns had stopped swinging, freezing the shadows on the wall.

"You're telling us the truth?" Jorge asked.

"I am . . ."

"You swear it?"

"On whatever you want . . . it's the truth."

"Look at his face," Morales said. "I believe him . . ."

Carvalho thought, "Has my face become that much a mirror to my thoughts . . . *my* face?" All his life he had guarded his emotions, kept them prisoner behind a rigid, unyielding mask. Even to his wife. Now a miner read his face in the half-dark of a tunnel.

"It's true?" Jorge put a hand on his shoulder.

Carvalho nodded again, wondering how many times they would ask that, how many of them would say the same words.

"Yes, it's true, it is true . . . now what do you want of me? Go ahead, I . . ." He raised his hands and lowered his head.

"Get up." Jorge was helping him up. "Watch your head." They had come up under a beam. The other miners were watching.

Morales handed him back his lighter.

"I'm sorry for you," Morales said.

"Don't be sorry for him," Jorge said. "He doesn't want that, do you?" He glanced at the tunnel roof. "You better go away, man. Go to Madrid. Get out of here. It won't be more than a few days. . . . No one will say anything."

Morales took him to the foot of the ladder.

"Go on . . ." He considered the ladder for a moment, the old man, now stooped and shrunken into himself, the coat open on his shoulders like a cloak of lead, weighing him down. What an old man, and how feeble he had become.

"Can you get up by yourself . . . ?"

"Yes." Carvalho could not look at the man. He had almost blown them all up. These men had their own wives, children, daughters, just as he had. Six of them altogether. How many wives and children did that make? And the tunnel was not even under the wall of the Alcázar yet.

Morales touched his arm. "Get out of here and don't ever come back. If you do . . ."

"I know."

"So don't ever come back here." He paused. "And look . . . even if you'd gotten the sticks, it wouldn't have made any difference. The other tunnel is too far away. You wouldn't have gotten the other tunnel, and they're as close as we are."

Carvalho began to climb silently. For some reason, the dizziness that had assailed him on his descent did not return. His hands curved firmly around the wooden rungs, and his feet struck powerfully on them, forcing him upward, until he could see the rim of light and a curious circle of stars at the mouth of the pit. He could hear the men above in the patio, grunting while they piled the dirt into wheelbarrows and carted it away. A pulley was creaking somewhere; baskets of dirt and rock were being raised from the other tunnel a few houses away.

He caught a glimpse of the figures of the miners below him, watching him climb. What drove them to dig, to destroy, to sacrifice . . . a man's brother's wife . . . and who knew what else? And in the years before, how many of them had lost brothers, wives, or children . . . and for what reasons? And had they thought then, as he did now, that no reason could be sufficient for such a sacrifice? Of course they had, even as he had ignored such things when they were not his own.

He looked at his hands; what liars they were, these long, strong fingers that were connected by muscle, by nerve—to nothing, to a soul that had rotted out from inside him, leaving only a void that he could fill with neither reasoning nor justification for anything he did now. He could hear Lachine's voice, surprisingly gentle sometimes, almost feminine, but never free of its glaze of irony: "This isn't the way . . . don't you realize?"

But what was the way? he wondered. In the end, wasn't it true that there was no way at all and that to think so for a second was the cruelest deception a man could practice on himself? But perhaps, at the same time, the most necessary. How else was a man to survive?

He looked below, then above. A ring of lanterns at the foot of the ladder; the miners, watching him. Above the patio walls the stars, a constellation he could not name. The stars spun, changed places, until he could not tell which was which.

With a shudder, he pulled himself over the top of the ladder and stood for a moment with his boots planted almost ankle-deep in the loose dirt.

No one paid any attention to him as he walked out again onto the Calle de Juan Labradors and back toward the Zoco. No one even asked him to say "phosphorous matches."

SEPTEMBER 15: *The Alcázar*

INFANTE DELGADO SAT BY the eastern wall of the ruined courtyard, scratching disconsolately in the dirt with his fingernails while his cousin watched, trying to think what to say.

Wooden pyres had been built around the yard in anticipation of a gas attack. The day before, a government biplane had succeeded in dropping a cluster of tear-gas bombs directly into the yard, the first direct hit since the siege had begun. The yard still reeked from the smoke of the fires that had been lit to drive off the gas. The piles of fagots, quickly rebuilt, made Esteban Barrera nervous. They looked too much like the pictures of the pyres on which heretics had been burned.

"Being well aware of the magnitude of our sins," Captain Herrera had said, "we have decided to expedite things and at the same time make sure they're done properly. It's a passion for detail one wouldn't have expected." Barrera had not known what he was talking about and had gone off muttering to himself. It was only later, when the thought of the *autos-da-fe* had occurred to him as well, that he had realized what the Captain had meant.

"It's no use," Infante complained, scraping at the flinty ground. "I'll never be able to sleep again. Not ever." He raised his eyes toward the patch of yellow sky visible above the four towers of the fortress. His eyes were red and sunken, his face blackened by the splotches of burnt cork he had worn since the day he had shot Ignacio Peralta. "The mark of Cain, what else," he had growled when Barrera had mentioned the smears.

Infante's boots had been reduced to an assemblage of torn leather strips, wires and old bandages wrapped about them to keep the rags in place on his legs. He seemed, of all the inhabitants of the Alcázar, the nearest to total disintegration. Over his shoulder, he persisted in carrying a blanket, like a cloak, even in the heat, and his uniform hung in shreds.

"The bastard," Infante mumbled, pointing an accusing finger at Rubén Góngora, the barber, whom he had spotted, asleep under the south arcade on a pile of ticking. "That one, he sleeps. What right has he got to sleep and not me?" He lowered his finger, ran his other hand angrily through his hair. "He sleeps . . . the bastard . . ."

Barrera looked away. What was he to do? All his attempts to convince his cousin that he had not in fact shot Ignacio Peralta had been in vain. True, Infante would agree, he had not been able to see clearly in the dark. True, it had been a great distance. True, there were hundreds of men in Toledo who were the same size and shape as Ignacio. "And so?"

"I know what I know, Esteban, and I know I killed him . . ."

There was a point, the driver knew from past experience, where pity will become anger and then disgust. Now, he could no longer bear the sight of his cousin's suffering. "He's doing it to himself, and there's no need . . ."

Now take the *teniente* Mercader, he thought. The man's head was laid open by a bullet, and there was no telling whether he would even survive. Yet there wasn't a complaint out of him. All he wanted was a little water now and then and a few words of reassurance. And what a lot the man must have to think of; maybe he was going to die, and for what? Barrera felt a twinge of guilt; Mercader had been wounded so that he,

Esteban Barrera, could get across the esplanade with a whole skin. There was that to think of, too. Guilt toward Mercader and a sense of frustrated loyalty toward Infante; God, what a mess. It was better not to think too much about it.

The firing had died down outside the walls as it so often did, as though to remind them all what a peaceful day outside the fortress could be like. The courtyard would fill at once with hundreds of wandering men, all with the same desperate look on their faces, aware that any second a shell might come crashing down on them.

"I just don't give a damn. I want to take a stroll," Jiménez the printer had insisted.

It was true. No one cared. They had gotten used to so many things. "We move through this chaos as though it were our natural environment," Major Punto had said ". . . just like the lions in the Retiro Park who have gotten so used to their cages that they wouldn't know what to do outside."

Barrera went over to his cousin, but could think of nothing to say. He glanced at his watch to cover his embarrassment. "It's time," he thought. "They're a little late today as a matter of fact . . . but they'll be starting up soon enough." The loudspeaker broadcasts now came at all hours, not just at sundown. The speaker trucks were moving closer all the time. The outer buildings of the "defense perimeter" had fallen to the militia's flamethrowers, and there was nothing between the garrison and the enemy but the walls of the Alcázar and the rubble that surrounded them.

It was enough to drive anyone mad. No wonder Infante couldn't sleep. Even without his nightmares, how could anyone sleep with the loudspeakers blaring raucous music all night long, spewing out speeches and exhortations calling for surrender until their very persistence caused a man to doubt his own motives for refusing to comply.

Delgado, his rifle in his lap, looked at the toes of his rotting boots and sniffed.

Just then a blast of music erupted outside in the street, the high stone walls lending it a harsh, primitive resonance.

"Christ's balls . . . a *fandango* . . ."

"If they had any decency . . ."

A hollow metallic voice interrupted the music.

"Do you hear me, you poor fools in there? Do you hear us? Can you remember what it's like to sleep in a bed? Can you? Well, we're sleeping in your beds with your wives and daughters. Why don't you come out and stop us, you capons . . ."

"Listen to them will you? The Virgin of Pilar herself . . . ," Delgado muttered, scraping the rifle butt in circles against the ground.

The metal voice continued: "Soldiers, listen to me. We have nothing against you. We don't blame you for what's happened. We were just like you ourselves until we killed all our officers . . . present company ex-

cepted, of course . . . and showed the rest of them how an honest Spaniard behaves . . ."

Barrera looked up toward the walls where some of the soldiers were
shouting and singing at the top of their lungs, trying to drown out the
speakers. Every so often someone tried to hit the loudspeaker itself, but
the range was too great.

"Do you want to go up there and take a few shots at them?"

"What's the use?" Infante said.

"You have our word," the voice on the loudspeaker continued, "Kill
your officers, the notorious Fascist pig Moscardó Ituarte, that hero who
would let his son be killed to save his own skin, and all the others like
him . . ."

Infante stood up suddenly. "That's too much. Moscardó shouldn't
stand for that kind of garbage. . . ."

The voice went on: "Bring us Moscardó Ituarte's head and you
won't have to worry about anything ever again. We'll put you out to pas-
ture à la Portuguese. . . ."

"You can be sure of that," Barrera said. His palms were sweating.
He'd seen a Portuguese bullfight once, the obscene ending when the bull,
very much alive, had been led out of the arena by a dozen cows. Did they
honestly think that they'd get anywhere with that kind of talk? They
were bigger fools than anyone had imagined if they did.

The loudspeaker blared again, this time with a clamorous music behind the voice.

"Come out and join us for supper, why don't you? We've got plenty
down here. We've got hams and suckling pigs, and plenty of beef too. As
much beans and rice as a man could ask for and the sweetest olives.
Wine? Do you want some wine? Or would you prefer a nice cold beer?"

"If they start on the cigarettes again, I'm going to make it a point to
kill one of them myself," Barrera groaned. He waved at Infante. A miracle. His cousin seemed so angry that he had forgotten his own misery.
"That crack about Moscardó's son . . . well, you can never tell what kind
of a banderilla will get the bull moving. . . ."

Delgado rose and lumbered after him, dragging his rifle like a club.

Possessed of a sudden energy which he could not explain, Barrera
took the steps at the double. His cousin climbed after him, breathing
hoarsely and swearing as his rifle bumped against the stones.

The sound of the loudspeaker was muffled by the walls. Someone
was carrying on about clean clothes and . . . damn their souls, about cigarettes too. By the time Barrera emerged at the first landing and took up
a position by the loopholes under the windows, the speaker had been replaced by yet another man with a still shriller voice who was again urging the soldiers to desert.

A dozen or so men, civilians and soldiers and Civil Guard as well,
lay along the wall, peering through chinks in the masonry or peeping
over the window ledge. A few had rifles but no one was firing. Someone

was taking bets on whether or not they would put on the record of the "Ride of the Valkyries" again. "It's their secret weapon," one man confided, loading his rifle. "And just you wait and see, they'll kill us all with that noise yet."

They were high enough so that they could see down into the street and yet not be seen by the snipers on the roofs across the way. The militiamen were becoming careless. The truck with the loudspeaker mounted on its back was in plain view at the end of the Cuesta, only partially hidden by part of a fallen wall. They could see a slice of the Zoco behind it and in the distance, the bristling spire of the cathedral.

Infante Delgado squinted, trying to make out the tiny figures clustered around the truck. He could see a man with a megaphone like that of a motion-picture director and could even see the wires leading from the truck into a nearby building, bringing out the electricity to power the amplifiers.

He stared out of the window. For days he had not looked outside of the building and the glare of the sun, the brilliance of the streets, all conspired to blind him. But most of all he was blinded by the sight of men moving freely under the sky, among the walls and houses, men who could go where they wanted to go, who could sleep when they wanted to sleep.

The music subsided as another man took the microphone. They could see him, standing up in the back of the truck, exposing himself to their fire, but knowing that there was no danger, that the range was too great. The man was wearing blue overalls, and he shouted happily into the microphone, his voice gushing out of the horn with an infuriating brassy cheer.

"Hey, brothers . . . you up there. Let a simple man talk to you, will you? You've got families out here, haven't you? Some of you left your sweethearts out here, didn't you? Well, no harm has come to them, I promise you . . . we don't do things like that. But you'll never see them again if you keep this up . . ."

Esteban Barrera's face became a mass of wrinkles; his forehead clamped down like a lid over his eyes. The voice sounded so familiar. Even the metallic distortion of the horn could not disguise it. If only the man were not so far away. The sun was slanting down, just so, and a nimbus clung to edges of the gap, making everything blurry. A movement nearby: his cousin. He watched as Delgado's fingers shifted from the ledge to the barrel of his rifle, began to slide slowly down toward the trigger. He stared into the street like a wild man.

The voice went on and Infante jerked as each word struck him.

"Now take me, for example . . . I've got relatives up there, and no one has shot me. It can be the same for you. Come out and surrender. Do the right thing. I promise that no one will be harmed if you surrender."

"Holy Mother . . . it's Ignacio . . . ," the driver thought. The loudspeaker voice exploded again: "Why take me, I'm a mechanic, that's all, and my brother-in-law is a Civil Guard, but I don't hold that against him. . . ."

"That swine . . . ," Infante Delgado hissed. His face had gone hard as a flint, his profile acquiring a terrifying sharpness against the square of sun in the window. His hand jerked to the stock of his rifle and before Esteban Barrera could scramble to his feet, Infante had hooked his finger through the trigger-guard and clamped the Mauser to his shoulder.

"That misshappen little pig, . . . that bastard, . . . he was faking all the time. He wasn't dead after all. . . ."

Barrera lunged across the few yards that separated him from his cousin, just as a shot from Infante's rifle slammed across the walls, echoing. Barrera fell short of his cousin, landing painfully on the points of his elbows.

Infante's body rocked with the recoil. He stood for a split second, swaying, then fell forward against the window frame as though he himself had been hit.

The boys who had been betting on which record the sound truck would play made a grab for Infante and pulled him away from the window before Barrera could get to his feet.

"For Christ' sake . . . how could you do such a thing . . . ?" Barrera shouted.

Infante's face was absolutely white, the color of lime. As the soldiers pulled him away from the window, he fell limply to the ground. Some of the other men scrambled over to see what was wrong.

"He wasn't hit, was he?" one of the boys asked.

Barrera dropped behind the window ledge and peered into the street.

At the end of the *calle,* the mechanic Ignacio Peralta lay sprawled next to the sound truck—on his back. When the bullet had struck him he had pitched forward over the cab of the truck and somersaulted twice, bouncing from the hood, then the front right fender. A splotch of bright red blood was plainly visible, even from that distance, over his heart. The others had run for cover. The driver was hunched down behind the wheel.

The microphone Peralta had been using was rolling slowly back and forth on the cobblestones of the Cuesta.

Barrera turned, staring at Infante, terrified, and absorbing every vibration of his cousin's gathering horror as if it were his own. The full shock of realization.

"That was . . . Ignacio . . . my God . . ." There was no question about it this time. What, he wondered, provokes God into such terrible jokes . . . ?

Delgado's eyes were now wide open. A Guard sergeant was pulling him across the floor like a sack of earth. Infanto's knees had already contracted toward his chest, as if he were trying to roll himself into a ball, to become as small as possible.

To hide from someone.

"AND YOUR DAUGHTER IS UP THERE with him?" Pascual Soler asked, crinkling his forehead in astonishment. "Why, I saw Mercader on the Zoco. You remember, when they brought out the priest and the woman who was killed . . ." Soler was sitting behind a table that had been set up in a room just off the main altar. He had been working for the Commission for two weeks now, and they had managed to preserve a good many works of art from destruction. Madrid was pleased, and the foreign reporters were mollified. Soler liked to think that it was because of his own efforts that so many frescoes and even the wooden St. Francis by Mena had been preserved but he knew it was simply that the militiamen had turned their anger on other targets. Nevertheless, it was good to think that one was doing something useful and, moreover, something that did not involve either injuring others or compromising oneself.

"There's no doubt about it. The only question is whether she was taken forcibly or went on her own . . . ," Carvalho said.

"Why should you care? She's there, that's all."

"I'd like to know, all the same," the Colonel replied. "And Mercader, now that I don't understand at all. I never would have believed it, and I still don't believe it, if you want the truth. But yet there he is. You saw him, you say. . . ."

Soler put his head in his hands so that his voice was muffled. Behind him, on the wall shelf stood a rank of images of saints of all sizes. "Yes, I saw him. And I wanted to speak to him, but something kept me from it. Barcenas was with me at the time, and I don't know what he would have done if I'd talked to the boy. Our friend Ruperto has let his revolutionary fervor go to his head to the point where he can't be counted on for the time of day anymore. I think, though, it was knowing about Mercader's father that stopped me. The boy would have asked me about him, and what could I have told him? Nothing. I don't understand it myself. None of this makes any sense. Even my being here, with all of these . . ." He turned halfway in his chair and stared at the wooden figures some of which towered five or more feet above him on the wall. "Do you know what they remind me of, Enrique? The dead, the mummies that the Mexicans bury standing up in their dry, hot air, so that they don't decompose and seem to be inviting you to die with them. I was in Mexico once, did you know that? I wrote about it for a magazine, an article that was meant to show what savages the Mexicans are, but I didn't succeed, and now I'm glad. How could we call anyone else savages, tell me? But there was one line I wrote that I've always remembered from that article . . . 'The smiling dead of Mexico who refuse to lie down, and the crystalline sugar-candy skulls, white as hen's eggs, that delight tiny children who are already learning to receive the love of death as that of their natural mother . . .' Do you think we're that way too, Enrique? I believe we are. . . ."

The wooden saints were caught in the peculiarly somber light streaming in from the windows at the rear of the room, a light like a yellow serum, that gave the wood a putrescent look that accorded almost exactly with that of natural flesh in decay. "We're that way too," Carvalho said, "not learning, though. We've learned. Didn't Lorca say something about the exaltation of death in this country . . . ?"

Soler nodded. "He said, 'A dead person in Spain is more alive when dead than is the case anywhere else—his profile cuts like the edge of a barber's razor.' These were his words, exactly. And he also said, 'Many Spaniards live between walls until the day they die, when they are taken out to the sun . . .' God, what a terrible judgment that is, Enrique, and how undeniably true."

A phone rang somewhere in the next room. A muffled voice, snapping sharp replies, then the click of the receiver. Soler rose. "Thank God, that wasn't for me. Madrid probably. They call ten times a day. It seems that every time some reporter for a foreign paper gets it into his head that his favorite painting has been destroyed, they feel they have to call us and make sure it isn't true. As if preserving a few pieces of canvas and wood could cancel out the rest of what's happening."

They walked down the aisle of the church, under the heavy stone carvings. There were smudges of soot on the ceiling. Someone had tried to fire the church during the first few days of the uprising, but the flames had done little damage, and now the church was guarded night and day.

"Every one of them seems to have his own particular favorite," Soler went on. "The French correspondents, all of whom are good Communists, by the way, are terribly concerned with Berruguete while the Germans seem to prefer the wrought-iron work of Domingo de Céspedos. The English seem mostly concerned with wooden figures, while the Cross of Lepanto seems to have everyone very excited. It's amazing. I don't pretend to understand it at all. . . ." They had come to the door of the church. A Guard was standing there, cleaning his rifle. He saluted, a gesture not seen too frequently around Toledo at that time, and the Colonel returned the salute with a laconic swing of the arm. They could see the Alcázar from where they stood, or at least its uppermost remains, two towers and the walls, heavily crenelated by artillery fire.

"And all the while," Soler said, gazing at the distant towers, "they dig and dig, and soon the most magnificent building in Toledo will go up in smoke. And for what? They could just as easily leave them all there to starve. They'd come out sooner or later."

The idea was strangely compelling; Carvalho tried to imagine how it would be to those up in the Alcázar if, one morning, the shelling stopped, the firing was stilled, and everyone below in the streets simply turned their backs and walked away, leaving them there to do whatever they wanted to do as long as they stayed put.

The Colonel spoke, hardly above a whisper. "I couldn't believe it when I first heard about the mine. But it's true. There's no doubt about it now."

Soler nodded. "I've seen it myself. One of the tunnels starts not far from here, and the miners go by all day. Asturians, most of them."

"I know. I've talked to some of them," the Colonel began, keeping the real, full truth at a safe distance. "And I wondered all the while whether they knew who I was. That would be a joke, wouldn't it? I mean, if some of the miners they've brought down were from Oviedo or Mieres or . . ."

Soler took his arm. "They're trying to get the women and children out. That's something."

"They won't come out. You know that."

"Yes, I know it. They're not like our plaster saints and our Riberas . . . they can't be rescued against their will, I'm afraid."

"If she's being held there against her will . . . perhaps they would . . ."

"If she went up with Mercader, then there's not a chance. When I saw him yesterday with the priest he had every opportunity to come over. There was a moment when I saw something like a wish to do it on his face. But, he didn't. He was even talking to one of the *milicianos,* smoking with him, when . . . that terrible thing happened with the woman."

They went back inside the church, to the room where Soler kept the wooden images and his telephone. The lawyer pointed to the instrument on the table.

"Who do I call? Tell me, Enrique, and I'll call. But what will they do? You know it as well as I do. Wood and canvas are one thing, human beings quite another. Isn't that a terrible thing to say? But look at me, I've become the living proof of it."

"Call Florez, or Ramón Linares . . ."

Soler sat down, his body seeming to deflate. "I'll try, of course. But it won't do any good."

"Captain Segurra thinks the idea of the mine is foolish," Carvalho said, a hint of desperation in his voice, as if what he said to Soler meant anything. "And there is a demolition expert with him who believes that all they'll accomplish is making the place even more invulnerable to frontal attack. I've spoken to Tierres, and he doesn't believe in it either . . . because of what will happen to the women and children, and all the propaganda afterward. There are so good many reasons . . . not to do it."

"There always are. And yet no one will stop it. They'll blow the mine even if God himself were to come down and sit on the cathedral roof and shake a fist at them."

Soler studied the face of a St. Andrew hiding in the shadows, just beyond the reach of the light coming in from the window. The shadows had so changed the aspect of its face that it seemed not only human but ready to speak as well. The expression was one of infinite, almost pleasurable suffering. The lawyer regarded the wooden saint with a look of compassion, almost of . . . friendliness. "We shall all come to our Achaia in time . . . and it makes no difference what it's called. . . ."

"Don't talk like that, for Christ' sake . . ."

Soler's hand went out to the telephone. "Do you want me to call Linares first, or Florez?" He lifted the receiver. "Enrique, it isn't going to help. If you keep this up here, this going around and trying to get them to stop the mine, you'll wind up against the wall, shot, or at the very least, in prison. That episode the other day with the police inspector didn't help matters any either. Oh, you don't have to explain it to me. I know how you felt. I can just imagine it. But to draw your pistol on the man? You have no idea how much power these people have. All of a sudden, they are the new rulers. Yes, believe me . . . you'll see. And none of the others will help you either. The Civil Governor, General Riquelme, Torroba and Tierres too, they all know what you've been doing. And the terrible part of it is that each one of them sympathizes with you . . . perhaps for a different reason . . . but sympathizes nonetheless. But none of them is going to move a finger to stop the mine. Ah, we do so many things in spite of ourselves. . . ."

The Colonel began to tremble. A viselike pressure fastened suddenly around his chest; he gave a sharp cry, and his head shot back. Then it passed. Soler was on his feet.

"It's nothing . . . ," Carvalho said hastily. Heavy beads of sweat had appeared on his head like a crown. Very deliberately, he took one of the last of his Havana cigars from his pocket and lit it, letting the smoke trail out of the sides of his mouth. "Only my heart, so Blas Aliaga says, and the heart should be . . . the least of my worries now, don't you think?"

Soler took his hands and held him fast: "Go to Madrid yourself, Enrique. Don't torture me by asking for something I know I can't do . . . or any of the others here. I'd save them all if I could. The ones in the Alcázar and the ones in Navalmoral who are being slaughtered by the Moors. And even the Moors themselves, who deserve saving as much as the next man. . . ."

He went on talking, his head in his hands and when he took his fingers away from his eyes, he was alone in the room with only the shadows of his wooden and plaster saints forming on the floor like a flood of night. The window trembled in a nimbus of late afternoon light. Under his feet he could feel the vibrations of shells landing somewhere. He no longer gave any thought to where the shells were coming down. It was enough that they were . . . somewhere. . . .

Carvalho walked up the street, borne along without volition. "Go to Madrid yourself." Of course, but for what? As long as he kept talking, arguing, even pleading, he kept alive the illusion that he might, in the end, accomplish something, somehow—by a miracle if one chose to call it that—convince someone who had the power to stop the mine. And all of this when he was not even sure Mercedes was still alive.

Jaime Mercader's face swam up before him like a sunspot, flaming. Mercader was alive. Soler had seen him. He tried to reason it out. What Portillo had said about being driven "mad," losing perspective. Could it be that he himself was responsible for what Mercader had done? He kept thinking of the boy's father, laid out under the dusty blanket in the car shed, and then of the flames exploding skyward, engulfing the shed, Mercader, everything. What would be more natural, he admitted, than for a man who is disillusioned by hypocrisy to turn completely away from what the hypocrite professes? But couldn't Jaime Mercader see that there was truth in what he had preached even if he himself had not had the strength to practice it without failing? That was the lesson of charity, that only time could teach, and even such as he had not learned it in time. A young man sees things with both a terrible clarity and a frightening simplicity: the world exists on two levels only, the right and the wrong. But how was one to explain to such a man that right was not always right nor wrong always wrong and that, in the end, the two were often synonymous? The argument of the cabalists came back to him; the concept had always fascinated him and often, while he was stationed in Morocco, he had sought out old Jews in the few synagogues that remained in the coastal towns, and disputed with them for hours. Since everything created by God held within it an element of holiness by virtue of its creation and since Satan, sin itself, was also created by God and was in fact only another aspect of God Himself, then it might be said that the two were one, and sin as holy as goodness. In everything lay the seed of its negation; hence each thing which existed on this earth was its opposite as well. How simple everything then became. A man could almost understand. . . .

But Mercader could not be expected to comprehend such things; an understanding of them came only with age, frustration—even despair.

If the young man was there in the Alcázar, if he died because of where he was, if he had been driven there by the Colonel's inability to somehow make it clear that he had not really betrayed the boy, was that to be yet another guilt that he would have to wear like a penitent's belt for the rest of his life? So many spikes in his flesh. . . . His heart, Aliaga would have said, had it been anyone else, was taking revenge on his soul.

To Madrid, then . . . for Mercedes, if she was still alive . . . for her soul and his own as well . . . if she was not. And for Francisco Mercader's son who even now would not understand what he was doing . . . if he were to know of it and might despise him even more for it . . . if he did.

SEPTEMBER 15: *The Alcázar*

HE KNEW ONLY THAT HE HAD LAIN for a very long time in a state halfway between consciousness and dreaming and that all through that time the one constant of his experience had been a painful throbbing in his head. At times he had decided that he was indeed dreaming all the while, for it would be impossible to truly have such pain and survive it, while at other times a familiar face would drift by, Mercedes' face or the face of the driver, Barrera. And when he would call out, he would receive an answer which came in such a voice that he could have sworn it was real and that he was not dreaming.

Toward the end of this time he began to recall certain things though he was not sure, again, whether they had been dreams or whether they had been real. There was the courtyard, full of people rushing back and forth and the smell of iodine very heavy; yet, of that scene he could recall having glimpsed clearly only the boots—mud-spattered and in some cases covered with blood. Boots and the sky above him which had been laced with flares and searchlights so bright that the stars had been eclipsed.

He remembered being taken through a corridor, backwards, and having seen the arches and the dead globes of the lighting fixtures that were without electricity pass over his head, always taking him by surprise because they came upon him from behind.

Of the operating room, he could recall only the boodstained carpet and the metal tables with legs like a giant insect, bent at odd angles as though the tables themselves were about to leap into the air and devour their victims whole. Bottles dangling from a stand and long coils of wire falling to the floor. A man, glimpsed for a second above him, sweating profusely, with a handkerchief tied around his forehead to keep the sweat out of his eyes and his sleeves rolled up above his elbows and with a look of exhausted fear in his eyes. Jaime had wanted to say to him, "Don't be afraid, it's me who's going to die . . . ," but he had said nothing because his mouth refused to obey his thoughts. The haze had closed in on him immediately, and now he was not even sure whether the man had been real. Yet he had seen the room before, the operating theater, the nuns who were trying to be nurses and the few harried doctors. He had always hurried by, not wishing to look too long at what went on within. Death was one thing; a man could meet it, hopefully, with some dignity when the time came. But disfigurement, gaping wounds, blood and—worst of all—the continuous moaning that proceeded from the operating theater, that was something else again.

Now he could not get the picture of the room out of his mind, and for that reason alone, conceded that he must have been there, that it had been real and the doctor's face with its staring eyes had been real too.

Gradually he began to see a little. For hours he had lain in a painful stupor, aware that he was awake but reluctant to force his eyes open for fear that he would find he could not see. Perhaps he had been blinded; that happened sometimes with a head wound. He had seen blind old Berbers wandering about in his mother's village, men who had been wounded in the twenties when Abd-el-Krim had nearly driven the Spanish Army out of Morocco. Children laughed behind their hands when the blind old men walked into things. The older men and women tried to help them but what, really, could they do?

After a time he knew that he had to try and he opened his eyes. To his surprise, he could see light, shapes, even faces. A line of packing cases swelled forward, then receded again in time to the pulsing of blood in his forehead. His temples ached terribly, and there was something tight around his head. He closed his eyes again, drifted contentedly back into sleep. The faces swept past him, changing their features as they whirled about like comets. Eyes, most of all; his own and those of Sebastián Gil. Through it all, he was aware of a vague tapping noise, like anvils being beaten miles and miles away. The sound grew louder, dimmed, sometimes almost to the point of silence, then rose again. No matter how thick the fabric of his dreams, the sound persisted.

When he awoke finally, the side of his head felt cold. In his sleep, he had been pressing his cheek against the cool rock wall of the room.

He had been placed on a cot, almost on the floor, in a long and narrow room with a low curved ceiling not unlike the rooms where the women had been sleeping. He knew that he must be deep underground, for there was no light at all except for the glow cast by a reeking lamp made of tin cans and rags that burned at the opposite end of the room. The gloom was at once both depressing and comforting. At the far end of the chamber a line of packing crates was stacked against the wall at irregular intervals. Below them, a number of cots had been placed, like his, low to the floor so that they seemed more like stretchers than beds. Striped gray mattresses lay empty on frames of rusted steel tubing. A few tattered pillows were heaped against the wall.

He squinted, trying to see who else was there. Most of the cots were empty. There were only six or seven wounded in the room besides himself.

Closest to him, he could make out a deathly pale man of about forty, in civilian clothes. The blanket had been raised over his right leg by a wire frame of some sort. He was whistling softly through his teeth; his skin was the color of cigarette paper that had been wet: gray, and exuding moisture. It was the man whose foot had been shot away. So . . . , they had gotten him back inside after all.

Nearby was a Civil Guard, identifiable as such by the cap which had been placed at the foot of his cot. He lay flat on his back, not moving.

On the farthest cot a man was sitting up, his arms wrapped around his drawn-up knees. His hands were tied at the wrists; the rope joining them coiled over the bandages that covered his hands. The other end of the rope was tied to a metal ring in the wall. On the floor below the ring there was a scattering of fresh mortar and rock chips; the ring had been driven into the wall just recently. The man was not moving, but was staring at the lamp the way an infant will stare fixedly at an object, trying to determine whether it is real and has anything to do with him.

The man with his arms around his knees was familiar. Jaime tried to think, but even that small effort produced an intolerable banging in his temples. As he began to slip off again into a dusty sleep, he remembered that it was the man who had gone running down the Comercio and into the machine-gun nest. Why had they tied his hands that way? Was it possible, after all, that they were not back in the Alcázar but in an Anarchist prison somewhere in Toledo? But the lighting fixtures and the corridors he remembered seeing. . . . It had to be the Alcázar. . . .

An intolerable heaviness seized him, almost driving away the pain in his head, and he sank back, his body going limp. Sleep overwhelmed him again, a troubled sleep ridden with burning, fragmentary images . . . more discontinuous visions than real dreams. . . .

He saw in his dream a horse he had watched being slaughtered the day before he had been wounded. . . . First he saw it as a living, snorting animal, prideful and stubborn . . . and then as a bloody carcass shackled by its hind legs to a beam in the stable . . . still identifiably a horse . . . still quivering with life. . . . Then, in a series of increasing frenzied visions, he saw the animal being skinned . . . its genitals being cut away . . . a gaping hole remaining . . . butchered . . . its organs emptied into bowls . . . its blood coagulating on the floor in a dense brown mass. . . . Then, only a skeleton . . . a wretched pile of yellow bones crumpled in a corner next to a tumble of harnesses. . . .

He awoke again. Had the dream taken a minute or a day . . . ?

The light in the room was as before, but for some reason it seemed darker. His eyes were not yet open; he sensed a shape moving between him and the source of the light.

"Jaime . . . ?"

Mercedes' voice.

He opened his eyes and made a move to touch her, but his arm fell back.

Was it the first time he had seen her face clearly? She looked even more pale, more wasted than he remembered. Her cheekbones stood out beneath tightly drawn, almost ivory skin; she gave the appearance of a Japanese bone carving. Her hair was intensely black, and her eyes wide and staring; the beauty of fever.

"Jaime . . . ?"

He had a feeling that he had spoken to her before and that perhaps he had already asked her the same question, but it was what came into his mind at once, and it fell from his lips without any thought or possibility of stopping it or recalling it.

"The radio . . . ?"

"It's working. Yes, I've told you that. . . ."

"And your father . . . ?"

"Yes."

Yes? What did she mean by . . . yes? She was looking at him as though she were merely repeating something that she had told him a hundred times. Yet, she was so gentle. It was a gentleness that caught him unprepared.

"They know then?" he said.

"Yes. And it doesn't matter."

"Tell me."

She drew a breath. "It was only a few words. A list of staff officers who had stayed with the Republicans."

"That's all?"

"No more than that. So now they know. We know."

She took a damp cloth and laid it on his forehead, just below the line of bandages. "You didn't have to do this, do you see?" she said. "It wasn't necessary."

"Aie . . . Mercedes, Mercedes. Don't say that. Everything is necessary if it's for. . . ." His voice trailed off.

She had been right before. "If it's for someone else," he was going to say, just as he'd said when he'd told her he was going. All right. Let it be. She tried not to look at the wound on his head, at the blood-caked bandages. She had grown up with wounds. Her father had been severely wounded when she was a child, and it had evoked more curiosity than fear. But Jaime's wound terrified her. She tried not to let it show.

"Did they find the wheat?" he asked.

She smiled. "That was a long time ago."

"Then . . . how long have I . . . ?"

"Two days."

"And the news about your father?"

"Two days ago, also."

Only two days ago. They hadn't done anything yet. But that didn't mean that nothing would happen. The Republicans had shot Moscardó's son, hadn't they? Why should they expect anything better . . . ?" Only two days. There was time yet.

"The radio . . . it didn't say anything else about him?"

"Only that he was alive, that he had offered his services to the Republic. There were a lot of names. They didn't talk about any one man. For all I know it might have been another Carvalho. It's possible."

Another Carvalho? Why not. Anything was possible, any macabre joke. Any absurdity. The world was full of Sánchezes, Ortizes, Torrobas, even Caballeros and Azañas; why not two Carvalhoes?

"How long have you been . . . here?" he asked, suddenly.

"Since they brought you down."

"Where are we? This place . . . ?"

"It's a storeroom, where they used to keep supplies. Can't you smell the chalk? There are old blackboards behind the packing cases. One of them was made in 1914. I saw it. Isn't that funny . . . ?"

"Why?"

"I was born in 1914. . . ." She smiled, and he managed to reach up and touch her face. She seemed so fragile he thought he might break her cheekbones just from the pressure of his fingers. A stabbing pain shot through his forehead, and he groaned and fell back on the pallet.

Across the way, the man whose foot had been shot away was whistling "La Cumparsita."

From behind, near the doorway, a soldier who was sitting on a low stool asked if there was anything he could do to help. Did they want the doctor? Mercedes thanked him; no, it wasn't necessary.

"Don't move around so much. You'll start to bleed again, Jaime . . . please . . . for my sake."

"For your sake only . . . everything," he said in a hushed voice. She didn't answer, only stared at him. Then a smile that was entirely differ-- ent from any he had ever seen on her mouth before curved her lips ever so slightly.

"How unfair it is . . . ," she murmured. . . .

She stayed with him for an hour or more, and they talked haltingly, in low voices, trying not to disturb the other wounded. Yet the others, those of them who were conscious, listened greedily, hanging on every word that passed between them, drawing sustenance, from the woman and the young man and what was between them. It was enough for the young cadet whose shoulder had been shattered to see that there was a woman there, ministering to someone, even if it wasn't he. It was enough for the man whistling "La Cumparsita" to know that there were young people who cared for each other, even if they did not care for him espe- cially. Only the Austrian seemed to take no notice; he continued to stare at the wall.

They had given her special permission to help in tending the wounded. There were not enough nuns now that the overflow of the wounded were being put in rooms in the lowest subcellars rather than in one central infirmary. A few of the woman had been allowed to assist, and there had been no problem in getting permission.

He was too tired to ask about the others. Talking with her had ex- hausted him beyond his expectations. After a while she left him and went for some food. There were enough rolls now, even though the meat was almost all gone. There were only two mules left, and the siege showed no signs of ending. Amado Leorza had thus far succeeded in raising Madrid only: "*Musica variada*"—José Calves de Rojas and a Sextet, grand opera, and medleys from "*Doña Francisquita*" and "*La Bruja*," The Pickens Sis- ters, and dance music relayed from Barcelona. News, to be sure, but nothing to raise any hope of relief. . . .

Yet, she had told him, just before he fell back to sleep, there were columns of smoke on the horizon to the northeast, and a few planes had been seen in the distance which the spotters declared were not of familiar manufacture and were most probably Italian. What did it mean? No one was willing to guess. If only Amado Leorza and his "assistants" would perform a miracle. One man was busy consulting a stack of religious trea- tises which had been discovered in a basement niche, trying to determine what saint one should pray to concerning radios.

The tapping continued, invading his thoughts, settling in and be- coming as much a part of his being as the muffled pulse of his heart. It lulled him to sleep. He dreamed again, this time that he was seated in a dark, stone room, facing a long table behind which stood a man in the uniform of a general, his chest covered with medals. The features of the general's face were hidden by the shadows of his peaked cap. Through a narrow window behind him, Jaime could see a wall in front of which stood a line of wooden stakes and nearby the figures of condemned men being led to execution. Shots, at regular intervals. The General took no notice. His lined face, his mustaches, and beard seemed familiar. For a long time the two conversed in low, mutually respectful tones, but there was a note of anger on both sides.

"Are you an Anarchist?"

"No sir. . . ."

"Are you a Communist, perhaps?"

"No, I am not a Communist."

"Do you belong to the POUM then?"

"No, not that."

"Then you are a Falangist, is that it?"

"No . . . not at all."

"A Socialist or a Monarchist? A Carlist? Come, now. . . ."

"None of those. . . ."

"Your grandfather was a . . . how shall I put it? . . . He threw bombs. He blew himself up, didn't he? The police archives are never wrong in these matters. . . ."

"No sir, no, that's not what happened."

"Come, come . . . you weren't there. How would you know what really happened . . . ?" A long silence, then the General leaned forward. "Just what is your allegiance then?"

"Allegiance?" Why did he have to have an allegiance? "Whatever you wish, General" . . . . The crack of rifles, regular as the ticking of a clock. . . . "I believe in nothing . . . that is, I will believe in whatever you wish. Nothing or everything or anything. . . ."

The General shook his head sadly. "An empty bottle soon fills up when it rains. Who is to say when and how the rains will come? No, we can't have too many empty bottles lying around. . . ."

Then, they led him outside and fastened him to a stake by the wall. The ground, he noticed, was foaming with black blood, as though underground streams of tar were boiling up through the surface. He did not resist; yet he could not help uttering one short cry as the rifle bolts slid back. It was a dream, he knew that, yet he had always believed that if one died in a dream, one's heart might really stop beating. . . .

He woke up instantly, the echo of his cry still resounding in the room.

"A nightmare?" the Austrian said from across the room, still sitting with his arms around his knees. "I should think so . . . we should all be having nightmares. But I don't. Isn't that extraordinary? I actually don't have nightmares."

The footless man tried to whistle again, but his lips were too dry and he cursed instead. His hands lay, white as altar cloths, on the edges of his rough blanket, twisting the threads.

"A little water?" he said, but no one heard him. The wounded Guard groaned and turned over, groaned louder and lay still.

"Yes," Vitolyn continued, "I ought to be dreaming, but now I don't see a thing. I think it's the dark, don't you?"

Jaime wondered whether it was worthwhile trying to answer the man or whether he would be quiet if he pretended not to have heard.

"A drop of water. Christ's wounds, there ought to be water . . . ," the man with the tented foot said. This time the soldier by the door heard him and came over with a dipper. When the soldier had gone back to the door, the footless man began to whistle again, off key and shrill, and to jerk his body in time to the tune. His fingers met each other on the surface of his blanket in a fantastic dance.

For a second, Jaime had the horrible sensation that it was not a hospital or infirmary at all but a madhouse; the Austrian with his bandaged hands, tied to the bed, a footless man whistling dance tunes, and himself with a crested turban of bandages. . . . "I must look like . . . a Berber . . . ," he thought without realizing what he was thinking. . . ." A Moor . . . no, it's not the same. . . ."

Little sounds filled the room. The Austrian became quiet again, fell to studying his bandaged hands. He would try to spread his fingers as far as he could, then rap with them on his knees until he winced from pain. Why he was doing that, deliberately hurting himself, Jaime could not understand. The man seemed to be pleased; the harder he struck his wounded hands, the more contorted his face, the more contented the smile that followed.

"A madhouse," Jaime thought, and his mind filled with pictures from Goya again. There was no lack of madhouse scenes in that artist's oeuvre, and every one of them that he had ever seen in his life flicked by in those few moments. Francisco Mercader had never liked Goya and had refused to allow reproductions of his drawings into the house. "A man who relished suffering that much, who could hang a picture of a man eating his own child in his dining room, no, that's not a man whose work I want here in my house." On one of his first trips to Madrid, Jaime had bought an entire set of the etchings, five volumes bound in red Florentine leather, at the book stalls under the walls of Retiro Park. The images he had found in those books had never ceased to haunt him from that day on.

Two cadets, only lightly wounded, played cards near the packing cases, arguing bitterly over their wins and losses.

"On this hand, I'll bet you my estates in *Los Cigarrales.* . . ."

"My olive groves, fifty acres, cheapskate . . . how's that?"

"Up the bet. I'll add my mill at Talavera. . . ."

As the hours passed, the boys began to wager the Cibeles fountain, the bridge over the Manzanares, the feet of Carlos V's statue, the Café Levante, anything that came to mind. And as each one won or lost a hand, the loss or the joy of ownership became at once real, painful. One of the boys would cry out: "Ai . . . what will you do with the whole Prado? You don't even like pictures. Give it back, damn you. . . ."

The game went on, and the Austrian continued to study his fingers.

Vitolyn saw that Jaime was awake. The two boys playing cards would not even look at him. The footless man was asleep. Apparently the Austrian had tired of torturing his hands.

"Do you know what they did to me?"

Jaime pretended to be asleep.

"Don't think you can fool me. I know, you're awake. . . ."

"All right." Jaime tried to sit up.

"No, don't do that. You'll just hurt yourself. Why should you do that?" He held out his hands, the fingers splayed.

"They stuck splinters under my nails and lit them," Vitolyn said. There was no resentment in his voice, only eagerness that someone should listen to him. "Can you imagine something so primitive? But that's what they did. Seven fingers altogether . . . I lit up like a Roman candle. . . ."

Jaime turned his head, and his temples burst from the movement. His eyes glazed: "Hold your head still, man . . . maybe it's worse than you think . . . you could kill yourself jerking about like that. . . ."

"Seven fingers," Vitolyn said. "Then why did they bandage all ten, do you imagine?"

Jaime said between his teeth; "They should have shot you. I was out there, I saw what happened."

"Yes, I know. I saw you on the stretcher when they brought us back in. That's why I chose to talk to you now. . . ."

"Well . . ." What kind of a lunatic was he? Yes, he should have been shot. If it hadn't been for him, "Sparrow" would have been all right, and the boy with the *duro* in his ear . . . there hadn't been much left of him either. The whistler . . . if he recognized him . . . if he remembered, would want to strangle him the first chance he got. You don't take the loss of a foot too lightly, especially if it can mean gangrene as well. . . .

"You're right of course. They should have shot me . . . but they didn't. It just shows how you can misjudge people. I thought they should have shot me. I told him so. The bald major, the one whose . . ." his voice trailed off and he began pulling at his rope. It was a thick length of manila hemp, the kind used to tether horses, and it had been knotted through the iron ring in the wall four or five times. The skin on Vitolyn's wrist was raw from chaffing, but he seemed not to notice it.

Vitolyn lowered himself from the cot, came crawling across the floor as far as the rope would allow him and remained there, crouched on the ground, five feet from Jaime's pallet. Jaime could not see him clearly without moving his head; his forehead pained him terribly. It occurred to him that he had not yet dared even reach up with his fingers to probe the wound, to see how bad it was.

"I'd always thought that you Spaniards were natural inquisitors," Vitolyn said, "that torture came easy to you all. How strange it is to realize the truth . . . and to know . . . ," he paused, licked his dry lips, ". . . to know how much suffering the torturers themselves must undergo, as well as the tortured . . ."

"Shut your mouth . . . ," Jaime said, trying to twist away, but he was as trapped by his wound as Vitolyn was by his long rope.

"The Captain who did it, I think it was as painful to him as it was for me. He did a strange thing at the start, do you know? He emptied his pockets on the table. A few books of matches, coins, a cigar cutter, and the like, some toothpicks. I think he hoped I'd be frightened enough trying to think what he was going to do so that he wouldn't have to do it. A very handsome man. I don't like to see handsome people suffer. It upsets the natural harmony of their faces. . . ."

Jaime closed his eyes; the man's voice took shape as a gray-green fog, just over his brain.

"He smoked a few cigarettes too. It smelled like rope or leaves . . . that doesn't work so well once you know they're not real . . . I almost started to laugh, he was trying so hard not to show how badly they tasted . . . but then he picked up the toothpicks, and I knew what it was going to be. All right, good. I was . . . do you want to know the truth . . . ? no, of course you don't, but you'll listen anyway . . . I was absolutely immobilized. I actually wanted him to do it. Can you imagine that? All I had to do was tell him where the tunnel was, and he would have let me go, but I wouldn't. I wanted him to use the toothpicks. Oh, he argued with me all right. Sly man . . . tried to wheedle it out of me, but I wasn't going to be put off. . . ."

Vitolyn closed his eyes. He could recall the scene so vividly, as though it had only been minutes before. . . . Captain Herrera leaning across the table counterfeiting the strictest of confidence, his gestures so transparent, yet his eyes disturbingly sincere. "No one wants to harm you, Anton. What good would it do?" . . . Vitolyn had shuddered and said nothing. He was not, at that moment, sure why it was that he was unable to answer . . . the words were trapped in his chest. He had been responsible for the death of a dozen men: Stoplinsky, Zipser, Roig, Paco the hunchback, and the soldiers in the plaza. But he had felt nothing at all. His anguish had been reflected in the eyes of Major Punto as they had brought him back into the courtyard that night. The despair, and the ultimate disgust in the Major's eyes as he looked hopefully for some sign of remorse and found none. The frustrated confessor whose penitent will not repent. "You are an animal," that glance had said. "You feel nothing. You are not a human being." The Major was right. A complete absence of feeling. He remembered thinking, "Even the Inquisition spared them if they repented. . . ." There were the Captain's black shadowed eyes in which he seemed to see focused to a point of dazzling fire the essence of that alien Catholic world in which he had become trapped. "Even at the stake . . . but to repent, they had to feel guilt first. . . ."

Vitolyn was speaking to Jaime, hardly aware of what he was saying. The boys near the packing cases had stopped their card game and were listening.

"What did they want me to do . . . get down on my knees and say a thousand *mea culpas?* . . . But I couldn't do it. I didn't . . . *feel* . . . guilty of anything. . . ." He had felt only an aching hollowness, as though all the vital organs had been ripped out of his body. Wasn't it the same way it had been with Baumgartner? If he'd admitted it, if he'd said, "Yes Helmut . . . it was a mistake," would it have made any difference? But the Captain was not Baumgartner, and there were no Zipsers there to sacrifice themselves.

"Pain," the Captain had said, "can break anyone. It's simply a question of degree." Vitolyn was repeating what the Captain had told him. "Can you imagine anything stronger than a man's belief in God? Yet . . . how simple it was for the Holy Office to obtain confessions of heresy. . . . Men confessed to what in their hearts they felt were the most blasphemous untruths. They denied their God, they informed on their wives, their children, their fathers and mothers. And all of this because of physical pain. Surely, when they went to the stake, they often recanted, but we can see the obvious irrelevance of that. . . ." But he hadn't seen it at all. Captain Herrera's words had proven just the opposite, that through pain one might find out the truth about one's self, be restored to a realization of a guilt which was otherwise too easily denied, which refused to surface, which needed a catalyst. . . .

Vitolyn said: "They took my hands and spread them on the table. I didn't resist it at all. Then they put the splinters under my nails and lit them. . . ." A distinct sensation of heat, a sudden needle of pain through two fingers; he could not tell which two, whether they were together or apart, only that they were both on the same hand. A rib-cracking pressure across his entire chest.

"The effect on my sphincter muscles was very interesting but, I'm proud to say, I didn't soil myself. . . ."

The Guards had held his hands down on the tabletop while the tiny points of flame chewed at his nails and the flesh beneath. He had not even been able to breathe deeply enough to support his own voice and instead of speaking had emitted short wheezing noises.

"And he kept shouting at me, 'This isn't necessary!' Can you imagine that? How little he understood. Why of course it was necessary. . . ."

They had done five, then six fingers, and he had not said a word. He had sat there, drawing in the pain, letting it go to work inside him, searching in his brain, his chest, for his guilt, dragging it up by the roots.

By the seventh finger, his feet had started to drum on the floor, and they had stopped, mistaking the kicking for capitulation. It was too late. The tension was broken. There was nothing to be gained by prolonging it . . . And he had been so near the climax. . . .

"I told them all about it then," Vitolyn said. "And they thought it was because of what they'd done to me. The Captain even said to me later, 'I'm sorry. . . .'"

Jaime had long since ceased to listen. There was a bright thread of pain running through the man's narrative that wound inextricably among his own wounds. But he could not pay attention. The throbbing in his head had grown muffled. His fingers moved aimlessly over the chest of his tunic, straying toward his head, even passing as far as his cheeks but always withdrawing before they made contact with the lower edge of the bandage.

"My little Moor," Mercedes had called him, when he had caught her glancing uneasily toward the winding of bandages that covered his head. How serious was it? He had no way of knowing. Of course no one would tell him; he expected that. But he had never been wounded before. How was he to interpret his symptoms? Approaching death or only a light scalp wound? The scalp bled so much. Full of tiny capillaries, giving the pretense of a deadly wound at the slightest scratch. "My little Moor," she had said, but her eyes betrayed her; something unsettling had flickered by in her eyes. But it could as well have been her hunger and exhaustion as his condition.

How long he lay there with his eyes closed, he had no way of telling. It was impossible to mark the passing of time by the sounds that pierced the drumming in his head for they were all the same. Endless repetition. The shrill, feeble whistle, the heavy breathing of the Austrian, the slap of playing cards on a crate. And above all, the tapping sounds. He lay there, trying to think what they might be, then drifting off, returning to consciousness only to find himself once again trying to identify the persistent, tapping noises. He could not even be sure of the direction they were coming from.

Did no one else hear them? Was he the only one?

Then, abruptly, the whistling stopped, and Jaime heard a grating noise. His eyes flickered open and without thinking, he tried to sit up. Someone was calling weakly from across the room, in pain, a hoarse voice.

"I want to dance . . . get me some . . . music. . . ."

The footless man was sitting up on his cot, waving his arms in the air, his face opaque with fever.

The soldier by the door went over and tried to quiet him. Vitolyn was off his cot, trying to cross the room and get through the door which the soldier had vacated. He had forgotten completely about the rope around his wrists.

He was caught up short ten feet from the wall and toppled over backwards just as the bewildered soldier had succeeded in pressing the footless man back down onto his cot.

"Hey, someone . . . get Dr. Sepulveda in here . . . This one is too much for me . . ."

Jaime, without thinking himself, tried to rise again. He flung his legs over the edge of the cot and leaned forward, trying to get to his feet. The Austrian was scratching at the floor a few yards away, pulling at the rope.

For a second, Jaime stood there, swaying, astonished that he had actually been able to rise, trying to brace himself against the wave of dizziness that was engulfing him. He thrust out his hands, seeking support, found none. Slowly, he doubled over and fell forward onto the floor.

The side of his head slammed against the stones and he uttered a cry of pain. He lay still for a moment, listening to the scrabble of footsteps and the agitated muttering of the soldier. He tried to catch his breath. The pain receded, and he felt the coldness of the stones under his ear, his cheek.

. . . the tapping sound again. It was there, under the stones.

His arms moved out cautiously. His movements now had nothing to do with his fall, the pain in his head, or the others in the room, but seemed controlled only by the sound coming up from beneath the floor. His hands opened on the stones as though to feel the tapping sound. There was no mistaking it. Hammers. Somewhere far below the surface of the earth, in the granite bowels of the Alcázar. Hammers and electric drills.

Someone was trying to lift him from the floor. He hunched his shoulders.

"Wait . . . be quiet."

"What is it?"

"The tapping . . ."

"We all hear that. . . ."

The Austrian's voice: "What is he saying about the tapping? I want to hear what he's saying. . . ."

"Quiet! . . ."

"The wound in his head," the soldier was saying to someone. "It's not so good. . . ."

Mercedes had come into the room again. He sensed her presence rather than saw her. What sensitive hearing. Her breathing. The sound blurred his sight, but his hearing, was now so acute . . .

"Hold on to me . . . ," the soldier was saying, his hands on Jaime's shoulders again.

Mercedes said, "It's the sappers, that's all. . . ."

"Who?" Jaime turned on his back, got his elbows under him and lifted himself to a sitting position.

"They're digging down there. They're digging for a mine, Jaime . . . it's been going on for a week," Mercedes said.

He let her guide him back to his cot. The Austrian remained where he was, on the floor, and no one bothered him.

"A mine? Are you sure. No, you don't have to answer me . . . I can hear it. That's it, a mine . . ." How could he not have known before?

She told him in hushed tones how they had first heard the sounds over a week before, in the women's quarters. No one had paid any attention until a soldier, also wounded, had gone into a delirium and started screaming that there was a huge rat under the floor. By the next morning, Lieutenant Rincón, an engineer, had organized a special party which was even now working in the lowest of the subcellars, trying to pinpoint the exact location of the mine and seal off the area. There was no doubt about the militia's intentions. They had been broadcasting it from the sound trucks for days, even repeating the priest's offer to let all the women and children out. The men, it seemed, were to have no choice. Either stay and be blown up or surrender and be shot. No one had left.

"There wasn't any point in telling you," Mercedes said.

"No, I suppose not. There's never any point in telling anyone anything." He heard his voice, full of bitterness. "I can't allow this . . . you . . . why should you . . . and your father, you say, on the outside . . . they'd permit you to . . ."

"I suppose they would . . ."

How difficult it is to judge one's fellow man, Jaime thought. He considered how badly he had judged Colonel Moscardó. To be sure, they had shot Luis, his son, and most men would find the simplest way to bear such an anguish would be to exercise a blind revenge. What would be easier than to turn on the daughter of a Colonel of the enemy camp? But he had not. Moscardó was in no way an extraordinary man; he gave all the outward signs of the most persistent mediocrity, but perhaps events had transformed him beyond the point where even he could recognize himself. Or perhaps they had simply weakened him to a point where he had not the strength for retaliation.

"Then . . . go, for Christ' sake, Mercedes . . . go . . ."

She shook her head and would not talk about it. It would not be so serious after all, she said finally; Lieutenant Rincón's engineering party would find and contain the mine area or the night sorties would locate the tunnel and blow it up. There was nothing to worry about. The important thing was not to become dispirited.

He looked at her, astonished that someone so weak could display such resolve. He found little enough in himself. The news of the mine had shaken him, and now he could think of nothing else. He had almost been willing to accept a personal death, a bullet aimed at him, a knife thrust at his throat. But a mine, blind and indiscriminate?

A whisper, from the floor. They had forgotten about the Austrian.

"I want to know exactly where it is."

"So does everyone else," one of the card players said.

The footless man pulled the covers under his chin and began to dribble.

"No. I must know," Vitolyn exclaimed. "I have a right."

"Listen to him . . ."

Vitolyn was on his feet, pulling at the rope with both of his bandaged hands.

"I must know exactly where it is. I have a right to know," he shouted. "You have to let me out of here . . . to find it . . ."

The footless man began to cry out, garbled, unintelligible syllables, while Anton Vitolyn wrenched at the rope and continued screaming. Mercedes' fingers dug into Jaime's arm so hard that he winced and almost tried to shake her off. The soldier at the door scrambled to his feet again and ran into the corridor.

In a moment, there was a clatter of boots in the corridor, and three men came in with the soldier: Dr. Sepulveda, a short man with a white smock and wearing sunglasses, Major Punto, and a Guard sergeant whom Jaime did not recognize.

"What's all the yelling . . . ?" the doctor demanded, trying to see through the dark lenses; they were the only glasses he had had with him when he had come to the Alcázar. Without them, he could not see at all.

"Is someone hysterical? Is that it?"

"This one. Look at him."

Major Punto squinted, not used to the gloom; he'd been in the yard, watching clouds. "Ahh . . . him . . . that one . . ."

"It's the mine. He's yelling about the mine."

"That's all right. The mine has us all frightened. We're human, after all. We *should* be afraid. That's nothing to worry about," the doctor said quietly to the soldier. "Don't you worry about the mine?"

"Me? . . ."

"You . . . of course."

"Yes, but I don't let on."

"So . . . ?"

No one was paying any attention to Vitolyn who was still shouting. The soldier protested: "But he's got everyone worked up. They were quiet before."

The footless man was trying to whistle "Isle of Capri" now and dragging one deep, rasping breath after another.

Vitolyn suddenly stopped shouting; his silence chilled everyone by its suddenness.

"He stays here," Major Punto said. "There's no place that's safe anyway. You, so what are you shouting for?"

"You don't understand me at all, do you?" Vitolyn asked with an ironic lilt to his voice.

"Eh? That you're afraid of the mine? Well, I understand that. I'm afraid too, but what can we do? No, you stay here . . . it's as safe as any place else. . . ."

"You, Major . . . it's your fault, all of this . . . ," Vitolyn said, ignoring the others. Jaime leaned forward, Mercedes' arm around his back, supporting him. The Austrian's face fascinated him; here was no state of hysteria, no collapse into terror. Quite the contrary.

"You have not dealt justly with me," Vitolyn said very calmly, holding out his hands. The rope dangled, falling across his feet. The Major's eyes followed the rope back to the ring on the wall. Jaime could see Dr. Sepulveda give the Civil Guard a questioning look; why had no one explained to him about the rope? What was the rope for and who was this man? And what had happened to his hands? He didn't remember treating anyone for burns on the hands.

Major Punto was taken aback. It seemed to him that everyone was watching him. His riding crop dangled from his hand, began to describe a nervous arc against his leg. It was like the day he had singled out the old man in the courtyard just after the airplane had dropped the food.

"Unjust?" he blurted out, feeling himself losing control. "What do you want, man? What would be just? Five men in the plaza, and who knows what before? I'll tell you what would be just . . . a bullet . . ."

"Yes, something. . . . anything so I know what I am and what is to happen to me. Not this . . . being ignored . . . treated like an animal. I am a human being, do you understand that?" He was shouting again. "Do you understand the difference between a human being and an animal? It's that a human being is held accountable for his acts . . ."

Punto stared at him, unable to reply.

"Judgment," Vitolyn insisted. "Whatever you want to do, I'll accept it . . . let me do it myself. Let me out of here . . . I'll see to it that . . ."

"What have I got to do with this? Why do you blame me . . . ?" Major Punto insisted. For him, there was no one else in the room; all the others had become paper cutouts pasted against the walls.

"I'll tell you why . . . you forgave me . . . you did *this,* but then you forgave me . . . ," he held out his hands. "Oh, I'll admit, it was a good start . . . but then you turned tail and ran and put me in here. . . . Well, I won't let you forget me this way. I won't let you forgive me. . . . Who gave you the right to forgive me?"

Dr. Sepulveda was pulling at the arm of the Guard. The soldier had stepped discreetly back.

"Do you think you're above judging me?" Vitolyn screamed. His face was flushed, and tears made white claw marks down his cheeks. "Pass sentence, damn you. . . . You haven't got the courage to do it, that's the trouble. . . ."

Punto brought his arm up. The riding crop. Swung it around, the thong slashing across Vitolyn's face.

The Austrian uttered a sharp cry, not of triumph but of surprise, then fell back. He trembled for a second, then seemed to regain his composure.

He touched his face, ran his index finger down the violet red welt that stretched from his right temple to his jaw.

"You see," he said. "It was so easy . . ."

"You bastard." Punto turned, wide-eyed, and shouted at the Civil Guard. "If he does this again, take him outside and chain him to the wall." Then he nodded toward Dr. Sepulveda who was standing there, shaking his head.

"Do you have any brandy?"

"Come to the operating room. I have some there." The doctor glanced at the Guard. "Needless to say, you will forget this incident at once. . . ."

The crop lay on the floor where Major Punto had dropped it, only a foot or so away from Vitolyn's feet. Without another word, Vitolyn walked back to his pallet, coiling the rope about his arm, and sat down.

"If he starts again, . . . take him out into the corridor and chain him up in the storage closet . . . remember," the Major said from the doorway.

It was not more than an hour later when Vitolyn suddenly sprang to his feet and began shrieking. No one could stop him. Yet the screaming seemed too regular, too orderly; there was about it a chillingly planned persistence. The soldier at the door went at once into the corridor and returned with two more men. They untied Vitolyn and dragged him out of the room.

The moment he had been taken into the corridor, he stopped screaming.

Jaime lay there, wishing that Mercedes would return and that she would explain so many things to him. What was happening, why . . . and most of all, how a man could act like a madman and yet seem at the same time the most sane of them all.

SEPTEMBER 16: *Madrid*

ALL OVER THE CITY ONE FELT the same thing; an intensely heightened awareness, a sharpening of every sense, as though some rare plague had stricken every inhabitant of Madrid, giving him the kind of frightening clarity and acuity of vision that marks the last minutes of so many fatal diseases. It was the English writer, Johnson, who had put it so well, Colonel Carvalho recalled: "Nothing concentrates a man's faculties so wonderfully as the prospect of being hanged in a fortnight."

Talavera de la Reina was a good deal less than a fortnight away, more like an hour and a half by car. The Fascists had taken it and were massing for the push on the capital; on September 8, Arenas de San Pedro had fallen.

The staff car had taken him directly to the Ministry of Navy and Air where Prieto had lately been installed, following the resignation of Giral as Premier and the formation of a new government under Largo Caballero. Ramón Linares, a protégé of Prieto's, had followed his mentor to the Ministry. Carvalho felt that he might receive a more sympathetic ear here than at the Ministry of War which Caballero had placed under his own personal control.

Linares, who had risen no higher than captain in the army, had served with Carvalho during the days of Abd-el-Krim. Would he remember him? And if so, would he do anything more than listen politely?

The building was cavernous, cold gray stone. Nothing had been done to give it the appearance of a government office; in fact it seemed as though great pains had been taken to give it a battlefield, improvisatory look. Carvalho was led up to Linares' office after only a few minutes' wait downstairs.

The room was not large, made smaller by a surfeit of gray-green filing cabinets and a clutter of maps which hid the pale yellow wallpaper almost entirely. A large window which reached almost up to the ceiling permitted a view of the Cibeles fountain where the water could be seen plashing contently against a slate-blue sky flecked with dots of cloud.

477

Linares, a short, wiry man with an impresario's wild head of hair and a razor-thin mustache, greeted him effusively. After all, they had met at so many occasions of state during the past years . . . Linares' hair was still black, and Carvalho gazed at him with suspicion . . . dye? There was not that much difference in age between the two men. Yet while Carvalho had taken on the aspect of a patriarch, Linares still seemed the boulevardier, a perfect type of slightly overaged *señorito*.

"Even now," Linares explained, "they are going about in the streets with the loudspeakers, shouting, "Send out the women and children, send out the women and children." What else can we do? Colonel Torado tries, we try, the Ministry tries, the foreign press tries, the government tries. But that stubborn ass Moscardó does not try. So, I ask you, what is there to do?" The way the man was talking, it seemed he had not heard Carvalho at all. To him, the matter was a study in abstracts: the destruction of a national monument, but after all, ". . . it was destroyed twice before, so in a manner of speaking, its destruction is as much a part of its existence as its existence is . . . isn't that so, Enrique . . . ?"

"But the women and the children," Carvalho protested. And in particular, his daughter. Had they given any thought to that, to what would happen to them when the mine went off?

"Of course we have. Weren't you listening to what I was just saying?" Linares said with a trace of annoyance. "We've asked them to come out. What more can we do?"

"Are you still a Catholic, Ramón?" the Colonel asked suddenly.

"I beg your pardon?" Linares blinked his eyes.

"I take it that you haven't gone in for the latest fashion and that you still consider yourself a Catholic?"

Linares hesitated as though trying to judge whether he was being baited or led into a trap.

"Yes, in a sense . . ."

"Then I take it also that you don't believe in suicide?"

"No . . . I still remain that much of a Catholic, certainly . . ."

"Then let me ask you, if you knew a man, say myself for instance, who had told you he was going to commit suicide, would you leave a loaded gun on his table?"

"Of course not . . . ," Linares frowned and pushed back his mop of hair. The room was very hot, and his forehead was covered with a film of sweat. The Colonel was right; there were traces of dye on Linares' fingertips when he lowered his hand.

"Well then," Carvalho said, "isn't that precisely what you're doing here with these women? You know they won't come out, and yet you're going ahead and letting them kill themselves . . ."

Linares smiled. "Nicely twisted. Bravo . . . but it isn't the same thing. Surely you see that?"

"No, I don't."

"We must break the resistance; the Alcázar must fall to us. . . ."

"Why?" One short syllable, thrown out like a shot.

"Why? Because the nation is watching to measure our resolve by this. The world, too, is watching. Surely . . ."

"To see five hundred women and children blown up?" Carvalho shook his head. "No, you know that isn't true. And you know what harm it will do you."

Linares got up and began pacing in front of the window. He gazed out at the fountain of the Cibeles and the peaceful splashing waters. Lines of lorries were moving down the street below, and a file of mules carrying enormous gray boxes of ammunition labored along the cobblestones.

"Why do you have to do it at all? What is the Alcázar? A pile of stone, that's all. What harm can these people do you? None, and you know it."

"Symbols, symbols, Enrique," Linares replied without turning around. "Men fight for banners, defend creeds they will never in their lives understand, and die for reasons that are beyond their comprehension if . . . in fact . . . they are reasons at all."

Carvalho stood up. Linares had not turned.

"I'm sorry Enrique . . . what can I do?"

Carvalho was already at the door. He was on the verge of thanking Linares for his time in his most ironic manner but simply said: "That's all then?"

"It is. *Salud,* Enrique."

"*Adios . . . ,*" Carvalho said, using the forbidden word with emphasis.

The last of the mules was passing as he stepped out of the front of the ministry building. Soldiers in steel helmets stood under the sun, the sweat pouring down their faces; others, in forage caps with the new red tassels hanging jauntily from them, walked about in twos and threes. Of the priests who in former times inhabited the city like flocks of starlings, none could be seen. Even the churches masqueraded behind layers of posters proclaiming patriotic slogans, paper soldiers gesturing with clenched fists in defiance of the armies massed for the attack just over the horizon.

There were others to see. Carvalho took from his pocket a small notebook in which he had inscribed a list of names: Florez, Arrondo, Azuela, López Sotomayer, Felipe Gelves . . . all of them men who had once been his friends. He stopped to let a troop of mounted *Asaltos* go by, their smart blue uniforms, peaked caps and boots a stark contrast to the disordered combination of "monos," pith helmets, regular army uniforms, and peasant straw hats that were the general rule on the streets of Madrid. Here, as in Barcelona, the women had been armed, and young girls marched with rifles too large for them to ever fire properly.

The lines on the paper of his note pad began to waver and to blur; the names wriggled like tiny blue worms. He tried to push the haze out of his eyes with the back of his hand. Without thinking of it, he dropped his hand to his collar to loosen it.

This was something new; no longer the pain and the vibrations but now a pronounced dizziness as well. What of it, he thought? Anyone will get dizzy if he stands in the heat long enough. You're old. That's the truth. Not like Raúl or even that fool Luccioni. They can stand about in the heat; you can't.

He sat on a bench on a broad avenue through which trees paraded as though they, not the soldiers, the *milicianos,* and the citizenry of the city, owned the way, the air, and the soil beneath. Pigeons fluttered down in whirls of wing-beats. Nearby a little boy was throwing crumbs into a blur of white and gray wings. Carvalho took a deep breath. That helped a little; his sight grew clearer. He experimented, drew in another, deeper breath. It seemed to steady him. The more oxygen, the better everything was. The lines of the note pad held still. But he could no longer remember how many of them he had seen. Was Linares the only one thus far, or had he talked to Felipe Gelves as well? Or López Sotomayer? He found, to his astonishment, that he could not remember.

Searching the pad for some key, he found one page on which he had scrawled an address. Or had he? The handwriting did not look like his own: "17 Calle Martínez de la Rosa." When had he written that? There were initials next to it, but he could make out only the letter *M.*

It was not hard for him to get a taxi. His uniform and his white beard were of such effect that the first cab that came by stopped for him and its passenger got out and offered him his place. No, it was hardly necessary, the Colonel replied, but if they were both going in the same direction . . .

He got in. His companion was a portly man who would at any other time have been wearing a hat. Now, even the *madrilenos* went hatless out of fear that someone might point an accusing finger at them. Now, why should a hat become . . . symbols . . . hadn't Linares said? . . . Hats.

The cab turned up the Gran Via, past the cafés which were doing a flourishing business and the motion-picture houses which were offering the latest American and English films.

"The only thing they send us," Carvalho's traveling companion observed, passing the Cino de la Flor which was playing *Las Mil y una Noches"* with Charles Boyer and Madeleine Carroll.

"The volunteers?" the Colonel said, surprised. "The Internationals?"

"You misunderstand me. The 'Internationals,' they 'come.' The films are 'sent.' There's a difference."

The Colonel remained silent, as did the driver. They passed a corner on which stood two lottery-ticket sellers. Was there still a lottery? Or had those poor old men been caught by the war with trays full of tickets to sell and gone right on, not understanding? Such things happened. Nearby, a woman was selling loose cigarettes from a box. Brands of every nationality except Spanish. Bright colors. Her eyes, dark circles.

They passed some buildings which had been hit during an air raid. The walls across the street were stitched with machine-gun bullets. The low flying planes not only dropped bombs but strafed as well, and as many had been killed by bullets as by shrapnel. Fumes rose, bluish against the afternoon sky. The cab turned a corner, and rows of massive stone buildings came into view. They had come out near the Plaza de Oriente. Then, for some reason, as though the driver had made a mistake, the cab swung back seemingly in the direction from which it had come. Streets had been marked "one way" to facilitate traffic, the portly man explained; it made it very difficult to get around, required odd, circuitous routes . . .

"Stop here," the Colonel called suddenly. The cab had just crossed the Calle Mayor, a few blocks above the Puerta del Sol. Carvalho pressed a few pesetas into his companion's hand.

"You can't win a civil war with Madeleine Carroll," he said, surprised at himself, yet the man invited nothing but such sarcasm; he got out and the cab moved away. A tram passed, bursting with passengers like an overripe fruit.

His arm had begun to ache. He took an odd pleasure in the effort it cost him to walk. The crowd thickened as he entered the Puerta del Sol. An armored car, blinded by its steel plates, lumbered across the plaza, its machine guns pointed at the shop windows, a man's head just visible on top, as though it had been cut off and placed there as a decoration. People walked about in front of the armored car as though it were not there.

Carvalho had crumpled the paper with the address in his pocket; he remembered now. It was the house where Señora Mercader was living. The number had come to him through Captain Segurra.

Pushing through the crowd was like trying to swim against coastal breakers; he leaned forward, pressing against the weight of bodies. Banners were hung all over the walls of the buildings around the Puerta del Sol, covering the windows of bookshops, of groceries, of restaurants.

He passed a theater which had until recently been showing *Zarzuela*. A blue and white poster, bordered with floral designs announced Serrano's *"Moros y Cristianos"* for that week, but the theater was closed. It had taken a bomb hit, and the windows were all shattered. Smoke trailed from within. Across the Manzanares River, Carvalho thought, that's where they'll get their music . . . Moors and Christians, to be sure.

He came to the War Ministry. The taxi ride had been foolish. He had not even been sure where he was going. 17 Calle Martínez de la Rosa? Mercader's widow? What could she say to him? The idea of even seeing her, much less talking with her, terrified him. He thought of his wife Amalia and how she might react under similar circumstances, of his daughter Inés and of Raúl, still in Paris, for whom all this was only newspaper headlines in French, political rallies, and conferences.

Suits of armor guarded the imperial staircases in the Ministry building, making the pale-faced guards seem insignificant by comparison. The carpets were thick underfoot and well cleaned. Yet there was a silence in the building, as though nothing anyone could say or do could ever adequately fill its cavernous spaces.

"López Sotomayer? Tell him it's Colonel Enrique Carvalho. . . ."

"I'll see, señor . . . one moment . . ." The clicking of telephone re-
lays, a nerve-racking buzzing.

Carvalho found himself climbing the staircase to the second floor. It
was difficult, and he experienced a sensation of mass concentrated in his
back that made climbing almost impossible. He had to stop to rest for a
moment; a corporal on guard at the landing helped him the rest of the
way. Carvalho was stricken with shame that a young man should have to
help him, physically. . . . What right did he have to ask for anything?
Was he being worn out that quickly? What a distance he had come from
the night on the quay at Santander.

"I'm sorry. Señor Sotomayer is in conference. . . ."

He jerked a thumb toward the attic. General Miaja's staff was meeting under the roof, in the broiling heat. Why there? Why not in the cool
stone-walled rooms?

The Colonel sat down gratefully and waited. Staff officers began
passing in the corridor outside. The meeting was breaking up. Voices
could be heard snapping into telephones. Jangling, drawers closing. The
arthritic sound of heavy file cabinets creaking open. In the street below,
someone was playing a concertina.

López Sotomayer came in without having been told that Carvalho
was waiting for him and stood in open-mouthed surprise in the doorway,
a look of embarrassment washing suddenly across his features; his face
was heavier than it had been when the Colonel had last seen him. The
man was a genius at tactics, at long-range planning. Carvalho wondered
what Sotomayer could possibly do with the front moving so rapidly,
whether he was up to what was required in such a situation. Sotomayer's
upper lids were enlarged, giving him a sleepy, dissipated look that was
completely in contrast to his real character. He was wearing a jacket with
a colonel's star pinned to the breast. A cigarette of dark tobacco dangling
from his lips.

Their greetings were odd, strained. Sotomayer's hand shook noticeably, but he invited the Colonel into his office all the same.

An open book of stamps lay on his desk; Carvalho remembered that
stamp-collecting was Sotomayer's passion, surpassing even his interest in
women. "The body will cease to respond in time," he had said once, "but
governments will continue to issue commemoratives, won't they?" Carvalho wondered whether the Republic had issued any commemoratives
since the uprising had begun.

Next to the stamp album was a packet of unsorted stamps, a glassine
envelope which bore the imprint of a philatelist near the Puerta del Sol.
Toilet articles lay on the window ledge; shaving soap—"Royal"
mentholated—razors, a towel. Sotomayer was evidently living in his office.
The couch had been made up as a bed, and a pair of trousers, badly
folded, hung over the end.

"Excuse me a moment," Sotomayer said. He retrieved the towel,
dabbed at his face. He had been sweating heavily. Then he ran a comb
through his tangled hair, patted on some brilliantine from a jar with a

stylized Indian on the lid. Reaching out to what had seemed an anonymous brown box on the ledge, he twisted a knob, revealed it as a radio. A string orchestra came on, playing light music. Not content with all of these preparations, López Sotomayer further insulated himself by taking a box of cigars from his drawer, offering one to the Colonel, and then lighting up himself.

Finally, he settled down in his chair and before Carvalho could speak, he waved a hand in the air, in a gesture of futility.

"I can guess why you're here," he began. He could not only guess, but he knew exactly. Linares had called him from the Naval and Air Ministry the moment Carvalho had left. But he hadn't needed to call at all. Word had been circulating for weeks about the Colonel's behavior in Toledo. "That you haven't been carted off to prison by now for all this defeatism is what's really astounding," Sotomayer said. "And that stupidity with Ibáñez. Yes, I know about that, too."

"Are you serious? Do you call this 'defeatism'? Trying to save one's own daughter from a useless death . . ."

"My dear friend, what death is not useless?"

"That's not what I mean . . . nor do I want to get into a philosophical debate with you." Something in Sotomayer's tone grated. It was as though he were intent upon putting the Colonel at once on the defensive and so staving off any requests Carvalho might make. That could mean only one thing: López Sotomayer was in a position to do something, knew what would be asked of him, and had already determined not to respond.

"I mean it, quite seriously. Believe me, I sympathize with you. Look, I've got children of my own, you know that. Two of the boys are on the front lines. The girls are working with the Auxiliaries, and it's all I can do to keep them from picking up rifles too."

"What does that mean?"

"It means, have you considered that your daughter went up there of her own free will? As I remember, she was no one to be told what to do. A very rebellious sort, wasn't she? Not like your older one at all."

"No, you're wrong. She could think, she could reason, and she was obedient . . ." the Colonel protested.

"She could reason, yes. You taught her and you taught her well. But obedient? Yes, as long as her concept of reason led her to the same conclusions as yours did. That was the case for a long time, wasn't it? But now, supposing that now . . ."

"You mean, supposing she's decided to be a Fascist? Impossible."

"But supposing nevertheless . . ."

"Are you trying to insult me?"

"No, I'm simply trying to make you see why what you've been doing is bound to have disastrous effects, for yourself if for no one else. . . ." He reached into his drawer. "Do you see this?" He held up a sheet of paper. "This is a record of what you've been doing the last few weeks. Do you know that both Major Barceló and now Colonel Torado have asked

that you be placed in 'protective custody'? Not to mince words, Enrique
. . . they want you arrested. Ibáñez insists that you are mixed up with
the POUM, and you know what that would mean for you . . . now . . .
Enrique, believe me when I tell you. For your own good . . ."

"In short," Carvalho cut him off, "you expect me to do what Colonel
Moscardó did?"

"What he *thought* he did . . . the son is still alive, of course. . . .
But, yes, precisely. That's what's expected, Enrique. Do you realize that
practically every other family in this country is divided against itself?
Cousins are slaughtering cousins, brothers butchering brothers. Fathers
and sons are torn apart, even mothers and daughters shake their fists at
each other. Which is more important—family or country? Ask yourself
that. The second without the first, yes, but not the first without the second." Sotomayer suddenly leaned across the desk, his fleshy face burning.
"There will be other families, but without the country, what of them?
Nothing . . . you know that and so do I. . . ."

Carvalho rose. "What has this to do with my daughter? For God's
sake . . ."

"Please, I'm trying to help you, don't you understand? Look at you.
Are you an old man? Of course not. And with your experience, you could
be a great help to us. Even General Miaja has asked after you. I swear,
he was astounded when he read these reports. But he persists. 'Can't we
convince that man to work with us?' he asks me. All right, I'll try. I'm
trying now. What a waste for you to be wandering about this way . . .
because of your past record, because your son Raúl who has been of such
help to us in Paris, because of the respect of your friends, you've been allowed to go on like this. But the time has come to put an end to it, don't
you think? The Moors are almost to the Manzanares. You know what
it's going to be like here in a few weeks, don't you? The bombing attacks
are increasing . . . everytime we go up there in the attic for a meeting, we expect a bomb to come crashing through the roof. I swear
it. . . ."

It was what he expected. Why should he feign surprise? Carvalho
folded his hands together to still their trembling, watched his knuckles
shake.

"Do you have any better cigars?" Carvalho asked suddenly, grinding
the cigar Sotomayer had given him under his heel.

"Eh? What was that?" Sotomayer's head jerked up, startled. "Cigars?"

"And you can turn the radio off now, too, if you like. I'm leaving."
He wrenched his note pad from his pocket and scrawled the name and
address of the Hotel Maravilla on a sheet of paper which he placed in
front of his astonished friend.

"This is where I can be found in Toledo if you choose to have me
arrested. As for my whereabouts in Madrid, I'm not sure how long I'll be
here or where, so you'll have to look for me if you can't wait."

He had been walking the streets for hours; he had taken off his insignia of rank and put the star in his pocket. He rationalized what he had done by saying that his arm pained him and that to have to salute so often was physically difficult for him. So many men in nondescript uniforms were wandering about the city. No one would notice an old man with a bristling white beard. The only trace of rank was the pinhole in his tunic.

The cafés were doing a thriving business. Men ate as though there would be no food at all the next morning. It was late, but he called both Florez and Arrondo. Neither was in. He took a whiskey and paid a great deal for it. For a moment he felt better. He looked out of the café window, past the crisscrosses of tape which had been spread on the panes to keep the glass from caving in if a bomb burst in the street, saw the streets filling with that unique russet shadow that marked Madrid's evenings in the summer. The buildings seemed to lean toward each other for support across the wide street. Trams went by, and in the distance the drone of planes could be heard, but they came no closer and no one in the café paid any attention to them.

He had something to eat and then went out again. The walls were covered with posters shouting ¡ No Pasaran! as though incantation could turn hope to fact.

The Plaza Mayor was as it always had been, another world, impervious to time. Dusty children skittered in the shadows. The smell of wet tiles and beer flowed up from cellars and out of doorways.

Women passed carrying bags of groceries, live chickens, bags of rice. Radios blared popular music and jaunty songs of defiance. Somewhere, down a street into which he could not see, he could hear men singing in a tough, tongue-cracking, unfamiliar language; the shuffle of booted feet. Men went by trundling wheelbarrows of lime and mortar. Lorries carrying sandbags were everywhere.

The streets grew more dense, the atmosphere thicker. It was as though all of Madrid were settling to the bottom of some huge pond, its mass concentrating in those ancient streets.

Calle Martínez de la Rosa, number 17. It was an old house but one with dignity, three stories high and not much different from his own home in Toledo. But the door had no iron eagle above the lock and hasp.

He knocked. A woman opened the door. When she saw his uniform, she stepped back, frightened.

"It's all right," he said hastily. "Is the Señora Mercader in?"

Xaviera, the only one of the household who had stayed with Francisco's widow, showed the Colonel into the dining room. Some of the furniture seemed familiar; had they actually been able to rescue some of the pieces from their Toledo house? Or was it just that he had seen such furniture in their home so many times before, in Morocco? It gave him a sense of displacement in time which added to his uneasiness. He was afraid to face her, yet she seemed the only person he could possibly talk to at that moment.

A noise in the hallway; slippered feet. Señora Mercader appeared, in a long white garment like the Moslem haik but not as voluminous. For some reason he had gotten it into his head that she might appear veiled, —a thing that he feared, for it would isolate her eyes and leave him vulnerable to their stare with no way to protect himself, no other feature of her face to focus on. But true to her Berber custom, she wore no veil but faced him waxen and unprotected. Her eyes, as he had feared, were wide and penetrating. She looked him up and down, trying in a glance to decipher the reasons for his appearance.

He held up a hand in greeting. She nodded and came into the room.

Xaviera had seated the Colonel in a chair at one end of the dining table. Señora Mercader took a seat at the opposite end. The expanse of polished wood between them caught the reflections of both faces, drew them out until they were long and sharp as knives.

What was there they could tell each other? It was plain to her from the Colonel's expression that he knew what had happened to Francisco, plain from the very fact of his being there. Equally plain that she had heard what had happened to his daughter, for her face bore an extra imprint of suffering, a compassion, that can only come when one takes into one's own heart the pain of another.

The Basque woman brought in two cups of chocolate without being asked.

For the first time, Señora Mercader spoke: ". . . or would you prefer coffee? We have some, I think . . ."

The chocolate was there. He would take that, thankful for anything that might warm his body. He sipped slowly, the sweet liquid almost gagging him. There was a photo not far off, on the window ledge; a gold frame that caught the last rays of the sun. The boy, Jaime.

She caught the direction of his gaze.

"He thought you were . . . ," she paused.

Carvalho shook his head. "Not after what happened . . ."

"Because of what happened . . . that proved it to me. No one could suffer as much if he had not . . . loved you as much as he did . . . more than his father, I think. . . ."

One thing she did not know: what happened to her son and his daughter. He told her, as quickly as he could. Everything that he knew. She did not seem shocked. Every gesture bespoke an intense weariness and, in a way, a kind of withdrawal, as though the dark apartment—he noticed now that there were no electric lights, only candles set in brass holders—were a cell in a convent. . . .

"So," she said, smiling in an enigmatic, pained way, ". . . we could blame each other for so many things, couldn't we? I for my son, you for your daughter. . . ."

"Blame . . . ?" He turned the word on his tongue. It seemed to have lost all meaning for him. A man can be blamed only for that which is within his power to avoid, he thought. No, that wasn't right either; one could exert an influence in so many ways, deflect events, alter them by something done even at a great distance in time or space. . . . Who was to say when a person had failed?

She told him of how she had been brought to Madrid after the burning of their home. At several points, she started to speak of the disaster itself but her eyes would cloud, and she would shake her head as though it were only a remembered fantasy and to tell it would be to tell a lie. And so she would not speak of it at all.

"I was hoping," she said, "that it might be possible to return to Ceuta. But . . . everything is so complicated now . . . I'm afraid . . ."

Did she know that Ceuta was in the hands of the military rebels? And if she knew, did it make any difference to this silent Berber woman?

He did not remember her looking so young. Ordinarily, suffering . . . loss would age a person. On Señora Mercader's face the mark of her pain was a disturbing, almost unearthly youthfulness. Her eyes were filled with the Moroccan highlands, its clouds and mountains, as her son's eyes had once been filled, toward the end, just before he had resigned his commission. Was it the mark of the Mercaders that at such moments they would reach back to the desert and draw it around themselves like a shroud? First the son, then the mother. It frightened him and at the same time gave him an unbearable feeling of calm. He found himself watching the woman's hands; her slender fingers moved so slowly over the surface of the table, caressing her own reflection, that they seemed to fade into the wood itself.

Looking at her hands, he thought of what he had said to Portillo the day before Emilio had been killed. He turned his own hands palms up on the table. "Do you still tell fortunes?" How little he knew her, and how well he had known her husband.

"No. Gypsies do that, not Berbers. We . . . understand our fate. There's no need to look into the future. What would it show us that we don't already know?"

Carvalho was silent. From the doorway, Xaviera was watching him intently. Suspicion or concern? he wondered, catching sight of her out of the corner of his eye.

The room was almost bare; not poor, because the few ornaments there were elegant and very valuable. But simple nevertheless. White predominated. It was as though with Francisco Mercader's death, his wife had begun an inevitable return to her origins and their simple customs.

She saw him looking at the bare walls, said, as if reading his mind, "There is no need for any of the things Francisco had. Most of them he brought here because of me, to assure me at least a small bit of what we had left. But I'm going back, you see, so there's no need." She paused, her lips trembling slightly. "But one thing, Enrique Carvalho, before I do go back and it is the end to my having been here . . . at all . . . tell me, what happened between you and my son? Not the fact of it, but *why*? . . . It caused him so much unhappiness that I should know. . . ."

He was astounded; she talked of going back, and of her son as though he were dead. With such finality, such an unnerving tranquillity. He protested: the boy was alive. Soler had seen him.

"And your daughter as well . . . but they're both really dead, aren't they? To think otherwise . . ." She glanced at the ceiling where mauve shadow obscured the delicate lines of the beams. The candles flickered. Carvalho became aware of an odor of damp wood.

"We accept things as they are," she said. "And as they are, they had to be . . . but we can still look for reasons. If we can change nothing, at least we can hope to understand . . ."

"If I could understand, I would gladly . . ." His fingers curled around the handle of the cup; suddenly it cracked under the pressure and the sharp china cut his finger. He stanched the blood with a rag. "Xaviera . . ."

The Basque, who had seen the accident from the doorway, brought a bowl of cool water. The blood curled like smoke in the water, making Carvalho dizzy. "If I knew," he mumbled . . . watching the blood. It seemed that he was seeing the Oviedo station, the railroad cars, and all the rest of it too, everything that had numbed him for the last twenty years.

"I'm glad you came here," the woman said. "Though it changes nothing, I am glad nevertheless. I think that in certain things I understood Jaime far better than did his father and . . . ," she smiled faintly, ". . . without the aid of words, Colonel, without words at all." She nodded. "He would have been glad to know you had come . . . and that you were as . . . confused as he was, as tormented by the same things, it seems."

When Carvalho had left the flat and was walking in the dark streets toward the Plaza Mayor and a searchlight beam was probing the murky sky for the rebel bombing planes that were coming in regularly every night from Sevilla, he remembered those words, in fact could not rid himself of them.

". . . that you were as confused as he was, as tormented by the same things . . ."

A siren wailed somewhere. From the depths of the city, a choir of klaxons wailed their response. Figures passed him, skulking in doorways, shrouded by the dark of the streets which was the same that night as it had been when Goya painted his *majos* wrapped in the cloaks and hidden beneath their sweeping hats, as when the Inquisition led its fragile lines of heretics chanting, wearing the *san bonito,* carrying their brooms and wands, symbols of their disgrace in God's eye . . . all of it, the same, nothing changed. The same, he thought, and the same confusion and the same torment. And has man been different for one second of eternity and can he ever aspire to be different, to achieve even the minutest understanding of what he himself does? "If we could understand that we understand nothing . . . and live with that knowledge . . ."

For the first time in as long as he could remember, he felt hot tears sliding down his cheeks, tracking under the whorls of white hair that rushed like a fire from his face. Tears for the boy, dead but not dead, who was somehow kin to him, and for his daughter as well who had been drawn into the tangle of his uncertainties and to whom he had passed on those uncertainties and with the same, inevitably tragic result.

He squinted, trying to flush out the tears but the supply seemed endless. At last, he relaxed and as he walked, let the tears flood his face.

A breeze was coming up the alleys from the Manzanares River, and it touched his cheeks, the tears, the damp tracks on his wrinkled skin. He felt cool and, in a strange way, refreshed.

SEPTEMBER 16: *The Alcázar*

OUT OF THE CORNER OF HIS EYE Jaime could see the doorway to the chamber. The young soldier had been playing cards with himself and had fallen asleep. Pepe was his name; everyone had gotten to know him, but no one would play cards with him because he took the game so seriously. Not at all like the two who had won and lost the Bank of Spain ten times over in the past few days. Even betting pebbles and losing upset Pepe, so he played by himself and often fell asleep over the game.

Twice Barrera had come down to the subcellar to see Jaime. "Christ, man, you'll be all right. I know you will," he would say and stand there by the cot with his hands twisted together, gazing down at Mercader with a look of infinite and irremediable sadness on his face.

"It's your cousin, isn't it?" Jaime asked weakly.

"And if it is. . . . ? Does it show . . . that much? Sure . . . it's him again."

"Is he dead?"

Barrera shook his head. "It's worse. He really did it this time, and I know. I was there and I couldn't stop him." And then he told Jaime the story of what had happened the day on the wall when Ignacio Peralta had died a second time. "He's gone mad this time, really mad. Dr. Sepulveda says he may never come out of it. He just lies there, all doubled up, like a baby, with his knees up to his chest." He stopped short and then said in a strained, weary voice, "I couldn't stop him. I tried but I couldn't move that fast, I just couldn't. You believe that, don't you, that I tried?"

Jaime reached up and took the man by the hands. For a moment they remained in that attitude, Jaime's fingers locked around the driver's wrists. It was the same, for those seconds, as it had been that evening when they had broken bread together on the flat rock by the Madrid–Toledo road. Through their fingers passed a compassion and reassurance that words could never have adequately expressed.

Barrera nodded and then he left. "You'll be all right, I know it, *teniente* . . . don't worry. Do you promise me, you won't worry?"

That had been three days ago. Barrera had not been back since.

The mule-fat lamp had long since burned out, and the greasy stink had faded, filming the stones with a thin, almost undetectable odor. Everyone was asleep. The first sign of approaching day filtering down through the corridors, a different light, cold and ashy in color.

Soon, Jaime thought, the artillery would start again. It was difficult to distinguish the bursting of shells from the drumming in his own head. Perhaps, after all, he was dying and it was simply that no one, not even Mercedes, would tell him. To have lost contact with everyone, with everything around him in this way made him more depressed even than the thought of approaching death. The sappers' drilling could be heard now and then, moving away like a giant insect thrumming beneath the stones. It was impossible to tell where they were. The Lieutenant with the stethoscope had come into the room a few times, once with his "crew" to take soundings, and Jaime had smiled but could find nothing to say to encourage him. How pointless it all seemed.

He groped about for the tin can that had been full of water the night before. The can was empty. His lips were dry and cracked, and he longed for a drink. His hand trailed over the edge of his cot, his fingers raking the ground. Finding a pebble, he rubbed it clean, put it in his mouth, under his tongue. For a moment his thirst eased and he was able to think of other things. Emptiness, he found . . . nothing.

Outside, in the corridor, it seemed to grow lighter by degrees.

The void receded, a giant orb of sun fading behind clouds. He recalled through it, the senseless cry of the Legionnaires . . . *Viva la muerte* . . . Of course, one should welcome death. Everything leads there. If a man makes a choice, he is trapped. If he doesn't, well then, he's trapped anyhow. He heard the laugh of the General from his dream. "An empty bottle soon fills up when it rains."

The footless man was sound asleep for the first time, his face like the profile on a coin, cast out of lead; his forehead glistened with beads of sweat. "Gangrene," someone had said, but the man went right on whistling "Isle of Capri" as though he might get there some day, and the boys at their card game looked away, embarrassed.

A sound. He turned his head. Mercedes stood there next to the sleeping soldier, a bottle of water in her hand. The bottle had once held soda, and the label was still there, bright orange, against the green glass. She saw that he was awake and came to him quickly.

"It was all I could find," she said in a whisper. "There's no food. Not even for the children now. . . ."

"It's all right . . . ," he said. How could he say anything else when it so obviously cost her almost all the energy she had left in her wasted body just to come down and tell him that she had nothing for him? He took the bottle and drank, then tipped the bottle on end and poured some water onto a cloth. She watched, puzzled and then tried to stop him as he put the cloth to her head.

"I should be doing that for you. . . ."

"It's all right," he said again. The cloth would revive her. For what?

he thought . . . "If resurrection comes, what will we find outside?"

Then: "Is there any news? The radio . . . ?"

She tried to smile. "A little comes through. Not much. Oh, Jaime . . . it's so awful to know that the troops are just a few miles away but that they may not get here before . . ."

He thought, "before what?" but asked instead, "Whose troops? Are we really going to be saved?"

She shook her head and looked as though she might begin to cry. But she bit her lip and gazed at him with an expression that struck so hard to his heart that it almost took his breath away. It was so unexpected. "You're right . . . ," she mused. "Whose? I don't know . . ."

He wished, suddenly, that Colonel Carvalho were there, standing right in that room, that he could speak to him. He felt an overwhelming urge to throw himself into the man's arms and beg him . . . for what? Only that he knew that whatever he asked for would be given. . . .

The morning in the pine forests above Oviedo, next to the stream, while the guards who had brought him up watched from the edge of a stand of dark-green pine, while Enrique Carvalho clambered up the steep bank of the stream, and then stood there looking at him, before he finally put his arm around Jaime's shoulder and said with a terrible weariness that betrayed more than anything his knowledge that he would in the end have come back no matter what, that he could carry his betrayal only so far. Now, Jaime wondered, had it been that way at all? Or was it possible that just as God required Judas in order that his play be carried out, that there was something in the scheme of his own life that required that betrayal, and that in doing what he did, Enrique Carvalho had somehow liberated Jaime from himself in the only way possible . . . ?

"I want to walk, Mercedes. . . ."

"No . . . no, you're not . . ."

"Yes. I want to," he said. "To see what's outside. . . ."

"We're three levels down. You'll never be able to get up the stairs. . . ."

"The wound is here," he said, touching his head, "not there . . ." his hand swept his legs. "Anything that I can still think to want, I can do. The weakness is . . . in the mind . . . not the body. . . ."

He swung his feet from the mattress, sat up with great effort, and gazed at her intensely.

He took the one-lensed binoculars from the foot of his bed. No one had stolen them.

Mercedes helped him to the door as best she could. The firing had not yet started. It was still very early and although the sky outside had lightened to a cottony gray, the sun had not yet come up. The corridor was murky.

"Let's go and see the sunrise," he said. "From the tower . . . is the tower still there?" He was seized with a sudden desire to gaze out onto the northern plains, to release himself from that claustrophobic vision of stone walls, low ceilings, and smoky shadows. She would come with him, to the tower and to the morning which would be, for him, its own liberation and in which they would share.

They climbed the stairs slowly. No one passed them on the steps. Muted sounds behind walls were their only companions: a child crying, a few threads of music dropped like arrows from an out-of-tune guitar, the rattling of pans, and the hidden hissing and steaming of water, of fire.

He closed his eyes, let her guide him. They climbed forever, mounting higher and higher and at the same time seeming not to move at all but to be remaining suspended, motionless, in his fever. It was no strain at all to climb. If only they could manage it without his having to open his eyes again. His head hung down, his chin against his breastbone, and he heard her start to say something a number of times, but each time she stopped, held onto him a little more tightly and continued climbing. He could hear her labored breathing, and though he knew how much it was costing her to come with him, what an impossible thing it was to ask of her, he kept on.

He could see daybreak without opening his eyes; suddenly everything around him became lighter, a sort of grayish orange color. The tiny creatures that moved across the insides of his eyes became lines of red and yellow against a field of squirming color that looked like blood or pus. . . .

"Jaime . . . ," she said.

"Are we there?"

"Yes. . . ."

He opened his eyes and all at once a sea seemed to rush through his head, pressing the sides of his skull outward like the walls of a bottle when its contents have frozen within it.

It was still there: the city, the plains. All of it.

"Have you ever seen the countryside from here?" he asked.

Mercedes shook her head. How many years had she lived in Toledo in her father's house and not once had she ever come up to the tower to look out at the city. It would have been so easy; her father had only to call someone at the Academy. But the thought had never occurred to her.

She looked out through a high-arched opening toward the river. There was no glass in the window; only an ogival shape of stone like the vault of a cathedral window. They were so high up that no one had bothered to barricade the window.

Shapes seemed to move on the hillside across the Tagus, but it was only the dawn breeze in the scrubby trees that dotted the slopes. The smell of cooking drifted along on the wind. Jaime wrinkled his nose, turned away, unable to bear the smell.

The sky to the west now seemed to bleed from a hundred wounds, like the polychrome Christs in the churches of Melilla; the clouds reddened, thick and clotted, weighted to the horizon by mourning. Above, the stars had already faded. It would be a clear day, as hot and ferocious as every day that had gone before. There would be no end to the heat, to the dust and the smell of the dry plains, the "bull-hide," as Lorca had called it once, stretched tight from the Manzanares to the Tagus, and withering under the sun.

"Look out there," he said after a time. "Do you see the towers . . . of Tetuán?"

She turned slightly to stare at him. Madrid lay in the direction of his gaze and Illescas, which was as far as anyone could ever see even on the clearest day. Even from the top of the cathedral. What had made him say . . . Tetuán? She shuddered to see the bloodstained bandages wound about his head. A trickle of fresh blood was running down his neck.

"No, no," he insisted, offended by her silence. "You can really see it if you look hard. There, just over the horizon. Don't you see them? Little bits of blue, the mosques. Like glass beads."

He felt her hands on his arms and struggled with an unbearable tenderness which he knew he had no right to feel.

"We could have gone there, you and I . . . to Ceuta . . . where all the white houses are piled up like pebbles to the sky. Very white and clean, my city of Tetuán . . ."

They seemed to float there on the horizon, just under the clouds, the white mounds of Ceuta and the mosques of Tetuán. "My father's house . . . we still had the house there. It was white too. He left it but we could have gone back there. . . ."

She reached out to touch his head, alarmed. He pushed her hand away, gently. "We all have a fever now. So it's nothing. Do you know what it is to have a fever under a real sun? The sun over Xauen is so hot . . . the houses are painted blue, so that they'll think they are cool and not notice . . ." His voice trailed off into a dry whisper, words she could not understand.

They waited. The heat grew more intense as the sun rose. His voice climbed, fell, began to trace singsong patterns in the air like the call of a muezzin. His fingers closed tightly over her hand. It was the first time he had ever done that, and she did not try to pull away.

". . . out there, the Riffs are in those hills, preparing themselves for the end of the world, chanting their secret prayers . . . don't be fooled, Mercedes . . . we should be saying those prayers . . . those same prayers. . . ." He raised his free hand to his forehead as though something pained him, closed his eyes. He seemed to be searching for something within himself.

Mercedes squinted into the light. There was smoke rising again to the northwest. She remembered what they had told her the night before, that the Legion was on those hills, and the Moors too. Could Jaime really see them? Hadn't he just said . . . the Riff?

"Those are the fires from Oropesa, and there, that over there is the smoke from Arenas de San Pedro. That's where the troops are . . . ," she said.

Oropesa? . . . Arenas de San Pedro? No, he knew what he was seeing. He knew the smoke from Berber fires when he saw it.

She said, "Radio Milan says that General Varela is over there, ready to take Marute. Do you think? . . ." she tried to suggest, to wean him away from his fantasy as gently as she could . . . let it come from him.

"Riff," Jaime said, smiling as the smoke rose like a lanyard wound into the sky toward Talavera de la Reina. "I've seen campfires like that . . . my mother's people. . . ," he was saying, but she could not hear the rest. It was hard for her to look at his face, and she cursed herself for allowing him to come up to the tower. He stood there, his face streaked by the rays of the slowly rising sun, staring out over the plains toward Madrid but seeing Tetuán, Ceuta . . . Xauen. . . . She waited, her heart pounding heavily, afraid to leave him. . . .

He had let go of her hand, but his fingers were still curved as though her hand was still there. His fingers were rigid. His face was drawn and bloodless . . . except for the steady trickle of dark red which proceeded from under the edge of the bandage, just over his left ear, and down under his collar.

She backed away from him; he seemed not to notice. "Come away," she said but he didn't hear her.

"Jaime! . . ." she was screaming, but he did not move, only holding one finger to his lips as though spearing silence on it and tasting it.

She knew she could not move him. Something had to be done. The sun was steaming up over the hills, and the firing would start soon. What if he would not move from the window, then?

She left the room and went down the stairs, her head reeling and her legs almost buckling under her from fatigue and hunger.

After a moment . . . and he did not realize at all, not once during that time, that he was alone . . . Jaime Mercader took the field glasses and brought them up to his eyes. Suddenly, the muddy brown hills grew sharp through the one lens. The tiny dots became distinct objects, rocks, olive trees, pine, shadowed ravines. He tried to imagine what it was like out there under the pall of smoke that blotched the western horizon.

Against the flat yellow expanse of plain, broken only by the occasional jut of a mesa, against a charred landscape which seemed freshly scorched by grass fires, that darker and more sinister cloud hovered like a live thing, sheltering a tremulous heartbeat of cannon.

He could see the Moors on their swift, frothing horses, clattering down the streets of Oropesa and Talavera de la Reina, with all the memory of their ancestors' fierce lust for that arid soil stinging in their nostrils. Come back to Castilla after five hundred years, their razor-sharp knives gleaming, their teeth white in the sun. And the chunking noise of artillery, the Legion's Schneiders coughing death into the bleached towns like a pestilence. The hooves of Africa striking sparks from the stones of Marute and Maqueda. Oropesa suffocating in its ashes while the Moors ranged through the ruins with their long knives. He saw the knives, the green turbans, and red fezzes, the white eyes like opals against the proud dark cheekbones, and could not dispel the vision of blood that followed in their passage. A purification, he thought, a purgation, and how well-deserved, how eagerly sought . . .

They were close. He could almost hear the sound of the hooves, the keening laments over their dead, the bang of rifles and the organic pulse of their drums at night over the campfires. How was it possible that he could gaze from that tower, see their smoky footprints on the horizon, yet despair of their ever reaching him, of their reaching Toledo, the Alcázar, of his ever seeing them ride through the Bisagra gate? And if they did, what then? Death comes in so many forms.

He moved the circle of the lens as far to the right as he could, trying to capture the city itself. Below, in the streets, the Anarchists and the Reds were sullenly preparing their weapons, all the while nervously listening to the whisper of cannon from Marute. And all the while the clank of the sappers' tools continued under the fortress. The bones of Amru and the ancient governors creaked in protest, showering the tunnels with ash and covering the electric cables with their skeletons.

What he dreaded most of all was silence, when the cannon would cease to boom and when the miners' tools could no longer be heard. He swung the lens hurriedly back along the rim of the far hill until he came upon a battery of artillery partly hidden in a clump of pine.

The lens was powerful. He could see the faces of the men quite clearly. Most of them were naked to the waist. They seemed to have just arisen, were wandering lazily about the encampment, stretching their arms above their heads, yawning. No one seemed to be concerned about the guns or the piles of ammunition just then picking up the first direct rays of the sun. A thin wisp of smoke rose. A breakfast fire flickered.

He turned the focusing screw, bringing the faces into even clearer view. The men were unshaven. They seemed at peace, as though they had just awakened on a camping trip. He looked from face to face, saw bearded, seamed peasant faces, intelligent faces, stupid faces, no different, in sum, from his own.

Suddenly he saw one man, and his heart thickened in his chest. He turned the focusing screw again. There was no mistake about it. He watched as the young man sat down beneath a scraggly pine and began to sip coffee from a steaming cup. His face was tilted back, toward the sun, and his features were clear and distinct.

He looked exactly like Jaime. The same eyes, the same hair, the same shape of head, the same mouth.

Ground haze rose and misted Jaime's view, then evaporated as if brushed away by the sun's intense rays. The man was still there, still with the same face. His own.

In that moment, Jaime Mercader felt as isolated as though he had been imprisoned in a cage woven of stars. He let the binoculars fall from his hands. They slapped against his chest, the impact transmuted into a stabbing pain in his head.

He thrust one hand up against the wall for support.

Mercedes, accompanied by Dr. Sepulveda and two other men came up into the tower room. Jaime sagged against the wall, barely able to keep himself upright.

"He has no more sense than a bull. Less even," Dr. Sepulveda was saying. "And you let him . . ."

Mercedes did not think it was necessary to answer nor did the doctor really expect her to say anything. He was used to making accusatory remarks and having them unanswered. After all, one had to blame things on some one other than God.

The doctor pulled off Jaime's bandages while the other two men held him up. The hair beneath the bandages was a mass of caked blood. A livid slash ran across his head, oozing serum. The skin was purple and puffed. The doctor shook his head and swore. One of the men crossed himself and Mercedes looked away.

"I'll do what I can for him," the doctor said. "With a few bottles of antiseptic, the right instruments, what I couldn't do? . . . but here, with nothing? . . ." He walked across the room, looked out of the window at the campfires on the opposite side of the Tagus. "It must have been like this a hundred years ago, more . . . when you could die from a scratch . . . and this is the twentieth century." He ground his teeth, then, hearing the girl's labored breathing, turned back. "We'll take care of you, too. Come now, don't protest. It has to be done. . . ."

"I don't want to leave him," she said quietly.

"All right. It doesn't matter."

The two men helped Jaime back down the stairs. He did not resist. His head hung down, his wild mat of hair falling over his forehead and the vine of blood winding darkly down his neck. His hands were white, like those of the angels over the cathedral altar.

From the direction of the Dehesa de Pineda came the boom of the first barrage of the morning, earlier than the cock's crowing, easily as futile.

A little plaster fell like a snow from the ceiling, settling on the floor just in time to catch Dr. Sepulveda's footprints.

SEPTEMBER 18, 3:30 A.M.: *Toledo*

SINCE SHORTLY BEFORE MIDNIGHT, the words had hovered in the air like the call of a medieval crier announcing the coming of plague:

"Leave your houses, leave your houses . . . on pain of death. Citizens of Toledo, you must leave your houses."

The distant metallic voices of the speaker trucks, withdrawing yard by yard into the alleyways and the narrow streets, echoing from the Moorish walls and in the hollows of blasted buildings:

". . . houses . . . houses . . . houses . . ."

". . . no one may remain . . ."

The sounds moved about the city, disembodied, forlorn, the grind of gears and hiss of tires on the few streets through which the trucks could still pass holding their own weird dialogue. Hand-held megaphones, horns, and the primitive amplification of cupped hands catching the shouts of the mad.

From house to house, the *milicianos* ran, wild-looking men in blue overalls, haunted by the shadows of a hungry death, and at each house where they passed and cut their signs and warnings into the icy air, there was an exodus.

Women emerged carrying bundles of bedding, clusters of pots and pans tied to sticks; bits of mirror reflected the glow of the fires burning around the Alcázar. People emerged carrying birdcages, tugging at sleepy dogs and herding chickens over the rubble. Old men in their under-shirts, grumpy and outraged at having been awakened yet another time, struggled into the streets, tugging at their trousers.

"So it's really going to happen . . ."

"Yes, we're going to do it at last."

"Don't say, 'we'. . . if you want to say that you're going to do it, go ahead but leave the rest of us out of it."

"As if they didn't deserve it . . ."

"But it's no way to do things. It isn't fair."

Sleepy-eyed children scattered in the streets like bits of wind-blown paper at a fiesta time.

"Leave your houses . . . ," the retreating speakers intoned, the voices less and less human as they grew more distant, themselves fleeing the city over the bridges of San Martín and Alcantara and into the hills.

The narrow streets and the foul, infested alleys, uncleared and un-cared for since the siege had begun, streamed with refugees, funneled them toward the Bisagra gate and out under the double-headed eagle, spread-winged over the portcullis . . . out to the northern plains.

Over the high stone bridges, San Martín, Alcantara, to the tree-speared, boulder-ridden hills, gray as elephant's hide during the day and now black and hunched in the night. *Los Cigarrales,* to the south, still smoking. Where the vineyard-owners had died, and apricot trees watched over the ashes of homes and piles of bones.

There was no reason to hush the cries of warning or to hide the rush of men and women out of the city. Some even pushed carts just as the *guardia civil* from the countryside had done two months before. All after-noon the loudspeakers had threatened and exhorted: "Send out the women and children, you fools . . . while you still can. Before the end. Before the mine. . . ."

"Send out the women . . . before it is too late . . ."

The night was moonless, the hills, from horizon to horizon, rough and humped as though there were something alive under the scraggly trees and rocks. A campanile tolled the hour: four A.M.

SEPTEMBER 18, 4:00 A.M.: *The Alcázar*

MERCEDES STOOD BY THE WINDOW opening, gazing into the gorge. Beyond the ring of fires, the hills lay wrinkled with cold. Most of the women had remained below in the areas marked off by Lieutenant Rincón's survey party. They huddled together in the darkness and had not even the breath to sing songs anymore. Only the children seemed not to understand what was happening, and the sound of their innocent voices made mothers weep. For a long while, Mercedes had hesitated, meaning to go at once to the room where Jaime Mercader still lay. But it had seemed to her that she must see the hills and the river, that she had to breath the night air if only for a minute or she would suffocate. Some of the women were being moved from one part of the fortress to the other; they passed through the corridors silently, like an exhalation, as rapid and driven as the wind-ravaged spirits of the Second Circle of Hell. Ever since the metal voices had begun crying in the streets, no one had dared speak above a whisper. Even those accustomed to command seemed to have lost their voices; no one told anyone else where to go. Yet everyone seemed driven. Mercedes felt the pressure of two huge hands on her back and she went where they pushed her, not caring.

Not far from where she stood, three soldiers were cleaning a machine gun. Captain Herrera leaned against the wall, concentrating on his facial tic, trying to make it stop. Every few seconds his cheek would quiver and he would curse at it. He longed for a cigarette. He too sensed the approach of death but what was terrifying about it was not the simple fact of its coming, but the shape in which it had chosen to appear. Perhaps precisely because of the handsomeness of his features and the many compliments which had always followed him all his life, he had a terrible fear of mutilation, a fear so strong that the torture of Anton Vitolyn had almost been beyond his ability to endure.

Mercedes looked across the gorge, trying to count the fires, gripped either side of the window frame with her hands so that she appeared for a second to be crucified against the distant hills.

Captain Herrera whistled to her urgently; he had not even the strength to shout. She turned her head.

"Don't do that, señorita . . . it's foolish. . . ."

"Is it any more foolish," she asked, "than what they're doing? Cleaning a gun? Now?"

"As you wish." Captain Herrera looked at the two soldiers. They seemed so busy. Cristóbal Herrera wondered if they thought at all about what the mine might do to them, what their bodies would look like after it was over? What was he to say to the girl? Could he deny the existence of the mine? He waited, let it pass.

There were massed footsteps in the corridor. Another group of women and children passed. Why was it, Mercedes wondered, that each group seemed to be going in a different direction?

The fires winked and flickered in the creases of the hills. Everything looked—almost gay, inviting. How strange it all seemed. She had forgotten what the sky looked like at night.

"It's so quiet out there," she said, trying to hear the voices that must be whispering to each other around those campfires.

"They may be getting ready for an attack. Who knows?"

"Or just watching. Wouldn't you watch if you were there? Or trying to keep warm. It must be freezing cold up there. How terrible for the children. It's so cold, even here . . ."

Hundreds of campfires flickered on the hillside just across the Tagus, lacing the air with trails of smoke, slightly darker lines that might have been trees but for their constant undulations; the entire sky seemed aquiver.

"Do you feel sorry . . . for *them?*" Captain Herrera asked. The two soldiers went on spreading oil over the firing lock of their gun.

"No," she said. "For that, you have to know that you're right yourself."

"I've always thought . . . if you'll pardon me . . . but I feel I can speak my mind. . . . I've always thought that God simply has made some people blind to certain things. It's not so much their fault as the fault of Divine carelessness."

"Does it make you feel better to believe that?" She had just noticed his tic and felt sorry for him. His whole face shook.

"I believe it because it's true," Captain Herrera said. "He . . . is careless about so many things. So many details are overlooked. Look here, señorita . . . do you know where General Varela is now? In Maqueda. Can you imagine that? Do you know how close Maqueda is to this . . . place?"

Mercedes nodded.

"Forty-two kilometers. An hour by truck, maybe two by tank . . ."

She said nothing. Her flesh seemed no protection at all now, and the cold cut through, stabbing into her bones. A cold beyond belief. The cold of a perfect vacuum.

"In two hours," Captain Herrera was saying, "how many times do you think a man can die?" He put a hand to his face. "I shouldn't have said that. Forgive me . . ." He walked out of the room, quickly. His breathing was stifled. He could not bear being alone and unless he was with someone who could tell him what a fool he was being, then he counted himself alone.

In a moment the soldiers had followed Herrera out of the room, leaving the machine gun in position by the window. The ammunition belts were already fitted into the breech and were spread out on the floor so that they would not tangle.

From hill to hill the fires had multiplied and to the north, on the plains toward Madrid, the flames flickered and wavered between outcroppings of rock. Out there, the people who had left their houses at the bidding of the loudspeaker trucks waited, boiling pots of coffee over campfires, huddling close under tarpaulins and tents made of blankets. Pitted with fires, the countryside appeared like a scene out of some medieval legend: a besieging army was drawn up on the fields surrounding the castle, the tents pitched, the watch fires smoldering. But here the men of that silent army were as miserable as those they watched. Low dark clouds scudded over the plains, and a sour wind drove the scent of boiling coffee against the walls of the fortress. The smell of the horse dung that fueled the fires came in heavy gusts, then passed, came again.

She turned and left the window, unable to bear the sight now, just as she had been unable to bear the darkness before.

Crates of books were piled along the corridor walls, barricades of Cervantes, Lope de Vega, and Benavente in place of sandbags. The air was damp with the smell of rotting wood and burnt gasoline; it infected the lungs like the most persistent cough. What a dismal smell, she thought. It's the odor of death itself . . .

As she descended the stairs she tried to force her thoughts outward and back. There had once been a particular bright and sunny day when her father had taken her to Madrid to see *Doña Francisquita*. Afterward they had sat at a tiny café near the Puerta del Sol drinking an almond-flavored drink . . . a film at the Bilbao . . . the North Americans, Joan Crawford and Robert Montgomery . . . the wire chairs outside the café. She had thought that her mother must have been jealous of her at that moment, and she felt not a little bit guilty. It had been just after King Alfonso had abdicated and fled the country. The air was heady with April and the Republic. The avenue, slanting upward, the tall buildings, but most of all her father, smiling, his beard neatly barbered and smelling of sandalwood.

Then she realized that the face in her imaginings was no longer that of her father; the lines had blurred, the features shifted, elongated, the beard melted away, and it was now Jaime Mercader's face. His eyes were closed and the bandages on his head were pure white. She shut her eyes, trying to drive the face away. It seemed to have no place there, at that moment.

She passed onto a landing, then into another sloping corridor, somewhat wider than the first. Rolls of concertina wire ran across the walls. Each time she brushed the prickly whorls, the entire length of wire began to shiver, filling the room with a faint, metallic scraping sound. The coils traversed the corridor, curved possessively around pillars and columns.

Ahead of her, in the shadows, she could see a team of ragged Civil Guard uncoiling the wires ahead of them, stretching them out and affixing them to the floor by means of spikes and wooden pegs jammed into the cracks between the blocks. The Guards were too weak to do more than stamp on the spikes with their bootsoles.

A torch flickered. Studded with barbs, the wire caught the feeble light and glowed faintly like the filament of a dying light bulb. An officer went by, a stethoscope dangling from his neck. Mercedes thought of slim fingers, about to strangle him. On his face a wistful smile lingered, as though he were trying to convince himself that he was pleased about something.

A group of women were pressed into an archway as small as a burial niche, silently watching. The Lieutenant moved about, scratching signs in the ground with a stick, and they watched him with a ritual fascination.

What was he doing? Marking off the safe areas? Mercedes was sure; it had to be that. What was there to protect? They were protecting Death, the honored visitor, from the prisoners of the Alcázar, the ragged and the wretched, the filthy and the infected. It must be so confusing for Death, she thought, here, in this place. . . .

A woman some place, chanting a prayer . . . then, amazingly, children's voices . . . children fighting over a ball and a trycicle. The sound of the child's voice transfixed her with a sudden, intense pain and brought back at once, for some reason, the image of the wounded Mercader.

She knew that she must be close now; the air had grown heavy and damp, and there was moss on the walls. She had come so deep.

There was no soldier guarding the door. She stepped inside. The only one left besides Jaime Mercader was the corpse of the man whose foot had been shot away; he had stopped whistling "Isle of Capri" a few hours before, but there was no place to bury him and no time even if there had been a place. The soldier at the door had gone to help man the walls.

"Even Dr. Sepulveda doesn't come here anymore," Jaime said. He tried to smile but his facial muscles seemed too stiff. "They've buried me already . . . that's it. . . ."

She tried to smile but the room looked so much like a mausoleum, a catacomb, that his words struck a fear into her which she could barely control. Piles of blankets lay over the cots; there were no men under them but the shape of the mounds seemed to imply that they were still inhabited by restless spirits. The only mound which harbored a human form covered a corpse and, for some reason, looked like a pile of blankets, nothing more.

"There wasn't anything to listen to down here so they all went off to try their luck somewhere else," Jaime said, raising himself on his elbows. "Listen, how quiet it is . . ."

"It's quiet outside, too. I was just looking out the window. . . ."

She told him about the encampments on the opposite bank of the river . . . on the plains . . . the fires . . . and the pots of coffee.

"So they're really going to do it," he said.

"You'll be safe enough here."

"I wasn't thinking of that," he replied. "What about you?"

"I'm safe where you are. . . ."

He took her arm, brought her down on the cot next to him. His bandages had been changed and he looked almost exactly as he had in her metamorphosized vision of her father a few moments before. His face was seamed by pain yet his eyes were fired with a secret laughter. Why wouldn't he share it with her? She felt so weak. . . .

"Close the door," he asked her. She got up and swung the door shut, then returned to him.

When she asked him why, he fell back onto the cot, his head at an odd angle on the pillow and said, "Because we've never been alone like this before, not for one second . . ."

"And now," she said. "Are we?" She was thinking of the body under the blankets. Jaime did not look where she was looking however, but stared up at the low-arched ceiling with its glistening slick of moisture, the few tiny splotches of moss or lichen.

"I suppose not. Your father, he's here, isn't he . . . ?"

She shook her head; she felt the same way, but she didn't want to talk about it. Time seemed suspended; every motion they made, every breath, was crystallized and frozen. The slow articulation of bone and soul strung out across the walls of the room like the frames of a motion picture, enlarged and all hung out, tracing each syllable, each gesture. It was all too clear, like something seen through a microscope.

He put his hands under his head, cradling himself while she poured him a cup of water.

"Do you remember the story about Queen Juana? She was Isabella's daughter . . ."

"Don't talk so much, Jaime . . . please. Have a drink of water, then let me talk to you. . . ."

"Listen, it's all right. I'm stronger than I was the other day. . . . That was a foolish thing to do, I know. Sometimes you think you're so much better than you actually are, but it's only because you're lying down. When you have to get up and prove it, that's a differ-ent story, isn't it? . . . well, all right, give me a drink, but only if you drink yourself. Did you know, the Jews drink from the same cup when they marry, then they smash the cup? . . ."

"It's tin," she laughed. "Do you want to try and smash it? Then you'll have to drink out of the bottle like a sailor . . ."

He sipped at the water; it was strong and medicinal. Dr. Sepulveda had been putting iodine into it. For some reason, the Alcázar seemed to have an almost unlimited supply of iodine.

"Queen Isabella's daughter, Juana," Jaime went on. "She was in love with the Austrian, Philip. He married her, you know, but there was a Portuguese woman . . ."

She could not help laughing. "What a time to be telling stories."

Jaime went on. "No . . . listen . . . it's important. You'll see why . . . so . . . Juana, she found out about Philip, of course, and she poi-soned him. Then she went crazy with remorse. Maybe you've seen the painting that Gasparo Cabrisas did of it . . . there used to be reproduc-tions all over, mostly in the taverns. For some reason people liked to look at it while they were drinking. . . . For years and years, she went out on the roads every night, a procession . . . it was all there in the picture, do you remember? In front, a troop of soldiers carrying torches dipped in pitch, black hoods, and cloaks. Really . . . dressed like demons . . . and behind, a crystal coffin carried by four mules with black cockades on their heads. . . . And then Queen Juana, the Mad, staring at Philip's face through the crystal lid. . . ."

She was suddenly serious. "Jaime . . . why are you telling me this . . . ?"

"I think I dreamed it, but I must have been thinking about it for a long time. . . . It's funny isn't it . . . sometimes you wake up realizing you've been masquerading in your dreams as a king or a saint or the worst kind of scoundrel . . . well, this time, I'm a mad queen. And in the coffin, you see . . . I can't get rid of the face either. . . ."

"My father?"

He nodded, and took her by the arm.

"Except now the face is blurred, and I don't think I see it so clearly anymore. If I knew that I would see him again . . . but it doesn't matter anymore, that's what I wanted to tell you. . . ."

"So . . ." She lowered her head. The light trembled on the wall, obscuring the outlines of their shadows.

"Mercedes . . . ," he said and she stiffened; it was the first time in such a long while he had used her name. He went on: "I have to ask you something, and you'll forgive me for asking it in such a stupid way but there isn't time or strength to do it any other way. Not as I'd like, but then none of this is . . . . Mercedes, tell me . . . do you love me? I have to ask that because I think that without knowing it or even . . . wanting it . . . I love you. . . ."

"I think," she said, "in the same way . . . yes, I do. . . ." She put her hands on his shoulders and looked into his eyes, frightened by the feverish glaze she found there.

"Isn't it absurd," he said slowly, "that such a thing should happen . . . here, of all places, and because of . . . all of this. . . ."

"There are so many things I can't understand. Any of it . . . so why should I be surprised about this? Yes, I do, I do love you, or at least I think that I do. It's the same thing. . . ."

"Yes," he said. He drew her down and folded his arms about her. His own body trembled from the effort, and she found she could barely breath. It felt as though, even in his weakened embrace, that her bones might snap.

"When I met you at my father's," he said, "all I wanted was to get as far away from you as I could, did you know that? And afterward, it was the same thing. . . ."

"But you came for me when you thought there was danger. . . ."

"No . . . I think I did that to hurt your father . . . again, you see . . . he was always there . . . and because he had done nothing for you, I had to do something, . . . to show him that I was a man where he was not . . . just as before. . . ."

"Jaime . . ."

"You see, he's still there. Now . . . just as before. . . ."

He shut his eyes.

"Not in this . . . ," she said against his cheek. Her own eyes closed, and she let her body press by its own weight against his.

"Do you know, in the films they always say something like, 'I've been wanting to say this for such a long time . . .' But I haven't. Not me. It's something that you realize all of a sudden, and you don't know why. . . ."

She placed a finger against his lips; they were cold and hard. He bent his head and kissed her.

She said, "The door is closed . . . there's no one . . ."

"Aren't you afraid . . . of the sin . . . ?"

"It would be a sin . . . if we didn't. We love each other, don't we? We've just said so. I want, once before I . . ."

It was his turn to quiet her. He pressed her hard in his arms, using all his strength. His hands moved over her body, and the feel of her wasted flesh under his hands terrified him; it was as though he was reaching through her skin and could touch her bones. Somehow, he sensed that she was watching him, could see his face, and he tried to appear as if touching her in such a way had aroused him . . . as it should. To lie, in charity to another, to one you loved, he thought . . . that's not a bad thing. Their clothing fell away . . . their bodies touched, sought warmth. . . . They twisted in each other's arms, trying to find the right way. A curl of smoke fumed from the sardine can on the table, now almost drained of oil.

The silence of the room magnified their breathing, the small sounds they made which so surprised them. . . .

"It's no good," he said after a while. "I'm . . . too weak. . . ."

"It's good enough . . . be quiet, Jaime . . . please. . . ."

"I can't . . ."

"Be quiet. . . ."

"No . . . I can't . . ."

But he did not get a chance to finish what he was saying, if in fact he ever knew what he was going to say.

At that moment, a miner from Mieres named Diego Santoro, who had never been in Toledo in all his life until the day before, pushed down on the button of a heavily wired detonating device. For a second his finger was frozen in the act, and he could force it farther down only with a hesitance, a regret which annoyed him intensely . . . for the shambles of the Alcázar still retained the power to instill respect, even awe, among those who had worked so hard to destroy her. But he found the impetus to complete his gesture, and the mine exploded beneath the west end of the Alcázar with a tremendous roar, lifting the tower and the entire western corner of the fortress a hundred feet or more into the air.

Jaime felt the shock of the explosion seconds before he heard it. The tin cup on the floor by the cot began to vibrate, then to clack loudly against the stones. A bottle on the same table as the lamp jumped about as if it were possessed. Jaime opened his eyes and in the few seconds left, he looked down over the curve of Mercedes' bare shoulder at his own hand, spread over her back. The fingers were vibrating, as was her back . . . his legs, everything. The wall suddenly took on the rhythm of the dancing bottle, the division between slabs began to blur and disintegrate. There was a sharp smell in the room, like a gust of boiling air from a furnace. Then, finally, the sound came, a great growling noise, that swelled instantly into an engulfing roar.

The walls of the chamber split with a groan as the ceiling rose over-head. The cots pitched sideways, spilling their contents onto the floor . . . blankets, straw, the corpse of the footless man, Jaime and Mercedes themselves.

The chamber itself seemed to be exploding outward, all in slow mo-tion like a scene in a trick cinema show.

The floor rose abruptly, throwing Jaime and Mercedes against the wall, their arms and legs still intertwined.

The roof of the chamber opened like hands released from prayer. A thousand tons of rock shot skyward, molding, expanding, then compress-ing again.

When the debris had finally cascaded back onto the western corner of the fortress, the chamber had become the bottom of a long pit that de-scended two stories deep into the subcellars of the building. Beams criss-crossing the bottom of the pit formed a bracing which prevented the walls from sliding down, while the walls themselves, sloped at a steep angle, formed an incline of broken beams, girders and brick, creating a long narrow funnel at the bottom of which lay what was left of the cham-ber.

At the very top of the pit, three large slabs of granite leaned one against the other, just above a twisted steel girder, sealing the top of the funnel. At two points, light entered briefly through spaces no more than a hand's breadth across.

From deep within a hundred such pits and cavities, geysers of smoke continued to erupt with volcanic pressure.

The pedestal upon which the statue of Carlos V had stood re-mained upright in the center of the yard. In the northeastern corner, the second and third story walls had been sheared away by the force of the explosion leaving the rooms gaping open like the rooms in a child's dollhouse. Below, a heap of broken stone and girders reached from the courtyard floor to a point high above the top of the second-story balcony.

Over the still-shuddering mounds that had replaced the northwest battlements, the sun began to rise grudgingly through the gray sky, burn-ing off the thick haze. The fortress high on its hill was ringed by an eddying mist through which only the upper walls and the remaining towers protruded. A great column of smoke thrust high into the glowing dawn sky, obscuring for a time even the sun itself.

Whistles shrilled and men shouted. Squads of militiamen carrying red banners, red and black banners, and no banners at all, began to move up the Cuesta del Alcázar to the final attack.

SEPTEMBER 18, 6:00 A.M.: *Toledo*

WITH THE DAWN, THE ALCÁZAR seemed to rise out of the earth itself, wreathed in a heavy mist which curled up and around the ruined towers as though to hide it and protect it. Tracer bullets, delicate and beautiful, flowed gracefully through the air and disappeared into the coils of gray mist. Slowly, the sun climbed over the distant horizon, sending out long feelers of gold to touch and disperse the haze. The sky above shone like polished slate, gray and cold. The bitter wind of the night before had died down, and now lay hidden in the gorges of the Tagus.

Carvalho had been there all night, standing on the edge of the crowd which had gathered to watch the explosion. A group of newsmen had come with their cameras and tripods and had set themselves up just to the side of the officials from Madrid. Touring cars and trucks were parked all over the field, and the buses that had brought so many of the curious from Madrid were parked at a distance, as though embarrassed by what they had done.

The olive trees of the Dehesa stirred in the wind, shaking their leaves with a mournful rustle.

Pascual Soler stood nearby, his head turned, looking northward rather than south. "It is like watching an execution. I will not look at it," he had said. But Carvalho knew that at the moment the mine went off Soler would turn and, just as all the rest, he too would look.

A dozen yards away stood the three men who had come the night before from Madrid with instructions to arrest him. They had come first to the Hotel Maravilla. The Colonel had expected them, and they had gone downstairs and sat together, all four of them, at a table in the bar where the reporters and correspondents were already gathering in anticipation of the detonation of the mine the next morning. The men had tried to explain why they had come and that it was not their fault. Surely it would be nothing serious, one of them had said; the Colonel's behavior required that certain measures be taken. That was all. Protective custody was a better term than arrest. The Colonel smiled and ordered beer for everyone though he himself did not drink but only ran his finger around the edge of the glass until it sang, a piercing whistle that pained one of the agents from Madrid visibly. Lachine had joined them and when he had discovered what was happening, he had gone off with one of the men, and when he had come back it was settled; they would wait until morning to take him back to Madrid. On his honor, he would not try to escape. Of course not. Escape to where? And for what?

Now the three men avoided looking at him as though to do so would be somehow to be implicated in the Colonel's personal tragedy in a way which would make them guilty of his own disastrous mistakes. One of the men was quite young; Carvalho wondered if he could possibly understand what was happening. No, it was probably just the other way around. He, like Jaime Mercader, probably understood far better than the older men. The young man seemed the most shamed of all by what was happening, and the Colonel found himself in the strange position of trying to comfort him, to make him understand that all that was happening was inevitable, and, so, carried with it no seal of guilt.

There were others he knew standing there in the field. Captain Segurra with a pair of binoculars. He had apologized for using the binoculars but he was to begin a covering barrage with his light artillery units as soon as the smoke cleared and the militia units from Madrid began moving up the streets to attack. Dr. Aliaga was there at the far end of the field, conspicuous in his white surgeon's jacket. Largo Caballero was there, wearing a windbreaker and a beret, surrounded by his staff, a forest of heads all ending in forage caps, all alike, faces white as chalk in the early morning light.

They were less than a mile away from the Alcázar. Over a hundred of them, standing like grave-markers in the lonely field of pine and olive trees.

A young man, whose face was disturbingly like his son Raúl's passed by; the same arrogant spring to his gait, the same permanent expression of contempt on his lips. The boy kept glancing at his watch impatiently. Carvalho felt like walking over and slapping his face.

A strange whirring seemed to be rising up from the ground. Colonel Carvalho looked around; it was coming from the newsmen who had set up their tripods and were already taking pictures, so as not to miss the exact moment of the explosion.

God, was it to be that soon? Carvalho was wearing a cloak which he had been given by Señora Mercader; it had belonged to Francisco and she had insisted that he take it. He pulled it more tightly around him but it did not cut the chill, only seemed to force it more deeply into his body.

Soler, muttering: "When they discouraged bullfights, I said . . . ah, the Republic *will* be civilized, they *will* bring enlightenment to this dark country, but . . . Lorca was right . . . it is a disgrace, this veneration of death. It goes too keep for us to ever root it out. We cannot have bullfights anymore, but we can have this instead. Oh, God, we are inventive." He spat into the dirt and ground the sputum under his heel as though it were something alive and vile.

"They're late," someone said; a disembodied voice.

"I'll bet it won't go off. Clumsy bastards that they are . . ."

"Those miners. The Asturians, they know how . . ."

"It won't go, you'll see . . ."

The voices rose like smoke; French, English. Even Spanish. The group of government officials seemed to have drawn in on itself. Largo Caballero was lost amid the forage caps and the brown jackets. To the east, in the distance, a few campfires still winked fitfully on the hills, and tiny trails of smoke rose almost straight into the air. There was no breeze. Nothing stirred; now the trees were silent, the leaves hanging as though cut out and pasted onto the air.

Captain Segurra lowered his binoculars.

"Not a sign," he said hurriedly. "Maybe it won't work." His voice fell to a whisper. "Not only for your sake, Colonel, but I hope to God it doesn't work. . . ."

Carvalho kept watching. He could see with his naked eye as clearly as any man could with field glasses. The distance collapsed before his gaze and every detail was clearer in his mind's eye than any lens could have made it. The walls towered above him, the fires smoldering within the windowless rooms. Girders, twisted like bones through a fracture. He saw it all and turned away Captain Segurra's offer of the binoculars.

From time to time he would gaze at the little knot of officials from Madrid. The Government. He had fought all his life for "the Government" and the order for which it stood, and now there was this. What excuse could he now find for Oviedo? It's necessary, he had told himself. The perpetration of minor cruelties, of lesser evils dissipates the energy, prevents the commission of major crimes. But was it true at all? How could he justify any of what he had done through his entire life? Now, suddenly, it seemed to him that he had been engaged for as long as he could remember in inflicting small wounds which remained to fester and infect others, rather than cutting clean and once and for all removing what had to be removed. The surgeon draws blood, to be sure, but he does so with quick, clean strokes. Why was he thinking in such terms? Operating rooms, knives, the smell of anesthetic? He realized that he was looking at Dr. Aliaga's distant, white-coated figure, standing alone against the gently sloping horizon, almost directly between himself and the Alcázar now slowly appearing out of a sea of ground haze. Compromise . . . let things take their course . . . line of least resistance . . . a little bloodshed to avoid a catastrophe and, always, that most elemental of all impulses, revenge for whatever ills have been done to you, only revenge twice as ferocious, twice as devastating as that which it revenges.

Everyone had stopped talking. Only the whirring of the movie cameras could be heard and the muted swearing of the cameramen.

Somewhere in the city, in Toledo, a man was poised over a detonator. It came to Colonel Carvalho that he did not even know what kind of mechanism they were going to use or how the mine had been laid.

Soler's hand was on his shoulder. The ticking of watches, greatly magnified, filled the air around him, the clicks sharp, like razors striking each other.

The shape of the fortress was clear, burned into the slate-gray sky; a mile or more away. The outlines grew sharp, touched only with a faint nimbus. The haze, washed away by the wind, rolled like foam down the sides of the gorge and disappeared into the Tagus. . . .

Then, suddenly, without warning and without sound, enormous puffs of white smoke began to rise from about the base of the fortress, round and soft as cotton balls. Slowly, they grew in size as they ascended. The towers nearest to them began to tremble, to sway. From the center of the Alcázar a jet of black smoke shot up into the air, a tunnel of smoke which gave the appearance of the cone of a cyclone. The entire tower, the northwest corner of the building, rose like a child's rocket, trailing flame and a wash of smoke, jetting up into the air where it suddenly stopped, poised as if it had changed its mind and then shattered in all directions. The masonry flew like pieces of cardboard, weightless, tumbling end over end, while steel girders and beams passed the descending fragments, still headed up into the air like a handful of thrown matchsticks.

Carvalho heard Pascual Soler saying something, his voice high, breaking, saw Captain Segurra reach out for the field glasses which he was still holding in his hands but which he had not brought up to his eyes . . . but somehow he could not make out what either of them were saying. The sounds came to him like the sounds made by birds hidden in a thick copse. The ground under his feet began to tremble. The shaking sensation flowed along his bones, setting his whole body to vibrating . . . his neck, his arms, his skull, and his brain as well. The air about his body pressed in on him; shock waves, he thought. Explosions always produce . . . such . . . waves. . . . Everything was muffled, soft, yet precise at the same time. He tried to look up. The smoke from the Alcázar seemed to cover everything. The exploding pieces of masonry, of stone and steel, hung there motionless in the sky. His chest tightened, his ribs clamping shut. The golden rays of the rising sun trembled across the sky, cutting the motionless fragments of the Alcázar into parallel lines which he could not join together into a whole. He blinked, felt himself burying his fists in his eye sockets, stared again, but the lines would not join. His body felt light, without substance. He was aware that his chest was not moving, that he had not taken a breath in . . . how long . . . everything hung, suspended.

He felt himself slowly pitch forward, gently, as though the air were a thick, viscous substance through which he could make his way toward the ground only with the greatest difficulty. There was a warmth, surging up from the ground to envelop him and then, suddenly, a shooting pain through his entire body. He heard himself cry out in an embarrassed, outraged voice.

The last thing he saw was the white-jacketed figure of Dr. Blas Aliaga running in great, almost comical bounds across the ground toward him.

Carvalho was dead before he struck the ground.

THE STEEP HILLOCKS OF RUBBLE left by the mine were even more impregnable than the walls had been before; the northwestern tower had erupted skyward in a geyser of stone and had come cascading down on the still unbroken walls that had formed the wings of the corner. A precipice had been formed, its walls slanting down into the Cuesta at an angle of over fifty degrees, almost impossible to scale in an assault.

The muffled sound of screaming rose up from the wreckage, from the subcellars where the women and children had been hiding. Their voices blended with the wind and the crackling of the fires, and were carried swiftly through the debris and away into the dawn.

A few pistol shots . . . and the vague, half-heard cries of officers trying desperately to rally their men in the smoke-congested corridors. Smoke rushed and rolled through the labyrinth of underground passages, strangling the Guards, the soldiers, everyone below.

Outside, squads of *milicianos* ran up the Cuesta toward the breach in the southwest wall, unaware of the unscalable mounds, the pits that lay waiting beyond.

Anton Vitolyn lay crumpled against the wall of the corridor directly opposite the closet in which he had been chained. His head rested against the exact spot of the wall at which he had stared for so long. The force of the explosion had crumpled the inner wall of the closet like tissue paper, and the iron rings to which his chains had been fastened had fallen away at once. A jagged chunk of plaster was still attached to one of the chains and lay next to his left leg. For days he had been listening to the tapping of the sappers and the sound of their drills, hoping that—somehow—he would be there, right over the mine when it went off. Then he would die in a memorable, clean, even meaningful way. The important thing was to avoid a disgusting, demeaning death such as had overtaken Sebastián Gil.

When the explosion had come, in the few seconds of consciousness that remained as he was catapulted across the hallway amid a shower of rock and plaster, as he realized what had just happened, he had thought: "Yes . . . oh God, there is justice after all. . . ."

Then came the pain-filled awakening and the gagging, humiliating coughing; he struggled for air, fighting for breath in spite of himself.

"I'm not dead . . . not . . . not . . . ," he cried out, choking on the smoke, bitter at the indignity of such a denial.

The sound of machine-gun fire joined with the distant snapping of rifles. Vitolyn found that the higher he lifted his head, the thicker was the smoke. In desperation he fell forward on the floor, his face pressed against the stones.

Suddenly he found that he could breathe again. A current of cool air swept across the corridor. Looking up, he saw figures hurrying across the mouth of the tunnel twenty yards ahead of where he lay. A glint of light flashed from a bayonet. A whistle shrilled outside.

After a few moments, he rose unsteadily to his feet. His head still buzzed from the blast and his eyes smarted and teared. Through a breach in the wall he could see figures gliding through the smoke in the courtyard, taking on new shapes even as he watched, like the pieces of glass at the end of a kaleidoscope.

Down the hall, there were others. A half-dozen soldiers, Civil Guard, he could not tell which, the smoke had blackened them so.

He turned away, hurried down the corridor.

Blackened figures, tattered figures, men and women splotched with white dust, stumbled through the corridors like ghosts frightened by specters even more terrifying than they themselves. From the courtyard above, came the crash of firing, the sound of men screaming like demons.

He found the stairwell, descended to the next level, then entered a familiar corridor. He had not even taken the trouble to think about what he was doing, to formulate in his mind the reasons for it, the justifications, the arguments against it; he was done with trying to think. It got a man nowhere. The only thing was to act instinctively.

There, by the storeroom door, a young soldier, a cadet, lay dead with a tiny puncture hole in his throat, his rifle still on his knees. Vitolyn stopped, regarded him with a muted feeling of pity mixed with envy . . . it was obvious that the boy had been killed as he sat there, probably dreaming of what his life would be like after the siege had been lifted. The bullet, or fragment of shrapnel, whatever it was, must have found its way through a narrow opening in the opposite wall across the tunnel; an accident, the purest of chance. The boy must have thought he was completely safe, sitting there.

The door to the prisoners' room was still closed, even though the bolt had been broken off by the explosion. Vitolyn paused to look at it as though to make absolutely sure that he was at the right place. A low murmuring could be heard on the other side.

He pushed the hanging bolt aside, opened the door a crack, and slipped into the dark, familiar room.

His eyes slowly became used to the gloom. The hostages sat against the wall. Lines of hunched, squatting men materialized out of the darkness; pale, bearded faces, open, staring eyes.

A trickle of light entered from the barricaded window just as it had on the day he had been first thrown into the room. A soft undersea luminescence filled the chamber. There were twenty or thirty men in the room. They had all seen him enter. Yet no one had moved. Did no one recognize him? Did no one remember?

He walked uncertainly to the center of the room, opposite the piled-up barrels. The air stank of sweat and excrement, so foul that the odor had become sweetish. He breathed it in, gratefully, expecting at any second a light of recognition to flicker in someone's eyes. The faces, in the half-light, seemed ghostly, almost translucent. A thread of smoke slipped in under the door, passed between his legs and hung just above the floor.

"Don't any of you remember me? . . ." he began, surprised by the dryness of his voice.

There was a slight, hesitant intake of breath, but no one moved. Heads turned neither toward him nor away.

"I . . . am Anton Vitolyn . . . I . . . killed . . . ," he began, pronouncing each word slowly and distinctly, so that there could be no mistaking what he said. . . . "I killed . . . César Roig."

No one stirred along the walls. Then one man looked away, another brushed an insect from his face.

Vitolyn's voice rose. "I killed César Roig . . . it's true, all of it . . . and I killed the hunchback, Paco Orsuña, too. . . . I drowned him in the swimming pool. . . ."

Still a silence, filled only with whistling, labored breath and, far-off, the rattle of gunfire and the dull plop of artillery shells falling somewhere along the river banks.

". . . it's worse than that," he continued, the pitch of his voice mounting with his excitement. "You must see it, you must . . . I'm one of you . . . I am Anton Vitolyn, from Vienna . . . I have been a member of the Communist party since 1929 . . . do you hear me? Since *1929* . . . but a traitor . . . that's why I killed Roig, to get away, to escape retribution for what . . . I did . . . I killed, you see . . . twice . . . and I stole . . . I was responsible for . . ."

He dropped Roig's papers at his feet. The smoke entering under the doorway curled over and through them, stirring the passport and identity card as a current of water might do.

"Don't any of you care?" Vitolyn shouted. "I've come back. . . . I'm giving myself up to you. . . ." He raised his arms above his head. "Punish me . . . ," he shouted. "For God's sake, punish me. . . ."

He saw that no one was listening. The men did not stir; each of them sunk in his own exhaustion, his own hunger and despair, looked away, inside himself, saw other things. Vitolyn remained where he was, shuffling his feet in panic, not knowing what to do, afraid of moving yet afraid at the same time of not moving.

Finally, one man looked up, his eyes filled with a weary disdain. "Sit down and be quiet . . . or else leave us alone. . . ."

Whistles outside, a furious burst of machine-gun fire, the shouts of men, then silence, as though the Alcázar had suddenly been lifted up by a giant hand and carried high into the sky.

Vitolyn stood immobile in the center of the room for many minutes, then walked slowly to the nearest wall and sat down. He took his place among the silent, filthy figures, breathing in their odor, rubbing against the shoulders nearest him, feeling, too, an uncertain warmth and the thin almost imperceptible throb of his own pulse and that of the man next to him as well.

"Will he ever speak to me?" Vitolyn wondered, and closed his eyes to wait.

DAWN SLIPPED UP FROM BEHIND the Sierra de Gredos and into the rain-laden sky. Thick convoys of black clouds skimmed low over the barren Castillian plains. The entire arc of sky visible across the Tagus from Talavera de la Reina on the west to Aranjuez on the east rolled with dense blackness, and at a distance it was impossible to distinguish the smoke rising from the battleground around Maqueda from the sky itself.

The air over Torrijos was ash-gray with cannon bursts where another rebel relief column was massing.

Above the Alcázar, the smoke continued to rise, greasy and heavy with the stink of burning gasoline. From deep within the ruins came the breath of hundreds of small fires, feeding the pall until it had blotted out everything and, trapped by the cooler air above, had begun to settle back into every crevice of the building. It flowed into corridors, down blasted stairwells, to the lowest dungeons and cellars of the Alcázar, three stories below the surface.

Jaime Mercader had been unconscious, and his dreams had been filled by a vision of black clouds shaped like angels' wings, all screaming at him from the sky with the shrill voices of furies. The fumes stole silently into the rock hollow where he lay, almost naked, and tortured his dreams, yet he did not wake until the agonies of these dreams at last broke the fragile walls of his unconsciousness.

He had been digging for days and no longer had any sense of time or even of purpose, knew only that stone after stone had yielded and the pit had deepened as he dug. He listened, waited, scratched at the loose shale, pushed back chunks of brick and mortar. His hands had whitened, then his arms, as though the blood had drained out of them. A few feet away lay the bandages that he had torn from his head; how long before was it now? His wound had bled freely again, and he had welcomed the bleeding. He had touched the blood, tasted it. It was his, and real. . . .

Darkness . . . no sense of day or night . . . only the steady roll of artillery and the far-away, unreal clatter of machine guns. He dug and dug, first stopping to rest, losing consciousness, then waking again. He could only guess at how long he had been unconscious each time by examining the blood on his hands. Had it dried? How hard was the crust?

He struck a match; the flickering light revealed Mercedes' silent figure a few feet away. He had a dim recollection of putting her clothing back on her as best he could, of trying to compose her in a posture of peace against the wall, as though she were only sleeping. A small black bruise over her forehead seemed the only wound. She would wake up soon enough; she had only been knocked unconscious as he had . . . he told himself this time and again. . . . He would talk to her, soothing her and telling her to sleep. "You need the rest . . . when you wake up, you'll be that much stronger . . . it's all right . . . I'm digging. There's no need for you to do anything . . . just sleep. It's good for you. . . ."

The water in the bottle she had brought with her had soured. He kept on digging, oblivious to the pain in his hands. He would stop to cough, shielding his face from the smoke when it flowed down the walls of the pit. At intervals he would pour out a little of the water and wet a cloth, put it to Mercedes' lips. Sometimes he would even try to open her mouth and make her drink; the water only dribbled away down her chin and ran into the hollow at the base of her neck.

He doubled his hands into fists and beat at the debris, dislodging only a few stones. Sooner or later, every brick that he had scraped up, every stone thrust aside mounted the sloping walls of the pit for a second, then slid back down again, forming a thick ring of debris around him.

He fell asleep in the newly formed hollow, woke again . . . his bones naked. Where was his flesh? How odd to feel one's bones on the outside. Only bones and transparent skin, tight as paper. He felt his skin crinkling as he moved. For hours he was tortured by visions of suckling pigs, broiled and split, platters of crawfish, lobster, and mussels, saffron rice moist and steaming. . . . Xaviera's lusty Basque soups . . . the heaping plates of *tadjin*. . . .

He dug, but the pit went no deeper.

He dug and slept, falling exhausted onto piles of stones. Above him, where the beams crossed and the slabs of broken rock leaned against one another, points of light moved about, disappearing as the clouds shifted back and forth over the face of the sun.

He dreamed of a field of bones, white as pottery shards. The field stretched as far as he could see, and at the end of it rose the shadow of El Escorial, strangely attenuated like the buildings in El Greco's paintings. But the palace itself was not there. Only the shadow, blotching the white landscape. A nearby tolling of monks' bells drove him almost mad.

He lay still, unsure whether the field of bones had not been in fact the bleached deserts of Morocco, the shadow of the purpled edifice, merely the shadow of the Riff mountains. He lay back, staring at the patch of light high above him, narrowing his eyes until the light itself began to pulse. There was no more smoke.

Now only bright sunlight and the silence of bones, of deserts.

A whorl of yellow, gold, silver sparks, sound and color as one. Morocco. When he closed his eyes, he could see light, when he opened them . . . only darkness. Everything was reversed, yet it did not seem strange to him at all. Why was he digging? Certainly, he had been digging for a long time, but had nothing to show for it. Mercedes seemed to be watching him and with approval too. Otherwise she would have said something; a sensible woman. A fine woman. Surely she would have said something if it was wrong to dig.

He closed his eyes, leaned against the incline he had created.

"To choose, to be able to choose . . . something . . . to choose not to choose . . ." He tried to stop himself from thinking . . . it was too painful. His head ached and he had forgotten about the wound, blaming everything on his thoughts. The pains transformed themselves in turn into vistas of boiling desert with clean, hard mountain peaks in the distance. The shouts of horsemen and the sea-thunder of hooves; all with a perfect clarity.

Open your eyes . . . nothing. Shale, rock, and Mercedes watching with closed eyes. He touched the stones next to her hand. They were hot and scorched his fingers. Where had he known stones that hot before? Only one place. Not even the plains between Toledo and Illescas had such stones.

The deep fever from his wound grew, yet he felt no real change. Each sensation passed naturally into the next. The pain in his head had become so much a part of him that he did not notice the increasing heat, the heaviness in his limbs. There was no mirror to show him the livid color of his temples, the purple inflamation that had spread wide over his head.

He listened, heard nothing. The hoofbeats were gone and the voice of the sun had faded to an echo. It seemed to him he was trapped in a great stillness where no one had ever existed except him. Not his father or his mother, not Enrique Carvalho, not even Mercedes who was there, a few feet away, a faintly amused smile on her silent face, as though death were at last revealed as a faintly ironic joke, nothing more.

The pit had become the fortress itself, the web of lines formed by the falling beams were the relief columns. "Trapped by it . . . ," he thought over and over again. "By what? There is no existence at all . . . nothing at all. . . ."

Suddenly he threw back his head and shouted:

"No . . . !"

There was no echo. A shaft of muted light fell from above, glancing off the side of the tin cup. Off another metal object, a rifle, half-buried in the debris. He had not noticed it before. He picked it up. It was old, yet familiar. He seemed to remember having seen such rifles before, in the hills, in gnarled brown hands, hung over blue Berber cloaks.

He took the rifle in his hands. There was delicate tooling along the barrel, a design of intertwined leaves and arabesques. No rust. Loosening the sling, he hung the rifle over his shoulder. His mother's people had used such rifles, he remembered, left to them by the fallen *Tercios,* the bewildered boys from Barcelona and Aragon who had trekked their lands under General O'Donnell's command, the conscripts from the alleys of Madrid who had left their bones to intensify the light of the deserts under the Riff.

He tightened the cinch so that the strap bit hard into his shoulder. He did not mind that; now the rifle would not fall. He rose shakily to his feet, testing himself, holding out his arms to seek his balance. He knew he must keep his eyes open; to close them meant to fall. Even for an instant. The pain in his head seemed to recede, replaced by a numbness that was almost . . . pleasant.

He began to climb along the side of the pit. There were moments when an upward movement would cause the pain in his head to flame suddenly, but he welcomed the fresh pain as a sign that he had not given over entirely to his delirium. Glancing back over his shoulder, he saw Mercedes, her head tilted back, a few droplets of water shining just above her collarbone. In that light her face had taken on an almost translucent, ivory color.

A few pebbles rolled down the incline. One struck Mercedes' outstretched hand. There was no sound. "She's too proud . . . after all, only a pebble . . . pride. Just like her father . . . pride. . . ."

He reached up, testing his next handhold. The walls of the pit were surprisingly steady. Tons of rock held each slab in place, anchored beams and fastened girders. Only the smallest stones gave way.

What was left of his clothing caught on the ragged edges of stone and tore; blood from the wound on his head, cracked open, the line of it flaming and dark under his hair, began to creep down his neck, and down his bare arms. He continued to climb. He was surprised; it was so easy.

Near the top, the sweat-drenched smell of the pit gave way to a sharp, penetrating odor, acrid as damp ash. A patch of brilliant blue sky grew out of what had been before only a faint point of light of indeterminate color.

Almost two stories below, haloed by the same shaft of light that had fallen on the rifle, Mercedes lay, the expression on her face unchanging in its utter tranquillity. Looking down made him dizzy, and he turned his head, fastened his gaze once again on the opening between the slabs of rock that covered the top of the pit, a fissure much wider than he had imagined it to be from below. A steel girder had fallen directly under the slabs. He would have to be careful; if he dislodged anything, it could easily fall on the girl. . . .

"You see, Colonel . . . do you see what I'm doing . . . ?"

The silence above frightened him. The bright-blue calm of the sky toward which he now drew nearer seemed to threaten much more than the dark pall of smoke he was accustomed to. No smoke drifted across the opening, no dust clouds whirled past. Only the faint whisper of a clear wind could be heard. The hiss of flame had faded, and the crack of rifle fire had been stilled. No explosions, no distant shouts. Could it be that he had gone deaf? Everything was so strange. His strength . . . where had he found the strength to make the climb? Dimly he recalled going up the stairs, watching the empty plains until . . . Dr. Sepulveda, the others . . . everything had faded . . . then the dark room again . . . and "Isle of Capri" . . . fading away. . . .

He was only a few yards from the top now, the girder and the opening to the sky.

The rifle swung loose for an instant, the butt striking a slide of shale from the slope. It rolled gently down the incline, was lost.

Jaime reached out a hand, took hold of the rock ledge at the opening, testing it to see if it would take his weight. A violent pain stabbed through his head, almost making him loose his grip. His fingers closed on the ledge. It was steady; the steel beam that spanned the top of the pit held fast.

Weak as he was, he had no doubt he could pull himself up; he reached out with his other hand and pushed off from the wall, leaving himself dangling from the ledge of rock like a pendulum bob. The rifle slipped on his shoulder, threatening to unbalance him. Then, gradually, he drew himself up through the opening. The rock held. A pebble skittered into the pit.

Jaime's head emerged through the opening, then his shoulders and the barrel of the rifle hung on his back. The sun whirled above him in a flat cloudless sky the color of glazed Portuguese tile. Shimmering air through which the September heat struck with merciless force. The sun seemed bloated, ready to burst and flood the earth with lava. With great care he turned his head. Hammers . . . slowly arched his back, pulled himself farther up so that only his feet still hung below the ledge.

The landscape was astonishing. It was so like his dream of the plain of bones, but here it was all gray and brown and black, not white. Massive falls of rock, broken slabs of granite and heaps of brick. Over it all, a white effluvium of mortar dust. To his right, a hill of bricks mounted to the skeletal remains of a wall. The west flank of the Alcázar seemed to have crumbled away, the victim of some leprosy that destroyed stone instead of flesh. All that was left was a no-man's land of rubble stretching all the way to the river embankment.

He crawled slowly on his hands and knees over the rock, toward the river. Beams and girders angled, charred and blackened by now silent fires. Broken tree stumps after a hurricane. He heard the sizzle of the sun on the stones. The air trembled, vibrated; he thought he heard the buzzing of swarms of flies such as had endlessly circled the villages beyond the valley of Oued Lau. But where were the oleander bushes, pale rose, and the sea? . . . Nothing . . . only the buzzing of the flies rising from the stones under his palms . . .

It was clear; he had emerged somewhere near the northwest corner of the Alcázar, directly next to the ruin of the north terrace. A few acacia trees thrust still leafy branches through the debris where the collapsed walls sloped down toward the burned-out buildings of the *gobierno*.

On the reddish hills to the north and east, across the Tagus, nothing moved but the shadows of a few low, swift clouds.

For a moment he struggled, almost losing his grip on the rifle; he fell face down on the stones, then got to his knees again. The sun haze seemed to dissipate, and he could see more clearly. Outlines became unusually precise, sharp. Shapes almost crystalline.

Far, far over the hills a flock of birds wheeled silently in the glassy sky, going nowhere, coming from nowhere.

He stared toward the gorge, thought . . . "Morocco . . . there's only some rocks and water between this stinking place and Ceuta. . . ." The words tumbled in his head. What right had anyone to deprive him of his frothing beaches, his forge-fire sunsets, and the immense cleansing openness of the deserts? Air so pure that a man almost lost his breath to breathe it? What right had any of them had, his father, Carvalho, Pelayo, Soler, any of them, to involve him in all of this? What he wanted was simple enough . . . to be left alone. To hell with their lies and their absurd pride . . . everyone knew where God was to be found and behind which tree lay paradise on earth, but wasn't it strange that God stubbornly stayed hidden and refused to show himself?

He turned sharply, almost losing his balance. The barrel of the rifle clanged against the stones, setting up an aching reverberation in his head which grew steadily into a din of wild, jubilant bells.

He tilted his head upward, got to his feet. The sun struck him across the eyes with stunning force. He felt strangely purified by the heat.

"I'm going to be free," he shouted, throwing his head back and staring open eyed into the sun. "Do you hear that? Do you . . . ?"

He voice echoed back softly from the gorge. Tears mixed with the blood on his face.

There before him rose the splendid hills of the Moroccan highlands. Lakes glittered, and he heard the sweet rush of cold, pure air about him. He strode happily forward toward the edge of the esplanade.

The steps of a great building seemed to lie under his feet . . . the Cortes . . . the Cathedral of Our Lady of Africa . . . the landscape before him assumed the phantom shapes of other, indescribable buildings. He lurched down the incline. The rubble gave way under his feet, propelling him toward the edge of the gorge.

He had never been more joyous. He was free, and there was no one in the world to stop him. The earth had been magically depopulated; only the mountains and the sun remained. . . . And Jaime Mercader, waving his ancient rifle over his head. . . . The sky rolled and sang. . . .

The hills and sky were there, exactly as he remembered them. The mountains stuck like the blades of spears into the flesh of the land. The sky, lemon yellow, the river whispering directly below him in the voice of the silver-breasted Martil.

But why did the sun vibrate so in the sky? Nothing would hold still long enough for him to make really sure of anything.

Suddenly, he stopped short and flung himself down in a half-crouch behind a boulder. Below, on the sloping mounds of rubble, far away where the hillside fell toward the edge of the gorge, there were dark specks stirring among the rocks, crawling slowly upward toward the breast of the slope where he now lay partly hidden.

He squinted; abruptly, tiny scarlet flames seemed to leap from among the rocks, to whirl into phantasmagoric shapes and then dissipate as quickly as they had come. He shouted after them, but they did not return his call.

The figures continued to crawl steadily toward him. Their forms clearer now, strangely bundled; brownish shapes with brown faces, their heads splashed with the red of their fezzes.

No one could climb like that. The hill was turning like a child's top. But the climbing figures hung on. . . . Inhuman. . . .

Jaime pressed against the boulder, his forehead pouring sweat. He could hear hoofbeats and shouts swarming inside his skull, yet he knew there was no sound. His hands were clammy on the rifle barrel.

He thrust out a hand to steady himself against the boulder and rose to a stoop, his head coming up over the edge of the rock. The figures advanced, and as he watched, they seemed to split and multiply, two where there had been one, four where there had been two before. The hills, the mountains, the lakes, all seemed to evaporate; only the clanging of bells remained.

He walked out from behind the boulder, out into plain view of the advancing red and black throng. His heart thrust against his ribs with an exuberance unlike anything he could remember since childhood. His head ached unmercifully. Blood ran thickly down his neck. His hair sprang wildly under a hot wind, rushing away from the wound.

Berbers . . . Moors . . . climbing the hills to meet him. He was home. Home and wherever he was had become one. He began to laugh, to shout incomprehensible things, words that he heard clearly enough inside his head but which burst from his lips distorted into gibberish and then, doubly torn by the wind, flew down the slope in lunatic syllables.

He waved the ancient rifle over his head, swung it so that it caught the sun and sent the reflections spinning down the hill like shards of broken glass. His finger was on the trigger. Shouting joyfully, he stumbled toward them.

The figures saw him, waited, poised on the burning shale. The sun pulsed above them. Jaime could see them clearly now, the nearer ones, a few hesitantly raising their weapons toward him.

His finger clamped down on the trigger of the rifle; the hillside shook with the explosion. A long puff of smoke shot skyward from the muzzle. As his mother's tribe had greeted him the first time he had ridden into the village, firing their muskets into the clouds. . . .

He would greet them. . . .

There was a sudden flash as though a grenade had gone off next to his head; the long rifle exploded. Flame burst from the lock and engulfed his eyes, drilling back down through his face, splitting his skull like an eggshell.

He fell headlong down the slope, smashed against a jagged bed of rock which caught him, held his naked body fast as though he were a butterfly pinned to a board.

The Moors scrambled to their knees, then to their feet and lunged forward as the silence returned. They continued up the hill. The Alcázar was before them, behind them the full weight of the relief column pouring across the hills bordering the river and from Maqueda and Torrijos to the north as well.

Toledo seemed quiet. Only the faint, dry rattle of an occasional rifle shot broke the stillness. Seedpods falling on tile . . .

It was very hot.

Moments later the first of the advance guard reached Jaime Mercader's body. He paused only an instant by the broken figure. The Moor kicked at it, rolling the corpse over, then saw that it had no face and kicked it back again onto its stomach. It was not good to look at things like that.

The Moor rubbed the sweat from his forehead and dried his hands on the sides of his scarlet fez. The others were already past him, up the hill and almost to the ruin of the esplanade.

There were supposed to be people in the fortress, the Moor remembered. He wondered whether any of them were still alive. The fortress was the important thing. People still up there? If there were, they must be great fools, he thought.

He brushed a fly from his ear and continued up the hill.

EPILOGUE /

Full Circle

Five loyalist airplanes heavily bomb Torrijos, Maqueda, and Barajas

Madrid prepares to fight Fascism in the Tajo sector

An enemy attack has been repelled in the Sigüenza sector, and in Talavera the objectives have been attained

El Sol

SEPTEMBER 29, 1936: *The Alcázar*

THREE SOLDIERS SAT ON THE PEDESTAL from which, once, the statue of Carlos V had looked proudly into the turret-riven square of sky above the Alcázar. Of the statue itself, little was left save a few fragments, an arm, the head, and a dozen chunks of unidentifiable white stone. One of the soldiers had drawn his knees to his chest and clasped them with his arms. The second kept his head lowered, his eyes focused on the ground; he could not bear the sudden light of the flashbulbs from the newsmen's cameras. He had been underground too long. Even the strong light of day was too much for his eyes. Yet he would not relinquish his place. The third man was not even watching the proceedings but rather was following the movements of a flock of birds dipping low over the destroyed archways.

Major Punto rubbed his eyes. The light from the flashbulbs irritated him too, caught him constantly by surprise although he knew that they would keep going off until General Franco was through speaking, until, perhaps, the grand tour of the Alcázar which was to follow had been completed. It was not the light but the suddenness of the flash that irritated him; the grinding of the newsmen's cameras was painfully magnified inside his skull. The correspondents continued to crank their cameras, oblivious to the Major's discomfort. The courtyard was crowded with Legionnaires, the Moors with their polished knives catching the sunlight, the survivors, dazed, too weak even to join in the cheers that had gone up when General Franco had entered through the main gate and exchanged greetings with Moscardó. A squad of demolition experts had gone first, poking about in the ground to make sure that no unexploded grenades lay in the General's path.

"Nothing is new in the Alcázar . . . ," the Colonel had repeated the same flat, expressionless words he had used the day before when General Varela had first entered the ruin of the Alcázar. Only this time, the Colonel, searching perhaps for some variety that would make meaningful what was otherwise only an absurd repetition of which he must have felt embarrassed, added, "You will find the Alcázar destroyed, señor, but its honor intact. . . ."

"Such honor as there is in simply surviving," Major Punto thought. It was all rehearsed, like a puppet play, a rerun of the previous day's events with minor accidental variations, staged solely for the benefit of the newsmen who had only now been allowed into the city. No one was there to watch it but the correspondents, the Legion, and the Moors. Only a few of the defenders of the building had remained.

A voice close by said, over the hubbub: "Bothers you, eh, the noise and all that?"

Punto turned his head. The man had spoken in a heavily accented Spanish . . . one of the correspondents . . . an Englishman.

"You're one of the ones who was . . . ," the man hesitated, as though the idea was too much for him, as though by saying it he might somehow inflict it on himself. A week's entombment . . . appalling. . . .

Major Punto looked at him, trying to catch his gaze directly and failing. The reporter did not want to look him in the eye, perhaps afraid of what he would see there. "Trapped underground . . . ?" Punto said, "Yes."

"Ten whole days, was it?" The reporter brightened. There he was . . . ten days, and yet he had survived, along with a dozen others.

Major Punto nodded disinterestedly.

The newsman seemed fascinated by the medal dangling from the left pocket of Punto's tunic. Punto's uniform was still in tatters; he had refused to change into the new uniform that had been offered him the day before. Instead, he had put the clean clothing into the case which previously had contained his records of the siege. The medal caught the sun, glinted brightly against the grimy cloth. "Perhaps that is why he stares," Punto thought, hoping that the man would not ask him the name of the decoration. He had no idea what it was called; the ceremony had passed over him like warm rain, its meaning evaporating as rapidly.

"Amazing," said the newsman, shaking his head. He wore a red beret donated by one of the Carlist *Requetes* who had come in with the Tetuán regulars. It sat at a comical angle over a face trying determinedly to look hard and windbitten but which succeeded only in giving the appearance of flaccidity. The man's clothing was an odd assemblage of military and civilian.

"Ten whole days," the man continued muttering in disbelief, "without food or water . . . ?"

"Men have gone longer without either," Punto said quietly. He could hear the regular rhythm of Franco's voice but could not quite make out the words. Was he interested in what the General was saying?

Punto was vaguely aware that the man was jotting things down on a little pad. "Let him . . . ," Punto thought, "we all keep our records, take our notes of what interests us. . . ."

General Franco was still talking; a small man with an anxious, alert squint. The collar of the shirt he wore under his plain tunic was much too large for him and hung loose around his neck. General Varela stood next to him without even a tunic on, only a Sam Browne belt across his uniform shirt, hatless. It was warm, hazy with sun. Flies buzzed, shuttling through the General's words. Colonel Moscardó stood nearby, as though waiting nervously for a cue in a play, the Cross of San Fernando already pinned to his tunic, the three stars on his cap polished more brightly than ever.

The English newsman continued to ask questions in a soft almost pleading voice, more concerned with Punto's experience than with anything Franco or Varela might be saying. His companions were taking all that down, as were the cameras, leaving him free to seek more intimate details.

The Englishman was almost a head shorter than the Major. Punto looked down. By his dress, his imitation soldiery, the man had proclaimed himself a fool. Punto said softly, "Will you write this down, just as I tell you? Yes, you will, so . . . write that I don't know how I survived. Just simply that, do you understand? I don't . . . know . . ."

"But surely, something . . ."

"There is nothing to tell. Absolutely nothing more."

The Englishman scribbled cursorily in his note pad, as though to walk away without writing something would be an unthinkable admission of defeat.

Punto turned away. In the shadows of the arcades a few people were stirring. For two days now, men and women had been struggling up from the caverns and tunnels, still unsure that it was really over, that the siege had ended. Men cried quietly to themselves without embarrassment in the shade of the broken archways while the Legionnaires and the Moors hunted through the streets and alleys of Toledo, routing out the last of the *milicianos* and Assault Guard left in the city, killing them off one by one. Even as the cameras whirred, a scattering of shots could be heard outside. Once, a long, high-pitched cry came unexpectedly from a house nearby, the sound of a man being gutted with a knife. The Moors were quiet, very busy. The Legionnaires used their rifles.

He remembered it all. "Lie still," someone had said to him . . . the surface, flooded with sunlight, blinding him . . . the image of the man below, waving, cheerful . . . a victory . . . his life. Alive again. After how long? At first they would not tell him. He had taken a canteen eagerly, then found that he was not really thirsty. They gave him food which he had eaten slowly, only a few bites at a time . . . "Enough, it will make me sick," and then, to the amazement of the soldiers who had rescued him, he stood, shaky for a moment, then surprisingly strong.

"Ten days . . . and look at him . . ."

Punto returned their astonishment with a puzzled look of his own, took a little more food. Someone had asked him his name, his rank . . .

it was impossible to tell from his uniform. . . . The insignia had fallen off. . . . He felt stronger. Another bite of food, then more water. He stood straighter.

"I can walk . . . it's all right. . . ." He thanked them and began to move about, cautiously, testing his legs.

"The light . . . ," was all he had said. A Legionnaire handed him a pair of heavy sunglasses. He put them on, at once felt better, less dizzy. All around, the death's-head emblems of the Legion, the dark Moorish faces. They stood back in awe, let him do whatever he wanted to do.

Now he was just as he had been the day the siege had begun; quite alone. Cristóbal Herrera was dead. . . . He had seen the body . . . one of the last to be killed. Dr. Sepulveda was already on his way to Madrid with the advancing troops. Even these he had only known slightly, like Jiménez the printer, Rubén Góngora, Lieutenant Rincón, all of them were gone. Everywhere he went, into the Zoco, littered with debris and corpses, onto the embankments . . . there was nothing.

The women and children were gone, returned to their homes, to what was left of their homes. Only a crowd of soldiers remained around the two generals and a weary Colonel with bloodshot eyes. The morning before someone had confirmed the death of Moscardó's son, Luis, killed not at the beginning of the siege but weeks later, in another city far away.

General Franco was still speaking, one hand raised high above his head as though he were grasping at something by means of which he might pull himself out from the circle of *Regulares* who surrounded him, their automatic weapons cradled loosely in their arms. . . . "Or grasping at the sun," Punto found himself thinking, "or at the ghosts of those poor demolished towers." He could still see them in his mind's eye, rising spiky and graceful into the blue sky. Now, there was nothing but rubble, and the soldiers, suspiciously eyeing the windows of the few buildings that could be seen over the shattered walls. The noise of the cameras, the sudden flashes of light from the photographers' bulbs, disturbed them, and they fidgeted nervously, anxious to have done with the ceremony and get outside again.

"The soldiers are all squinting," Punto thought, looking about. "But our people all have their eyes wide open, as though they've seen too much already." He watched them for a moment through his dark glasses. "The African sun . . . it's that perpetual squint." He could see Varela's round, almost cherubic face from where he stood. The General was squinting, too, fingering his holstered pistol.

Punto turned away. No one even looked after him, though only an hour before he had been, for a brief moment, the center of all attention. As he traversed the rubble-strewn yard, following the path cleared by the demolition experts, the scattering of soldiers moved silently out of his way.

The General's voice . . . more shots, very distant, and the roaring of planes as a flight of bombers rushed in low formation over the Alcázar. "For the newsmen," he thought. He stopped to watch as the cameras all swung skyward, away from the gesticulating General.

The main gate was open. As he passed through it onto the ruin of the esplanade, a Moor standing guard smiled and waved, his teeth very white against the oiled blackness of his skin. A long curved knife gleamed in his belt. For some reason, the Moor's smile reminded Punto of the patronizing smile of the Captain to whom he had handed over his reports the day before. They had been there in his room, undamaged by the blast or the final assaults, just where he had left them. Even the brief-case was unscarred. Some entries in pencil, others in pen . . . some written in large capital letters, block capitals such as a child might make. He had no recollection of having done such a thing but there they were, unquestionably in his own hand.

The Captain's tone had been highly impersonal; he was obviously not concerned with Punto, but only with the information contained in the briefcase and the uses to which it might later be put. Punto had waited patiently while the younger man had leafed slowly through the piles of papers.

"Is there anything else?"

"Why . . . I . . . ? Something else?" The Captain stammered, taken aback by the brusqueness of the Major's tone.

"Well then?"

"Excuse me, Major, I must be sure . . . this is all very important. You yourself understand that, of course. . . ."

"They contain a wealth of information, Captain. Whole pages on the sanitary problems of disposing of the dead which are created by having no place in which to bury them. . . . Read the reports, Captain, then if you have any questions you wish to ask me. . . . I understand I am to be quartered at the Hotel Castilla with Colonel Moscardó's staff."

"I'm sure," replied the Captain, embarrassed without quite knowing why, angry at the same time. "Everything will be read. I can assure you . . . we owe you a great debt for having kept such a record. There are not many who, under such circumstances would . . . that is . . ."

"What you mean to say is that there are not many men who would under . . . such circumstances. . . . have thought it important to fill hundreds of pages with such trivia? What an utter fool such a man must be. Is that it, Captain?"

The Captain had stared, speechless, indignant.

"May I go now?" Punto had said.

"You don't have to ask my permission. You outrank me, Major. . . ."

"Of course," and he had smiled and walked away. "Let the wind take the papers; let the wind take them all." He could not have cared less.

"All this in the Moor's smile," he thought, picking his way down the esplanade. Bodies still lay about, blood blackening on outstretched hands and masking faces. "How many more such little things will remind me of other little things in the days to come?"

He circled the Alcázar. Inside, he could still hear the General's voice echoing, the amplified whirring of the cameras, the occasional shouts of encouragement.

A number of vehicles were drawn up on the esplanade: trucks, a few open-backed officers' cars, and an ambulance. The wounded were being loaded into the ambulance by a group of Moors and a few nurses. Next to the ambulance stood a truck which had been fitted out with a grill-work back, almost like a prison grating. Punto recognized the driver, Barrera, who was standing at the back of the truck. Inside, behind the grating, was the man's cousin, the Civil Guard, Delgado. He and a number of others who had gone mad or were in shock from their ordeal were being taken to a special hospital in Burgos. Barrera had gotten permission to drive the truck.

The Major waved to him as he passed, and the driver tried to smile, to wave back, but succeeded only in forcing a grotesque grin across his face that made him appear at once both pitiful and foolish.

Major Punto looked away; he had heard the story about the driver's cousin and what had happened on the wall that day. What could a man say? In a way, wasn't that worse than dying yourself? Yet he wondered what he would say if someone gave him such a choice. . . .

He walked on, trying to shut out the broken singing that was coming from inside the back of the truck. He wondered if the madmen had been manacled and what would happen if they attacked each other during the trip.

As he passed down the Cuesta and into the empty Zocodover, he lit a cigarette. A sign hung from a battered shop window: *pescados*. . . . Beneath it a body in gray civilian clothes sprawled face down, his back stitched with bullet holes. Another man lay nearby, also dead, on his back, his arms thrown lazily out as though he were peacefully sunbathing.

Punto passed through the plaza, aimlessly turned up a steeply rising alleyway. A group of Legionnaires, all with rifles at shoulder arms, was just then descending the street, coming directly toward him. A lieutenant saluted him as the group passed. Punto returned the greeting, continued trudging up the street, then stopped at a rise where the alley leveled out. Ahead of him, on one side, ran a row of shuttered houses, their small windows covered by iron grilles; a blank wall, purple with shade, flanked the street on the other side.

All along the foot of the wall lay the bodies of men, twenty or thirty of them, their hands tied behind their backs. Some were blindfolded. Thick rivulets of fresh blood trickled along the crevices between the stones.

The men were filthy, bearded, wasted, even as he was. He approached more closely. The vengeful rays of the moribund September sun struck down between the buildings with all the ferocity of a man aware of impending death and determined to destroy everything around him before he dies. Punto took a handkerchief from his pocket, tied it around his forehead and let the flap hang back to protect his bare scalp, then moved closer. He recognized some of the dead men.

The hostages who had been held alive in the Alcázar all through the siege had just been shot.

Slowly, he walked the line, looking down at the corpses. Flies had begun to buzz over the warm blood. Some men lay face down, others were twisted about so that he could see their features. He stopped and knelt before one man, undid the blindfold, turned the body over on its back with his foot. It was the Austrian, the mark of Punto's riding crop still dark across his cheek.

The expression on Vitolyn's face was strange, a contorted mixture of emotions, as though it had started out as a smile of contentment, then, as the bullets had torn into him, had changed to a look of disbelief, the horrified expression of a man who realizes both that he has made a terrible mistake and that the mistake is irreversible. There were five bullet holes in Vitolyn's chest and one in his throat. He must have died almost instantly, yet there had been enough time for his expression to change. Punto studied the lines of the Austrian's face for a moment.

"They won't change," he thought. "No matter how long I watch . . . God, what a look to die with . . . but the muscles are already stiff . . . no, it's his face . . . leave him alone. . . ." He had to tear his gaze away. "How stupid. As though he might change that . . . look . . . simply by being there. . . ." He tried to understand how Vitolyn had come to be with the hostages again, how he had died in such a way, and with such an inexplicable look on his face. It was beyond understanding, all of it. He raised himself from his kneeling position, still looking down at the Austrian's corpse. He saw only the welt left by his riding crop.

Major Punto leaned against the wall and lit a cigarette, drawing the smoke into his lungs in deep, greedy draughts. He looked again up and down the line of huddled bodies and felt a violent trembling seize him for a moment, a desire to run back down the street and grab hold of the young Legion Lieutenant who had commanded the firing squad. What right had they, he thought? "After all those months . . . these men, as well as we, were entitled to live."

Suddenly he felt a sharp pain in his fingertips; unnoticed, his cigarette had burned down to the end. He dropped the smoldering butt and it rolled along the stones, fizzled out in a puddle of blood. He began to walk up the steep street again, toward a house that suddenly emerged from the shadows which engulfed the rest of the area, exploding in a bright shaft of almost golden stone. A colored awning, fringed with tassels hung from the second floor above a tiny iron-railed balcony. A pot of flowers stood tranquilly on the balcony railing. Overhead the sky was bright blue, glassy. As he walked, a white puff of cloud whisked swiftly across the open patch of sky. The sun shifted and quite as suddenly, the house fell under an arc of lavender shadow.

Punto stopped. The street branched off to his left. He could go straight ahead or continue up toward the patch of sky. He chose the darker turn, found himself in another narrow alleyway, walled by balconies, jutting windows.

As he walked on aimlessly, he felt his isolation like a wound. Even before, during the weeks preceding the relief of the siege, he had been beset by doubts, a nagging indifference. The sight of the brisk young men of the Legion, the turbaned Moors, the shots, the bodies . . . all of this confirmed, vivified painfully that nascent doubt.

He passed more buildings where sudden, unexpected gaps in the solid lines of walls let sunlight through to break the expanse of shadow. "Sombra y sol. . . . The entire city . . . like the ring . . . death played out according to tradition, according to our unique love of it, the honor we render it."

Already, the new conquerors of Toledo had set to work with buckets of whitewash, painting over the slogans of the FAI, and the legends scrawled over the walls by the Communists. One wall he passed bore a gentle poem about orange blossoms. . . . The words of a popular song? he wondered. They, too, had been partially obliterated by a sweep of the brush, but the whitewash had been thin and the words were still visible.

Other posters had followed . . . pots of black paint, brushes heavy as with tar, new slogans on the barely dry walls, walls cradling streets still running with blood. How many had been killed? he wondered as he walked, lighting another cigarette.

"How different are they, these men who bring back to us what we expelled four hundred years ago, the blood of Africa. . . . Who are they and what . . . what . . . what do they want of me?" He would never be able to answer that question, nor find his own place in the mosaic of death now being pieced together around him. It occurred to him that he had had no real idea of what they, the besiegers had been like, what they had thought, how they had felt. Had they been the embodiment of the now obliterated slogans? Or rather the simple lines about orange blossoms that still remained, despite the whitewash? In his memory, they had become simply an endless cracking of rifles, a thud of artillery, blood, hunger, and senselessness. There was nothing human about them, he thought, but they had, at least, the saving grace of anonymity. The men who had freed him and who now claimed him had faces, their eyes fixed tight in the "African squint." Yet they were as much a mystery to him as any of the faceless riflemen who had fired at him all summer from the distant rooftops of the Santo Cruz. Nowhere had he found that trace of sympathy in either thought or action that he knew he needed. "Where, my God, where will it be? Can it be?" Yet he was there among "them," the other "them" this time, a hero with a medal on his tunic. How little he understood those men who had but hours before extolled his bravery, his true "Spanish" courage . . . which consisted, he thought with sad amusement, in lying inert at the bottom of a hole for an entire ten days. . . . "Perhaps the real courage is in doing . . . nothing . . . ," he thought. A phrase passed through his mind: "For fear of doing something wrong, he often settled for doing nothing at all . . ."

A priest passed across the street far ahead of him, a musty figure, his cassock suddenly caught in a breeze. Then he disappeared into a house. Like a figure out of his past.

It was like being a child again. . . . Children's games . . . you line up with your friends, and you pick sides . . . and unless you are a special friend of the one who is picking sides, who knows where you wind up? It is a matter of chance . . . unless you are very, very good at the game. Then both sides want you . . . but once you are on a side, then everything is expected . . . loyalty, devotion, endless energy. Even sacrifice. Death. And if you refuse to play, then everyone turns on you. Coward. You cannot refuse to play. To play, that is a condition of existence . . . forget whether the game is worth playing or not."

It was noon. Quiet. Men and women watched from doorways. Some who had been hiding in cellars for months were now seeing the sun for the first time. Others had now taken their place in hiding. It had not occurred to Punto before, but even outside the fortress there had been those who had been as besieged as he himself.

The heat was at its peak. Heavy, acrid odors, intensified by the heavy September sun, rose up and brought tears to his eyes.

The street broadened. For a second, he felt reluctant to enter the new, wider passage. More bodies? The Moors had killed anyone whose shoulders bore the bruises of a rifle butt. Were there other hostages who had been slaughtered?

But there was nothing, only three young *Regulares,* hardly out of their adolescence. They wore their uniforms with a blinding pride, a fierce arrogance. They knelt by a blank wall next to a gutted storefront. Painting the wall. A bucket of black paint. Brushes moving swiftly over the wall. Huge black letters.

¡ARRIBA ESPAÑA! the letters said.

Major Punto shook his head and walked on.